DC COMICS
YEAR BY YEAR
UPDATED EDITION

LONDON, NEW YORK, MELBOURNE,
MUNICH, AND DELHI

Senior Editor Laura Gilbert
Editors Pamela Afram, Hannah Dolan, Tori Kosara
Proofreader Julia March
Design Manager Robert Perry
Designers Nick Avery, Nathan Martin,
Mark Richards, Samantha Richiardi, Satvir Sihota
Design Assistant Rhys Thomas
Design Manager Ron Stobbart
Publishing Manager Catherine Saunders
Art Director Lisa Lanzarini
Publisher Simon Beecroft
Publishing Director Alex Allan
Senior Production Editor Jennifer Murray
Production Controller Kara Wallace
Indexer Lindsay Kent

This updated edition published in 2014
First published in Great Britain in 2010 by
Dorling Kindersley, 80 Strand, London WC2R 0RL
A Penguin Random House Company

001–275048–Sep/14

A CIP catalogue record for this book
is available from the British Library.

DORL33523

ISBN: 978-0-2410-1585-8

Color reproduction by Alta Images in the UK
Printed and bound in China by Hung Hing

DK Publishing would like to thank:
Benjamin Harper at Warner Bros. Consumer Products; Adam Schlagman, Christopher Cerasi, Steve Korté, John Morgan, Frank Pittarese, Dylan Runco, Georg Brewer, Allan Asherman, Jay Kogan, Roger Bonas, and Michael Wooten at DC Entertainment; Ryan Sook for the stunning jacket artwork; Paul Levitz for the wonderful foreword; Mark Waid for looking over this book with a keen eye; Ian Levine for giving us access to his amazing comic book collection; Jon Hall for design assistance; Jo Casey, David Connifey, Elizabeth Dowsett, Aditi Ghosh, Shari Last, Lisa Stock, and Victoria Taylor for editorial assistance; Nicholas Bland for the datelines.

In memory of Roger Bonas.

Discover more at
www.dk.com

DC COMICS
YEAR BY YEAR
UPDATED EDITION

Written by Alan Cowsill, Alex Irvine, Matthew K. Manning,
Michael McAvennie and Daniel Wallace
Additional writing by Alastair Dougall and Chris Cerasi

CONTENTS

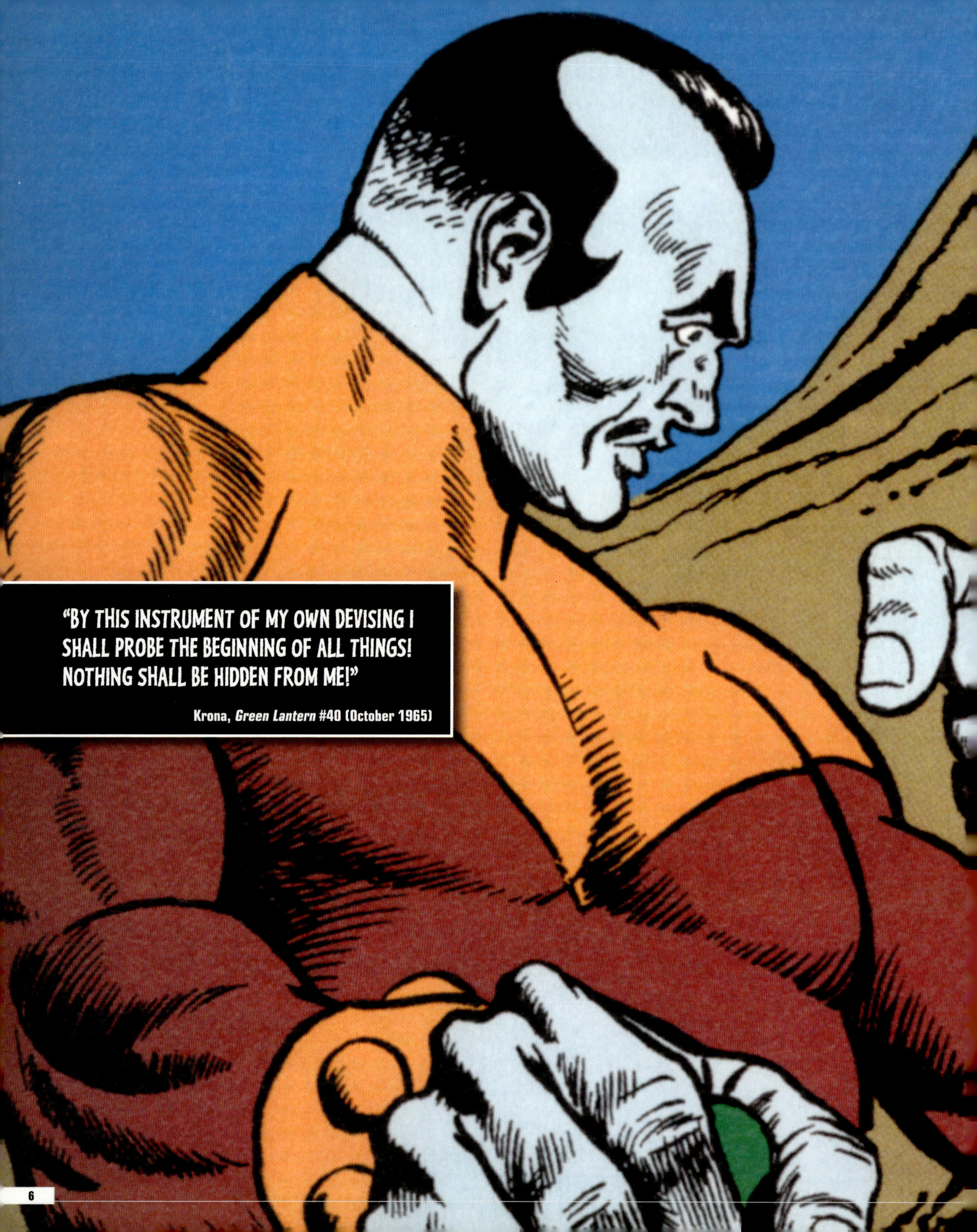

"BY THIS INSTRUMENT OF MY OWN DEVISING I SHALL PROBE THE BEGINNING OF ALL THINGS! NOTHING SHALL BE HIDDEN FROM ME!"

Krona, *Green Lantern* #40 (October 1965)

FOREWORD

It's all Krona's fault.

Looked at one way, Chronos, the ancient Greek god of time, was the beginning of Western civilization's preoccupation with the measurement of years, decades, and the passage of our days that has been our obsession ever since. Without Chronos, there would be no time, no time measurement, and no way to march through DC's history year by year.

Or looked at as a lexicographer might, we took from the Greek word "chronos" the root for our words that talk about time, and hence we have this chronicle, neatly divided into a chronology of DC's seventy-five years.

But to shift to a completely DC vernacular, the blame falls on Krona, not Chronos. Yes, there's a DC villain actually named Chronos, and there are brief appearances by the titan Cronus, but when you finish studying this volume, you'll know that Krona is the renegade immortal who unleashed evil into the DC Universe by daring to study the beginnings of time itself. And without the battle between good and evil, what stories would we have had to tell?

Such minutiae are the tiny building blocks of the complex mythology that DC's talented writers, artists, and contributors have built over seven decades, entertaining young and old alike in every medium of the imagination. From Malcolm Wheeler-Nicholson's daring concept of producing an original comic book instead of merely reprinting newspaper comics, a cascade of over 40,000 comics have flowed, and from them hundreds of hours of cartoons, radio and television shows, films, and live performances, each building on the prior contributors' work and adding new dimensions of their own. Our readers have been endlessly interested not simply in the tales we tell, but how they fit together, and how they have been created… all topics that will be amply touched upon in this mammoth volume. And if learning more about the chronicle of DC just whets your appetite for more stories and more information about what has gone on behind the scenes at this incredible creative factory, don't be surprised. I've had the good fortune to spend most of four decades in DC's halls, and the list of questions I still want to ask is far longer than the one whose answers I've learned. I only wish you have half the fun I've had as a reader, writer, editor, publisher—and once or twice, as a character in these stories.

Dive in: start with the year when you first discovered comics, or perhaps the year when you were twelve (sages have suggested that's our personal "Golden Age" of comics or other types of genre entertainment). Dig deeper to find the trails that led to the world you loved… or to the more recent comics that have sprung from the fertile ground seeded earlier. Or just close your eyes, flip the tome open at random, and welcome to the chronicle of DC's universe. I hope you never leave.

PAUL LEVITZ

INTRODUCTION

It's been a long time coming. For seventy-five years, DC Comics has been at the forefront of graphic art. For many, Superman's first appearance in the legendary *Action Comics* #1 in June 1938 signified the birth of super heroes. *DC Comics Year by Year: A Visual Chronicle* takes you from the very start of the company, before—if, for a moment, you can consider such a desolate world—Superman and Batman even existed, right up to the present day, when DC's comic books top best-seller lists all over the world, and their heroes and villains have become some of the most iconic characters of all time.

This book isn't just a brief history of America's greatest and longest running comic publisher; it's a month-by-month chronicle, charting the major (and minor) publications and events from seventy-five years of DC Comics. It covers the events of the Golden Age of comics (1938–1955), the Silver Age (1956–1969), and the Bronze Age (1970–1979), right on through to the Modern Age (1980–present). It travels from Earth-2 to Earth-1, to the Antimatter Universe and back again to provide a comprehensive record of the people and circumstances that have shaped the DC Universe.

DC Comics Year by Year also includes titles from companies that eventually became part of the DC family, from the *All Star Comics* of the 1940s through to Captain Marvel's first appearance in *Whiz Comics* #2 (February 1940), right up to the greatest moments of the WildStorm imprint, established in 1999. The articles are richly illustrated with covers and artwork and are set against a chronology of real-world events, allowing DC's seventy-five-year evolution to be charted in a historical context.

A team of top comic book historians and writers have been scouring comic shops, their collections, other people's collections, and the sacred DC vaults, to present *DC Comics Year by Year* to a waiting world. Whether it's the first appearance of Slam Bradley in *Detective Comics* #1 (March 1937); the trend for funny animal stories in *Real Screen Comics* #1 (Spring 1945); tales of heartbreak in *Romance Trail* (1949–1950); the debut of Ace the Bat-Hound (*Batman* #92, June 1955); or Morpheus' return to the Dreaming in *The Sandman* #1 (January 1989), all genres are covered, detailing not only a timeline of the world's greatest heroes but a chronicle of one of the most successful artforms of modern times.

Just a quick note about cover dates, though. It is all but impossible to pinpoint the release dates of early comics. They go back to a more innocent time when comics were sold on newsstands and in drugstores, when they would go on sale at least three (and sometimes four) months before the cover date. The cover date itself was originally to indicate to the vendor when unsold comics or magazines could be removed from shelves and sent back to the publisher. Although cover dates don't tell the whole story, they do act as a guide and offer a method for sequencing the books while maintaining continuity between various titles.

But that's just four-color semantics; the comic books themselves are the real stars of the show. So get ready for a trip through comic book history, from the Golden Age through to the present day. Just turn the page and you'll be… up, up, and away!

1930s

The Great Depression cast its long shadow across the economies of the world. In Germany, the century's most infamous dictator, Adolf Hitler, rose to power. Beset by economic hardship and the threat of world war, the public looked for distraction, for entertainment, for amusement.

Motion pictures, buoyed by the coming of sound, entered a golden age. Pulp magazines ruled printed entertainment and, with stars like the Shadow and the Phantom Detective, provided templates for the comic book super heroes to come. The pulps influenced artists such as Batman creator Bob Kane and employed future DC editors including Harry Donenfeld and Jack Schiff.

Science fiction also promised a brighter tomorrow. In Cleveland in 1932, Jerry Siegel and Joe Shuster launched *Science Fiction*, a mimeographed amateur magazine. The third issue featured a story titled "The Reign of the Superman," which told of a penniless joe who gained mental powers and tried to take over the world. Siegel and Shuster soon developed a more ambitious and imaginative take on the Superman character, styling him as the orphaned son of a distant world with abilities far beyond those of mortal men.

Meanwhile, the first comics were being born. In 1933, salesman M. C. Gaines of Eastern Color Printing realized that the broadsheet pages of Sunday newspaper comics could be folded into a more appealing and child-friendly size, roughly seven by ten inches. This resulted in the giveaway comic *Funnies on Parade*. *Famous Funnies* followed in 1934, with a cover price of ten cents.

As competitors jumped on the fast-rolling comics bandwagon, a retired cavalry officer named Major Malcolm Wheeler-Nicholson made the moves that would create DC Comics. A prolific pulp writer, he founded National Allied Publications in 1934 based on his faith in the new medium. The fledgling company would survive several stumbles before birthing twin legends in Superman and Batman at the close of the decade, heralding the Golden Age of Comics. After the 1930s, comics were here to stay.

"YOU NEEDN'T BE AFRAID OF ME. I WON'T HARM YOU."

Superman, *Action Comics* #1 (June 1938)

1935

"LAUGHTER IS THE UNIVERSAL ANTIDOTE FOR THE BLUES."

Promotional copy in *New Comics* #1

DC'S GENESIS

It all started here for DC Comics. Malcolm Wheeler-Nicholson, a former military officer and pulp writer, had founded National Allied Publishing in 1934 and in 1935 he launched the first-ever comic book devoted to new material: *New Fun*. Before *New Fun*, comic books reprinted popular newspaper comic strips, but Wheeler-Nicholson's tight budget meant he could not afford to purchase reproductions of the lucrative syndicated strips. So ironically, Wheeler-Nicholson was forced to allow original storytelling to flourish. In *New Fun*, the notion that writers and artists had a place to sell their wares inspired many dreamers, including two young creators from Cleveland: writer Jerry Siegel and artist Joe Shuster. After publishing four issues of *New Fun*, Wheeler-Nicholson packaged them into his first reprint book and added a second title, *New Comics*, to the National Allied lineup.

FEBRUARY

Disney lost the rights to Oswald the Lucky Rabbit to Universal, and responded by creating their own character—Mickey Mouse.

DAWN OF A DYNASTY
***New Fun* #1**

Wheeler-Nicholson's National Allied Publications planted its flag on the emerging comics scene with the release of *New Fun*. Subtitled "The Big Comic Magazine," it was literally larger than its competition, measuring in at a tabloid-sized 10 × 15 inches (25.4 × 38.1 cm). *New Fun* even had comics on its cover, with the first issue's twelve panels introducing readers to the cowboy heroics of Jack Woods.

Although Wheeler-Nicholson was hoping to compete with 1934's trailblazing *Famous Funnies* (published by Eastern Color Printing), he started off at a steep disadvantage. Not only was *Famous Funnies* full-color throughout, but it had already locked up the rights to reprint some of the most popular comic strips from the nation's newspapers, like "Mutt & Jeff" and "Dixie Dugan." *New Fun* began with black-and-white interior pages and a heavy reliance on new material. The inability to license surefire hits didn't help at the outset, but it did make *New Fun* a pioneer at supplying original content—a critical template to follow as the industry began to mature out of the repackaging and reprinting business.

The features in *New Fun* #1 ran the gamut from humor ("Caveman Capers") to literature ("Ivanhoe") to spy intrigue ("Sandra of the Secret Service"). Among the few licensed characters to appear in the title was Universal Pictures' Oswald the Lucky Rabbit, co-created by a young Walt Disney in the 1920s. The comic also carried advertising, another unusual move for the time. In its original, historic incarnation, *New Fun* lasted for six issues, and incorporated a few interior color pages starting with issue #3.

IN THE REAL WORLD...

January: Elvis Presley is born in Tupelo, Mississippi.
February: Airplanes are banned from flying over the White House.

OCTOBER

TWO NEW FACES

***New Fun* #6**
Two new characters, Henri Duval and Dr. Occult, debuted in *New Fun* #6—yet neither would prove to be as important as the writer and artist team who put them on the page in the first place. Writer Jerry Siegel and artist Joe Shuster had finally succeeded in breaking into the comics industry.

New Fun only published original material and Malcolm Wheeler-Nicholson needed a fresh supply of talent. While Henri Duval wasn't exactly Superman (for whom Siegel and Shuster had received a host of rejections), the team's work was finally being published. The Siegel and Shuster byline framed "Henri Duval, Famed Soldier of Fortune," but on "Dr. Occult, the Ghost Detective" the two adopted the pseudonyms of Leger and Reuths. The swashbuckling musketeer Duval didn't cut a memorable figure and only lasted four installments. However, Dr. Occult, whose mystic powers were limited only by the writer's imagination, proved to have a little more life. In his first outing, Dr. Occult rescued a victim from a vampire by means of a potent talisman.

Dr. Occult, the Ghost Detective uses a mystic symbol to defeat a vampire and rescue a damsel in distress.

NOVEMBER

DON'T MISS THE FUN
The Big Book of Fun Comics
The experiment that was *New Fun* had not yet imploded, so Wheeler-Nicholson sought to expand his readership while minimizing the costs needed to secure writers and artists for original material. The result was *The Big Book of Fun Comics*, a standalone, forty-eight-page reprint of *New Fun* #1–4 with a cardboard cover. The special comic was advertised in regular issues of *New Fun*, though the idea of an "annual" consisting of reprinted material did not survive this first installment.

DECEMBER

WHEELER-NICHOLSON DOUBLES DOWN

***New Comics* #1**
With *New Fun* already out on newsstands, Wheeler-Nicholson didn't waste any time in adding a second title to his line. *New Comics* appeared in a smaller format than *New Fun*, one that was similar in size to what are now considered standard comic book dimensions.

Featuring a cover by Vin Sullivan, *New Comics*' varied features included the humor offerings "Sir Loin of Beef" and "Jibby Jones," alongside adventure outings "Gulliver's Travels" and "17-20 on the Black." While this particular title was in fact destined for success (after evolving into *Adventure Comics* in November 1938 it remained in publication until September 1983), it was nevertheless a poor time for Wheeler-Nicholson to overextend himself, given his mounting debts.

"Jibby Jones" was a two-page humor feature within ***New Comics* #1**. Drawn by Vin Sullivan, the feature was largely visual and without dialog.

ALSO THIS YEAR: Harry Donenfeld, soon to play a key role in DC's history, headed up Culture Publications, home of the suggestive pulp magazines *SPICY DETECTIVE* and *SPICY MYSTERY STORIES*...

March: Porky Pig makes his debut in Looney Tunes' animated short *I Haven't Got a Hat*.
March: Hitler announces German rearmament in violation of the Treaty of Versailles.
September: Howard Hughes sets a world airspeed record of 352 mph (566 km/h).
November: Parker Brothers releases the board game Monopoly.

1936

"WHAT LOOKS BETTER TO YOU, KIDNAPPING OR A MURDER CHARGE? DO AS I SAY AND YOU'LL GET A LIGHT SENTENCE!"

Steve Carson, *New Comics* #2

FINDING A FOOTHOLD

Despite the world being in a brutal economic depression in 1936, Jesse Owens' performance at the Berlin Olympics proved that the real world had a place for heroes. Meanwhile, in popular culture, the Green Hornet and the Phantom defined the image of the costumed crime fighter. In comics, Malcolm Wheeler-Nicholson hoped to launch a new title, *Detective Comics*, but the need to secure funds for it forced the title into 1937. During this time, Whitney Ellsworth and Vin Sullivan worked for Wheeler-Nicholson as editors, with both occasionally taking on writer and artist duties. Other contributors included Jerry Siegel and Joe Shuster, who introduced "Federal Men" in *New Comics* and "Calling All Cars" in *More Fun Comics* while continuing the adventures of Henri Duval and Dr. Occult. They also continued to strike out in their efforts to sell Superman.

JANUARY

TOUGH GUYS FROM THE FBI
***New Comics* #2**

Amid the relentless bad news of the Great Depression, America had become fascinated with J. Edgar Hoover's FBI. Super heroes did not yet exist in comics, but the industry was casting about for reliable moneymakers, and adventurers and law-and-order types were beginning to make headway. In the second issue of *New Comics*, Jerry Siegel and Joe Shuster introduced "Federal Men," starring FBI agent Steve Carson, who investigated kidnappings and other federal crimes above the reach of local law enforcement. In subsequent issues, the feature spawned a Federal Men fan club for young readers called the Junior Federal Men.

FEBRUARY

ALL CHANGE
***More Fun* #8**

After only six issues, *New Fun* underwent a name change to *More Fun*, although it would only remain as such until issue #8. The change helped distinguish the comic from the recently launched *New Comics*, but it would finally gel as *More Fun Comics* with issue #9 in March. This final rechristening also coincided with a new slimmed-down size, which corresponded to what modern audiences would recognize as a standard comic book size.

JULY

COPS IN COMICS
***More Fun Comics* #11**

Increasingly prolific contributors Jerry Siegel and Joe Shuster used this issue to launch their latest feature, "Calling All Cars." Their two-page tale introduced police officer Sandy Kean, who drove a police car equipped with a radio—a noteworthy occurrence. The feature was later renamed "Radio Squad," and it is likely that Siegel was influenced by the newspaper comic strip "Radio Patrol," which dated from 1933. Also in this issue was an exhortation for young readers to join "the growing army of youngsters who are enrolling in the Worldwide Fun Club." Members were mailed a Fun Club button and given a secret password and countersign to identify fellow members.

IN THE REAL WORLD...

February: The first hero to wear a skin-tight costume and mask, the Phantom, makes his first appearance in U.S. newspapers.

NOVEMBER

SUPER-OCCULT?

***More Fun Comics* #15**

Jerry Siegel and Joe Shuster's mystic detective Dr. Occult began a multi-part storyline in this issue, in which the spell-caster donned a blue costume and red cape—an ensemble quite familiar to modern eyes. In addition, Occult exhibited super-strength and the ability to fly. The powers weren't necessarily far-fetched for a figure that could draw upon a limitless well of magic, but it was becoming increasingly obvious that Siegel and Shuster (still writing under the pseudonyms of Leger and Reuths on Dr. Occult features) were starting to incorporate elements from Superman, their still-unsold dream character.

DECEMBER

DETECTING A DETECTIVE

***New Comics* #11**

In the final pages of this issue, an advertisement hailed the launch of *Detective Comics*. "Just what you ordered!" blared the sales copy. "A high-stepping detective magazine in pictures!" Writers such as Tom Hickey, Sven Elven, and Bill Patrick—largely overlooked today—received top billing, while the up-and-coming writer and artist team of Jerry Siegel and Joe Shuster appeared in the listings almost as an afterthought. Interestingly, the ad's reproduction of *Detective Comics* #1's cover bore a "December 1936" date, but delays would shift the issue to March 1937—robbing Wheeler-Nicholson of the cross-promotion he obviously hoped to engender with the advertisement.

The morally dubious character Basyln appears in "The Blood Pearls," a story in *New Comics* #11.

Malcolm Wheeler-Nicholson didn't know if his new title would find an audience.

A giant robot attacks New York City in *New Comics* #10's (November) "Federal Men" feature, as writer Jerry Siegel and artist Joe Shuster begin to indulge their sci-fi cravings.

ALSO THIS YEAR: Masked hero the Green Hornet made a splash with a popular radio program, exhibiting soon-to-be super hero staples such as a secret identity and a sidekick... Jungle crime fighter the Phantom debuted in newspapers across the country, wearing tights and a mask that would partially inspire the design of Bob Kane's Batman...

July: The Spanish Civil War begins when Nationalist troops under the command of General Francisco Franco rise against the existing Republican government.

August: The 1936 Summer Olympics open in Berlin, Germany, and mark the first live television coverage of a sports event in world history.

1937

"KNIVES FLASH! FISTS FLY! ALTHO' OUTNUMBERED, SLAM IS HAVING A SWELL TIME!"

From Slam Bradley, *Detective Comics* #1

CHANGE IN OWNERSHIP

Malcolm Wheeler-Nicholson's bold entry into the comics market continued to meet mixed results. *New Comics* and *More Fun Comics* hadn't yet found a consistent audience in the emerging industry, and Wheeler-Nicholson's desire to launch a third title forced him to face the reality of finding a partner with deeper pockets. His distributor, Harry Donenfeld, had by 1937 agreed to go into business with him for the release of *Detective Comics*, and together with Donenfeld's business advisor Jack Liebowitz they founded Detective Comics, Inc. The company's initials, emblazoned on the covers of all its comics by 1940, made everyone aware of the DC brand. However, Wheeler-Nicholson didn't remain a part of Detective Comics, Inc. for long. Money issues forced him out by the end of the year, and Donenfeld and Liebowitz moved to secure his assets.

CHARTING A NEW COURSE

***New Adventure Comics* #12**
New Comics received a makeover with issue #12, becoming *New Adventure Comics*, its symbolic cover featuring a fresh-faced Baby 1937 ushering out Father Time's past relics. While still stuffed with short humor strips, including "Hard Luck Harry," *New Adventure Comics* increasingly emphasized action in faraway lands through such features as "Castaway Island" and "The Vikings."

Rounding out issue #12 was another installment of "Federal Men," though readers could have been forgiven for puzzling over its bizarre sci-fi twist. Unapologetic science-fiction fans writer Jerry Siegel and artist Joe Shuster had shoehorned in a professor who explained the "future of scientific crime detection." This framing device gave the two a license to delve deep into their favorite obsession, telling a tale set in the year 3000 that involved ray guns, rocket ships, and star pirates. It also starred an "ace sleuth" named Jor-L (a name later to be recycled as that of Superman's father).

The sci-fi characters in this story closely resemble the robot-building scientists from Siegel and Shuster's "Federal Men" tale in *New Comics* #10 (November 1936).

Interplanetary investigator Jor-L is held at ray-gunpoint by the Bandit Queen in the year 3000 CE.

IN THE REAL WORLD...

February: The first successful flying car, Waldo Waterman's Aerobile, makes its initial flight.

MARCH

IT ALL STARTS HERE

***Detective Comics* #1**

The launch of *Detective Comics* defined Wheeler-Nicholson's young comics company and set it on an ascendant path within the industry. Unfortunately, cash flow problems meant that Wheeler-Nicholson wasn't able to enjoy it for long. However, his smart decision to partner with businessmen Harry Donenfeld and Jack Liebowitz on *Detective Comics* guaranteed that his company's third title would at least be solvent, and the editorial decision to have all the stories revolve around a single theme helped distinguish it from its newsstand competition.

Issue #1 featured a striking cover by Vin Sullivan and several action-mystery stories that used Chinese stock villains, including Wheeler-Nicholson's own feature, "The Claws of the Red Dragon." Minor DC character Speed Saunders made his first appearance in the issue as a special operative of the harbor police. But *Detective Comics* #1 is most notable for the debut of two new features from the young writer/artist team of Jerry Siegel and Joe Shuster: "Bart Regan, Spy" and, particularly, "Slam Bradley." Slam was a muscle-bound scrapper and freelance police investigator capable of hoisting his enemies and using them as baseball bats to knock down even more thugs. His huge strength and gruff attitude were lightened somewhat by the addition of his comic sidekick, Shorty. The powerful, dark-haired Slam bore some resemblance to the character that would later become the Man of Steel, and Siegel admitted that the Slam Bradley feature included "some of the impact we'd planned to use later in Superman." By this point the pair had seen such little interest in their pet project that Siegel may have been willing to strip the concept for usable parts. With its mix of energetic offerings *Detective Comics* was a hit, and has remained in continuous publication ever since.

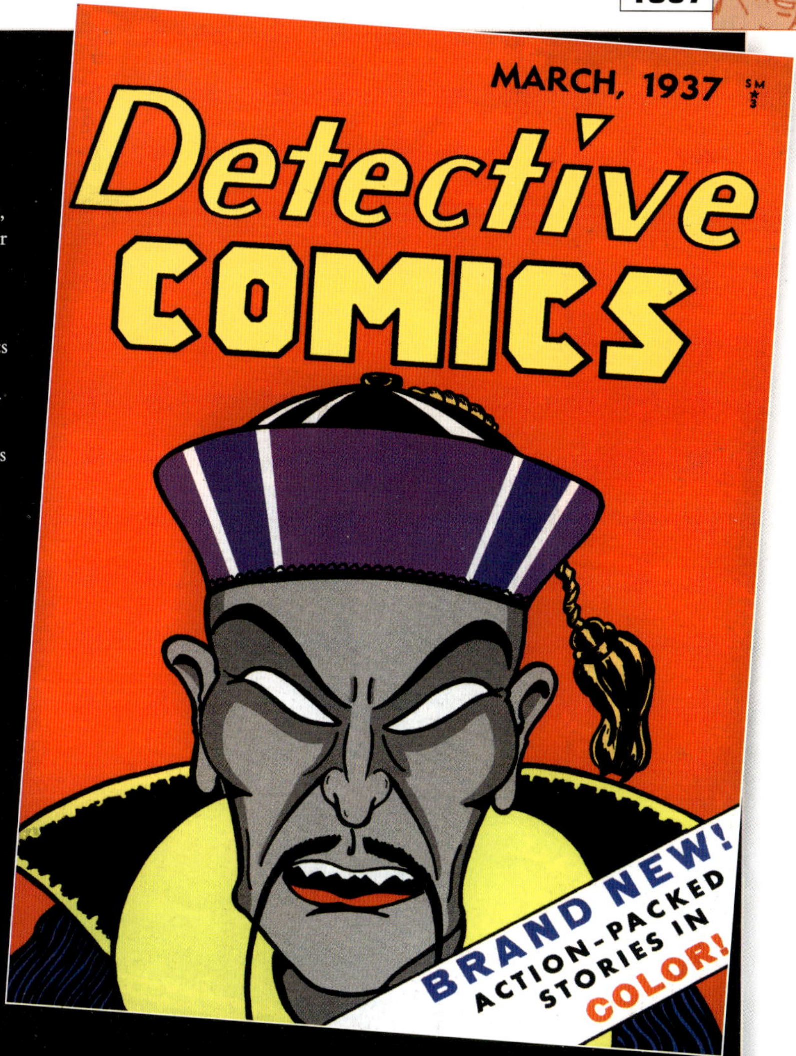

Cyril Saunders, better known by his nickname "Speed," is a federal agent assigned to the harbor police force.

Disguised as an army officer, secret agent Bart Regan takes an opportunity to use his spy skills so he can get closer to a beautiful foreign agent.

Slam Bradley, a handsome and well-built freelance police investigator, saves the wealthy heiress Rita Carlisle from Chinese crooks in his first adventure.

ALSO THIS YEAR: *DETECTIVE COMICS* #2 in April emphasized Slam Bradley, perhaps recognizing two rising stars in writer and artist team Jerry Siegel and Joe Shuster... Jerry Siegel continued selling his "Superman" concept, pitching it for *TIP TOP COMICS*, published by United Features Syndicate, but racked up yet another rejection...

March: William Henry Hastie becomes the first African-American federal judge.
June: Wallis Simpson marries the former Edward VIII of the United Kingdom.
September: George Allen & Unwin, Ltd. of London publishes the first edition of J. R. R. Tolkien's *The Hobbit*.

NATIONAL HEROES

NEW FUN #5 (August 1935)
This panel shows the Super Police setting the world of 2023 to rights. *New Fun*, which also starred characters such as Sandra of the Secret Service, Oswald the Rabbit, and Buckskin Jim, was National Allied Publications' first title.

LUCKY WE STILL HAVE OUR HELMETS ON!!

1938

"SUPERMAN! CHAMPION OF THE OPPRESSED—THE PHYSICAL MARVEL WHO HAS SWORN TO DEVOTE HIS EXISTENCE TO HELPING THOSE IN NEED!"

Superman's introduction, *Action Comics* #1

SAY HELLO TO SUPERMAN

The comics business was struggling to survive, but Jack Liebowitz had a premonition that comic books had untapped potential. "I had a feel for it, that it was a good field," he said. When Malcolm Wheeler-Nicholson went bankrupt, Leibowitz and business partner Harry Donenfeld acquired his share of the company on behalf of Detective Comics, Inc. They purchased *More Fun Comics* and *New Adventure Comics*, bringing the company's total to three (with *Detective Comics*). Another change at the company was the departure of Whitney Ellsworth, which left Vin Sullivan as sole editor.

The industry needed a hero, and Superman arrived at just the right time. With the launch of *Action Comics*, Jerry Siegel and Joe Shuster finally saw their brainchild in print, and readers responded with rave reviews. Superman became the first comic book megastar and proved that comics were more than a fad. The Golden Age of Comics was born.

JUNE

BIRTH OF THE SUPER HERO

***Action Comics* #1**

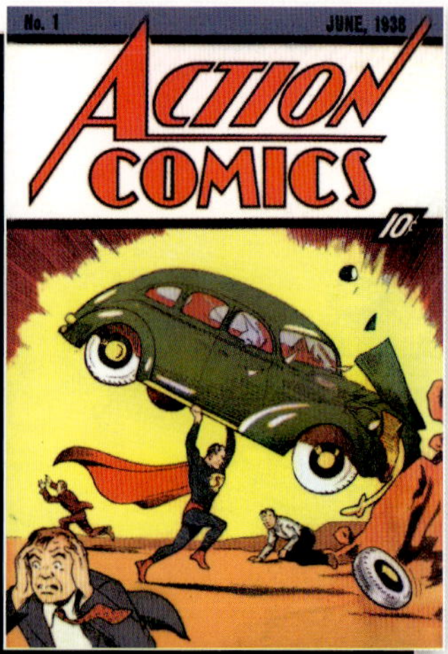

DC launched its fourth title, *Action Comics*, in the summer. Joining *More Fun Comics*, *New Adventure Comics*, and *Detective Comics*, the new title supplied exciting stories that lived up to the promise of its name. And while the exploits of manly adventurers such as Chuck Dawson, Scoop Scanlon, and Pep Morgan may have seemed like a safe bet to snag readers, it was the lead feature, "Superman," that proved to be something special.

"All this time we really felt that we had something that was very different, something that the public would really take to its heart," said Superman writer Jerry Siegel who, together with artist Joe Shuster, finally put their favorite character in the hands of readers. It was editor Sheldon Mayer, working at M. C. Gaines' McClure Syndicate, who suggested Superman to DC as a potential filler feature for *Action Comics*.

The first story included a short introduction in which Superman was described as able to "leap ⅛th of a mile, hurdle a twenty-story building, raise tremendous weights, [and] run faster than an express train." He was also blessed with such invincibility that "nothing less than a bursting shell could penetrate his skin." The planet Krypton was seen but not named, and Clark Kent worked as a reporter for the *Daily Star* (the *Daily Planet* wouldn't appear until November 1940, in *Superman* #7). Reporter Lois Lane was established, chasing a Superman story, but she rejected Clark as a "spineless, unbearable coward." The story ended with the prophetic signoff: "And so begins the adventures of the most sensational strip character of all time." Of this, Siegel said "That may sound a little conceited, but actually, that's the way we felt about the character."

Superman takes an opportunity to demonstrate his super-strength when he tackles a villain to save a woman from execution.

IN THE REAL WORLD...

March: The *Anschluss*: German troops occupy Austria and annexation is declared the following day.

JULY

SUPERMAN'S SECOND STEP

***Action Comics* #2**

Superman was missing in action on the cover of *Action Comics*' second issue, a sign that editor Vin Sullivan never expected the new character to become a blockbuster right out of the gate. Another curiosity within the issue was an instance in which Clark Kent mailed a packet of photos taken in a warzone directly to the "Evening News, Cleveland Ohio." Because Clark and Lois had already been established as colleagues at the *Daily Star*, this reference was an apparent tip of the hat by Cleveland natives Jerry Siegel and Joe Shuster to their hometown newspaper. Elsewhere, super hero Tex Thompson took a bizarre turn, gaining a comic sidekick and battling an Asian Cyclops.

OCTOBER

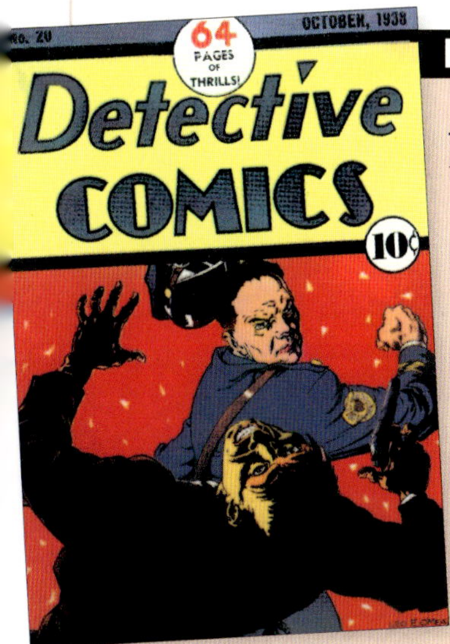

MASKED JUSTICE

***Detective Comics* #20**

Alongside more typical fare like "Larry Steele, Private Detective" came the debut of the Crimson Avenger, the first masked crime fighter in comics. Not exactly a super hero, this befriender of the helpless from writer/artist Jim Chambers wore a heavy overcoat, head-topping fedora, and a simple domino mask, and carried a gas gun. But like Superman, the Crimson Avenger had a secret identity—that of newspaperman Lee Travis, who used his position to get the latest scoops, following up on those that required a bit of vigilante justice. The character also shared some similarities with popular 1930s radio star the Green Hornet, including an Asian sidekick named Wing (mirroring the Green Hornet's Kato) and a fast car. The Crimson Avenger earned modest popularity among readers, taking over the cover on *Detective Comics* #22 in December. He reappeared in the comic on a semi-permanent basis until the mid-1940s, and became a founding member of the Seven Soldiers of Victory.

Armed with a gas gun, Lee Travis as the Crimson Avenger confronts a crooked district attorney to expose his underhanded deals.

NOVEMBER

A LASTING CHANGE

***Adventure Comics* #32**

DC's second-oldest series, which began as *New Comics* and then became *New Adventure Comics*, underwent a third name change—but this one stuck. The first installment of *Adventure Comics* included a mix of features, including humor offerings (Don Coyote, Professor Doolittle) and now-forgotten action heroes (Tom Brent, Dale Daring) alongside Hollywood gossip, brainteasers, and sports tips. But the work of emerging creators could still be seen in its pages, including Siegel and Shuster's "Federal Men" and Bill Finger and Bob Kane's "Rusty and His Pals."

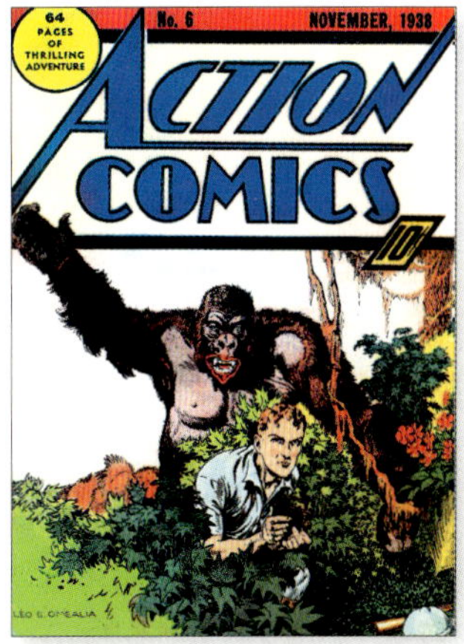

JIMMY OLSEN'S QUIET ENTRANCE

***Action Comics* #6**

The Man of Steel's future pal Jimmy Olsen made his first appearance within this issue of *Action Comics*, although he was identified only as an "inquisitive office-boy." Though lacking red hair, other elements of the character that would become Jimmy Olsen were already in place, including his tenacious curiosity and his trademark bow tie. The same story also predicted Superman's popularity as the subject of spin-off merchandise. A greedy promoter released a range of products (including an automobile called the "Superman streamline special") all apparently endorsed by the Man of Steel, before Superman revealed the deception.

The bow tie is the only immediately recognizable element, but this office boy soon became the familiar Jimmy Olsen.

ALSO THIS YEAR: ***MORE FUN COMICS* #31 in May featured an ad depicting the iconic cover of the upcoming *ACTION COMICS* #1, making this Superman's first appearance in print... June's *ACTION COMICS* #1 saw the debut of the top-hatted magician Zatara and the Western-themed Tex Thompson (who later adopted the costumed identities of both Mister America and the Americommando)...**

July: Howard Hughes sets a new record by completing a ninety-one-hour airplane flight around the world.

October: Orson Welles' radio adaptation of *The War of the Worlds* is broadcast, causing panic in various parts of the United States.

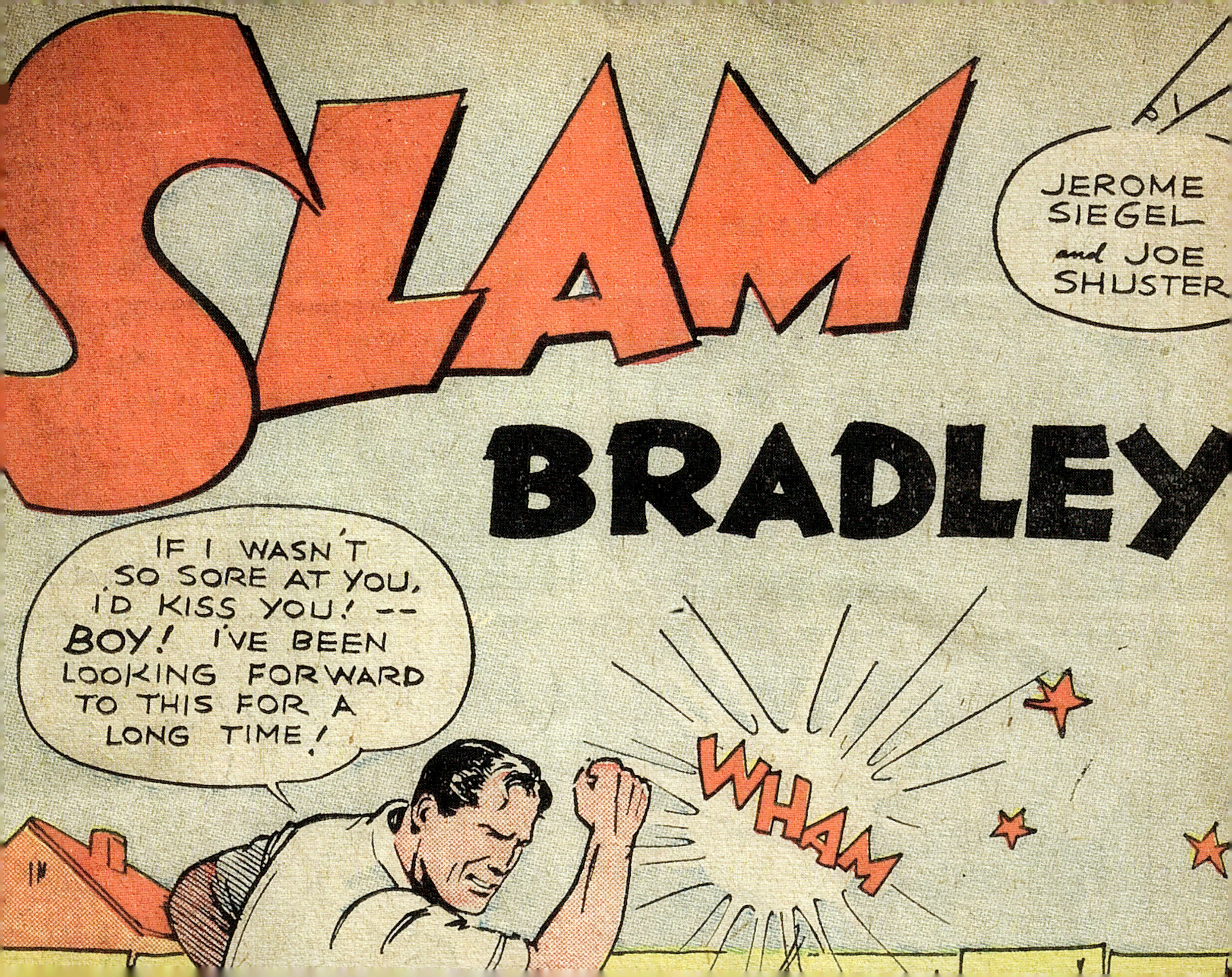
SLAM BRADLEY
BY JEROME SIEGEL and JOE SHUSTER
IF I WASN'T SO SORE AT YOU, I'D KISS YOU! -- BOY! I'VE BEEN LOOKING FORWARD TO THIS FOR A LONG TIME!
WHAM

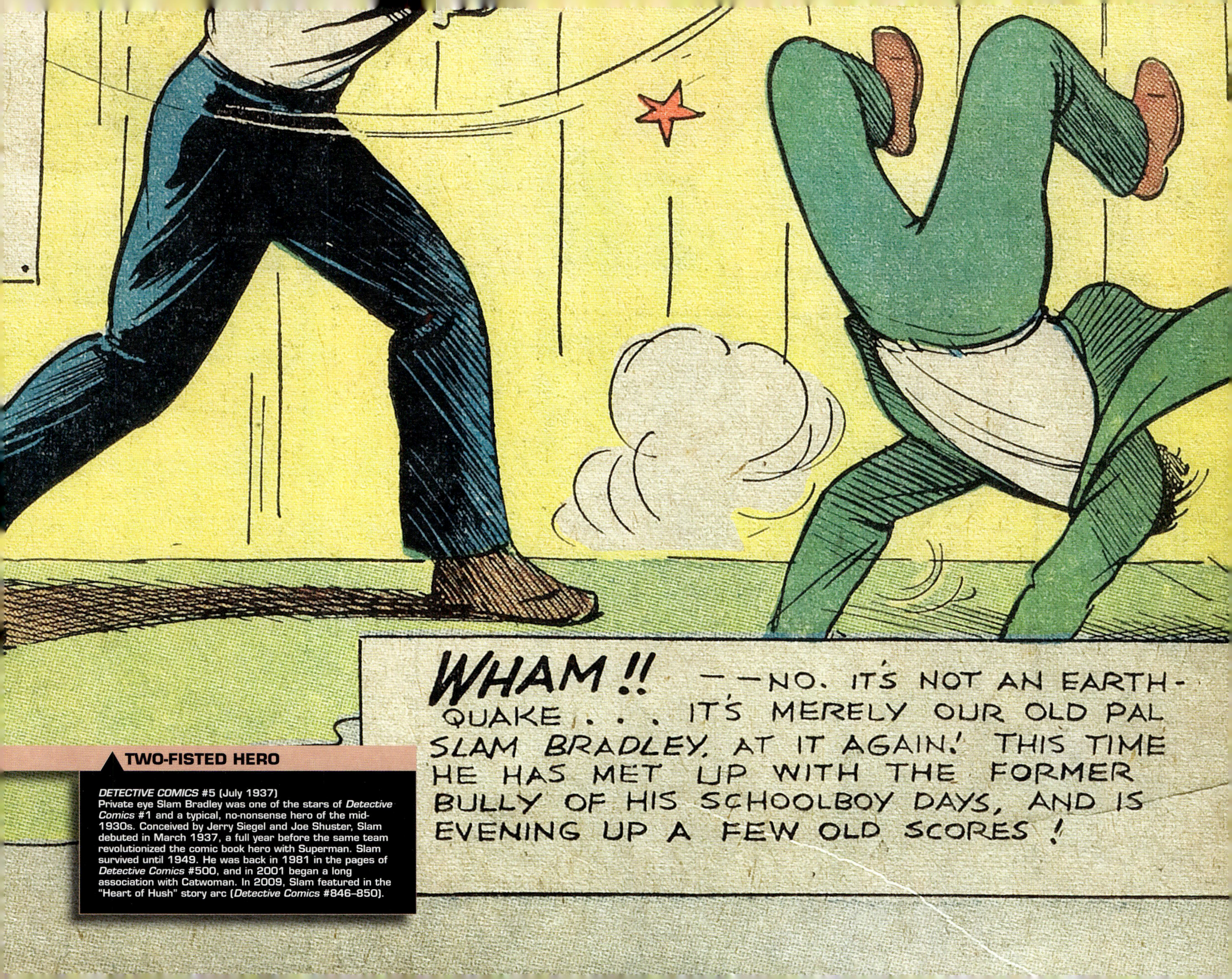

TWO-FISTED HERO

DETECTIVE COMICS #5 (July 1937)
Private eye Slam Bradley was one of the stars of *Detective Comics* #1 and a typical, no-nonsense hero of the mid-1930s. Conceived by Jerry Siegel and Joe Shuster, Slam debuted in March 1937, a full year before the same team revolutionized the comic book hero with Superman. Slam survived until 1949. He was back in 1981 in the pages of *Detective Comics* #500, and in 2001 began a long association with Catwoman. In 2009, Slam featured in the "Heart of Hush" story arc (*Detective Comics* #846–850).

1939

"I MUST BE A CREATURE OF THE NIGHT. BLACK, TERRIBLE... A BAT!"

Batman, *Detective Comics* #33

DARK KNIGHT'S DEBUT

Emboldened by the runaway success of Superman, DC business manager Jack Liebowitz partnered with publisher M. C. Gaines (who brought with him his sharp young editor, Sheldon Mayer) to launch a new line of comics under the All American Publications banner. All American existed side-by-side with DC, the two companies enjoying a friendly relationship that eventually extended to sharing characters among their titles.

The Golden Age was now in full swing as *All-American Comics*, *Movie Comics*, and *Mutt & Jeff* hit newsstands from All American. Over at DC, Superman got a solo series and moved into newspapers, but the year's biggest news was editor Vin Sullivan's acquisition of writer Bill Finger and artist Bob Kane's new hero—a masked vigilante called the Batman. "It seemed like an interesting character," said Sullivan. "I don't think anybody realized that it would develop into what it has become today."

JANUARY

IN NEWSPAPERS THIS MONTH: The "SUPERMAN" newspaper strip is launched, featuring the Man of Steel's first complete origin, years after Siegel and Shuster had tried and failed to drum up interest...

APRIL

A LAUNCH AND A GAMBLE
***All-American Comics* #1**

All American Publications, DC's sister company owned by Jack Liebowitz and M. C. Gaines, announced itself with the debut issue of *All-American Comics*. Edited by Sheldon Mayer, the title contained newspaper reprints and puzzle pages alongside original material such as Mayer's own "Scribbly," the semi-autobiographical adventures of a boy cartoonist. The features "Hop Harrigan" and "Red, White, and Blue" also debuted in this issue.

MAY

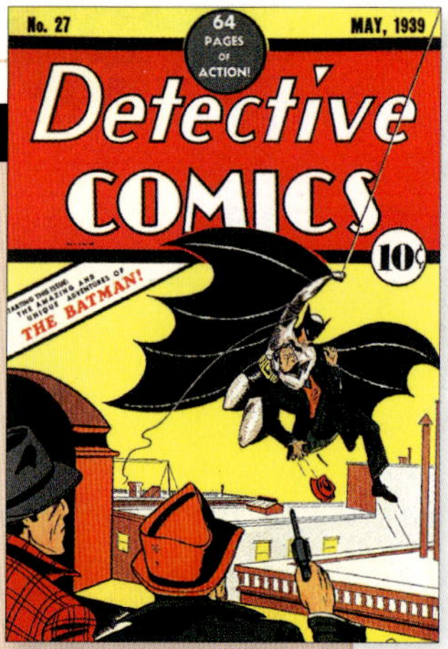

THE DEBUT OF BATMAN

***Detective Comics* #27**

DC's second superstar debuted in the lead story of this issue, written by Bill Finger and drawn by Bob Kane, though the character was missing many of the elements that would make him a legend, such as the Batmobile. However, even as a work in progress Batman possessed an iconic power, with a costume the color of shadow, a distinctive silhouette marked by triangular "bat ears," and blank slits in place of his eyes.

Introduced in his civilian identity as bored socialite Bruce Wayne, Batman demonstrated a ruthless streak, and dispatched thugs with grim satisfaction. ("A fitting end for his kind," he announced, after punching a crook into a vat of acid.) Police Commissioner Gordon was the only member of Batman's supporting cast to appear in his debut. Writer Gardner Fox took over from Finger for a few subsequent installments of the feature and introduced such gadgets as the Batarang and the Batgyro (a helicopter/airplane hybrid).

Dodging a gunshot, the Batman punches murderous chemical-company worker Alfred Stryker (the first criminal to face the wrath of the Batman) and sends him flying into an acid tank.

IN THE REAL WORLD...

June: In Bombay, Mohandas Gandhi begins to fast in protest against the autocratic rule in India.

JUNE

THE MAN OF STEEL HAS MADE IT

***Superman* #1**

Superman's runaway popularity as part of *Action Comics* earned him his own comic. This was a real breakthrough for the time, as characters introduced in comic books had never before been so successful as to warrant their own titles.

Issue #1 was a curious combination of original material and reprints from *Action Comics*, opening with an expanded origin tale that established Clark's adoptive parents as Mary and Jonathan Kent, good-hearted Earthlings who found his space capsule, turned him over to an orphanage, and later adopted him. Jonathan Kent instructed his son to use his powers "to assist humanity" before he and his wife died, establishing Superman's motivation to look out for the little guy. In the issue's second tale, writer Jerry Siegel and artist Joe Shuster told how Clark got his job at the *Daily Star* newspaper. After Clark's initial job application to the *Daily Star* was rejected, Superman stopped a lynching and Clark called the newspaper with the story. Superman then nabbed the real culprit of the murder that sparked the lynching and dropped mid-story into a reprint of the opening tale from *Action Comics* #1 (June 1938).

The issue's remaining content included familiar tales from *Action Comics* #2–4 (July–September 1938), as well as a two-page prose story (to benefit from a lower postage rate permitted for periodicals with literary merit). Not missing a single opportunity to cross-promote, *Superman* #1 came packed with plugs for *Action Comics* and the "Superman" newspaper strip, as well as an ad that urged all "red-blooded young Americans" to join the Supermen of America and receive a membership certificate, a button, and a secret code to decrypt messages directly from Superman. A "Meet the Creators" feature closed out the fun, with photos and biographies of Siegel and Shuster.

In only a few panels, *Superman* #1 recapped Superman's extraterrestrial origins, his stint in an orphanage, and his amazing abilities. Superman's history had originally been told in *Action Comics*.

JUNE

COMICS SAMPLER

***New York World's Fair Comics* #1**

Superman came to life at the New York World's Fair after DC hired actor Ray Middleton to wear a costume for personal appearances. Fans visiting the fair could also snap up a ninety-six-page comic, bound in a cover featuring Superman, for the low price of twenty-five cents. The Man of Steel was the obvious hook, but DC undoubtedly hoped to attract new readers by providing a variety of features from its full array of comics. Features included stars Slam Bradley, Zatara, and Scoop Scanlon, and the issue also housed the first appearance of the Sandman, who moved to *Adventure Comics* for issue #40 the following month.

Superman's growing popularity saw him starring in multiple titles, with *World's Fair Comics* joining Superman's regular titles, *Action Comics* and *Superman*.

SUPERMAN'S FIRST FLIGHT

***Action Comics* #13**

Superman was presented with his first opportunity to demonstrate true flight in *Action Comics* #13. It was a brilliant but paralyzed scientist named the Ultra-Humanite who gave him that opportunity on his debut appearance. The head of a "vast ring of evil enterprises," the Ultra-Humanite tried to dispose of Superman with a rotating saw. The blade shattered on contact with the Man of Steel's skin and the villain fled in an airplane, whereupon Superman leapt into the sky, colliding with the fleeing aircraft and bringing the Ultra-Humanite down in flames.

ALSO THIS YEAR: Writer Gardner Fox and artist Bert Christman established the gas-masked and trench-coated Sandman in *ADVENTURE COMICS* #40 in July, marking the start of his long comics career... The premier issue of *MUTT & JEFF*, released by All American Publications in Summer, gave artist Bud Fisher's popular newspaper characters their own series... In November's *DETECTIVE COMICS* #33, a two-page story titled "The Batman and How He Came to Be" recounted the Dark Knight's tragic origin... Superman gained a new power in November's *ACTION COMICS* #18 and it would come to be one of his most famous—X-ray vision...

September: A German battleship opens bombardment on a Polish military base, firing what are, according to many sources, the first shots of World War II.

December: The movie *Gone with the Wind*, starring Vivien Leigh and Clark Gable, premieres at Loew's Grand Theater in Atlanta, Georgia.

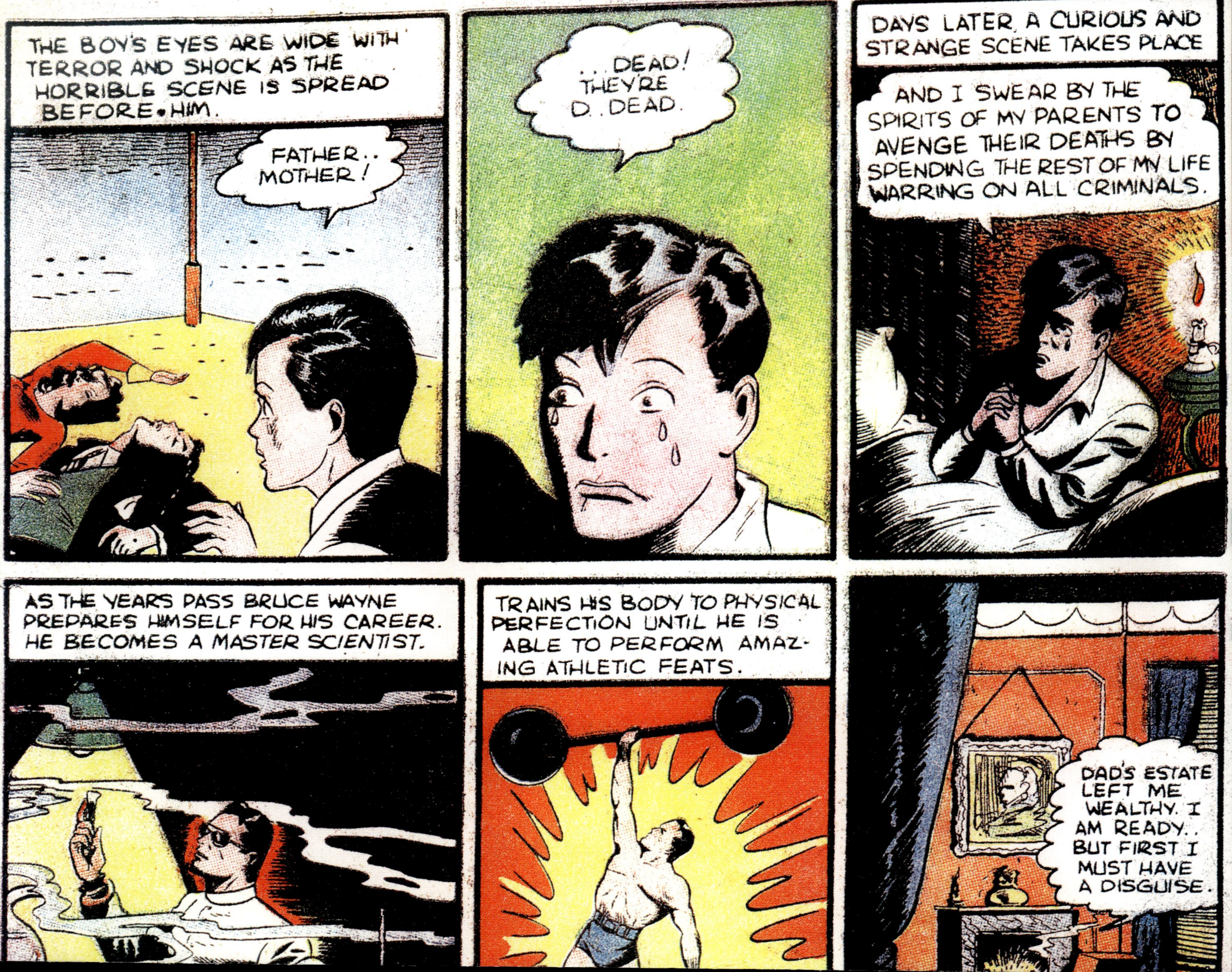
THE BOY'S EYES ARE WIDE WITH TERROR AND SHOCK AS THE HORRIBLE SCENE IS SPREAD BEFORE HIM.
FATHER.. MOTHER!
...DEAD! THEY'RE D..DEAD.
DAYS LATER A CURIOUS AND STRANGE SCENE TAKES PLACE
AND I SWEAR BY THE SPIRITS OF MY PARENTS TO AVENGE THEIR DEATHS BY SPENDING THE REST OF MY LIFE WARRING ON ALL CRIMINALS.
AS THE YEARS PASS BRUCE WAYNE PREPARES HIMSELF FOR HIS CAREER. HE BECOMES A MASTER SCIENTIST.
TRAINS HIS BODY TO PHYSICAL PERFECTION UNTIL HE IS ABLE TO PERFORM AMAZING ATHLETIC FEATS.
DAD'S ESTATE LEFT ME WEALTHY. I AM READY.. BUT FIRST I MUST HAVE A DISGUISE.

BIRTH OF THE BATMAN

DETECTIVE COMICS #33 (November 1939)
Batman's tragic origin story, in which a mugger guns down Bruce Wayne's parents as the family walks home from a movie, gave the new hero depth and motivation for his crusade against crime. This first version of a tale that has been retold many times introduced a story titled "The Batman Wars Against the Dirigible of Doom."

1940s

THE 1940S BEGAN with a world at war and ended with the promise of peace. On the battlefield and on the home front, a generation found its identity in the tumultuous events of World War II. The discovery of atomic energy created a sense of unease, promising futuristic wonders even as it threatened the annihilation of entire cities.

The popular culture of the 1940s reflected the reality of global conflict. Every radio program, movie serial, and newspaper strip offered an escapist outlet for the overworked factory laborer, but their plots often featured real-world Axis villains—as if fighting Hitler in the cinema might herald his defeat in Berlin.

Comic books followed suit as they entered their Golden Age. Riding high on a wave of popularity generated by the debuts of Superman and Batman, DC Comics matured from a publisher of standalone stories into the caretaker of a shared universe. The decade saw the introduction of heroes like Wonder Woman, Robin, and Aquaman, and the debuts of villains like Lex Luthor, the Joker, and Two-Face; the 1940s also made room for pioneering incarnations of Green Lantern and the Flash. Most DC super heroes used their fantastic abilities to aid the war effort by fighting Nazi spies and Japanese saboteurs.

The super hero boom became a mixed blessing for DC. It attracted tough competition as rivals pushed characters like the Sub-Mariner and Captain America, and wartime rationing reduced the availability of the paper used to print the super heroes' colorful adventures. During the decade's latter half, DC moved away from costumed heroes in an effort to find the next big thing. Comic books with romance, western, teen humor, crime, and funny animal themes appeared, meeting with mixed success on the newsstands. The Golden Age of super hero comics was beginning to near its end, but the world-building achieved during the 1940s paved the way for a heroic Silver Age resurgence in the following decade.

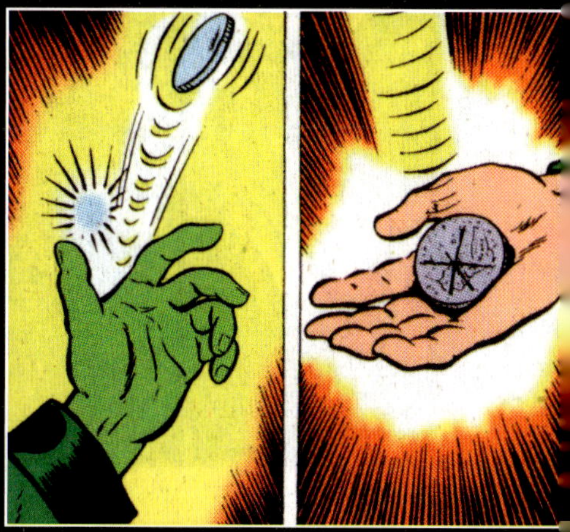

"A COIN SPINS HIGH... DROPS INTO A PALM..."

Two-Face, "Half Man Half Monster," newspaper comic strip (June 1946)

1940

"THEY CAN'T KEEP ME HERE! THE JOKER WILL YET HAVE THE LAST LAUGH!"

The Joker plans his escape from prison, *Batman* #1

EXPLOSION OF CHARACTERS

Superman and Batman were now established as DC's cornerstone characters, but 1940 was the year that the company birthed an entire universe. Batman became more than a grim vigilante with the humanizing addition of Robin, and the Joker and Catwoman set the tone for the bizarre villains that would come to populate Gotham City. Superman gained his own arch-nemesis in Lex Luthor and added a successful radio program to his list of achievements. With the departure of Vin Sullivan, Whitney Ellsworth returned to DC as editor and oversaw an explosion of creative energy. New characters included the Flash, the Red Tornado, Hawkman, Green Lantern, Doctor Fate, Hourman, the Atom, and the Spectre, and the inauguration of the Justice Society of America proved that these fresh faces could share the same space.

JANUARY

TRIPLE THREAT

***Flash Comics* #1**

DC shattered the sound barrier with the debut of the Flash, a blindingly fast mystery man written by Gardner Fox and drawn by Harry Lampert. University researcher Jay Garrick gained amazing speed after inhaling the vapors of "hard water," and donned a costume featuring a winged helmet inspired by the god Mercury. Unlike most super heroes, Jay revealed his secret identity to his girlfriend, Joan Williams.

In the same issue Gardner Fox wrote the first story featuring Hawkman, who wore a hawk's-head helmet and a winged harness that allowed him to fly. In a story drawn by Dennis Neville, antiquities collector Carter Hall realized he was the reincarnation of Prince Khufu of ancient Egypt, and located the modern-day resurrection of his lost love Shiera while fighting his nemesis, Hath-Set.

Flash Comics scored a third hit with Johnny Thunder, star of a humorous feature about a boy raised in the distant land of Badhnisia and blessed with the ability to raise an all-powerful, genie-like Thunderbolt upon saying the words "Cei-U." Because the phrase sounded similar to "Say, you" in English, the dim-witted but good-natured Johnny Thunder often accidentally summoned the Thunderbolt to comic effect.

After he is exposed to exotic fumes in a chemical accident, Jay Garrick gains the power of super-speed. He first shows off his new power on a football field before assuming the identity of the Flash.

FEBRUARY

GANGWAY FOR CAPTAIN MARVEL!

***Whiz Comics* #2**

Fawcett Publications brought in its own rival to Superman with issue #2 of *Whiz Comics* (issue #1 was created for advertising solicitation and was never sold to the public). Distinctively drawn by C. C. Beck and written by Bill Parker, Captain Marvel was the super-heroic identity of young Billy Batson, who transformed into the red-garbed titan by shouting the magic word "Shazam!" Captain Marvel became an instant hit with the comics-buying public—and attracted the attention of DC's lawyers.

IN THE REAL WORLD...

February: Tom and Jerry make their debut in the one-reel animated cartoon *Puss Gets the Boot*.

THE SPECTRE SPEAKS
***More Fun Comics* #52**

Writer Jerry Siegel and artist Bernard Baily introduced a new hero in the form of the Spectre, a "supernatural being whose mission on Earth is to stamp out crime and enforce justice." When Detective Jim Corrigan crossed a mob boss, he found himself sealed in a cement-filled barrel and thrown off a pier. In the afterlife, Corrigan was granted the ability to return to Earth to avenge all wrongs. Later tales saw Corrigan assume the white-and-green appearance of the Spectre and demonstrate near-omnipotent powers of retribution.

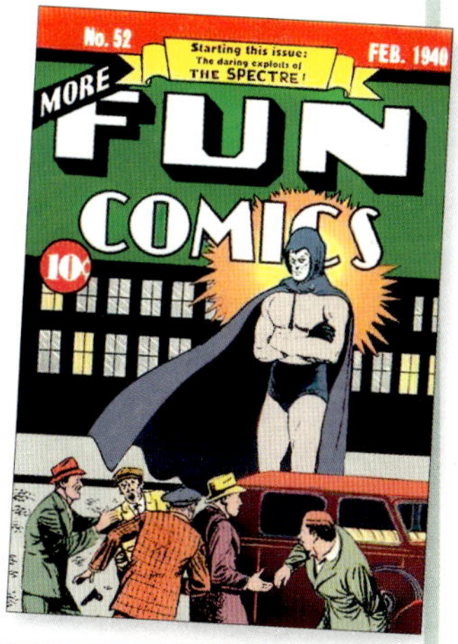

ON RADIO THIS MONTH: Superman moved on from comics and newspapers to conquer radio too, in *THE ADVENTURES OF SUPERMAN* radio show. Within its first few months, the radio show had popularized its famous intro: "Faster than a speeding bullet! More powerful than a locomotive! Able to leap tall buildings in a single bound! Look! Up in the sky! It's a bird! It's a plane! It's Superman!"...

APRIL

SUPERMAN MEETS HIS MATCH
***Action Comics* #23**

Superman had encountered few recurring villains, but the debut of the brilliant scientist known as Luthor was a sign of things to come. Not yet identified with the first name Lex—and with a head of red hair instead of his distinctive bald pate—Luthor nevertheless proved that his brains were more than a match for Superman's brawn in his first issue, written by Jerry Siegel and drawn by Joe Shuster. Luthor's scheme to manipulate a war between two countries ended with his apparent death in a crash, but the mad genius would soon be back to plot his revenge.

THE DYNAMIC DUO IS BORN
***Detective Comics* #38**

The cover said it all: "The sensational character-find of 1940.... Robin—the Boy Wonder!" Writer Bill Finger and artist Bob Kane justified any hyperbole in this issue, for with the introduction of Robin, Batman's world changed forever. Dick Grayson was a circus performer orphaned when gangster Boss Zucco murdered his parents, and Bruce Wayne—struck by the similarity to his own childhood tragedy—agreed to take the boy in as his ward. After training together to hone their combat and crime-fighting skills, Batman and Robin hit the streets and brought Zucco to justice.

SPRING

DANGEROUS FOES
***Batman* #1**

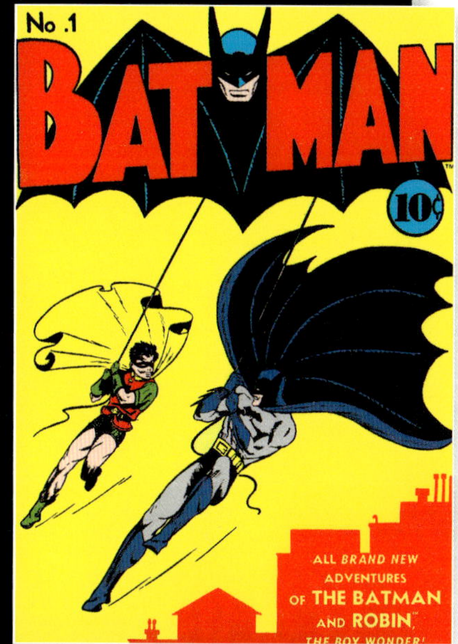

The first issue of Batman's self-titled comic, written by Bill Finger and drawn by Bob Kane, represented a milestone in more ways than one. With Robin now a partner to the Caped Crusader, villains needed to rise to the challenge, and this issue introduced two future legends: the Joker and Catwoman.

After a two-page recap of Batman's origin (taken from *Detective Comics* #33, December 1939), the Joker stalked onto the scene with his chalk-white face, leering grin, and trademark purple suit. Cheerfully murdering victims page after page, the Joker proved facile with a gun, a knife, and a unique poison that pulled the corners of each victim's mouth into a ghoulish death-rictus. Batman and Robin were able to put a stop to the Harlequin of Hate's rampage and put him behind bars, but he returned in a second story later in the same issue. After the Joker was stabbed in the heart, he delivered a mad, memorable farewell ("Ha ha ha! The Joker is going to die! Laugh, clown, laugh!"), but fortunately for readers, he came back to life in the hospital ambulance, guaranteeing a return engagement.

Catwoman, here known only as "the Cat," debuted as a jewel thief hoping to steal the necklace of a wealthy heiress aboard a luxury yacht. Robin went undercover to protect the item, and he and Batman were forced to use their fists to put away several gunmen during their mission. The Cat remained a more subtle opponent, but Batman's detective skills allowed him to see through the makeup that disguised her as an old woman and caught the would-be thief. The Cat tried to lure Batman into a life of crime, and naturally he refused—yet he did nothing to prevent the Cat's escape from custody, leaving Robin to wonder if his partner had become smitten by this wicked new kitten.

The Joker's greatest weapon is his unpredictable lunacy. Batman proves victorious on their first meeting, but the Joker's later reappearances would enshrine him as the Dark Knight's arch-enemy.

March: Adolf Hitler and Benito Mussolini meet at Brenner Pass in the Alps and agree to form an alliance against France and the United Kingdom.

May: Winston Churchill becomes prime minister of the United Kingdom.

May: The very first McDonald's restaurant opens in San Bernardino, California.

JUNE

THE CRIMES OF CLAYFACE
***Detective Comics* #40**

The list of Batman's enemies grew longer with the debut of Clayface, a masked villain revealed to be an ex-actor and expert makeup artist. In a story by writer Bill Finger and artist Bob Kane, the embittered thespian Basil Karlo adopted the identity of Clayface to commit a string of murders on a movie set. The character only appeared once more, but he provided the basis for a reinterpreted Clayface with shape-shifting abilities during the Silver Age.

UNCLE SAM WANTS YOU
***National Comics* #1**

With war raging in Europe, patriotism remained on the upswing in America. DC rival Quality Comics introduced the ultimate expression of the nation's identity in the form of Uncle Sam, a super hero modeled after the famous World War I recruiting poster by James Montgomery Flagg. Uncle Sam was a soldier killed in the Revolutionary War whose soul became infused with the Spirit of Liberty, and his first appearance was written and drawn by Will Eisner. He was one of the characters DC acquired from Quality Comics when the company folded in the mid-1950s.

JULY

GREEN LANTERN SHINES
***All-American Comics* #16**

Railway engineer Alan Scott underwent an unexpected career change into the costumed hero Green Lantern in a story by artist Martin Nodell (using the pseudonym "Mart Dellon") and writer Bill Finger. When a rival engineering company derailed a train to kill everyone on board, Scott was saved by the green energies of a mysterious glowing train lantern he had held onto during the crash. The lantern spoke to him and revealed that it originated from a "green flame" meteor that had fallen to Earth in ancient China. When the meteor rock was first discovered by a lantern-maker, its green flame spirit had intoned, "Three times shall I flame green! The first—to bring death! Second—to bring life! Third—to bring power!" The glowing meteor rock had been carved into a lantern by the time Scott discovered it, and two-thirds of its prophecy had been fulfilled. So when the lantern flamed green for a third time, it brought great power upon Scott. It instructed him to fashion a piece of the lantern into a ring that gave him the powers of flight and intangibility, and at this, Alan Scott became the super hero named Green Lantern. He brought the train saboteurs to justice, and by the story's last panel, he appeared in a colorful crime-fighting costume.

Green Lantern creates a solid wall of blazing light to thwart an attack from the train saboteurs, demonstrating just how much power his new ring has given him.

SUMMER

BEST OF THE BEST
***All Star Comics* #1**

In an attempt to piece together a hit from unrelated parts, editor Sheldon Mayer merged features from *Adventure Comics* (Sandman, Hourman), *More Fun Comics* (the Spectre, Biff Bronson), *All-American Comics* (Ultra-Man, Red, White, and Blue), and *Flash Comics* (the Flash, Hawkman) into the all-new *All Star Comics*. The first issue's cover featured panels that appeared to be torn out of its constituent comics, and showed depictions of Sandman, the Flash, the Spectre, and Gary Concord the Ultra-Man (who, by comparison, seemed a bit out of his league). In true egalitarian fashion, each source title in *All Star Comics* was represented by exactly two features, and in an editor's letter readers were asked to mail in a coupon indicating which three characters they would like to see join the lineup and which three characters they would like to get the boot. The revolving door implied by this "content by democracy" setup didn't entirely take hold, as the comic changed its focus with issue #3 (in winter) by introducing the Justice Society of America. Consequently, the Biff Bronson, Ultra-Man, and Red, White, and Blue features—the only ones with protagonists not represented in the JSA—were quickly eclipsed in popularity.

IN THE REAL WORLD...

May: The Auschwitz-Birkenau concentration camp opens in Poland.
June: Vichy France and Germany sign an armistice at Compiegne.
July: The Democratic Party begins its national convention in Chicago, and nominates Franklin D. Roosevelt for an unprecedented third term as president.

OCTOBER

THE ATOM: PINT-SIZED PUGILIST
***All-American Comics* #19**

Writer Bill O'Connor and artist Ben Flinton revealed the Atom in a short, six-page story, though the non-superpowered character soon went on to bigger things. Al Pratt was a college student mocked for his short height and weak physique. When he was dumped by his girlfriend after proving useless against a mugger, Al hooked up with a boxing trainer to hone himself into fighting shape. He then donned a brightly colored costume with a face-concealing mask and saved his ex from kidnappers under the guise of the Atom.

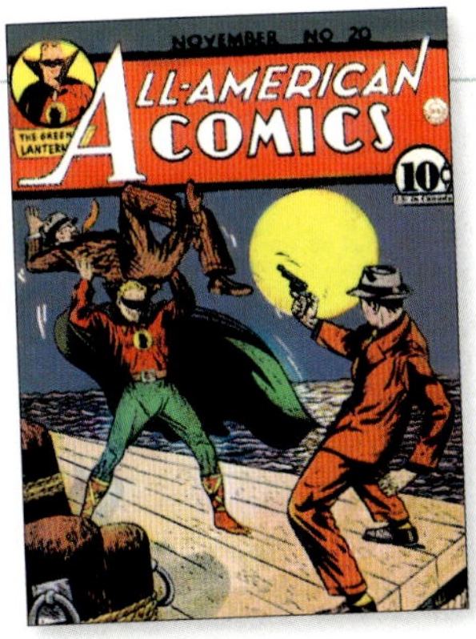

NOVEMBER

THE RED TORNADO BRINGS HUMOR
***All-American Comics* #20**

The Red Tornado was the first outright super hero parody at DC, and she was also one of the company's first prominent female characters. Written and drawn by Sheldon Mayer as a back-up character in his Scribbly the Boy Cartoonist feature, Ma Hunkel was a working mother in a rough New York neighborhood and was inspired by Green Lantern's example to become a super hero herself. In her four-page debut story, Ma Hunkel donned long underwear and covered her head with a cooking pot to become the eponymous Red Tornado. Immediately popular, the Red Tornado soon dominated Mayer's Scribbly stories.

RIGHT AWAY, MISTER WHITE
***Superman* #7**

Perry White muscled his way into comics in a story by writer Jerry Siegel and artist Joe Shuster, replacing George Taylor as Clark Kent's gruff but good-hearted boss. The character had originated in *The Adventures of Superman* radio show earlier in the year and moved into comics from there, though his first name wasn't provided to readers until issue #10 in May 1941. Among the other changes to Superman lore during 1940 was the renaming of Metropolis's newspaper from the *Daily Star* to the *Daily Planet*.

"NICE WORK, CLARK! THAT SCOOP ON LASH'S ARREST WAS A HUMDINGER!"

Perry White, *Superman* #7

WINTER

THE JSA COMES TOGETHER
***All Star Comics* #3**

If individual super heroes were popular with readers, what kind of reaction would you get if you united eight of them? DC took the "greatest hits" premise of the comic to its logical conclusion in *All Star Comics* #3 by teaming the Flash, the Atom, Doctor Fate, Green Lantern, Hawkman, Hourman, Sandman, and the Spectre under the banner of the Justice Society of America for an ongoing series of shared adventures.

Written by Gardner Fox and featuring a variety of artists, the JSA's first tale opened with another character, *Flash Comics*' Johnny Thunder, complaining at being left out of the festivities. Johnny's inadvertent wish attracted the attention of his genie-like Thunderbolt, who whisked Johnny to the JSA's secret meeting. Johnny listened in as each member related a memorable escapade from his adventuring career, a premise that served as an introduction for new readers and provided a rich variety of art styles from illustrators as diverse as the cartoony Sheldon Mayer and the hyper-detailed Sheldon Moldoff. The Flash told of retrieving treasure from a sunken galleon, Hawkman remembered the time he fought creatures that couldn't be burned by fire, and the Spectre revealed the secrets of his first battle against the evil Oom.

At the end of the issue, the Justice Society received a summons from the FBI and the Flash rushed off to see how the team could serve its country. Before long, the JSA would be fighting foreign agitators and would provide the template for the following year's Seven Soldiers of Victory.

Johnny Thunder is annoyed that he's been left out of the JSA, so much so that his powerful Thunderbolt takes him to gatecrash their first meeting.

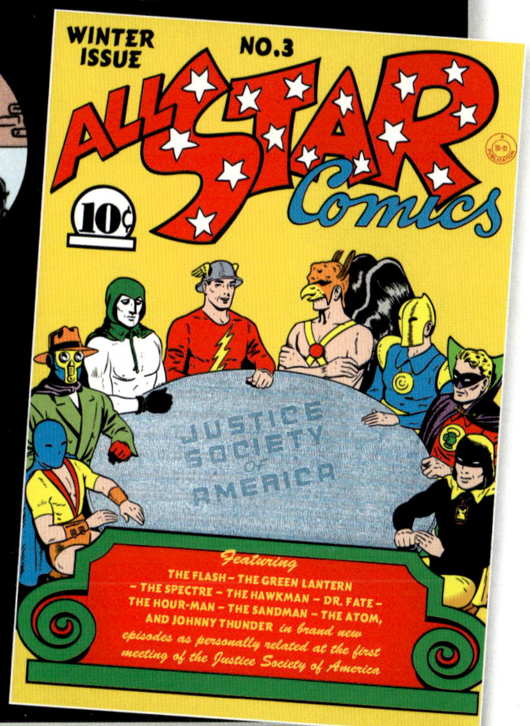

ALSO THIS YEAR: Superman's telescopic vision and super-breath were introduced in January's *ACTION COMICS* #20… March saw *ADVENTURE COMICS* #48 introduce Hourman, who possessed superpowers for sixty minutes at a time… The DC bullet "A DC Publication" first appeared on issues with April cover dates… Writer Gardner Fox helped usher in the yellow-helmeted mystic known as Doctor Fate in May's *MORE FUN COMICS* #55, illustrated by Howard Sherman…

August: Leon Trotsky is assassinated with an ice axe in Mexico.
September: The Blitz: Nazi Germany begins to rain bombs on London.
December: The Chicago Bears, in what will become the most one-sided victory in National Football League history, defeat the Washington Redskins 73–0.

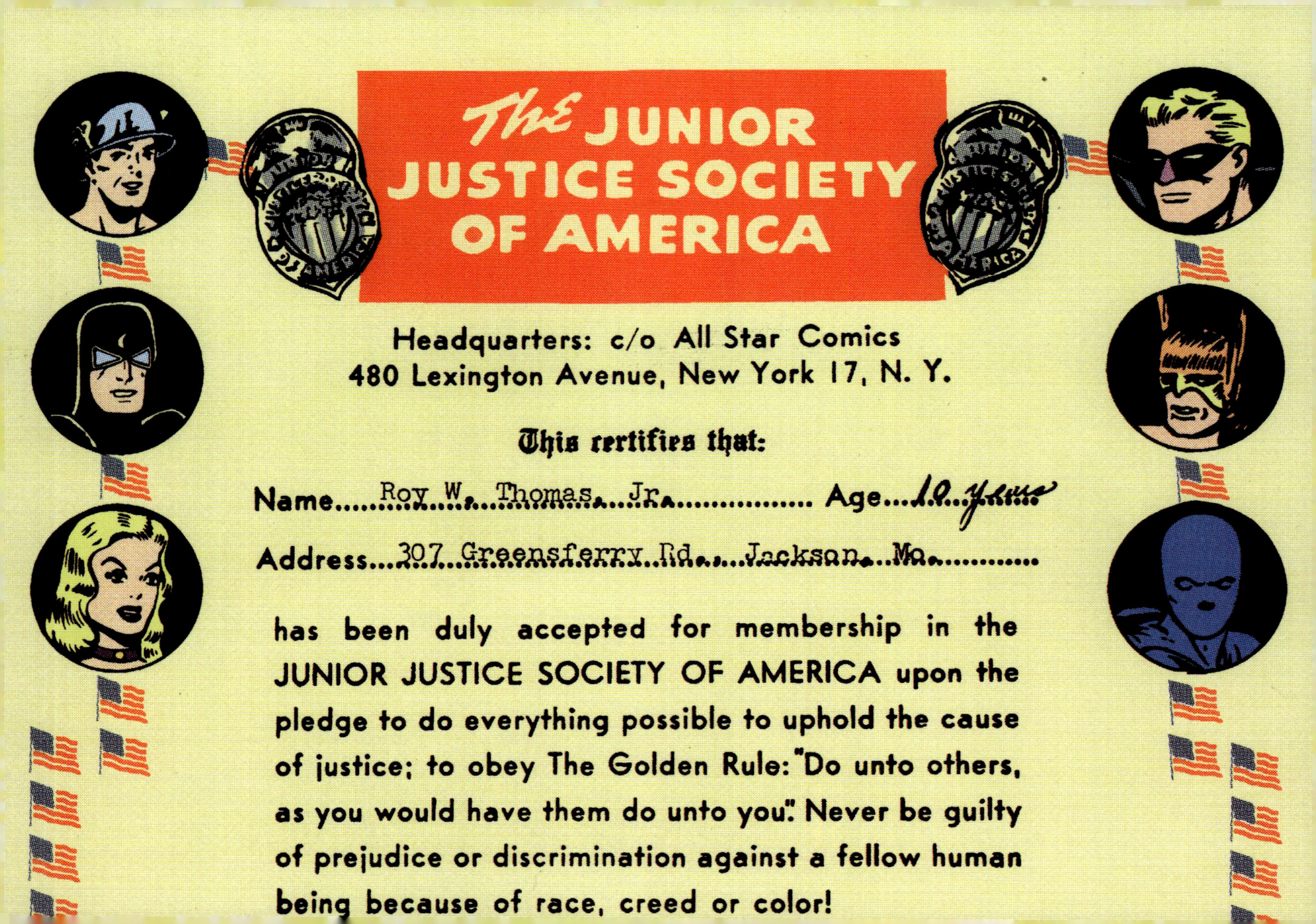

The JUNIOR JUSTICE SOCIETY OF AMERICA

Headquarters: c/o All Star Comics
480 Lexington Avenue, New York 17, N. Y.

This certifies that:

Name....Roy W. Thomas, Jr.............. Age...10 years

Address...307 Greensferry Rd., Jackson, Mo...........

has been duly accepted for membership in the JUNIOR JUSTICE SOCIETY OF AMERICA upon the pledge to do everything possible to uphold the cause of justice; to obey The Golden Rule: "Do unto others, as you would have them do unto you." Never be guilty of prejudice or discrimination against a fellow human being because of race, creed or color!

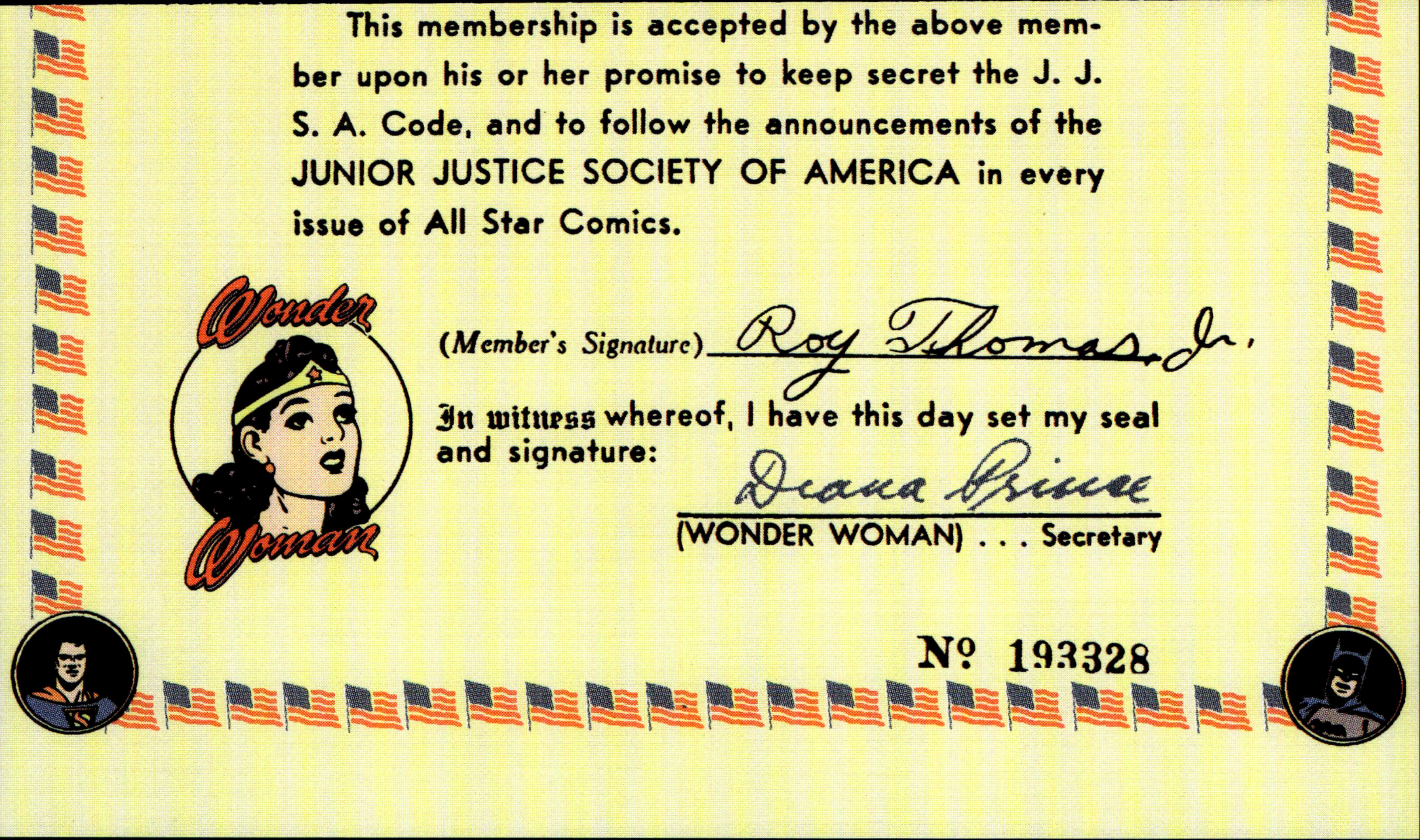
This membership is accepted by the above member upon his or her promise to keep secret the J. J. S. A. Code, and to follow the announcements of the JUNIOR JUSTICE SOCIETY OF AMERICA in every issue of All Star Comics.

(Member's Signature) Roy Thomas, Jr.

In witness whereof, I have this day set my seal and signature:

Diana Prince
(WONDER WOMAN) . . . Secretary

Nº 193328

JOIN THE JSA!

JUNIOR JSA CLUB KIT CERTIFICATE (1942) DC Comics prided itself on its strong bond with its readers. An 8½ x 11 in (21.6 x 28 cm) certificate, signed by Wonder Woman Diana Prince and featuring an inspiring, patriotic wartime message, awaited young fans who joined the Junior Justice Society of America between 1942 and 1944.

1941

"MOST AMAZING OF ALL THE SECRETS OF THE SEA IS THE STORY OF AQUAMAN, WHO, LIKE A WATER-GOD OF OLD, DWELLS IN THE DIM UNKNOWN DEPTHS OF THE OCEAN!"

Aquaman's introduction, *More Fun Comics* #73

SUPER HEROES ABOUND

It was a year of expansion for DC, as the company added new titles from *All-Flash* to *Star Spangled Comics* and gave Green Lantern his own title. Mort Weisinger joined the staff as an Associate Editor and quickly went to work filling out the company's stable of characters, writing the introductory adventures of Johnny Quick, the Vigilante, Green Arrow, Speedy, Aquaman, and the Seven Soldiers of Victory. Other stars stepping onto the DC stage included Starman, Doctor Mid-Nite, and the Star-Spangled Kid, whilst rival companies including Quality Comics and Fawcett Comics kept up the pressure and familiarized readers with hit creations from Plastic Man to Captain Marvel Jr. By the end of the year, the Japanese attack on Pearl Harbor had brought the U.S. into World War II. As the nation's mood switched from shock to fierce determination, the war became an increasingly frequent backdrop for super hero adventures.

APRIL

DC'S FINEST HEROES
***World's Best Comics* #1**

With ninety-six packed pages and DC's three biggest stars sharing the cover, *World's Best Comics* promised a galaxy of stories for the low price of fifteen cents. The basic format had been a success under the name *New York World's Fair Comics*, which had been tested at the fair in 1939 and 1940. The new ongoing title, renamed *World's Finest Comics* with issue #2, featured heavy-hitters Superman and Batman, mid-list stars Zatara, Johnny Thunder, the Crimson Avenger, and Red, White, and Blue, and all-but-forgotten curiosities such as Punch Parker and Lando, Man of Magic.

A STARMAN IS BORN
***Adventure Comics* #61**

Writer Gardner Fox and artist Jack Burnley presented the new costumed hero Starman in this issue. Known as Ted Knight in his civilian identity, the science hero gained the abilities of flight and energy manipulation from his handheld "gravity rod." He wore a red-and-yellow costume accented with a green cape and a finned helmet. Starman received a plum cover position for his first outing, which saw him pitted against the evil Dr. Doog to contain the destructive energies of a revolutionary invention, the Ultra-Dynamo.

SEPTEMBER

QUICKLY MAKING HIS MARK
***More Fun Comics* #71**

In a story by Mort Weisinger within *More Fun Comics*' back-up pages, the Flash gained a rival in fellow super-speedster Johnny Quick. Born under the name Johnny Chambers, the hero gained his powers after discovering an ancient speed formula written on a piece of Egyptian papyrus. By speaking the formula aloud (written in the comics as "3X2(9YZ)4A"), Johnny could gain the speed of lightning. The unique gimmick of a mathematical mantra set him aside from other heroes of the era, though Johnny Quick never unseated Doctor Fate as *More Fun Comics*' leading attraction.

AT THE MOVIES THIS MONTH: A series of *SUPERMAN* animated shorts, created by Fleisher Studios and released by Paramount, appeared in movie theaters…

IN THE REAL WORLD…

January: President Franklin D. Roosevelt delivers his "Four Freedoms" speech in the State of the Union address.

OCTOBER

PATRIOTIC HEROES ASSEMBLE
***Star Spangled Comics* #1**

The U.S. hadn't yet joined the war in Europe when *Star Spangled Comics* debuted, but the fighting raged on and enemy saboteurs made for fertile story fodder. Star-Spangled Kid had appeared in *Action Comics* #40 in September, but this story by writer Jerry Siegel and artist Hal Sherman introduced his adult sidekick, Stripesy, and their civilian identities of spoiled rich kid and dim-witted chauffeur. Together, the pair battled Nazi spies to serve their country.

JIMMY'S DEBUT
***Superman* #13**

Jimmy Olsen made his first appearance as a named character in this issue. The red-haired cub reporter and photographer looked up to the more experienced Clark Kent and Lois Lane as career role models. He was also a friend of Superman and could summon his help at the push of a button. This debut comics appearance followed his April 1940 introduction in *The Adventures of Superman* radio show, though a similar *Daily Planet* employee had already popped up in *Action Comics* #6 (November 1938) but remained unnamed.

NOVEMBER

STRAIGHT TO THE POINT

***More Fun Comics* #73**

Writer Mort Weisinger and artist George Papp ushered in the era of Green Arrow by foregoing a traditional origin story and joining the brand-new hero and his sidekick Speedy in the middle of what appeared to be a lively adventuring career, subtly implying to readers that this was an established, popular feature and not one still finding its legs. As his *nom de guerre* implied, the Green Arrow was a Robin Hood-like vigilante who could solve any dilemma with the application of archery. This included stringing a line between two rooftops for a high-wire balancing act and firing shafts into a wall to create an impromptu ladder.

The last story of the issue (also written by Weisinger) introduced Aquaman, King of the Seven Seas. Aquaman wasn't the first underwater hero—DC's rival Funnies Inc. had introduced the character Namor the Sub-Mariner in their publication *Marvel Comics* #1 in 1939—but he filled a niche among DC's costumed adventurers. Featuring the artwork of Paul Norris, the story showed off Aquaman's array of powers including super-strength, the ability to breathe underwater, and an understanding of the language of ocean creatures.

Aquaman makes a big impact on his debut by battling Nazis who try to sink a refugee ship.

ALSO THIS MONTH: The DC bullet logo was changed to read "A Superman-DC Publication" on the covers of all issues dated from November…

DECEMBER

FEEDING TIME FOR THE PENGUIN
***Detective Comics* #58**

One of Batman's most peculiar foes first appeared in this issue, and naturally he brought his trademark umbrella with him. The Penguin was a squat dandy with a beaked nose and a tuxedo; not the sort of character to raise the suspicions of the police or even Bruce Wayne. Yet, in this story by writer Bill Finger and artist Bob Kane, he murdered a gang leader with a shotgun concealed in his umbrella and took over the crook's criminal operation. Using his wits, the Penguin framed Batman as a thief, but he couldn't outsmart the Caped Crusader for long.

WINTER

THE SEVEN SOLDIERS REPORT FOR DUTY
***Leading Comics* #1**

Writer Mort Weisinger helped unveil the Seven Soldiers of Victory, DC's second super hero team, a year after the company inaugurated the concept with the Justice Society of America. Most of the Seven Soldiers had newly minted pedigrees, with many of those written by Weisinger himself. The lineup consisted of the Crimson Avenger (from *Detective Comics*), Green Arrow and Speedy (of *More Fun Comics*), the Shining Knight (from *Adventure Comics*), the Star-Spangled Kid and Stripesy (the patriotic duo from *Star Spangled Comics*), and the gun-toting Vigilante (a new star in *Action Comics*).

ALSO THIS YEAR: April's *ALL-AMERICAN COMICS* #25 saw the costumed hero Doctor Mid-Nite make his first appearance… In Summer, the Flash received a second comic, *ALL-FLASH*… In August, DC's rival Quality Comics introduced notable characters like Blackhawk and Miss America in *MILITARY COMICS* #1 and Plastic Man, Firebrand, the Human Bomb, Mouthpiece, and the Phantom Lady in *POLICE COMICS* #1… In Fall's *GREEN LANTERN* #1, the ring-slinging hero received his own series with story and art duties handled by Bill Finger and Mart Nodell… In December's *WHIZ COMICS* #25, DC's competitor Fawcett Comics brought in Captain Marvel Jr., a younger counterpart to their most popular character, Captain Marvel…

May: In Berlin, Konrad Zuse presents the Z3, the world's first programmable, fully automatic, working computer.

December: The Japanese Navy launches a surprise attack on the United States' fleet at Pearl Harbor, drawing the United States into World War II.

DC GOES TO WAR

With the nations of the world locked in global conflict, the customary comic book depictions of super heroes fighting gangsters and mad scientists no longer seemed relevant. As Americans witnessed the fall of France and the Battle of Britain in 1940, World War II became an increasingly common backdrop in comics stories. Reflecting the headlines, patriotic Captain X used his flying skills to aid the Royal Air Force against the Luftwaffe, while the Star-Spangled Kid and Stripesy battled Nazi spies on U.S. soil, foiling sabotage attempts on factories and dams.

World War II took center stage after the United States joined the war following the Japanese raid on Pearl Harbor in 1941. Soldier-heroes, including the trio Red, White, and Blue and the undead men-in-uniform of the Ghost Patrol, became popular. Even kids got in on the action in the form of the Boy Commandos and the Newsboy Legion.

Established heroes such as Superman and Batman fought Axis infiltrators, too, and the covers of their comics frequently exhorted Americans to rally around the flag and oppose the twin menaces of Adolf Hitler and Emperor Hirohito. On one cover, Batman overcame his antipathy toward firearms (a legacy of the shooting of his parents by a mugger) to present an army G.I. with a fresh rifle. On another, the Dynamic Duo soared into action on the back of a giant eagle while urging their readers to buy war bonds and stamps. Other comic book publishing companies took a similar approach to that of DC. Quality introduced the patriotic Uncle Sam and the aviator hero Blackhawk, while Fawcett created the ultimate Aryan villain with Captain Nazi.

Sacrifice was an ever-present theme for readers on the home front, with gas rationing, meat coupons, and scrap drives (selling trash for cash) defining the new reality. For DC, paper shortages reduced the page length and publication frequency for many of its titles. Some of the company's foremost creators, including Jerry Siegel and Jack Kirby, joined the armed forces. Comic book heroes bore the hardships with good cheer, pitching in to plant victory gardens and saluting the personnel of the army, navy, and marines as the *real* heroes. In addition, DC placed its expertise at the disposal of the government, publishing a number of public information leaflets and pamphlets.

The end of the war came in 1945 with Victory in Europe Day and Victory over Japan Day. The end of paper rationing coincided with the start of a larger economic boom that saw the U.S. reach new heights as a world power. The popularity of DC's super heroes, however, was on the wane, a trend that would continue until their dramatic resurgence during the middle years of the following decade.

Left: A wartime public information pamphlet published by DC Comics.
Main pictures: Superman looks on approvingly as a female fan realizes that members of the U.S. Armed Forces are the real heroes of the war on the cover of Superman #29 (July 1944).
On the cover of World's Finest Comics #11 (Fall 1943), the Dynamic Duo join Superman to plant a victory garden.

No. 11
FALL ISSUE
15¢
WORLD'S FINEST COMICS
A SUPERMAN DC PUBLICATION
VICTORY GARDEN
ONIONS
PEAS

1942

"FOR HEAVEN'S SAKE, DON'T GIVE ME THE CREDIT. IT BELONGS TO THAT BEAUTIFUL GIRL—WONDER WOMAN!"

Steve Trevor, *Sensation Comics* #1

THE AMAZON ARRIVES

This was Wonder Woman's year, as the Amazon Princess headlined the new title *Sensation Comics* and earned her own self-titled comic. The brainchild of psychologist William Moulton Marston—who joined DC in an advisory capacity before writing his own stories—Wonder Woman was an unusual sight in an industry full of male super heroes. Meanwhile, DC scored a coup by luring to their ranks the popular artist and writer team of Jack Kirby and Joe Simon, who this year introduced the Newsboy Legion, the Guardian, and the Boy Commandos. Jerry Siegel wrote Robotman, and other characters including Mister Terrific and Wildcat also debuted. Superman starred in a prose novel and acquired a maddening opponent in the Prankster, while Batman scored a new enemy in Two-Face. But with the Battle of Midway raging in the Pacific and gasoline rationing starting in the U.S., it was the war that shaped the lives of readers and creators alike.

JANUARY

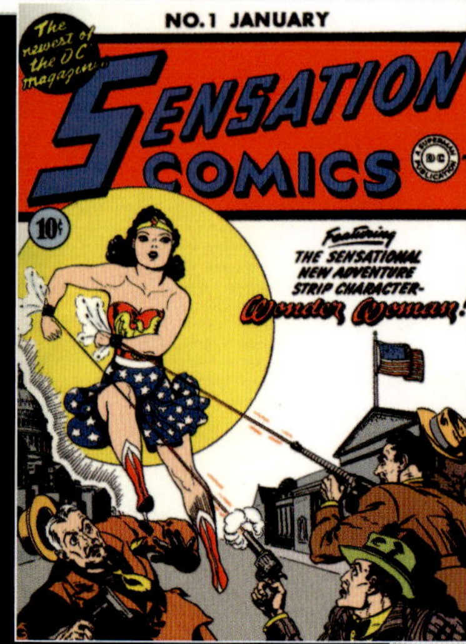

WONDER WOMAN WOWS
***Sensation Comics* #1**

Psychologist William Moulton Marston joined the ranks of the heavyweight comics creators with Wonder Woman, as his creation took the lead in *Sensation Comics* following a sneak preview in *All Star Comics* #8 the previous year. Marston had wanted to introduce a strong female super hero into comics to even the battlefield in a male-dominated world. "It seemed to me, from a psychological angle, that the comics' worst offense was their blood-curdling masculinity," wrote Marston, in a 1943 issue of magazine *The American Scholar*. "A male hero, at best, lacks the qualities of maternal love and tenderness which are as essential to the child as the breath of life." The cover of *Sensation Comics* #1 was drawn by Jon Blummer (who worked on the Hop Harrigan of *All-American Comics*), though Harry G. Peter handled the interior illustrations of Wonder Woman, establishing an exaggerated style that would come to define the character.

The *All Star Comics* preview had introduced U.S. Army captain Steve Trevor, who crashed on the Amazon outpost of Paradise Island and earned the attentions of Diana. The inaugural *Sensation Comics* story picked up the narrative with Diana's mission to return Steve Trevor to the world of men. Inspired by her mother Queen Hippolyte and carrying the blessings of the goddesses Aphrodite and Athena, Diana traveled to the United States in her invisible jet, wearing a costume seemingly inspired by the Stars and Stripes but revealing enough to earn her the condemnation of local busybodies. As Wonder Woman, Diana demonstrated enhanced strength, incredible speed, and amazingly precise reflexes. To keep an eye on the hospitalized Steve Trevor, Wonder Woman purchased the identity of Diana Prince and took a job as a nurse.

The following issue of *Sensation Comics* fleshed out Diana's supporting cast by introducing her friend Etta Candy and the Holliday Girls from nearby Holliday College. An immediate hit, Wonder Woman earned her own title before the end of the year and joined the Justice Society of America in *All Star Comics* #11 in June.

Wonder Woman needs no help from tough U.S. Army captain Steve Trevor to fight off a crowd of gun-wielding thugs on her first visit to the world of men.

IN THE REAL WORLD...

January: The first American forces arrive in Europe in Northern Ireland.
February: Princess Elizabeth registers for war service.

JANUARY

MORE GOLDEN AGE HEROES
***Sensation Comics* #1**

Mister Terrific and Wildcat made an impact among the back-up features of *Sensation Comics* #1. As written by Charles Reizenstein and drawn by Hal Sharp, Terry Sloane was a genius and athlete who was utterly bored with life, but he found renewed purpose by living out the motto "fair play" as Mister Terrific. Writer Bill Finger and artist Irwin Hasen's Wildcat was Ted Grant, a boxer accused of murdering his opponent in the ring. He donned a panther-like outfit to bring the true killers to justice.

APRIL

A BIG WELCOME TO SIMON AND KIRBY
***Adventure Comics* #73**

Hot properties Joe Simon and Jack Kirby joined DC after developing Captain America at rival Timely Comics. After taking over the Sandman and Sandy, the Golden Boy feature in *Adventure Comics* #72, the writer and artist team turned their attentions to Manhunter with issue #73. Their version of Manhunter seemed to be a different creation than the Paul Kirk Manhunter who had previously starred in the comic, but subsequent issues merged the two creations for consistency. The pairing of Simon and Kirby created a real buzz throughout 1942, but Kirby would be drafted into the war the following year.

STAR-SPANGLED DEBUTS
***Star Spangled Comics* #7**

Joe Simon and Jack Kirby took their talents to a second title with *Star Spangled Comics*, tackling both the Guardian and the Newsboy Legion in issue #7. Jim Harper, a policeman in Suicide Slum, picked up the golden shield of the Guardian for a secret crusade against crime. Impressed by the spirit of local orphans Gabby, Scrapper, Big Words, and Tommy Tompkins, known as the Newsboy Legion, Harper became their legal guardian. The same issue unveiled Robotman, by writer Jerry Siegel and illustrators Leo Nowak and Paul Cassidy. The saga of a human trapped in a robot body was surprisingly lighthearted, thanks in part to his comic sidekick Robotdog.

"I PROBABLY LOOK LIKE A COMIC MAGAZINE SUPER HERO, OUT TO GRAB CRIME BY THE HORNS!"

The Guardian, *Star Spangled Comics* #7

AUGUST

TWO FACES OF EVIL
***Detective Comics* #66**

The nightmarish Two-Face debuted as Batman's antagonist in this story by writer Bill Finger and artist Bob Kane. Gotham City's district attorney (called Harvey Kent, though later renamed Dent) was disfigured after mobster Boss Moroni threw acid on half of his face. Driven mad by his horrific appearance, Two-Face determined his future actions by flipping a misprinted silver dollar with two head sides. When the scarred side (scratched by Dent) came up he took actions to strengthen his hold on the underworld, but on other flips Two-Face performed good deeds.

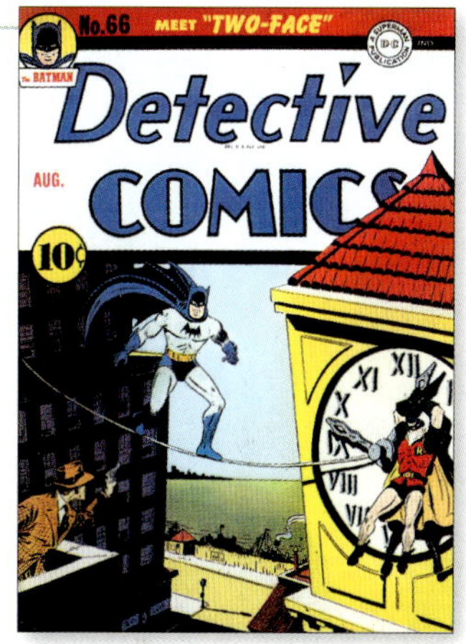

WINTER

SIMON AND KIRBY'S NEW CREATIONS
***Boy Commandos* #1**

The inaugural issue of *Boy Commandos* represented writer Joe Simon and artist Jack Kirby's first original title since they started at DC (though the characters had debuted in *Detective Comics* #64 in June). The Boy Commandos was a military squad of orphaned kids from diverse backgrounds: American-born Brooklyn, France's André Chavard, Jan Haasen of the Netherlands, and Brit Alfie Twidgett. Issue #1 saw the Boy Commandos liberate Jan's village from the Nazis under the supervision of Captain Rip Carter.

MORE PAGES, MORE ADVENTURES
***Comic Cavalcade* #1**

The new anthology title *Comic Cavalcade* weighed in at a hefty ninety-six pages and bore the promise of "a galaxy of America's greatest comics." Dedicated to the characters from the All-American Publications lineup, it featured the Flash, Green Lantern, and Wonder Woman on every cover and included an array of guest-stars in its back-up features, including Hop Harrigan, Scribbly, Wildcat, and the Ghost Patrol. *Comic Cavalcade* also represented a milestone in Wonder Woman's popularity, adding a fourth title to her repertoire in addition to *Wonder Woman*, *Sensation Comics*, and *All Star Comics*.

ALSO THIS YEAR: Wonder Woman's magic lasso made its first appearance in June's *SENSATION COMICS* #6… "Can Superman be fooled?" asked the cover of August's *ACTION COMICS* #51, which heralded the first appearance of the mischievous Prankster… Writer Al Bester and artist Stan Kaye's eight-page story in *ADVENTURE COMICS* #77 in August marked the first appearance of the young know-it-all Genius Jones… Following her appearances in *ALL STAR COMICS* and *SENSATION COMICS*, Wonder Woman was quick to receive her own self-titled solo title in Summer… December saw the release of the novel *THE ADVENTURES OF SUPERMAN* by George Lowthner, narrator and scripter for the Superman radio show of the same name…

June: On her thirteenth birthday, Anne Frank makes the first entry in her new diary.
July: The Oxford Committee of Famine Relief (OXFAM) is founded.

November: The movie *Casablanca* premieres at the Hollywood Theater in New York City, starring Humphrey Bogart and Ingrid Bergman.

SENSATION COMICS #7 (July 1942)
Wonder Woman was the first-ever female super hero. The character was conceived by psychologist William Moulton Marston not only to represent the modern, liberated woman, but to save humankind: "There isn't love enough in the male organism to run this planet peacefully," he wrote.

AMAZON SENSATION

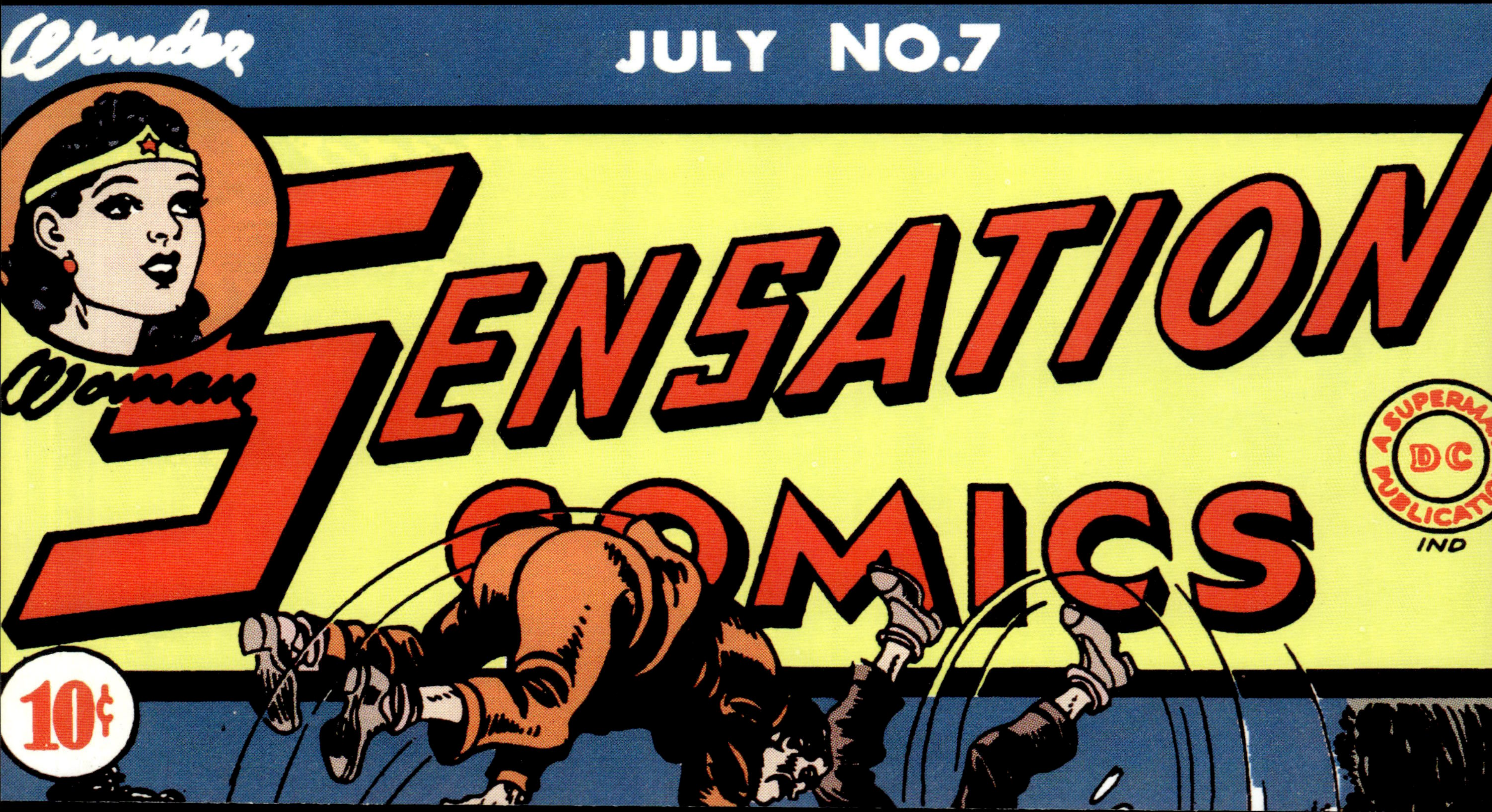

INTERNATIO
MILK
COMPAN
LET'S GO! U.S.A.: KEEP 'EM FLYING!

1943

"YOU MAY CALL ME ALFRED, WITHOUT THE 'MISTER,' AND IT'S I WHO WILL DO FOR YOU! YOU SEE, I'M YOUR NEW BUTLER!"

Alfred introduces himself to Bruce Wayne, *Batman* #16

WARTIME SACRIFICE

World War II rolled on, providing story fodder for the comics while at the same time reducing the availability of the paper on which they were printed. Wartime paper restrictions required DC to cut back the page counts of several of its books, and characters like Sandman and Doctor Fate lost their back-up features as a result. Other titles, including *Adventure Comics*, were reduced in frequency. Superman co-creator Jerry Siegel was inducted into the armed forces, so other writers took over story duties for the Man of Steel's adventures. Meanwhile, the mythology of Superman was deepened with the introduction of kryptonite in *The Adventures of Superman* radio program. Wonder Woman picked up new foes, while Green Lantern coined a memorable oath. Batman leapt into newspaper pages and a movie serial, and welcomed unflappable butler Alfred Pennyworth into his world.

APRIL

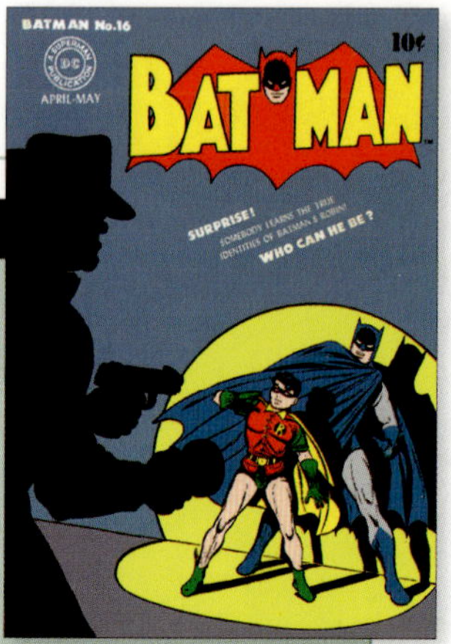

HERE COMES ALFRED

***Batman* #16**

Batman and Robin got some help in their crusade against crime with the arrival of butler Alfred in a thirteen-page back-up story by writer Don Cameron and artist Bob Kane. Intended as a comic-relief character, Alfred (who was later given the surname Pennyworth) arrived in Gotham City on the boat from England and immediately ran afoul of thugs who tried to steal his valise. Batman and Robin rescued the Briton and were stunned when he later arrived at their mansion, announcing his intent to serve in his father's footsteps as the Wayne family's butler. A self-styled amateur detective, Alfred quickly worked out the secret identities of his new employers and rescued them from their latest predicament. Batman declared "You're one of us now, Alfred!" and just like that, the Dynamic Duo became a trio. Initially portrayed as portly and clean-shaven, Alfred was redesigned later in the year to better resemble William Austin, the lean and mustachioed actor who played him in the *Batman* movie serial. Alfred's loyalty to Batman and Robin remained unimpeachable, though his initial efforts at becoming a super-sleuth often caused headaches for the more experienced crime fighters. This aspect of Alfred's personality was toned down as the character eventually became less comedic.

Bungling Alfred is determined to be of use to his masters as a detective, studying hard and looking the part.

AT THE MOVIES THIS MONTH: Advertised as "A Hundred Times More Thrilling on the Screen!," the fifteen-part movie serial *BATMAN* was released, starring Lewis Wilson as Batman and Douglas Croft as Robin...

JUNE

DOCTOR PSYCHO'S DEFEAT

***Wonder Woman* #5**

In the environment of the early 1940s, Wonder Woman carried the banner for female heroes largely on her own; a point not lost on her creator and writer William Moulton Marston. In the fifth issue of her self-titled series, drawn by Harry G. Peter, the Amazonian faced the diminutive Doctor Psycho, who obeyed the commands of Wonder Woman's arch-foe the God of War to stop the women of the United States from assisting the war effort. Posing as the spirit of George Washington, Doctor Psycho urged America's women to leave their factory posts and return home, but he was defeated by Wonder Woman and her friends the Holliday Girls in this clear-cut tale of female empowerment.

ON RADIO THIS MONTH: Kryptonite was introduced on *THE ADVENTURES OF SUPERMAN* radio show as a substance that emitted radioactivity hazardous to Superman's health...

IN THE REAL WORLD...

March: Rodgers and Hammerstein's *Oklahoma!* opens on Broadway, heralding a new era in "integrated" stage musicals.

SEPTEMBER

THE TOYMAN WANTS TO PLAY
***Action Comics* #64**

In writer Don Cameron and artist Ed Dobrotka's "The Terrible Toyman," a quirky toy maker used his bizarre playthings to commit crimes. As Superman's super-strength made him a tough opponent to beat in a one-on-one slugfest, comics writers often introduced colorful troublemakers like the Toyman who served mainly to annoy the title character. The Toyman's cover appearance was a good example of this, as he pogo-sticked his way out of Superman's reach.

FALL

CHEETAH UNSHEATHES HER CLAWS
***Wonder Woman* #6**

As one of the few woman super heroes in comics, Wonder Woman frequently faced off against female villains as writer William Moulton Marston fleshed out her Rogues Gallery. A memorable villain was the Cheetah, introduced on a dynamic cover by artist Harry G. Peter. Priscilla Rich, jealous of Wonder Woman after meeting her at a charity event, adopted the costumed identity of the Cheetah and stole the charity's money in an attempt to frame the Amazon Princess. Although the Cheetah appeared to die, she staged a comeback later in the same issue and went on to become one of Wonder Woman's most iconic enemies.

As the Cheetah, Priscilla Rich lacks superpowers but is deadly with a knife.

IN NEWSPAPERS THIS MONTH: Under the title "BATMAN AND ROBIN," a daily strip appeared in newspapers across America. Both the daily and Sunday installments were initially written and drawn by Bob Kane...

IN BRIGHTEST DAY

***Green Lantern* #9**

Green Lantern created a catchphrase for the ages in this issue, with the first reading of what would become the official Green Lantern oath. In a tale by writer Al Bester and artist Martin Nodell, Alan Scott charged his mystical power ring by reciting "In brightest day, in blackest night, no evil shall escape my sight! Let those who worship evil's might beware my power—Green Lantern's light!" Green Lantern's ring needed recharging every twenty-four hours, and while an oath wasn't a necessary requirement, it did add a certain level of formality to proceedings.

This wasn't the first time that Alan Scott had spoken an oath. In his first appearance in *All-American Comics* #16 (July 1940), he had used "And I shall shed my light over dark evil, for the dark things cannot stand the light, the light of the Green Lantern!" He also tried out other variations including "My rays strike the darkest corner, banishing all wickedness!" (in *All-American Comics* #45, December 1942) and "As the green rays strike forth into darkness, so may all black evil be exposed and driven away!" (in *All-American Comics* #47, February 1943). Such variety wasn't uncommon in early super hero comics, as creators tried to find that magical connection with readers. However, it was the "In brightest day, in blackest night" oath that proved to have true staying power, as it was resurrected by Alan Scott's successor, Hal Jordan, during the Silver Age of Comics.

WINTER

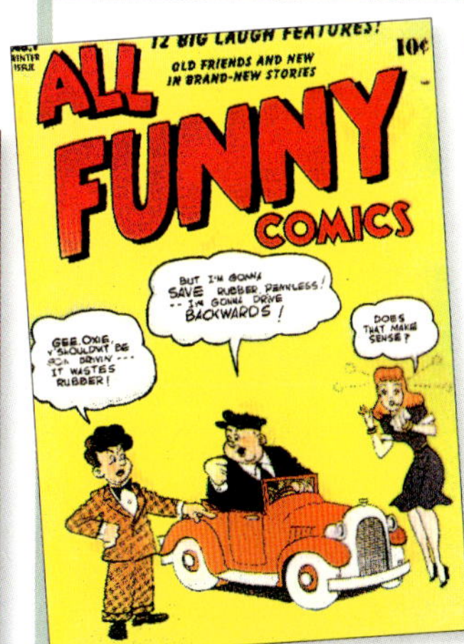

WHAT'S SO FUNNY?
***All Funny Comics* #1**

Inside the optimistically titled *All Funny Comics* were twelve different humor features assembled by editor Bernie Breslauer. Pulling together as many joke characters as possible, *All Funny Comics* raided some of its sister titles to enlist Genius Jones (from *Adventure Comics*), the good-natured detectives Dover and Clover (from *More Fun Comics*), and the perennially broke policeman Penniless Palmer (from *Star Spangled Comics*). Original characters introduced in *All Funny Comics* included Hayfoot Henry, Two-Gun Percy, and Buzzy.

ALSO THIS YEAR: December's *GREEN LANTERN* #10, written by Alfred Bester, with art by Martin Nodell, saw Green Lantern discover that his adversary, Vandal Savage, was an immortal who had existed since ancient times. Savage's cunning left him in a position to become one of the DC Universe's greatest masterminds...

July: Battle of Kursk: The largest tank battle in history begins.
September: General Eisenhower announces the surrender of Italy to the Allies.

December: The Great Depression officially ends in the United States and the Works Progress Administration is closed.

1944

"MR. MXYZTPLK! AN ODD NAME! I'D HATE TO BE THE STONE CUTTER WHO WILL HAVE TO ENGRAVE IT ON YOUR TOMBSTONE!"

Superman to Mister Mxyztplk, *Superman* #30

VARIETY IN COMICS

With continuing wartime paper shortages, the page counts of DC's titles were cut back further than in the previous year. This wasn't good news for super heroes hoping to make an impact with readers, and characters dropped from their back-up features included the Crimson Avenger (in *Detective Comics*), Manhunter (in *Adventure Comics*), and Tex Thompson the Americommando (in *Action Comics*). Wonder Woman made her debut in the newspapers and Green Lantern gained a new enemy in Solomon Grundy, while Superman dealt with the pranks of an extradimensional sprite named Mr. Mxyztplk. A focus on comedy seemed to be a welcome distraction from the war, so DC launched new titles in the funny animal and teen humor genres. Religious comics adapting Bible stories also hit the market as DC made efforts to diversify its line.

SUMMER

THE ANIMALS ARRIVE

***Funny Stuff* #1**

Although super heroes were still DC's bread and butter, the company made a preliminary entry into the funny animal market with the first issue of *Funny Stuff*. Edited by Sheldon Mayer, the anthology title showcased a number of new animal humor features. These included Rufus Lion, Blackie Bear, Bulldog Drumhead, and also McSnurtle the Turtle, who could change into a super hero called the Terrific Whatsit.

SEPTEMBER

AN IRRITATING IMP

***Superman* #30**

Writer Jerry Siegel promised that readers had never met anyone more unusual than the "absurd being known as Mr. Mxyztplk," and his debut back-up feature in *Superman* #30 proved his point. After a strange little man in a bowler hat was struck down by a passing truck, he raised himself from the dead and drove a waiting ambulance up a skyscraper wall before a crowd of astonished onlookers. After this ambulance stunt, Mr. Mxyztplk brought a statue to life, erected a highway in the middle of a lake, and forced the mayor of Metropolis to bray like a donkey. Possessed with powers that could put Superman to shame, the troublesome Mr. Mxyztplk cared only for pranks and harmless mayhem. Assuring Superman that he "hadn't had so much fun in ages," Mr. Mxyztplk revealed his origin as a court jester from another dimension who could only be forced to return home if he spoke his own name backward. Superman tricked the imp into blurting it out, and he vanished—but the story's last panel contained an appeal from Siegel and artist Joe Shuster for readers to send in postcards if they wanted to see further adventures starring Mr. Mxyztplk. Much like the Toyman, Mr. Mxyztplk served merely to irritate the Man of Steel. He remained the most straightforwardly comic character in the Superman books, and later underwent a slight name change to just "Mxyzptlk."

Mr. Mxyztplk is a trickster whose superpowers more than match Superman's, and the impish villain loves to torment Superman with them.

IN THE REAL WORLD...

June: D-Day commences with the landing of 155,000 Allied troops on the beaches of Normandy, helping to liberate France from Germany.

OCTOBER

INSPIRATION ON THE NEWSSTAND

***Picture Stories from the Bible* #1**

The Bible had heroes, villains, and amazing feats, so its content proved well-suited to the comic medium. The first DC series to feature biblical tales had appeared back in 1942. Titled *Picture Stories from the Bible*, it adapted stories from the Old Testament including those of Moses, Abraham, the prophet Elijah, and the classic underdog match-up of David and Goliath. The 1944 version, labeled "New Testament Edition" on the cover, told tales from the life of Christ. Don Cameron illustrated the series, which offered forty-five pages of religious education for only ten cents.

After emerging victorious from a battle with the devil in the desert, Jesus is attended to by angels.

SOLOMON GRUNDY, BORN ON A MONDAY

***All-American Comics* #61**

Green Lantern faced a monstrous foe in *All-American Comics* #61. Solomon Grundy was a zombielike strongman who was able to withstand the energy beams of Green Lantern's mystical power ring. His origin, recounted in a story by writer Alfred Bester and artist Paul Reinman, involved the corpse of a murdered man, Cyrus Gold, and his reanimation in the depths of a swamp. Gold received his moniker from some hobos—they nicknamed him Solomon Grundy after the children's nursery rhyme character who was born on a Monday, which was the only detail Gold could remember about his former self.

DECEMBER

GIANT-SIZED FUN

***The Big All-American Comic Book* #1**

Given the demand for paper during wartime, finding a 128-page comic of all-new material on sale for twenty-five cents was a welcome discovery. *The Big All-American Comic Book* was a standalone issue edited by Sheldon Mayer and starred characters from the All American Publications lineup, including lead heroes Wonder Woman, Hawkman, and The Flash alongside lesser lights such as Scribbly, the Whip, and Little Boy Blue. It was published by William H. Wise and Company, an outside publisher with access to paper stockpiles.

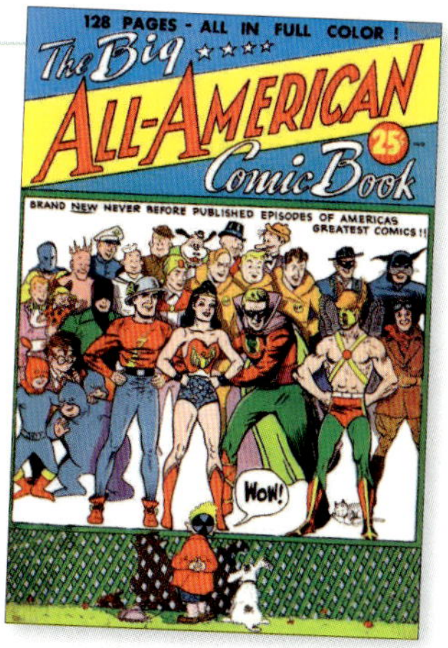

WINTER

OUR FAVORITE TEENSTER

***Buzzy* #1**

By the middle of the 1940s, DC's competitor MLJ Magazines had hit paydirt with *Archie Comics* and the adventures of its titular teen, so DC moved to claim its own piece of the market with the launch of its first dedicated teen title, *Buzzy*. Billed on the cover as "The rib-tickling misadventures of America's favorite teenster," the series starred Buzzy Brown, a scrawny youth with a fondness for swing music. Between pursuing the affections of the sweet Susie Gruff and fending off the schemes of his rival Wolfert, Buzzy barely had time to lead his hepcat five-piece combo and listen to the latest stacks of wax. Artist George Storm captured Buzzy and the other denizens of the town of Cupcake Center in whimsical, stylized curves, creating a unique look that complemented the punchy scripts of Alvin Schwartz. Many adventures brought Buzzy into conflict with Susie's short-fused father Popsy, though Buzzy remained unflappably cheerful no matter what predicament he faced. Introduced as a back-up feature in *All Funny Comics* the previous year, Buzzy was the only *All Funny Comics* experiment to be spun off into his own ongoing title and paved the way for DC's subsequent teen launches.

In one of their first adventures, Buzzy and his hepcat five-piece combo jam at a local zoo for an elephant named Betsy, who happily jumps along to their "jungle jive."

ALSO THIS YEAR: In May, Wonder Woman joined Superman and Batman in the pages of newspapers with her own daily strip… Lois Lane took a more prominent role in the *SUPERMAN* comic with the first appearance of her own back-up feature in May's *SUPERMAN* #28… Giganta, an ape artificially evolved into the form of a redheaded woman, made her first appearance in *WONDER WOMAN* #9 in summer…

August: IBM presents the first program-controlled calculator, the Automatic Sequence Controlled Calculator, to Harvard University.

November: Franklin D. Roosevelt wins re-election over Republican challenger Thomas E. Dewey, becoming the only U.S. president to serve for a fourth term.

1945

"WHAT WAS SUPERMAN LIKE BEFORE HE GREW TO MAN'S ESTATE—WAS HE JUST AN ORDINARY BOY, OR WAS HE A SUPERBOY?"

Superboy's introduction, *More Fun Comics* #101

DC CONSOLIDATES

1945 saw differences between DC and All American Publications result in a brief period in which the All American titles (including *All-Flash*, *Green Lantern*, and *Comic Cavalcade*) bore an "AA" logo on their covers. The DC-created heroes Starman and the Spectre were also removed from the Justice Society of America in All American's *All Star Comics*. However, the disagreement was over by year's end after DC acquired the All American titles and characters, meaning further developments in the DC Universe would now proceed under one roof.

The creation of Superboy this year provided a new window for telling stories about the Man of Steel, and Hawkman became a stronger hero under the steady hand of artist Joe Kubert. Meanwhile, DC broadened its humor offerings on the newsstand, aiming at the funny animal market with the launch of new title *Real Screen Comics* and a new direction for *Leading Comics*.

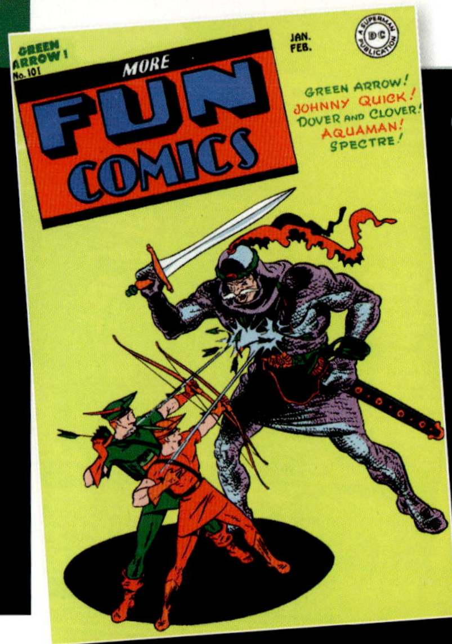

JANUARY

MEET SUPERBOY
***More Fun Comics* #101**

In 1945, Superman reigned as DC's most popular character while child sidekicks such as Robin and Sandy the Golden Boy had made an impact with readers. In *More Fun Comics* #101, DC combined both winning factors with a novel twist by introducing the character of Superboy as a new feature.

The idea of telling the adventures of Superman before he reached adulthood had occurred to writer Jerry Siegel back in 1941, but his proposed series starring Superman "before he developed a social conscience" didn't go anywhere. This short, five-page strip in *More Fun Comics* #101 was written by Siegel but published while he was away during the war, and it was illustrated by Joe Shuster. It introduced Superboy at the approximate age of eight after first retelling the story of his father Jor-El's rocket, the explosion of his home planet of Krypton, and young Kal-El's adoption by the kindly Kents.

The Kents, whose first names went unknown in this story, adopted the boy after finding him in an orphanage and did not appear to be related to the "passing motorist" who had rescued him from his Kryptonian rocket. As he grew, young Clark Kent's muscles came in handy for carrying firewood, but it was only after rescuing a man pinned beneath a truck that Clark realized his extraordinary powers might bring unwanted attention to his adoptive family. The last panel of the feature depicted Clark Kent in his alternate identity of Superboy, sporting a miniature version of the familiar red, blue, and yellow of Superman's costume.

Superboy proved a hit character and returned in the very next issue of *More Fun Comics*, this time scripted by Don Cameron with continued art duties from Shuster. In light of the popularity of his appearances in *More Fun Comics*, DC moved Superboy to a lead spot in *Adventure Comics* #103 in April the following year.

Having escaped the destruction of his home planet, young Clark Kent demonstrates his amazing powers on Earth. Although introduced as a novelty, Superboy would prove to be nearly as popular as his adult incarnation.

IN THE REAL WORLD...

January: The Red Army liberates more than 7,000 remaining prisoners from the Auschwitz and Birkenau concentration camps.

FEBRUARY

HAWKMAN MEETS KUBERT

***Flash Comics* #62**

Artist Joe Kubert began his most memorable work on the gravity-defying super hero Hawkman in this issue. Kubert had joined DC in 1943 and contributed the pencil work on *Leading Comics* #8's Seven Soldiers of Victory feature in Fall of that year. He had also contributed to *Action Comics* and *Sensation Comics* before turning to Hawkman. *Flash Comics* #62's nine-page story "The Painter and the $100,000," written by Gardner Fox, marked the start of a long and fruitful run between illustrator and character. Although Kubert had tackled the Winged Wonder before in 1944's *The Big All-American Comic Book* and as a member of the Justice Society of America in *All Star Comics*, it was his work on the Hawkman feature in *Flash Comics* that became one of DC's signature outputs of the decade.

APRIL

FOCUS ON THE MONOCLE

***Flash Comics* #64**

This issue saw writer Gardner Fox and illustrator Joe Kubert present the Monocle, a new villain with a unique method of committing crimes. Jonathan Cheval was an expert in optics who used lenses—including those in his own distinctive monocles—to focus destructive energy rays. Although stopped by Hawkman in his debut story, the Monocle was set for return appearances. He became representative of the "gimmick villain," a staple of the super hero genre and a common sight among the colorful Rogues Galleries of heroes such as Batman, Superman, and the Flash.

As the Monocle, optics expert Jonathan Cheval develops a number of monacles that can emit different types of energy. He usually operates the powerful devices while holding them to his eye.

SPRING

FROM THE SMALL SCREEN

***Real Screen Comics* #1**

Animated cartoons were big business on movie screens, and lots of publishers hoped that success could translate onto the pages of comic books. However, DC rival Dell Comics had already cornered the market by securing the rights to print comics using the characters from Disney (Mickey Mouse), MGM (Tom and Jerry), Warner Bros. (Bugs Bunny), and Walter Lantz (Woody Woodpecker). Undeterred, DC editor Whitney Ellsworth licensed the characters of Charles Mintz' Screen Gems Studio from their distributor, Columbia.

The resulting funny animal anthology, *Real Screen Comics*, starred the Fox and the Crow, who had debuted in the 1941 cartoon short "The Fox and the Grapes." The confrontational Crow and the upper-crust Fox were next-door neighbors, and their incessant quarrels secured them a recurring feature slot, plus the majority of the *Real Screen* covers. Other features in the Bernie Breslauer-edited title (technically named *Real Screen Funnies*, but only for its first issue) included Tito and his Burrito, starring a Mexican boy and his pet donkey (from 1942's short "Tito's Guitar"), and the canary-and-cat duo Flippity and Flop (from 1944's "Dog, Cat, and Canary").

In a twist on the predator-prey relationship, the Crow is much pushier than the Fox.

SUMMER

DC LETS THE FUR FLY

***Leading Comics* #15**

Leading Comics began as a showcase for super heroes, but as public tastes shifted away from men in tights, it became a testing ground for DC's deeper involvement in the funny animal genre. Perhaps emboldened by the previous year's launch of *Funny Stuff*, DC announced this new direction to readers with the cover line, "They walk! They talk! They're just like humans! But they're all animals—and they're a riot!"

ALSO THIS YEAR: Marine hero Neptune Perkins made his debut in *FLASH COMICS* #66 in August. He had one further appearance in *FLASH COMICS* until revived by writer Roy Thomas in 1984's *ALL-STAR SQUADRON* #33... In December, DC rival Fawcett Comics debuted Black Adam in *MARVEL FAMILY COMICS* #1 as a villainous counterpart to the virtuous members of the Marvel family...

August: The United States drops atomic bombs on Hiroshima and Nagasaki in Japan.
October: The United Nations is founded.
November: Trials against Nazi war criminals begin in Nuremberg.
December: Twenty-eight nations sign an agreement creating the World Bank.

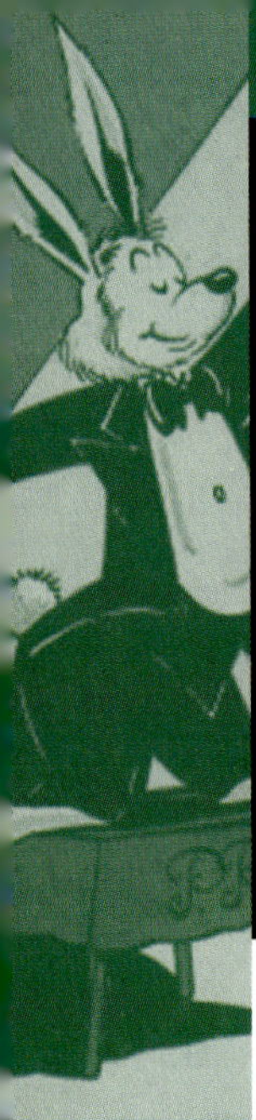

1946

"THE BEST-KNOWN SYMBOL IN COMICS PRESENTS *ANIMAL ANTICS*—CHOCK FULL OF NEW FUNNY FEATURES!"

Promotional copy for *Animal Antics* #1

KEEPING IT LIGHT

With the war a thing of the past in 1946, paper quotas were no longer a concern and DC increased the frequency of many of its titles, including *All-American Comics*, *Green Lantern*, and *World's Finest Comics*. All American Publications was now firmly a part of DC's new official name, National Comics Publications, Inc., with Sheldon Mayer editing the former All American titles alongside Whitney Ellsworth, who edited the comics that had been with DC all along.

The nuclear bomb became ingrained in the public consciousness as the U.S. entered the Atomic Age, and Superman helped usher in the cautious optimism of the post-war era. But people seemed ready to laugh again, so DC launched *Animal Antics* and *Funny Folks* to claim a larger share of the funny animal market. The company also repositioned *More Fun Comics* as a humor title, reflecting the mood that comic books should sometimes be comic in tone.

MARCH

IT'S A ZOO IN HERE
***Animal Antics* #1**

A new DC funny animal title joined the newsstands alongside *Funny Stuff* and *Real Screen Comics*. The inaugural issue of *Animal Antics* starred Presto Pete, a magician's rabbit who performed his own tricks with disastrous results. Other characters getting their tryout in the issue included Walrus Whopper and Sheriff Corky. However, it was Otto Feuer's Raccoon Kids who proved so well-liked that they would take over as *Animal Antics*' lead feature with issue #6. The comic was renamed *Raccoon Kids* in 1954.

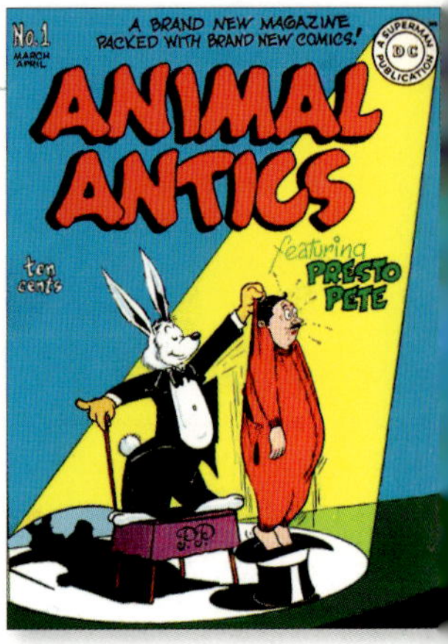

LAUGHING IT UP
***More Fun Comics* #108**

With the announcement "NOW! *More Fun Comics* is loaded with more fun than ever!," DC's oldest title underwent a radical theme change. Now completely focused on humor, *More Fun Comics* pushed aside super heroes like Superboy and Aquaman, who were moved to *Adventure Comics*. Under editor Jack Schiff, Genius Jones the Answer Man moved in (from *All Funny Comics* and *Adventure Comics*), receiving a warm welcome on the cover from mainstays Dover and Clover. Other features in *More Fun Comics*' revamped lineup included the Gas House Gang, Rusty, Cabbie Casey, and Cunnel Custard.

MEET CURT SWAN
***World's Finest Comics* #21**

In an early example of his work for DC, Curt Swan took on art duties for the Boy Commandos in the twelve-page story "Brooklyn and Columbus Discover America," written by Jack Kirby. Swan was a U.S. Army veteran who had spent much of his service with the military newspaper *Stars and Stripes*. In *World's Finest Comics* #21, the artist honed a clean and simple style of expressive character lines. Swan got his first opportunity to draw the Man of Steel in March 1948 in *Superman* #51, and would go on to become one of Superman's most iconic artists during the Silver Age of Comics.

AT THE MOVIES THIS MONTH: Columbia Pictures released a fifteen-part *HOP HARRIGAN* movie serial starring William Bakewell as pilot Hop, Sumner Getchell as his mechanic Tank Tinker, and Jennifer Holt as girlfriend Gail Nolan. Its chapters bore such adrenaline-infused titles as "Plunging Peril" and "The Chute that Failed." The popular aviation hero Hop had first appeared in *ALL-AMERICAN COMICS* #1 in April 1939...

IN THE REAL WORLD...

January: Project Diana bounces radar waves off the moon proving that communication is possible between Earth and outer space.

APRIL

SUPER HEROES RELOCATE

***Adventure Comics* #103**

Following *More Fun Comics*' change in focus the previous month, the displaced super heroes Superboy, Green Arrow, Johnny Quick, Aquaman, and the Shining Knight were welcomed by *Adventure Comics*. Although the move suited the comic's title, it sadly meant the end of Mike Gibbs, Guerilla, and the high-profile Sandman. The Sandman, whose adventures had been in print since 1939, would not appear again in comics until a revival with the Justice Society of America in the 1960s.

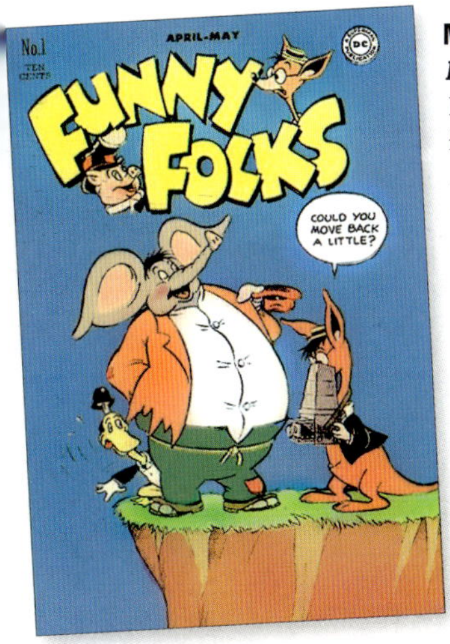

MORE CRITTERS JOIN THE PARTY

***Funny Folks* #1**

Editor Sheldon Mayer launched yet another funny animal title. Like the newly launched *Animal Antics*, the features in *Funny Folks* were originals, not based on characters from animated movie shorts. With a cover showcasing Sweeney and Willie, the first issue included features from Funny Fez, Cheepy, and the animals of Wobbly Creek. But it was Nutsy Squirrel, by writer Woody Gelman and artist Irving Dressler, who became the breakout star. Nutsy was as outlandish as his name implied, and his unhinged antics amused readers enough for the title to be renamed *Nutsy Squirrel* with issue #61 in 1954.

Nutsy Squirrel's anarchic slapstick came from the same tradition as contemporary cartoon stars Bugs Bunny and Daffy Duck.

JUNE

ON RADIO THIS MONTH: A storyline in *THE ADVENTURES OF SUPERMAN* radio show centered on the Ku Klux Klan, earning praise for addressing the nation's social conscience. "Clan of the Fiery Cross" included secret Klan passwords and countersigns passed on to the program's writers by activist and author Stetson Kennedy...

OCTOBER

ATOMIC AGE SUPERMAN

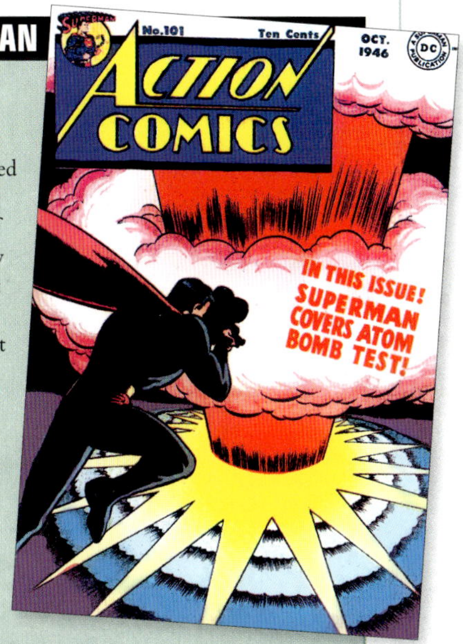

***Action Comics* #101**

A stunning cover by Wayne Boring heralded a tale that played on the conflicted post-war zeitgeist surrounding the use of nuclear weapons. The story, by J. Winslow Mortimer, with art by George Roussos, saw a cabal of crooks cook up a formula that drove their victims—including Superman—insane. The Man of Steel wreaked havoc until an atomic blast at a U.S. military test site in the Pacific knocked the sense back into him. The story's narration described the explosion as a "man-made holocaust," and Superman's first clear-headed action was to photograph a second blast at close range as "a warning to men who talk against peace."

This issue's atomic test was based on the recent Operation Crossroads, in which the U.S. had detonated two nuclear bombs at Bikini Atoll in the Pacific. These were the first atomic explosions since the 1945 destruction of the Japanese cities of Hiroshima and Nagasaki to end the war. To the American readers of *Action Comics*, nuclear destruction may have represented victory and power. The idea of nuclear power as a force to be used for good mirrored Superman himself, who possessed near-unlimited power yet exercised it with the utmost self-restraint. But within several years, Russia had cultivated its own nuclear stockpile and Cold War paranoia took hold of the nation.

NOVEMBER

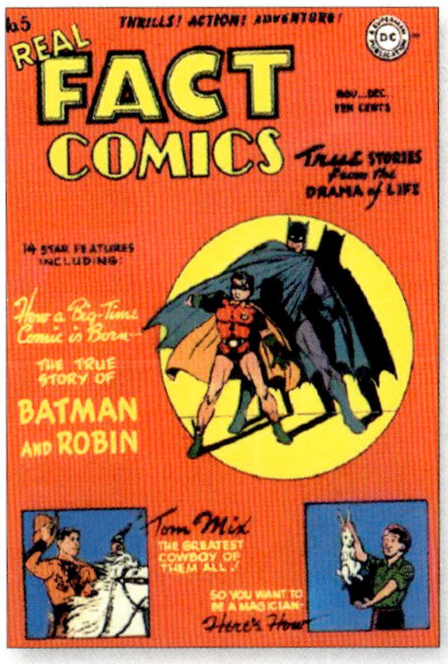

THE FACTS ARE IN

***Real Fact Comics* #5**

Although its cover was devoted to a fanciful biography of Batman creator Bob Kane, titled "The True Story of Batman and Robin," the most notable thing in issue #5 of *Real Fact Comics* was its glowing portrayal of actor, singer, and athlete Paul Robeson. In an era well before the Civil Rights Movement—and devoid of black comic book heroes—the issue wrote of Robeson, "He already, by example, has taught the world as well as his race that color has nothing to do with greatness."

ALSO THIS YEAR: In November, the "BATMAN" newspaper strip ended after a run of three years, bringing Batman creator Bob Kane back to the comic books. "What made Batman powerful were the big splash pages I'd create at the beginning of the stories," he explained. "[In the newspaper] I didn't have enough room to expand on the action."...

June: In a referendum, Italians decide to turn Italy from a monarchy into a republic.
July: Bikinis go on sale in Paris for the first time.

October: Mensa International, the high-IQ society, is founded in the United Kingdom.
December: Frank Capra's movie, *It's a Wonderful Life*, is released in New York.

SECRETS OF THE BATCAVE

REAL FACT COMICS #5 (November 1946)
"True Stories from the Drama of Life," "How a Big-Time Comic Is Born," "The True Story of Batman and Robin"—these were just some of the features promised on the cover of *Real Fact Comics* #5, part of a twenty-one-issue series that took fans behind the scenes of DC Comics and its character universe. One of issue #5's highlights was a tour of the Batcave conducted by Batman creator Bob Kane!

WAYNE HOME
LAB
ELEVATOR
WORKSHOP

1947

"MEET THE MOST FASCINATING CROOK OF ALL TIME! THE BLACK CANARY! THOUGH AN ENRAGED UNDERWORLD WOULD HAVE GIVEN A FORTUNE FOR HER IDENTITY, NOBODY KNEW WHO SHE WAS!"

Black Canary's introduction, *Flash Comics* #86

IDEAS AND EXPERIMENTS

A new generation of artists including Alex Toth, Joe Kubert, and Carmine Infantino began to set a new house style at DC in 1947, employing dynamic figures and clear panel staging. Super heroes began to decline in popularity but DC did everything it could to keep them in readers' hearts, with Robin breaking away from Batman to embark on a solo career and the Black Canary making a splash with her debut in *Flash Comics*. Even the super-villains got in on the act, pooling their sinister talents to form the Injustice Society of the World and menacing the heroes of the Justice Society of America. DC also experimented with new genres this year, launching the romance/humor title *A Date with Judy*, while *Real Fact Comics* took on a futuristic slant by creating a vision of tomorrow.

JANUARY

HELLO TOMORROW
***Real Fact Comics* #6**
Space hero Tommy Tomorrow, the first man to reach Mars, debuted in this issue of *Real Fact Comics*. The series had begun as an experiment to relate both historical biographies and the "strange but true" tales that dominated the newspaper feature *Ripley's Believe it or Not*. Tomorrow's inaugural tale of his journey to the red planet and back, drawn by Howard Sherman, was a fanciful dramatization of what writer Jack Schiff claimed to be a future vision of human space travel.

FEBRUARY

ROBIN IN THE SPOTLIGHT

***Star Spangled Comics* #65**
The first solo Robin series began with what the cover promised would be "a thrilling new series of smash adventures." Readers seemed to agree, and Robin held this spot for five years until *Star Spangled Comics* published its last issue in March 1949. Robin's ten-page introductory tale, "The Teen-Age Terrors," by J. Winslow Mortimer centered on the Boy Wonder going undercover to infiltrate a crooked reform school. Because of his youth, Robin provided certain storytelling opportunities that Batman did not, and subsequent adventures often paired him with kids his own age, including a boy movie star in issue #66 and a group of child geniuses in issue #67.

DC had placed an increased focus on kid heroes since the mid-1940s, with the likes of Superboy, Genius Jones, and the Boy Commandos emerging from it. Ironically, it was one such feature, the Newsboy Legion, that had fallen by the wayside in the pages of *Star Spangled Comics* in order to make room for Robin. On the cover of *Star Spangled Comics* #64 in January, the Newsboy Legion could be seen adrift at sea, forlornly clinging to a life preserver as a potential rescue ship steamed away from them and toward the horizon. The metaphor could not have been more poignant, as the Newsboy Legion did not appear again in comics until their surprise revival in October 1970, when they were featured in *Superman's Pal, Jimmy Olsen* #133.

IN THE REAL WORLD...
February: Edwin Land demonstrates the first "instant camera," the Polaroid Land Camera, at a meeting of the Optical Society of America.

HAM ON A ROLL
***Leading Comics* #23**

Piggy prankster Peter Porkchops seized the *Leading Comics* cover position from Roman Emperor Nero Fox on his debut. This proved to be a wise move for editor Bernie Breslauer, since Peter had potential and was headlining his own title within three years. Illustrated by Otto Feuer (known for his work on the Raccoon Kids and Dodo and the Frog), Peter's first story saw him vex his neighbor Wolfie in a familiar setup for repeatable comic gags. This issue also heralded a "flock of brand new animal friends," including Puss 'n' Pooch and Doodles Duck.

JUNE

A TOMAHAWK REVOLUTION
***Star Spangled Comics* #69**

The historical hero Tomahawk burst onto the scene in the ten-page back-up story "Flames along the Frontier," illustrated by Edmond Good. Although Tomahawk tapped into many of the themes found in Western titles, his adventures were set a century earlier during the time of the American Revolution. After Native Americans captured settler Tom Hawk and taught him their ways, he vowed to fight injustice as Tomahawk. He even acquired a sidekick when he helped a young boy, Dan Hunter, stop a group of vicious men from smearing the reputation of a local tribe.

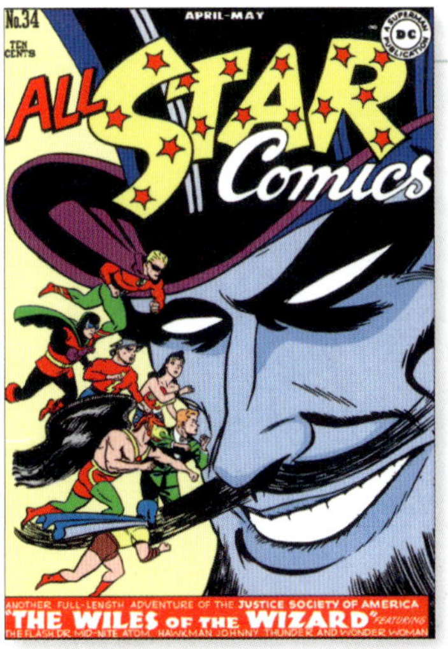

APRIL

GARDNER FOX SIGNS OFF
***All Star Comics* #34**

Gardner Fox penned his last story about the Justice Society of America in this issue. The writer, who scripted the group's very first adventure in *All Star Comics* #3 (January 1941), introduced an ill-tempered illusionist called the Wizard who was convinced that the JSA were fakes posing as do-gooders in order to plan criminal deeds. The Wizard made enough of an impact with readers that he was brought back for the debut of the villainous Injustice Society of the World in October (issue #37).

MAY

WONDER GIRL?
***Wonder Woman* #23**

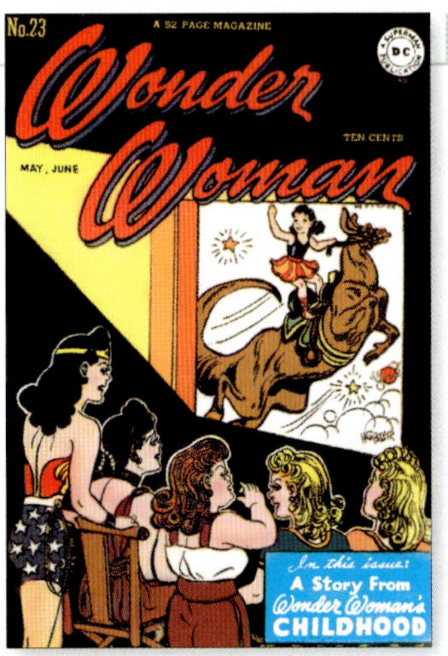

If Superman could have a Superboy backstory, why couldn't Wonder Woman have a Wonder Girl? That may have been writer William Moulton Marston's reasoning when he penned the twelve-page "Wonder Woman and the Coming of the Kangas," with art by Harry Peter. The flashback tale was narrated by Amazonian Queen Hippolyte to the visiting Holliday Girls, and depicted a young Wonder Woman in a fight against the aliens of Nebulosta and their airborne sky kangas. Although Diana was not specifically named "Wonder Girl" in the story, it opened the door for writer Robert Kanigher to explore the narrative possibilities of a child version of Wonder Woman when he revisited the concept in the 1950s.

AUGUST

THE BLACK CANARY
***Flash Comics* #86**

With the obvious exception of Wonder Woman, female comic book heroes in the 1940s tended to have short shelf lives—a fact made worse by the overall post-war decline of the super hero genre. One notable exception was the Black Canary.

Debuting as a supporting character in a six-page Johnny Thunder feature written by Robert Kanigher and pencilled by Carmine Infantino, Dinah Drake was originally presented as a villain trying to steal a priceless sapphire. Her plan was thwarted by Johnny Thunder, but Dinah managed to evade her captor. Artist Carmine Infantino drew Dinah as a bombshell beauty so attractive that even Johnny Thunder spent most of his story smitten by the newcomer. The Black Canary's costume added an undeniable jolt of sex appeal, consisting of fishnet stockings, high-heeled boots, a bustier, and an open jacket. She also wore a domino mask but dropped the face covering after her first appearance.

Also jettisoned in subsequent adventures was Black Canary's ambiguous moral positioning, as she became more of a straightforward hero and teamed up with private investigator Larry Lance to solve crimes. Johnny Thunder, however, still became her victim—the Black Canary kicked him out of the pages of *Flash Comics* starting in issue #92 (February 1948). She would perform the same trick over on *All Star Comics* in June 1949, replacing him in the Justice Society of America with issue #41.

The Black Canary uses her striking good looks to bamboozle men, but her skills as a fighter and investigator are second to none.

April: Jackie Robinson, the first African-American baseball professional, signs a contract with the Brooklyn Dodgers.

August: After more than 150 years of British colonial rule, India becomes an independent nation. Jawaharlal Nehru takes office as India's first Prime Minister.

OCTOBER

INJUSTICE FOR ALL

***All Star Comics* #37**

The Justice Society of America had pioneered the concept of the super hero team back in *All Star Comics* #3 (January 1941), and this issue enjoyed doing exactly the opposite. In Robert Kanigher's story, featuring art by Irwin Hasen and Joe Kubert, a cabal of villains united as The Injustice Society of the World and took revenge on the JSA's assembled do-gooders.

The scoundrels came from other DC adventures, including the quick-witted Thinker (from *Flash Comics*), the cunning Gambler and immortal Vandal Savage (from *Green Lantern*), as well as the mystical Wizard, time-traveling Per Degaton, and psionically gifted Brain Wave from *All Star Comics*. Together, the Injustice Society created an army of prison escapees and forced the JSA to split up. They then captured the heroes but were undone by Green Lantern's clever subterfuge.

The issue's cover by Irwin Hasen depicted the members of the Injustice Society carving up a map of the U.S. and assigning their names to each part. This provided a visual metaphor for their violent greed and a handy cheat sheet for new readers who might not have been familiar with their names. The Injustice Society later returned in *All Star Comics* #41 (June–July 1948).

The Injustice Society drops recruitment leaflets on a prison shortly before freeing all of its inmates. Vandal Savage is the mastermind behind the plot.

INFANTINO AND FLASH

***All-Flash* #31**

The first Carmine Infantino art of the Flash character appeared in this issue's twelve-page adventure "The Secret City." Infantino had recently worked on the Injustice Society tale in *All Star Comics* #37 and before that on the Ghost Patrol and Johnny Thunder stories in *Flash Comics* (with the Black Canary's introduction in August's *Flash Comics* #86 representing his first published work for DC). But it was Infantino's work on the Flash that would become the cornerstone of his career.

Unfortunately, very little time remained for anyone to make an impact on readers using the Jay Garrick version of the Flash. *All-Flash* would be canceled with the following issue, and *Flash Comics* had less than two years left before giving up the ghost. In these pages, however, Infantino showed a gift for character expression with his economical use of lines. In depicting a character with super-speed, the artist developed methods for conveying blur and other tricks of visual shorthand. Infantino set himself up for a long career at DC, which would lead into his role in the Silver Age revival of the Flash as a new character named Barry Allen (with Jay Garrick reappearing as an occasional guest star).

YOUR DATE'S HERE!

***A Date with Judy* #1**

As comics began to diversify beyond super heroes, DC hoped to strike gold with *A Date with Judy*, which combined elements of teen, humor, and romance comics all in one title. Licensed from a long-running radio show of the same name, the series centered on the teenaged Judy, her boyfriend Oogie Pringle, and her frustrated father. Jack Schiff edited the stories, with Graham Place providing the art. Billed on its cover as "Radio's famous coast-to-coast favorite," *A Date with Judy* soon found its audience and settled in for a thirteen-year run.

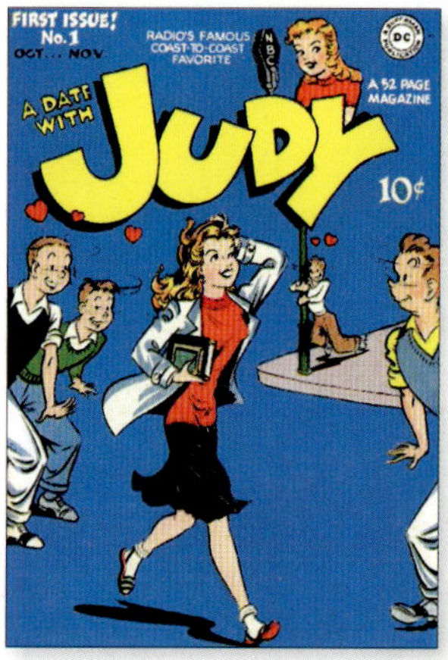

ALEX TOTH

***Green Lantern* #28**

This issue featured some of the earliest DC work by talented young artist Alex Toth. Both "The Fool Comes to Town" and "The Tricks of the Sportsmaster" were representative of Toth's skill with character illustration and his use of panels to advance the flow of visual storytelling. A recent art school graduate, Toth got his professional start at DC and before long found a niche in reinvigorating the Western comics genre. Alongside other newcomers such as Joe Kubert and Carmine Infantino, Toth helped bring a fresh look to the pages of DC.

IN THE REAL WORLD...

September: The National Security Act creates the Central Intelligence Agency (CIA).
October: Civil war begins in Kashmir, leading to the Indo-Pakistani War of 1947.
November: Princess Elizabeth, daughter of King George VI, marries Prince Philip, the Duke of Edinburgh at Westminster Abbey, London.

NOVEMBER

A THORNY ISSUE

***Flash Comics* #89**

Writer Robert Kanigher and artist Joe Kubert presented a female twist on Robert Louis Stevenson's *Dr. Jekyll and Mr. Hyde* with the Thorn, who made her first appearance in a twelve-page story within this issue. The Thorn was the villainous alter ego of the harmless Rose Canton, who gained superpowers to match her killer alternate personality when she transformed into the Thorn. Jay Garrick used his wits and speed to survive his encounter with the Thorn, but she returned once more in *Flash Comics* #96 (June 1948). The Thorn then entered a decades-long hibernation before her revival in the 1970s.

"HA HA! I WONDER WHAT THE FLASH WOULD THINK IF HE KNEW THE ROSE AND THE THORN ARE ONE!" The Thorn, *Flash Comics* #89

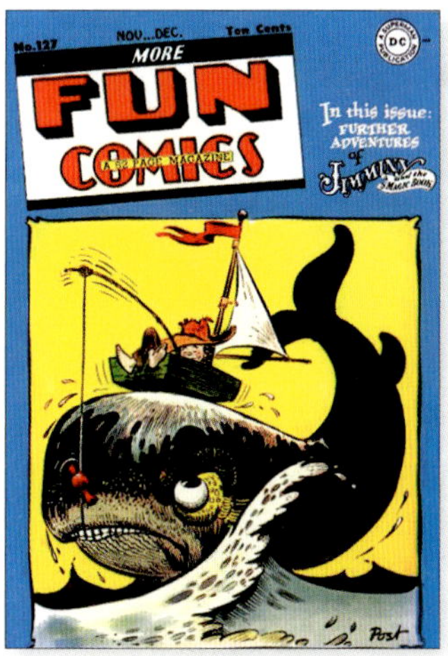

END OF AN ERA

***More Fun Comics* #127**

DC's longest-running title came to an end as *More Fun Comics* published its final issue. The series, which began as *New Fun Comics* back in 1935, had made countless changes in an effort to keep up with readers' changing tastes. Most recently, the title had scaled down comedy features like Dover and Clover and Genius Jones in favor of the imaginative Jimminy and the Magic Book, from writer Jack Mendelsohn and artist Howard Post. The story of a boy who traveled to other times, places, and realms via his book's pages debuted in issue #121 (April 1947), but it could not save the title from cancelation.

INTRODUCING DOC AND FATTY

***All Funny Comics* #20**

Continuing its experimentation with the humor medium, *All Funny Comics* focused its attention on a new feature starting in this issue. Doc and Fatty were two comedic con men given an unbelievable gift—the ability to travel back to other eras of history. This premise was introduced in the issue's lead story, "A Trip Thru Time," by writer/artist Howard Sherman, and on the cover, which featured a gag as old as Egypt itself. In later adventures, the pair met such notorious figures as Captain Kidd and Ali Baba, but they couldn't prevent *All Funny Comics*' cancelation with issue #23.

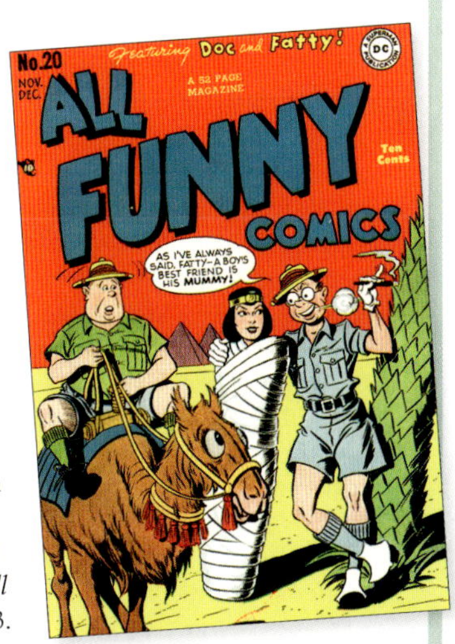

DECEMBER

THE CANARY FLIES THE NEST

***All Star Comics* #38**

In a sign of the character's growing popularity, Black Canary made her first appearance outside of *Flash Comics* in a feature by writer Robert Kanigher and artist Alex Toth. Faced with the apparent murders of the members of the Justice Society, Black Canary teamed up with Wonder Woman to restore the heroes and solve the crime. By the story's end, Black Canary was considered for JSA membership, but wouldn't officially join until *All Star Comics* #41. The character she replaced in the team, Johnny Thunder, was her costar in her introductory *Flash Comics* appearances.

TWO VILLAINS, TOO LATE

***All-Flash* #32**

Although writer Robert Kanigher and artist Lee Elias introduced a pair of new villains to *All-Flash* in this issue, the series couldn't stem the ebbing popularity of the super hero genre and issue #32 became its last. In true gimmick-villain fashion, the Fiddler fought his enemies using malevolent emanations from his violin, while Star Sapphire possessed the power to challenge the Flash in his dreams. The Star Sapphire concept proved durable, however, and provided an idea seed for the 1960s revamp of Green Lantern during the Silver Age.

CRIME DOESN'T PAY

***Gang Busters* #1**

DC hoped it could beat slumping sales trends with its first dedicated entry into the crime comics genre. To minimize risk, DC licensed an established property—the *Gang Busters* radio program, which had been on the airwaves since 1935 (originally under the name *G-Men*). Edited by Jack Schiff, the *Gang Busters* comic focused on FBI cases and standalone crime stories. The first issue included tales titled "Murder Was My Business" and "The Case of the Iron-Clad Alibi." Later issues featured photo covers, a practice becoming increasingly common in the late 1940s.

ALSO THIS YEAR: Catwoman proved her potential as a villain by making her first cover appearance in a story in April's *DETECTIVE COMICS* #122... Readers made the acquaintance of the Gentleman Ghost in a nine-page Hawkman story within October's *FLASH COMICS* #88, written by Robert Kanigher and illustrated by Joe Kubert...

November: The United Nations General Assembly votes to partition Palestine between Arab and Jewish regions resulting in the creation of the State of Israel.

December: American playwright Tennessee Williams' play, *A Streetcar Named Desire*, opens on Broadway.

1948

"OUT OF THE OLD WEST ON A HORSE THAT STREAKS ACROSS THE PLAINS LIKE LIGHTNING AND WITH SIX-GUNS THAT ROAR LIKE THUNDER APPEARS A NEW AMERICAN CHAMPION!"

Johnny Thunder's introduction, *All-American Comics* #100

COMIC BOOK COWBOYS

This was the year of the Western comic. DC made a splash with the launch of *Western Comics,* and *All-American Comics* was transformed into *All-American Western*. New characters who hailed from the frontier included Nighthawk and an all-new Johnny Thunder. DC branched further into the crime genre with *Mr. District Attorney,* and broadened its line of teen offerings with *Leave it to Binky* and a relaunch of the boy cartoonist Scribbly in a title of his very own.

Super heroes were clearly on their way out, a fact driven home when Green Lantern was upstaged by a dog in his own comic. Yet Superman and Batman continued going strong, with Superman celebrating the tenth anniversary of his debut in *Action Comics* and Batman receiving some colorful additions to his Rogues Gallery in the form of the Riddler and the Mad Hatter.

JANUARY

COMICS GO WEST
***Western Comics* #1**

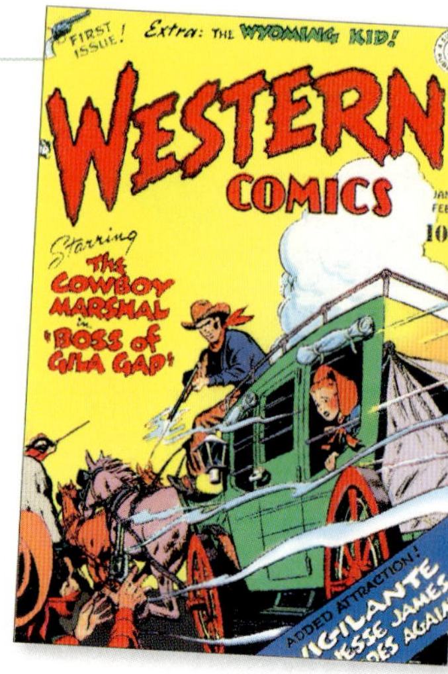

The introduction of *Western Comics* stood as proof of DC's commitment to the Western genre. Its first issue introduced new characters including the Wyoming Kid, Cowboy Marshal, and Rodeo Rick, but the Vigilante may have seemed most familiar. The bandana-masked hero had already earned his place among the Seven Soldiers of Victory following his introduction in *Action Comics* #42 (November 1941). Although his adventures took place in contemporary times, the Vigilante's costume helped him fit in among the stars of *Western Comics*.

LAYING DOWN THE LAW
***Mr. District Attorney* #1**

Like its contemporary *Gang Busters*, the crime comic *Mr. District Attorney* was licensed from a popular radio show. The radio version had been on air since 1939 and DC was quick to advertise its popular pedigree with a cover banner reading "Based on radio's No. 1 hit!" Its subject was the tough-talking (and nameless) District Attorney, an implacable and callous force for justice who fought ugly crooks with colorful names like "Smoke-Rings" Thompson and the Pittsburgh Kid. *Mr. District Attorney* came along at the right time to catch a wave of crime comics and lasted for sixty-seven issues.

AT THE MOVIES THIS MONTH: Movie distributors had been trying to say "Up, Up, and Away" to a Superman movie deal for years, and Columbia Pictures finally got the project off the ground. The fifteen-part *SUPERMAN* serial was directed by Thomas Carr and starred Kirk Alyn as Superman and Noel Neill as Lois Lane. As a cost-saving measure, Superman's flying shots were achieved through hand-drawn animation...

FEBRUARY

TEENAGE TROUBLES
***Leave it to Binky* #1**

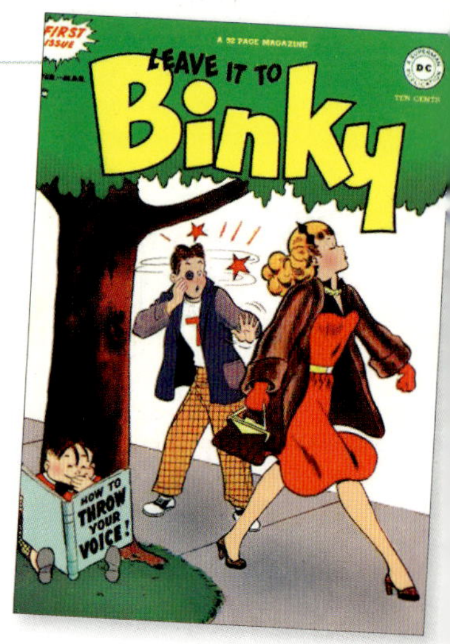

Another teen title joined DC's lineup. *Leave it to Binky* centered on the hapless Binky Biggs and his efforts to date the beautiful Peggy, despite the interferences of his troublemaking younger brother "Little Allergy." Edited by Sheldon Mayer, with art by Bob Oksner, *Leave it to Binky* followed in the footsteps of DC's 1944 launch of the teen title *Buzzy*. Both titles reflected the fact that competitor Archie Comics Publications had turned teen comics into big business through its namesake title *Archie Comics* and its popular freckle-faced hero.

IN THE REAL WORLD...

January: Warner Bros. Pictures shows the first color newsreel.
January: Indian leader and pacifist Mahatma Gandhi is assassinated.

GOING TO THE DOGS
***Green Lantern* #30**

The debut of Streak the Wonder Dog in a story by writer Robert Kanigher and artist Alex Toth wasn't a good sign for Green Lantern. Perhaps inspired by another popular German Shepherd, Rin Tin Tin, Streak was popular from the outset. Even on this issue's cover, Green Lantern was just a spectator, watching as Streak got the laugh by depositing a bone at the local bank. Streak took over the cover of issue #34 in September, but he couldn't save his master's series from cancelation the following year.

JULY

A MILESTONE FOR THE MAN OF STEEL
***Superman* #53**

Superman's origin was retold—and slightly revamped—for this special tenth anniversary issue, which commemorated the character's first appearance in 1938's *Action Comics* #1. Writer Bill Finger and penciller Wayne Boring related how Jor-El failed to save Krypton and sent his son to Earth. After finding Clark, the Kents took him to an orphanage and later adopted him. The Kents were named John and Mary, and both died before Clark left Smallville for Metropolis (with Clark's career as Superboy not mentioned at all). It would be several years before the Kents received the enduring names of Jonathan and Martha.

AUGUST

THE BOY CARTOONIST GROWS UP
***Scribbly* #1**

Scribbly Jibbet, the boy cartoonist written and drawn by Sheldon Mayer, received his own title in 1948 after years of appearances in *All-American Comics* and *Comic Cavalcade*. *Scribbly* was the beneficiary of a teen comics boom that also saw the launch of *Leave it to Binky*. The series still contained Mayer's work but now focused more on romance and Scribbly's attempts to get a steady job, with the previously regular guest-star Red Tornado notably absent from its pages. During the fifteen-issue run of *Scribbly*, the Scribbly character also appeared in a few back-up stories in *Leave it to Binky* and *Buzzy*.

OCTOBER

RIDDLE ME THIS

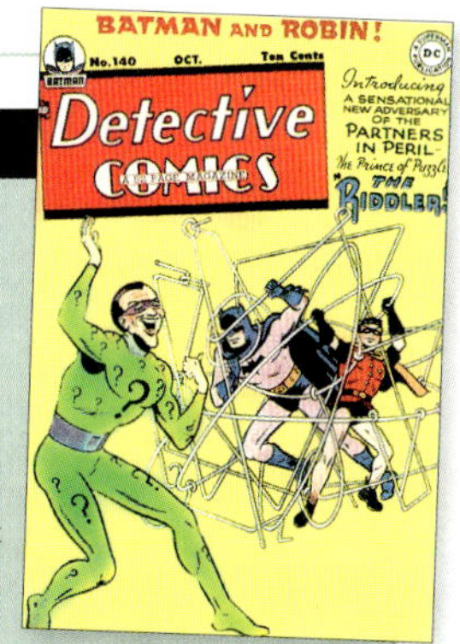

***Detective Comics* #140**

The Riddler debuted as a perplexing foe of Batman in a story by writer Bill Finger and artist Dick Sprang. The brilliant Edward Nigma stayed one step ahead of his competitors by using "riddles, jigsaws, acrostics, and all types of puzzles to perplex the Dynamic Duo." As the Riddler, Nigma donned a costume speckled with question marks and left clues to his crimes all over Gotham, including a crossword puzzle on the side of a building, heavy-wire brainteasers capable of crushing a man, and a jigsaw so huge it could only be assembled inside a sports stadium.

Despite Batman's reputation as a brilliant detective, the Riddler's enigmas left him a step behind, and he and Robin found themselves trapped inside a glass maze at the end of the Riddler's debut adventure. Batman forced his way out of the maze before a bomb destroyed it, which seemingly killed the Riddler—but a question mark floating in the harbor left the door open for future appearances from the Prince of Puzzles.

The Riddler believes he has fooled Batman and Robin, but soon learns that even he can be outwitted.

AT THE MOVIES THIS MONTH: *ACTION COMICS* star Congo Bill appeared in new movie serial *CONGO BILL* from Columbia Pictures, with Don McGuire in the title role…

NOVEMBER

WESTWARD HO
***All-American Western* #103**

All-American Comics became *All-American Western* with this issue, and Johnny Thunder leaped out from a backdrop of comic pages on the cover to announce the radical transition. At the movies, Westerns were hotter than ever, and DC hoped to cash in on the craze. In addition to Overland Coach and Foley of the Fighting Fifth features, the issue included the first appearance of Minstrel Maverick—a singing cowboy who used his guitar as his weapon.

ALSO THIS YEAR: Otto Binder wrote the first appearance of Merry, Girl of 1000 Gimmicks in *STAR SPANGLED COMICS* #81 in June… Western gunslinger Johnny Thunder, who was curiously unrelated to the former JSA member Johnny Thunder, debuted in a story by writer Robert Kanigher and artist Alex Toth in *ALL-AMERICAN COMICS* #100… Charles Paris drew the first appearance of Western hero Nighthawk in *WESTERN COMICS* #5 in September… Inspired by Lewis Carroll's *Alice in Wonderland*, the Mad Hatter joined the other costumed freaks of Gotham City on his debut in October's *BATMAN* #49…

April: The World Health Organization is established by the United Nations.
June: Albert I is the first monkey to be launched into space from New Mexico.
December: The United Nations General Assembly adopts the Universal Declaration of Human Rights.

1949

"I'M GOING TO KEEP ON ASKING YOU UNTIL YOU MARRY ME!"
"I HOPE THAT DAY WILL COME SOON, DARLING!"

Steve Trevor and Wonder Woman, *Sensation Comics* #94

LOVE IS IN THE AIR

With the end of the decade, the mood of comics had shifted to romance. DC moved to dominate the field with three new titles: *Romance Trail, Girls' Love Stories*, and *Secret Hearts*. There was also a lovelorn reworking of *Sensation Comics*. As comics emphasized traditional gender roles and the courtship dances of eligible suitors, even Superman got in on the act, marrying Lois Lane in his newspaper strip. *Miss Beverly Hills of Hollywood* helped DC establish a tie with celebrity culture, along with a number of other celebrity comics based on stars Alan Ladd, Jimmy Wakely, and Ozzie and Harriet. Although Green Lantern, Flash, and the Boy Commandos saw their comics end this year, Superman received a boost with the introduction of a dedicated Superboy title.

MARCH

COMICS GO GLAMOROUS

***Miss Beverly Hills of Hollywood* #1**
An odd entry into the field of celebrity comics, this title featured Miss Beverly Hills and her interactions with real-life Hollywood guest-stars including Alan Ladd and Wanda Hendrix. Beverly had a newspaper reporter boyfriend named Will Shire (a play on Los Angeles' Wilshire Boulevard) and most stories revolved around her desire to meet movie stars and become a star herself. The series blended the celebrity, humor, and romance genres with mixed results, and sadly only made it to issue #9.

SUPERBOY STEPS UP

***Superboy* #1**
Superboy had been making appearances as a lead feature in *Adventure Comics* since early 1946, but he finally debuted in his own series with this issue. Any Superman fans who were unfamiliar with the "adventures of Superman as a young boy" concept may have been reassured by the fact that the adult Man of Steel himself presented the lead story of *Superboy* #1, as a narrative flashback to his childhood.

The first issue saw Superboy help protect a Smallville friend after a psychic predicted her death, battle the troublesome Boy Vandals, and compete in a talent competition against a new rival named Mighty Boy. In the issue's "how-to" feature, called "Superboy's Workshop," readers could learn how to make a rocket plane and how to make a telephone out of two cans and a piece of string. The *Superboy* series featured the writings of the likes of France E. Herron and William Woolfolk and proved a success, lasting for over thirty years.

Even when challenged by rivals like Mighty Boy or faced with natural disasters, Superboy maintains a cheerful spirit.

IN THE REAL WORLD...

January: The first Volkswagen Beetle to arrive in the United States, a 1948 model, is brought to New York by Dutch businessman Ben Pon.

MAY

THE LIGHT DIMS FOR GREEN LANTERN

***Green Lantern* #38**

In a sign of the end of the Golden Age of Comics, *Green Lantern* ended its run with a story by John Broome and Irwin Hasen. To add insult to injury, Green Lantern was nowhere to be seen on the cover of *Green Lantern* #38, as his crime-fighting pet, Streak the Wonder Dog, hogged the spotlight. The Green Lantern story scheduled for the nonexistent issue #39 was put on the shelf for years until it was printed during the 1960s revival of the hero.

AT THE MOVIES THIS MONTH: The fifteen-part movie serial *BATMAN AND ROBIN* is released, starring Robert Lowery as Batman and Johnny Duncan as Robin and centering on a plot by the hooded villain the Wizard...

JULY

LAUNCHING INTO LOVE

***Romance Trail* #1, *Girls' Love Stories* #1, *Secret Hearts* #1**

When it came to romance, DC put its heart on the line by launching no less than three new series. First up was *Romance Trail*, a Western-themed romance billed to be "as romantic as an Arizona sunset." The first installment featured a photo cover of singing cowboy star Jimmy Wakely (who would receive his own series later that year), but *Romance Trail* only lasted six issues. *Girls' Love Stories* also featured a photo cover, this time bearing the pathetic plea, "It was like tearing my heart in two—yet I couldn't hate him!" The stories were overheated epics of emotional abandonment, summed up with quotes such as "I aimed at the target, and the arrow pierced my heart!" Yet *Girls' Love Stories* must have been doing something right, finding an audience and publishing steadily until 1973. In September, *Secret Hearts* rounded out the trio. Its first issue featured the DC bullet on its cover but that logo disappeared in subsequent installments as the title tried to set itself apart from traditional DC Comics fare. Promoted with the promise of "52 romantic pages," *Secret Hearts* enjoyed a run that lasted decades.

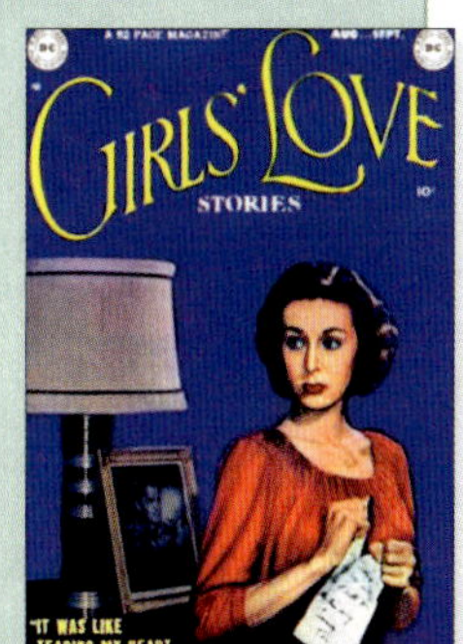

IN NEWSPAPERS THIS MONTH: Clark Kent and Lois Lane were married in a "SUPERMAN" story by Alvin Schwartz and Wayne Boring. Their union would last for two years until it was retroactively undone by calling it a dream...

NOVEMBER

THE FIRST SUPERGIRL

***Superboy* #5**

Although the cover bore the promise "In this issue—Superboy meets Supergirl!," the Supergirl in question was not the figure who would come to make her mark during the Silver Age of Comics. Instead, the story centered on young Queen Lucy of the mythical Latin American nation of Borgonia, who was an excellent athlete but possessed no superpowers at all. When Smallville's mayor asked Queen Lucy to perform athletic feats at a local benefit, a smitten Superboy used his super-breath to make it appear as if she could leap great distances and used his powers of flight to let her join him in the sky.

ROY RAYMOND, TV DETECTIVE

***Detective Comics* #153**

Television was a new medium in 1949, and this issue saw the debut of Roy Raymond, adventurer and star of the fictional TV program "Impossible—But True!" In his first adventure, drawn by Ruben Moreira, Roy traveled to the Amazon to investigate reports of a valley that caused travelers to suddenly grow old. Setting the pattern for future stories, Roy uncovered secret shenanigans and exposed the site as a hoax. The feature was initially named "Impossible—But True" but later became "Roy Raymond, TV Detective."

POCKET FULL OF KRYPTONITE

***Superman* #61**

Kryptonite finally appeared in comics following its introduction in *The Adventures of Superman* radio show back in 1943. In a story by writer Bill Finger and artist Al Plastino, a mysterious swami appeared to weaken Superman with a hex. However, the Man of Steel determined that the cause of his weakness was a piece of meteorite rock placed within the swami's turban. He traced the rock back through time in a ghostlike form, viewing Krypton's destruction and his own rescue as a baby by the Kents. Superman now possessed knowledge of his Kryptonian origins and was at last aware of why he was the strongest man on Earth.

ALSO THIS YEAR: *FLASH COMICS* crossed the finish line with issue #104 in February... DC rode the coattails of a movie celebrity with *THE ADVENTURES OF ALAN LADD* #1 in October... Licensed from the popular comedy radio show, *THE ADVENTURES OF OZZIE AND HARRIET* was launched in October... The Boy Commandos rocketed away on the cover of their final issue, November's *BOY COMMANDOS* #36... *SENSATION COMICS* started to focus entirely on romance with issue #94 in November...

February: The Arthur Miller play *Death of a Salesman* opens in the Morosco Theater, New York, and runs for 742 performances.

April: Éire leaves the British Commonwealth and becomes the Republic of Ireland.
July: The de Havilland Comet, the first jet-powered airliner, makes its maiden flight.

1950s

AT THE BEGINNING of the 1950s, super hero comics were in the middle of a post-World War II decline. Genre titles proliferated while super hero comic stagnated, with few exceptions. War comics, relatively unpopular during the long years between Pearl Harbor and Nagasaki, took off again and the beginning of the Space Age brought about a surge in the number of science-fiction titles. Western and crime titles also saw huge growth, while super hero books languished.

Toward the middle of the decade a long-simmering public debate over comic books and their influence on American youth came to a boil. The moralism and witch-hunting tendencies of the 1950s drove the infamous Kefauver hearings, at which psychologist Fredric Wertham became the eternal nemesis of comics fans and EC Comics' William Gaines made a name for himself by trying to defend the good taste of an image of a severed head. The Comics Code Authority put an end to the excesses of horror and crime comics, sending a clear signal to the industry that comics, like everything else in Cold War America, were supposed to be God-fearing, anti-Communist, and family-friendly.

This signaled a return to costumed heroes. By the tim 1960 loomed on the horizon, the super hero comic was in the ascendancy again, back from the dead after creators learned to work with the CCA (which Werthan dismissed as a half-measure). Sgt. Rock, the Phantom Stranger, J'onn J'onzz, Krypto the Super-Dog, the Legion of Super Heroes, and the Bottle City of Kandor, among other debuts, permanently altered the landscape of the DC Universe. The 1950s that we all know—the half-decade of "Duck and Cover," *Sputnik*, DiMaggio, Marilyn, and the birth of rock'n'roll—was in full swing. A new generation of creators had revitalized old heroes, or created new ones, and comics' Silver Age had dawned

"STAND BACK CRYLL... WE'LL MAKE THIS OUR OWN DOOR! THIS VACUMIZER WILL SCOOP OUT A HOLE TO HIDE US... WHILE I USE A THERMOBLAZE ON THE WALL ITSELF!"

Space Ranger, *Showcase* #15 (August 1958

1950

"I NEVER SAW A BABY STAND SO FIRM OR WALK SO WELL AT HIS AGE!"

Martha Kent, *Superboy* #8

SCI-FI TIMES

The 1950s were to be a science-fictional decade, as the public's interest in new technologies and space travel grew. DC's first title in the science-fiction genre, *Strange Adventures*, debuted with an adaptation of a new science-fiction movie. *Sensation Comics* changed its focus from romance to science fiction and introduced the new hero Astra, Girl of the Future. Meanwhile, an early version of the prison dimension later known as the Phantom Zone appeared in a Superman movie serial.

This was also the year that comedian Bob Hope began his adventures in comics, as DC began to license celebrity images. Super hero comics were now declining in popularity but readers were introduced to Superboy as a Superbaby, and later saw Lana Lang walk into his life. While over in *Batman*, the dawn of the Jet Age was marked with a redesigned Batplane, and Batman and Robin met their Arthurian counterparts.

FEBRUARY

HAVE TUX, WILL TRAVEL
***The Adventures of Bob Hope* #1**

Super hero comics were on the decline, so DC decided to obtain licensing rights to use celebrity images. The first of these was *The Adventures of Bob Hope*, written by Cal Howard, with art by Owen Fitzgerald. The series followed the (mis)adventures of "America's favorite funnyman" for 109 issues, the last four of which were drawn by Neal Adams, who would later make his mark on the Batman and Superman comics. The lead stories followed the hapless Hope through comedic sagas blurbed by teasers like "A haunted house—a heavenly honey—and a horrified Hope add up to a HILARIOUS ADVENTURE!" Supporting tales focused on other celebrities of the day—issue #1 included a story featuring Rhonda Fleming, Hope's costar in the 1949 movie *The Great Lover*.

MAY

MEET SUPERBABY
***Superboy* #8**

In the *Superboy* series, young Clark Kent had primarily appeared as a teenager, but *Superboy* #8 introduced a toddler version of the Man of Steel. In a story written by Bill Finger and drawn by Curt Swan, "Superbaby" wore a red-and-blue costume sewn by Martha Kent from the super-strong blankets that had swaddled him on his journey to Earth from Krypton. Like any other toddler, little Kal-El spent his days exploring his surroundings and getting into trouble—but his secret superpowers often raised the stakes, creating comic havoc.

JULY

AT THE MOVIES THIS MONTH: The fifteen-part movie serial *ATOM MAN VS. SUPERMAN*, distributed by Columbia Pictures, featured something called "The Empty Doom" in its eighth chapter. The Empty Doom was a prototype for the Phantom Zone, a prison dimension for Krypton's worst galactic criminals that would not appear in comic books until 1961's *ADVENTURE COMICS* #283...

AUGUST

DESTINATION ADVENTURE!
***Strange Adventures* #1**

DC picked up on renewed public interest in science fiction by launching its first comic in the genre, the anthology series *Strange Adventures*. The series kicked off its 244-issue run with an adaptation of the first color science-fiction movie, *Destination Moon* (released that same month), written by Gardner Fox and drawn by Curt Swan. Issue #1 also saw the first appearances of "science detective" Darwin Jones, by scripter David Reed and artist Paul Norris, and child of space Chris KL-99, from legendary sci-fi author Edmond Hamilton and artist Howard Sherman.

IN THE REAL WORLD...

January: The International Police Association (IPA), the largest police organization in the world, is formed.

SEPTEMBER

TOMAHAWK'S RANGERS
***Tomahawk* #1**

After ongoing back-up appearances in *Star Spangled Comics* and *World's Finest Comics* during the late 1940s, "America's favorite frontier hero" Tomahawk was awarded his own title. *Tomahawk* was set in the period of the American Revolution and narrated the adventures of soldier Tom Hawk (or Thomas Haukins) as he fought under George Washington through the French and Indian War, and then the Revolution. Hawk, drawn by Bruno Premiani, was adept with his namesake weapon, fluent in any Native American language he encountered, and the valiant leader of the fighting force, Tomahawk's Rangers.

QUEEN OF SMALLVILLE

***Superboy* #10**

Superboy met the girl next door in *Superboy* #10, when the spunky redhead Lana Lang made her first appearance. In a story written by Bill Finger, with art by John Sikela, Lana quickly became infatuated with her Smallville neighbor, Clark Kent, almost as much as she was with local super hero, Superboy. The inquisitive teen was a dogged pursuer of Superboy's identity from the outset, and her debut issue saw her first (failed) attempt to discover it.

As Clark Kent's childhood sweetheart, Lana Lang acted much like a younger version of Superman's love interest Lois Lane, becoming convinced that Clark Kent and Superman were the same person and spending much of her time trying to prove this theory. Later, Lana appeared in various 1960s stories (particularly in *Superman's Girl Friend, Lois Lane*) to serve as foil for Lois Lane, triangulating Clark Kent between two strong and ambitious women.

The teenage Lana was given special powers in *Superboy* #124 (October 1965) when a chance interaction with an insect-like alien left her with a ring that granted her the power to assume the partial form of any insect. As the Insect Queen, Lana had a series of adventures in *Superboy* and *Adventure Comics* before Clark, in an ironic twist, discovered her secret identity. Lana Lang was later awarded the position of reserve member of the Legion of Super-Heroes after she rescued four Legionnaires, including Superboy, on a Legion mission in *Adventure Comics* #355 (April 1967).

Lana Lang rescues an insect-like alien trapped under a tree. The grateful creature then rewards her with special powers.

OCTOBER

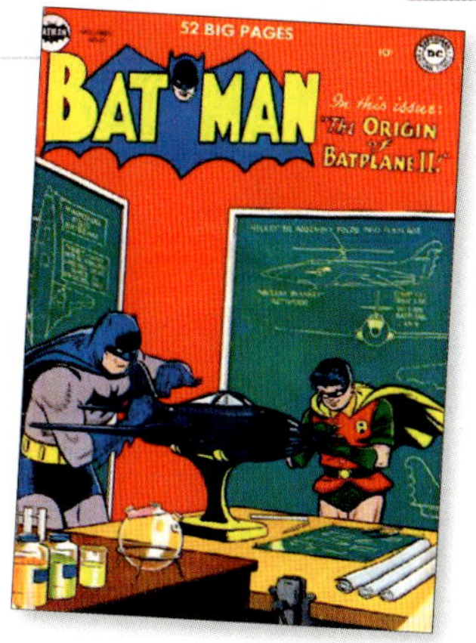

THE BATPLANE TAKES OFF
***Batman* #61**

Writer David Reed and artist Dick Sprang premiered an extensively redesigned version of the Batplane in *Batman* #61. The first fixed-wing version of the Batplane had debuted in *Batman* #1 (Spring 1940), but the Batplane II was much sleeker, as befitted a customized Wayne Aerospace product. Gone was the bat-head design on the front of the earlier version's fuselage; now the Batplane was aerodynamic, jet-propelled, and ready for anything. The cover of this issue featured the Dynamic Duo working on a scale model of the plane, and inside readers discovered that it came complete with "television, radar, crime lab, [...] 'vacuum blanket,' Batmarine, ejectors, [and] the Bat-Beam."

DECEMBER

ANOTHER DYNAMIC DUO
***Batman* #62**

An Arthurian version of Gotham's Dynamic Duo, Knight and Squire, made their first appearances in *Batman* #62. Writer Bill Finger and artist Dick Sprang were behind the father-and-son duo of Percy and Cyril Sheldrake, who teamed up with the Caped Crusader and the Boy Wonder to take down a nest of neo-Nazis at Stonehenge in "The Batman of England." Later, after Percy's death, Cyril would become the Knight and train a new Squire.

REINDEER GAMES
***Rudolph the Red-Nosed Reindeer* #1**

DC began an annual tradition of producing a *Rudolph the Red-Nosed Reindeer* Christmas special. Following the success of the famous song (released in 1949), DC licensed the character and put Rudolph at the center of a series of lighthearted adventures. Rudolph's holiday festivities included everything from pulling a stuck Santa out of a chimney to running on a treadmill to power a complex, Rube Goldberg-inspired contraption that painted a series of last-minute toys for Santa. The Christmas Special would continue until 1962, and then return from 1972–77.

ALSO THIS YEAR: In February, the dating and marriage-themed comic *GIRLS' ROMANCES* began. The title was without a DC logo as it was jointly published by the National Romance Group... In September, Astra, Girl of the Future began her run as a recurring feature in *SENSATION COMICS* #99, as the title shed its romance focus and turned to science fiction. The girl "telecaster" from the far future moved through time and space on a series of adventures...

August: American swimmer Florence Chadwick crosses the English Channel in 13 hours and 22 minutes, breaking the world record.

October: The comic strip "Peanuts" by Charles M. Schulz is first published in U.S. newspapers.

1951

"I WAS BORN JUST AS AN UNKNOWN, BRILLIANT COMET FLASHED ACROSS THE SKY... SO I WILL BE CAPTAIN COMET!"

Adam Blake (Captain Comet), *Strange Adventures* #1

SUPER HERO SLUMP

Super hero comics, once so popular, fell on hard times in 1951, and it was Western, mystery, and science-fiction comics that came forth to replace them. DC's super hero anthology *All Star Comics* changed its focus to Western-themed tales, becoming *All Star Western*. The company launched its second science-fiction anthology title, *Mystery in Space*. And by the end of the year, another anthology title, *House of Mystery,* made its debut with stories centering on all things supernatural.

Despite most super heroes proving unpopular, Captain Comet—DC's first mutant hero—managed to make a big impact in *Strange Adventures*. Meanwhile, Superman's continuing success was marked on the big screen with his first-ever feature film, *Superman and the Mole Men*, which also saw the debut of George Reeves as the Man of Steel.

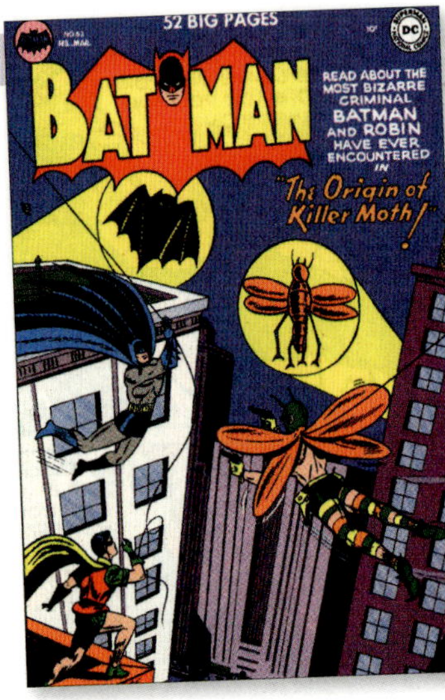

FEBRUARY

DEBUT OF KILLER MOTH
***Batman* #63**

Batman #63 kicked off with the origin story of a new Batman villain: the Killer Moth. Once a prisoner known only by his prison number, 234026, the Killer Moth wanted to become the "anti-Batman." Upon his release from prison, he donned a garish winged costume, constructed a "Mothcave," assumed the false identity of Cameron van Cleer, and became the patron saint of Gotham City's underworld. The Killer Moth soon clashed with Batman and Robin and used his "Mothmobile" to capture the Dynamic Duo, but they quickly escaped and set up a showdown on the 1,000-foot-high Gotham Bridge. During the climactic battle, the Killer Moth fell off the bridge and disappeared… until *Batman* #64 the following month, that is.

The Killer Moth builds a high-powered Mothmobile to rival Batman's own Batmobile, then uses it to capture Batman and Robin.

APRIL

***ALL STAR WESTERN* RIDES INTO TOWN**
***All Star Western* #58**

As super hero comics continued to decline in popularity, many of them mutated into Western, crime, and horror titles. The super hero omnibus *All Star Comics* was one such series, becoming *All Star Western* as of issue #58. With work by artists Gil Kane, Carmine Infantino, and Alex Toth and writer Robert Kanigher, among others, *All Star Western* would run for ten years as a bimonthly title and feature such ongoing characters as the Trigger Twins (who starred in the inaugural issue), Johnny Thunder, and Madame .44. After a hiatus during the 1960s, *All Star Western* returned for eleven issues in 1970–72, during which run the DC readership was first introduced to the menacing, tormented loner who called himself Jonah Hex.

IN THE REAL WORLD...

March: Hank Ketcham's best-selling comic strip "Dennis the Menace" appears in newspapers across the U.S. for the first time.

APRIL

RACING INTO SPACE

***Mystery in Space* #1**

Although the early 1950s were difficult years for super heroes, they were boom years for science-fiction comics, so DC took its opportunity to launch its second title in the genre, *Mystery in Space*.

The new title kicked off a 110-issue run with a classic pulp-fiction-style sensational cover, featuring the dramatic rescue of a damsel from certain outer-space death. Each issue of *Mystery in Space* contained a variety of material, mixing popular-science articles and public-service announcements ("Know Your Country!"; "Be Your Self—Your Best Self!"; "Be Sure of Your Facts!") with ongoing storylines and non-series tales, a format that was established from the outset. *Mystery in Space* #1 included a Knights of the Galaxy cover story by Robert Kanigher and Carmine Infantino, along with three standalone science-fiction tales, two informative text articles, and a public-service announcement by Superman entitled "Human Rights for All."

Mystery in Space would run until September 1966, and by its end had introduced such recurring feature stars as Space Cabbie, the Star Rovers, and Hawkman (who was launched in his own title in 1964)—but the series' signature character was without doubt the space hero Adam Strange. After moving to *Mystery in Space* from *Showcase* at issue #53 (August 1959), Strange would come to dominate the title, appearing in forty-eight straight issues before skipping one and taking his final bow in issue #102 (September 1965).

JUNE

A FIRST FOR MUTANTS

***Strange Adventures* #9**

In an attempt to revive readers' interest in super heroes, writer John Broome and artist Carmine Infantino introduced "Tomorrow's Man of Destiny", Captain Comet, in *Strange Adventures* #9. After a childhood in which he discovered abilities ranging from telepathy to a form of clairvoyance, Adam Blake met the scientist Emery Zackro and learned that he was a mutant, his genome transformed by the radiation of a comet that had passed Earth at his birth. Professor Zackro then mentored Adam as he became the super hero Captain Comet. With a ship and weapons courtesy of the professor's tinkering, Captain Comet—DC's, and possibly comics', first mutant hero—would appear in thirty-eight issues of *Strange Adventures* (until issue #49 in October 1954), fighting enemies ranging from destructive aliens to homicidal flowers.

NOVEMBER

AT THE MOVIES THIS MONTH: Following on from the success of the two previous *SUPERMAN* movie serials, George Reeves debuted as the Man of Steel in the first Superman feature movie, *SUPERMAN AND THE MOLE MEN* (costarring Phyllis Coates as Lois Lane)...

DECEMBER

HOUSE OF HORRORS

***House of Mystery* #1**

Like DC's popular science-fiction comics *Mystery in Space* and *Strange Adventures*, *House of Mystery* was a wide-ranging anthology title, but what made it different was that its content was mostly horror-themed. *House of Mystery*'s debut issue offered tales of the supernatural from classic horror (such as cover story "Wanda was a Werewolf") to articles debunking spiritualism ("Exposing Voices from Beyond"). The meat of the series' early issues was occult stories mixed with crime thrillers, plus the occasional foray into science fiction.

However, when the Comics Code Authority was formed in 1954 in response to public concerns about "inappropriate" content in comics, horror-themed storylines featuring supernatural entities like werewolves and vampires were banned. *House of Mystery* was therefore forced to gradually re-focus itself as a suspense and science-fiction title.

House of Mystery was revamped once more in the Silver Age of Comics, changing its focus to super heroes as of issue #143 in June 1964. In this guise, *House of Mystery* would give the super hero Martian Manhunter his first run as a lead feature from #143–155 (June 1964–December 1965) after years as a back-up feature in *Detective Comics*.

The House of Mystery was a location that existed within the DCU, although its origins remained unknown and its dimensions shifted constantly. In the late 1960s, the biblical Cain was introduced to reside over the house as an "Able Care Taker" with issue #175 (August 1968). The same issue saw *House of Mystery* return to its horror roots under the editorial direction of EC Comics veteran Joe Orlando, as the comics industry began to edge away from the Comics Code Authority.

House of Mystery remained in the horror genre for the rest of its run, which lasted up to issue #321 (October 1983). Before the series ended, *House of Mystery* #290 (March 1981) introduced Andrew Bennett, the anguished vampire hero of the serialized story "I…Vampire." During this period, under the editorial direction of future Vertigo chief Karen Berger, the title showcased the artistic talents of Berni Wrightson and Sergio Aragones, among others. After the final issue of the series, the House of Mystery remained as a location, reappearing as a key location in the Dreaming of Neil Gaiman's *The Sandman* (1989).

ALSO THIS YEAR: Celebrity comic *THE ADVENTURES OF ALAN LADD* came to an end with issue #9 in February. The title followed the exploits of the popular movie star Alan Ladd, but it failed to win enough readers to last beyond its two-year run… The decline in popularity of super hero comics led to the adventure series *ALL STAR COMICS* ending its run at issue #57 in February, ironically with a story entitled "The Mystery of the Vanishing Detectives"…

July: Judy Garland opens the first of fourteen concerts in Dublin, Ireland.
August: *The Catcher in the Rye* by J. D. Salinger is first published.
October: New York Giants' Bobby Thomson hits a game-winning home run against the Brooklyn Dodgers, in one of the greatest moments in Major League Baseball history.

1952

"OUT OF THE SWIRLING MISTS OF NOWHERE LOOMS A MYSTERIOUS FIGURE TO SHIELD THE INNOCENT FROM THE DARK FORCES OF EVIL..."

The Phantom Stranger's cover introduction, *Phantom Stranger* #1

POST-WAR DC

By 1952, the United States had been sending troops overseas for twelve years, with the most recent conflict, the Korean War, slowly beginning to grind to a halt. War had been very much a part of life for comics readers, and most had been affected by it in some way. Although war comics had been relatively unpopular during World War II, 1952 was a boom time for the genre, with *Our Army at War*, *Star Spangled War Stories*, and *The Adventures of Rex the Wonder Dog* all making their debuts.

Television was a new cultural phenomenon that was spreading across America's suburbs by 1952, and this was the year that *The Adventures of Superman* made its TV debut, bringing the Man of Steel to the small screen.

Perhaps the most notable comics character to emerge this year was the mysterious entity known as the Phantom Stranger, who kept everyone guessing from the start.

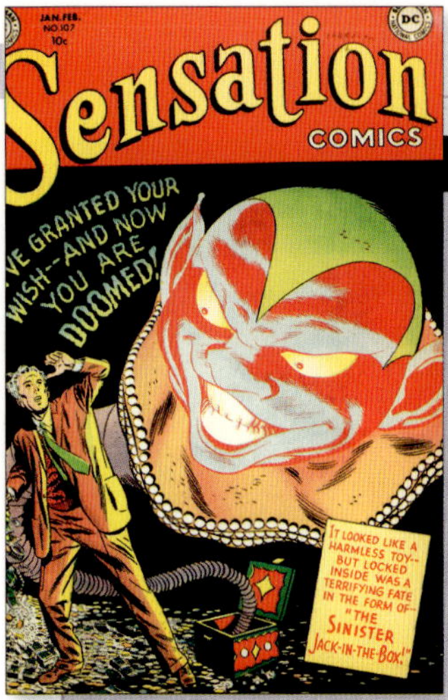

JANUARY

PERILOUS ADVENTURES

***Sensation Comics* #107**

Sensation Comics started life as a super hero title in 1942 and gave Wonder Woman her first cover on its debut issue. For most of *Sensation Comics*' run the lead feature remained Wonder Woman, but from issue #107 the theme of the comic changed as the mysterious adventurer known as Johnny Peril took center stage.

Little was known about Johnny Peril, and even his name was likely to be an alias. What readers did know was that Peril was a high-risk adventurer who got involved in mysteries of an unusual nature. He had first appeared in *Comic Cavalcade* #22 in August 1947 before his move to *Sensation Comics*. In his first issue as a lead feature, Peril starred in a supernatural tale entitled "The Sinister Jack-in-the-Box," which was drawn by legendary artist Alex Toth.

At issue #110, *Sensation Comics* changed its name to *Sensation Mystery* to better represent its new focus. Johnny Peril remained the lead feature of the comic until its demise six issues later in July 1953. The tenacious Peril would live beyond *Sensation Mystery*, however, reappearing during the 1970s in a more substantial role as an "adventurer of the weird" in the horror anthology series *The Unexpected*.

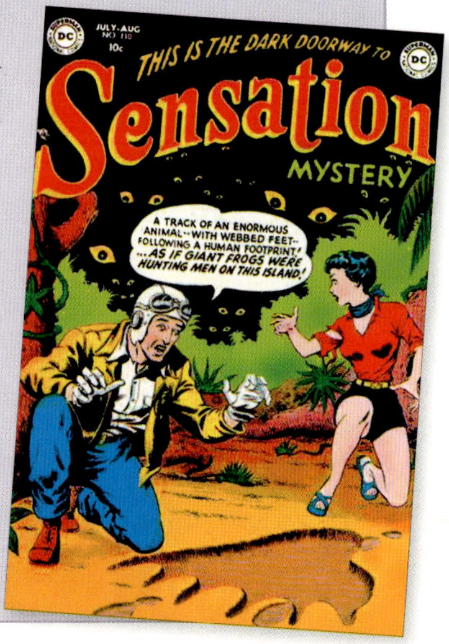

A WONDER DOG'S LIFE

***The Adventures of Rex the Wonder Dog* #1**

Rex the Wonder Dog leaped into comics with his own bimonthly series, kicking it off with an adventure following the "Trail of the Flower of Evil," written by Robert Kanigher and Alex Toth. Possibly named after a canine silent-movie star of the 1920s, Rex the Wonder Dog had been selected by a U.S. Army doctor to be test subject for a super-soldier serum which gave him incredible strength, speed, stamina, and intelligence. After serving in World War II and Korea, the white German shepherd came home with his handler Major Dennis and embarked on a forty-six-issue run of heroic adventures, ranging from serving as a small-town sheriff to bullfighting and solving interstellar crimes.

IN THE REAL WORLD...

January: *The Today Show* premieres on U.S. TV channel NBC.
February: In England, Elizabeth II becomes queen upon the death of her father.

AUGUST

STRANGER IN TOWN

***The Phantom Stranger* #1**

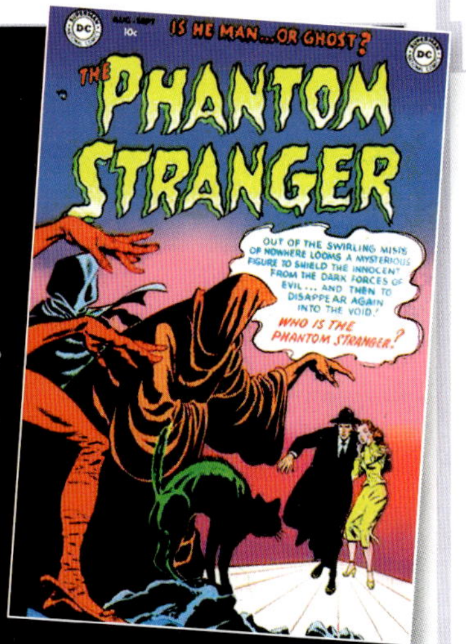

The Phantom Stranger is unusual in comics history because his true name and origins have never been decisively revealed. Is he a fallen angel? Is he the son of Superman and Wonder Woman? No one knows. From his first appearance in the six-issue miniseries bearing his name, the Phantom Stranger has been a figure of pure mystery.

In his first series, the Phantom Stranger often made his appearances to debunk supernatural-seeming events, and the inaugural issue established this theme from the outset with stories like "The Haunters from Beyond" and "When Dead Men Walk" from writer John Broome and artist Carmine Infantino. The first saw a woman almost driven to suicide when she was haunted by ghosts, but a mysterious stranger stopped her and quickly proved that the "ghosts" were just two people in disguise trying to steal the woman's inheritance. In the second, three men died in a plane crash and their spirits returned to haunt those they left behind, but the Phantom Stranger revealed that the "hauntings" were in fact the work of an embezzler trying to cover up a theft. In both stories, the Phantom Stranger always seemed to know more about situations than the other characters expected, and he was the only thing that remained unexplained by the end. The Phantom Stranger always disappeared just as quickly as he came, and left everyone wondering "Who is the Phantom Stranger?"

After this six-issue introduction, the Phantom Stranger went on a seventeen-year hiatus, reappearing in February 1969 in *Showcase* #80 (February). A new *Phantom Stranger* title then began in June that year, with the original miniseries providing reprint material for the first few issues before the title went on to develop the character into a powerful occult figure in his own right. The Phantom Stranger evolved through this series and over several more into one of the most powerful and enigmatic beings in the DC Universe.

Three men die in a catastrophic plane crash and they each seemingly return to haunt those they left behind, before the Phantom Stranger exposes the hauntings as a hoax.

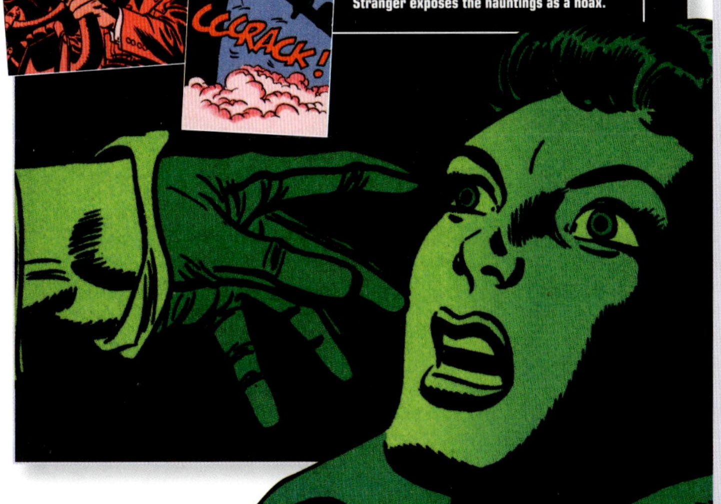

AUGUST

THE GRUNTS-EYE VIEW

***Our Army At War* #1**

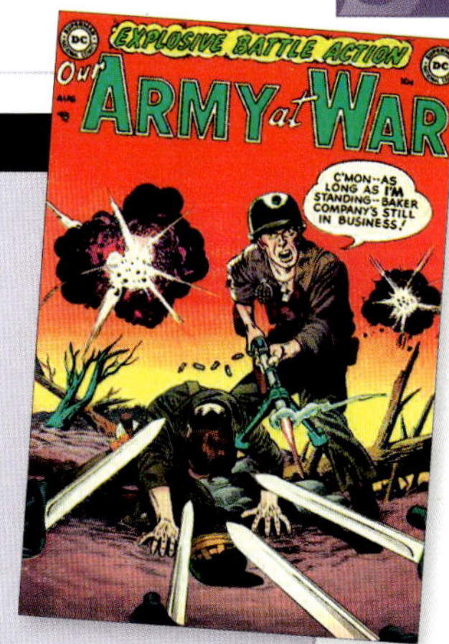

DC's latest title, *Our Army At War,* emerged at the forefront of a wave of war-themed comics that swept the industry in the early 1950s. After 1954, war comics proved popular not only with readers; the Comics Code Authority was happy to approve gung-ho war stories at a time when tight restrictions were placed on other comics. By that time, *Our Army at War* was already on duty ahead of its competition.

The comic's stories took place primarily in World War II and Korean War settings. They were nearly always focused on the way war looked from the ground, with stories like "Dig Your Foxhole Deep," by writer Robert Kanigher and artist Irv Novick, appearing in the first issue. The everyday heroism of the infantryman—or even the mess sergeant—formed the core of *Our Army at War*.

The title eventually became best known for launching the toughest master sergeant ever to come out of Pittsburgh—one Frank Rock. First written by Robert Kanigher and drawn by Joe Kubert, Sgt. Rock and his unit, Easy Company, debuted in issue #81 (April 1959). From then on, *Our Army at War* increasingly focused on Sgt. Rock and Easy Company, and was eventually renamed *Sgt. Rock* as of issue #302 in March 1977.

SEPTEMBER

ON TV THIS MONTH: The first episode of *THE ADVENTURES OF SUPERMAN* aired in September, bringing the Superman feature-movie star George Reeves to the small screen for six seasons...

NOVEMBER

FLAMING ACTION ON FIGHTING FRONTS

***Star Spangled War Stories* #3**

Star Spangled Comics had brought adventure stories to the reading public since October 1941, but its name change to *Star Spangled War Stories* turned the focus of the title to war-themed characters and stories. *Star Spangled War Stories* was initially intended to be a retitling of *Star Spangled Comics* and continued the numbering of its predecessor from issue #131. However, that only lasted until issue #133, when DC rebooted the numbering so that the first *Star Spangled War Stories* issue was #3. The title would, over the next 200 issues, become the primary home of German anti-hero Enemy Ace and the mysterious Unknown Soldier, and it was retitled *The Unknown Soldier* as of issue #205 (May 1977).

ALSO THIS YEAR: July saw the debut of another celebrity-themed title, *THE ADVENTURES OF DEAN MARTIN AND JERRY LEWIS*. The series typically involved Jerry Lewis's misapprehensions regarding his attractiveness to bevies of young ladies and Dean Martin, as always, was right there to provide his trademark martini-dry commentary...

July: Maria Eva Duarte de Perón, known as "Evita," dies of cancer at the age of thirty-three. During her life she championed women's suffrage in Argentina.

September: The first open-heart surgery is performed at the University of Minnesota.
November: The United States successfully detonates the first hydrogen bomb.

1953

"THERE IS THE SCENT OF EVIL IN THE WIND—A SCENT MIGHTIER THAN ANY I HAVE EVER KNOWN!"

Rex, *The Adventures of Rex the Wonder Dog #11*

A NEW DIMENSION

In 1953, Sir Edmund Hillary and Tenzing Norgay proved that seemingly miraculous feats were not restricted to comic books when they displayed extreme strength and endurance in reaching the summit of Mount Everest.

Dinosaurs and gorillas appeared in greater numbers of DC comics, as did stories reflecting the growing concerns about nuclear war. In 1953, with the communist nuclear threat looming, the U.S. continued to develop its nuclear arsenal, conducting atomic tests in Nevada. *The Adventures of Rex the Wonder Dog* addressed these fears in September and fulfilled a public service role by giving civilians instructions to follow in case of an attack.

And let's not forget a signature phenomenon of the early 1950s: 3-D. Following the popularity of 3-D movies like *Bwana Devil*, *Man in the Dark*, and *House of Wax*, both Batman and Superman had 3-D comics in 1953.

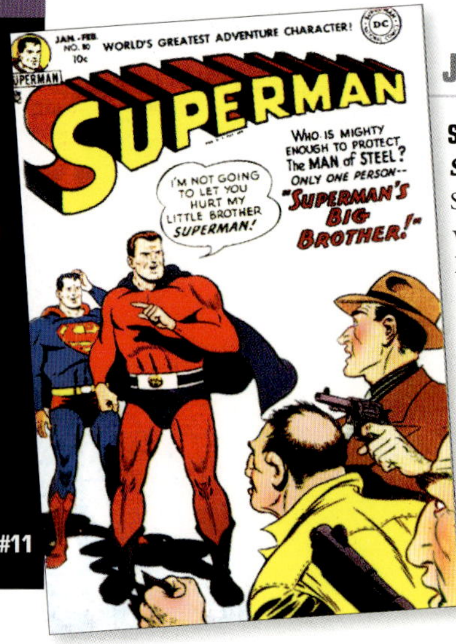

JANUARY

SUPERMAN'S FAMILY
***Superman* #80**

Superman's first taste of finding family was in "Superman's Big Brother" by writer Edmond Hamilton and artist Al Plastino. Superman found an unconscious man, Halk Kar, with no memory and a note from Superman's father, Jor-El, that led him to believe Halk was his brother. But Superman was puzzled over Halk's lack of superpowers when they teamed up to fight crime. After Halk regained his memory, it emerged that he was not a Kryptonian (or Superman's brother), but a Thoron: His rocket had crashed on Krypton and was sent on to Earth by Jor-El.

JUNE

GEE WHIZ
***Whiz Comics* #155**

Longtime home of Captain Marvel and the crime-fighting frontier archer Golden Arrow, Fawcett Publications' *Whiz Comics* came to an end with issue #155. After a twelve-year lawsuit with National Comics Publications over Captain Marvel's copyright infringement of Superman, Fawcett settled out of court and agreed to cease its Captain Marvel comics. Faced also with the decline of super hero comics, they soon closed their entire comics division. As well as Captain Marvel, *Whiz Comics* was known for introducing the Egyptian sorcerer Ibis the Invincible, the adventuresome seaman Lance O'Casey, and the original Spy Smasher. Several of its characters, including Captain Marvel, were later revived by DC.

AUGUST

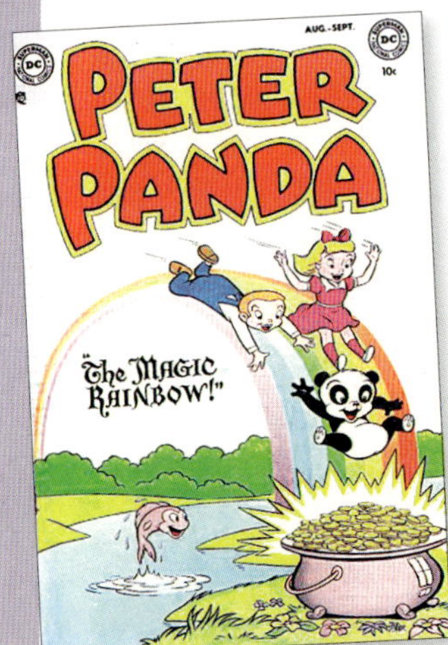

WATCH OUT FOR FOXY DAN!
***Peter Panda* #1**

Not all 1950s comics were full of super heroes, occult mysteries, or star-spanning adventures. Some were gentle kids' fantasy titles like *Peter Panda*. Starting with this first issue drawn by Rube Grossman and believed to be written by Sy Reit, Peter and his friends Dronald Dragon and Jimmy and Janie Jones embarked on a thirty-one-issue series of escapades. Peter and his friends rarely met actual bad guys; rather harmless schemers like Foxy Dan. Most stories were fractured fairy tales or funny-animal capers, many involving dragons from Dronald's neighborhood—which, reinforcing the series's kid-friendliness, wasn't too far from Mother Goose's house.

IN THE REAL WORLD...

April: James D. Watson and Francis Crick publish their discovery of the DNA double helix.

SEPTEMBER

REX VERSUS REX!

***The Adventures of Rex the Wonder Dog* #11**

Rex the Wonder Dog faced a T. rex in "Rex, Dinosaur Destroyer" by writer Robert Kanigher, penciller Gil Kane, and inker Sy Barry. The story, which combined early nuclear-age anxieties and incipient dinosaur mania, told how Rex found a dinosaur whose world had been revealed by a nuclear explosion. The canine kept the dino-villain at bay outside a cave and ducked inside as a second test vaporized the T. rex and resealed the opening to its world. This story is also notable for its "Duck and Cover"-style attitude toward the dangers of nuclear war and panel of instructions for readers on what to do in the case of a nuclear attack.

DECEMBER

MONKEYING AROUND

***Strange Adventures* #39**

"The Guilty Gorilla", by writer John Broome and artist Murphy Anderson in *Strange Adventures* #39, was a foray into the intelligent-gorilla craze that flourished in DC comics in the 1950s. In this story, Captain Comet took a break from his usual interplanetary adventures and stayed home in Midwest City to break up a criminal syndicate run by a super-intelligent gorilla.

By December 1953, comics readers had already met several gorillas, including Man-Ape the Mighty, with whom Captain Comet switched minds, and Gorilla Boss, who had the brain of mobster George Dyke. Broome himself would return several times to the gorilla theme, notably in the *Strange Adventures* classic, "The Human Pet of Gorilla Land" from issue #108 (September 1959). In this story drawn by Carmine Infantino, gorillas were masters of civilization who were given a human to keep as a pet. Elsewhere in *Strange Adventures*, apes usurped humanity's role as explorers of space, as in "Gorillas in Space" (issue #64, January 1956).

Later, DC gorillas also included Congorilla, who was originally a human called Congo Bill; the Flash's arch-enemy, Gorilla Grodd; Superman's foes, Titano the Super-Ape and the Ultra-Humanite; the super-villain Monsieur Mallah; and Taro the Gorilla Witch—the mix of a jungle explorer, a gorilla, and a potion. Transforming into apes wasn't limited to walk-on characters; before the craze subsided, even Jimmy Olsen and Superboy had become apes.

DECEMBER

AMAZING 3-D ACTION

3-D Batman

Exactly one hundred years after Wilhelm Rollman first demonstrated the anaglyphic method of creating 3-D images using glasses with one red and one blue lens, the Dynamic Duo leapt off the page in *3-D Batman*. The comic tapped into the 3-D trend that was popular in movie theaters at the time.

Shipped with a bat-shaped pair of 3-D glasses, the comic reprinted 3-D versions of three stories: "The Fowls of Fate" from *Batman* #48 (August–September 1948), "The Interplanetary Aquarium" from *Action Comics* #127 (December 1948), and "The Robot Robbers!" from *Batman* #42 (August–September 1947).

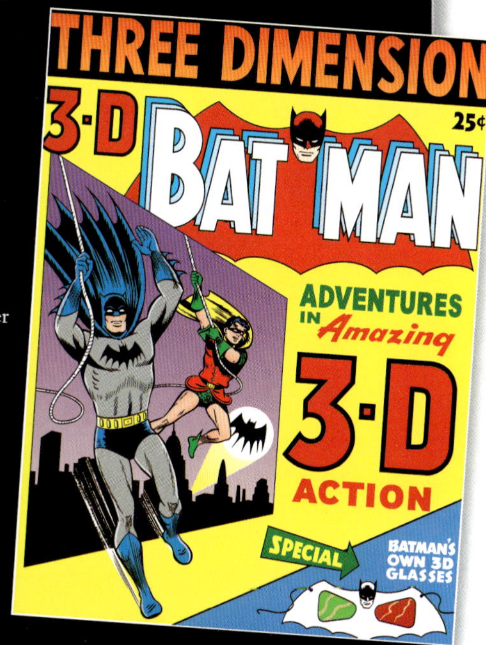

In the same year, Superman also appeared in a 3-D issue, under the banner "startling 3-D life-like action!" Like its Batman counterpart, *Superman 3-D* offered three reworked stories: "The Man Who Stole the Sun" from *Superman* #48 (September–October 1947), "Origin of Superman" from *Superman* #53 (July–August 1948), and "The Man Who Bossed Superman" from *Superman* #51 (March–April 1948). The stories varied in tone from the opener, written by Jerry Siegel and drawn by Curt Swan, in which Lex Luthor caused a planetary crisis, to the closer's lighthearted story of a gangster who wins a day as Superman's boss and lives to regret it, also drawn by Curt Swan.

3-D comics never caught on in any big way, but these two books have become reminders of an age when anaglyphic images jumped not just out from the movie screen, but up from the printed page as well. Both were reprinted after 1953, *3-D Batman* in 1966 and 1990 and *Superman 3-D* in 1998. In both cases, the later reprints—from ages when anaglyphic 3-D was no longer quite the miracle it had seemed in 1953—featured more action-oriented covers than the originals, which had relied on the sheer novelty of 3-D to sell.

ALSO THIS YEAR: Along with the closure of Fawcett's comics division, *CAPTAIN MARVEL ADVENTURES* ended with issue #150, in which Captain Marvel made his last Golden Age appearance. "Captain Marvel's Wedding," written by Otto Binder and drawn by C. C. Beck, gave readers the witchy Theo Hagge, who very nearly trapped the World's Mightiest Mortal into marrying her. A second story, "The World of Too Many Sivanas," also drawn by C. C. Beck, featured the final Golden Age appearances of the wizard Shazam and Captain Marvel's arch-nemesis, the World's Wickedest Scientist, Dr. Thaddeus Bodog Sivana...

June: The coronation of Queen Elizabeth II in Westminster Abbey.
April: Ian Fleming publishes his first James Bond novel, *Casino Royale*.
June: The first Chevrolet Corvette is built at Flint, Michigan.
December: The first color television set goes on sale for about $1,175.

1954

"BUT IT MEANS... I'LL HAVE TO PLAY SUPERMAN!"

Batman, *World's Finest Comics* #71

LEGAL RESTRICTIONS

The world of comic book publishing experienced enormous change in 1954. The simmering anti-comics movement gained a scientific voice in psychiatrist Fredric Wertham and his book, *Seduction of the Innocent*, which warned against the dangerous effects of violent comics on young people. A Senate Subcommittee on Juvenile Delinquency followed, chaired by anti-crime crusader Senator Estes Kefauver, resulting in the Comics Code Authority, which regulated the content of comics like never before.

Meanwhile, within the world of DC Comics, Superman and Batman started working together in *World's Finest Comics*; Jimmy Olsen got out of the *Daily Planet* newsroom to set off on his own adventures; and readers were presented with Congo Bill, a new African explorer-hero dedicated to protecting indigenous peoples from the threats of exploitation.

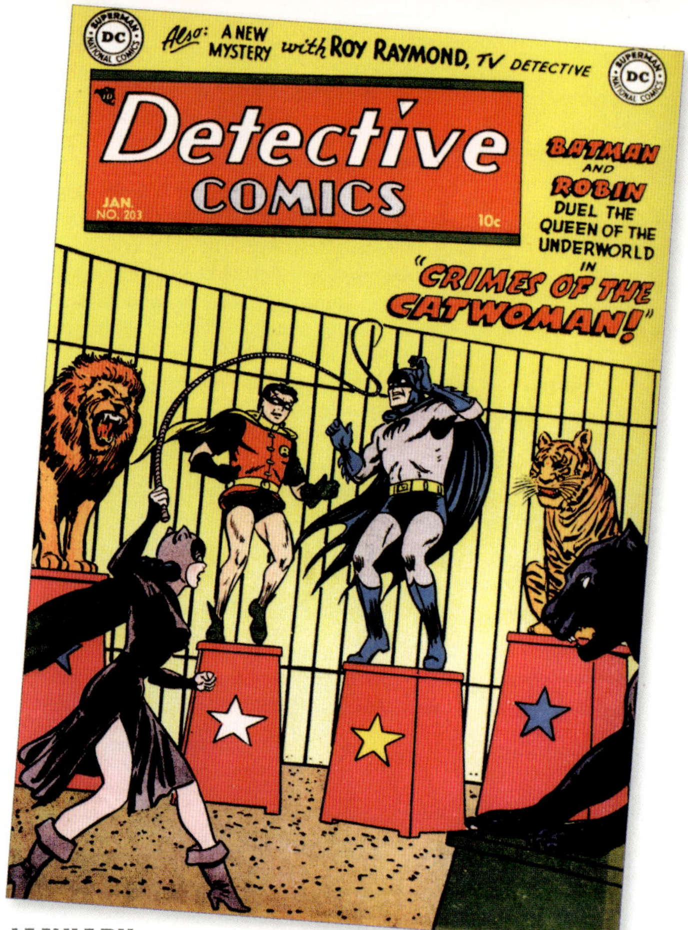

JANUARY

MOVE OVER, ROBOTMAN
***Detective Comics* #203**

Detective Comics #203 saw Captain Compass replace Robotman for a second time. The crime-fighting sea captain had first pushed the mechanical body with a human brain to *Detective Comics* from *Star Spangled Comics* #83 (August 1948). Now Captain Compass took over Robotman's *Detective Comics* slot at issue #203, with the story "The Great Ocean Showboat," written by Otto Binder and drawn by Joe Certa. Captain Compass continued his sea-faring adventures in *Detective Comics*, solving mysteries and preventing crime on the ocean wave, until issue #224 (October 1955).

FEBRUARY

CASSIDY HOPS ALONG TO DC COMICS
***Hopalong Cassidy* #86**

Following the decision taken to close the comics division of Fawcett Publications in 1953, *Hopalong Cassidy* came to DC with issue #86. This issue of the comic, based on the popular *Hopalong Cassidy* films, told three cowboy stories: "The Secret of the Tattooed Burro," "The Brand of Hate," and "The Lucky Lawman" by the writers Gardner Fox and Don Cameron and artist Gene Colan. The comic for America's Favorite Cowboy stayed with DC for the remaining fifty issues of its run.

IN THE REAL WORLD...

February: The first mass vaccination of children against polio begins in Pittsburgh, Pennsylvania.

JULY

TOGETHER IN ONE ADVENTURE

***World's Finest Comics* #71**

Although the covers of *World's Finest Comics* had teased co-appearances of Batman and Superman for years, the first joint adventure of the two in the comic occurred in issue #71, in the story "Batman—Double for Superman," written by Alvin Schwartz, pencilled by Curt Swan, and inked by Stan Kaye.

The Man of Steel and the World's Greatest Detective had actually met for the first time in *Superman* #76 (May–June 1952), where they learned each other's secret identities and forged a relationship that would last—with its share of tension—through the coming decades. The story of their first meeting, "The Mightiest Team in the World," written by Edmond Hamilton and drawn by Curt Swan, was a lighthearted caper in which Superman and Batman, who happened to be sharing a stateroom on the ocean liner *Varania*, thwarted a diamond heist on the high seas. They also worked together to preserve Superman's secret identity from the suspicions of Lois Lane: Batman assumed a disguise as Clark Kent and, with Lois, met Superman. There followed a friendly competition for the attentions of Lois Lane (which Robin won, to the surprise of both heroes).

In *World's Finest Comics* #71, "Batman—Double for Superman" recapped their first meeting, and further complicated the issue of Lois Lane sniffing around the two heroes' identities after she saw Clark becoming Superman. To shake her off the trail, Superman and Batman swapped identities to convince her she had seen Superman becoming Bruce Wayne. The action of the story centered around the pair recovering a stolen piece of kryptonite in danger of being sold off to the highest bidder in gangland.

With the ice broken, the two heroes appeared regularly together in *World's Finest Comics*, setting the stage for the story "Superman and Batman's Greatest Foes" in issue #88 (June 1957). In this story by writer Edmond Hamilton, penciller Dick Sprang, and inker Stan Kaye, fans got their fondest wish: Superman and Batman teaming up against their arch-nemeses, Lex Luthor, and the Joker. A helter-skelter story followed, switching locales between Metropolis, Gotham City, and the ocean floor, where an army of Mechano-Men, manufactured by the villainous duo, prepared dastardly schemes. The climactic confrontation took place as the Mechano-Men smashed into a bank vault, accompanied by their creators—only to have Superman swoop in and lasso the robots while Batman and Robin put the clamps on the Joker and Luthor.

Superman and Batman pull on each other's costumes to cover up a blunder and keep Superman's identity a secret from Lois Lane in *World's Finest Comics* #71.

AUGUST

AFRICAN GUARDIAN

***Congo Bill* #1**

The intrepid explorer Congo Bill, who had first appeared in *More Fun Comics* #56 (June 1940), got his own title with *Congo Bill* #1. He, along with his leopardskin-clad sidekick Janu the Jungle Boy, protected Africa's people and wildlife against exploitation. Later, Bill would become the super hero Congorilla by transferring his consciousness to the body of an ape called the Golden Gorilla. Although *Congo Bill* only lasted seven issues, it set the stage for Congorilla and Golden Gorilla storylines that would unfold across different titles for decades.

SEPTEMBER

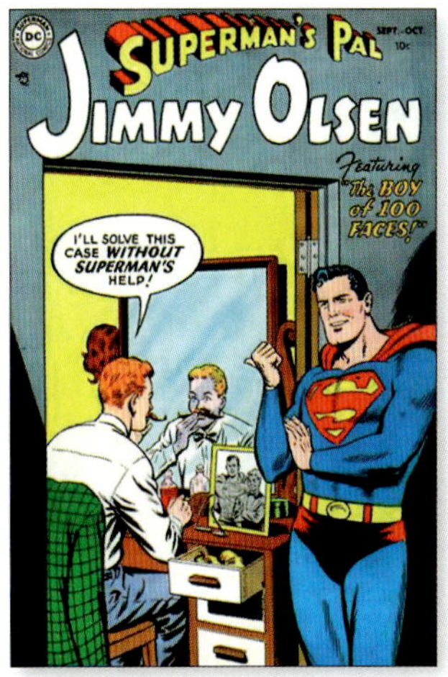

THE MANY FACES OF JIMMY

***Superman's Pal, Jimmy Olsen* #1**

Former *Daily Planet* copy boy Jimmy Olsen got his own adventures in *Superman's Pal, Jimmy Olsen* #1. A comic remarkable for its inventiveness and longevity, it ran for 163 issues. The lead story of issue #1, "The Boy of 100 Faces," was written by Otto Binder and drawn by Curt Swan. It followed Jimmy as he disguised himself to infiltrate the criminal gang of Deuce Dorgan. Along with colleague Jumbo Jones, Jimmy succeeded in getting into Dorgan's hideaway—but was caught and had to call on Superman for help.

OCTOBER

MORE WAR STORIES

***Our Fighting Forces* #1**

The public's appetite for war comics kept growing, and new titles were needed to fill the void left by those canceled in light of the new Comic Code Authority restrictions. Enter *Our Fighting Forces*, an anthology that would feature Gunner, Sarge, and their dog Pooch (Rex the Wonder Dog's brother); the *Dirty Dozen*-inspired Hunter's Hellcats, who ran on the cover from issues #106–122 (April–December 1969); and, of course, the Losers, who took over the cover slot from #123 (February 1969) until *Our Fighting Forces* hung up its boots with issue #181 (October 1978).

ALSO THIS YEAR: Dim-witted, crazy Nutsy Squirrel took over as the star of the funny animal comic *HOLLYWOOD FUNNY FOLKS*, when it was renamed *NUTSY SQUIRREL* #61 in October. As the popularity of funny animals declined, the title ended with issue #72 (November 1957)...

May: English athlete Roger Bannister runs the first four-minute mile.
June: The words "under God" are added to the United States Pledge of Allegiance.
November: The first *Godzilla* movie premieres in Tokyo, Japan.
December: The first Burger King restaurant opens in Miami, Florida.

THE COMICS CODE

"All scenes of horror, excessive bloodshed, gory or gruesome crimes, depravity, lust, sadism, masochism shall not be permitted."
The Comics Code, 1954.

Concerns about the effects of comic books on impressionable minds had been voiced as early as 1941. Comics companies had responded with a form of self-censorship, but this did not satisfy their critics. This opposition lacked scientific backing, however, until psychologist Fredric Wertham entered the fray. Wertham had studied juvenile delinquency since the 1940s and, noting the popularity of comics among delinquents, he concluded that reading comics *created* delinquency. He published his claims in 1954 in a denouncement of popular culture titled *Seduction of the Innocent*. Extracts began to appear in *Ladies' Home Journal* during 1953.

Wertham gained the ear of Senator Estes Kefauver, whose Senate Subcommittee on Juvenile Delinquency had been concerned about the influence of comic books since 1950, and Wertham became a star witness at the committee's 1954 hearings on comic books and delinquency. The other star was EC Comics Publisher William Gaines, who had pioneered the horror comic with titles such as *Crypt of Terror,* starting in 1950. The two men struck sparks, and the conflagration burned EC to ashes.

Born out of the Kefauver hearings, the Comics Code Authority (CCA) prohibited most depictions of violence as well as any supernatural phenomena. It also instituted restrictions regarding sex and the portrayal of authority figures. Wertham made some pointed allegations about what he saw as problems with DC's characters, and DC took steps to make its flagship characters more family-oriented. Although the Comics Code was not legally binding, opinion was on its side. Mainstream comics thus came into line with the rest of American popular culture at that time: they became wholesome.

The CCA killed off crime and horror comics, but did not entirely stifle creativity. Among the writers, artists, and editors displaced by the loss of these titles was *MAD* Magazine's Harvey Kurtzman. He proved an important influence on the underground comics artists of the 1960s, some of whom would find mainstream success with DC during the 1980s and 1990s when the influence of the Code began to wane. (Nowadays most comic book publishers ignore the Code altogether, although DC submits some super hero titles for approval.)

In the end, the profusion and then suppression of horror, crime, and supernatural comics in the years after World War II had a number of unforeseen effects on the industry—and on comics readers. A generation of (mostly) boys grew up on William Gaines' four-color EC creepfests and, when they became writers, they took their revenge on Wertham by pushing boundaries even further than Gaines could have imagined.

Wertham has become one of comics' favorite whipping boys, but he was also a force for progressive causes. His work may have killed off EC, but it indirectly helped pave the way for Vertigo Comics in 1993.

Left: The CCA stamp appeared on the covers of mainstream comics. It was designed by DC logo designer and letterer Ira Schnapp. Main picture: Superman was unfairly singled out by Fredric Wertham as being a fascist.

1955

"OH, BOY! NOW I'VE GOT A PET, JUST LIKE THE OTHER FELLOWS!"

Superboy, *Adventure Comics* #210

FAMILY VALUES

In comics, as elsewhere in the mid-1950s, the focus was on the family. Superman storylines, in particular, began to focus on family-oriented issues. Both Superboy and Batman got pet dogs, and Superboy was forced to confront criminal threats to the Kents. And in *Detective Comics*, J'onn J'onzz, bereft of his family, became a regular.

Adventure stories were also popular, with two new anthology series released this year: *The Brave and the Bold* and *My Greatest Adventure*. *The Brave and the Bold*'s team-up stories would be incredibly popular in coming years, bringing Batman together with a rotating array of the DC Universe's most memorable characters.

The heyday of the Golden Age super hero had long passed, but change was on the horizon. In 1955, DC was on the cusp of the Silver Age, when a new generation of super heroes would flourish within the pages of its comics.

JANUARY

A BIG ADVENTURE

***My Greatest Adventure* #1**

The anthology series *My Greatest Adventure* began an eighty-five-issue run with the stories "I was King of Dagger Island" drawn by Leonard Starr, "I Hunted a Flying Saucer" drawn by Bill Ely, and "My Cargo Was Death" drawn by John Prentice. All three were edited by Whitney Ellsworth. The series would become most notable for introducing a misfit band of maybe-super heroes, the Doom Patrol, in issue #80 (June 1963). As of issue #86 (March 1964), the series changed its name to *Doom Patrol*, and retained the same numbering until its end at issue #121 (October 1968).

MARCH

THE SUPER-DOG FROM KRYPTON!

***Adventure Comics* #210**

Superboy was reunited with his dog in "The Super-Dog from Krypton" by writer Otto Binder and artist Curt Swan. Superboy found the dog in a rocket, along with written records, proving the dog was Krypto, his canine companion from when he was a baby. Superboy's father, Jor-El, had used the dog as a test passenger when experimenting with escape rockets as the destruction of Krypton approached. Although Krypto set off before Jor-El dispatched Superboy, his rocket wandered off course, so he arrived on Earth when Superboy was already a teenager.

Arriving on Earth, Krypto, like all Kryptonians, acquired super powers. His abilities, including flight, super-strength, invincibility, and X-ray vision, were similar to Superman's but weaker, as they were proportionate to a dog's body. Krypto acquired a cover for his secret identity by dying a patch of his all-white fur brown to disguise him as Skip, the Kents' family dog. To turn back, he could burn off the dye with heat vision.

In early stories, Krypto was a smart and loyal dog, but he gradually acquired human-level intelligence and began thinking in full sentences. When Superboy grew up and moved to Metropolis, he left Krypto behind in Smallville because he felt the big city was a bad place for a dog.

Superboy was delighted at being reunited with Krypto the Super-Dog, but was a bit overwhelmed with all the giant-sized "gifts" the dog kept fetching him.

IN THE REAL WORLD...

April: Winston Churchill resigns as Prime Minister of the United Kingdom.
August: The first edition of the *Guinness World Records* book is published.

JUNE

HERE, ACE!

***Batman* #92**

Once Superman had a dog, Batman got one too, in "Ace, the Bat-Hound!" In the story by writer Bill Finger and artist Sheldon Moldoff, Batman and Robin found a German shepherd called Ace, when his owner, an engraver named John Wilker, was kidnapped by counterfeiters. Once rescued, Wilker left the dog with Bruce Wayne. Ace had a distinctive diamond-shaped marking on his forehead that had to be disguised lest he give away the link between Bruce Wayne and Batman. One black mask later, Ace the Bat-Hound was born, and he would fight at the Dark Knight's side through the Silver Age.

AUGUST

FROM SILENT KNIGHT TO DARK KNIGHT

***The Brave and the Bold* #1**

The anthology series *The Brave and the Bold* focused on adventure tales from past ages. The first issue introduced a number of new characters, most notably the Silent Knight—a youth named Brian Kent who discovered his trademark suit of armor, sword, red helmet, and red shield in "Duel in Forest Perilous," by writer Robert Kanigher and artist Irv Novick. He would appear throughout the years that followed in a number of different titles, and was possibly an ancestor of Superman's adoptive father, Jonathan Kent. In the early issues, other regular characters included the non-superpowered quartet the Suicide Squad; super hero team the Justice League of America; the police officer Hawkman; and the shapeshifting Metamorpho. Batman made his series debut in *The Brave and the Bold* #68 (November 1966) and quickly became the title's staple character, replacing the rotating array of characters.

OCTOBER

SUPERBOY LEAVES HOME?

***Adventure Comics* #217**

A two-part story ran in *Adventure Comics* #217 and #218, a rare occurrence at the time as most stories began and ended in the same issue. The two parts, "Superboy's Farewell to Smallville" and "The Two Worlds of Superboy" were both by writer Otto Binder and artist Curt Swan. Death-row inmate Duke Mason threatened to kill the Kents and reveal Superboy's identity so Superboy made plans to return to Krypton with his real parents, Jor-El and Lara Lor-Van. Once Mason went to the electric chair, it was revealed that leaving Earth was a ruse by Superboy, and the people seen in Smallville were only pretending to be his parents.

NOVEMBER

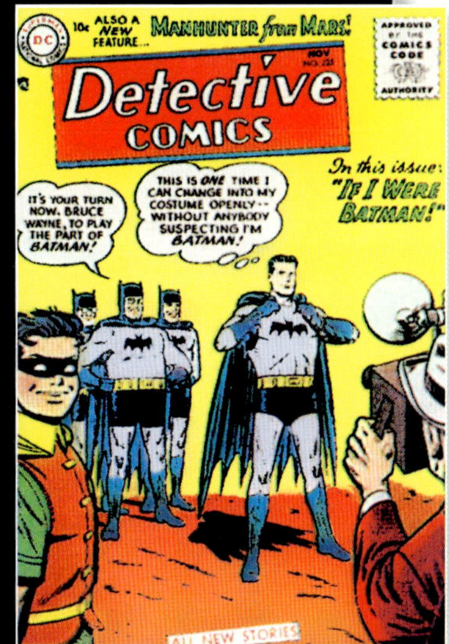

MARTIAN MAN-HUNTER!

***Detective Comics* #225**

After a teasing appearance in *Batman* #78 (August–September 1953), the Martian called J'onn J'onzz debuted as a regular feature in *Detective Comics* #225. "The Strange Experiment of Dr. Erdel," by writer Joe Samachson and artist Joe Certa, gave the origin for the lonely Martian Manhunter.

Saul Erdel, a mostly self-educated Colorado scientist, archaeologist, and general tinkerer, discovered some odd bits of machinery and after much trial and error constructed what he believed to be a beam that would transmit matter. Aiming it at Mars, Dr. Erdel brought J'onn J'onzz across space and time, from ancient Mars to present-day Earth. J'onn used his Martian shapeshifting abilities to assume a human appearance. The shock of these events proved fatal to Dr. Erdel, who collapsed in the lab.

Now stuck on Earth, J'onn observed the culture and created the identity of John Jones, a crime fighter and investigator in Apex City. His only way of getting home, he realized, was to wait until Martian technology advanced sufficiently for a Martian mission to make contact with Earth. While waiting, he resolved to bring Earth closer to one of Mars's great advancements: the abolition of crime. J'onn's powers varied according to the desires of different writers before stabilizing over time; one consistent weakness was a vulnerability to fire, which was congenital to the Martian race in J'onn's earliest appearances. J'onn would be a near-constant back-up presence in *Detective Comics* until the early 1960s, as well as an important member of the Justice League of America. In addition, he and the Green Arrow would inaugurate the super hero team-up format of *The Brave and the Bold*, in issue #50 (November 1963).

A tall green Martian, J'onn J'onzz shapeshifted into a human to blend in on Earth. He used the concentration of mind over matter to extract gold from the sea in order to barter with in Earth society.

ALSO THIS YEAR: January's *DETECTIVE COMICS* #215 saw the debut of two vigilante super heroes, Legionary and the Native American Man-of-Bats. Dark Ranger, an Australian bush ranger also debuted in the issue. Although he had no superpowers, he was skilled at using his jetpack and pulse pistol...

September: Actor James Dean is killed when his Porsche 550 Spyder collides with another automobile at a highway junction near Cholame, California.

December: Rosa Parks is arrested for refusing to give up her seat on a bus to a white person, and the Civil Rights Movement begins.

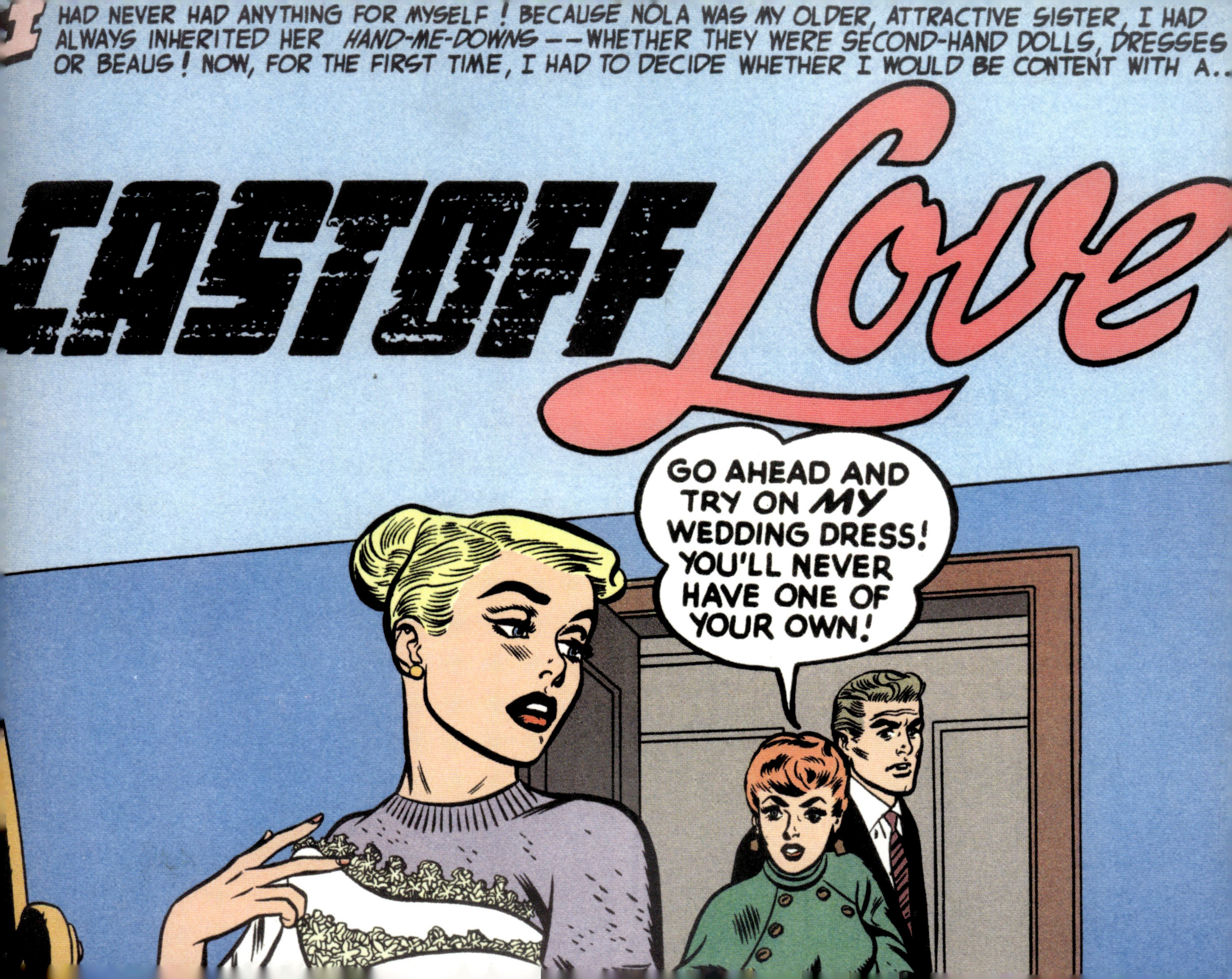
I HAD NEVER HAD ANYTHING FOR MYSELF ! BECAUSE NOLA WAS MY OLDER, ATTRACTIVE SISTER, I HAD ALWAYS INHERITED HER HAND-ME-DOWNS -- WHETHER THEY WERE SECOND-HAND DOLLS, DRESSES OR BEAUS ! NOW, FOR THE FIRST TIME, I HAD TO DECIDE WHETHER I WOULD BE CONTENT WITH A...
CASTOFF Love
GO AHEAD AND TRY ON MY WEDDING DRESS! YOU'LL NEVER HAVE ONE OF YOUR OWN!

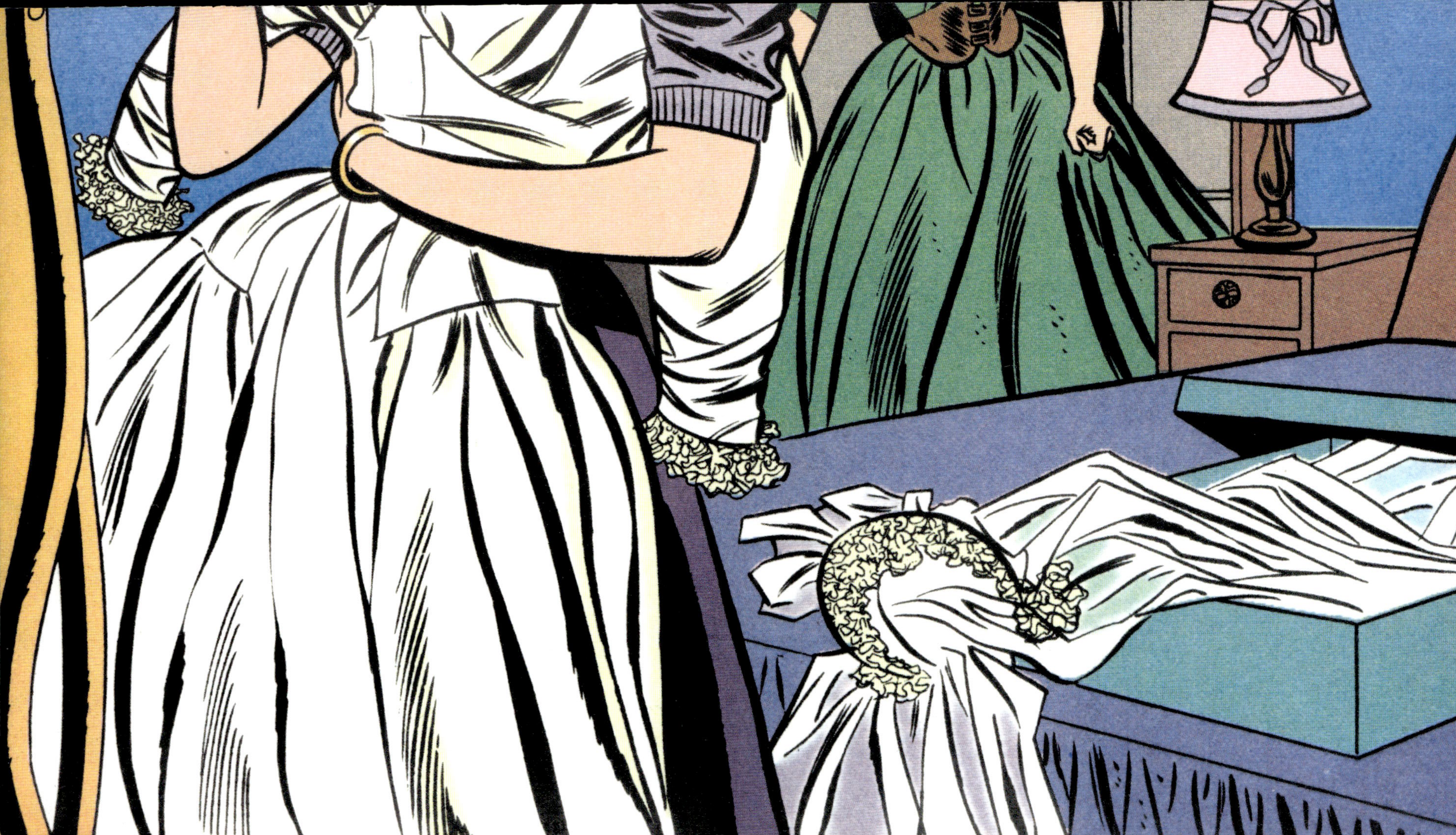

SUBURBAN BLISS

GIRLS' LOVE STORIES #27 (February 1954) During the late 1940s, the public tired of super-heroics. *Girls' Love Stories* was DC's first foray into the increasingly popular romance genre. Befitting the nervous political atmosphere of the Cold War, these stories' heroines rejected passion and thrills in favor of settling down to a life of suburban domesticity with "Mr. Right."

1956

"THERE MUST BE SOME WAY I CAN USE THIS UNIQUE SPEED TO HELP HUMANITY! HMMM—THIS GIVES ME AN IDEA!"

Barry Allen, *Showcase* #4

THE SILVER AGE

1956 ushered in a new era at DC, which would spread across the entire comic book industry. *Showcase* would become DC's most reliable testing ground for new characters, and the arrival of the second incarnation of the Flash in issue #4 is considered to be the official start of the Silver Age of comics.

The Silver Age was characterized by the revival of super heroes as the reading public's enthusiasm for Westerns began to wane. Golden Age characters were reworked and new heroes were created. Revamped characters retained their names, but acquired new costumes and identities. In new origin stories, superpowers tended to have "scientific" rather than magical roots.

Meanwhile, the first painted covers on comics lent the flimsies a new artistic weight (although it would be decades yet before comics were taken seriously as an artistic genre).

FEBRUARY

ALL-AGES ADVENTURE
***Tales of the Unexpected* #1**

As part of a new breed of science-fiction adventure cut from the more wholesome cloth demanded by the Comics Code Authority, *Tales of the Unexpected* began. Its 104-issue run led with the cover story "The Cartoon that Came to Life," by writer Otto Binder and artist Bill Ely, in which a drawing of a Martian Dragon-Man comes to life. Whether offering body-switching gorilla stories, strange technology, or weird mystery, the series provided all-ages adventure. With issue #40 (August 1959), the series became home to Rick Starr, Space Ranger who protected the solar system of the 22nd Century with his shape-changing alien sidekick, Cryll.

MARCH

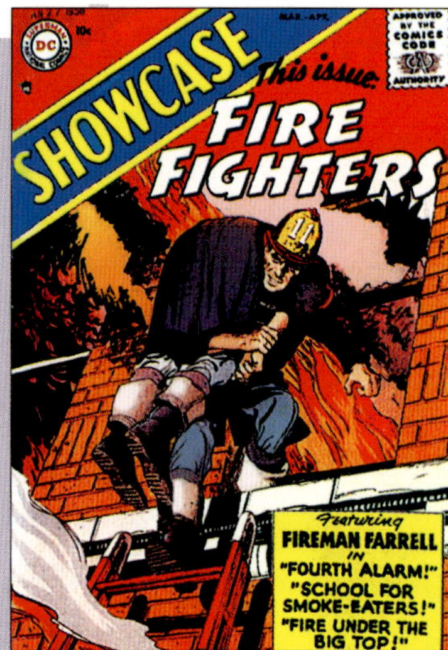

SHOWTIME FOR *SHOWCASE*
***Showcase* #1**

Showcase kicked off its twenty-two-year run with an unusual choice of feature: stories about Fireman Farrell. Although admired by many boys, firefighters never caught on in comics—unlike cowboys, astronauts, and police officers, who were staples—and Farrell was no exception. The series later introduced, among others, Challengers of the Unknown, Adam Strange, Hawk and Dove, Space Ranger, Rip Hunter, the Metal Men, and the Inferior Five. But it was perhaps best known for kicking off new versions of some of DC's most enduring characters, including the Green Lantern, the Atom, and the Flash.

JULY

THE BATWOMAN!
***Detective Comics* #233**

In the story "The Batwoman" by writer Edmond Hamilton and penciller Sheldon Moldoff (as Bob Kane), Bruce Wayne took notice of a young admirer who—he and Robin soon discovered—was fighting crime while wearing a bat-costume very similar to the one the Dark Knight wore. Concerned, in a paternalistic 1950s way, that Kathy Kane might be getting into more than she could handle, Batman tried to dissuade her. But plucky Kane knew what she wanted and went on to have a crime-fighting career of her own, until her assassination on the orders of Batman's arch-enemy Rā's al Ghūl. in *Detective Comics* #485 (September 1979).

IN THE REAL WORLD...

February: Elvis Presley enters the United States music charts for the first time with "Heartbreak Hotel."

OCTOBER

A FLASH OF SILVER

***Showcase* #4**

Showcase produced several kinds of story in its first few issues, but one stood out from the others: issue #4's "Mystery of the Human Thunderbolt," by writer Robert Kanigher and artist Carmine Infantino. It told the origin of Barry Allen, the Fastest Man Alive, who became the second incarnation of Golden Age hero the Flash.

Barry Allen was a midwestern boy whose life was tinged with trauma at an early age, when his father was convicted of murdering his mother. A comics fan, he voraciously read the adventures of Jay Garrick, the original Flash (this metafictional angle on the Flash's origin story was, if not the first of its kind in super hero comics, very early in the tradition). Barry also displayed an early interest in chemistry, becoming a police scientist in Central City and dating reporter Iris West (who later became his wife). A lightning strike on his lab gave him a chemical bath that left him with the gift of super-speed, as he discovered the next day when he was able to save Iris from an accidental shooting.

As Barry grew into his new gift, he put his chemistry skills to work creating a miniaturized suit. It fitted inside a ring he wore on his finger, and could grow to full size in reaction to nitrogen present in the air. Naming himself for his childhood idol, Barry Allen became the Flash, a role he would inhabit for the next thirty years, serving as a founding member of the Justice League of America. Along the way he would meet his predecessor, Jay Garrick, who was a resident of the parallel world Earth-2. After Iris's murder by Doctor Zoom, and Barry's accidental killing of Zoom, he retired into the future, returning only during the large-scale crossover event *Crisis on Infinite Earths* (1985), in which he appeared to have died.

The Scarlet Speedster chases after the Turtle Man, the Slowest Man on Earth. The criminal had tried to shoot dead Flash's girlfriend, Iris West, while making a getaway from a bank raid.

DECEMBER

TELLING SECRETS

***House of Secrets* #1**

The mystery-suspense anthology series *House of Secrets* began the eighty-issue run of its first incarnation in December.

The title retained features of other anthology series, such as one-page public-service announcements from prominent super heroes, occasional text pieces, and one-page filler gags. Although it had a fairly steady stable of writers and artists, including Jack Kirby—who wrote early tales such as "The Cats Who Knew Too Much" and "The Hole in the Sky" and also drew several of the series's early covers—it had some recurring characters, such as the supernatural sleuth Mark Merlin and the super-villian Eclipso.

A number of early stories were later reprinted in *The Unexpected* in the late 1960s. Many stories would also be reprinted in the incarnation of *House of Secrets*, which would be resurrected in the 1960s as a companion to a new version of the horror-mystery-suspense anthology, *House of Mystery*. The story introductions in *House of Secrets* were narrated by Abel, whereas Cain hosted the stories of *House of Mystery*. The Swamp Thing, the monster made from vegetative matter, made his first appearance on the cover of issue #92 of the revamped *House of Secrets* in July 1971.

RIDING INTO THE SUNSET

***Frontier Fighters* #8**

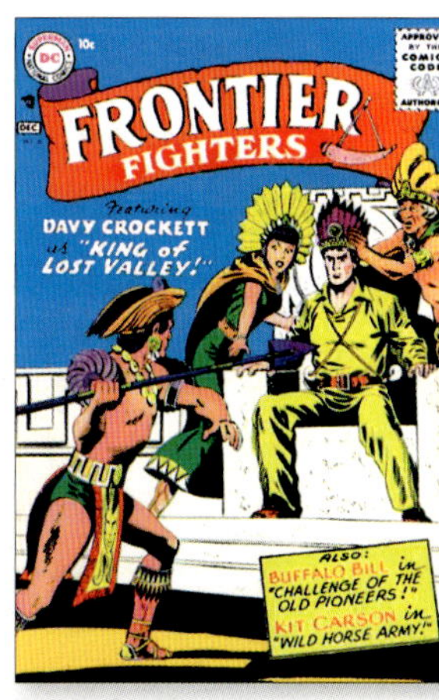

Issue #8 was the final *Frontier Fighters*. Western heroes Davy Crockett, Buffalo Bill, and Kit Carson had all appeared in every issue. Each cover featured Crockett, whose stories led off seven of the eight issues; issue #7 began with the Kit Carson story, "The Treasure of Death Valley." In the final issue, Crockett found himself "The King of Lost Valley," drawn by Bob Brown; Carson took on "The Wild Horse Army," drawn by Howard Sherman; and Buffalo Bill wrapped up with "The Challenge of the Old Pioneers," drawn by Joe Kubert. All three stories were edited by Whitney Ellsworth.

ALSO THIS YEAR: Two children's titles began: *SUGAR AND SPIKE* and *THE THREE MOUSEKETEERS*... In July, *JACKIE GLEASON AND THE HONEYMOONERS* began and was DC's first TV show license... Also in July, *ALL AMERICAN MEN OF WAR* #35 featured the first painted cover, by Jerry Grandenetti....

April: Actress Grace Kelly marries Rainier III, Prince of Monaco.
September: An IBM team led by Reynold B. Johnson invents the hard disk drive.

October: Baseball player Don Larsen of the New York Yankees pitches the only perfect game in World Series history, in a game against the Brooklyn Dodgers.

SUPERMAN DC NATIONAL COMICS
10¢
SHOWCASE presents
DEC. NO 23
APPROVED BY THE COMICS CODE AUTHORITY
GREEN LANTERN
NOT EVEN GREEN LANTERN'S MIGHTY POWER RING CAN STOP ME FROM SETTING OFF THIS ATOMIC BOMB EXPLOSION!

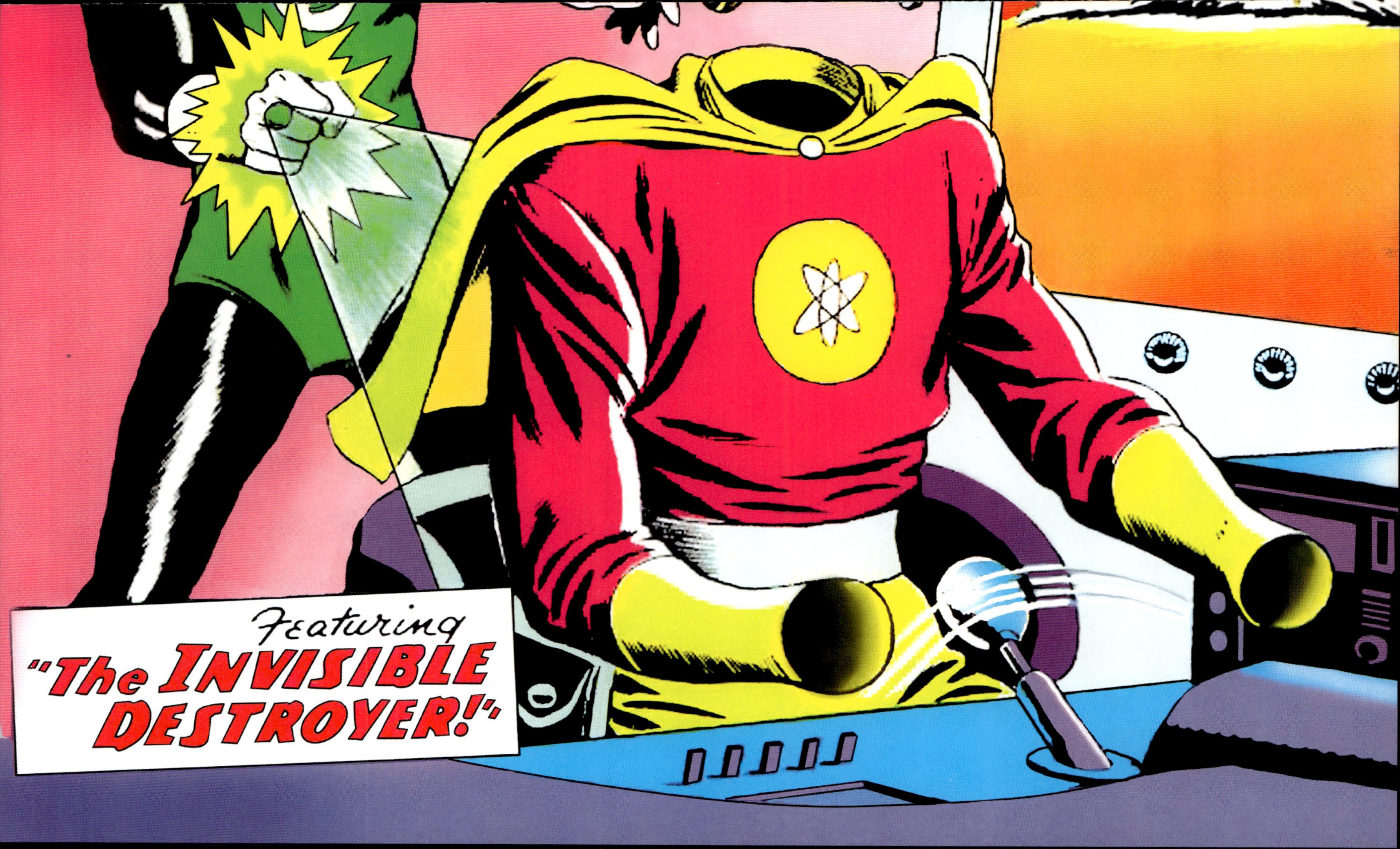

WORLD SAVED!

SHOWCASE PRESENTS GREEN LANTERN #23 (December 1959)
Fear of "the bomb" was a preoccupation of the 1950s. Green Lantern was one of many heroes who faced that threat. When the Invisible Destroyer fed on radiation and set off an atom bomb to make itself invincible, Green Lantern's Power Ring rendered the blast no more powerful than that of a firecracker.

1957

"ANYTHING OUT OF THIS WORLD IS OUR SPECIALTY!"

Ace Morgan (Challengers of the Unknown), *Showcase* #6

SPACE AGE HEROES

The word of the year for 1957 was *Sputnik*. The 184-pound (83.5 kg) sphere launched by Russia was the first artificial satellite and a wake-up call to the United States, jump-starting the space race that culminated with the *Apollo 11* Moon landings twelve years later. It also galvanized the imaginations of a generation of children, laying the groundwork for the next waves of comics and science-fiction writers.

Exemplifying the comics industry's current taste for science-fiction-style plots involving extraterrestrials and fantasy creatures, Jack Kirby scored a hit with his first solo project for DC: a quartet of adventurers called the Challengers of the Unknown, who would seek out such threats.

Elsewhere in comics, Superman discovered his father was a Superman before him, the Flash got chills when he met a new nemesis, and Lois Lane tried out for her very own comic.

JANUARY

ON TV THIS MONTH: George Reeves appeared as Superman on television show *I LOVE LUCY*. Its star, Lucille Ball, put on a Superman suit in the episode, probably becoming TV's first Supergirl...

FEBRUARY

ON BORROWED TIME

***Showcase* #6**

The immortal creative team of Joe Simon and Jack Kirby had parted ways in 1955, and in the aftermath, Kirby's first solo project was a test run of a non-super hero adventure team called Challengers of the Unknown. Appearing for the first time in *Showcase* #6, the team would make a few more *Showcase* appearances before springing into their own title in May 1958.

The Challengers were Rocky Davis, Red Ryan, Ace Morgan, and Prof. Haley (with frequent appearances by "honorary Challenger" June Robbins). After surviving a plane crash and deeming themselves to be living on borrowed time, they decided to fight evil menaces wherever they found them. In their first adventure, "The Secrets of the Sorcerer's Box," they met a challenge posed by the sorcerer Morelian: to open the four chambers of a magical box inscribed with the legend "Contained in me, find immortality." The Challengers defeated a stone giant, a freezing sun, and a strange "Whirling Weaver" from three of the chambers before Morelian opened the final chamber himself, finding a ring he thought would make him immortal. He flew away in his airplane but was killed when it crashed right onto the magical box. The Challengers then understood that the ring was just one more test, and the box itself was what conferred eternal life. Morelian had destroyed the very thing he sought.

Having miraculously survived a plane crash, the Challengers take risks no-one else would—like tackling a stone giant.

MAY

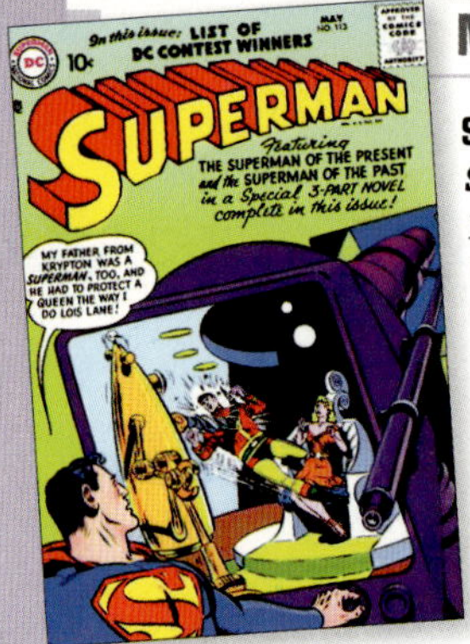

SUPERMAN PAST, SUPERMAN PRESENT

***Superman* #113**

Most 1950s comics contained several stories, so a book-length Superman tale was a novelty. Superman's "3-part novel," by writer Bill Finger and artist Wayne Boring, featured Superman's father, Jor-El, acting like a Superman before Kal-El ever did. Superman found a helmet containing "mind-tapes" from the past that had recorded Jor-El's exploits. Queen Latora of the planet Vergo knew that Krypton was doomed due to its unstable uranium core, so she planned to destroy the planet before it destroyed itself and use its uranium to prolong the life of Vergo's cooling sun. Jor-El put a stop to the queen's plan, but at the story's end, Superman resolved to help her because his father never could. He sent uranium to Vergo's sun, saving Queen Latora's world.

IN THE REAL WORLD...

January: Hamilton Watch Company introduces the first electric watch.
March: Dr. Seuss's book *The Cat in the Hat* is published.

JUNE

SILVER AGE SERGEANT
***Sgt. Bilko* #1**

Continuing a trend of licensing TV properties, DC premiered its comic adaptation of sitcom *The Phil Silvers Show*, popularly known as "Sgt. Bilko." The comic closely tracked the show's ongoing story of Sergeant Ernie Bilko, the man in charge of the motor pool at a Kansas U.S. Army base. Bilko concocted madcap schemes to get out of working and to relieve his fellow soldiers of their money. Colonel John T. Hall played the unwitting pushover, and Private Duane Doberman always seemed to be around as Bilko's straight man. Doberman would later get his own title, *Sgt. Bilko's Pvt. Doberman*, which began in July 1958.

DEEP FREEZE
***Showcase* #8**

Showcase #8 introduced one of the Flash's recurring nemeses: Leonard Snart, otherwise known as Captain Cold. This visor-clad villain, presented in a story by writer John Broome and artist Carmine Infantino, did time in prison thanks to the Flash ending his crime spree and had schemed against the Flash since his release. When he experimented with cyclotron emissions, speculating that they might interfere with the Flash's super-speed, Snart accidentally hit upon a freeze gun that could stop the Flash in his tracks. Thus Captain Cold was born. He continued to develop his sub-zero talents to fight against both Barry Allen and the men who were to become the Flash after him.

Captain Cold's freeze gun freezes objects to absolute zero. However, the Flash moves too quickly to be frozen, so Captain Cold freezes the road to make the Flash lose his footing.

AUGUST

LOIS LANE, ADVENTURER
***Showcase* #9**

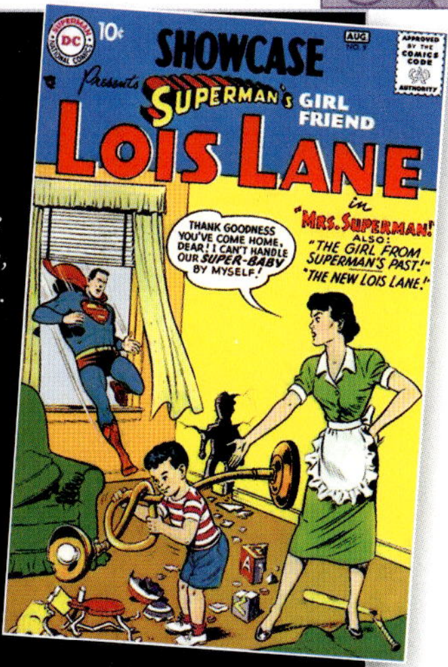

The future title *Superman's Girl Friend, Lois Lane* got a tryout in issues #9 and #10 of *Showcase*, when Lois Lane stepped in as the lead feature.

The debut story in *Showcase* #9, "The Girl in Superman's Past," by writer Jerry Coleman and artist Al Plastino, introduced Lois Lane to Superman's old flame Lana Lang. After some initial friction, the two inquisitive women realized they had a common curiosity: the strange parallels between Clark Kent and Superman. Lois and Lana began a friendly competition to see which of them Superman liked more and set "traps" to test his preference. Their schemes became progressively more outlandish, but Superman could not be outwitted. Superman similarly played Lois and "Con" Conners off against each other to protect his identity in the issue's second story, "The New Lois Lane" written by Otto Binder and drawn by Ruben Moreira, while Lois dreamed of being Superman's wife in "Mrs. Superman" also written by Binder, with art handled by Al Plastino.

Showcase #10 in October featured a cover story by writer Otto Binder and artist Wayne Boring, "The Forbidden Box from Krypton," in which Lois's inquisitiveness proved to have a serious Pandora-style downside. In opening a box of Kryptonian artifacts, she inadvertently gave herself superpowers. "The Jilting of Superman," by the same writer and artist team, then followed Lois' efforts to make Superman jealous by pretending she was married.

In general, these introductory stories put together the aesthetic of 1950s romance comics—emphasizing heartbreak, uncertainty, and forgiveness—with super hero flair, which Superman could always be relied on to provide. Although Lois had previously appeared in her own series of back-up stories called "Lois Lane, Girl Reporter," in *Superman* #28–42 (May 1944–October 1946), her investigative inclinations had been played more humorously than in the *Showcase* stories. Lois would get her own series, *Superman's Girl Friend, Lois Lane*, in April 1958.

Superman's past and present loves, Lois Lane and Lana Lang, try to find out which one of them Superman prefers. In their final test, the women pretend they are both in mortal danger to see who he saves first.

ALSO THIS YEAR: In April, DC's romance comics gained their own heart-shaped variation of the bullet logo... In November, art imitated life when *THE ADVENTURES OF DEAN MARTIN AND JERRY LEWIS* became *THE ADVENTURES OF JERRY LEWIS* at issue #41 after the break-up of the comedy duo...

May: Brooklyn Dodgers owner Walter O'Malley agrees to move the team from Brooklyn, New York to Los Angeles, California.

October: The Soviet Union launches *Sputnik 1*, the first artificial satellite to orbit the earth.

A THRILLING "FOLEY of the FIGHTING FIFTH" ADVENTURE
SUPERMAN DC NATIONAL COMICS
APR. MAY NO.12
ALL AMERICAN
Western
10c
SUPERMAN DC NATIONAL COMICS
WE'VE BEEN WAITIN' FOR THIS, THUNDER! YOU'RE A PERFECT TARGET! HAW HAW!

HOME ON THE RANGE

ALL-AMERICAN WESTERN #12 (April 1952)
Westerns, with their blend of black-and-white morality, escapism, and nationalism, were all the rage in the 1950s. *All-American Western* was just one of DC's titles to capitalize on the trend. Johnny Thunder was a schoolteacher by day and a six-gun-shootin' crime fighter by night who rode a horse called Black Lightning.

1958

"THOSE KIDS, WITH ONLY ONE SUPERPOWER EACH, CAN DO SUPER-FEATS EQUAL TO ANY OF MINE!"

Superboy, speaking about the Legion of Super-Heroes, *Adventure Comics* #247

DC BLASTS OFF

1958 was a major year for DC Comics. It saw the debuts of characters and teams that would become comic book greats, including Adam Strange, Bizarro, the Legion of Super-Heroes, Brainiac, and Space Ranger. Not only that, the Challengers of the Unknown got their own book and Superman discovered that he wasn't the only surviving being from Krypton.

The 1950s had seen a proliferation of science-fiction comic book titles, but the space bug really took a hold in popular culture following the establishment, in 1958, of NASA and the coining of the word "aerospace." The obsession with space thoroughly penetrated many of DC's titles, with Batman visiting other planets and Tomahawk encountering aliens.

In another important development, letters columns began to appear in DC titles, inadvertently creating organized comics fandom.

JANUARY

ALIEN BATMAN
***Detective Comics* #251**

Throughout 1958 Batman encountered aliens from different planets and dimensions. He even became an extraterrestrial himself—or so it was believed.

In "The Alien Batman" in *Detective Comics* #251, by writer Edmond Hamilton and artist Sheldon Moldoff, reporter Vicki Vale got a photo of what she thought was Batman as an alien. But it turned out that this Batman was a hoax created by gangsters to discredit the real Caped Crusader in the eyes of Gothamites.

A month later, in *Batman* #113's lead story "Batman—Superman of Planet X" by writer Ed Herron and artist Dick Sprang, the Caped Crusader found himself transported to Zur-En-Arrh, a planet where he discovered himself to have powers equivalent to Superman's on Earth. He used them to assist his alien counterpart, Tlano, in repelling an invasion of striped costume-wearing robots before returning to Earth.

To the horror of two innocent bystanders, Batman appears to reveal himself to be an extraterrestrial. It is later proved to be an elaborate fraud.

FEBRUARY

TIME-TRAVELING TOMAHAWK
***Tomahawk* #54**

The science-fiction trend sweeping through DC in the late 1950s wasn't limited to super hero titles. Even the Revolutionary War guerrilla Thomas Haukins—or Tomahawk—had his share of strange adventures during this period. Tomahawk would encounter a host of odd creatures and phenomena, beginning with artist Bob Brown's "The Lost Tribe of Tiny Warriors" in *Tomahawk* #54. These would include dinosaurs, time travelers, invisible Indian raiders, crashed alien spacecraft, a sea monster, the Frontier Sorcerer and the Indian Sorceress, and "The Fabulous Frontier Chimp!"

IN THE REAL WORLD...

February: Twenty-three people are killed when British European Airways Flight 609 crashes in what becomes known as the Munich Air Disaster.

APRIL

THE HEROES ARE LEGION
***Adventure Comics* #247**

The Legion of Super-Heroes would become one of DC's most enduring and popular groups despite their humble beginnings, in a story by writer Otto Binder and artist Al Plastino. They were futuristic, they were young, and they stuck together. For the youthful comic-reading audience of the late-1950s super hero renaissance, the Legion was the perfect team.

They started out as a group of curious young time-travelers—Cosmic Boy, Lightning Boy, and Saturn Girl—who headed back to early 20th Century Smallville to meet the icon they regarded as the first super hero of all: Superboy. The trio invited young Clark Kent to return with them to the 30th Century and become a member of their "special club" called the Legion of Super-Heroes. Once he got there, there was a catch: Clark had to compete against all three members of the Legion to be initiated into the group. After failing all of the challenges, Clark realized that the test was fixed. It was really just an initiation ritual. The Legion had already decided that they wanted him to be in the team. Superboy got a medallion for his trouble—and, of course, a membership.

With that, their adventures began, and the original Legionnaires' identities were fleshed out. Cosmic Boy was Rokk Krinn, with powers over magnetic fields; the electrically powered Lightning Boy (who soon became Lightning Lad) was Garth Ranzz; and Saturn Girl was Imra Ardeen, a telepath from the moon Titan. Readers were told that the group formed after the trio prevented the assassination of the telepathic tycoon R. J. Brande. Brande agreed to finance their activities if they defended the nation of the United Planets. Over time, the Legion's membership increased, eventually requiring regular tryouts for aspiring new teammates, and its equipment grew more sophisticated. The mandate of the Legion, however, remained the same: to protect the United Planets across time and space and adhere to the principles set out in the group's constitution.

The Legion of Super-Heroes' members use their powers to slow down a getaway rocket while Superman looks on in awe at their combined abilities.

APRIL

LOIS STEPS OUT
***Superman's Girl Friend, Lois Lane* #1**

Following her successful test run in the pages of *Showcase* #9 and #10, Lois Lane got her own title, *Superman's Girl Friend, Lois Lane*, in which Superman was ever the prankster. In the cover story of issue #1, "The Witch of Metropolis" by writer Otto Binder and artist Kurt Schaffenberger (who provided art for the entire issue), Lois had an encounter with toxic fumes that turned her into a hideous-looking woman, and left her convinced she was a witch. A sly Superman played along until the effects of the fumes wore off. Two back-up stories gave readers different sides of the plucky reporter and continued showing off Superman's mischievous side. In "The Bombshell of the Boulevards," written by Jerry Coleman, Lois impersonated a movie star to get an interview with an ambassador, while in "Lois Lane, Super-Chef," written by Binder, Superman played tricks on Lois as she worked in a restaurant.

MAY

KIRBY'S CHALLENGERS
***Challengers of the Unknown* #1**

The paranormal explorers, the Challengers of the Unknown, got their own title, following their test run beginning in *Showcase* #6 (February 1957). The first issue's cover and all interior pencils were by Jack Kirby, who also wrote both stories, "The Man Who Tampered with Infinity" and "The Human Pets."

The first story pitted Rocky, Red, Prof, Ace, and June against Olan Tagorian, who created mutant monsters with the aid of stolen laboratory equipment. The Challengers dispatched Tagorian's beasts with his own teleportation machine before capturing Tagorian himself and destroying his mountain base, which was very similar to what would become the Challengers' own headquarters, Challenger Mountain. The second story was a gag in which the Challengers become an alien child's playthings—until its parents found out.

This issue set the tone for the seventy-six that were to follow. In the Challengers' adventures, the non-super hero adventure comic reached its peak. The team would later reappear in three new self-titled series (in 1991, 1997, and 2004), varying widely in tone, the last of which was written by Mark Waid and restored the Challengers to their pulp-adventure roots.

Prof, Rocky, and Red wrestle an alien monster before it can attack fellow Challenger Ace.

March: The 30th Annual Academy Awards® ceremony takes place. *The Bridge on the River Kwai* wins seven awards, including Best Picture.

April: Unemployment in Detroit reaches twenty percent, marking the height of the Recession of 1958 in the United States.

MAY

A NEW ORIGIN
***Wonder Woman* #98**

Wonder Woman's origin story and character was given a Silver Age revamp, courtesy of writer Robert Kanigher and artist Ross Andru. This issue retold the story of the contest that had been initiated by Athena and sponsored by Hippolyta to determine which of the Amazons would be sent to "Man's World," after army intelligence officer Steve Trevor crashed on Paradise Island. Orana, the red-haired Amazon, challenged Diana for the title of Wonder Woman. Her challenge was unsuccessful and a triumphant Diana returned to Earth with Trevor, adopting the identity of Diana Prince, Trevor's new secretary. Orana would later become Wonder Woman briefly, until her death in issue #251 (January 1979) at the hands of Warhead.

Diana Prince, now Wonder Woman, demonstrates her remarkable powers by exerting pressure on a penny and transforming it into a bridge.

JUNE

TV MYSTERIES
***The New Adventures of Charlie Chan* #1**

Comic adaptations of TV shows were common in the late 1950s and June saw another hit the shelves. *The New Adventures of Charlie Chan*, based on the short-lived syndicated TV show, began its six-issue run, care of writer John Broome and artist Sid Greene. Stalwart detective Charlie Chan confronted weird menaces with the bumbling assistance of Number One Son, solving "The Secret of the Phantom Bells" and "Charlie Chan's Invisible Clue" in issue #1. In later issues Chan traveled far and wide, helping the Mounties investigate "Trail Across the Sky" and the Appalachians probe "The Case of the Hillbilly Detective."

JULY

BRAINIAC'S BOTTLE CITY
***Action Comics* #242**

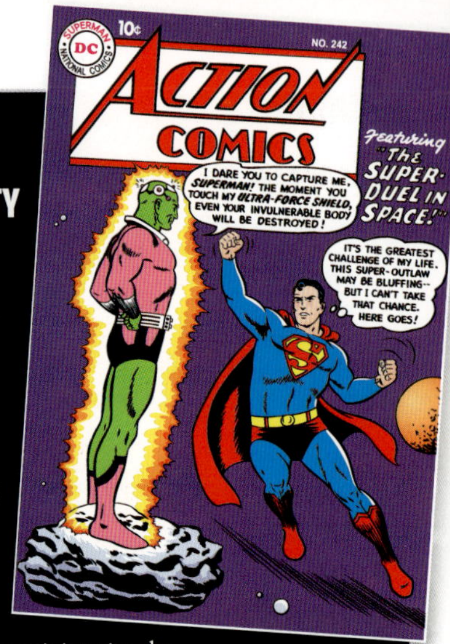

The mythology of Krypton expanded dramatically with the introduction of the evil Brainiac and the Bottle City of Kandor in the *Action Comics* #242 story "The Super-Duel in Space," written by Otto Binder and artist Al Plastino.

As guests aboard the first manned flight into space, Lois Lane and Clark Kent spied a UFO. Superman's X-ray vision revealed it to be the vessel of the tyrant humanoid Brainiac, who intended to miniaturize the cities of Earth and capture them in glass bottles, so that back on his depopulated home world of Bryak he would have subjects to rule.

Clark slipped out of the spaceship, making it appear as if he had evacuated back to Earth, though he actually transformed into Superman. Taking on Brainiac, Superman discovered that even he wasn't strong enough to contend with Brainiac's advanced technology. Superman allowed himself to be miniaturized along with Metropolis so he could board Brainiac's ship. Escaping from the bottle Metropolis was housed in, Superman discovered that one of the other bottles contained a miniaturized version of Kandor, once the capital of Krypton. Even in miniature, the existence of Kandor told Superman that he was no longer the last of the Kryptonians. Getting inside the bottle, Superman met the scientist Kimda. Kimda explained that Brainiac's Hyper-Ray could return the cities to their normal size.

As Brainiac put himself into suspended animation for his long return voyage, Superman took control of the Hyper-Ray and returned the cities of Earth to normal size. However, with only one charge left in the Hyper-Ray, he realized that he could restore himself or Kandor. Just as Superman was about to restore Kandor, Kimda deliberately crashed his spaceship into the controller button. This action returned Superman to his regular size and kept Kandor in miniature so that Earth would not lose its super-protector. Sending Brainiac on his way, a saddened Superman placed the bottle containing Kandor in the Fortress of Solitude, hoping that someday he would be able to restore it to its normal size.

When Brainiac labels the Man of Steel "Puny-Man," Superman is overcome with anger and rips a huge chunk out of a planetoid, proving Brainiac's moniker is far from accurate.

IN THE REAL WORLD...

May: Arturo Frondizi becomes President of Argentina.
May: F-104 Starfighter sets a world speed record of 1,404.19 mph (2,259.82 km/h).
June: Charles de Gaulle is brought out of retirement to lead France by decree for six months.

AUGUST

SPACE RANGER ON PATROL
***Showcase* #15**

DC decided it was time to mix sci-fi and adventure by trying out some new space heroes. The first of these was Richard Starr, Space Ranger, who debuted in *Showcase* #15 in stories by writer Edmond Hamilton and artist Bob Brown. Allied Solar Enterprises scion Starr used his money and influence to fight interplanetary crime in his spaceship *Solar King* in the 22nd Century. He was helped on by his girlfriend Myra Mason and the alien Cryll. A damsel in distress, Myra often contributed to adventures by being imperiled, as seen on this cover, where she was frozen inside a Paralybeam by the nefarious Shann-Men. Occasionally, Space Ranger would leave his base in the Asteroid Belt—and the 22nd Century—to pitch in on adventures in the 20th Century, working with the JSA and Green Lantern.

SEPTEMBER

DEAR SIR
***Superman* #124**

This issue of *Superman* was the first DC comic to include a letters column that would become a regular feature, though readers' letters were published in issue #3 of *Real Fact Comics* in July 1946. The letters page in *Superman* became known as the "Metropolis Mailbag." Letters from fans would gradually replace the one- or two-page text stories that had served as filler in previous years across various comics. As readers began to develop a forum, comics fandom was born.

CHECK THE CALENDAR
***Detective Comics* #259**

Detective Comics #259 saw the first appearance of Julian Gregory Day, otherwise known as the Calendar Man. In "The Challenge of the Calendar Man," written by Bill Finger and drawn by Sheldon Moldoff, Day arrived in Gotham City to front a series of magic shows and pull off a number of criminal plots. Each crime saw the Calendar Man don a costume linked to a season—Winter, Spring, Summer, Fall, and Monsoon. Later, in *Batman* #312 (June 1979) he would link his crimes to days of the week, and in 1996–97, he would be a suspect in the "Long Halloween" murders.

OCTOBER

BIZARRO WORLD
***Superboy* #68**

A book-length story by writer Otto Binder and artist George Papp took up the entirety of *Superboy* #68. Bizarro was a copy of the Boy of Steel, created by a malfunctioning prototype duplicator ray, who possessed the same powers as Superboy. This copy seemed clumsy and unable to control his powers, but he was well-intentioned. Battling him, Superboy met his equal—until Bizarro destroyed himself by coming into contact with debris from the ray. More durable Bizarros would also appear in the DCU.

DECEMBER

MORE STRANGE ADVENTURES
***Showcase* #17**

Emerging from the same editorial meeting that gave birth to Space Ranger, Adam Strange debuted in a three-issue trial starting with *Showcase* #17, which was written by Gardner Fox and featured art by Mike Sekowsky. An archaeologist in remote South America, Adam ran straight into a teleportation device called the Zeta Beam while fleeing hostile natives, and ended up on the planet Rann—an origin that neatly fitted together the tropes of the classic adventure story with those of newer science-fiction-style adventures. While on Rann, Strange met scientist Sardath, inventor of the Zeta Beam. Sardath explained the teleporting properties of the beam, and also explained that it would eventually wear off, returning Strange to Earth. Strange, who had fallen in love with Sardath's daughter Alanna, returned to Earth reluctantly, until he could ride the Zeta Beam back to Rann again. Reappearing on that planet regularly, he would pursue his affections for Alanna while also defeating those that threatened Rann before the Zeta Beam would lose its efficacy and teleport him home.

In Strange's first adventure, the danger to Rann came from an alien race of Eternals who threatened the city of Kamorak. Strange and Alanna helped the scientists of the city Samakand trap the Eternals in a fourth-dimensional prison. A second invasion saw Adam armed with what would become his trademark ray gun and jet pack.

Space adventures might be familiar to Alanna, but for Adam Strange they are voyages of discovery.

ALSO THIS YEAR: In June's *ACTION COMICS* #241, Superman's Fortress of Solitude was seen for the first time. The story "The Super-Key to Fort Superman," by writer Jerry Coleman and artist Wayne Boring, revealed the secrets of the Fortress, including a laboratory, an exercise room, and an alien zoo...

August: The King Of Pop, Michael Jackson, is born in Gary, Indiana.
October: Pope John XXIII succeeds Pope Pius XII as the 261st pope.
December: Tallies reveal that, for the first time, total passengers carried by air exceeds total passengers carried by sea in transatlantic service.

1959

"THE SARGE! STANDIN' LIKE A ROCK!"

Easy Company officer,
***Our Army at War* #81**

SUPER HEROES RETURN

The popularity of the super hero was already on the upturn, but in 1959 things really began to take off. DC continued to revamp heroes who had dwindled in popularity. The year saw the debut of a new Green Lantern, Hal Jordan, who would go on to become one of the Silver Age's true greats. DC introduced new heroes, too, the most important of whom was Supergirl, from Superman's home planet of Krypton.

1959 was also the year of the monkey, if only in the American cultural imagination. Able and Miss Baker, a rhesus and squirrel monkey respectively, became the first animals to survive spaceflight and were celebrities upon their return to Earth. Gorillas had already appeared in comics, but this year DC introduced primate stalwarts Congorilla and Gorilla Grodd. In fact, it was a banner year for debuts, including Kid Flash, Bat-Mite, the Suicide Squad, and Sgt. Rock. Things were looking up.

JANUARY

CONGO BILL BECOMES CONGORILLA
***Action Comics* #248**

The decline of the traditional adventure comic in favor of more other-worldly adventures might have had dire consequences for intrepid explorer Congo Bill. However, writer Robert Bernstein and artist Howard Sherman gave Congo Bill a new direction in *Action Comics* #248. Bill became the beneficiary of witch doctor Chief Kawolo's dying gift: a magic ring that, when rubbed, enabled him to place his consciousness inside the body of the giant Golden Gorilla. A sceptical Bill didn't believe in the ring's powers until he was trapped in a cave-in and gave the ring a try out of desperation. It worked and the people of Africa had a new protector: Congorilla.

FEBRUARY

A FEMALE BLACKHAWK
***Blackhawk* #133**

Wth *Blackhawk* #133, the Blackhawk Squadron finally welcomed a woman to their ranks—Zinda Blake—courtesy of editor Jack Schiff and artist Dick Dillin. Blake was determined to be a member of the famed World War II team of ace pilots. She made her first attempt to join the group by rescuing member Olaf Friedriksen from the villainous Scavenger. Turned down for team membership due to her gender, Zinda went on to rescue the entire company of men from the Scavenger, after which they couldn't really keep her out! Known as Lady Blackhawk, she would go on to join the all-female Birds of Prey in 2004.

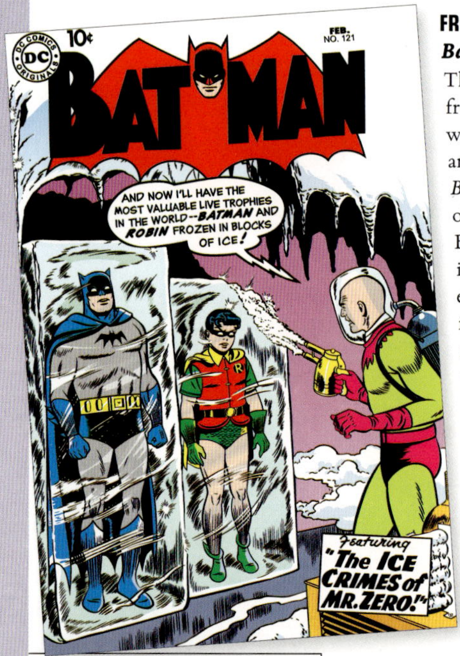

FROM ZERO TO ANTIHERO
***Batman* #121**

The Dynamic Duo battled the frosty foe Mr. Zero in a story written by Dave Wood and with art by Shelton Moldoff in *Batman* #121. When ice-obsessed Mr. Zero froze Batman and Robin in blocks of ice to pull off a heist, Batman escaped and bathed the villain in steam, which made him normal again. This character was an interesting example of other media feeding back into the comics. The 1960s *Batman* TV series, starring Adam West, included the character of Mr. Zero but renamed him Mr. Freeze. Later comic book incarnations of the ice-cold villain would adopt the new name.

IN THE REAL WORLD...

January: Motown Records is founded by Berry Gordy, Jr.
February: Fidel Castro becomes Premier of Cuba.

MARCH

MEET GUNNER AND SARGE
All American Men of War #67

War comics had rarely featured recurring characters, but writer Robert Kanigher and artist Ross Andru changed that with the introduction of U.S. Marines Gunner MacKay and Sarge Clay in *All American Men of War* #67. In most of Gunner and Sarge's stories, Gunner was the decoy while Sarge gave the orders. They were always together as they fought their way across the Pacific, and were joined by a German shepherd dog, Pooch, before becoming part of the first incarnation of the special forces team, the Losers. Later, Pooch would be revealed as Rex the Wonder Dog's brother.

MAN IN THE MIRROR
The Flash #105

In February 1949, *Flash Comics* had been canceled with issue #104. However, the 1950s had seen a revival of the super hero, and in *Showcase* #4 in October 1956 a Silver Age version of the Flash had appeared. In March 1959, *The Flash* was back, care of writer John Broome and artist Carmine Infantino. The series continued the numbering from *Flash Comics* and gave Barry Allen his own title. Issue #105 also debuted the Mirror Master, one of the Flash's greatest adversaries. Sam Scudder had a gift for enhancing mirror technologies to create illusions. He began to use his skills for criminal means, creating holograms, exploring teleportation via mirror, and trapping people inside mirrors. The Mirror Master and the Flash would tangle until his death in *Crisis on Infinite Earths* #10 (January 1986).

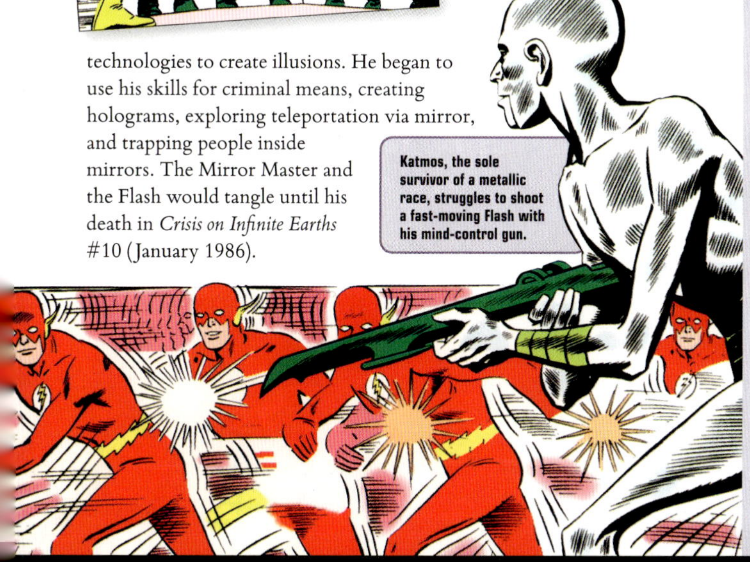
Katmos, the sole survivor of a metallic race, struggles to shoot a fast-moving Flash with his mind-control gun.

APRIL

THE ROCK OF EASY COMPANY
Our Army at War #81

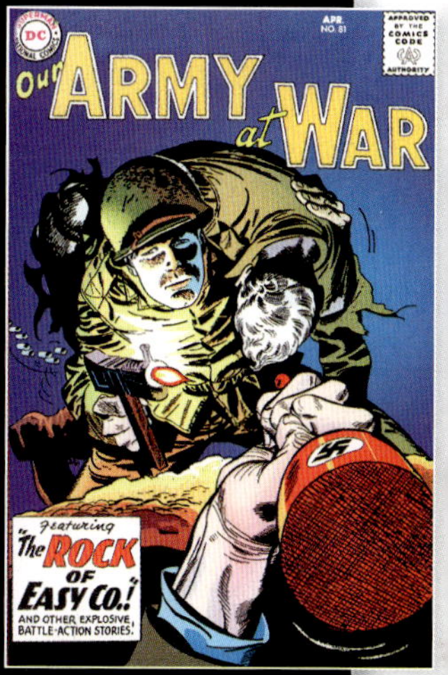

Sgt. Rock, one of DC's longest-running and most popular war characters, made his debut in *Our Army at War* #81. This courageous character would outlive all other DC war figures, persisting well past the heyday of the military comic.

In "The Rock of Easy Co.!" written by Robert Kanigher and Bob Haney, with art by Ross Andru, the reader was introduced to Sgt. Frank Rock of Easy Company (or Sgt. Rocky as he was then known). The solid-as-a-rock sergeant was a deadeye marksman and a fearsome hand-to-hand fighter, but his greatest asset was his indomitable will. In his first outing, he and his company fought the Nazi Iron Captain, ending in hand-to-hand combat between the captain and a triumphant Rock.

Sgt. Rock's Easy Company took part in almost every major action in the European theater, and along the way the biography of Rock unfolded. A native of Pittsburgh, he enlisted after Pearl Harbor and landed with the army in North Africa, working his way up to the rank of Master Sergeant and adopting that grade's chevrons on his uniform and helmet. Writer Kanigher let it be known that Rock's war experience was in part modeled on the legendary 1st Infantry Division, the Big Red One. Additionally, Rock's dog tag number, 409966, was popularly said to be Kanigher's own.

When Sgt. Rock's popularity became apparent, he made an appearance in *Showcase* #45 (August 1963). This would usually be a prelude to the launch of a new title featuring the character in question. But in this case, the Rock of Easy Company stayed with *Our Army at War*—until issue #302 in March 1977, when that title officially became what it really had been for some time: *Sgt. Rock*.

The Nazi Captain may rule his soldiers with an iron fist but he is no match for Sgt. Rocky, who handles his Browning machine gun as if it weighs no more than a toy gun.

March: The Barbie doll makes its debut at the American International Toy Fair in New York. American businesswoman Ruth Handler is credited with the creation of the doll.

April: Recording sessions for Miles Davis' seminal album *Kind of Blue* take place at Columbia's 30th Street Studio in New York City.

MAY

PIED PIPERS AND GORILLAS

***The Flash* #106**

Two popular villains debuted in *The Flash* #106, in stories by writer John Broome and artist Carmine Infantino. "Menace of the Super-Gorilla" saw Barry Allen battle Gorilla Grodd, a hyper-intelligent primate who could manipulate new technologies. Grodd planned to take over Gorilla City but was stopped by Allen. In "The Pied Piper of Peril," Hartley Rathaway, who was born deaf, became obsessed with the powers of sound after his hearing was restored. Developing a flute that could hypnotize or paralyze, he hired himself out to criminals as the Pied Piper and became Allen's nemesis.

IT'S SUPERGIRL!

***Action Comics* #252**

When Krypton exploded, it was thought that the only survivors were the miniaturized residents of the bottle city of Kandor and Superman. *Action Comics* #252 revealed that there was another survivor—Supergirl. Kara Zor-El (Supergirl) crashed to Earth, having been sent there by her parents who hoped the planet would be a safe place for her to grow up in. Superman saw the Kryptonian rocket approaching and was reminded of the time when, as Superbaby, he was sent to Earth by his parents. Superman was shocked to find out that the passenger of this rocket was in fact his cousin, Supergirl, whose journey paralleled his own. He was even more surprised to discover that Krypton's Argo City survived the destruction of Krypton until a meteor shower destroyed the protective shield Supergirl's father had built around it.

Superman set Kara up with a secret identity as Linda Lee and placed her in Midvale Orphanage. In early issues, Supergirl used her super-strength and super-speed to rescue plummeting airplanes and save tribes from fire-breathing serpents. However, she was forced to operate in secret until Superman felt she had control of her powers. Supergirl appeared across several titles until she sacrificed her life to save the multiverse in *Crisis on Infinite Earths* #7 (October 1985).

Action Comics #252 also saw the debut of the cyborg villain Metallo, who would become one of Superman's ongoing nemeses, eventually using kryptonite to power his own heart.

Supergirl returns to Midvale Orphanage after making a late-night secret patrol of her new town. She hopes she can become Midvale's "guardian angel."

A SPEEDY RECOVERY

***Adventure Comics* #260**

In the back pages of *Adventure Comics* #260 (where Green Arrow spent most of his time in the 1950s and 1960s), Speedy, the Green Arrow's sidekick, was worried that the Arrow was training a replacement. The orphan Roy Harper (Speedy) came to the Green Arrow's attention by winning an archery contest and was taken on by the Emerald Archer as his right-hand man. In a story by writer Robert Bernstein and artist Lee Elias, the Green Arrow explained that, rather than looking for a new sidekick, he was helping some would-be crime fighters. Speedy and Green Arrow would stick together, through Roy's adventures with the Teen Titans, the Outsiders, and the JLA.

A MITE CONFUSING

***Detective Comics* #267**

The impish Bat-Mite made his first appearance in *Detective Comics* #267, care of writer Bill Finger and artist Sheldon Moldoff. Bat-Mite traveled from another dimension to show his admiration for Batman. But Bat-Mite wasn't content simply to watch his hero; he wanted to help and use his magical powers—including invisibility and possibly power over three-dimensional reality—to make Batman's operations more interesting. Batman found him annoying, and at times a real danger, but there was no getting rid of this determined imp.

JUNE

MASTERS OF TIME

***Showcase* #20**

Time-traveler Rip Hunter and the Time Masters—brother and sister Corky and Bonnie Baxter, and Bonnie's boyfriend, Jeff Smith—made their debut in *Showcase* #20. The Time Masters were ready for any trans-historical adventure in their trusty Time-Sphere. They were also aided by the Encyclo-Matic, which gave the team all the historical information they needed to ensure a successful journey. "Prisoners of 100 Million B.C.," by writer Jack Miller and artist Ruben Moreira, in *Showcase* #20 saw the Time Masters head back to the age of the dinosaurs. After a few *Showcase* appearances, Rip Hunter moved into his own title and later joined the Forgotten Heroes.

IN THE REAL WORLD...

May: British Empire Day is renamed Commonwealth Day.
June: A new government of the State of Singapore is sworn in by Sir William Goode.
July: Charles Ovnand and Dale R. Buis become the first Americans killed in action in the Vietnam War.

SEPTEMBER

SUICIDE MISSION
***The Brave and the Bold* #25**

Since August 1955, *The Brave and the Bold* had graced the newsstands, telling adventure tales of knights and princes. That changed with issue #25, when the series was reinvented as a title that would test out new characters.

In "The Three Waves of Doom," a story that filled *The Brave and the Bold* #25, writer Robert Kanigher and artist Ross Andru introduced the Suicide Squad, a band of World War II-era military misfits. Led by Rick Flag, the team was sent out on the missions that weren't worth sacrificing other soldiers for, hence its name. Working with Flag in the Squad's initial incarnation were Jess Bright, Dr. Hugh Evans, and Rick's girlfriend, Karin Grace. In its first adventure, the Squad fought a horned monster on dry land and in the air. Subsequent tales included battles with giant snakes, dinosaurs, and the cyclops Polyphemus.

Later the Suicide Squad developed into a sort of "Dirty Dozen" for incarcerated super-villains who were willing to take on dangerous missions in return for reduced or commuted sentences. Also known as Task Force X, the Suicide Squad carried out its missions at the direction of Rick Flag's son. Based in Belle Reve prison in Louisiana, the team was outfitted with explosive bracelets to ensure that they carried out their orders. A still later version of the Squad was started up by Sgt. Rock, as part of his occasional post-war career in black operations.

Having fought a frenzied monster, the Suicide Squad's Rick Flag and Karin Grace look to the future. They set about planning the first manned flight into space, aboard *Rocket Hope One*.

OCTOBER

SOS GREEN LANTERN

***Showcase* #22**

After difficult times for super hero titles in the mid-1950s, DC had decided to revamp a number of characters to inject new life into the genre. Writer John Broome and artist Gil Kane ensured that Green Lantern got his turn in October's *Showcase* #22.

In the issue's first story, "SOS Green Lantern," Abin Sur, the Green Lantern of Space Sector 2814, suffered mortal injuries in a desert spaceship crash. Just before he died, Sur ordered his Green Lantern power ring to find a successor. Miles away, test pilot Hal Jordan found himself—and the flight simulator he was occupying—transported by a flash of green light. Hal learned that Abin Sur's ring had decreed that he would succeed Sur. Accepting the role and the responsibility it entailed, Jordan became the first human Green Lantern.

The remaining two stories in *Showcase* #22—"Secret of the Flaming Spear" and "Menace of the Runaway Missile"—set the tone for the Green Lantern adventures that were to follow, seeing Jordan swiftly save an airplane from crashing and stop a runaway missile. The reader also learned that an impurity in the Green Lantern power ring meant that Hal was vulnerable when faced with the color yellow.

Both stories also focused on Jordan's personal life. "Secret of the Flaming Spear" introduced Carol Ferris, Hal's occasional love interest, who would later become Star Sapphire, the Green Lantern's adversary. In "Menace of the Runaway Missile," Hal's duties as Green Lantern forced him to break off a date with Carol early, setting up the ongoing tension between his Green Lantern duties and his personal life.

Showcase #22 was also Abin Sur's debut. This was not Sur's first encounter with the Jordan family, having met one of Hal's ancestors in 1860s U.S.A.

COVER STAR
***Pat Boone* #1**

Pop star, actor, and wholesome 1950s icon, Pat Boone made his first DC appearance in *Superman's Girl Friend, Lois Lane* #9 (May 1959), where he granted an interview to the *Daily Planet*, much to the delight of fan Lois Lane. Later in the year, Boone got his own series, offering a mix of biographical pieces and fictionalized accounts of the life of a beloved celebrity. The series lasted for five issues.

ALSO THIS YEAR: In August, after a three-year hiatus, Mr. Mxyzptlk, an imp from the Fifth Dimensional world of Zrfff, returned to plague the Man of Steel in *SUPERMAN* #131. Mr. Mxyzptlk's practical jokes could only be stopped by forcing him to say or spell his name backward. The mischievous super-villain would appear regularly throughout the 1960s...

August: United States satellite *Explorer 6* transmits the first pictures of Earth from space.

November: MGM's widescreen, multimillion-dollar, technicolor version of *Ben-Hur* is released and becomes the studio's greatest hit so far.

1960s

Like all great stories, the seventh decade of the 20th Century was defined by a strong beginning, middle, and end. Furthermore, the decade laid the foundations for a society ruled by the "Baby Boomers" —the generation born after World War II.

A continuation of the conservative ways of the 1950s characterized the early 1960s, with young Baby Boomers inhabiting a flawed but nonetheless optimistic world. By the middle of the decade, The Beatles and other pop stars influenced the younger generation's tastes and attitudes, while television and other media encouraged new fashions, radical lifestyles, and independent thought. As a result, the late 1960s gave rise to a counterculture that challenged the status quo, and sought to change a world riven by social unrest and the violation of civil rights.

The 1960s' metamorphoses were reflected in the titles that DC Comics published—particularly those under the editorial direction of Julius Schwartz, who carried on the Silver Age renaissance of super heroes from the preceding decade. As the Space Race between the U.S. and the Soviet Union gathered pace, Schwartz echoed readers' fascination with science fiction and adventure, placing not only the stars within their grasp, but parallel worlds and extradimensional realities as well.

In the mid-1960s, Schwartz assigned writer John Broome and artist Carmine Infantino to modernize Batman, revamping his look and, most important, the tone of his stories. By the end of the decade, Schwartz, Infantino, artist Joe Kubert, and other pioneers had overseen one of comics' most significant transformations—turning larger-than-life champions into characters that readers could more realistically aspire to emulate and identify with.

"AN UTTER IMPOSSIBILITY! THE RED TORNADO—ALONG WITH THE JUSTICE SOCIETY—ARE DEAD!"

Professor T. O. Morrow, *Justice League of America* #64 (August 1968

1960

"THERE'S NO TIME TO WASTE! I MUST SUMMON THE JUSTICE LEAGUE TO AN EMERGENCY MEETING!"

Aquaman, *The Brave and the Bold* #28

A BRAVE NEW WORLD

At the dawn of a new decade, the Silver Age was already firmly underway. Anthology titles such as *The Brave and the Bold* were proving popular. The wildly successful revitalization of the Flash and Green Lantern had cemented the idea that older comic book concepts could be made new again. And the utterly fantastic had become the norm, as DC traveled across galaxies, back in time, into the far-off future, and beneath the farthest ocean depths for thrilling tales of adventure and heroics.

Regardless of the where or when, however, what mattered most to readers were the who and how. The Justice League of America brought together the World's Greatest Heroes to combat threats larger than any member could handle alone, and completely reinvented the super hero team dynamic. The enemies also grew more powerful in nature or cosmic in scope, upping the stakes for everyone involved.

FEBRUARY

DEEP (SEA) PURPLE
***Adventure Comics* #269**

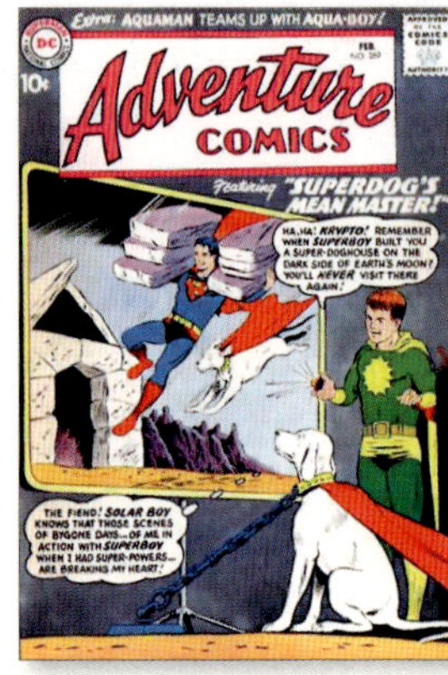

Everyone needs a friend, even the King of Atlantis, so writer Robert Bernstein and artist Ramona Fradon provided a lifelong pal for Aquaman in a back-up tale in this issue. The Sea King found a young Atlantean boy—identified as such by his purple eyes—who was exiled from the city due to his fear of marine life. The boy was dubbed Aqualad, and through Aquaman's guidance, he eventually accepted that fish were friends, not foes. In return, he helped his mentor to rescue a plane in distress by telepathically instructing dozens of luminous fish to create an emergency landing strip. His phobia conquered, Aqualad was returned home to Atlantis, though he quickly decided that he much preferred swimming side-by-side with Aquaman.

POWER COUPLE
***Superman's Girl Friend, Lois Lane* #15**

Superman's lookalike cousin Van-Zee sought Lois Lane's heart, but Lois rejected him, so writer Otto Binder and artist Kurt Schaffenberger matched Van-Zee with heiress Sylvia DeWitt instead. The two married and moved to Venus, where they settled down with their super-twins. The couple suffered a rocky moment when Van-Zee created a serum that gave Sylvia superpowers. Sylvia's super-vision spotted Lana Lang kissing Superman on Earth, and she mistook him for her husband and left him. However, Superman and Lois explained the mix-up, and the couple reconciled.

Van-Zee and Sylvia DeWitt may look like Superman and Lois Lane, but their love for one another and their super-children is like no other.

IN THE REAL WORLD...

January: Actress Joanne Woodward receives the first star on the Hollywood Walk of Fame.

MARCH

A LEAGUE OF THEIR OWN

***The Brave and the Bold* #28**

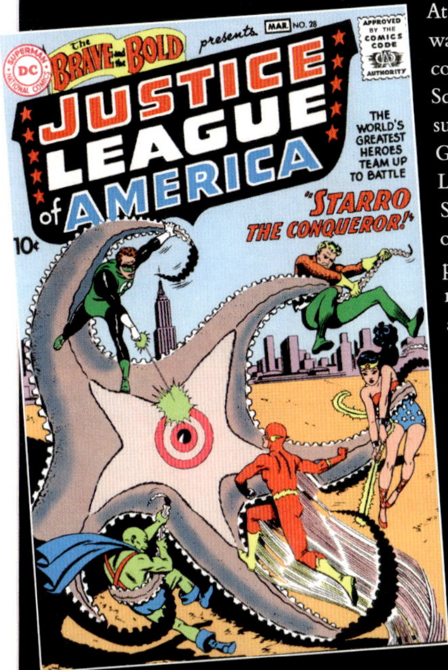

At a time when the super hero was a minority breed in comics, editor Julius Schwartz had repopulated the subculture by revitalizing Golden Age icons like Green Lantern and the Flash. Now, Schwartz wanted to take it one step further: he would pair these heroes with other members of their class for adventures that no hero could handle alone. To do this, he recruited writer Gardner Fox and artist Mike Sekowsky, and together they came up with the Justice League of America, a modern version of the legendary Justice Society of America from the 1940s. Fox altered the name because he thought fans of Major League Baseball and the National Football League would better identify with a Justice League. And it appears he was right—readers immediately took to the idea of seeing heroes interacting with each other while combating vast, cosmic-level threats.

With a lineup consisting of Aquaman, Wonder Woman, Martian Manhunter, the Flash, and Green Lantern—plus cameos from Superman and Batman—the Justice League of America proved its collective mettle against the menace of Starro the Conqueror in their inaugural issue. A massive alien invertebrate, Starro resembled the common Earth starfish—it even hinted that starfish were its distant relatives as it transformed three of them into Starro-like deputies—but it possessed formidable celestial powers, including the ability to control minds.

After meeting in their cavernous Secret Sanctuary, the JLA split into teams to combat the starfish deputies now doing Starro's bidding. They succeeded, though defeating Starro itself was difficult. In fact, the key to the team's victory resided not with the heroes themselves, but with a happy-go-lucky teenager named Snapper Carr. Snapper had mysteriously remained unaffected while Starro's agents controlled Happy Harbor's inhabitants. Before long, the Flash and Green Lantern uncovered the reason why: while maintaining his parents' front lawn, Snapper's clothes had been covered in lime, and this is what had made him impervious to Starro's power. Gathering as much lime as possible, the JLA doused it across Starro's entire body, imprisoning the tentacled terror inside a hard, white shell. The heroes celebrated their victory by welcoming Snapper into their ranks, making him an honorary member of the Justice League.

Justice Leaguers Wonder Woman, Martian Manhunter, the Flash, and Green Lantern battle Starro the Conqueror's mind-controlled starfish, transformed into the tentacled terror's own image.

MARCH

INTRODUCING CAPTAIN ATOM

***Space Adventures* #33**

Donning a suit designed to protect ordinary humans from potential radiation, Captain Atom was born in a tale by artist Steve Ditko and writer Joe Gill. Military scientist Allen Adam's body was vaporized after he was launched in an experimental rocket ship. Miraculously, Allen reformed his own body and found that he now harnessed the very power of the atom from within. With military ties and a nuclear arms race in full swing, Captain Atom was widely considered to be the definitive Cold War hero.

APRIL

BALD TO THE BONE

***Adventure Comics* #271**

This tale by Superman co-creator Jerry Siegel and artist Al Plastino revealed the never-before-told origin of the villain Luthor, and his first name as well: Lex. The DC Universe was shocked to learn that a teenaged Lex was once the Boy of Steel's biggest fan. In fact, he even rescued Superboy from a kryptonite meteor, and they became instant friends. Unfortunately, history dictated that the two pals had to part ways, as surely as Lex's mane had to part from his scalp. Lex inadvertently started a fire inside his lab while creating a protoplasmic life form and cooking up an antidote for the deadly irradiated rocks from Superboy's lost planet of Krypton. The Boy of Steel arrived in time to snuff out the blaze with his super-breath, but he accidentally knocked an acid compound into the protoplasmic form, creating a gas that made Lex's hair fall out.

Forever follicly challenged and mentally unhinged by the accident, a vengeance-driven Luthor eventually tried destroying Superboy with the kryptonite meteor that first brought them together. The Boy of Tomorrow survived by using his super-breath to inhale the last drops of Luthor's antidote, and he hoped that his former friend would see the error of his ways. Instead, Lex's hatred remained, and would eventually make him Superman's greatest enemy.

In one of comics' unlikeliest moments, Superboy and a teenage Lex Luthor meet and become instant friends after Luthor rescues the Boy of Steel from a kryptonite meteor.

"YOU RAT!... THE GAS FUMES MADE MY HAIR FALL OUT! I'M BALD!"

Lex Luthor, *Adventure Comics* #271

March: The United States announces that 3,500 American soldiers will be sent to Vietnam to fight in the Vietnam War.

April: The United States launches the first weather satellite, TIROS-1.
April: *Ben-Hur* wins Best Picture at The 32nd Annual Academy Awards®.

APRIL

MONDO BIZARRO WORLD
***Action Comics* #263**

When Superman visited the dead planet inhabited by Bizarro and the woman of his nightmares, Bizarro Lois Lane, writer Otto Binder and artist Wayne Boring introduced an entire world filled with the backward beings, living amid foul, dilapidated conditions. Ever the noble hero, Superman sought to help the population by providing extreme home makeovers, only to suffer his own reversal of fortune: home improvement was actually a crime for which he had to stand trial! In the following issue, to avoid being found guilty (or is it not guilty?) and converted into a Bizarro, the Man of Steel helped turn the "perfectly" round-shaped Bizarro World into a square shape, and was released by the "ungrateful" Bizarros.

MAY

FOSSIL FEUDS
***Star-Spangled War Stories* #90**

Beyond the high quality of its story and art, what was most notable about this initial installment of "The War That Time Forgot," by writer/editor Robert Kanigher and artist Ross Andru was that it was the first cross-genre story to blend war comics with science fiction. In the series' first Jurassic joust, a patrol was sent to the Island of Armored Giants to investigate the disappearance of two prior patrols. It wasn't long before the soldiers uncovered the prehistoric parties behind the disappearances, and Tyrannosaur terror ensued.

ELONGATED ARM OF THE LAW
***The Flash* #112**

Editor Julius Schwartz, writer John Broome, and artist Carmine Infantino introduced the Elongated Man, a stretchable super-sleuth who quickly became the Flash's rival for Central City's affection. Motivated by a lifelong fascination with Indian rubber men, Ralph Dibny identified and ingested elements from a fruit extract, giving him incredible stretching abilities. The Scarlet Speedster initially believed the hero was behind several high-profile robberies, until the Elongated Man convinced him of his innocence. Together, the duo captured the real thieves, becoming fast friends in the process.

JUNE

AN ATOMIC KNIGHTS' TALE
***Strange Adventures* #117**

"The Rise of the Atomic Knights," ushered in by scribe John Broome and illustrator Murphy Anderson, transported fans to a post-World War III Earth ravaged by atomic radiation. While facing a bleak, apocalyptic future, soldier Gardner Grayle, teacher Douglas Herald and his sister, Marene, twins Wayne and Hollis Hobard, and scientist Bryndon Smith discovered six suits of radiation-resistant medieval armor. Donning the suits and dubbing themselves the Atomic Knights, the sextet sought to restore civilization one city at a time, starting in the Midwest of America, where they brought down the tyrannical Black Baron and opened his massive food stores to a starving populace.

In their suits of radiation-resistant armor, the newly formed Atomic Knights lead the charge against the Black Baron and others who overrun a post-apocalyptic Earth.

JULY

ARTIFICIAL ANTAGONIST
***The Brave and the Bold* #30**

An obsessive fear of death prompted criminal genius Professor Ivo to seek immortality, though it was his android creation Amazo that cemented his insane legacy. Amazo was designed to absorb the powers and abilities of Justice League members Green Lantern, the Flash, Wonder Woman, Martian Manhunter, and Aquaman. Becoming a one-man Justice League, Amazo managed to defeat the heroes but fortunately remained thankfully unaware of their weaknesses, including the inability of Green Lantern's ring to affect anything yellow. This gave the Emerald Gladiator the opening he needed to save his teammates, who together stopped Ivo and rendered the android inert, thanks to writer Gardner Fox and artist Mike Sekowsky.

IN THE REAL WORLD...

May: U.S. President Dwight D. Eisenhower signs the Civil Rights Act of 1960 into law.
May: The first functional laser is demonstrated by T.H. Maiman in the U.S.
May: An American U-2 spyplane is shot down over the Soviet Union.
July: Harper Lee's novel *To Kill a Mockingbird* is published.

AUGUST

TAKING CHARGE
***Green Lantern* #1**

Almost a year after being deemed worthy of carrying the Green Lanterns' precious Battery of Power in *Showcase* #22 (October 1959), test pilot Hal Jordan had earned the right to fly solo in his own ongoing series. Writer John Broome and artist Gil Kane, having chronicled the first adventures of the Silver Age Green Lantern during his massively popular three-issue run in *Showcase*, were charged with not only continuing the Emerald Warrior's exploits, but expanding his importance on a cosmic level—and they wasted no time in doing so. In the historic first issue, Green Lantern traveled to Calor, "The Planet of Doomed Men," to save its solely male inhabitants from the Dryg, a gargantuan creature with the power to fire bolts of will-sapping energy. Following a brief but intense struggle, the hero managed to literally put the creature on ice, trapping it within a glacier. What made the story particularly noteworthy to fans, however, was that it recounted Green Lantern's origin while introducing the hero of Space Sector 2814 to his "bosses" on Planet Oa, the Guardians of the Universe—even though they initially wiped Hal's memory of the meeting.

A far more local—albeit equally dangerous—foe would plague Green Lantern and Coast City in the issue's second tale, when a scientist's hypno-ray enabled him to control others to do his criminal bidding. Before long, the emerald ring-wielder would end the marionette machinations of the "Puppet-Master"—though the incident would force Hal Jordan to realize that he faced a far more difficult task in pulling the heart strings of his love and employer, Carol Ferris, who only had eyes for Green Lantern.

On the planet Calor, Green Lantern Hal Jordan has a difficult time mustering up enough willpower to stop the Dryg, a sixty-foot creature that weakens its enemies with overpowering mental blasts.

NOVEMBER

ALIEN CHESSMASTER
***Justice League of America* #1**

Despero gave the World's Greatest Heroes a run for their money in the first issue of their ongoing series. The three-eyed tyrant possessed telepathic abilities and an array of super-weapons, including a chessboard that doubled as a dimensional transporter. Despero turned the JLA into literal chess pawns and sent them to different worlds, but his plans of galactic conquest were thwarted by honorary member Snapper Carr, who used an energy absorber to render the alien inert.

DECEMBER

TOSSING HIS NAME AROUND

***The Flash* #117**

Good super-villains make life miserable for heroes; great super-villains come back time and again with ever more inventive new ways of doing so. So what could be better than an Australian-born antagonist who takes petty thievery to new extremes with the aid of gimmicked boomerangs?

Writer John Broome and artist Carmine Infantino kept even the Flash off-balance when they introduced George "Digger" Harkness and his hand-held rebounding weaponry. Shrewd as he was skilled, Harkness launched his criminal career when he took a job at the Wiggins Game Company, which had been looking for a mascot to market the company's boomerangs. Becoming Captain Boomerang, the criminal tailored his handheld arsenal to accomplish different tasks. He was also intelligent enough to misdirect the Fastest Man Alive, making Flash believe that he had been caring for his elderly parents, who turned out to be his crooked cohorts in disguise. Though the Flash would escape a giant boomerang deathtrap and put the crooked criminal behind bars, it would not be long before Captain Boomerang returned to plague both the hero and Central City.

Captain Boomerang casts the Flash into space on a rocket boomerang designed to re-enter Earth's atmosphere and plunge straight to the ocean floor.

ALSO THIS YEAR: Writer Jerry Siegel and artist Jim Mooney couldn't help Supergirl join Chameleon Boy, Invisible Kid, and Colossal Boy as members of the Legion of Super-Heroes in August's *ACTION COMICS* #267... *SHOWCASE* #27 in August saw Dane Dorrance, Biff Bailey, Judy Walton, and Nicky Walton dive into underwater adventures as the Sea Devils, by writer/editor Robert Kanigher and illustrator Russ Heath...

August: Alfred Hitchcock's thriller *Psycho* is released in movie theaters.
September: Cassius Clay wins the gold medal in boxing at the 1960 Summer Olympics.

December: Two civilian airliners collide over Staten Island, New York City, killing 128 passengers and crew on both planes along with six people on the ground.

1961

"HOW CAN YOU POSSIBLY CLAIM TO BE THE FLASH, BARRY ALLEN—WHEN I—JAY GARRICK—AM THE FLASH—AND HAVE BEEN SO FOR MORE THAN 20 YEARS?!"

The Golden Age Flash, *The Flash* #123

DRAWING PARALLELS

In 1961, the world was a tumultuous place. The Cold War had grown colder, the competitive race to space kicked into full throttle, and the movement toward racial integration was a source of conflict and consternation. Yet even as superpowers and societies struggled to come together, DC (whose official company name was National Periodical Publications, Inc. as of this year) specialized in the merging of worlds. Aliens and humans worked as one for the good of humankind. Scientists harnessed the power of the atom to explore worlds too small to be seen by the human eye. And the discovery of parallel Earths brought DC's present face-to-face with its past, positing a future filled with unforgettable characters, cosmic adventures, and untold potential. At a time when the real world became more insular and uncertain, DC provided the best form of escapist entertainment.

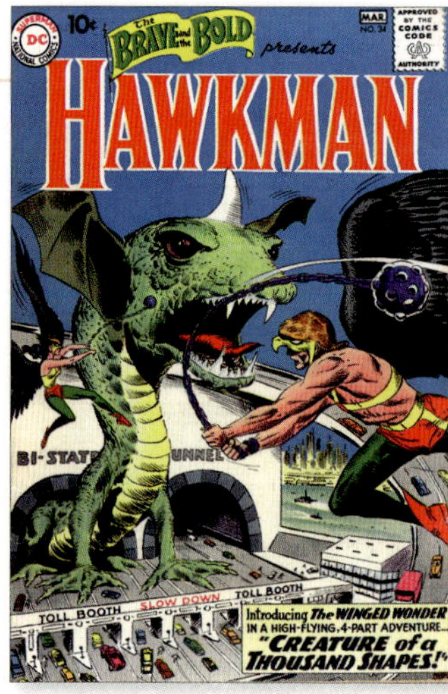

MARCH

BIRDS OF A FEATHER
***The Brave and the Bold* #34**

DC's Golden Age renaissance soared to new heights with the return of Hawkman and Hawkgirl. Writer Gardner Fox and artist Joe Kubert, who had crafted many of the Hawks tales of the 1940s, ushered in a pair of Winged Wonders that, costumes aside, were radically different from their Golden Age predecessors. For one thing, they hailed from a distant world. For another, they were this era's first married manhunters.

Thanagarian police officers Katar and Shayera Hol had traveled to Earth in pursuit of Byth, a thrill-seeking thief with the ability to radically alter his shape. The duo were set up with new identities as the Midway City Museum's new curators, and "Carter and Shiera Hall" familiarized themselves with Earth's culture—particularly its ancient weaponry, which they adopted into their Thanagarian arsenal. The Hawks' new tools proved useful against Byth. Using drug-tipped maces they captured their criminal prey and sent him back to Thanagar. But their desire to learn more about Earth and its policing methods prompted the lovebirds to remain in Midway City.

APRIL

ENTER BAT-GIRL
***Batman* #139**

Young Betty Kane assumed the costumed identity of Bat-Girl in this tale by writer Bill Finger and artist Sheldon Moldoff. Assisting Batman, Robin, and Batwoman in the hunt for King Cobra and the Cobra Gang, the teen employed keen detective skills to locate the villains' hideout. Though she was captured and imprisoned, the resourceful Bat-Girl created bat shapes from carbon paper and funneled them through an exhaust vent to alert the heroes to her whereabouts. She was then quickly freed and the remaining gang members were taken into custody.

IN THE ZONE
***Adventure Comics* #283**

Inside a sealed cache of weapons that crash-landed on Earth, Superboy found a projector that cast him into the Phantom Zone. This interdimensional realm trapped Krypton's criminals in an invisible state until they completed their prison sentences, which had commuted to a seeming eternity when the planet was destroyed. Superboy escaped his own banishment by using his super-thoughts to send a message to Pa Kent on how to free him. However, he wouldn't do so before writer Robert Bernstein and artist George Papp had introduced him to the Kryptonian militant, General Zod.

IN THE REAL WORLD...

January: John F. Kennedy becomes the thirty-fifth U.S. President.
April: The Bay of Pigs Invasion of Cuba begins; it fails by April 19.

AUGUST

ROTTEN TO THE CORPS

***Green Lantern* #7**

On "The Day 100,000 People Vanished," the Guardians warned Hal Jordan of the culprit responsible: Sinestro, a renegade Green Lantern who had been stripped of his power and banished to the Antimatter Universe of Qward. In this tale by scribe John Broome and artist Gil Kane, Jordan surrendered himself for the safe return of Valedale's people when he realized Sinestro's agenda was to capture him and exploit his power ring's weaknesses. While trapped inside a yellow bubble encasement, Green Lantern used his ring to move the carbon dioxide particles he exhaled to speed up a clock's hands. Sinestro believed that the ring's twenty-four-hour charge had expired, until Jordan defeated him with just minutes of power to spare.

SEPTEMBER

A WAY WITH WORLDS

***The Flash* #123**

This classic Silver Age story resurrected the Golden Age Flash and provided a foundation for the Multiverse homes from which he and the Silver Age Flash would hail. It was fitting that the historic meeting between the two Flashes would be crafted by writer Gardner Fox and artist Carmine Infantino, who had both chronicled the adventures of the Golden Age Flash in the 1940s. The creative duo sent Silver Age Flash, Barry Allen, through an interdimensional rift to a parallel Earth, where he would meet the childhood idol he had read about in *Flash Comics*. Allen's timing couldn't have been better: Jay Garrick, now twenty years older, had just decided to come out of retirement in the midst of a mysterious crime wave in Keystone City—a string of thefts by his old arch-enemies the Thinker, the Shade, and the Fiddler.

The Flashes became fast friends and tracked down the dastardly trio to the Keystone City Museum, where they thwarted the villains' plan to steal rare gems. The experience motivated Jay Garrick to remain out of retirement, while Barry Allen returned home to track down *Flash Comics* writer Gardner Fox and tell him of the fantastic adventure he just shared with his "creation."

The Flashes dance helplessly under the control of the Fiddler's music, allowing the villain and his cohorts to carry on with their jewel heist.

OCTOBER

(RE)BIRTH OF THE ATOM

***Showcase* #34**

The Atom was the next Golden Age hero to receive a Silver Age makeover from writer Gardner Fox and artist Gil Kane. Ray Palmer was not provided with a costume in *Showcase* #34, but there was no mistaking that a giant hero resided within the scientist who discovered how a dwarf star fragment could alter his size and weight. In his origin story, Palmer became trapped inside a cave during a spelunking expedition, prompting him to risk using the potentially lethal fragment to shrink down in size. Luckily it worked, and Palmer freed his fellow hiking club members and lawyer girlfriend, Jean Loring.

Ray Palmer converts star fragments into a crystal that shrinks objects. By using it on himself, and fashioning a digging device from an engagement ring, Palmer rescues his hiking club during a cave-in.

DECEMBER

BREAKING THE MOLD

***Detective Comics* #298**

Scribe Bill Finger and artist Sheldon Moldoff reshaped the face of evil with the second—and perhaps most recognized—Clayface ever to challenge the Dark Knight. Immersing himself in a cave's radioactive pool of protoplasm, treasure hunter Matt Hagen was suddenly able to shape himself into any form he imagined. Such malleable malevolence would only last forty-eight hours, however, before Hagen needed to re-saturate himself in the pool—a drawback that Batman and Robin ultimately exploited to apprehend the shapechanger.

ALSO THIS YEAR: In January's *SUPERBOY* #86, writer Robert Bernstein and artist George Papp introduced Clark Kent to Pete Ross, who four issues later discovered Clark's super-secret… In April, writer Jack Miller and artist Ross Andru placed Rip Hunter in his very own series to fight dinosaurs in *RIP HUNTER, TIME MASTER* #1… May's *G.I. COMBAT* #87 saw Confederate General J.E.B. Stuart guide Lt. Jeb Stuart and the Haunted Tank on their first adventure by scribe Bob Haney and artist Russ Heath… By summer, DC reprinted the genesis of many of its heroes in the eighty-four-page special, *SECRET ORIGINS*…

October: Baseball player Roger Maris hits his record-breaking sixty-first home run.
November: The Joseph Heller novel *Catch-22* is published.

December: The Vietnam War officially begins as the first American helicopters arrive in Saigon along with 400 U.S. Army personnel.

1962

"IF WE METAL MEN FAIL—THE WORLD OF HUMANS WILL BE DOOMED!"

Lead, *Showcase* #37

HEROES AT LARGE

In 1962, amid growing Cold War tension and social changes, the world was in need of heroes. Fortunately, comic book champions continued to emerge in the DC Universe. Aquaman surfaced in his own series after decades of defending the oceans as a back-up feature. Supergirl, having spent years as an emergency secret weapon, was formally introduced to the world in her own right. And while some protagonists materialized to fight for justice on four legs, others were born from natural elements.

Their presence came at the right time. Fresh ideas were needed as advancements in technology provided the first live trans-Atlantic television signal and man successfully orbited Earth. Such scientific wizardry would also feature in the insurgence of new villains for DC's heroes, from the illuminant evil of Dr. Light to the malevolent trickery of Abra Kadabra.

FEBRUARY

NEW DEPTHS

***Aquaman* #1**

More than twenty years after first surfacing, the King of the Seven Seas had earned his own ongoing series. Writer George Kashdan and artist Nick Cardy immediately pushed Aquaman into the deep end of the oceanic pool with an adventure that pitted him and Aqualad against Fire-Trolls that had been freed by an undersea volcanic eruption. The issue also introduced the duo to Quisp, a magical water sprite whose people lived beneath the ocean beds and were also threatened by the overheated ogres.

Quisp made certain that Aquaman and Aqualad literally came up short when they tried to prevent the Fire-Trolls from attacking a U.S. missile base. Sensing that they were in mortal danger, he shrank the heroes down in size, but failed to consider that they would then have to battle normally small land creatures while struggling to find life-sustaining water. Tricking a pelican to drop water on them, the revived duo eventually grew back to size, then used a freezing solution to cool off the Fire-Trolls before the villains could execute their plan to overtake the planet. After having Quisp shrink down the now-frozen ogres, Aquaman and Aqualad returned them to their volcanic point of origin and sealed up the fissure.

Flying fish enable an airborne Aquaman to cool off the Fire-Trolls with a freezing solution, while water sprite Quisp shrinks down the hotheaded ogres.

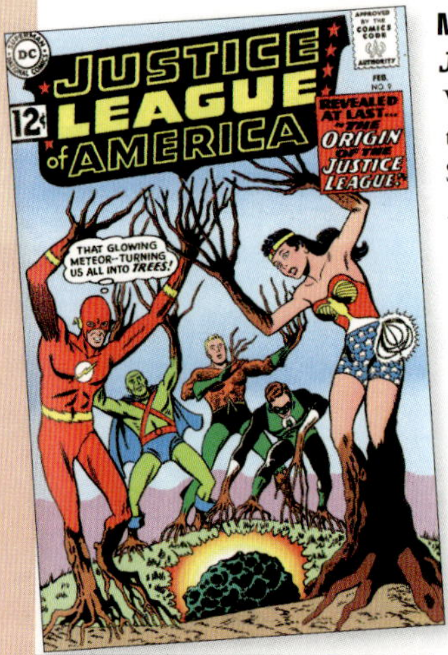

MAKING THE BAND

***Justice League of America* #9**

While celebrating their anniversary as a team, the Justice League shared their origin with Snapper Carr and new member Green Arrow. When representatives of the planet Appellax sought to conquer Earth, they drew the individual attentions of the Flash, Green Lantern, Aquaman, Wonder Woman, and the Martian Manhunter. Despite singular success against the aliens, the champions fell one-by-one to Appellaxian the Wood King. Only by combining their abilities would the heroes overcome their foe—a conclusion that was also reached by Superman and Batman, who jointly thwarted the alien in the end.

IN THE REAL WORLD...

January: New York City introduces a subway train without a crew.
April: *West Side Story* wins the Academy Award® for Best Picture.

APRIL

ALLOYED FORCES

***Showcase* #37**

Writer/editor Robert Kanigher and artist Ross Andru put a then-modern-day spin on robots with the exploits of comics' first "heavy metal" group, the Metal Men. These weren't caterpillar-track automatons with flailing grappler arms as seen in the television show *Lost in Space*. Instead, they were sleek, human-looking, self-aware androids that could determine right from wrong, with conflicting emotions that sometimes stirred up as much trouble for them as their adversaries.

Noted scientist Will Magnus had crafted his personable "artificial intelligents" with a device called the Responsometer, which mirrored the characteristics and substance commonly associated with each metal he used to create his robots. His first success came in the form of Tina, a platinum-based beauty who could elongate her shape at will. When a prehistoric flying manta ray with radioactive eye blasts was awakened and threatened to destroy Earth, Dr. Magnus quickly created companions for Tina—Iron, Tin, Gold, Mercury, and Lead—and sent his Metal Men to save the day.

Realizing that the manta ray thrived on radioactivity, Tina bound the creature while Lead's body completely encased it, effectively cutting it off from its life force. Sadly, the Metal Men's victory came at the expense of their artificial lives, though there was another underlying reason behind their demise. The heroes' genesis in *Showcase* #37 was a result of overnight manufacturing by Kanigher and Andru, to repair a scheduling glitch that had been created when the Atom grew into his own ongoing series. However, because the alloyed adventurers proved so popular with fans, the creative duo tapped Dr. Magnus to salvage their parts and rebuild them for several more stories in *Showcase*, and ultimately their own series the following year. Though death proved to be a regular occurrence for the Metal Men, fan popularity provided them with a lifetime warranty that, to this day, has remained in effect.

Dr. Magnus' platinum-based creation, Tina, spins a very convincing case as to why he should let her accompany the Metal Men on their first mission.

MAY

ABRA KADABRA, DISSIN' PEERS

***The Flash* #128**

A failed stage magician from the 64th Century, Abra Kadabra debuted in this story by writer John Broome and artist Carmine Infantino. He quickly garnered notice in Central City as a master thief, utilizing a hypno-ray to paralyze crowds and commit robberies. Pulling off the ultimate "disappearing act," Abra Kadabra sent the Flash off to another world, but the Scarlet Speedster's fast feet launched him back home where his quick thinking enabled him to upstage the magician with his own hypno-ray.

JUNE

AN ILLUMINATING ADVERSARY

***Justice League of America* #12**

In a tale written by Gardner Fox, with art by Mike Sekowsky, Dr. Light's first was almost the JLA's last. The luminous lawbreaker used his light device to transport the team individually to dimensions that played to their personal weaknesses and rendered them powerless. But Dr. Light didn't realize Superman and Batman had exchanged costumes, allowing the Man of Steel to escape and rescue the other members. While the reunited team pursued light-created duplicates of their foe, Green Lantern feigned his own death until he could find and power down the real Dr. Light.

OCTOBER

THE WEAKER SEX?

***Green Lantern* #16**

In his first confrontation with Star Sapphire, Green Lantern didn't realize he was actually battling his lady love, Carol Ferris. As was revealed by scribe John Broome and artist Gil Kane, the alien warrior women known as the Zamarons had forced Carol to become their new queen due to her uncanny resemblance to their late ruler. They granted her a royal Star Sapphire gem, giving her incredible power, then ordered her to prove herself as their new leader against Green Lantern. But when Carol failed to best the Emerald Gladiator, she was stripped of her powers and any memories of the Zamarons.

ALSO THIS YEAR: In January's *ACTION COMICS* #285, written by Jerry Siegel, with art by Jim Mooney, Superman's Kryptonian cousin Kara Zor-El was finally revealed as Supergirl to a very receptive Earth… July's *THE ATOM* #1 saw the Mighty Mite come up big against the Plant Master in the first issue of his own series, written by Gardner Fox, with art by Gil Kane… In *TOMAHAWK* #81 in August, writer Ed Herron and artist Fred Ray ensured that frontier heroine Miss Liberty made a star-spangled debut…

August: The South African government arrests Nelson Mandela and charges him with incitement to rebellion.

October: Escorted by federal marshals, the first black student, James Meredith, registers at the University of Mississippi.

SUPERMAN DC NATIONAL COMICS
12¢
MAR.
NO. 10
APPROVED BY THE COMICS CODE AUTHORITY
JUSTICE LEAGUE of AMERICA
Featuring THE WORLD'S GREATEST SUPER-HEROES in
"The FANTASTIC FINGERS of
NOW THAT I HAVE THE ENTIRE JUSTICE LEAGUE AT MY FINGERTIPS, NOTHING CAN STOP ME FROM CASTING MY

1963

"WE'RE GOING TO KEEP IN TOUCH! THERE'S NO TELLING WHEN WE MAY BE CALLED UPON TO JOIN FORCES AGAIN!"

Hawkman of Earth-2, *Justice League of America* #22

WORLDS IN CRISIS

In 1963, Martin Luther King, Jr. had a dream, the assassination of President John F. Kennedy was an all-too-real nightmare, and people around the world were waking up from what had once been regarded as an innocent age. Comics, meanwhile, were enduring their own upheavals a year after an industry-wide decision to increase all cover prices from 10 to 12 cents. Anthology comics showed dramatic declines in sales, so DC turned to super heroes—the least impacted by the price increase—to boost those titles. The Doom Patrol came to the rescue of *My Greatest Adventure*, while Eclipso took up the main living space within *House of Secrets*.

Caped crime fighters also faced looming significant changes, however. The inaugural meeting of two of Earths' greatest super hero teams opened a veritable Multiverse of story possibilities, and set the stage for what would amount to DC's ultimate crisis decades later.

JANUARY

STRUCK BY LIGHTNING
***Adventure Comics* #304**

The Legion of Super-Heroes faced its greatest tragedy to date when Lightning Lad sacrificed his life to save Saturn Girl from Zaryan the Conqueror. Written by Jerry Siegel, with art by John Forte, the demise of the Legion co-founder was a first not only for the Legion fan base, but for mainstream comics in general. From that moment, there were no guarantees that recognized super heroes wouldn't perish in the line of duty. By the same token, Lightning Lad was resurrected later that year in *Adventure Comics* #312, which provided another guideline for comics today: death isn't necessarily the end.

Lightning Lad rescues Saturn Girl and Earth from Zaryan the Conqueror, but is fatally struck down by a freeze-ray emanating from the villain's destroyed spacecraft.

MARCH

TURNING YELLOW
***The Flash* #135**

In this tailor-made tale by writer John Broome and artist Carmine Infantino, Kid Flash got a new look. The story followed Kid Flash as he alerted his mentor of motion, Barry Allen, to super-weapons sent by Ryla of Korydon, who was trying to stave off the Makryds' invasion of Earth. While the Flash inspected one of the weapons, a "mind-over-matter" device, the unit projected the designs he contemplated for a new Kid Flash costume onto his protégé. A radical departure from the Scarlet Speedster's suit, Kid Flash's new yellow-and-red look made him instantly more recognizable to fans, even as the two now-distinct Flashes worked in unison to rescue Earth and Ryla's dimension from the Makryds.

IN THE REAL WORLD...

March: The Alcatraz Island federal penitentiary in San Francisco closes.
May: The Coca-Cola Company debuts its first diet drink, TaB cola.

APRIL

CLASSIC, ILLUSTRATED
***Showcase* #43**

It was a comic book first: British publisher Gilberton Publications, who produced the series *Classics Illustrated*, approached DC Comics about publishing its adaptation of Ian Fleming's bestselling novel *Dr. No* in the U.S. The movie of the novel was a box-office smash in the U.K., so DC agreed to publish the James Bond story illustrated by Norman J. Nodel. They did so as part of the *Showcase* anthology series, four months before the movie opened in theaters in the U.S. Needless to say, Agent 007 went on to celluloid immortality.

JUNE

DOOM FROM THE START

***My Greatest Adventure* #80**

As the cover to *My Greatest Adventure* #80 appropriately stated, the Doom Patrol were figures reborn from disaster to form "the World's Strangest Heroes." Made up of the size-altering Elasti-Girl (Rita Farr), the irradiated "living mummy" that contained Negative Man (Larry Trainor), and the human brain trapped within an android body known as Robotman (Cliff Steele), this embittered group of social exiles was gathered together by a wheelchair-bound scientific genius who at first was known only as "The Chief" (Niles Caulder). Their mission: to battle past the personal tragedies that made them "exiles from the human race… to save a world that had rejected them."

Writers Arnold Drake and Bob Haney, joined by artist Bruno Premiani, had an objective of their own in producing the first-ever adventures of the Doom Patrol: to create a super hero title for editor Murray Boltinoff amid a fledgling period for anthology comics such as *My Greatest Adventure*. Fortunately, both the Doom Patrol and its creative team succeeded with comic fans. Six issues after the group bested the megalomaniacal mastermind General Immortus, *My Greatest Adventure* was rechristened *The Doom Patrol*. And although the team has been through numerous incarnations since its first "greatest adventure," their legacy has endured to the present day.

The Chief convinces Rita Farr, Cliff Steele, and Larry Trainor that despite being labeled outcasts, they can use their abilities to help others and "experience adventures more incredible than any human has ever known!"

AUGUST

THE FIRST CRISIS

***Justice League of America* #21–22**

The first-ever meeting between the Justice League of America and the legendary Justice Society of America was a momentous event. The fact that it was penned by Gardner Fox, who chronicled the JSA's adventures in the 1940s, made it even more remarkable. Most historic, however, were the stakes involved: an ever-evolving plane of parallel dimensions, each with a version of Earth. The Multiverse was flourishing, and comics were changed forever.

The two-part "Crisis on Earth-One!" and "Crisis on Earth-Two!" saga represented the first use of the term "Crisis" in crossovers, as well as the designations "Earth-1" and "Earth-2." In it, editor Julius Schwartz, Fox, and artist Mike Sekowsky devised a menace worthy of the Worlds' Greatest Heroes: the Crime Champions, a coalition of super-criminals from both Earths. The villains swapped identities (and Earths) to defeat and imprison the JLA, and the team summoned the JSA to help. The two teams switched Earths to pursue the Crime Champions, but the villains had set a trap that neutralized all of the heroes within outer-space jail cells. Using their rings to shrink down and free themselves from their prison, the dual emerald warriors released their teammates, whose combined might would quickly prove too much for the Crime Champions to overcome.

The Crime Champions are no match for the collective might of the Justice League of America and Justice Society of America, who agree to keep in touch despite residing on parallel Earths.

SEPTEMBER

RUNNING IN REVERSE
***The Flash* #139**

This issue saw 25th-Century criminal Eobard Thawne use his era's advanced science on an old Flash costume. The suit gave Thawne reverse super-speed, which he used to travel to the past and commit crimes. The Flash halted him by burning off the suit's chemicals protecting Thawne from air friction, but he couldn't stop writer John Broome and artist Carmine Infantino from introducing a new recurrent villain in "Professor Zoom."

ALSO THIS YEAR: In August's *HOUSE OF SECRETS* #61, writer Bob Haney and artist Lee Elias used a black diamond to transform Dr. Bruce Gordon into "Eclipso, The Genius Who Fought Himself"… As told by scribe John Broome and artist Gil Kane, an experiment gone awry turned Neal Emerson into a real negative influence as the Master of Magnetism, Doctor Polaris, in June's *GREEN LANTERN* #21…

August: Martin Luther King, Jr. delivers his "I Have A Dream" speech on the steps of the Lincoln Memorial to a 250,000-strong audience.

November: United States President John F. Kennedy is shot dead in Dallas, Texas; Vice President Lyndon B. Johnson becomes the thirty-sixth President.

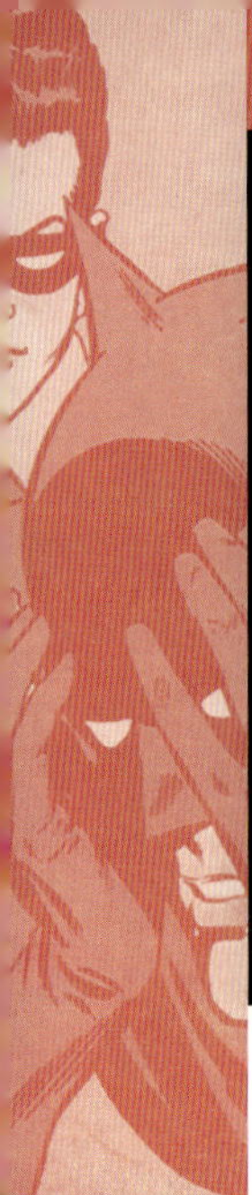

1964

"LIKE ALL ADULTS, YOU FORGET THAT YOU WERE ONCE A TEEN-AGER, TOO!"

Kid Flash, *The Brave and the Bold* #54

BREAKING NEW GROUND

Bob Dylan put it best in his classic 1964 song: "The Times They Are A-Changin'." The Rolling Stones launched their debut album, while Beatlemania ran rampant across America and the Billboard charts. Toy manufacturer Hasbro recruited G.I. Joe for duty, while the U.S. Congress authorized sending American soldiers off to fight in Vietnam. Comics, too, were changing with the times. Batman underwent a major streamlining in look and direction. Robin and other super hero sidekicks ventured off on their own as advocates for fellow teenagers who were being pushed around by "square" adults. Zatanna debuted to search for her missing authority figure, and a Brotherhood of Evil formed with a shared penchant for destruction. Some bonds, such as love and marriage, proved more powerful than the ocean depths, while others linked by parallel universes weakened at the discovery of an Earth overrun with champions of injustice.

FEBRUARY

A TIME TO DREAM
***Adventure Comics* #317**

Several firsts highlighted this issue. Its title now included "Featuring Superboy and the Legion of Super-Heroes," and writer Edmond Hamilton and artist John Forte made the first-ever reference to the nefarious Time Trapper. Meanwhile, new Legionnaire Dream Girl, a Naltorian precognitive whose dreams prophesized the future, secretly orchestrated the age regression and expulsion of seven of her teammates to prevent their foreseen deaths. Upon discovering that the "dead" heroes were actually android duplicates, a relieved Dream Girl left the Legion to hone her skills, but not before she renamed a teammate. Lightning Lass had gained new gravity-defying powers when she was de-aged by Dream Girl, and was henceforth Light Lass.

MAY

NEW LOOK BATMAN

BATMAN'S NEW LOOK
***Detective Comics* #327**

Precisely twenty-five years and 300 issues after his debut, the Dark Knight received a much-needed facelift from new Batman editor Julius Schwartz, writer John Broome, and artist Carmine Infantino. With sales at an all-time low and threatening the cancelation of one of DC's flagship titles, their overhaul was a lifesaving success for DC and its beloved Batman.

Broome's story saw the Dynamic Duo doused with a phosphorus isotope that enabled a criminal to temporarily immobilize them. It was an ideal representation that the surreal "sci-fi" yarns that permeated the Batman titles over the past several years had given way to slick action, clever mystery-solving, and emotional storytelling. Meanwhile, the sleek artistic elements that Infantino had already made famous in *The Flash* achieved an even more immediate impact in this story. Batman's costume was more stylized, most notably with a yellow ellipse now surrounding his Bat-emblem. Robin looked like a hip teenager of the time, and the Batmobile was transformed into a sporty two-seat roadster. Even Gotham City had been redesigned, with this issue depicting an artsy, Greenwich Village-style Gotham Village.

Batman is forced to strike a pose in his new-look costume when master criminal Frank Fenton uses chemicals to render him and Robin immobile.

IN THE REAL WORLD...

February: The Beatles vault to the #1 spot on the U.S. singles charts for the first time with "I Want to Hold Your Hand."

JUNE

SERVICES RENDERED

***Detective Comics* #328**

Only one issue into Batman's overhaul, loyal butler Alfred bit the dust in this story by writer Bill Finger and artist Bob Kane. Alfred died honorably, driving himself into the path of an oncoming boulder that was bound for Batman and Robin so that the Dynamic Duo could live to incarcerate the Tri-State Gang. However, the story was proof positive for Batman fans that sweeping changes were underway—changes that even Bruce Wayne and Dick Grayson would have to adjust to. Before they could mourn the loss of their faithful manservant, Dick's Aunt Harriet Cooper arrived at the doorstep of Wayne Manor and insisted on staying to take care of the two bachelors.

EVIL SHOWS ITS HAND

***Green Lantern* #29**

Scribe John Broome and artist Gil Kane split this issue into two stories—and split Green Lantern in half during its first tale. William Hand, introduced in a cameo by Kane, informed readers of a power light he invented to collect remnant energy from Green Lantern's power ring. As Black Hand, William used that energy to divide the emerald champion in two, sending half of him to another dimension. However, before the rest of him disappeared, Green Lantern's ring attached a mirror reflection onto his missing half. Seeing his adversary whole again caught Black Hand momentarily off-guard—long enough for Green Lantern to hand out justice and restore himself.

JULY

TITANS TAKE CHARGE

***The Brave and the Bold* #54**

Granted, they were never given a team name when scribe Bob Haney and artist Bruno Premiani spun them up against Mr. Twister. However, this first team-up of Robin, Kid Flash, and Aqualad came to be classically regarded as the inaugural story of the Teen Titans, a teenage variation of the popular Justice League of America.

The impetus that brought together these Justice League sidekicks—a vocal generation gap between "wild and unruly" youths and "un-hip" adults—was indicative of the period's genuine social revolution, where teenagers rebelled against older authority figures. In this story, the mayor's son had invited Robin, Kid Flash, and Aqualad to take part in a youth rally in Hatton Corners. However, the heroes arrived to discover the teenagers had been abducted and the adults terrorized by Mr. Twister, a bizarre blowhard in control of the elements, who demanded reparations that he believed were due to generations of his family.

Working in unison, the teen trio weathered Mr. Twister and his violently stormy disposition. Upon rescuing the teenage population from their enslavement on nearby Goat Island, they fought off Mr. Twister's torrential tirades, which included fire raining from the sky and a flood threatening to drown all of Hatton Corners. Ultimately deducing the source of their foe's power, Robin ensnared Mr. Twister's staff to end the threat once and for all. More importantly, watching the heroes work together prompted Hatton Corners' estranged generations to reconcile their differences.

Though clearly intended as a "Junior Justice League" spinoff, the subject matter beyond the Teen Titans' first adventure together became as much a part of what the Teen Titans themselves were about at that time. They, like the generation they represented, were finding their way in the world, and trying to do so without necessarily following the paths of their protagonist predecessors.

Robin, Kid Flash, and Aqualad arrive at a youth rally and are shocked to hear that all Hatton Corners' teenagers have been abducted by Mr. Twister.

February: Muhammad Ali is crowned the heavyweight champion of the world.
March: In New York City, Malcolm X says that he is forming a black nationalist party.
April: The Ford Mustang is officially unveiled in the United States.
May: Pablo Picasso paints his fourth *Head of a Bearded Man*.

JULY

ONCE A GREEN LANTERN…

***Green Lantern* #30**

In a story by writer John Broome and artist Gil Kane, the Guardians assigned Hal Jordan to persuade Korugar's Green Lantern, Katma Tui, not to resign. Katma feared her sense of duty was compromised after falling in love with Imi Kann, a scientist who had aided her against a giant amoeba. Unconvinced, Jordan recreated the threat, putting both himself and her fiance in seeming danger. Katma instinctively raced to save Jordan first, and their combined rings' might destroyed the amoeba. Jordan's ring then created an emotion meter, which confirmed that Katma's loyalty as a Green Lantern superseded her love for Imi Kann.

AUGUST

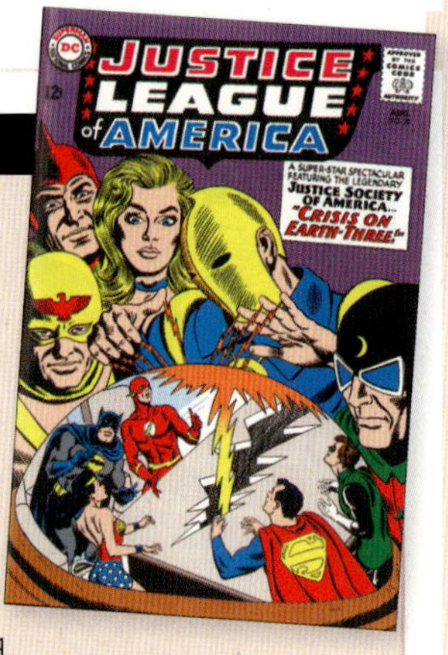

SYNDICATED TRIP

***Justice League of America* #29**

Ultraman, Superwoman, Power Ring, Johnny Quick, and Owlman: together, they were the Crime Syndicate of America, the World's Greatest Villains on Earth-3. It was a planet much like Earth-1, except that its people and historic events were direct opposites. Writer Gardner Fox and artist Mike Sekowsky crafted a tale in which the Crime Syndicate, who felt unchallenged on its own turf, ambushed the JLA on Earth-1. The villains would have lost, but they used Power Ring's mystic weapon to transport everyone to Earth-3, where the disoriented heroes were defeated.

Realizing that each team was stronger on its own world, the Crime Syndicate announced that it would prove its superiority by fighting the JLA on neutral territory—Earth–2. Leaving the JLA members imprisoned within their own Secret Sanctuary on Earth-1, the villains traveled to Earth–2 where they got rid of likely allies for the JLA by tricking the Justice Society into defeat on its own planet. However, when the Crime Syndicate fought the Justice League on Earth-2, the heroes just managed to prevail against their warped mirror images.

While debating over what to do with the now-captured Crime Syndicate, the Justice League discovered that the Justice Society had been trapped in a prison set to blow up both Earth-1 and Earth-2. In the end, the JLA safely freed their Earth-2 counterparts, then banished the defeated Crime Syndicate to a bubble between worlds.

On Earth-3, a parallel Earth where every super-being is a criminal, the Crime Syndicate of America (Johnny Quick, Power Ring, Superwoman, Ultraman, and Owlman) overpowers its polar opposite, the Justice League of America.

NOVEMBER

ZATANNA'S SEARCH

***Hawkman* #4**

It was unheard of for one storyline to continue throughout multiple comic book titles over several years. That changed when the young magician Zatanna began searching for her missing father, Zatara. Her first appearance, presented by scribe Gardner Fox and artist Murphy Anderson, ultimately conjured up the era of the crossover, and emphasized the effectiveness of continuity in comics.

It was rather ironic that a beautiful mage in fishnets who cast spells by speaking backward would be responsible for such progressive storytelling. Yet, with the penned guidance of Fox, Zatanna enlisted the aid of Hawkman and Hawkgirl, the Atom, Green Lantern, Elongated Man, and Batman (whom she would later admit she secretly helped him while disguised as a witch in 1965's *Detective Comics* #336) within their individual titles during their own solo adventures. Although she made some progress by the conclusion of each encounter, her quest kept sending her in another direction—and into the pages of another DC title.

After nearly three years, the search for Zatara ended in *Justice League of America* #51, when Zatanna, joined by mystical duplicates of the heroes who had helped her previously, rescued her father from the evil elemental Allura. It was a happy ending for the two magicians, and an exciting beginning for comics.

Hawkman and Hawkgirl are mystically drawn to China and Ireland by the magician Zatanna, who is rendered immobile after splitting herself in two to widen the search for her missing father, Zatara.

IN THE REAL WORLD…

July: President Lyndon B. Johnson signs the Civil Rights Act of 1964 into law, abolishing racial segregation in the United States.

August: The final Looney Tune, "Señorella and the Glass Huarache," is released before the Warner Bros. Cartoons division is shut down by boss Jack Warner.

DECEMBER

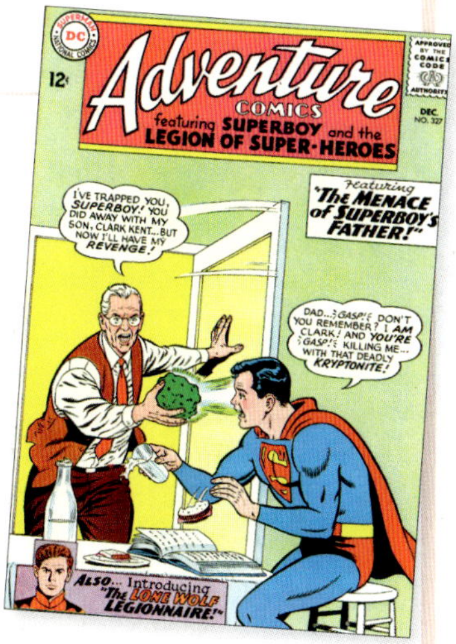

WOLF IN THE FOLD?

***Adventure Comics* #327**

While the Legion of Super-Heroes quelled rampaging beasts at an interplanetary circus, writer Edmond Hamilton and artist John Forte introduced them to Karth Arn, a super-strong acrobat calling himself "Lone Wolf." Suspicious of Arn's antisocial behavior, the Legionnaires soon tied him to several thefts on the planet Zoon. There, the heroes met with Brin Londo, who explained that Arn was an android built by his late father that had turned to crime. When Lone Wolf confronted Brin, however, the Legionnaires discovered that "Brin" was actually Karth Arn, who had convinced an amnesiac Brin Londo that he was the android. Cleared of wrongdoing, the real Brin was eager to remain with the Legion—though not as "*Lone* Wolf." The hero soon adopted the moniker of Timber Wolf.

Legionnaire Brainiac 5 reveals that Lone Wolf is not the android criminal Karth Arn, but an amnesiac Brin Londo, whose identity has been stolen by the artificial being.

G.I. JURY

***Showcase* #53**

Less than nine months since G.I. Joe ushered in the era of the action figure, Hasbro's incredibly popular war hero enlisted for some action in the pages of *Showcase*. G.I. Joe's two-issue run focused on land, sea, and air representations of the toy soldier franchise, with the first issue reprinting stories from *G.I. Combat* #52, #59, and #60 of the late 1950s. The tales were introduced in a framing sequence that called for a battle prize to be awarded by "The Battlefield Jury" of readers, written by editor Robert Kanigher, with art by Joe Kubert (who also provided the cover) and Irv Novick. Who won? The kids who read this issue and asked for a G.I. Joe for Christmas, naturally.

ALSO THIS YEAR: The World's Strangest Heroes took over the numbering for *MY GREATEST ADVENTURE* with *THE DOOM PATROL* #86 in March, so writer Arnold Drake and artist Bruno Premiani provided them with equally eccentric adversaries in "The Brotherhood of Evil"... The maddening genius of Thomas Oscar (T.O.) Morrow set the Scarlet Speedster and Emerald Gladiator on the "Trail of the False Green Lanterns," in March's *THE FLASH* #143... In May, Katar and Shayera Hol debuted in their own series, *HAWKMAN*, by writer Gardner Fox and artist Murphy Anderson...

DECEMBER

WEDDING SPLASHERS

***Aquaman* #18**

For generations, the idea of a super hero getting married seemed like comic book anathema. So it was rather fitting that Aquaman would be the first to swim against the tide of traditional storytelling and take the plunge—quite literally—in his own series.

To be fair, the hero needed convincing by his best pal, Aqualad, in the prose of writer Jack Miller enhanced by the artistic genius of Nick Cardy. After all, no sooner had Aquaman been informed that Atlantis had named him as its new king than he was instructed to find a nice Atlantean girl and marry her. So he did what every good person who had just been simultaneously made royalty and ordered to marry would do—he fled, leaving ripples of white foam in his wake.

The new king did have a special someone, though: the undersea queen from another dimension named Mera. However, their relationship was about to hit choppy waters. Mera gave up her home and her powers just so she could be with Aquaman, but he felt forced to reject her, believing that Atlantis's laws prevented him from marrying a non-Atlantean. A heartbroken Mera then turned to Oceanus, the man who had joined her in abandoning their dimension, then stripped her of her powers when she rebuffed his feelings. Using his hard water powers to create an army, Oceanus conquered Atlantis and, with Mera apparently by his side, imprisoned Aquaman and Aqualad for some time.

Thankfully, when it mattered the most and her true love was in mortal danger, Mera rescued Aquaman and helped him overtake Oceanus. As a reward—and through Aqualad's advice—the Sea King made Mera an honorary Atlantean, which subsequently made her eligible to marry Aquaman. On the star-studded last page of this watermark issue, with best man Aqualad and heroes such as Robin and the Justice League of America in attendance, Aquaman and Mera became the first super hero couple to be pronounced husband and wife in a DC comic.

Mera is heartbroken that Aquaman, by law, can marry only an Atlantean woman. Fortunately, the newly appointed King of Atlantis names her an honorary Atlantean and pops the question.

September: The Bond movie *Goldfinger* opens in the U.K.
October: The 1964 Summer Olympics are held in Tokyo.
October: Dr. Martin Luther King, Jr. receives the Nobel Peace Prize.
November: The British House of Commons abolishes the death penalty for murder.

1965

"FAREWELL, BATMAN AND GREEN LANTERN! YOUR 'TIME' HAS COME!"

Time Commander, *The Brave and the Bold* #59

WINDS OF CHANGE

Super heroes were always DC Comics' livelihood. Any character who had a cape, mask, or cool power began to dominate the pages. Golden Age champions like Green Lantern and Doctor Fate continued re-establishing their costumed careers. Current defenders like the Flash and Aquaman started families, while newcomers like Metamorpho and Buddy Baker tried to balance adventuring with a normal life.

Although DC's aim was to provide readers with escapist entertainment, the company also recognized its target audience and the importance of popular trends. Young costumed crusaders like the Teen Titans and Beast Boy took on more prominence as counterculture became influential in the real world. Meanwhile, an acknowledgment of emerging fashion trends and the significance of pop-culture became prevalent within the company's humor and romance titles.

JANUARY

IN HIS ELEMENT, MAN
***The Brave and the Bold* #57**
When it came to offbeat super heroes, scribe Bob Haney and artist Ramona Fradon were truly in their element. Business tycoon Simon Stagg and his Neanderthal servant, Java, had trapped soldier of fortune Rex Mason inside an ancient pyramid and subjected him to the mystical rays of the Orb of Ra. This, combined with Haney and Fradon's collaborative chemistry, resulted in Mason becoming Metamorpho, the man who could transform his body into any element. Hitherto shallow, Mason's character grew and deepened not only from the harrowing experience, but from the chemistry he shared with Stagg's beautiful daughter, Sapphire, who encouraged Metamorpho to use his powers for good.

FEBRUARY

HAMMER TIME
***Our Army at War* #151**
DC teased that it dare not show "the blazing enemy" on the cover of this landmark issue, which presented a very different look at war through the eyes of Enemy Ace Rittmeister Hans von Hammer. Writer/editor Robert Kanigher and artist Joe Kubert based von Hammer on German WWI pilot Manfred von Richtofen a.k.a. the "Red Baron." Featuring amazing aerial artistry, the Enemy Ace's battles in the 1918 skies were unlike anything yet seen in a war comic. However, the stories' main impact came from von Hammer, who was grounded by the anguish of claiming so many lives.

MAY

ENIGMATIC RETURN
***Batman* #171**
Nearly eighteen years had passed since the Riddler last tried to stump Batman and Robin. Therefore, when writer Gardner Fox and artist Sheldon Moldoff released Edward Nigma from prison, the villain insisted that he had reformed. In truth, the conniver of conundrums tried to discredit Batman and Robin with riddles that suggested he was perpetrating a crime, only for them to arrive and discover he had done nothing illegal. The heroes thwarted the Riddler, but the prince of puzzles was bound to return with more brainteasing bafflers.

IN THE REAL WORLD...

February: Malcolm X is assassinated in New York City.
April: *My Fair Lady* wins eight Academy Awards®, including Best Picture.

MAY

BOLD NEW DIRECTION

***The Brave and the Bold* #59**

The Brave and the Bold had seen several incarnations. First, it was an anthology series that focused on heroes from another age, such as the Silent Knight. By issue #25, it had evolved into a tryout venue, like DC's *Showcase*, with issues focusing on the Suicide Squad, the JLA, and Metamorpho, among others. By issue #50, *The Brave and the Bold* developed into the ultimate team-up book.

The Brave and the Bold #59 added one final element to the team-up theme, when writer Bob Haney and artist Ramona Fradon partnered Batman with Green Lantern. This, along with the fact that Batman would become a mainstay throughout the rest of the series, led fans to consider *The Brave and the Bold* the official Batman team-up book.

Using a time-shifting hourglass, criminal John Starr discovered the Caped Crusader's secret identity. He then took over Batman's identity and fooled Green Lantern into energizing him with his power ring so that he could go on a crime spree. Before they could stop him, Starr (now the Time Commander) sent Green Lantern twenty-four hours into the past and Batman twenty-four hours into the future. However, the heroes managed to smash the Time Commander's hourglass, and used Green Lantern's ring to wipe away the Time Commander's memories of Batman's identity.

SEPTEMBER

THE ANIMAL UNLEASHED

***Strange Adventures* #180**

Although it would be several months before Buddy Baker would take on the moniker of Animal Man, it was in this issue that he developed animal powers.

Writer Dave Wood and artist Carmine Infantino sent Buddy on a hunting trip, where he came into contact with an exploding alien spaceship. The blast irradiated Buddy, and enabled him to temporarily acquire the abilities of any animal within his reach—as he would demonstrate in hand-to-paw encounters with an elephant, gorilla, and tiger. When Buddy confronted the alien whose craft gave him his powers, Buddy realized the alien could also borrow animal abilities. He forced the creature to inherit the traits of scared mice, and the alien scurried off a cliff to its doom.

Strange Adventures #184 (January 1966) would bring out the animal in Buddy Baker once more, though it wasn't until *Strange Adventures* #190 (July 1966) that Buddy adopted the blue-and-gold costume by which he would be recognized, as well as the name "A-Man." He wouldn't go by the familiar alias of "Animal Man" until *Strange Adventures* #195 (December 1966).

Buddy Baker springs like a tiger and punches like a gorilla to fell an elephant.

JULY

WONDER GIRL, INTERRUPTED

***The Brave and the Bold* #60**

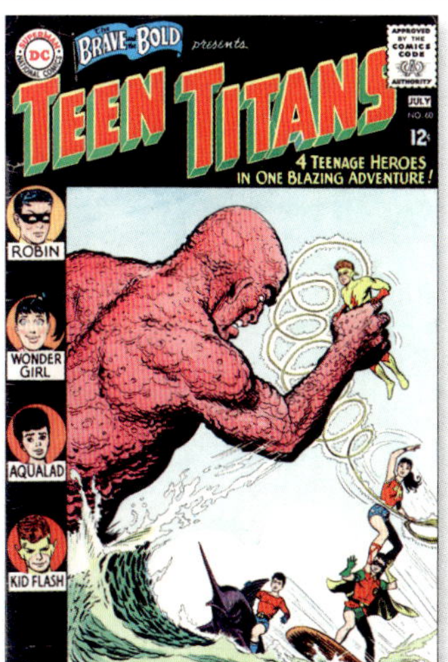

Writer Bob Haney and artist Nick Cardy added another member to the ranks of the newly formed Teen Titans: Wonder Girl. Nothing was known about this new heroine as she bid farewell to Queen Hippolyta and Wonder Woman on Paradise Island, nor would any details be shared for another four years. The truth is, this teen Amazon was the result of mistaken identity by the issue's creative team. There had been a Wonder Girl in earlier issues of *Wonder Woman*, but she was a teenaged Princess Diana, not a separate character.

NOVEMBER

BEAST BOY OF BURDEN

***The Doom Patrol* #99**

Garfield Logan didn't impress the Doom Patrol after he broke in and littered their headquarters with lion pawprints, bird feathers, gorilla hair, and elephant tusk chips as Beast Boy. Still, writer Arnold Drake and artist Bob Brown saw something in the green-skinned delinquent who could take on the form of animals. Beast Boy was made to guard the Duchy of Dusenberg's crown jewels during a parade. Jewel thieves disguised as policemen were prepared for the Doom Patrol, but not for Beast Boy, who transformed into an eagle, an ape, and a dog to thwart them.

ALSO THIS YEAR: In June, *GIRLS' ROMANCES* #109, drawn by Gene Colan, featured dreamy versions of the Beatles sighing over Penny, who confused reality with fantasy… In October's *AQUAMAN* #23, Aquababy was born. The bundle of doom was given dangerous mental powers, care of writer Bob Haney and artist Nick Cardy… October saw the Golden and Silver Age Green Lanterns come to blows in *GREEN LANTERN* #40 when writer John Broome and artist Gil Kane unleashed immortal scientist Krona…

April: The first Students for a Democratic Society (SDS) march against the Vietnam War draws 25,000 protestors to Washington, D.C.

August: The Beatles perform the first stadium concert in the history of rock, playing at Shea Stadium in New York.

1966

"THIS IS ONE FIGHT I DON'T DARE LOSE! TO THE VICTOR GOES IRIS WEST AS HIS BRIDE!"

The Flash, *The Flash* #165

POP CULTURE SHOCK

In the comic book world, 1966 was the Year of the Bat. The TV launch of *Batman* was a pop-culture phenomenon, with celebrities clamoring to appear on the series. Well-read Batman enthusiasts and casual viewers alike enjoyed the emphatic "Pow!," "Biff!," and "Zowie!" that splashed across their TV screens in vibrant color. Seeing comic book characters come to life—and become relevant to a larger audience—made it cool to be a Batman fan.

Of course, Batman and Robin weren't DC's only champions to enjoy a great year. The Man of Steel flexed his muscles on Saturday morning TV and in musical form on Broadway. The Flash stopped running away from commitment, the teen movement grew titanic in strength, and DC adorned the top of its titles' covers with a black-and-white checkerboard pattern to help them stand out on newsstands.

JANUARY

DIALING IT UP A NOTCH

***House of Mystery* #156**

The villainous Thunderbolt organization messed with the wrong number when writer Dave Wood and artist Jim Mooney put young Robby Reed in touch with the mysterious H-Dial. After finding the device in a cavern near his home in Littleville, Robby decoded the unit's alien characters and dialed the equivalent of the letters H-E-R-O. Each time he did this, Robby transformed into a random new hero imbued with new powers. Using the device to become Giantboy, the Cometeer, and the Mole, Robby thrashed the Thunderbolt members afflicting his town.

ON TV THIS MONTH: *BATMAN*, starring Adam West and Burt Ward, began airing on ABC-TV on January 12 and became a sensation. The series ran until March 1968...

FEBRUARY

THE TEEN SCENE

***Teen Titans* #1**

The Teen Titans earned their own series after successful tryouts in both *The Brave and the Bold* and *Showcase*. Scribe Bob Haney and artist Nick Cardy promptly dispatched Robin, Aqualad, Wonder Girl, and Kid Flash to the South American land of Xochatan as the newest members of the Peace Corps.

Their mission was twofold. First, the teens had to help build a dam and school. Second, they were to protect the superstitious villagers and Peace Corps representatives from strange happenings, including a giant conquistador robot that tried to destroy the site.

The Teen Titans soon trapped the robot inside a large pit they dug up, but the real threat surfaced when the now-completed dam began flooding an ancient pyramid. Strange beast-gods nearly destroyed the teens before they apprehended the man responsible for their creation: an embittered land owner calling himself El Conquistadore. Upon capturing the villain, the Titans ended the monstrous threat and saved the village, completing their inaugural mission to better the world—and themselves.

Wonder Girl, Aqualad, Kid Flash, and Robin attempt to locate the giant robot conquistador.

IN THE REAL WORLD...

January: Indira Gandhi is elected Prime Minister of India.
February: A spacecraft makes the first controlled landing on the Moon.

SPIRITED RETURN

***Showcase* #60**

Almost twenty years had passed since Jim Corrigan was last able to summon the Spectre within him. Fortunately, scribe Gardner Fox and artist Murphy Anderson recruited the ethereal entity in time for #60 of *Showcase*.

The Spectre re-emerged when his human host, Corrigan, now a captain of detectives, was targeted by mob gangs while investigating a dead millionaire's stolen fortune. Corrigan's inquiries uncovered the reason for the Spectre's decades-long imprisonment: Azmodus, an astral evildoer who rendered himself and the Spectre inert when he possessed his own host, petty crook Paul Nevers. Azmodus had been freed upon Nevers' death, enabling the Spectre to resurface from Corrigan and engage in a clash that ended when the detective knocked out the Azmodus-controlled Nevers.

The Astral Avenger was more powerful than ever; his opponents found themselves on the receiving end of hurled planets, moons, or whatever was handy. However, the Comics Code's presence restrained the vengeful spirit that first possessed Jim Corrigan in 1940. The Spectre's mean streak would not return for many years.

While the human hosts of Spectre and the spirit demon Azmodus battle on Earth, a super-sized Spectre takes his war with Azmodus to the astral plane.

MARCH

DISASTER STRIKES

***Green Lantern* #43**

Major Disaster debuted in March, care of scripter Gardner Fox and artist Gil Kane. Crook Paul Booker stumbled upon engineer Thomas Kalmaku's casebook, containing the identities of Green Lantern and the Flash. Booker, now calling himself Major Disaster, hired scientists to devise a contraption that created deadly natural catastrophes. It also transferred Green Lantern and Flash's abilities to one another, though their powers soon reverted back to their rightful owners. Disaster was to strike Booker himself—while powering up his device, he forgot to wear insulated gloves and electrocuted himself.

ON STAGE THIS MONTH: ***IT'S A BIRD, IT'S A PLANE, IT'S SUPERMAN!*** **opened on Broadway in March 1966. Starring Jack Cassidy as the villainous Max Mencken, Patricia Marand as Lois Lane, and Bob Holiday as Superman, with music by Charles Strouse and lyrics by Lee Adams, the musical lasted 129 performances before closing in July…**

MAY

GET A CLUE

***Detective Comics* #351**

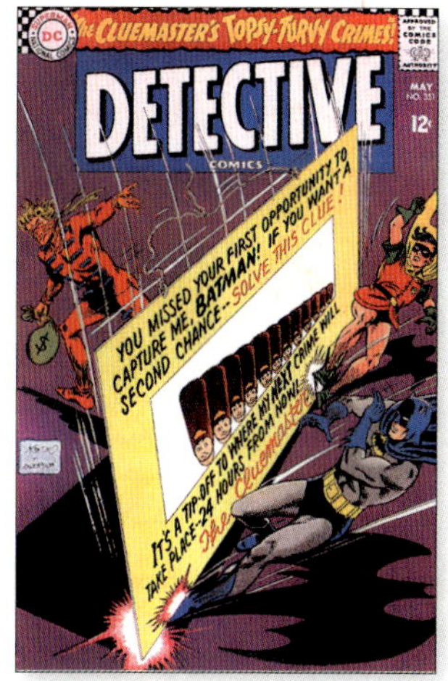

In May, writer Gardner Fox and artist Carmine Infantino unleashed the Cluemaster on Batman and Robin. A master criminal who left clues to stump authorities, the Cluemaster believed he could negate the Dynamic Duo's effectiveness if he uncovered their identities. Meanwhile, after Dick Grayson's Aunt Harriet discovered the Batcave, she began to suspect Bruce and Dick were the cowled crimebusters. Bruce showed Harriet a doctored film of himself and Dick meeting Gotham City's guardians, convincing her she was wrong. This also foiled the Cluemaster's efforts, leading the crook to trace the Batmobile to a bogus Batcave the heroes had set up to capture his gang.

JUNE

INFERIORITY COMPLEX

***Showcase* #62**

Writer E. Nelson Bridwell and artist Joe Orlando knew what was in a name when they unleashed the Inferior Five in Megalopolis. A quintet of ham-fisted heroes sired by more capable members from the Freedom Brigade, these chumpish champions consisted of the jester-garbed, sub-ninety-seven-pound leader, Merryman; the incredibly beautiful, strong, and unbelievably Dumb Bunny; an overinflated frequent flyer in the Blimp; the mighty and uncoordinated Awkwardman; and White Feather, an aimless archer with trembling hands. Despite their deficiencies, the Inferior Five overcame every obstacle to defeat mad scientist Gregory Gruesome and his henchman, Hermes.

White Feather, the Blimp, and Merryman try to halt Dr. Gruesome's crime car. Unfortunately, Megalopolis needs heroes but has to make do with the Inferior Five!

April: The opening of the United Kingdom Parliament is televised for the first time.
May: The legendary album *Pet Sounds*, by The Beach Boys, is released.
June: The Supreme Court of the United States rules that the police must inform suspects of their rights before questioning them.

JUNE

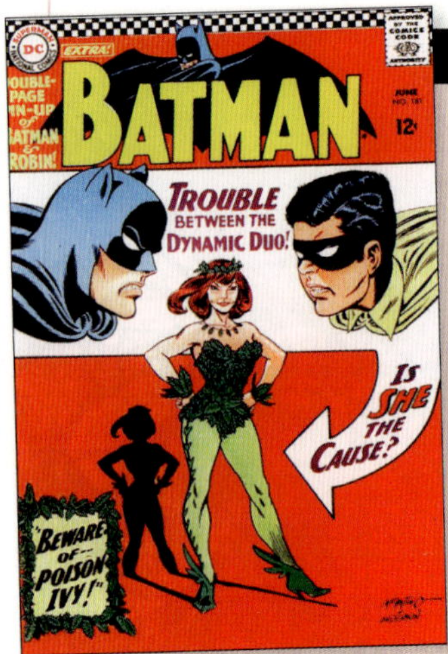

POISON IVY CREEPS UP

***Batman* #181**

Poison Ivy first cropped up to plague Gotham City in issue #181 of *Batman*. Scripter Robert Kanigher and artist Sheldon Moldoff came up with a villain who would blossom into one of Batman's greatest foes.

Botanist Dr. Pamela Isley was an alluring antagonist who itched to be recognized as the city's Queen of Crime. She quickly established herself as such after crashing a pop-art show at the Gotham City Museum, where her toxin-laced lipstick left Batman smitten while she escaped. As the Caped Crusader tried to fight off the effects of her chemical charms, Poison Ivy began to act like a Venus flytrap, luring her opposition—Dragon Fly, Silken Spider, and Tiger Moth—into an ambush that weeded them out of further competition.

With Robin's help, Batman repelled Poison Ivy's almost irresistible advances. However, the seductive stalker left a lasting effect on the Caped Crusader that flourished two issues later, when she took total control of his mind while she was in jail. Robin again helped Batman snap out of her spell, this time leaving the root of Poison Ivy's evil dormant for many years. Later, Dr. Pamela Isley branched out as an eco-terrorist of extreme measures.

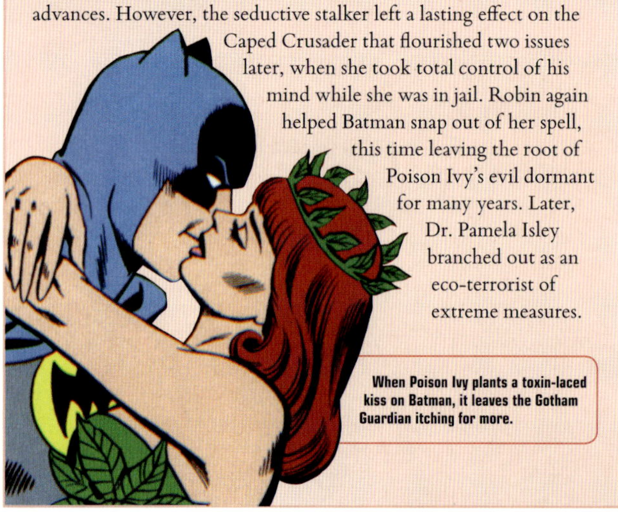

When Poison Ivy plants a toxin-laced kiss on Batman, it leaves the Gotham Guardian itching for more.

JULY

THE MOD SQUAD

***Swing with Scooter* #1**

Through the latter half of the 1960s, DC made a concerted effort to attract the teenage reader. This included turning to lighter fare with the likes of Scooter, a Paul McCartney-esque musician who left England and his group, the Banshees, to start a new life in Plainsville, U.S.A. Crafted by writer Barbara Friedlander and editor Jack Miller, with art by Joe Orlando, Scooter himself was fashioned as a Modernist with a love for tailored wear and Italian motor scooters.

JIM SHOOTER'S FIRST STORY

***Adventure Comics* #346**

In his first-ever published story, fourteen-year-old Jim Shooter admitted four new members into the Legion of Super-Heroes, made one of them a spy, and produced one of the 30th Century's greatest recurring threats in the warlike Khunds. Pencilling the story "One of Us is a Traitor!" Shooter introduced Legion fans to Princess Projectra, Ferro Lad, Karate Kid, and Nemesis Kid. In the following issue, Nemesis Kid was revealed as the traitor secretly aiding Warlord Garlak's attack of Earth's defense towers. Though he'd relinquish the art chores in later titles, Shooter's long, memorable tenure as one of the Legion's greatest writers was officially underway.

AT THE MOVIES THIS MONTH: Following the success of the television series, 20th Century-Fox released a feature-length film version of *BATMAN* on the big screen on July 30. Adam West and Burt Ward reprised their roles as Batman and Robin, and preserved world peace against the Joker (Cesar Romero), the Riddler (Frank Gorshin), the Penguin (Burgess Meredith), and Catwoman (Lee Meriwether)...

AUGUST

PURPLE DRAIN

***Action Comics* #340**

With a story written by Jim Shooter and drawn by Al Plastino, the Parasite entered Superman's life after research plant worker Maxwell Jensen exposed himself to isotopes from biohazardous materials. The energies turned Jensen into the Parasite—a purple-skinned, faceless being with the ability to sap the strength, intelligence, and life force of anyone near him. Likening himself to an atomic furnace that needed replenishment, the Parasite leeched onto the Man of Steel as his power source. However, he miscalculated how much power he could siphon from Superman, whose Kryptonian-based energies forced the Parasite to overload and burst.

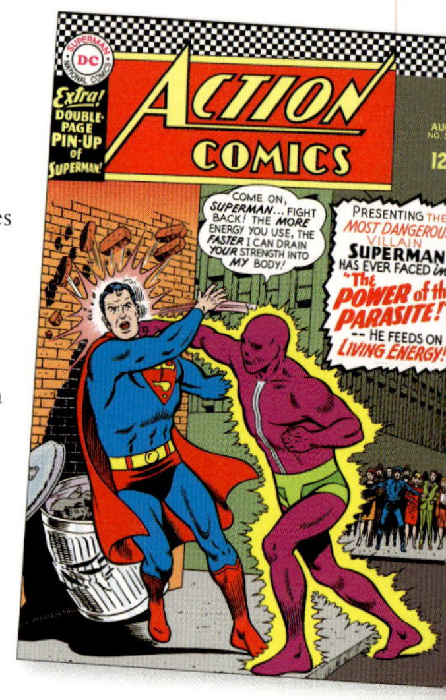

> **"I DRAINED HIM OF HIS STRENGTH... AND HIS MIND, TOO! I'VE BECOME A SORT OF PARASITE!"**
>
> Maxwell Jensen (The Parasite), *Action Comics* #340

SEPTEMBER

ON TV THIS MONTH: In September, kids tuned in to CBS-TV on Saturday mornings for the Filmation-animated *THE ADVENTURES OF SUPERBOY* and *THE NEW ADVENTURES OF SUPERMAN*. *SUPERBOY* lasted until 1969, while *SUPERMAN* continued airing until 1970 ...

IN THE REAL WORLD...

July: England beats West Germany 4–2 to win the 1966 FIFA World Cup at Wembley.
August: The Doors record their self-titled debut album.
September: *Star Trek* makes its TV debut with its first episode, "The Man Trap."
October: In American Football, the AFL-NFL merger is approved by the U.S. Congress.

NOVEMBER

SHOTGUN WEDDING

***The Flash* #165**

Barry Allen and Iris West's wedding day was DC's third marriage ceremony in the past two years. The 1960s had seen Elasti-Girl wed Mento and Aquaman marry Mera. Barry and Iris's wedding, however, was the longest anticipated. Iris still had no idea that her intended was actually the Fastest Man Alive—or that he almost wouldn't make it to his own wedding.

Writer John Broome and artist Carmine Infantino were the team behind the nuptials in the story "One Bridegroom Too Many!" Professor Zoom, a.k.a. the Reverse-Flash, abducted and imprisoned Barry inside a 25th-Century energy cell. Then, with no one the wiser, Zoom turned Barry's electric shaver into a matter distributor so he could assume the guise of his adversary—and his place at the wedding altar.

Luckily, the Scarlet Speedster used his costume ring's chemical formula to produce a shrinking effect on his cell energy walls. He vibrated out of the cell and raced back to the present, just in time to super-speed Zoom out of the church before he could utter "I do." After a fast and furious confrontation, an enraged Flash pummeled Zoom, returned him to his own time, and completed the wedding ceremony he had almost missed.

The happiest day of his life aside, Barry Allen decided to keep his alter ego a secret from his new bride. Throughout the Golden and Silver Ages, it was one of the most typical conundrums faced by super heroes in love—one that often destroyed a romance. Barry finally stopped running away from the problem in *The Flash* #174 (November 1967), and told Iris the truth as the couple celebrated their one-year anniversary. He needn't have worried; Iris revealed that she discovered Barry's secret on their wedding night, and in fact had heard about it numerous times throughout the year as Barry talked in his sleep!

Iris West and her wedding guests look on in astonishment as the Flash snatches the man who seems to be Barry Allen away from the altar.

DECEMBER

ON THE REBOUND

***Plastic Man* #1**

Plastic Man was once Quality Comics' signature super hero of the Golden Age, but he had yet to flex his malleable DC muscles a decade after the company acquired rights to the character. Resilient as his name might suggest, though, Plastic Man put his best foot far forward in 1966. After being called up briefly by Robby Reed in the "Dial H for H-E-R-O" feature in July's issue #160 of *House of Mystery*, Plastic Man finally starred in his own series.

Written by Arnold Drake with art by Gil Kane, "the slyest, slippery-est, slinky-est super hero of them all" was targeted by Dr. Dome, a helmeted heavy who utilized weapons devised by the nefarious Professor X. With the aid of Dome's seductive daughter, Lynx, and Fawnish, the disgruntled butler of Plastic Man's rich girlfriend "Mike," Dome and Professor X made many attempts to end Plas' elasticized life. Ultimately, though, they just couldn't cut short the long arm of the law. Plastic Man apprehended Professor X, while Dr. Dome and the others remained at large for future battles.

Plastic Man—who was revealed as the Golden Age Plastic Man's son, Eel O'Brien, Jr.—wouldn't enjoy an extended run, however. After only ten issues, Plastic Man unfortunately bounced into creative limbo for a decade.

BAD SPELLER

***Detective Comics* #358**

Batman was hopelessly entranced within "The Circle of Terror" rendered by new villain Spellbinder, and produced by scripter John Broome and artist Sheldon Moldoff. Pop art painter Delbert Billings used optical illusions and hypnotic weaponry to forge a life of crime for himself. The Spellbinder's greatest masterpiece was to force Robin to rescue a hypnotized Batman on two separate occasions, though the Spellbinder went to that canvas once too often. The cowled crime fighter's will enabled him to shake off the trance during a third encounter, and Billings spent a long spell inside prison.

ALSO THIS YEAR: In January's *ADVENTURE COMICS* #340, one of Triplicate Girl's selves was killed by the robot Computo in a story by writer Jerry Siegel and drawn by Curt Swan... In June's *JUSTICE LEAGUE OF AMERICA* #45 scripter Gardner Fox and artist Mike Sekowsky helped the JLA defeat Shaggy Man... Aquaman's half-brother, Ocean Master, debuted in October's *AQUAMAN* #29...

November: Former Massachusetts Attorney General Edward Brooke becomes the first African-American elected to the United States Senate since the Reconstruction era.

November: Jack L. Warner sells Warner Bros. Pictures to Seven Arts Productions. The company eventually becomes Warner Bros.-Seven Arts.

TEEN DREAMS

The "Swinging Sixties," with its kaleidoscope of viewpoints and attitudes, was the spectacular reaction to the preceding decade's faith in the status quo. Although youthful idealism and optimism turned to social and political turmoil by the decade's end, the prevailing mood of the period was enthusiastic and positive.

Fittingly, the super heroes ruled comics, as they had done since the beginning of comics' Silver Age (1956-1969). DC introduced a multiverse of parallel worlds to give their heroes a limitless playground. So-called "tryout" comic books like *Showcase* and *The Brave and the Bold* presented new heroes and villains. Fantastic abilities, costumes, and accessories made revitalizations of characters such as the Flash, Green Lantern, Hawkman, and the Atom enormously popular. And if one champion wasn't enough for fans, there was now the Justice League of America, who carried on in the Golden Age tradition of the Justice Society of America. Land, sea, air, space… super heroes were everywhere.

Romance comics, on the other hand, declined in popularity, now seeming hilariously old-fashioned. Nevertheless their stylistic influence and innocence permeated advertising and pop art circles. Roy Lichtenstein's famous *Drowning Girl* was a reworking of artist Tony Abruzzo's splash page for the story "Run for Love" from DC's *Secret Hearts* #83 (November 1962).

DC's war titles enjoyed renewed popularity. Writer Robert Kanigher and artist Russ Heath revved up the Haunted Tank in *G.I. Combat* #87 (May 1961), while Kanigher and artist Joe Kubert offered a unique perspective of combat through World War I's "Enemy Ace" from Germany—Hans von Hammer—in *Our Army at War* #151 (February 1965). The books' grittier art and stories—many of which decried war—were a departure from the rest of DC's output, especially once anti-war sentiment escalated during the conflict in Vietnam.

By the mid- to late-1960s, comics' primary audience consisted of teenagers with disposable income. DC began focusing on younger heroes with whom their audience could better relate. When the Teen Titans weren't out fighting bad guys, they were much like the teenagers of the period, rebelling against older authority figures. They, like many of the teens portrayed in their adventures, were unwittingly caught up in a social revolution.

During this time, DC Comics was also undergoing something of a revolution. The massive success of the *Batman* TV series in 1966 encouraged the publisher to mirror some of the show's comical, camp style by lightening the tone of many of its titles. Go-go checkerboard strips adorned the tops of DC's covers to convey a "hipper" feel; illustrations became more humor-oriented, or featured pop-culture celebrities like The Beatles, to connect with the readership.

This levity didn't last, as the counterculture movement took a hold of society. Reflecting this change, DC would revamp many titles and radically alter its approach to its heroes and their stories.

Left: A gang impersonates pop sensations The Flips to go on a crime spree in Teen Titans Annual *#1 (1967). Main picture: Diana gives up the title of Wonder Woman and reinvents herself in order to save boyfriend Steve Trevor from a murder rap in* Wonder Woman *#178 (October 1968).*

ELVI'S
BOUTIQ

1967

"IF I CAN'T HOLD A MOUSE IN MY HAND—HOW CAN I GRAB A KILLER?"

Boston Brand, *Strange Adventures* #205

NEW OPPORTUNITIES

With its titles still consisting of predominantly classic super hero adventures, DC began to look to attract a hipper, older audience that wanted their comics to follow suit. However, the company was still enjoying the Silver Age it had ushered in, and wasn't quite ready to move its characters toward a more insecure world.

Nevertheless, change was inevitable. New editorial director Carmine Infantino hired artist-editors like Joe Kubert, Joe Orlando, and Dick Giordano to emphasize visual direction. He also recruited up-and-coming creators—among them, Neal Adams, whose striking imagery would mark the beginning of a brand new age in dynamic storytelling.

Although the results of this new direction weren't immediately evident, 1967 would produce some standouts—such as Boston Brand and Batgirl—that would remain popular.

JANUARY

MILLION-DOLLAR DEBUT

***Detective Comics* #359**

Nine months before making her television premiere on *Batman*, a new Batgirl appeared in the pages of *Detective Comics* and would become one of the more popular characters to emerge from the Silver Age of comics. Yet the idea for the debut of Barbara Gordon, according to editor Julius Schwartz, was attributed to the television series executives' desire to have a character that would appeal to a female audience and for this character to originate in the comics. Hence, writer Gardner Fox and artist Carmine Infantino collaborated on "The Million Dollar Debut of Batgirl!"

Barbara Gordon was a brainy librarian with a brown belt in judo. She was nothing like her teenage predecessor, Betty Kane, who relished being a hero; in fact, the daughter of Police Commissioner Gordon only donned a Batgirl costume for a policeman's masquerade ball. However, when she stumbled upon a attempt on the life of millionaire Bruce Wayne by Killer Moth, Barbara sprang into action, fending off the attackers and feeling a crime-fighting spirit awaken within her.

That spirit awakened again following what appeared to be Wayne's murder at the hands of the Killer Moth. Unfortunately, Batgirl soon discovered that "Wayne" was a dummy set up by Batman and Robin to draw out Killer Moth, and her arrival had interfered with the operation.

Though dejected, Batgirl quickly made amends for her rookie mistakes, tracking Killer Moth to his hideout and rescuing the Dynamic Duo from a gravity-free chamber that made them helpless targets. She had been wearing perfume during their previous tussle and some had rubbed off on Killer Moth. She was even able to scent down the criminal mastermind when he attempted to evade capture.

The Caped Crusader told the impressive Batgirl that he would welcome her help wherever the need arose, though she wasn't the type to wait for an invitation. Furthermore, she was intent on refuting perceptions of the "weaker sex," and refused to take a back seat to anyone. Although she partnered with TV's Dynamic Duo for only one season, Batgirl became a regular fixture in future comic book adventures.

Librarian Barbara Gordon prepares a special outfit for the Gotham City Policeman's Masquerade Ball, but instead uses it to battle Killer Moth's gang and begin a crime-fighting career as Batgirl.

IN THE REAL WORLD...

January: In Super Bowl I, the Green Bay Packers defeat the Kansas City Chiefs 35–10 at the Los Angeles Memorial Coliseum.

JANUARY

FIVE FOR FIGHTING

***Adventure Comics* #352**

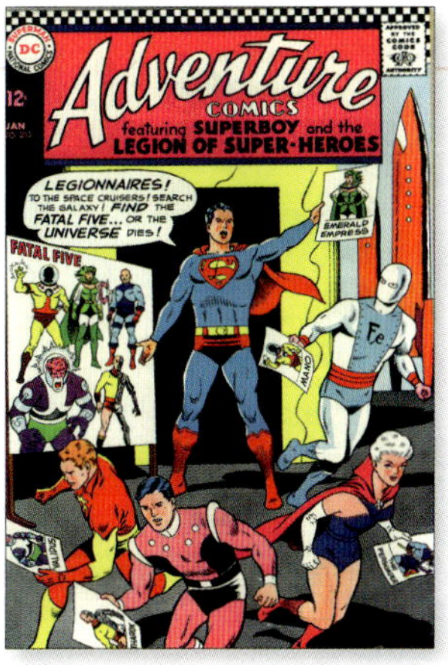

With the cloud-like Sun-Eater threatening to devour the Milky Way's sun, the Legion of Super-Heroes had its work cut out. With many of its members on other missions, the Legion was desperate for help and enlisted a quintet of the galaxy's greatest criminals: the half-robot, all-inhuman genius Tharok; the atomic axe-wielding Persuader; Validus, a behemoth that projected bolts of mental lightning; Mano, whose right hand had the antimatter power to destroy a planet; and the Emerald Empress, mistress of the powerful Emerald Eye. Tharok's Absorbatron bomb would ultimately destroy the Sun-Eater's power, but writer Jim Shooter and artist Curt Swan unleashed an even greater menace when the Fatal Five decided to stay united in the years ahead.

Legion of Super-Heroes member Sun Boy avoids the lightning bolts emanating from Validus' skull, though he's not sure how he'll convince the giant to help the Legion combat the Sun-Eater.

FEBRUARY

JUNGLE WARRIOR

***Showcase* #66**

Africa found itself a helmeted, loinclothed champion of mammals when scribe Bob Haney and artist Mike Sekowsky presented B'wana Beast. After his plane crash-landed on Mount Kilimanjaro, Mike Maxwell drank mysterious cavern water that granted him great strength. He also befriended the gorilla Djuba, who gave Maxwell a helmet that enabled him to communicate and control animals, and actually fuse them together into a chimera.

As B'wana Beast, Maxwell protected Africa against the likes of Hamid Ali, an immortal poacher who used robotic monstrosities to do his dirty work. Having thwarted Ali during his two consecutive issues of *Showcase*, B'wana Beast conquered a loyal following among DC readers.

JUNE

GUPPY LOVE

***Aquaman* #33**

Aqualad found romance under the sea when scripter Bob Haney and artist Nick Cardy introduced him to fellow young Atlantean Tula, also known as Aquagirl. The two got along swimmingly, to the point that Aquagirl convinced Aqualad to leave Aquaman's side and party at the underwater disco of Doctor Dorsal—whose hypnotic eels turned the young lovers and other teens into criminals. The pair eventually were shocked out of their hypnosis and returned to Atlantis.

DOUBLE FEATURE

***Blue Beetle* #1**

The first issue of Charlton Comics' short-lived *Blue Beetle* featured Blue Beetle and the debut of the Question, two heroes who would leave an indelible impression on the DC Universe for years to come.

Eight months after Ted Kord assumed the scarab as Blue Beetle in a back-up feature of *Captain Atom* #83, writer/artist Steve Ditko and co-writer "D. C. Glanzman" (who was actually Ditko) launched the Blue Beetle into his own series. This Beetle didn't possess superpowers. Instead, Kord was a brilliant inventor whose gadgets—chief among them, a bug-shaped aircraft and a gun that fired blinding light and compressed air blasts—powered his wisecracking war against crime. In his inaugural issue, the Blue Beetle dispatched the Squids, a costumed gang equipped with suctioning devices that enabled them to climb walls.

In this same issue, Ditko introduced Vic Sage, a hard-hitting TV reporter for World Wide Broadcasting Co., and his faceless alter ego, the Question, to Hub City's criminal underground. Using a chemical gas to apply and remove a special skin mask created by his mentor, Aristotle Rodor, Sage was able to conceal his features completely while operating outside the law. As the Question, he made his first mark by apprehending gambling ringleader Lou Dicer and his accomplice, WWB executive Jim Lark—on whom Sage blew the whistle during his next broadcast.

June: The Beatles release *Sgt. Pepper's Lonely Hearts Club Band*, a chart-topping album that would be nicknamed "The Soundtrack to the Summer of Love."

October: Thurgood Marshall becomes the first black U.S. Supreme Court Justice.
October: The revolutionary Che Guevara is executed in Bolivia.

JULY

QUICK ON THE DRAW

***The Adventures of Jerry Lewis* #101**
It is almost laughable that one of the medium's most influential artists broke into DC Comics drawing the misadventures of a comedian and also a gut-wrenching war tale. Yet it also bears testimony to the vast artistic range of Neal Adams.

Adams commandeered his first DC work as a penciller/inker with "It's My Turn to Die," a nine-page back-up tale written by Howard Liss for *Our Army at War* #182 in July. The story centered on a World War II army captain who had broken under the pressure of sending patrols to their deaths. Adams' renderings captured the anguish felt by Captain Sanders and the resolve Sanders showed to lead a defensive stance against attack.

The following month, *The Adventures of Jerry Lewis* #101 perfectly illustrated how Adams was equally adept at delivering the art of laughter. In his first full-length story for DC, he provided writer Arnold Drake's space odyssey "Jerry the Astro-Nut" with a photo-realistic flair not seen in comics. Later Adams would bring his talents over to the company's mainstream super hero titles, starting with covers for *Superman's Girl Friend, Lois Lane* and *Action Comics*.

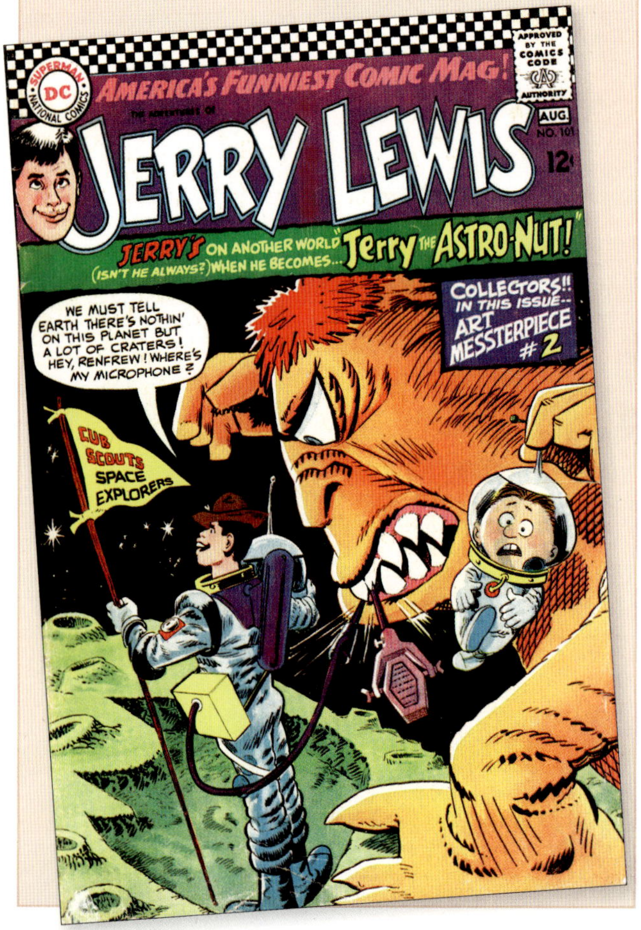

AUGUST

ON YOUR MARKS...
***Superman* #199**

Since the dawn of comics' Silver Age, readers have asked, "Who's faster: Superman or the Flash?" Writer Jim Shooter and artist Curt Swan tried answering that question when the Man of Steel and the Fastest Man Alive agreed to the U.N.'s request to race each other for charity. Unfortunately, two criminal organizations wagered heavily on the contest, with each side picking a winner and setting up traps to slow down the competition. Superman and the Flash never broke stride while thwarting the criminals' plans, though the race to the finish line would end in a dead heat.

Who is faster: the Flash or Superman? There's no clear winner in their first-ever race, and the question is unanswered even to this day.

SEPTEMBER

ON TV THIS MONTH: Filmation's animated series, *THE SUPERMAN/AQUAMAN HOUR OF ADVENTURE*, began airing Saturday mornings on CBS-TV on September 9. The show lasted through 1968 and featured the vocal talents of Bud Collyer as Superman and Marvin Miller as Aquaman...

OCTOBER

DANGEROUS SEA PREDATORS
***Aquaman* #35**
Although it was Black Manta's debut in the DC Universe, Aquaman instantly considered him one of his fiercest enemies. Manta demonstrated why when he poisoned the dome that protected Atlantis, keeping Aquaman preoccupied long enough for the villain to abduct the Sea King's son, Arthur, Jr. However, Ocean Master, Aquaman's half-brother, had his own plans for Atlantis. He defeated Black Manta, ensuring the safe return of Arthur, Jr. Black Manta would often resurface to plague Aquaman before killing Arthur, Jr. in *Adventure Comics* #452 (August 1977).

IN THE REAL WORLD...

November: U.S. President Lyndon B. Johnson secretly meets with prestigious leaders in the U.S. ("the Wise Men") to find ways to get the American people behind the Vietnam War.

November: Carl B. Stokes is elected Mayor of Cleveland, Ohio, becoming the first African-American mayor of a major United States city.

OCTOBER

DEADMAN LIVES

***Strange Adventures* #205**

In a story by scribe Arnold Drake and artist Carmine Infantino, circus aerialist Boston Brand learned there was much more to life after his death. The rather callous Brand was shot by a sniper and fell to his demise while performing in midair under his cadaverous "Deadman" guise. Yet his astral form was quickly awakened by the Hindu spirit goddess Rama Kushna, who allowed Brand's spirit to remain earthbound as Deadman until he caught his killer, a man with a hook for a right hand.

Beginning his investigation at the Hills Bros. Circus, Deadman discovered that he was not only invisible to the living, he could also enter their bodies and completely possess them. He chose to inhabit the body of the good-hearted but simpleminded strongman, Tiny. Despite uncovering and breaking up an in-house narcotics-smuggling operation as Tiny, Brand found no clues that could lead him to "the Hook." He now had no choice but to embark on a long journey in search of his killer.

Besides offering a gripping, surreal mystery with plenty of action, Deadman's quest was truly groundbreaking in the medium. Deadman's origin tale was the first narcotics-related story to require prior approval from the Comics Code Authority. In addition, Neal Adams, the artist who succeeded Infantino with the second issue, would soon become an industry legend.

Adams had already garnered widespread acclaim for his innovative covers on the likes of *Our Army At War* and *Action Comics*. Yet his darker, detailed renderings and innovative layouts complemented Deadman and *Strange Adventures* with an even more radical new look in comics. In many ways, Adams' personal evolution as an illustrator—and as a writer, since he'd later assume the scripting chores from plotter Infantino and editor/scripter Jack Miller—practically shadowed every intangible step Deadman took toward locating "the Hook."

Boston Brand plummets to the ground, shot by a mysterious hook-handed assailant as he performs his circus trapeze act; then opens his eyes, astonished to find he has seemingly survived both the bullet and the fall.

DECEMBER

SPIRITUAL GROWTH

***The Spectre* #1**

The Spectre's triumphant Silver Age resurrection spirited DC's higher powers to grant the Astral Avenger his own series, care of writer Gardner Fox and artist Murphy Anderson. U.S. ambassador Joseph Clanton became possessed by his ancestor, an 18th-Century pirate whose time displacement created a megacyclic force that overpowered even the Spectre. Unable to thwart Captain Skull from traveling back in time and seizing control of his evil ancestors, the Spectre traveled to another solar system where he browbeat the buccaneer out of Clanton's body.

POP GOES COMICS

***Teen Beat* #1**

Recognizing how teen music magazines were attracting a huge fan base, DC Comics made its own admirable attempt to garner that same audience. Editor Jack Miller launched the first issue of *Teen Beat*, a twelve-cent magazine with various features and speculative gossip focusing on the likes of the Beatles, Moby Grape, Jefferson Airplane, and The Mamas and the Papas, among others. The issue was presented "In Groovy Color," but, with the exception of the cover and interior illustrations, it was actually the backgrounds to black-and-white photos that were presented as such.

Commenting throughout many of the features was "Teeny," an illustrated teenage girl who provided her innermost thoughts and predictions regarding her favorite bands. In the first issue, the mod redhead lamented over growing rumors of the Monkees breaking up, although they wouldn't do so until some time after the issue came out. She also prophesized monster success for several up-and-coming musical groups, though the only one of her predictions to come true was that of the Bee Gees. Unfortunately, Teeny couldn't foresee that *Teen Beat* would last only one more issue—which was renamed *Teen Beam*—before being cancelled.

Cass Elliot, Denny Doherty, Michelle Phillips, and John Phillips from The Mamas and The Papas feature in *Teen Beat*.

ALSO THIS YEAR: In *BLACKHAWK* #228 in January, writer Bob Haney and artist Dick Dillin ushered in a new era for the Blackhawks... In March's *THE PEACEMAKER* #1 the pacifist headlined his own series, by writer Joe Gill and artist Pat Boyette... Aquaman advisor Dr. Vulko debuted in September's *THE BRAVE AND THE BOLD* #73 in a story by scribe Bob Haney and artist Sal Trapani...

December: Christian Barnard carries out the world's first heart transplant at Groote Schuur Hospital in Cape Town.

December: Professor John Archibald Wheeler coins the term "black hole."

December: *The Graduate*, starring Anne Bancroft and Dustin Hoffman, is released.

IMAGINING SUPERMAN

SUPERMAN SKETCHES BY CURT SWAN
Swan began drawing Superman full time in 1955 and defined the character for the next thirty years. These Silver Age sketches present the "Strange Visitor from Another Planet" as clean-cut and strong, but also as a sensitive, emotional, approachable hero. Swan commented: "I drew him to look like a nice guy, someone you'd want on your side."

1968

"I'M LEAVING METROPOLIS TO START A NEW LIFE... ONE THAT *DOESN'T* INCLUDE *YOU*!"

Lois Lane, *Superman's Girl Friend, Lois Lane* #80

SOCIAL INSECURITY

Contradictions abounded in 1968. Peace movements escalated nearly as much as riots throughout America, and the assassinations of the peacemakers Martin Luther King, Jr., and Robert F. Kennedy only led to further upheaval.

Great unrest also befell comics. The traditional super heroes were no longer "in" with their audience—they were too good to be true in a less-than-perfect world. So, DC Comics tried to bridge the gap between the real and unreal. Lois Lane stopped waiting for Superman to sweep her off her feet, and Princess Diana tried to right wrongs without her Amazon abilities.

Teenaged heroes also played a part. Two brothers Hawk and Dove personified both war and peace while "flower power" took a hold of a freakish mannequin called the Geek, resulting in controversy over the counterculture subject matter within DC's own offices.

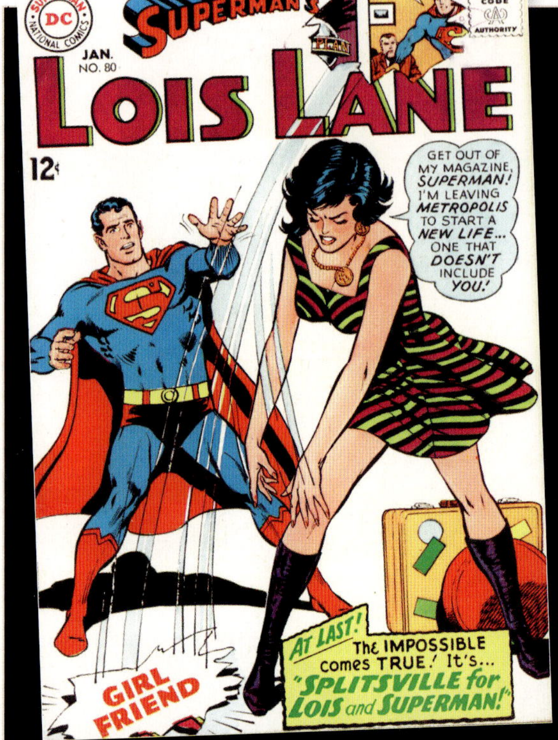

JANUARY

CHANGING LANES

***Superman's Girl Friend, Lois Lane* #80**

DC realized that its loyal comic book audience had begun maturing, so it was time for the company's characters to move forward. That included the *Daily Planet*'s intrepid reporter Lois Lane who, after thirty years of pining and scheming for Superman's affections, became one of the greatest beneficiaries of this ethos.

Lois Lane loved Superman, but she grew tired of waiting for him to come to his senses and marry her. At least, that's how scripter Leo Dorfman and artist Kurt Schaffenberger presented her dilemma in the story "Get Out of My Life, Superman!"

In a symbolically bold first move, Lois tore the term "Girl Friend" off her own cover (though it would reappear the following issue). She started trading in her generic blouse-and-pencil-skirt combinations for a "mod" wardrobe filled with printed dresses, go-go boots, miniskirts, and hot pants. Most important of all, Lois stopped looking up in the sky, waiting for her Superman to save her. When she had a problem, she dealt with it herself.

Not every facet of her metamorphosis took place in one issue. It was a gradual process that began when her dream Kryptonian missed her birthday party. Lois, concluding that she would never become Mrs. Superman, moved to Coral City, changed her last name to "Lorne," and took a job as a nurse, where she found romance after saving the life of astronaut Rand Kirby.

Despite going so far as to become engaged to Kirby, Lois soon realized that she not only still loved Superman, but that he had similar feelings for her. After exposure to an experimental gas gave her temporary ESP, Lois learned how Superman feared that she would become a target for his enemies if they ever married. Lois eventually called off her engagement to Kirby and returned home. From this point on, Lois and her Man of Steel were on an equal footing.

IN THE REAL WORLD...

April: Dr. Martin Luther King, Jr. is shot dead in Memphis, Tennessee, sparking riots in major American cities for several days afterward.

MARCH

A NEW LIGHT

***Green Lantern* #59**

John Broome's script and Gil Kane's renderings debuted a character who would one day become a Green Lantern—Guy Gardner. According to a device that recorded the dying Abin Sur's final thoughts, the power ring had located two men worthy of succeeding him as the Green Lantern of Sector 2814, but it selected Hal Jordan because he was closer to the crash that killed Sur. Viewing an alternate timeline, Jordan witnessed Gardner prove himself a worthy emerald-clad champion and struck up a friendship with him.

APRIL

BEWARE THE CREEPER

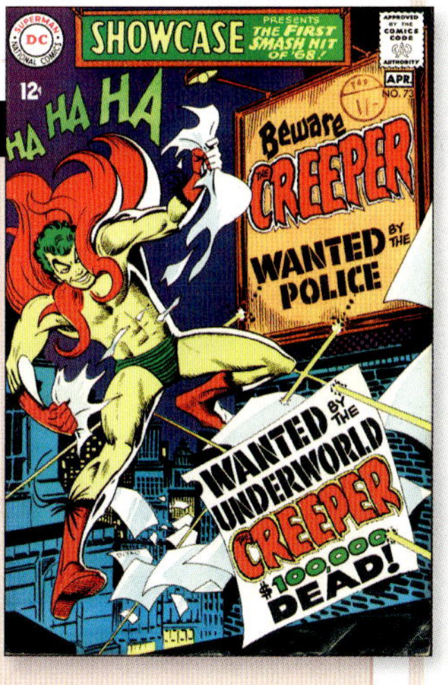

***Showcase* #73**

Ousted TV personality Jack Ryder hadn't planned on working for a security agency or combating communists. However, writer/artist Steve Ditko and co-scribe Don Segall gave him more than the last laugh as the garishly garbed Creeper, one of DC's quirkiest protagonists.

Ryder had adopted yellow makeup, a green wig, and red sheepskin to crash a mobster's costume party and locate the kidnapped Soviet scientist Emil Yatz. Criminal Angel Devilin's gang had abducted Yatz, and he was being shipped back home by communist spy Major Smej. Ryder was stabbed by the mobsters just as he found Yatz, but Yatz promptly gave Ryder a serum to heal his wounds and boost his energy to superhuman levels. He also implanted a device inside the wound, enabling Ryder's creepy attire to materialize and disappear with the click of an activator dial.

Yatz was shot dead by the mobsters, but Ryder's odd appearance, disturbing behavior, and maniacal laughter helped him to dispense with the criminals and spies. Authorities wrongly branded the Creeper as a crook, even though the underworld had felt his wrath, which he would begin doling out again in his own series two months later.

Professor Yatz hides an activator within the wound of his rescuer, a creepily garbed Jack Ryder.

MAY

WORLD'S FINEST PAIRING

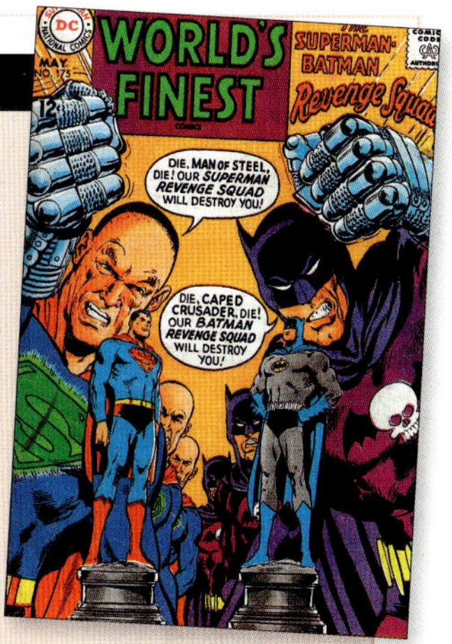

***World's Finest Comics* #175**

1968 was the year when Neal Adams and Batman's fates became forever intertwined. The two first "met" when the artist provided the January cover to *The Brave and The Bold* #75, which featured Batman fighting the Spectre, another DC character with whom Adams had become associated. After rendering the Batman-featured March covers to *The Brave and The Bold* #76, *World's Finest Comics* #174, and *Batman* #200, Adams tackled his first interiors with Batman on Leo Dorfman's script for "The Superman–Batman Revenge Squads" story in *World's Finest Comics* #175.

This story departed from the dark style that fans had until now associated with Adams' version of the World's Greatest Detective. The Superman and Batman revenge squads joined forces just as Superman and Batman had squared off in their annual contest to test each other's skills. The villains thought they had successfully destroyed Batman and Superman by rigging the trophies each of them won with bombs. However, the villains were apprehended and learned that the World's Finest tandem had already discovered the bombs and staged it so it seemed like the bombs had been detonated. Nevertheless, Adams' art clearly demonstrated that he was born not only to draw Batman, but was also quite expert at rendering the Man of Steel, Jimmy Olsen, Robin, the Flash (who made a cameo), and just about any other DC champion he chose.

Batman's specially treated kryptonite gloves give him the upper hand against Superman during their annual skill-testing contest.

June: U.S. presidential candidate Robert F. Kennedy is shot at the Ambassador Hotel in Los Angeles, California by Sirhan Sirhan; he later dies in hospital from his injuries.

June: James Earl Ray is arrested for the assassination of Dr. Martin Luther King, Jr.
August: Russia and members of the Warsaw Pact invade Czechoslovakia.

MAY

SECRETIVE SEXTET
***Secret Six* #1**

Writer E. Nelson Bridwell and artist Frank Springer brought together six individuals who all possessed special skills and dark secrets, and were all being blackmailed into the service of the faceless Mockingbird. The Secret Six was made up of boxing champion Tiger Force, nuclear physicist August Durant, illusionist Carlo di Rienzi, mistress of disguise Lili de Neuve, pilot and stuntman King Savage, and femme fatale Crimson Dawn. The Secret Six's first mission was a success, with the team stopping villain Zoltan Lupus from demonstrating his weapons of mass destruction.

PRIME TIME
***The Flash* #179**

"The Flash: Fact or Fiction?" was the question scribe Cary Bates and artist Ross Andru posed following the Fastest Man Alive's encounter with the Nok. In feeding off the Flash's aura, this hurricane-type creature cast him to a parallel world—ours—where he and other super heroes existed solely within comic books. Trapped on "Earth-Prime," the Flash knew only one man could possibly help him: DC Comics editor Julius Schwartz, who provided the Scarlet Speedster with the necessary resources to build a cosmic treadmill to help him return home.

Barry Allen changes into his Flash outfit, convincing editor Julius Schwartz that he is more than just a comic book character.

JUNE

BIRD-EYE VIEWS
***Showcase* #75**

Brothers Hank and Don Hall were complete opposites, yet writer/artist Steve Ditko, with scripter Steve Skeates, made sure the siblings shared a desire to battle injustice as Hawk and Dove. Aggressive militant Hank (Hawk) and pacifist Don (Dove) joined forces when their father was injured by a local mob. Don's wishes to help his father were answered by a disembodied voice, which granted the pair special powers. Although they bickered all the way, Hawk and Dove rescued their father—who then condemned the costumed duo as vigilantes.

AUGUST

RAISING CAIN
***The House of Mystery* #175**

As the Comics Code Authority's strict upkeep began coming into question in the late 1960s, editor Joe Orlando decided that *The House of Mystery* was in need of renovation. So, he pulled up the floorboards that had been worn out by super hero adventures over the past several years and refurbished the series to its horror anthology roots. Cain became the "Able Care Taker" and resided in the House of Mystery—just a short walk across the graveyard from the House of Secrets—from where he would introduce nearly every tale of terror for the next fifteen years.

The House of Mystery reopens its doors to supernatural tales with "The House of Gargoyles," by scribe Bob Haney and artist Jack Sparling. A group of curious children witness a murderous sculptor meeting his fate at the claws of stone behemoths, who are the parents of Cain's pet gargoyle.

"THE GARGOYLES WILL KILL YOU! YOU WILL NEVER ESCAPE THEM ! NEVER...NEVER...NEV-...!"

The dying words of Francois, the sculptor – "House of Gargoyles"

SEPTEMBER

THE ODD COUPLE
***Showcase* #77**

Writer John Albano and artist Bob Oksner injected pretty primitive humor into the classic "beauty and the beast" concept when they opened the O'Day and Simeon Detective Agency for business. Angel O'Day was a stunning sleuth who was partnered with Sam Simeon, a gorilla with an eye for details.

The Angel and the Ape's first case involved caging a zookeeper-turned-spy before he acquired the secret plans to a theme park ride. In December, the buddies spun off into their own series.

ON TV THIS MONTH: The *BATMAN/SUPERMAN HOUR*, produced by Filmation for CBS-TV, debuted on September 14. It was the Caped Crusader's first animated series...

IN THE REAL WORLD...

September: Mattel's Hot Wheels toy cars are introduced.
September: *60 Minutes* debuts on television channel CBS in the U.S.
October: Police strike civil rights demonstrators with batons in Derry, Northern Ireland, marking the beginning of the Troubles.

OCTOBER

DOOMED PATROL

***The Doom Patrol* #121**

Editor Murray Boltinoff and artist Bruno Premiani appeared in *The Doom Patrol*'s last issue to urge readers that the team's fate was in their hands. Only a miracle could save the Doom Patrol. With the Doom Patrol's powers neutralized on a Caribbean island, Brotherhood of Evil member Madame Rouge and Nazi Captain Zahl demanded that the team choose between saving their own lives or those of the fourteen innocent residents that formed the population of Codsville, Maine. In unison, the heroes told their enemies to fire away at them. One explosion later, and the Doom Patrol was no more.

COMIC BOOK GEEK

***Brother Power, The Geek* #1**

The medium didn't appear to be ready for Brother Power, the Geek, envisioned by writer Joe Simon and artist Al Bare. Simon's mod re-imagining of Frankenstein's monster—a mannequin turned reclusive hero-philosopher—was a trip that lasted only two issues. Bizarrely, though, the latter of those issues actually sold better than the first, and the debate as to why Brother Power fizzled out has continued to this day.

On the run from a biker gang called the Mongrels, flower children Nick and Paul squatted inside an abandoned tailor shop, where a bolt of lightning struck a dummy dressed in oil-soaked, bloodstained clothes. The dummy sprang to life and, through extraordinary displays of power, rescued the two hippies from the returning Mongrels. Teaching the animated mannequin how to speak their hip language, Nick and Paul welcomed the Geek as one of their own. With that, Brother Power's journey of self-discovery began… and abruptly ended.

From the Geek's inception, when he was originally conceived as the "Freak," internal constituents within DC had feared that Simon's rag-tag protagonist endorsed drugs and the hippie counterculture. So, before Brother Power could spread his peace-loving word for a third issue, the series was brought to a halt.

Brother Power makes an impact with the hippie scene, encouraging him to run for Congress in favor of "Love, Peace… Flower Power!"

OCTOBER

NEW AND… IMPROVED?

***Wonder Woman* #178**

DC publisher Carmine Infantino wanted to rejuvenate what had been perceived as a tired Wonder Woman, so he assigned writer Denny O'Neil and artist Mike Sekowsky to convert the Amazon Princess into a secret agent. Wonder Woman was made over into an Emma Peel type, and what followed was arguably the most controversial period in the hero's history.

The collaborators' first issue put Diana Prince's transformation into motion, even though it focused primarily on her wardrobe. When testimony by Wonder Woman landed her friend Steve Trevor in jail for a murder he didn't commit, her alter ego tried blending in with the local hippie culture to find the eyewitness who could clear his name. Diana succeeded, and realized that she needed to better connect with the people she protected.

Those changes exploded in the following issue, after Queen Hippolyta informed her daughter that Paradise Island was relocating to another dimension in order to replenish the Amazons' dwindling mystical energies. Shockingly, Diana opted to renounce her powers and costume so that she could remain on "Man's World," and help Steve thwart the terrorist machinations of the mysterious Dr. Cyber, including one that had Cyber sending bomb-rigged toys to the children of America's leaders.

Though powerless, Diana quickly built a new life for herself, opening a boutique and undergoing training under the tutelage of I Ching, a blind martial-arts expert she befriended. Unfortunately, it wasn't enough for the radically altered Wonder Woman, who wouldn't stop Doctor Cyber before the villainess saw to the murder of Steve Trevor.

For the next five years, Diana's adventures lauded the versatile spirit and independent strength of the modern woman more than her physical wonders, although some feminists argued that the "depowering" of Wonder Woman had greatly diminished the character.

Relinquishing her Amazon abilities and costume, Diana Prince trains her body and mind to turn herself into a very different Wonder Woman.

ALSO THIS YEAR: In March's *BATMAN* #200, writer Mike Friedrich and artist Chic Stone had the Caped Crusader and Robin fearful of the Scarecrow until loyal Alfred recapped their origins and urged the pair to give the Scarecrow reason to fear *them*… Writer Sergio Aragonés and artist Nick Cardy served up the offbeat Western hero Bat Lash in August's *SHOWCASE* #76… Writer Jim Shooter and artist Wally Wood helmed November's *CAPTAIN ACTION* #1, based on Ideal's popular action figure…

November : Republican Richard M. Nixon wins the U.S. presidential election, defeating the Democratic candidate, Vice President Hubert Humphrey.

November: Yale University announces it is going to admit female students.
November: The Beatles release their *White Album*.

1969

"THIS WORLD IS COMPOSED OF MANY THINGS THAT ARE LEFT UNEXPLAINED!"

The Phantom Stranger,
The Phantom Stranger #1

CHAMPIONS REDEFINED

1969 was a year of landmarks: the Woodstock Festival featured three days of peace and music; President Richard Nixon launched his policy of "Vietnamization," intended to allow the withdrawal of American troops; and more than 238,000 miles (38,300 km) from Earth, the astronauts of *Apollo 11* took one giant leap for mankind.

In DC Comics, however, things were different. The decline of comics' Silver Age continued to tarnish DC's circulation, despite its merger with Warner Bros.-Seven Arts. DC canceled nine series—including *The Atom and Hawkman*—and cover prices for titles increased to fifteen cents.

However, the age of experimentation was taking effect. Before man walked on the Moon, the Man of Steel came to Earth and experienced the Vietnam War, while familiar faces like Batman and Green Arrow redefined themselves in time for comics' next age.

MARCH

BEWITCHING
***The Witching Hour* #1**
During DC's latest foray into horror/mystery titles, editor Dick Giordano conjured up a triumvirate of witches to host an anthology series produced by some of comics' biggest names. For the first issue, writer/artist Alex Toth provided a framing sequence (with an epilogue drawn by Neal Adams) that introduced readers to cronish Mordred, motherly Mildred, and beautiful maiden Cynthia—as well as their bumbling pet zombie, Egor. Each witch then brewed a potent blend of horror and dark humor crafted by Toth, writer Denny O'Neil, and artists Pat Boyette and Jack Sparling. It was an effective spell that would entrance a loyal audience long into the next decade.

APRIL

NEW HOUSE DWELLERS
***House of Mystery* #179**
"The Man Who Murdered Himself" in *House of Mystery* was writer Marv Wolfman's inaugural horror yarn, and the first DC story illustrated by Berni Wrightson (who left the "e" off his first name to distinguish himself from a famous diver). In the story, narrated by "care taker" Cain, an estate in 1882 was haunted by the ghost of a man who killed himself. Fans of the comic didn't know it, but they were witnessing the earliest effort of two greats who would become renowned for their tales of terror and suspense.

MAY

RELUCTANT ROCK HERO
***Showcase* #82**
Starting with this issue and continuing through the next two, the *Showcase* series distinguished itself with the word "Preview" on the cover. The series focused on Nightmaster, by writer Denny O'Neil and artist Jerry Grandenetti. Rock singer Jim Rook was transported to the magic-ruled dimension of Myrra, where he learned he was a descendant of the warrior Nacht. When the evil Warlocks abducted his girlfriend, Rook took hold of his ancestor's Sword of Night and became Myrra's protector. The Nightmaster would last for only three issues.

IN THE REAL WORLD...

January: Australian media baron Rupert Murdoch purchases the largest-selling British Sunday newspaper, *The News of the World*.

THE SOLDIER OF STEEL

***Superman* #216**
While U.S. involvement in the Vietnam War continued, writer Robert Kanigher and artist Ross Andru crafted a story that took Superman straight to the battlefield. Whereas DC's war comics primarily took place during the two World Wars, this issue marked the first time that any DC publication had sent one of its heroes into Vietnam. The overall story provided little social commentary regarding the war itself. Nevertheless, "The Soldier of Steel" story was a landmark moment in the Man of Steel's history—and was topped off with a rare *Superman* cover by artist Joe Kubert.

Superman involved himself in the conflict when U.S. soldiers flooded the offices of the *Daily Planet* with letters asking for his help. Clark Kent and Lois Lane enlisted as a medic and nurse, respectively, to acquire stories from the soldiers' points of view. However, it wasn't long before Superman was dispatched to rescue the troops and a local orphanage from enemy forces—chief among them, Johnny Morely, a meek U.S. soldier who was forced by the evil Dr. Han's medical herbs to transform into the monstrous King Cong. The Man of Tomorrow eventually isolated the raging giant long enough for the herbs to wear off, enabling Morely to help rescue troops that were under fire.

When Clark Kent goes on assignment to cover the Vietnam War as an enlisted man, so does Superman, who makes short work of enemy tanks advancing toward American GIs.

STRIFE ON MARS

***Justice League of America* #71**
In less than a year on the *Justice League of America* series, scribe Denny O'Neil and artist Dick Dillin had made major changes to the team. Two issues after Wonder Woman left the JLA, the Martian Manhunter did the same. J'onn J'onzz had been embroiled in a civil war against Commander Blanx, who wanted to destroy the Martian race. With the team accompanying him back to Mars, J'onn defeated Blanx in one-on-one combat. However, the surviving Martians fled, and J'onn decided to leave the JLA to search the galaxy for his people.

JUNE

A STRANGER COMES

***The Phantom Stranger* #1**
Sixteen years after he faded into obscurity, the Phantom Stranger rematerialized in *Showcase* #80 (February 1969) before making his way back into his own series. Yet this dark traveler, whose true name, origins, and mission remained unknown, was very different from the one who disappeared in 1953. The original Stranger was a debunker of the supernatural, but this one was drawn toward it, and possessed formidable powers of his own to combat it—on the occasions when he chose to involve himself in such affairs.

The inaugural issue, like *Showcase* #80, contained a new story that framed around reprint tales from both the Stranger's original series and *Star Spangled Comics*, featuring Dr. Terrence Thirteen, also known as the Ghost-Breaker. The Ghost-Breaker made a career out of disproving arcane activity and spent many issues of the series trying to reveal the Phantom Stranger as a charlatan. Although he never succeeded, he proved proficient at unveiling other unknowns and mysteries—albeit, ironically, with the help of the Stranger.

Such was the case in "Defeat the Dragon Curse… or Die!," a story scripted by Mike Friedrich with renderings by Bill Draut. The Phantom Stranger and Dr. Thirteen's paths crossed in San Francisco during Chinese New Year, when friends of the Ghost-Breaker were seemingly killed by the ancient dragon curse of Ching Hi Fu. Eventually, the duo uncovered the real culprit to be a Ching Hi Fu worshipper, who destroyed modernized buildings he considered disrespectful to his Chinese heritage.

With each issue of the series, this incarnation of the Phantom Stranger progressed even further into the paranormal protagonist he is today—an all-knowing guide and narrator through the darkness. That evolution came about through the work of some of comics' most reputable talents, including writers like Robert Kanigher, Gerry Conway, and Len Wein, and artists such as Neal Adams and Jim Aparo.

The first issue of *The Phantom Stranger* also includes a reprint of the "When Dead Men Walk" story from the original 1952 series with revised art.

January: Elvis Presley begins recording what becomes his landmark comeback sessions for the albums *From Elvis in Memphis* and *Back in Memphis*.

February: The Boeing 747 makes its maiden flight.
May: John Lennon and Yoko Ono begin their "Bed-In" in Quebec, Canada.

AUGUST

WHO IS WONDER GIRL?
***Teen Titans* #22**

Four years after the debut of Wonder Girl, writer Marv Wolfman and artist Gil Kane disclosed her origins. They revealed that she was a seemingly orphaned infant whom Wonder Woman rescued from an apartment building fire. Raised on Paradise Island as Queen Hippolyta's foster daughter, she was given powers identical to Wonder Woman by scientist Paula von Gunther's healing device, the Purple Ray. After the Amazons relocated to another dimension, Wonder Girl took the name Donna Troy and moved into a New York apartment. She also gave herself a new hairstyle and costume, both of which she would wear for twenty years.

CAIN AND ABEL
***DC Special* #4**

A year after Cain took over *House of Mystery*, writer Mark Hanerfeld and artist Bill Draut introduced readers to Abel, the stuttering, softhearted brother who was temporarily staying with him in *DC Special*. It was evident that a fraternal friction existed between this duo, even as they narrated tales of terror to children who were holding the zombie Egor hostage in exchange for stories. Abel never earned any respect from his brother or anyone else—not even from Goldie, the imaginary girlfriend to whom he always told his stories. Yet it didn't stop him from reopening *House of Secrets* with issue #81, following the series' three-year hiatus.

Kids looking for Halloween tales get more than they bargained for, thanks to storytellers Cynthia, Cain, the Mad Mod Witch, Judge Gallows, and Abel.

SEPTEMBER

SEEING RED
***Showcase* #85**

Born into a white family but raised by Native Americans, the flame-maned, pale-skinned Firehair didn't readily assimilate with either culture in the 19th-Century Southwest. However, writer/artist Joe Kubert's tales of racial and social discordance, steeped in grease pencil and Native American folklore, was a natural fit within a comic book that tested bold new concepts. Firehair realized he would have to walk the Earth to find true acceptance.

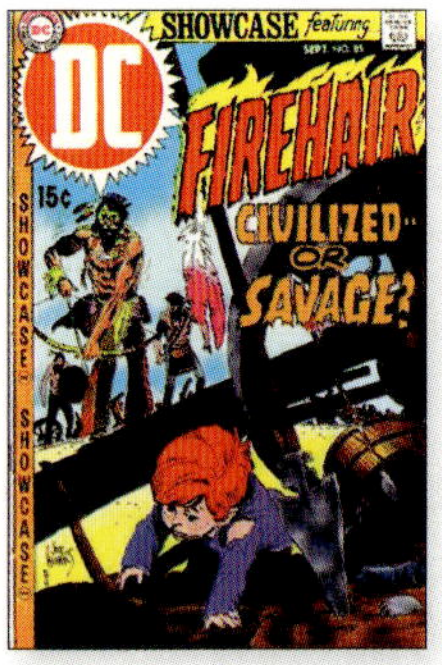

SEPTEMBER

SHARPENING UP
***The Brave and the Bold* #85**

He may have a revamped look, but the Green Arrow's archery skills remain as reliable and familiar as ever.

Since his inception in 1940, many had considered Green Arrow a Batman imitation. Like the Dark Knight, the Green Arrow was rich, skilled, partnered with a young ward, and known to sport motif-themed gadgetry. So when writer Bob Haney paired Green Arrow with Batman to find out why a senator had been shot, artist Neal Adams targeted the Emerald Archer for a radical redesign that ultimately evolved past the surface level.

The story presented identity crises for both Bruce Wayne and Oliver Queen following an assassination attempt on Wayne's friend, Senator Paul Cathcart. Wayne was set to fill his friend's seat and provide the passing vote on a crucial anti-crime bill. Queen, meanwhile, was at a crossroads over whether or not to give up his bow and arrow, believing that he could serve the greater good as the financier behind the construction of New Island, a second Gotham City.

Queen and Wayne each revealed their secret identities to a mutual friend—Senator Cathcart's psychiatrist son, Edmond. When Edmond was abducted by Miklos Minotaur, Queen's chief rival for New Island's construction contract and the figure behind the Senator's assassination attempt, Batman and Green Arrow collaborated to rescue their friend before voting on the bill took place.

Beyond this well-crafted story, the most significant aspect of this issue was Adams' depiction of Oliver Queen's alter ego. He had rendered a modern-day Robin Hood, complete with goatee and mustache, plus threads that were more befitting an ace archer. And where the new look began, Green Arrow's new personality soon followed. Though he was still a wealthy capitalist in this story, corporate corruption soon forced Queen into bankruptcy. In effect, this created a hero who became socially conscious of the world's problems and one who would try to solve these problems when he partnered with Green Lantern in *Green Lantern/Green Arrow* #76 (April 1970).

IN THE REAL WORLD...

June: The Stonewall Riots in New York City mark the start of the modern gay rights movement in the U.S.

July: The world watches in awe as Neil Armstrong takes his historic first steps on the Moon.

NOVEMBER

BORN LOSERS

***G.I. Combat* #138**

The crew of the Haunted Tank was the first to cross paths with the Losers, a Special Forces group made up of members who had lost more than a few men under their command. Scribe Robert Kanigher and artist Russ Heath turned these self-described Losers—including "Navajo Ace" Johnny Cloud of the U.S. Army Air Force, Marines Gunner Mackey and Sarge Clay, and Captain William Storm, a PT boat commander with a prosthetic leg—into a fighting force that meshed as one. Accompanied by their canine mascot Pooch, this collection of lower-tiered characters with incredibly bad luck went on to become some of DC's most beloved war heroes.

PRETTY BIRD CALLING

***Justice League of America* #75**

November saw Black Canary both relocate and develop her "canary cry." After Black Canary's husband, Larry Lance, sacrificed himself to save her from the astral antagonist Aquarius, Black Canary relocated to another world. The crime-fighting beauty, at the behest of writer Denny O'Neil and artist Dick Dillin, left the JSA on Earth-2 to join the JLA on Earth-1. Some JLA members thought the non-powered heroine might not handle their enemies, but she silenced all questions with an ultrasonic scream that floored them. It was the first time that Black Canary had exhibited her "canary cry."

THE MADNESS OF JEAN LORING

***The Atom and Hawkman* #45**

It was the final issue of *The Atom and Hawkman*, but just the start of a pattern of mental instability for Ray Palmer's then-fiancée, Jean Loring. As revealed through Denny O'Neil's script and Dick Dillin's art, Jean was driven mad by the Jimberen, a subatomic race that believed she had descended from their Earth-born queen. The Atom (Palmer) shrank himself and Hawkman to confront the aliens, only for both to become slaves of the new Queen Jean. Eventually, the heroes freed Jean from the aliens' grasp, but her sanity would not be restored until *Justice League of America* #81 (June 1970).

DECEMBER

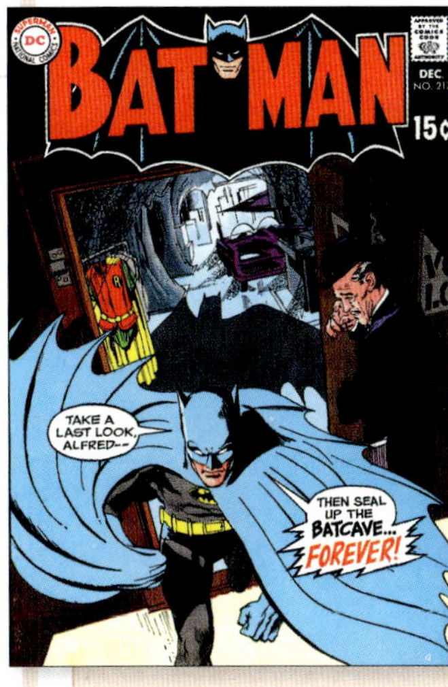

THE DARKER KNIGHT

***Batman* #217**

When Dick Grayson moved out of Wayne Manor to begin college, writer Frank Robbins and artist Irv Novick orchestrated a chain reaction of events that forever altered Batman's personality.

Within minutes of Dick's goodbye, Bruce Wayne and Alfred sealed off the Batcave, moved out of Wayne Manor, and made their new home in a penthouse apartment atop the Wayne Foundation. Wayne decided that Batman would return to the darker persona that struck terror into the criminals now hiding behind phony respectability. Wayne also replaced his playboy image with that of a benefactor and the founder of V.I.P., a foundation to help the victims of crime.

Bruce's first client was Dr. Susan Fielding, whose husband had been fatally shot while removing a bullet from a wounded man. A disguised Batman spread word around Gotham City's underworld that Fielding could identify the killer, prompting the killer's return to the scene of his crime. While preventing an attempt on Fielding's life, Batman caught a slug in the arm, which he had the doctor extract immediately so they could compare it with the bullets that killed her husband and wounded the other man. All three were a match, allowing police to identify and apprehend the real murderer, gangster "Stub" Sartel.

A tearful Dick Grayson heads off to college, prompting Bruce Wayne to make major changes for himself and his alter ego.

TRAITOR IN THE RANKS

***Justice League of America* #77**

As told by writer Denny O'Neil and artist Dick Dillin, the JLA suffered heartbreak at the hands of Snapper Carr. Tired of being the JLA's mascot, Snapper was swayed by the words of "John Dough," an everyman intent on making America more normal. With Snapper's help, Dough captured Batman, disguised himself as the Caped Crusader, and nearly convinced the U.S. government that the heroes had plotted a coup. The real Batman escaped and exposed the everyman as the Joker. Meanwhile, a disgraced Snapper resigned from his JLA honorary membership.

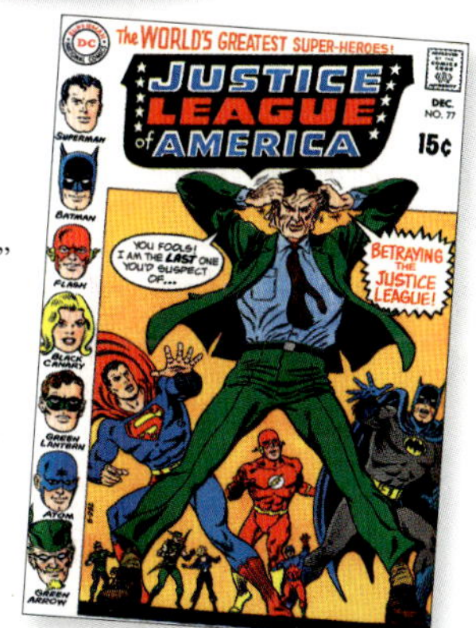

ALSO THIS YEAR: In July's *THE ATOM AND HAWKMAN* #43 the Winged Wonder rescued Hawkgirl from the Gentleman Ghost, who materialized for the first time in twenty years thanks to writer Robert Kanigher and artist Murphy Anderson… In *CHALLENGERS OF THE UNKNOWN* #69 (September) scripter Denny O'Neil and artist Jack Sparling got Corrina Stark to join the Challengers…

August: The Woodstock Festival is held in upstate New York, featuring some of the top rock musicians of the era.

November: Regular color television broadcasts begin on BBC1 and ITV in the U.K.

November: Soccer great Pelé scores his 1,000th goal.

1970s

By the 1970s, society was in the grip of an identity crisis. The turmoil of the late 1960s had spilled over into the new decade. The Watergate scandal, the Vietnam War, an oil crisis, and stagflation (severe inflation, sparse growth) had engendered a growing distrust of government and big business. Civil and women's rights were burning issues throughout the first half of the 1970s, fuelling a sense of hostility, alienation and frustration felt by many.

Thankfully, the decade's youth eventually moved away from rebelling against the past and began building a better tomorrow. The 1970s witnessed IBM's birth of the floppy disk and Intel's launch of the first microprocessor. Global concern for the environment wa seeded during the world's first-ever "Earth Day," even a nuclear energy emerged as an alternative resource.

Furthermore, the 1970s—its many problems aside—pushed cultural boundaries in all kinds of ways. New voices in soul, punk, and pop music emerged, though it was disco that defined the decade's sound, trends, and social behavior. Ernö Rubik, a professor of architecture in Budapest, Hungary, turned his cube-shaped geometry model into the world's most popular puzzle.

As DC Comics entered its Bronze Age, it was immersed in its own identity crisis, which continued throughout the 1970s, despite the fact that the company's titles were at their most innovative and socially relevant. There were progressive titles like *Green Lantern/Green Arrow* and the revamping of icons like Batman and Superman, while a "King of Comics," Jack Kirby, wrote and illustrated his "Fourth World" series, comprising *The Forever People*, *Mister Miracle*, and *New Gods*. Unfortunately, flagging sales, rising costs, and a paper shortage threatened to depose DC as the foremost name in comics. The company had to take significant steps to rediscover itself before heading into the next decade. Along the way, the company also found strong leadership in new Publisher Jenette Kahn, dynamic new storytelling methods, and exciting new formats.

"THE NEW GODS WIELD GREATER POWER—FOR IN OUR DAY, IT'S WE WHO LIVE IN THE DARK SHADOW OF THE OUTCOME!"

Narrator, *New Gods* #1 (March 1971

1970

"SOMETHING IS WRONG! SOMETHING IS KILLING US ALL...! SOME HIDEOUS MORAL CANCER IS ROTTING OUR VERY SOULS!"

Green Arrow, *Green Lantern/Green Arrow* #76

FINDING RELEVANCE

By the Seventies, the Silver Age was unofficially over. While the world's socially progressive values pushed through the declining counterculture movement of the 1960s, sales and reader interest in super heroes waned. So the medium turned to new writers, artists, and editors who had more of an interest in topical issues and the "real world." Thus began the medium's Bronze Age.

The launching point of the Bronze Age was never pinpointed to one particular title or creative team, though DC Comics was clearly a significant contributor to the era. The creative tandem of Denny O'Neil and Neal Adams ushered in "relevant" comics with their run on *Green Lantern/Green Arrow*. And iconic storyteller Jack Kirby shocked the comics world when he departed from DC's competition, then came to DC to herald a new way of storytelling—starting with *Superman's Pal, Jimmy Olsen*.

FEBRUARY

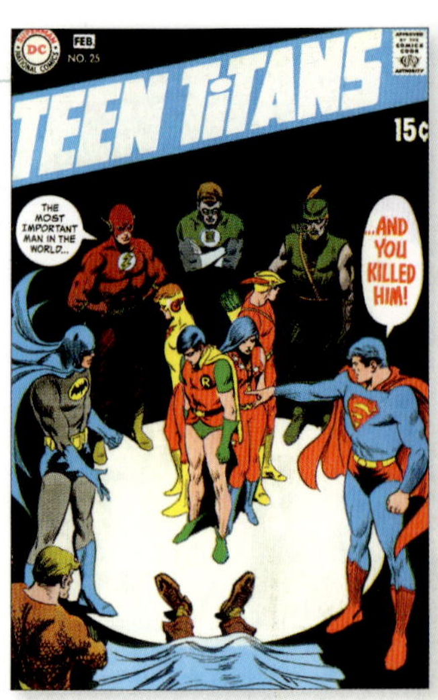

GROWING PAINS
***Teen Titans* #25**

Tragedy initiated a new era for the Teen Titans, as told by scribe Robert Kanigher and artist Nick Cardy. At a local disco, a precognitive named Lilith warned that Robin, Wonder Girl, Speedy, Kid Flash, Hawk, and Dove would "open the door for death." She was right—amid a riot at a nearby peace rally, the Titans' reckless attempt to stop a gunman resulted in the fatal shooting of peace activist Dr. Arthur Swenson. After drawing harsh criticism from the Justice League for their part in the killing, the downtrodden youths found a supportive hand in the world's richest man, Mr. Jupiter. He appealed to the Titans (minus Robin, who decided to go off to college and pursue his own career) and Lilith to forego their powers and costumes and join his secret government-sponsored training project for teenagers.

Hoping to discover themselves following tragedy, Teen Titans Kid Flash, Wonder Girl, Speedy, Hawk, Dove, and Lilith give up their costumes and superpowers for a while.

APRIL

LICENSE TO DRIVE
***Hot Wheels* #1**

DC's collective foot floored the pedal after acquiring the rights to publish a comic based on Mattel's enormously popular Hot Wheels die-cast car line. The company even hired Alex Toth to draw it, since the legendary artist had designed the line's characters for a Saturday-morning cartoon show. Toth's inaugural issue with writer Joe Gill chronicled turbo-charged teen Jack Wheeler and his Hot Wheels pit crew matching horsepower against Dexter Carter and his Demons. The comic ran out of gas after only six issues, but Toth's aerodynamic storytelling fueled a series that took licensed tie-ins in a bold new direction.

IN THE REAL WORLD...

February: Black Sabbath's self-titled debut album, often regarded as the first true heavy metal album, is released.

APRIL

HARD-TRAVELING HEROES

***Green Lantern/Green Arrow* #76**

Real-world politics has always gone hand-in-hand with comics and their creators' own personal perspectives. Yet this was never more creatively expressed than when writer Denny O'Neil and artist Neal Adams paired the liberal Green Arrow with the conservative Green Lantern.

While the heroes shared the color green in their names, their respective points-of-view infused a grey area to problems that, until then, had often been regarded in black-and-white terms in comics. Liking Adams' redesign of the archer's look in September 1969's *The Brave and The Bold* #85, and having stripped Oliver Queen of his fortune in *Justice League of America* #75 later that year, O'Neil saw Green Arrow as an ideal counterculture representative to oppose Green Lantern's role as an intergalactic "establishment cog." Together, under the editorship of Julius Schwartz, O'Neil and Adams tackled a plethora of real-world topics that helped launch comics' more socially relevant Bronze Age.

In issue #76, Green Lantern thought he was doing his job when he stopped a disgruntled Star City teen from harassing businessman Jubal Slade. Green Arrow, however, decried Green Lantern's actions, pointing out that the businessman Green Lantern had rescued was actually a fat cat slumlord planning to tear down the teenager's apartment building. Both heroes took different approaches in trying to convince Slade not to go through with his plans, though together they brought the slumlord to justice after he orchestrated a hit on Green Arrow.

On Oa, the Guardians chastised Sector 2814's protector for resorting to means that were not in line with being a Green Lantern. However, when Green Arrow challenged them to come to Earth and get a better understanding of humanity, the Guardians acquiesced, and sent one of their own to accompany the heroes on a cross-country journey through America.

Introducing the Bronze Age theme of racism to this issue, an elderly man asks Green Lantern why he has never before helped black people. A shaken Hal Jordan is unable to answer.

A SOLDIER'S STORIES

***Our Army at War* #218**

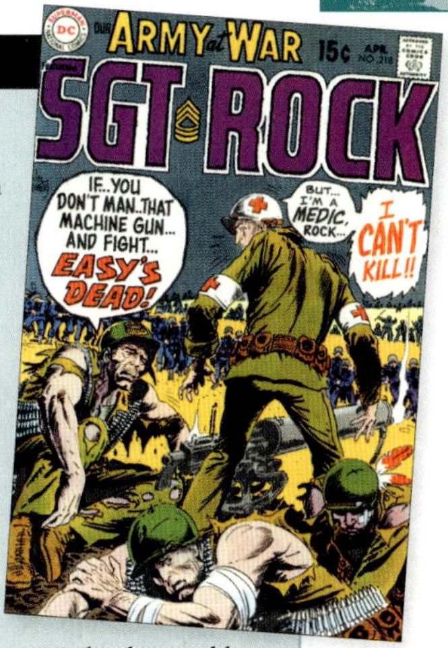

When editor Joe Kubert hired Sam Glanzman as the artist on *G.I. Combat*, he ensured that the Haunted Tank stories had a firmly grounded influence throughout much of the 1970s. However, it was Glanzman's semi-autobiographical tales in *Our Army at War* that brough a harrowing realism to World War II that few war comics have matched.

During the war, Glanzman had been stationed aboard the USS *Stevens*, a *Fletcher*-class destroyer for the United States Navy. Though he illustrated many war stories for Charlton Comics throughout the 1950s and '60s, it was only after he started working at DC that he would convert his personal journal of experiences aboard the USS *Stevens* into war tales he wrote and drew. He started with a story that recounted a novice seaman's baptism by fire during an air attack.

"The *Stevens* meant so much to me," Glanzman once told *Military Officer* magazine. "In a sense, that's the only reason I went into comic books – I wanted to honor my ship and the men who served on her." Glanzman did indeed honor his fellow soldiers, producing more than sixty powerful accounts that dealt with different aspects of the war and captured the humanity of soldiers from all sides.

Our Army at War featured realistic and harrowing accounts of soldiers' experiences in action during World War II.

INNER-CITY TITAN

***Teen Titans* #26**

The inaugural adventure of the non-powered, non-costumed Teen Titans introduced one of DC's first African-American heroes, Mal Duncan. Written by Robert Kanigher with stellar artwork from Nick Cardy, the Titans' new benefactor, Mr. Jupiter, assigned them to obtain jobs, room, and board in Hell's Corner. In this tough, inner-city neighborhood, the teens clashed with a street gang called the Hell Hawks, but they also found a fighting ally in Mal, who later defeated the gang's leader in a boxing duel. Though he had no powers, Mal's noble spirit immediately earned the respect of the Titans, who invited him to become part of Mr. Jupiter's top-secret training project for teenagers.

March: The Nuclear Non-Proliferation Treaty goes into effect.
March: ***The New English Bible***, a new translation of the Bible, is published.

April: President Richard Nixon signs the Public Health Cigarette Smoking Act into law, banning television advertisements for cigarettes in the United States.

JUNE

FRIGHT AT THE MUSEUM
***Detective Comics* #400**

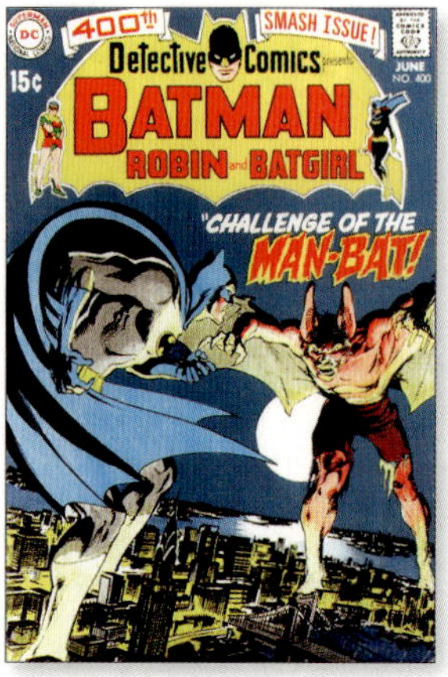

Ultra-stealthy thieves the Blackout Gang had expected Batman to track them down to the Gotham Natural History Museum, but neither they nor the Dark Knight anticipated scripter Frank Robbins and artist Neal Adams to issue the "Challenge of the Man-Bat!" Museum zoologist Kirk Langstrom's secret experiment—using a bat gland extract to concoct a serum that would enhance people's auditory abilities—exceeded his wildest expectations when he tested it on himself. His senses became hyper-enhanced, while his features steadily deteriorated into that of a winged "Man-Bat." Though he aided Batman in lighting up the Blackout Gang, a distraught Langstrom quickly flew off, leaving the Dark Knight to wonder if he had met a new friend or foe.

JULY

TOME OF THE UNKNOWN SOLDIER
***Star Spangled War Stories* #151**

Ironically, this war anthology series found its most recognizable face when Joe Kubert wrote, drew, and edited the first of a slew of "unknown tales of valor… of a man who no one knows—but—is known by everyone!" The Unknown Soldier was familiar to readers with his gauze-bandaged features, the result of being horribly disfigured by a hand grenade that also killed his brother. However, he was a master of disguise and proved instrumental in countless missions throughout World War II. Seven years and fifty-four issues later, the series would change its title, renaming itself *The Unknown Soldier* in honor of the "Immortal G.I."

The Unknown Soldier, posing as a U.S. Air Force pilot assigned to bomb Tokyo, is attacked by a guerilla leader in China.

SEPTEMBER

THE OLD WEST RIDES ANEW

***All-Star Western* [second series] #1**

Although the Western comic's popularity had waned with the coming of the Silver Age, editor Dick Giordano ushered the genre into a new era with the return of *All-Star Western*. Revived after its cancelation nine years prior, the first issue reprinted several classic Pow-Wow Smith tales, but also promised to introduce readers to "a new breed of blazing Western adventure" with issue #2.

Scripter Robert Kanigher lived up to the issue's hype with the debuts of Outlaw and El Diablo. His first story, with artwork by Tony DeZuniga, forced Rick Wilson to abandon his dream of becoming a Texas Ranger like his father. While running with a nefarious group of outlaws known as the Fenton Gang, a stagecoach robbery-turned-murder forced Wilson to become an unwilling outlaw, evading the father he idolized. Kanigher and artist Gray Morrow presented a weirder Western tale from Mexico in the issue's other story, which saw the mysterious El Diablo thwart a stagecoach robbery and aid a pregnant woman in giving birth. What made El Diablo so intriguing, however, was the hero's unique secret identity. Bank teller Lazarus Lane was in a coma after being struck by lightning, and awoke only when El Diablo was needed.

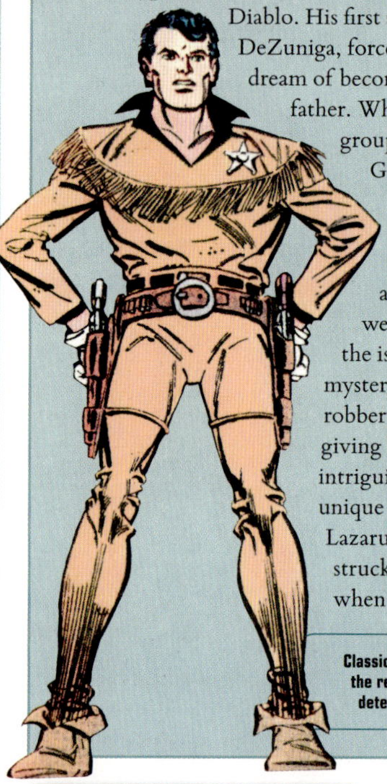

Classic Western hero Pow-Wow Smith kicks off the revival of *All-Star Western* with tales of his detective work as a Native American sheriff.

DASHING PAST 200
***The Flash* #200**

New series artist Irv Novick and writer Robert Kanigher scattered the number 200 throughout this landmark issue of *The Flash*. Foreign spy Dr. Lu brainwashed the Scarlet Speedster into believing that she was his wife, Iris, and that he was picking up a can of hairspray for her. In reality, Flash was unknowingly attempting to assassinate the president of the United States with a laser gun. Thankfully, he snapped out of it just in time after a kiss from Dr. Lu revealed the taste of her lipstick, which wasn't Iris's brand. The Flash sped to Lu's island hideout and rescued his real wife who had been held captive. He then raced around the island 200 times, forcing Lu's explosive missiles to alter their course and obliterate the location.

IN THE REAL WORLD…

June: The United States Military appoints its first female generals.
June: Brazil defeats Italy 4–1 to win the 1970 FIFA World Cup.
September: Rock legend Jimi Hendrix dies in London from alcohol-related complications.
October: Soviet author Aleksandr Solzhenitsyn is awarded the Nobel Prize for Literature.

OCTOBER

JACK KIRBY'S PAL

***Superman's Pal, Jimmy Olsen* #133**

With an entire "Fourth World" saga on the horizon, it was astonishing that the first DC cover to proclaim "Kirby is Here!" was one of DC's poorer-selling titles. Since no ongoing creative team had been slated to *Superman's Pal, Jimmy Olsen*, "King of Comics" Jack Kirby made the title his DC launch point, and the writer/artist's indelible energy and ideas permeated every panel and word balloon of the comic.

Morgan Edge, Galaxy Broadcasting's underhanded media mogul and current owner of the *Daily Planet*, assigned Jimmy to accompany the Newsboy Legion (offspring to the original Newsboy Legion from World War II). Together they traveled to the Wild Area and Habitat, a super-scientific commune for the biker gang known as the Outsiders. Meanwhile, Edge arranged for the criminal organization Intergang to carry out a hit-and-run on Clark Kent in case he asked his "friend" Superman to interfere with Jimmy's assignment. Thankfully, Intergang failed and Superman tracked down Jimmy, who had just bested the Outsiders' leader in combat to take over the biker tribe. Jimmy insisted that Superman did not interfere as he and the Outsiders prepared to ride the otherworldly Zoomway and uncover the mystery behind the mighty Mountain of Judgment. All this, and Kirby's cliffhanger had only scratched the surface on the interlocking series that ultimately formed his "Fourth World" universe.

As the creative legend himself explained in the letter column of this landmark issue, Kirby saw *Superman's Pal, Jimmy Olsen* and his return to DC as a sign of unprecedented times ahead. "This is the place to be, in order to watch the medium lock into our turbulent times and fish for the future," he wrote. "For in that future, comics should be bigger than ever, and the forerunner of newer and more stimulating trends."

Once just a cub reporter and Superman's pal, Jimmy Olsen is now a man of action who is capable of defending himself.

EVERY ROSE HAS HER THORN

***Superman's Girl Friend, Lois Lane* #105**

Rose Forrest had a split personality. Her prickly other half, the Thorn, swore to avenge the murder of her policeman father at the hands of the criminal organization the 100. Although Thorn appeared in the issue's first story as Lois Lane's rescuer, the second feature uncovered the roots of Rose Forrest/Thorn's identity, as told by writer Robert Kanigher and artist Ross Andru. Whenever Rose slept, the vicious, vengeful Thorn awoke and hunted Metropolis's notorious criminal cartel. Neither Rose nor Thorn ever learned of each other's existence, though both retained a strong connection to their father's partner, Detective Daniel Stone.

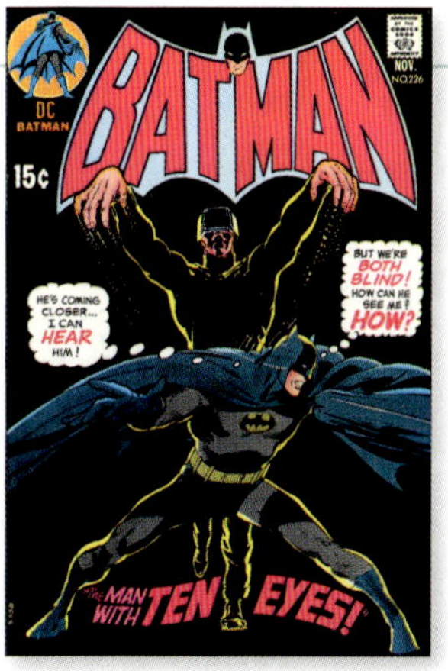

NOVEMBER

THE EYES HAVE IT

***Batman* #226**

Scripter Frank Robbins and artist Irv Novick gave Batman two handfuls of trouble in this issue. A former member of the U.S. Special Forces, Philip "Three-Eye" Reardon was a security guard caught in a warehouse vault explosion after Batman mistook him for a thief. The explosion rendered Batman temporarily sightless, but Reardon was permanently blinded. Fueled by revenge, Reardon underwent radical surgery to connect his optic nerves with each of his fingertips. As the Ten-Eyed Man, Reardon nearly handed Batman a fatal blow, but the Dark Knight disabled one of the abusive appendages and blinded the other with his cape.

DECEMBER

DARKSEID'S RISE

***Superman's Pal, Jimmy Olsen* #134**

He appeared in the issue's second-to-last panel, on a monitor, to chide his minion Morgan Edge. Yet one of Jack Kirby's greatest creations instantly made his ominous presence felt. In Kirby's second issue since returning to DC, Darkseid's debut forever changed the DC Universe and set the writer/artist's "Fourth World" opus fully into motion. According to Kirby historian Mark Evanier, the Lord of Apokolips was modeled physically after actor Jack Palance, though his style and substance "were based on just about every power-mad tyrant Kirby had ever met or observed."

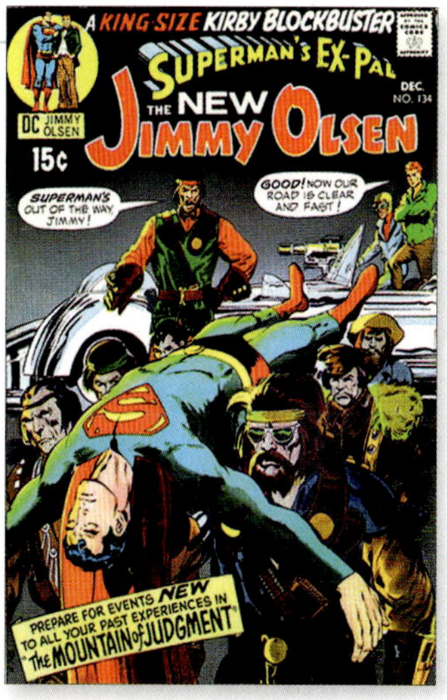

ALSO THIS YEAR: A decidedly darker Batman appeared in January's *DETECTIVE COMICS* #395, writer Denny O'Neil and Neal Adams' first-ever Batman collaboration… The familiar circular DC logo gave way to a simple, rectangular box with "DC" accompanied by the name of the series or its featured character…

November: A tropical cyclone hits the densely populated Ganges Delta region of East Pakistan (now Bangladesh), killing an estimated 500,000 people.

December: The North Tower of the World Trade Center is topped out at 1,368 ft (417 m), making it the tallest building in the world.

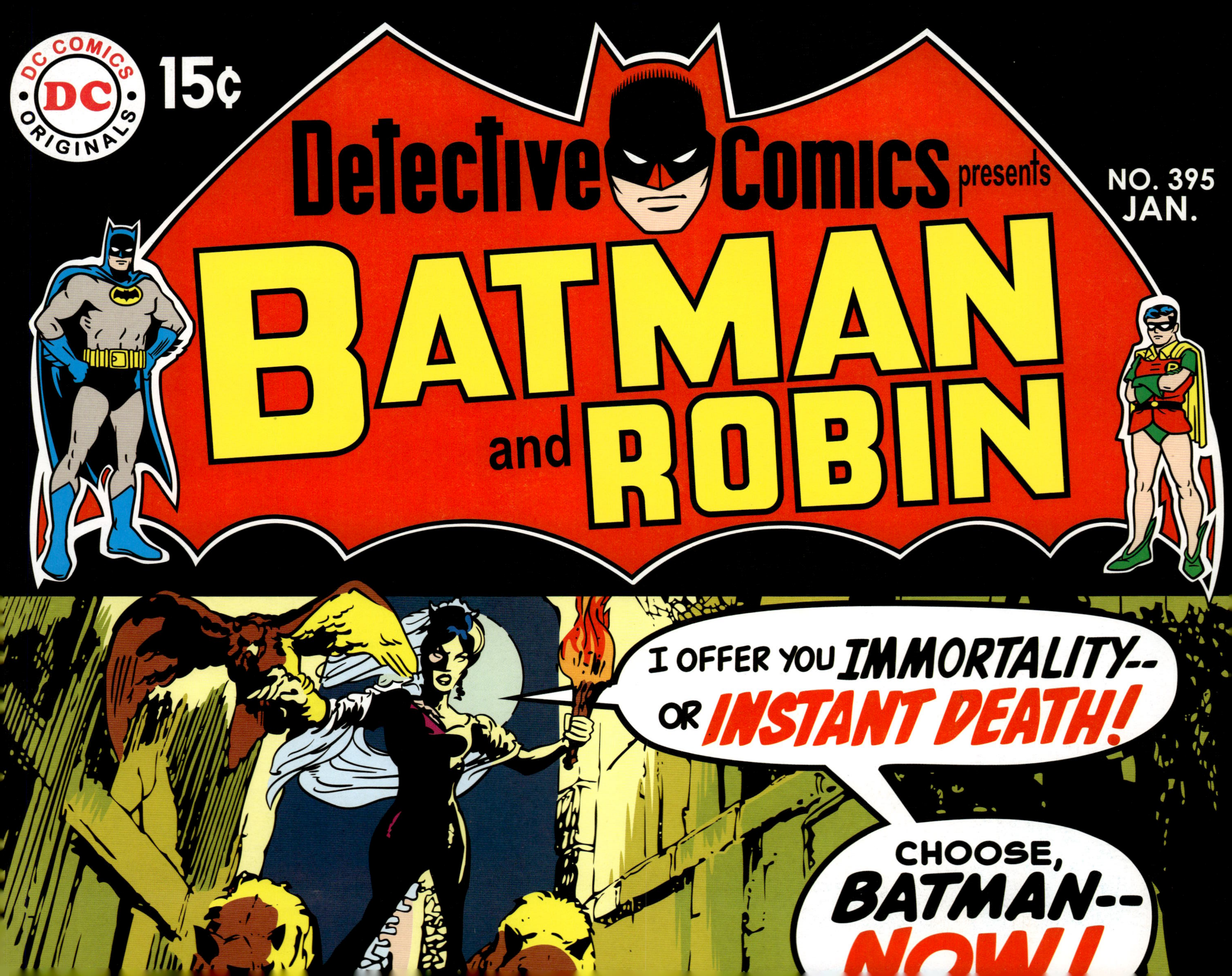
DC COMICS ORIGINALS
DC
15¢
Detective Comics presents
BATMAN and ROBIN
NO. 395
JAN.
I OFFER YOU IMMORTALITY-- OR INSTANT DEATH!
CHOOSE, BATMAN--

GOTHIC MAKEOVER

DETECTIVE COMICS #395 (January 1970)
Artist Neal Adams and writer Dennis O'Neil rescued Batman from the cozy, campy cul-de-sac he had been consigned to in the 1960s and returned the Dark Knight to his roots as a haunted crime fighter. The cover of their first collaboration, "The Secret of the Waiting Graves," was typical of Adams' edgy, spooky style.

1971

"I HAVE HEARD THE WORD—IT IS BATTLE!"

Orion, *New Gods* #1

GODS AND MOBSTERS

It was a year of tremendous excitement for DC Comics as the company appointed editorial director Carmine Infantino as its new publisher. Although decreasing sales and inflation dictated a hefty cover price increase from 15 to 25 cents, Infantino saw to it that extra pages containing classic reprints and new back-up features were added to DC titles.

Moreover, under veteran guidance, a wealth of emerging young storytellers generated new ideas and renewed excitement in DC's existing line. Superman joined Batman under the editorial umbrella of Julius Schwartz, whose creative collaborators produced unforgettable changes and enemies for the comic book world's finest icons. And all of this occurred while Jack Kirby, having laid down basic groundwork in *Superman's Pal, Jimmy Olsen*, introduced his "Fourth World," a celestial opus steeped in science fiction and mythology.

JANUARY

KRYPTONITE NEVERMORE
***Superman* #233**

New editor Julius Schwartz, new scripter Denny O'Neil, and regular artist Curt Swan removed the Man of Steel's greatest weakness from the face of the Earth. When an experiment utilizing green kryptonite as an alternative energy source went awry, it transformed the irradiated fragments from Krypton into harmless iron. However, making the Man of Steel seemingly unstoppable was actually part of a grand scheme to de-power him. The failed experiment also gave life to a three-dimensional sand-based impression of Superman, and over the next several issues it permanently drained the hero of a third of his power.

APRIL

TITLE WAVE
***Aquaman* #56**

Aquaman's series ended as abruptly as writer Steve Skeates and artist Jim Aparo finished off "The Creature that Devoured Detroit!" The "creature" was algae that grew at an uncontrollable rate thanks to a satellite that emitted perpetual artificial sunlight. Don Powers, a former police scientist-turned-vigilante known as the Crusader, had launched the satellite to render criminals incapable of hiding at night and to offset his own increasing blindness. Such literal and figurative shortsightedness led to Powers accidentally falling to his death, while Aquaman ended the ecological danger Powers had created by breaking into the scientist's lab, barricading the door from several guards, and triggering the satellite to self-destruct.

Aquaman fights his way past security to blow up a satellite that has created a growing algae problem.

IN THE REAL WORLD...

February: A new stock-market index called the Nasdaq debuts.
February: Motorcyclist Evel Knievel sets a record by jumping nineteen cars.

APRIL

THE FOURTH WORLD

***Forever People* #1, *New Gods* #1, *Mister Miracle* #1**

As the writer, artist, and editor of the "Fourth World" family of interlocking titles, each of which possessed its own distinct tone and theme, Jack Kirby cemented his legacy as a pioneer of grand-scale storytelling.

DC Comics' "King" launched *Forever People* first, featuring a group of "cosmic hippies" from New Genesis. Aboard their Super-Cycle, Mark Moonrider, Big Bear, Serifan, and Vykin the Black journeyed through a "Boom-Tube" to Earth in search of group-member Beautiful Dreamer, whom the evil Darkseid was holding prisoner. The hippy youths overpowered Darkseid's Gravi-Guards by using their living computer, Mother Box, to summon the powerful being Infinity Man. After rescuing Beautiful Dreamer, the Forever People opted to remain on Earth to oppose Darkseid.

The Forever People weren't the only ones who were Earth-bound, though it took the warrior Orion a few detours to get there in *New Gods* #1. Kirby briefly chronicled how the death of the Old Gods had split their world in two, forming the idyllic utopia New Genesis and the sadistic, dystopian Apokolips. At the behest of his foster parent Highfather and the fiery, handwritten word of the cosmic consciousness known as the Source, Orion set forth to Apokolips, where he battled a slew of Parademons, the rabid Dog Cavalry, and Darkseid's son, Kalibak the Cruel. He also freed several Earthlings who had been abducted by Darkseid and, after hearing Darkseid was on Earth, opened a Boom Tube to Metropolis. There, Orion would prepare to combat Darkseid, who was eventually revealed as his father.

Thaddeus Brown and Oberon watch as Scott Free demonstrates the abilities that will one day define him as the world's greatest escape artist, Mister Miracle.

In Kirby's final "Fourth World" series, *Mister Miracle*, Scott Free was already on Earth having fled Apokolips and the cruel orphanage that raised him to become part of Darkseid's army. By chance, Scott encountered Mister Miracle, an aging escape artist named Thaddeus Brown. Scott worked alongside Brown and his dwarf assistant Oberon to fend off thugs from the criminal organization Intergang, led by Steel Hand. When Brown was murdered by a Steel Hand-hired sniper, Scott used the technological advancements he had brought with him from Apokolips to bring Steel Hand to justice. He then decided to assume the identity of Mister Miracle so that his mentor's legacy would live on.

MAY

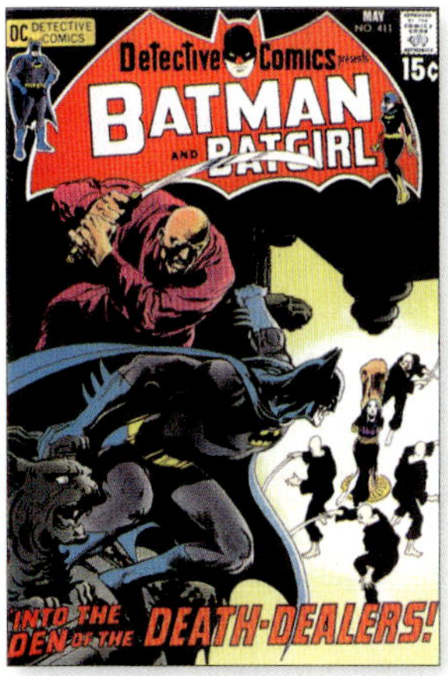

DADDY'S LITTLE GHUL

***Detective Comics* #411**

Before Batman first encountered one of his greatest adversaries, Rā's al Ghūl, he met his daughter, the lovely but lethal Talia. Writer Denny O'Neil and artist Bob Brown put the Dark Knight in pursuit of Dr. Ebenezer Darrk and his League of Assassins. When Batman was overwhelmed by the League's numbers, he was placed in a prison cell with Talia, who Darrk had taken hostage. The pair escaped, but when Darrk made one last attempt at killing Batman, Talia shot Darrk and sent him reeling into the path of an oncoming train.

JUNE

"THE DEMON'S HEAD"

***Batman* #232**

Writer Denny O'Neil once stated that he and artist Neal Adams "set out consciously and deliberately to create a villain… so exotic and mysterious that neither we nor Batman were sure what to expect." Who they came up with was arguably Batman's most cunning adversary: the global eco-terrorist named Rā's al Ghūl.

Rā's, whose name is Arabic for "the Demon's Head," enlisted Batman's help to locate his daughter Talia who, along with Robin, had been abducted by a cult called the Brotherhood of the Demon. The duo worked together to uncover clues that sent them to various locations around the world, their search concluding in a sanctuary within the Himalayan Mountains. There, they rescued Robin and Talia, but it was then that Batman revealed that he had known all along that Rā's had orchestrated the cult kidnappings, though he couldn't determine why. Rā's explained that he had been testing Batman, for he was seeking a worthy successor to someday lead the Brotherhood, as well as a suitable husband for his daughter.

Batman would decline both offers, and thus began his endless rivalry with Rā's. For hundreds of years, Rā's would resurrect himself in life-restoring chemical pools called Lazarus Pits, determined to one day purge the evils humanity has rendered on the planet.

March: Boxer Joe Frazier defeats Muhammad Ali at Madison Square Garden.
March: *The Ed Sullivan Show* airs its final episode on American TV.
May: Amtrak begins an inter-city rail passenger service in the United States.
July: Jim Morrison, lead singer of The Doors, is found dead in his bathtub in Paris.

JULY

AN "UGLY" SITUATION

***Superman's Pal, Jimmy Olsen* #139**

In one of Jack Kirby's strangest tales, Jimmy Olsen met real-world funnyman Don Rickles' costumed likeness, "Goody" Rickels, and Intergang boss Bruno "Ugly" Mannheim. When Ugly abducted Jimmy, the Guardian, and Goody, he hosted a nice sit-down dinner at gunpoint, where he forced his "guests" to dine on food laced with poison. Jimmy and friends would find an antidote before they succumbed to the poison's effects, though Mannheim would continue to rear his "Ugly" head for years to come.

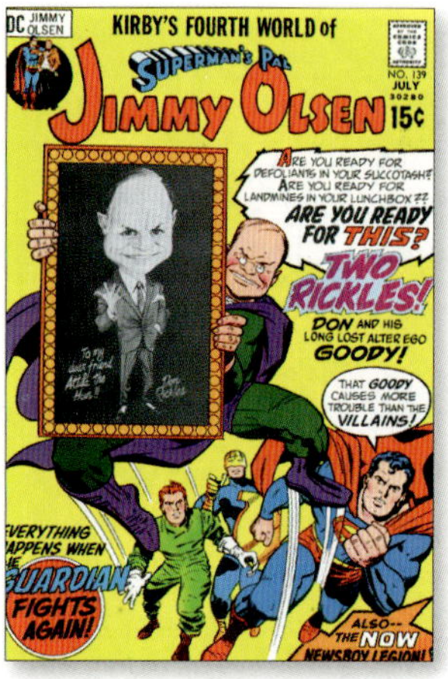

ROOTED IN SUSPENSE

***The House of Secrets* #92**

It was a simple, eight-page gothic tale of romance, betrayal, and tragedy that became one of the best-kept *The House of Secrets* and served as the key fertilizer for one of DC's most beloved tragic figures. "Swamp Thing" was the name of Len Wein and Bernie Wrightson's turn-of-the-century tale, and its popularity with readers led a modernized version of the character into his own series a year later.

Here, the monstrosity formerly known as Alex Olsen lumbered toward a house inhabited by Linda, the love of his life, and Damian, his best friend who claimed Linda's hand months after he murdered and buried Alex in the marsh. The narrative thoughts of Alex, Linda, and Damian recounted their separate tales of love and duplicity until Damian, growing fearful that his wife suspected his treachery, attempted to murder her. The Swamp Thing intervened and crushed the life out of his former friend, but he had no vocal chords to explain his actions or who he was to calm a screaming Linda. Heartbroken, he returned to the marsh, thinking that "if tears could come – they would!"

Swamp Thing crashes through a window to stop the murder of his love, Linda.

SEPTEMBER

ADDICTION HITS HOME

***Green Lantern/ Green Arrow* #85–86**

It was taboo to depict drugs in comics, even in ways that openly condemned their use. However, writer Denny O'Neil and artist Neal Adams collaborated on an unforgettable two-part arc that brought the issue directly into Green Arrow's home, and demonstrated the power comics had to affect change and perception.

The emerald duo first confronted the problem after Green Arrow Oliver Queen was mugged by some strung-out teenagers, one of whom shot him with a crossbow. Recognizing the arrow as one of his own, Queen enlisted Green Lantern to help track down his ward, Speedy, who had been missing for some time. Upon finding Roy Harper associating with the same youths, Green Arrow believed his protégé had been working undercover on his behalf. He was even grateful when Harper rescued him and Green Lantern from a confrontation with drug pushers, which resulted in a drug-induced psychotic episode for the ring-wielder. However, that all changed back at the archer's apartment, where he discovered Roy in the process of shooting up. Unable to cope with his charge being a heroin junkie, Queen threw Roy out of his home.

Green Lantern and Green Arrow would track down and incarcerate the pushers' main supplier, a pharmaceutical CEO named Salomon Hooper, while Roy, with the support of Dinah Lance (Black Canary), went cold turkey to kick his habit. Harper confronted his guardian, explaining that he sought refuge in heroin due to Queen's neglect of him, then argued that society needed to stop attacking the symptom (youths hooked on drugs) and focus more on the disease (the drug suppliers).

A shocked Green Arrow physically vents his disbelief and outrage that his ward, Roy Harper, has become a heroin user.

IN THE REAL WORLD...

July: The 26th Amendment to the United States Constitution, formally certified by President Richard Nixon, lowers the voting age to eighteen.

August: The U.S.S.R. and India sign a twenty-year friendship pact.

September: A cyclone in the Bay of Bengal, in Orissa State in India, kills 10,000.

OCTOBER

KIRBY SPEAKS OUT

***Spirit World* #1, *In the Days of the Mob* #1**

Even amidst the dawning of his "Fourth World" opus, Jack Kirby pushed the proverbial envelope in a series of upscale, provocative magazines aimed at mature audiences. Believing that new formats were necessary for the comic medium to continue evolving, Kirby oversaw the production of what was labeled his "Speak-Out Series" of magazines: *Spirit World* and *In the Days of the Mob*.

The cover copy on *Spirit World* #1 summarized the magazine's tales of "Prophecy! Reincarnation! Haunting! Black Magic!" hosted by paranormalist Dr. E. Leopold Maas. Meanwhile, the inaugural issue of *In the Days of the Mob* featured a framing sequence in Hell with host Warden Fry, and then targeted some of the underworld's biggest guns, including Al Capone, Pretty Boy Floyd, and Ma Barker.

Besides producing most of the writing and artwork for both titles, Kirby also experimented with photo collages and fumetti (photo novels) to tell his stories.

Sadly, these unique magazines never found their desired audience. Newsstands had no idea where to position the tabloid-sized titles, which DC published in black-and-white under a "Hampshire Distributors, Limited" imprint. There would be no second issues of these dramatic departures from Kirby's otherwise cosmic odysseys, despite both titles already having completed stories—many of which would appear in various DC titles in the years ahead.

FOR BARDA OR WORSE

***Mister Miracle* #4**

Mister Miracle battled supervillain Doctor Bedlam with the aid of a voluptuous figure from his past. The volcanic-tempered Big Barda was raised in Granny Goodness' orphanage, like Scott Free, and became leader of Darkseid's female task force. However, it was evident from the way she demolished Bedlam's forces that Barda would do anything to protect Scott. Jack Kirby reportedly modeled the Barda after actress and singer Lainie Kazan, while the dynamic between her and Mister Miracle took tongue-in-cheek inspiration from Kirby's relationship with his wife, Roz. It was therefore understandable that Mister Miracle eventually became Barda's husband.

WAR GETS WEIRD

***Weird War Tales* #1**

With the Comics Code Authority relaxing its decades-long stance on censoring the use of monsters and the undead in mainstream comics, DC placed an emphasis on the horror of combat with *Weird War Tales*. The hybrid genre series was hosted by Death, who appeared in new military garb every issue to present gritty tales of combat with overtones of suspense, science fiction, and paranormal activity. Produced by a who's who of war comic greats, including series editor Joe Kubert, writer Robert Kanigher, and artists Alex Toth and Russ Heath, the series' 124-issue run also introduced readers to cult favorites like the Creature Commandos.

FEAR OF COMMITMENT

***The Dark Mansion of Forbidden Love* #1**

DC merged genres with this occult-gothic romance anthology edited by Dorothy Woolfolk and Ethan Mordden. The first issue, drawn by Tony DeZuniga, followed a woman's investigation into a friend's death as she uncovered sinister spousal secrets and an alarming number of murdered in-laws hidden throughout her marital mansion. Sadly, there just wasn't enough love for the series or *The Sinister House of Secret Love*, its companion title that debuted a month later. The honeymoon lasted only three years for both series.

APPARITIONS ABOUND

***Ghosts* #1**

Disbelievers of spooks and spirits were challenged on the cover of every issue of *Ghosts* to read "True Tales of the Weird and Supernatural." Each installment of the horror anthology series featured stories with surprise twist endings designed to send shivers down the spine. Contributors of the first issue included writer Leo Dorfman and artists Nick Cardy, Jim Aparo, Sam Glanzman, Tony DeZuniga, and Carmine Infantino. *Ghosts* obviously converted a large number of non-believers, as the series haunted newsstands for eleven years and 112 issues.

ALSO THIS YEAR: In November's *JUSTICE LEAGUE OF AMERICA* #94, the League of Assassins assigned the marksman Merlyn to kill Batman, as told by scripter Mike Friedrich and artist Dick Dillin... In December, *MISTER MIRACLE* #5 writer/artist Jack Kirby placed Mister Miracle in a very tight spot, inside Virmin Vundabar's Murder Machine, to rescue Big Barda from Apokolips's surgeon of sadism...

December: Pakistan attacks Indian airbases, beginning the Indo-Pakistani War of 1971.
December: The U.S. dollar is devalued for the second time in history.
December: In the longest game in NFL history, the Miami Dolphins eventually beat the Kansas City Chiefs.

KEEPING IT REAL

Super heroes remained the staple of comic books during the 1970s. The world these heroes inhabited, however, drastically altered from the simpler one of the 1960s. With rock music, television, news, film, and theater more open, permissive, and subversive than ever before, comics began to confront darker, more mature themes and subject matter.

DC Comics understood how different things had become. It was no longer enough for a hero to simply beat up bad guys. Readers wanted their champions to endure problems like their own, with no quick solutions, using powers far beyond those of mortal men.

Like its heroes, DC's villains evolved throughout the decade. Maniacal menaces still abounded; some, like the Joker, Kobra, and the Secret Society of Super-Villains even earned their own series, while Darkseid established himself as the greatest threat both to man and New God. For the most part, however, wearing outlandish costumes and boldly stating evil plans to anyone willing to listen became a thing of the past. The "big bads" now consisted of extreme eco-terrorists, drug kingpins, slumlords, crooked land developers, C.E.O.s, and politicians.

This more socially relevant brand of villainy was best depicted through writer Denny O'Neil and artist Neal Adams' groundbreaking work on 1971 *Green Lantern/Green Arrow*. Though the duo had also been recognized for returning Batman to his Dark Knight roots, their pairing of a model space-cop (Green Lantern) with an outspoken anarchist (Green Arrow) at first seemed the creative equivalent of matching a square peg with a round hole. However, this super hero odd couple provided the perfect point/counterpoint balance between combating alien threats and society's evils. Benefitting from the recent liberalization of the Comics Code, O'Neil and Adams' depiction of Green Arrow's ward, Speedy, as a heroin addict (*Green Lantern/Green Arrow* #85–86, September and November 1971) remains one of comics' seminal and most hard-hitting stories.

This grittier, more realistic approach to storytelling and art didn't translate into sales; in fact, DC endured its greatest crisis as a publisher in the 1970s, due to inflation-fueled costs, a bad economy, and other factors. However, these obstacles motivated the company to take chances creatively. Under the guidance of publisher Carmine Infantino, then Jenette Kahn, DC developed a multitude of titles and characters designed to appeal to a variety of tastes. Readers witnessed the revival of the "Big Red Cheese" Captain Marvel (*Shazam!* #1, February 1973); the rise of a Warlord on a lost world (*1st Issue Special* #8, November 1975); and the creation of new urban street heroes (*Black Lightning* #1, April 1977) and nuclear-powered protagonists (*Firestorm, the Nuclear Man* #1, March 1978). It didn't seem so at the time—especially amid a rash of cancellations that threatened the company's continued existence—but this veritable explosion of innovation would propel DC into one of its greatest-ever decades.

Left: Neal Adams' dramatic cover of Green Lantern/Green Arrow *#86 (November 1971) was an explicit warning against the dangers of heroin. Main pic: the storyline pulled no punches in its depiction of the misery of Speedy's addiction.*

1972

"NEVER SHOW YORE BACK TO A MAN AIMIN' TO KILL YA..."

Jonah Hex, *All-Star Western* #10

BLAZING A TRAIL

Despite its renewed excitement, and a mid-year cover price decrease to 20 cents, DC's line of super hero comics was experiencing uneven sales results in 1972. *Green Lantern/Green Arrow*'s revolutionary run took a four-year hiatus due to lowering sales, while two-thirds of Jack Kirby's much-heralded "Fourth World" titles were canceled after only a year.

Fortunately, the company picked up steam—and readers—with a return to once-beloved genres. Recent revisions made to the Comics Code Authority had provided fewer restrictive mandates regarding horror elements and themes that were more adult-oriented. This immediately opened the creaking door for DC to launch a myriad of suspense, mystery, and horror titles, and the Code's revisions also gave the Western comic a desperately needed resurgence—with a DC twist. DC also found success by purchasing the rights to Edgar Rice Burroughs' most famous creation, Tarzan.

JANUARY

GREEN LANTERN'S BRILLIANT BACK-UP
***Green Lantern/Green Arrow* #87**

An injury to Guy Gardner prompted the Guardians of the Universe to recruit African-American architect John Stewart as Green Lantern Hal Jordan's new back-up. Initially, Jordan didn't much care for Stewart's hostile attitude toward authority figures. However, the substitute Green Lantern proved his worth during a rally held by racist politician Jeremiah Clutcher. He rescued a police officer from a gunman, then proved how Senator Clutcher staged his own assassination attempt to bolster his bid for the presidency. Stewart went on to become one of the Green Lantern Corps' most valued members.

FEBRUARY

FLASHMAN AND THE FURIOUS
***Mister Miracle* #6**

Even the world's greatest escape artist couldn't elude Jack Kirby's marvelously underhanded entrepreneur, Funky Flashman. Donning a fake wig and beard, the conman promoter sought to become Mister Miracle's tour manager. He quickly relinquished the position, however, after Mister Miracle and his friends fended off an attack from the Female Furies. Thinking he could still profit from Mister Miracle, Funky stole his former client's Mother Box. However, this brought upon him the full wrath of the Female Furies, who were tracking their enemies' whereabouts through the living computer.

MARCH

TERRA-MAN FROM THE SKIES
***Superman* #249**

Scripter Cary Bates and artist Curt Swan chose an inopportune time for Superman to meet Terra-Man, a spaghetti Western-garbed menace who rode a winged horse and wielded lethal alien weaponry. The Man of Steel's powers were temporarily out of control due to a genetic bout of deep sorrow that Kryptonians suffered every sixth solar cycle. Fortunately, Superman caught an atomic bullet with his mouth and shot it back into Terra-Man's gun, forcing the weapon to backfire. A back-up tale by Bates and artist Dick Dillin explored Terra-Man's origin and accounted for his lifelong hatred of aliens.

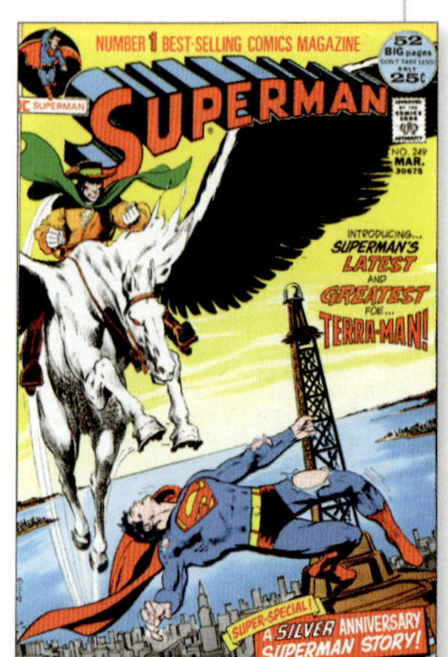

IN THE REAL WORLD...

January: The British Army kills thirteen unarmed nationalist civil-rights marchers in Derry, Northern Ireland ("Bloody Sunday").

MARCH

THE JOY OF HEX
***All-Star Western* #10**

The Western comic had all but ridden off into the sunset, until the arrival of Jonah Hex gave the genre a new face. It was a scarred, horribly disfigured face, but a much-needed one regardless.

A tale written by John Albano and drawn by Tony DeZuniga immediately presented the bounty hunter as a cold-blooded killer. Garbed in a worn Confederate Army uniform, Hex was said to be somewhat modeled after the literary gunslinger of the movie *Shane* and Clint Eastwood's "The Man with No Name" in Western movies. His disfigured facial features were a visual representation of Cain and Abel, with a good side and a bad side. The townspeople of Paradise Falls feared that if they got on Hex's bad side, they wouldn't live long enough to see his better side. Yet they weren't afraid of hiring him to rid the town of Big Jim and his raiders, who terrorized townsfolk by grabbing their land to sell to railroad owners. One by one, Hex gunned down his prey, collecting $100 per head, before eliminating Big Jim himself. He then surprised the town's chief businessmen by donating some of his bounty to pay off the property tax owed by a local widow and her son, whom he had encountered earlier.

Unfortunately, the business owners had an even uglier side than Hex, and refused to sell the "savage" a property on the outskirts of town. Meanwhile, the widow he had just aided threatened to kill him for being a bad influence on her son, who wanted to ride with Hex. The bounty hunter dissuaded the boy from following him, then rode off to his next destination… alone.

An instant hit with fans, Jonah Hex quickly overshadowed the other stars of *All-Star Western*. The series was renamed *Weird Western Tales* two issues later, with the gunslinger riding front and center as the main attraction.

The disfigured bounty hunter Jonah Hex heads off for his latest job—ridding Paradise Falls of Big Jim and his land raiders.

APRIL

THE APE-MAN COMETH

***Tarzan* #207**

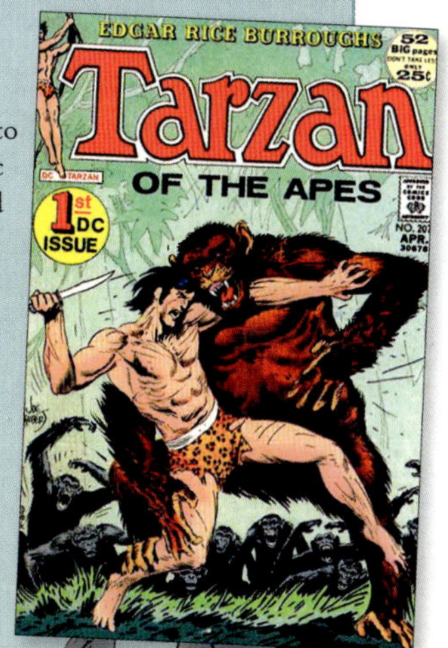

Tarzan enjoyed a prolific period in comics when DC acquired the rights to novelist Edgar Rice Burroughs' iconic ape-man. Much of that success should be attributed to writer, artist, and editor Joe Kubert, a lifelong Tarzan fan whose gritty, expressive style was perfect for the jungle hero.

Kubert's initial issues on *Tarzan* were a faithful adaptation of Burroughs' 1912 novel *Tarzan of the Apes*. After chronicling the origins of the hairless lord of the jungle, Kubert mixed in original Tarzan exploits with further Burroughs adaptations, including *The Return of Tarzan* and *Jungle Tales of Tarzan*.

Other Burroughs creations accompanied the ape-man on his transition to DC, including the title hero of *Korak, Son of Tarzan*. Korak's series also featured tales from Burroughs' *Carson of Venus*, while early issues of *Tarzan* showcased adventures with John Carter, Warlord of Mars, and stories based on *Beyond the Farthest Star*.

Tarzan is a man who can handle rampaging animals, but he longs to share his life with his love, Jane.

DRAWN TO THE LEGION
***Superboy* #184**

After more than a year as Murphy Anderson's background inker, Dave Cockrum landed his big DC break as the *Legion of Super-Heroes'* artist. By this point, waning interest had relegated the Legion to the back pages of *Superboy*. However, Cockrum's debut story, which was written by Cary Bates, quickly established an exciting new vibe for the super-team. Cockrum would go on to redesign the entire 30th Century, including the Legionnaires' costumes and their headquarters.

April: The U.S. and the Soviet Union join some seventy nations in signing an agreement to ban biological warfare.

May: The Magnavox Odyssey video game system is demonstrated, marking the dawn of the video-game age.

JULY

A BUG'S LIFE
***The New Gods* #9**

Writer/artist Jack Kirby presented New Genesis in a morally questionable light by having its New Gods repel a lowlier species. When a society of humanoid bugs raided the New Gods' supply depots out of necessity, the colony's Prime One charged the bug Forager to mediate an alliance with the New Gods. However, a pro-Apokolips bug called Mantis usurped Prime One to wage war against New Gods Lightray and Orion on Earth. Before ritually sacrificing himself to the colony's ruling "All Widow," the deposed Prime One implied that Forager might actually be a New God, then encouraged him to Boom Tube to Earth and make peace with Mantis' foes.

AUGUST

DESTINY'S GUILE
***Weird Mystery Tales* #1**

DC's latest horror anthology didn't enjoy as long a life as the company's other *Weird*-themed titles. However, the host that was first presented in a framing sequence by scribe Marv Wolfman and artist Bernie Wrightson would provide endless creative material for Neil Gaiman's *The Sandman* series decades later. Cloaked in a dark robe and cowl, Destiny's stories came from a large book chained to him, containing events past, present, and future. Despite his blindness, nothing escaped his notice—except, perhaps, the fact that the biblical Eve would replace him as the series' host after fourteen issues.

A VICTORIOUS RETURN
***Justice League of America* #100**

Through an impromptu team-up of the JLA and the Justice Society on Earth-2, writer Len Wein and artist Dick Dillin ushered in the return of DC's Seven Soldiers of Victory. When the villainous Iron Hand threatened to destroy Earth-2 with a similarly named giant appendage, a magical entity called the Oracle urged that victory resided within the decades-missing Soldiers, who had defeated a similar menace with a Nebula Rod before being scattered through time. Over the next three issues, the Soldiers were recovered and reunited by the JLA and JSA. However, stopping the Iron Hand required the Soldier Red Tornado to sacrifice himself.

SEPTEMBER

RISE THE DEMON!
***The Demon* #1**

While his "Fourth World" opus was winding down, Jack Kirby was busy conjuring his next creation, which emerged not from the furthest reaches of the galaxy, but from the deepest pits of Hell. Etrigan was hardly the usual Kirby protagonist battling unspeakable evil, most likely because he *was* evil, though he was often forced to ally with the forces of good by his human guise, Jason Blood.

The series' premiere presented the Demon's origins, which dated back to the final days of Camelot. Merlin the magician had summoned Etrigan to battle the hordes of King Arthur's half-sister, the sorceress Morgaine le Fey, who sought everlasting life from Merlin's tome of spells, the Book of Eternity. Yet as the fall of Camelot appeared imminent, Merlin housed his demon guardian inside the form of a man until needed again. That need would not arise until the 20th century, when demonologist Jason Blood, possessing no knowledge of his demonic self, was tricked into locating Merlin's crypt and reading aloud the rhyming incantation that revived the demon. The deception was orchestrated by a dying Morgaine le Fey, with whom Etrigan would resume his battle before she collected Merlin's Book of Eternity.

Etrigan integrated with DC's mainstream titles, particularly the monster- and horror-themed series that were enjoying their renaissance. However, the Etrigan-Blood duality offered a one-of-a-kind spin that only Kirby could craft. While most comics stories had humans possessed by demonic entities, Kirby reversed the roles with Etrigan, whom Merlin imprisoned within a human vessel. *The Demon* lasted only sixteen issues, but the character of Etrigan has remained a major character in the DC Universe to this day—especially where a good rhyme or devilish deed is concerned.

Confronted by the forces of the sorceress Morgaine le Fey inside Merlin's crypt, Jason Blood utters words from an ancient inscription that free Etrigan, his imprisoned malevolent spirit: "Gone! Gone! The form of Man! Rise, the Demon Etrigan!"

IN THE REAL WORLD...

August: Dictator Idi Amin declares that Uganda will expel 50,000 Asians with British passports to Britain within three months.

September: Eleven Israeli athletes at the 1972 Summer Olympics in Munich are murdered when members of Arab terrorist group Black September invade the Olympic Village.

NOVEMBER

LAST BOY ON EARTH

***Kamandi: The Last Boy on Earth!* #1**

Comic book enthusiasts initially believed Jack Kirby's *Kamandi: The Last Boy on Earth* was DC's way of capitalizing on the popularity of the recent *Planet of the Apes* movies. However, Kirby had already introduced a similar concept and characters for *Alarming Tales* #1 (1957), where mankind had been made extinct in a future ruled by intelligent dogs, rats, and tigers. Coupling the premise with his unpublished 1956 newspaper strip, "Kamandi of the Caves," Kirby's Last Boy on Earth roamed a world that had been ravaged by the "Great Disaster" and taken over by talking animals.

DARK GENESIS

***Swamp Thing* #1**

Following his debut in *House of Secrets* #92 in 1971, the Swamp Thing grew into his own series, albeit with a reimagining of his origins by writer Len Wein and artist Bernie Wrightson. The nefarious Conclave organization strong-armed Dr. Alec Holland to surrender his bio-restorative formula, designed to stimulate plant growth. When Holland resisted, he was blown up in his lab in the Louisiana bayou. Engulfed in flames, the scientist ran into the swamp, which interacted with the bio-restorative formula and generated a marsh-encrusted colossus with Holland's memories. The Swamp Thing couldn't prevent the murder of Holland's wife, Linda, but he would deliver violent retribution against her killers.

(SUPER)GIRL POWER

***Supergirl* #1**

Following a decade of back-up action and three years headlining *Adventure Comics*, Supergirl finally starred in her own series. For the inaugural issue, scribe Cary Bates and artist Art Saaf enrolled Linda Danvers in college. Following the murders of two of her fellow students, Supergirl surmised that drama instructor Basil Rasloff was the killer, for the victims were all in theatrical revivals of films Rasloff had made famous. Supergirl prevented Rasloff's next murder before capturing the deranged instructor. For ten issues, the Maid of Might continued flying solo, albeit with the occasional help of guest stars like Zatanna and Prez, until DC opted to merge her title with several others into the eponymously titled Superman Family.

DECEMBER

A CHANCE ENCOUNTER

***Action Comics* #419**

Starting as a back-up feature in the pages of *Action Comics*, scribe Len Wein and artist Carmine Infantino introduced Christopher Chance, a master of disguise who would turn himself into a human target—provided you could meet his price. Chance wasn't cheap, but he *was* the best. Assuming the identity of chemical tycoon T.C. Newman, Chance set himself up as an assassin's target on a train to San Francisco. Eventually deducing that the killer was disguised as a train conductor, Chance fought the killer atop the train, finally using the emergency brake to send the assassin to his demise.

WONDER WOMAN'S LIB

***Wonder Woman* #203**

The banner atop this issue's cover proclaimed "Special! Women's Lib Issue." In a controversial story by ultramodern sci-fi writer Samuel R. Delany and artist Dick Giordano, readers were prompted to ask: was the issue in favor of the women's movement or against?

The story reunited Diana Prince with her former boutique shop assistant, Cathy Perkins, who was now part of a women's liberation group. When Philip Grandee, a rich department store owner, paid Diana to model his new liberated women's clothing line, Cathy's group advised against it. Explaining how Grandee paid his all-female staff poor wages and bought goods from sweatshops, they asked Diana to join their cause. After Grandee paid thugs to break up the group and abduct Cathy, Wonder Woman did help the group and brought Grandee to justice, though it was a mixed victory. A contingent of ladies stormed into a group meeting to complain how Wonder Woman's actions had closed Grandee's store and left many women unemployed.

A story was proposed to follow up on this dangling storyline. However, with another radical new direction looming for Wonder Woman, it was never published.

Diana Prince springs into action when Mr. Grandee's guard dogs go on the attack.

ALSO THIS YEAR: In September's *THE FLASH* #217, while writer Len Wein and artist Irv Novick helped Barry Allen figure out how Professor Ira West's computer split him into five Flashes, scribe Denny O'Neil and artist Neal Adams put Green Lantern on the trail of his buddy Green Arrow, who disappeared after accidentally killing a gang member… Filmation's *THE BRADY KIDS*—Greg, Marcia, Peter, Jan, Bobby, and Cindy—shared adventures with Superman and Wonder Woman in their respective animated TV series…

October: The first publication reporting the production of an artificial DNA molecule marks the birth of modern molecular biology methodology.

November: The last executions by guillotine in France take place in Paris.
December: International Human Rights Day is proclaimed by the United Nations.

1973

"CRIMINALS... RUNNING AWAY FROM THE POLICE! I SEE THINGS HAVEN'T CHANGED MUCH IN THE TWENTY YEARS I'VE BEEN AWAY!"

Captain Marvel, *Shazam!* #1

LIGHTNING STRIKES

DC enjoyed an abundance of success in 1973, even if it wasn't reflected by a spike in sales. Other factors dictated the publisher's triumphs, not the least of which was the licensing of several of DC's characters for television. With the World's Greatest Heroes and the renderings of lead character designer Alex Toth, Hanna-Barbera launched the popular cartoon super-team *Super Friends*. Another hit came from DC's utterance of a single word: "Shazam!" The result was a lightning strike that charged a generation of readers to discover a marvel that hadn't been seen in twenty years. Even better, Captain Marvel also brought along his family, friends, and foes. The third factor boiled down to DC's growing diversity in characters, creators, and stories. By year's end, readers had been introduced to a re-powered Wonder Woman, a teenaged president, a Demon child, a resurrected hunter, and even Superman, Jr. and Batman, Jr.

JANUARY

ARCANE SCIENCE
***Swamp Thing* #2**

Attacking the moss-matted mutation of Alec Holland, a horde of misshapen "Un-Men" transported him to the Transylvania castle home of their creepy creator—the immortality-obsessed Anton Arcane. Arcane offered to use his mystic soul jar to restore Holland's human form in return for Swamp Thing's powerful body. However, upon learning that Arcane wanted to destroy a nearby Balkan village, the defiant Swamp Thing knocked the mad scientist out of a tower window. The Un-Men loyally followed Arcane to his seeming death, though scribe Len Wein and artist Bernie Wrightson left Swamp Thing some company: Arcane's brother Gregori, aka the Frankenstein's monster-modeled Patchwork Man, and the woman who would become Swamp Thing's soul mate, Abigail Arcane.

FEBRUARY

BACK IN POWER
***Wonder Woman* #204**

After nearly five years of Diana Prince's non-powered super-heroics, writer/editor Robert Kanigher and artist Don Heck restored Wonder Woman's… well, wonder. Diana was left a hospitalized amnesiac when a sniper struck her in the skull after killing her mentor, I-Ching. Despite her injury, Diana's homing instinct kicked in and she commandeered a military craft to make her way to Paradise Island. There, the Amazons restored her powers and memories and Diana resumed her role as Wonder Woman.

A rooftop sniper guns down Diana Prince's mentor, I-Ching. In his final moments, a tearful Diana says farewell to the father she never had.

IN THE REAL WORLD...

January: The United Kingdom, the Republic of Ireland, and Denmark enter the European Economic Community (now the European Union).

FEBRUARY

WITH ONE MAGIC WORD
Shazam! #1

Ending his hiatus from comics since the early 1950s, Captain Marvel made a triumphant return in his own all-new, ongoing franchise. One word—*Shazam!*—revived the "Big Red Cheese" and allowed him to re-emerge in print for the first time ever as a character in a DC Comics publication.

Beginning in 1941, DC had engaged in a years-long legal dispute with Fawcett Publications, the original home of Captain Marvel and his alter ego Billy Batson. DC had alleged copyright infringement for Captain Marvel's similarities to its iconic flagship character, Superman. Sadly, not Solomon's wisdom, Hercules' strength, Atlas' stamina, Zeus' power, Achilles' courage, or Mercury's speed could hasten or eclipse the litigation. The lawsuits dragged on for years, until finally, in 1952, Fawcett agreed to never again publish the character, putting Cap out of print.

A Silver Age renaissance of super hero comics thankfully forged an opportunity for the Marvelous mortal to be reborn. In 1972, DC acquired the rights to Captain Marvel and in 1973 they launched the series *Shazam!*, which re-established the Captain Marvel mythos. The premier issue's cover featured the returning Captain Marvel alongside Superman himself—ironically delivering closure for the two alike characters so long debated. Responsible for resurrecting the lightning-charged champion, writer Denny O'Neil and original artist C.C. Beck together explained Cap's absence. The entire Marvel Family and other key characters had been snared within a compound-created globe of suspendium for twenty years—as had their captors, the Sivana Family, due to a mishap. That is, until this most fortuitous of events, which bore their ultimate liberation from the time freeze and reactivated the series' cast and the World's Mightiest Mortal.

No longer trapped within the Sivana Family's globe of suspendium—or the twenty-year litigation between Fawcett Publications and DC Comics—a jubilant Captain Marvel takes to the skies once more.

MARCH

FANTASTIC LORE

Sword of Sorcery #1

Fantasy became a DC Comics reality when writer/editor Denny O'Neil and artist Howard Chaykin brought forth a new comic based on novelist Fritz Leiber's adventurous and virtuous warriors of myth, Fafhrd the Barbarian and the Gray Mouser. After making their comics debut less than a year earlier in *Wonder Woman* #201–202, the heroic pair of towering brute Fafhrd and cunning thief Mouser ravaged the medium in *Sword of Sorcery*.

O'Neil and Chaykin's collaborative effort featured precise adaptations of Leiber's work, including the story "The Price of Pain Ease" in the first issue, as well as original tales. With these storytelling masters working together, DC produced a flawless portrait of two very dissimilar companions on a bold, nomadic journey. Welcoming adventure of all kinds, the seven-foot, sword-swinging Fafhrd and his far more diminutive, sorcery-trained companion, Mouser, traveled the most rugged terrain of the mythical world of Nehwon.

Comic book loyalists and fans of the fantastic converged to read of Fafhrd and the Gray Mouser's conflicts with beasts, plunderers, wizards, and much more until *Sword of Sorcery*'s final issue in December 1973.

Fritz Leiber's adventurers, Fafhrd the Barbarian and the sorcery-trained Gray Mouser, find trouble everywhere they journey throughout Nehwon.

LITTLE HELLION
The Demon #7

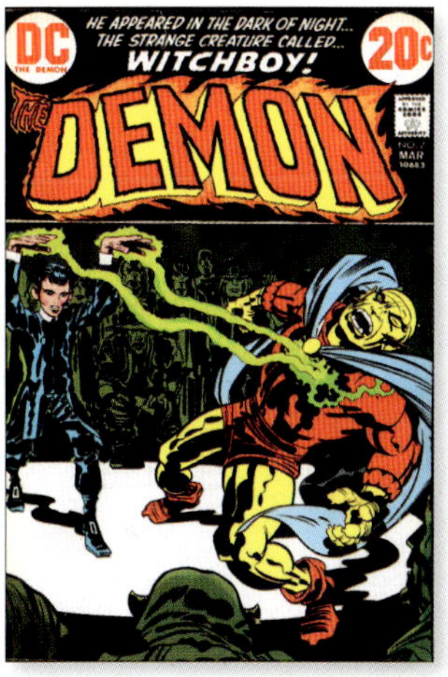

Growing up is tough for most kids, but Klarion the Witchboy made it pure hell for Jason Blood and Etrigan in *The Demon* #7. As told by Jack Kirby, the permanently prepubescent mage and his mystical cat Teekl fled their "beyond country" home and sought sanctuary from "Uncle" Jason (there was no relation). Although Klarion was powerful enough to control Blood and Etrigan, he needed them to rescue him after being captured and put on trial by his own people. Etrigan then cast Klarion and Teekl to an unknown place where they could do no harm, though it wasn't far enough to stop the rotten kid from turning up again and making himself a nuisance in future issues.

January: Elvis Presley's concert in Hawaii, the first worldwide telecast by an entertainer, is watched by more people than the Apollo moon landings.

March: Pink Floyd's landmark rock album *The Dark Side of the Moon* is released.
April: The first handheld cellular phone call is made in New York City.

AUGUST

SEEDED IN MYSTERY

***Adventure Comics* #428**

Very little was known about the Black Orchid, even after writer Sheldon Mayer and artist Tony DeZuniga presented her so-called "origin issue" in *Adventure Comics*. Black Orchid's true identity would remain a secret during her three-issue stint. While she rescued District Attorney Ken Ransom from hired killers and gathered evidence against the crooked politicians who killed his brother, readers garnered only these few facts: she was super-strong, nearly invulnerable, able to fly, and a master of disguise.

MIRTHY KILLING

***Batman* #251**

After decades as an irritating prankster, Batman's greatest enemy re-established himself as a homicidal harlequin in this issue. Joker Venom and explosive cigars were part of the maniac's wrathful repertoire used against members of his former gang. When Batman rescued the last henchman from a shark tank within the Joker's aquarium hideout, the Joker almost evaded capture, but in typical slapstick fashion he slipped in sand. All kidding aside, this classic tale by writer Denny O'Neil and artist Neal Adams introduced a dynamic that remains to this day: the Joker's dependence on Batman as his only worthy opponent.

ON TV THIS MONTH: Hanna-Barbera animated the adventures of Superman, Batman and Robin, Wonder Woman, and Aquaman with the launch of ABC-TV's Saturday morning show *SUPER FRIENDS* (which assumed a multitude of names throughout its thirteen-year run)...

Black Orchid's "origin issue" reveals little about the masked hero, but she does seem to enjoy shaking a group of hitmen out of their vehicle.

SEPTEMBER

COMMANDER-IN-BRIEF

***Prez* #1**

Teenage President of the United States Prez Rickard didn't enjoy a long term in comics. However, scripter Joe Simon and artist Jerry Grandenetti gave him plenty to tackle in four issues, the first of which chronicled his rise to power. Satirical, subversive, and downright surreal, the issue posed the quandary of politics corrupting youthful idealism, with Prez being endorsed for a senate seat by the crooked Boss Smiley. Thankfully, Prez discovered the truth about his benefactor and the youth of America rocked the vote, making Prez "The Man."

"WHEN I WAS BORN, MY MOM SAID, 'SOMEDAY THIS BABY WILL BE PRESIDENT.' SO SHE NAMED ME PREZ."

Prez Rickard, *Prez* #1

OCTOBER

EARTH-X MARKS THE SPOT

***Justice League of America* #107**

The annual Justice League-Justice Society get-together resulted in scribe Len Wein and artist Dick Dillin transporting both teams to the alternate reality of Earth-X. There, Nazi Germany ruled after winning a prolonged World War II and only a group of champions called the Freedom Fighters remained to oppose the regime. Together with the JLA and JSA they halted the Nazis' dominance over Earth-X's population, with the JLA's Red Tornado discovering and disabling the regime's sentient computer. This finally gave the Freedom Fighters autonomy to rebuild their world.

PLOP! CULTURE

***Plop!* #1**

Edited by Joe Orlando with contributions from comics' finest creators, *Plop!* was truly "The Magazine of Weird Humor!" Hosted by Cain, Abel, and Eve, the bizarre anthology's first issue showcased the hilarity of dungeon life in writer/artist Sergio Aragones' "The Escape!"; monster-sized amusement with scribe Frank Robbins, artist George Evans, and "Kongzilla"; ghost-plagued TV reception from Sheldon Mayer and Alfredo Acala in "The Message"; and tasty amphibian retribution in "The Gourmet," by writer Steve Skeates and artist Bernie Wrightson. From the lavish covers of Basil Wolverton and Wally Wood to one-page gags and stories too peculiar for even the likes of a *MAD* magazine, *Plop!* lived—and, after twenty-four issues, died—by its own macabre rules.

IN THE REAL WORLD...

June: Soviet leader Leonid Brezhnev addresses the American people on television, the first Soviet leader to do so.

September: In "The Battle of the Sexes," Billie Jean King defeats Bobby Riggs 6–4, 6–4, 6–3 in a televised tennis match at the Astrodome in Houston, Texas.

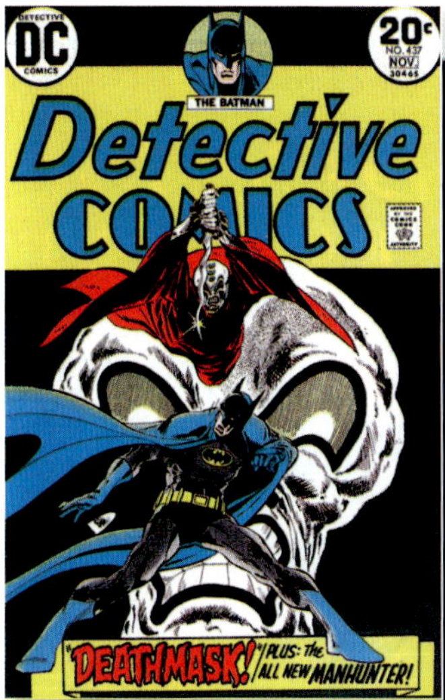

NOVEMBER

MANHUNTER REBORN
***Detective Comics* #437**

When writer Archie Goodwin replaced Julius Schwartz as the editor of *Detective Comics*, he also placed an inspired new spin on the Golden Age Manhunter. Together with exciting new artist Walt Simonson, Goodwin executed seven flawless tales that chronicled Paul Kirk's hunt for the world's deadliest game.

His Golden Age background aside, this incarnation of Manhunter boasted a uniqueness both in his munitions (which included a Katara dagger and Mauser firearm) and his costumed appearance. Intended as a visual foil to *Detective Comics'* premier champion, Batman, Manhunter wore bright hues of red and white—a stark contrast to the Dark Knight's grim, cool shades of grey. Furthermore, the skilled weapons specialist wore his proficiency on the chest of his high-pointed shoulder shroud, where rested the symbol of another key component to his arsenal: Shuriken throwing stars.

In this issue, readers were reintroduced to Paul Kirk through Christine St. Clair, an Interpol agent assigned to track down the former big-game hunter. Believed dead since the 1940s, Kirk had actually been preserved via cryogenics and, thus, resurrected by a clandestine society known as the Council. Augmented by his superior healing ability, Kirk's intensive martial arts training made him the perfect weapon, yet he was never more than a pawn for the Council to play its despotic hand.

The most prolific product of the Council's efforts became its greatest foe, as the moral Manhunter rebelled, vowing to terminate the clan and their plot to generate the ultimate military for their own wicked gain. The battle concluded in issue #443, with Manhunter and the Batman teaming together at last to defeat the Council. Although the story ended with the demise of Paul Kirk, Manhunter's award-winning revival earned undying acclaim for its talented storytellers.

Thirty years after his death, Paul Kirk is revived by the mysterious Council to stalk the world's most dangerous game as Manhunter.

NOVEMBER

SERIAL THRILLER
***The Shadow* #1**

Writer Denny O'Neil and artist Mike Kaluta presented their atmospheric interpretation of writer Walter B. Gibson's pulp-fiction mystery man of the 1930s. In the series' inaugural issue, the Shadow posed as wealthy socialite Lamont Cranston in order to trick Wall Street broker Osgood Bamber into confiding in him. By doing so, the Shadow and his crime-solving partner Margo Lane foiled a robbery orchestrated by the villain.

DECEMBER

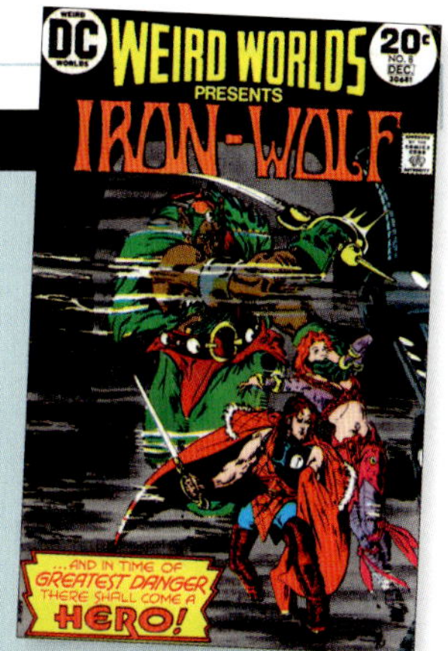

CHAYKIN'S CURTAIN CALL

***Weird Worlds* #8**

As the cover of *Weird Worlds* #8 proclaimed, in a time of greatest danger, there came a hero. With sword tight in grip, Iron-Wolf, a Shakespeare-inspired space traveler, exploded into the realm of comics, combating creatures of all kinds and rescuing a slew of damsels from a most grim demise. Immediately after the debut tale by acclaimed artist Howard Chaykin and co-scripter Denny O'Neil, Iron-Wolf became the lead protagonist in the *Weird Worlds* franchise, which highlighted the intergalactic outlaw's heroic bouts with leviathans, ogres, and other equally grotesque repulsions.

However, Iron-Wolf's final battle would take place after only three installments. Between dwindling sales and the fact that the title's earlier Edgar Rice Burroughs-based features had not proved cost-effective, DC discontinued publication of *Weird Worlds* with its tenth issue in November 1974. The series would be one of Chaykin's final long-term undertakings with the company, until his return on *World of Krypton* six years later.

The outlaw Iron-Wolf has no superpowers, but he is a master swordfighter and skilled gunman.

ALSO THIS MONTH/YEAR: Scribe Bob Haney and artist Dick Dillin introduced the DC Universe to an alternate timeline starring the World's Finest offspring in January's *WORLD'S FINEST COMICS* #215... ERG-1 vied for Legion membership in June, though according to writer Cary Bates and artist Dave Cockrum in *SUPERBOY* #195, the future Wildfire had a self-destructive ability that made him "The One-Shot Hero!"...

November: The U.S. Congress overrides President Richard Nixon's veto of the War Powers Resolution, which limits presidential power to wage war without congressional approval.

December: Spanish Prime Minister Luis Carrero Blanco is assassinated in Madrid by the terrorist organization ETA.

1974

"MY HALF OF DUO DAMSEL IS MY BRIDE-TO-BE! YOU CAN'T TURN HER OVER TO THE VILLAINOUS STARFINGER!"

Bouncing Boy, *Superboy starring the Legion of Super-Heroes* #200

SINNERS AND LOSERS

Inflation was a growing problem in 1974, and skyrocketing costs had been affected by global shortages in fuel, energy, and raw materials—the last of which included the lifeblood of publishers: paper. To help combat its own growing costs, DC Comics condensed the width of its books, and reduced the total amount of books produced by more than 25 percent. A portion of that drastic drop-off, however, was attributed to a huge increase in 100-page super-spectaculars and giants. For example, marrying Superman's supporting cast into one *Superman Family* series saved publishing costs on three individual titles alone.

Furthermore, the company slightly modified its logo, adding the words "The Line of DC Super Stars," of which there remained many. Among them was a more terrifying incarnation of the Spectre than readers were used to; a One Man Army Corps; and a group of World War II Losers.

JANUARY

SNOOZE ALARMIST
***The Sandman* #1**

The legendary tandem of writer Joe Simon and artist/editor Jack Kirby reunited for a one-shot starring the Sandman. Unlike the titular crime-buster they regularly partnered on for *Adventure Comics* in the 1940s, this Sandman was the mythological master of the Dream Dimension. Aided by the nightmarish Brute and Glob, he protected young Jed Paulsen and our reality from the computer-brained menace General Electric. Despite the issue's popularity, it would be Simon and Kirby's last collaboration. The series continued featuring Kirby and other creators before being put to bed in 1976.

From inside his Dream Dome, the Sandman closely monitors the nightmarish activity that threatens young Jed Paulsen as he sleeps.

FEBRUARY

NEW PLAYER-HATER
***Action Comics* #432**

Jack Nimball was a small-time player in crime until he usurped the mantle and methods of the Toyman from retired predecessor Winslow Schott. Writer Cary Bates and artist Curt Swan gave Superman all the "fun" he could handle with the savvy new Toyman in *Action Comics* #432, until Schott interceded. Getting his game on one more time, the former Toyman aided the Man of Steel in ending Nimball's playtime.

Nimball didn't enjoy too many play dates in Superman lore; Schott murdered him and reclaimed the Toyman name in *Superman* #305. However, Nimball's incarnation of the Toyman would enjoy a longer animated life with the Legion of Doom on ABC-TV's *Challenge of the Super Friends*.

IN THE REAL WORLD...

February: The long-running daily comic strip "Sazae-san" is published in Japanese newspaper Asahi Shimbun for the final time.

FEBRUARY

SOMETHING "BORROWED"

Superboy starring the Legion of Super-Heroes #200

A milestone event that represented a growing maturity in the 30th Century's teenaged super-team, Bouncing Boy and Duo Damsel became the first Legionnaires to tie the knot. The wedding planners were writer Cary Bates and artist Dave Cockrum, whose tale-telling tenure had reinvigorated the Legion. Amid new costumes, new members, and re-envisioned galaxies, the team's popularity had soared to the point that Superboy had become a guest star in his own series, even for his landmark 200th issue.

That said, the Boy of Steel would play a significant hand in the issue's story. Bouncing Boy discovered that he was losing his self-expanding ability, but rather than feel deflated, Chuck Taine popped the question to his sweetheart(s), Duo Damsel, who answered him with an enthusiastic yes. The happy couple would experience one significant hitch before getting hitched, however: Duo Damsel had become half the woman she once was. Her duplicate was believed killed by a monstrous bird of prey, but the truth came to light during the wedding ceremony. Legion nemesis Starfinger burst in, holding the other Duo Damsel as his captive. Forcing the Legionnaires to surrender their half of Duo Damsel, Starfinger tried to use Duo Damsel's cloning ability to create a legion of Starfingers. However, his first effort was actually Superboy in disguise, who knocked out the villain and allowed the separated Damsels in distress to rejoin. The happily wed couple then left the Legion, though the void they left would be filled by the popular Legionnaire Wildfire two issues later.

Surrounded by fellow Legionnaires amid the beautiful backdrop of Nix Olympica on Mars, Luornu Durgo (Duo Damsel) and Chuck Taine (Bouncing Boy) are finally proclaimed husband and wife.

THE GREATS OF WRATH

***Adventure Comics* #431**

Four years since his last appearance in a DC title, the Spectre re-materialized in the pages of *Adventure Comics*. This time, however, he brought along an all-out wrathful disposition, delivering punishments that not only fit the crimes, but arguably exceeded them.

In an interview in *The Amazing World of DC Comics*, editor Joe Orlando attributed a mugging in New York City to the Spectre's latest incarnation. The crime had filled Orlando with a "feeling of helplessness and anger" that inspired his "Walter Mitty idea of fantasy revenge." Therefore, he recruited writer Michael Fleisher and artist Jim Aparo to help the Spectre exact such reprisal against criminals.

Fleisher and Aparo's run lasted only ten issues, yet it was widely regarded as some of their finest work, and the character's seminal period. It has been argued that the series' horrific tone was the reason for its brevity. The debut story demonstrated the Astral Avenger's gruesome notions of payback when he melted a murderous armored car robber's gun, then his hands, followed by the rest of him, like wax.

The Spectre's new warped idea of retribution leads to him melting a killer's gun, then the killer himself.

MARCH

ON TV THIS MONTH: Cathy Lee Crosby donned a star-spangled jumpsuit and protected Man's World in an unlikely *WONDER WOMAN* TV-movie pilot, which aired on ABC-TV...

MAY

ONE BIG, HAPPY FAMILY

***Superman Family* #164**

DC's 100-page Super Spectaculars were proving popular, so DC said goodbye to *Supergirl*, *Superman's Pal, Jimmy Olsen*, *Superman's Girl Friend, Lois Lane*, and housed the characters together in *Superman Family*. Continuing the numbering from where *Superman's Pal, Jimmy Olsen* ended, the series featured classic reprints with new tales in the lead spot. The series' 100-page format was short-lived, and its characters would come and go, but *Superman Family* as a whole stayed strong, lasting eight years and a total of fifty-nine issues.

February: The United Kingdom general election results in an almost dead heat, but Labour Party leader Harold Wilson becomes Prime Minister again by a narrow margin.

April: ABBA wins the annual Eurovision Song Contest in Brighton, England.
June: The Universal Product Code is scanned for the first time.

MAY

WILD BEAUTY
***Rima, the Jungle Girl* #1**

Hot topics like environmental activism in the real world provided ideal timing for Rima, the Jungle Girl to swing into comics. Her series chronicled the adventures of the statuesque Venezuelan "bird girl" and Abel, the explorer she loved. *Rima, the Jungle Girl* lasted only seven issues, with Robert Kanigher credited as writer for the final three. However, editor Joe Kubert's gorgeous covers, plus the untamed beauty of South America's wildlife and flora, as accentuated by famed Filipino artist Nestor Redondo, were unforgettable.

JUNE

A BALANCED ASSAULT

***Justice League of America* #111**

Through the words of scripter Len Wein and the art of Dick Dillin, the masked menace of Libra established himself as a grave threat to the World's Greatest Heroes. First, he gathered Poison Ivy, the Tattooed Man, Chronos, Shadow Thief, Mirror Master, and the Scarecrow to form the original Injustice Gang of the World. Then, from their own satellite headquarters orbiting Earth (opposite the JLA's, of course), Libra insisted that the gang's evil would balance the scales, and that they would succeed as a team where individually they had failed.

What the Injustice Gang didn't know, however, was that their leader had been using them for his own insidious purposes. Knowing his team would fall before the might of the Justice League, Libra supplied them with an energy device that rendered the JLA members unconscious. Then, holding the heroes captive in Injustice Gang headquarters, Libra siphoned half of their powers and abilities, finally turning his energy device on the entire universe in order to make himself a god. Libra succeeded all too well—in fact, his device absorbed so much energy that his body couldn't sustain it. Libra evaporated into nothingness, while the Justice Leaguers were forced to siphon back their powers in the following issue.

Superman's powers have been sapped by an energy device created by the mysterious Libra.

JULY

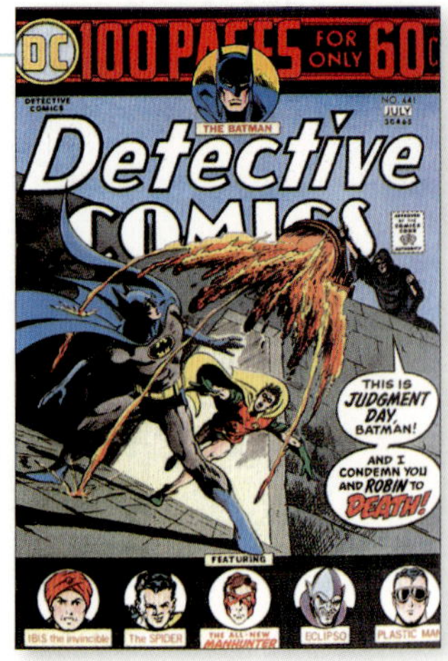

JUDGE, FURY, AND EXECUTIONER
***Detective Comics* #441**

Justice was blind in this tale by writer/editor Archie Goodwin and artist Howard Chaykin, during which a gavel-waving menace called the Judge kidnapped and attempted to slay Robin. The villain's motive was revenge. Years earlier, in a summer resort, Batman's struggle with a masked killer had ended with a stray bullet that caused the Judge's daughter to lose her sight. Evading multiple death traps around the now-abandoned resort, Batman rescued Robin and captured the Judge, who was finally revealed as the killer who had accidentally blinded his daughter.

FANBOYS UNITE!
***The Amazing World of DC Comics* #1**

Recognizing its hardcore fan base, DC published the inaugural installment of its new mail-order "pro-zine"—an in-house fanzine that celebrated the company's diverse history, interviewed top creators and editors, and promoted current and upcoming projects. Staffed mostly by DC's editorial assistants, the premier issue included an interview with Joe Kubert; traveled back to the 1950s and the set of TV's *Adventures of Superman*; and ran Jack Kirby's ten-page "Murder, Inc.," a story intended for the unpublished second issue of Kirby's *In the Days of the Mob*. Lasting four years and seventeen issues, The Amazing World of DC Comics was considered the perfect source for DC fans who always wanted more.

AUGUST

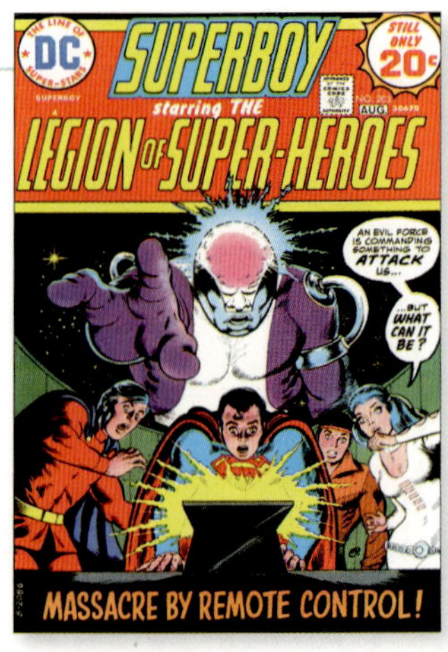

WE NEVER SAW IT COMING
***Superboy Starring The Legion of Super-Heroes* #203**

With the unenviable task of replacing a departing Dave Cockrum, one of the most popular artists ever to draw the Legion of Super-Heroes, Mike Grell's first issue on *Superboy Starring The Legion of Super-Heroes* killed off one of the team's most beloved members. Grell and writer Cary Bates caught both the Legion and its fans off guard when the monster Validus invaded Legion headquarters and wreaked havoc. Lyle Norg, a.k.a Invisible Kid, deduced that Validus was being controlled by Legion arch-foe Tharok, even though components from the villainous cyborg's electronic brain seemingly lay dormant within the team's headquarters. Tragically, Validus crushed Invisible Kid just as he destroyed the components.

"G-GOT TO DESTROY THE BRAIN... IT'S THE ONLY WAY TO SET VALIDUS FREE FROM ITS EVIL CONTROL!"

Invisible Kid, *Superboy starring the Legion of Super-Heroes* #203

IN THE REAL WORLD...

August: French acrobat Philippe Petit walks across a high wire slung between the twin towers of the World Trade Center in New York City.

August: President Richard Nixon becomes the first U.S. President to resign from office, in a move to avoid being impeached in response to his role in the Watergate scandal.

SEPTEMBER

ON TV THIS MONTH: *SHAZAM!* **became the popular word on Saturday-morning television in Filmation's first live-action series, which starred Captain Marvel and ran on CBS-TV until 1977...**

OCTOBER

THE BUDDY SYSTEM
***OMAC* #1**

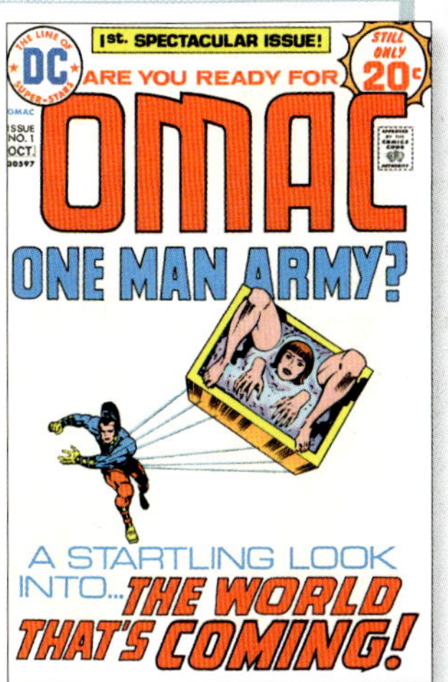

In *OMAC*'s first issue, editor/writer/artist Jack Kirby warned readers of "The World That's Coming!," a future world containing wild concepts that are almost frighteningly real today. Buddy Blank, a nondescript employee at Build-A-Friend factory Pseudo-People, Inc., was chosen by the Global Peace Agency to restore calm in a world that could not afford violence. Transformed into a super-peacekeeper named OMAC (One Man Army Corps) by a sentient satellite, Blank destroyed Pseudo-People, Inc.—and his love, Lila, the "Build-A-Friend" woman who he was shocked to find was literally made for him.

When Buddy Blank is transformed into an unstoppable One Man Army Corps, he discovers that his employer Pseudo-People, Inc. is sending out its "Build-A-Friend" models for assassinations.

NOVEMBER

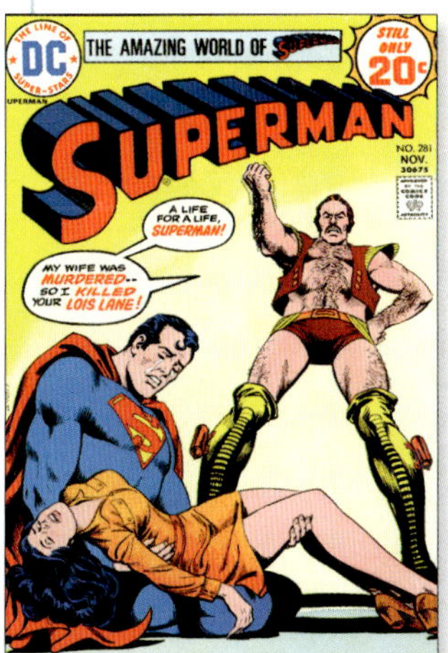

HYPER-ACTIVE IMAGINATION
***Superman* #281**

Fans of John Boorman's 1974 sci-fi film *Zardoz*, starring Sean Connery in revealing red spandex, could appreciate writer Cary Bates and artist Curt Swan's inspiration for Vartox of Valeron. A hyper-powered protector from another galaxy, Vartox came to Earth after the death of his wife, Elyra, who had been psychically linked to a Metropolis woman gunned down by robber Frank Sykes. A "time-scanscope" revealed that Vartox's attempts at retribution would lead to the accidental death of Lois Lane. So, he extradited Sykes to his world, then aged him six decades within minutes, making justice incredibly swift.

NOVEMBER

LOSERS WIN WITH KIRBY
***Our Fighting Forces* #151**

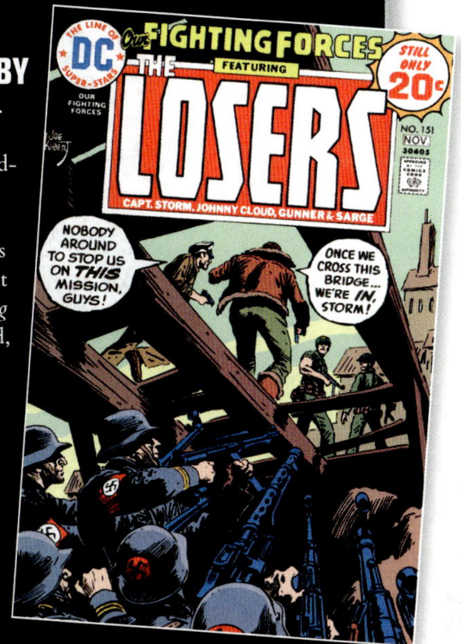

While he developed a plethora of unforgettable new characters, mind-boggling concepts, and lavish new worlds, Jack Kirby also took on a group of established DC characters that had nothing to lose. The result was a year-long run of *Our Fighting Forces* tales that were action-packed, personal, and among the most beloved World War II comics ever produced.

Kirby clearly identified with Captain Storm, Johnny Cloud, Gunner, and Sarge—and he made certain that his readers did as well. Some debated that Kirby's perspective wasn't necessarily in line with the foursome's originally distinct Special Forces backgrounds. What really mattered, however, was the skill with which Kirby imbued his most personal military experiences in World War II within his Losers stories, which featured a quartet of seemingly unremarkable soldiers who represented those whose lives were defined (or lost) by moments not of their own choosing.

In the Losers' first mission under Kirby, the unit rescued a concert pianist hiding among the Nazis as a general's maid. Two issues later, inspired by Private First-Class Rodney Rumpkin's love for sci-fi comics, they devised a bogus "Devastator" weapon to fool the Nazis and dissuade them from unleashing their giant cannon, "Big Max."

In a text piece following his first issue, Kirby conveyed how he saw the Losers as "a 'people' thing. A small squad of 'everymen' caught up in the crushing tide of events, pushing their 'know-how' to the limit in a wild effort to survive."

The Losers (Johnny Cloud, Sarge Clay, Gunner Mackey, and Capt. Storm) go in search of a missing pianist.

ALSO THIS YEAR: The newly re-powered Diana Price took on twelve assignments to prove she should rejoin the Justice League, the first of which she received in June's *WONDER WOMAN* #212... In June's *SUPERMAN* #276, the Man of Steel was forced to "Make Way for Captain Thunder!"...

October: "The Rumble in the Jungle" takes place in Kinshasa, Zaire, where Muhammad Ali knocks out George Foreman in eight rounds to regain the heavyweight title.

November: Ronald DeFeo, Jr. murders his parents and his four siblings in what is later known as "The Amityville Horror House" massacre.

1975

"... SKARTARIS! A STRANGE NAME FOR A STRANGE WORLD!"

Travis Morgan, *1st Issue Special* #8

A SERIES OF FIRSTS

The paper shortage of 1974 had forced all comic book publishers to raise the cover price of comics to twenty-five cents, and DC to reduce its story count to eighteen pages. But, after a year of drastically reduced publishing, DC publisher Carmine Infantino did an about-face, launching sixteen new titles in 1975.

One word summed up Infantino's decision to expand DC's output: competition. Although comics' two giants—DC and Marvel—would actually collaborate on a joint publication for the first time ever with *MGM's Marvelous Wizard of Oz*, during the rest of the year, rivalry was fierce.

Intent on increasing its market share, DC executives attempted several daring experiments, including giving a maniacal murderer his own series in *The Joker*, and publishing an ongoing title made up solely of first issues to gauge and retain readers' interests.

APRIL

SAMACHSON'S LOST STORY

***Adventure Comics* #438**

An unpublished Seven Soldiers of Victory story finally saw print as a backup feature in *Adventure Comics* #438—three decades after it was written. Noted scientist and author Joseph Samachson had penned his last Soldiers story in 1945, when the super hero team were a regular feature in *Leading Comics*.

Back then, an editorial decision to change *Leading Comics* into a funny animal book had cast its victorious stars into comic book limbo, and forced Samachson's tale, "Land of Magic," to languish in DC's inventory for the next several decades. Yet when the Soldiers resurfaced in *Justice League of America* #100–102 (August–October 1972), *Adventure Comics* editor Joe Orlando recognized a Golden Age opportunity. He published Samachson's story in installments, in which the Soldiers were transported into strange, cartoonish realms within the Land of Magic before reuniting. Teeming with Samachson's whimsical sense of humor and adventure, this Seven Soldiers tale from the Golden Age was a lost treasure no more.

Wing joins with the Seven Soldiers of Victory: (clockwise) the Shining Knight, the Vigilante, Stripesy, the Crimson Avenger, the Star-Spangled Kid, Green Arrow, and Speedy.

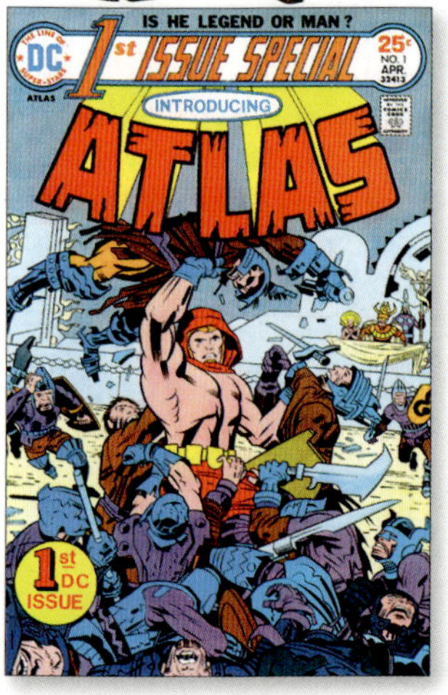

IT'S A FIRST

***1st Issue Special* #1**

Recognizing that first issues attracted more readers, DC launched *1st Issue Special*. The series experimented with new characters and concepts and every installment was an issue #1. Debuting with Atlas the Great, writer and artist Jack Kirby didn't shrug at the chance to put his spin on the well-known hero. Unlike the Greek god, Kirby's warrior hailed from the Crystal Mountain. He was also the sole inheritor of the fabled mountain's power—especially as he was the lone survivor of the land, which had been ravaged by the Lizard King Hyssa, against whom Atlas swore revenge.

IN THE REAL WORLD...

January: The Altair 8800 is released, sparking the microcomputer era.
January: *Wheel of Fortune* premieres on U.S. television channel NBC.

MAY

DRAGON'S DEN
***Richard Dragon, Kung-Fu Fighter* #1**
While Bruce Lee demonstrated his Jeet Kune Do in the movies, DC produced a new series starring martial arts expert Richard Dragon. Richard Dragon, *Kung-Fu Fighter* was based on the 1974 novel *Dragon's Fists* by "Jim Dennis" (the shared pseudonym of comic book writer Denny O'Neil and artist Jim Berry). With art by Leo Duranona, the series adapted Dragon's origins—as a young thief, reformed and trained in the martial arts—for the DC Universe.

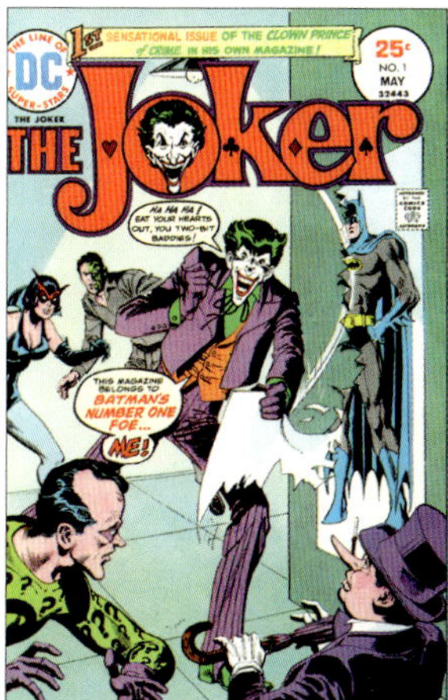

YOU MUST BE JOKING

***The Joker* #1**
It may have been an unusual idea at the time, but writer Denny O'Neil and artist Irv Novick decided to feature a villain in his own comic book series. *The Joker* lasted only nine issues, but in seven of the issues the homicidal harlequin literally got away with murder.

The premiere issue subjected Two-Face (Harvey Dent) to "The Joker's Double Jeopardy" after criminal Señor Alvarez broke Dent out of Arkham Asylum to help him steal a priceless coin collection of Spanish doubloons. When Alvarez and Dent thought the grinning Joker was too inferior to liberate, the insulted madman used an oversized helium balloon to take off on his own… and then meted out some payback with a smile. His ol' "acid-filled cream pie in the face" gag left the arrogant Alvarez writhing on the floor.

Two-Face, meanwhile, nearly had the killer clown in stitches after trying to cut him in half with a circular saw. But the Joker rallied, and used adhesive on his own coat to secure Two-Face until the police arrived. When Commissioner Gordon turned up, he delivered the story's punchline: The stolen doubloons were counterfeit.

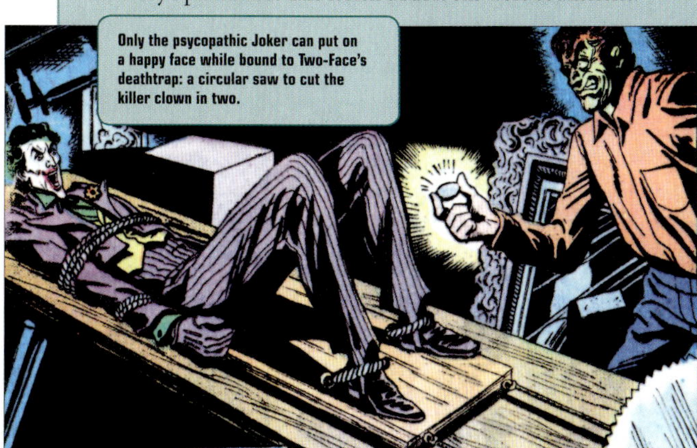
Only the psycopathic Joker can put on a happy face while bound to Two-Face's deathtrap: a circular saw to cut the killer clown in two.

JUNE

AN AVENGER IS BORN
***Justice, inc.* #1**
DC again translated pulp fiction into comics with a revival of the icy-eyed 1930s hero, the Avenger. Writer Denny O'Neil and artist Al McWilliams adapted the novel *Justice, Inc.* by "Kenneth Robeson" (a.k.a. writer Paul Ernst). Globetrotting millionaire adventurer Dick Benson declared war on crime following the murder of his wife and daughter. The trauma had turned his skin and hair ghost-white. Jack Kirby rendered the Avenger's comic-book exploits starting with issue #2. Sadly, though, *Justice, inc.* was unfairly swift, lasting a total of four installments.

THE CAVEMAN COMETH
***Tor* #1**
In conjunction with DC's launch of fantasy/adventure titles, writer and artist Joe Kubert revived Tor, the caveman whose legend began in the early 1950s. Tor was now a more experienced caveman, and Kubert a far more seasoned storyteller. His powerful visuals provided authoritative narration as Tor recalled his younger years and the challenges of manhood—challenges that conveyed man's primitive, instinctive nature. Kubert's revival of *Tor* lasted six issues, though the series' sheer power and brilliance has transcended time.

CURSE OF THE CLAW
***Claw the Unconquered* #1**
David Michelinie's pen and Ernie Chan's pencils and inks provided the magic for this fantasy series that introduced Claw the Unconquered, a barbaric outlander with a deformed, claw-like right hand. The appendage, often covered in a crimson gauntlet, had been afflicted by a generations-old curse that Claw roamed the lands of Pytharia to end. Of course, that meant doing away with evildoers and despots in the process, including the ruler who murdered Claw's father, Prince Occulas of the Yellow Eye. *Claw the Unconquered* was a brave effort for nine issues, until it could no longer stay the hand of cancelation.

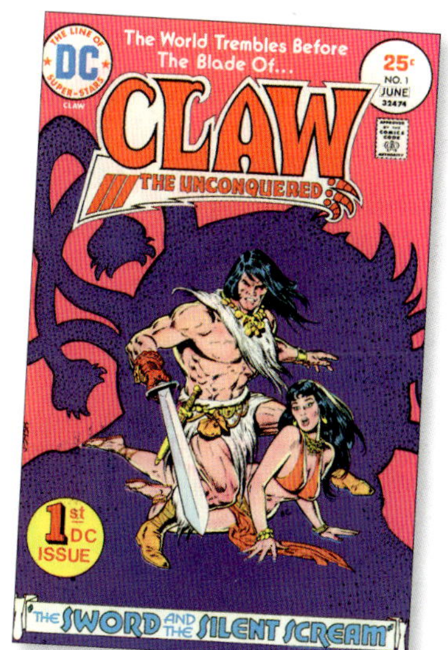

"HIS NAME IS VALCAN—THOUGH HIS DEFORMITY HAS EARNED HIM THE FEARED TITLE OF—CLAW!"

Miftung, *Claw the Unconquered* #1

February: The Haicheng earthquake, the first successfully predicted earthquake, kills 2,041 and injures 27,538 in Haicheng, Liaoning, China.

March: Charlie Chaplin is knighted by Queen Elizabeth II.
April: Bill Gates founds Microsoft in Albuquerque, New Mexico.

JULY

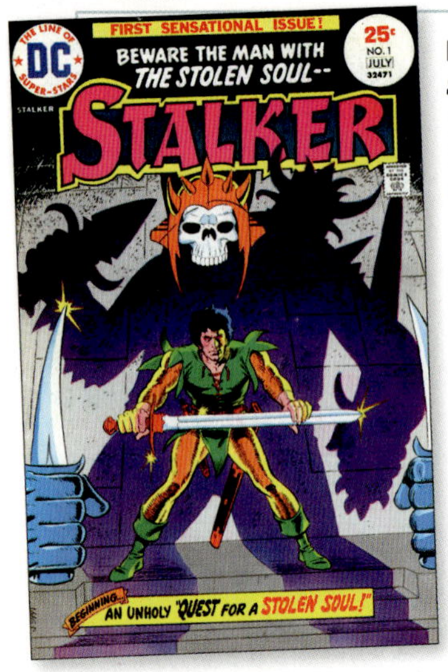

LOST SOUL
***Stalker* #1**

This sword-and-sorcery title by scribe Paul Levitz and artist Steve Ditko epitomized the credo "Be careful what you wish for." The series' anti-hero was a nameless wanderer whose dreams of becoming a warrior brought him first slavery, then worse. Dgrth, the demon lord of warriors, answered the boy's prayers, granting him unparalleled combat skills, plus a hunter's gifts and name—in exchange for his soul. As Stalker the Soulless, the youth came to realize that smiting his enemies brought him no joy, for he had been stripped of his humanity. From that point, the young hunter's target became the demon that made him.

PREHISTORIC MAMA'S BOY
***Kong the Untamed* #1**

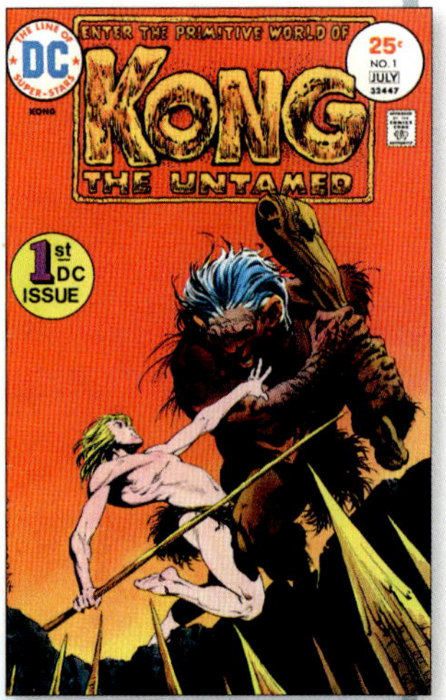

Writer Jack Oleck and artist Alfredo Alcala focused on a primitive, powerful theme with which to depict the prehistoric warrior Kong in his debut issue: a growing son's bond with his mother. That bond gave Attu the strength to protect her newly born son from Trog the One-Eyed, who feared that the infant would someday rise to take his place as tribal leader. The child's blond hair was unusual among the dark-headed people, referencing a legend about a blond, unbeatable warrior called Kong, and Attu named him for this hero. Exiled from Trog's clan, Kong grew up fending for himself and his mother, until the evil Trog murdered Attu and ignited another primitive theme that would dominate the remainder of the series: retribution.

Young Kong and his mother, Attu, watch as Trog the One-Eyed battles those who dare challenge his leadership of the clan. Kong has no idea that it is his destiny to become tribal leader.

AUGUST

MANHUNTER REVISITED

***1st Issue Special* #5**

Though *1st Issue Special* was primarily DC's forum to introduce new characters and storylines, editor Jack Kirby used the series as an opportunity to revamp the Manhunter, whom he and writer Joe Simon had made famous in the 1940s.

The original Manhunter, Paul Kirk, had met his demise two years earlier, so Kirby turned to Mark Shaw, a discouraged public defender who believed that the legal system had been corrupted. Shaw's uncle put him into contact with the Grandmaster, leader of the arcane Cult of the Manhunters. Swearing his allegiance, Shaw trained in the crime-fighting sect's methods and weaponry, and then assumed the outfit and power baton to become the new Manhunter.

Kirby's Manhunter, however, didn't earn a spot in an ongoing series. Instead, Shaw and the crime-fighting cult played a bigger role in the pages of *Justice League of America* in 1977, when it was revealed that the Manhunters were the original galactic law-enforcers, prior to the Green Lantern Corps.

Adopting the arcane skills of the Manhunters, public defender Mark Shaw protects his uncle from the gangster called "The Hog."

SEPTEMBER

ON TV THIS MONTH: Premiering September 6 as part of CBS-TV's Saturday morning lineup, Filmation's *THE SECRETS OF ISIS* became America's first weekly live-action program to star a female super hero...

OCTOBER

FAMILY KNIGHT
***Batman Family* #1**

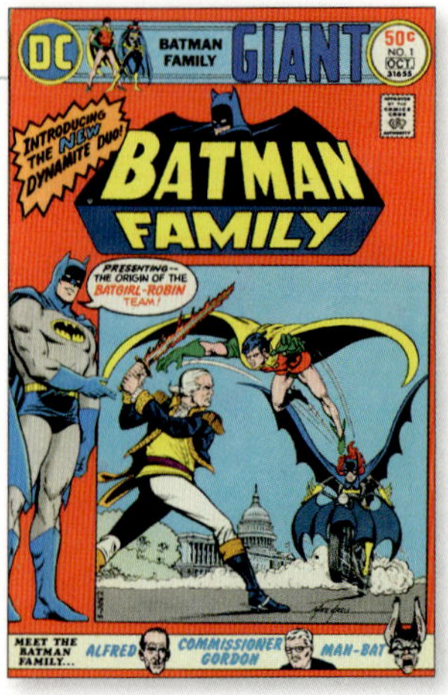

As part of its new "Giant" line of titles, DC launched *Batman Family*, with its memorable debut of the Batgirl–Robin team. Scribe Elliot S! Maggin and artist Mike Grell unleashed "The Invader from Hell," Benedict Arnold himself. Batgirl and Robin fought off the disgraced general until his frustrated boss—the devil—returned him to his Hadean dwellings. In victory, Batgirl and Robin shared a moment that would someday blossom into a romance—though it wouldn't be realized in the series' twenty-issue run.

IN THE REAL WORLD...

May: Junko Tabei becomes the first woman to reach the summit of Mount Everest.
June: In a referendum, the United Kingdom votes to stay in the European Community.
September: Rembrandt's painting *The Night Watch* is slashed a dozen times at the Rijksmuseum in Amsterdam, The Netherlands.

CROSSING OVER TO OZ

***MGM's Marvelous Wizard of Oz* #1**

The Yellow Brick Road from Munchkin Land to the Emerald City was also wide enough to accommodate DC and Marvel as they produced their first-ever joint publication. In fact, their shared adaptation of MGM's *The Wizard of Oz* would pave the way for many more future company crossovers.

The 1939 classic movie, based on the novel by L. Frank Baum and starring Judy Garland, had enjoyed a resurgence in recent years, with repeated television airings and an upcoming toy launch. Such attention had not gone unnoticed by DC or Marvel, with both sides ready to compete with each other for the publishing rights.

Thankfully, brains, courage, and heart prevailed, as DC and Marvel executives agreed to collaborate on a tabloid-sized, MGM-authorized treasury edition. Roy Thomas scripted a faithful, seventy-two-page adaptation of Dorothy Gale's adventure, while John Buscema's artwork depicted the landscape of Oz in lavish detail.

The Cowardly Lion, the Tin Man, the Scarecrow, and Toto accompany Dorothy as she meets the "great and powerful" Wizard of Oz.

NOVEMBER

OFF THE CHAIN

***Hercules Unbound* #1**

Old-school mythology clashed with a post-apocalyptic future when an atypically clean-shaven Hercules awoke four weeks after World War III, the star of his own series. He broke free of his enchanted bonds to rescue a blind teenager, Kevin, and his dog, who were being terrorized by an enraged sea creature. Doing so also freed the anti-gods from their prison, including Hercules' nemesis, the god of war, Ares. *Hercules Unbound* featured powerful writing from Gerry Conway plus stellar artwork by José Luis García-López throughout its twelve-issue run.

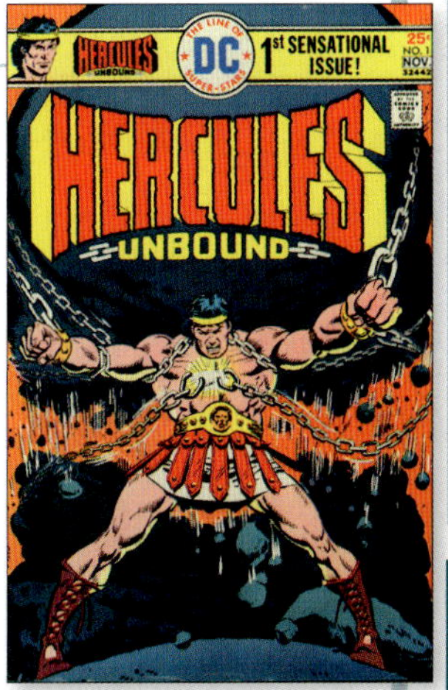

ON TV THIS MONTH: Wonder Woman, played by Lynda Carter, fought against the Axis forces in World War II when ABC-TV debuted the live-action series *THE NEW ORIGINAL WONDER WOMAN*...

NOVEMBER

ENTER THE LOST WORLD

***1st Issue Special* #8**

Writer/artist Mike Grell elevated the sword-and-sorcery genre to new heights with the Warlord.

For years, Skartaris was a realm that existed in Grell's mind as a comic strip called "Savage Empire." The plan had always been to release a series about the adventures of Travis Morgan (whose goatee, contrary to popular belief, was modeled after Grell's, not Green Arrow's), until a decision was made to launch the saga in the pages of *1st Issue Special*. Ironically, the single-issue origin tale would become one of that title's only two features to spin-off into its own series.

Grell based Skartaris within the Arctic Circle, where Lt. Col. Morgan of the U.S. Air Force was forced to jettison from his dying aircraft. He landed in a strange, tropical land bathed in perpetual sunlight and populated by dinosaurs, otherworldly creatures, and Tara, a warrior from the city of Shamballah. Morgan also became acquainted with Deimos, a high-priest in the city-state Thera, who sacrificed innocent people as part of his plan to rule Skartaris. Morgan and Tara defeated attackers sent by Deimos to kill them and fled into the wilderness. From that moment, Morgan's destiny as the Warlord, and his quest to liberate the people of Skartaris, began. His own epic adventure series began in February 1976, and sprawled thirteen years and 133 issues.

Abandoning his failing Air Force jet, Lt. Colonel Travis Morgan finds himself on a world within a world—the savage empire of Skartaris.

ALSO THIS YEAR: Scribe Michael Uslan and artist Ricardo Villamonte introduced the broadsword-bashing hero of Anglo-Saxon myth in May's *BEOWULF, DRAGON SLAYER* #1... In August's *JUSTICE LEAGUE OF AMERICA* #121 Adam Strange said "I do" to his long-time love, Alanna, in a story by scripter Cary Bates and artist Dick Dillin in attendance... With a heavy heart, writer Joe Simon edited the final issue (#208) of the first romance comic—*YOUNG ROMANCE*—in December, a labor of love he started with artist Jack Kirby more than twenty-eight years earlier...

October: Juan Carlos I of Spain becomes acting Head of State after dictator Francisco Franco concedes that he is too ill to govern.

November: Spanish dictator Francisco Franco dies in Madrid, Spain.

November: The Irish Republican Army is outlawed in the United Kingdom.

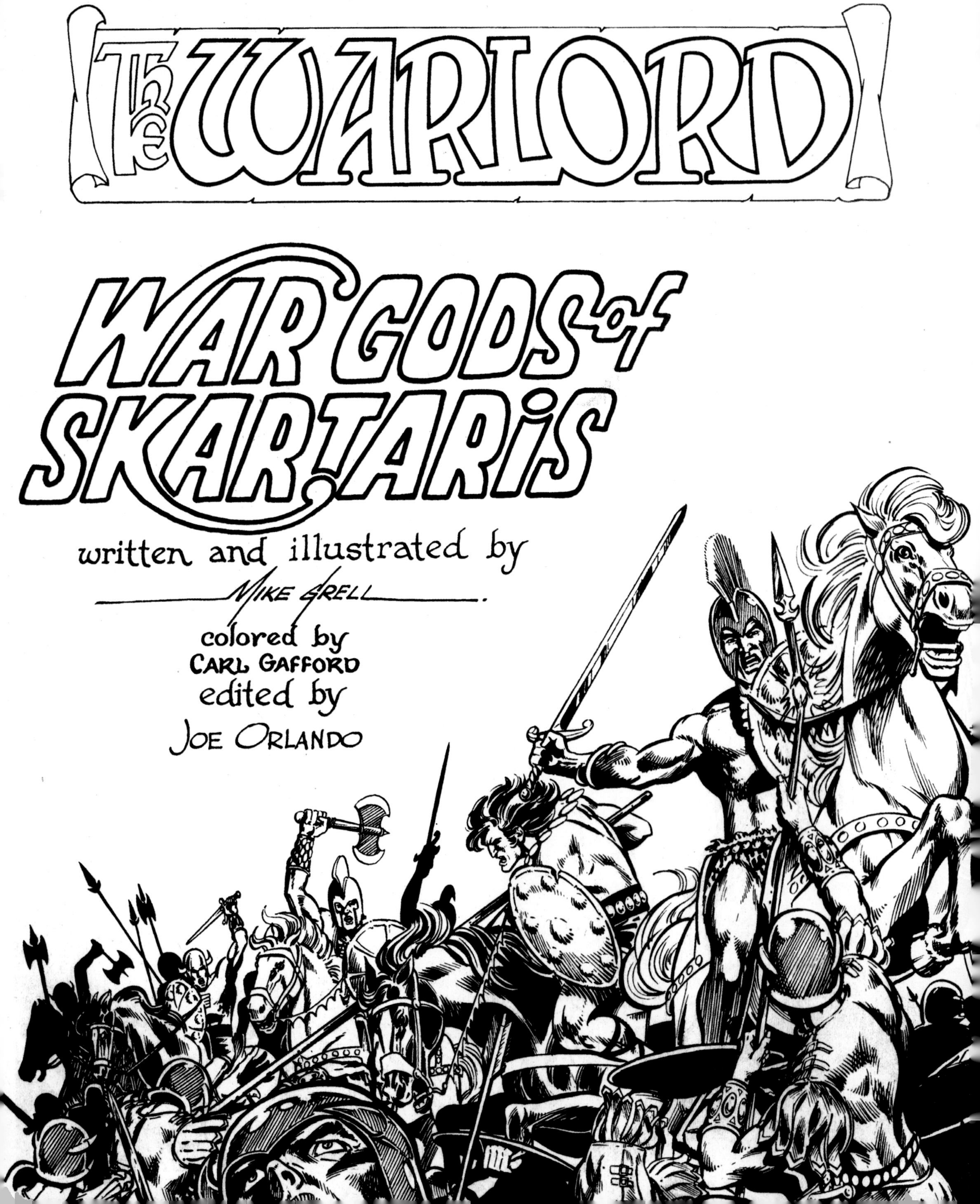
The Warlord
War Gods of Skartaris
written and illustrated by
Mike Grell
colored by
Carl Gafford
edited by
Joe Orlando

THE WARLORD #3 (October 1976)
Spectacular action set pieces, as exemplified by this inked splash page, as well as scantily clad maidens, dinosaurs, and mythical beasts, helped gain *The Warlord* a cult following during the 1970s and 1980s vogue for sword and sorcery. Written and illustrated by Mike Grell, the title debuted in February 1976.

1976

"THAT DOES IT. EVEN A SUPERMAN CAN BE PUSHED SO FAR!"

Superman, *Superman vs The Amazing Spider-Man* #1

BRAND NEW BLOOD

During America's 200th birthday, Jimmy Carter was elected president, Apple Computers opened its doors, and children's publisher Jenette Kahn replaced Carmine Infantino as publisher of a struggling DC Comics.

With comic book cover prices raised to thirty cents and story pages decreased to seventeen, there was little wonder as to why eleven titles were canceled almost as quickly as twenty-one new series were added. Kahn, however, welcomed the challenge and was eager to let everyone know that big changes were on the horizon for DC Comics, the now-official name of the company previously known as National Periodical Publications, Inc.

Meanwhile, DC cornered the market with comic book adaptations of TV shows—*Super Friends* was even based on DC characters. There was also the ultimate crossover, between Marvel's wall-crawler and DC's Man of Steel.

JANUARY

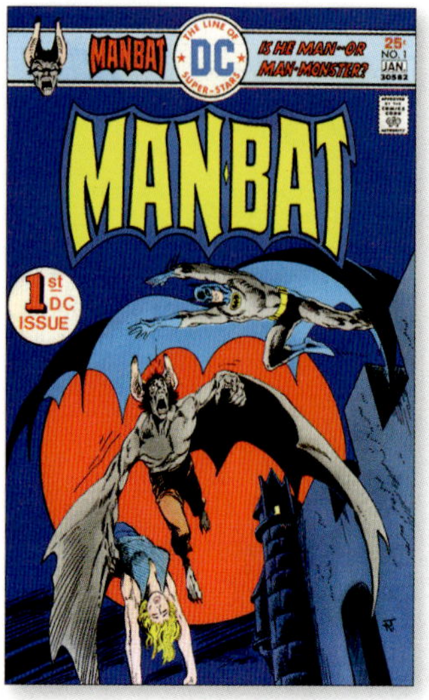

KNIGHT FLYER
***Man-Bat* #1**
Thanks to his appearances in *Detective Comics* and *Batman*, Man-Bat's popularity soared to the point where writer Gerry Conway and artist Steve Ditko launched the flying mammal into his own series. Kirk Langstrom swooped in to save his wife, Francine, whom the sorcerer Baron Tyme turned into the vampire She-Bat. After fighting Batman to convince him of Tyme's involvement, Man-Bat tracked the sorcerer to Antioke University. A struggle ended in a fire that seemingly killed Tyme. Man-Bat didn't fare much better; his series ended after two issues.

GODDESS OF DESTRUCTION
***Richard Dragon, Kung-Fu Fighter* #5**
Writer Denny O'Neil and artist Ric Estrada matched up martial arts hero Richard Dragon with dangerous beauty Lady Shiva in January. Naming herself after the Hindu goddess of destruction, Shiva was once Sandra Woosan, whose sister Carolyn had been killed while under Dragon's protection. Criminal businessman and arch-enemy of Dragon, Guano Cravat, convinced Shiva that Dragon was Carolyn's murderer, even though one of his own lieutenants had actually committed the foul deed. Shiva demonstrated her killer martial arts skills in battle with Dragon, until he convinced her of his innocence and helped her take down Cravat.

Richard Dragon's adversary reveals herself to be Sandra Woosan, sister of a woman whom Dragon supposedly killed. Before long, she becomes renowned as assassin Lady Shiva.

IN THE REAL WORLD...

January: The first commercial Concorde flight takes off.
March: Harold Wilson resigns as Prime Minister of the United Kingdom.

FEBRUARY

THE SUPER SQUAD

***All Star Comics* #58**

In a single issue, writer/editor Gerry Conway launched new adventures for the Justice Society of America, added a younger element to the team, and revived a series that had not been published in more than a quarter of a century. Along with artist Ric Estrada, Conway also introduced the DC Universe to the cousin of Earth-2's Superman, Kara Zor-L a.k.a. Power Girl.

When a series of unlikely geological catastrophes threatened to destroy the world, the seasoned JSA super-team split up to contain the disasters. Along the way, the JSA was surprised to find help in the form of three young super heroes, Robin, the Star-Spangled Kid (now wielding Starman's cosmic rod), and Power Girl, in her debut role.

Combining their forces, the heroes located and defeated the source behind the global catastrophes: longtime nemesis Brain Wave, who'd been given a new, more powerful body by another JSA adversary, Per Degaton. Deciding to remain with the Justice Society, the younger heroes became the team's new auxiliary detachment, the Super Squad.

The Justice Society's Flash and Wildcat meet a new ally who stops a volcano from erupting in Peking: Superman's cousin, Power Girl.

THIS SAVAGE WORLD

***The Warlord* #1**

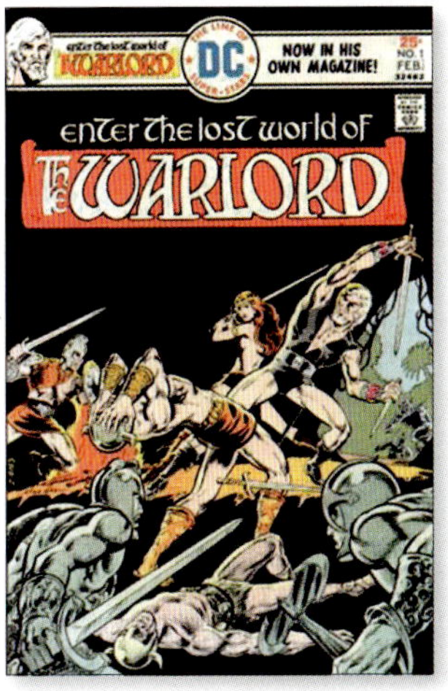

Writer/artist Mike Grell returned to Skartaris, the land of eternal light, and unveiled the first of the Warlord's exploits in his own series. Recapping what transpired in *1st Issue Special* #8 (November 1975), the story found Tara training Travis Morgan in the ways of combat as they journeyed to her land, Shamballah. They were soon captured by slave raiders, until Morgan freed Tara and urged her to flee. Because of his defiance, Morgan was sentenced to a slow and painful death, although he would survive and be reunited with Tara before long.

MARCH

WHAT A SUPERMAN WANTS

***Superman* #297**

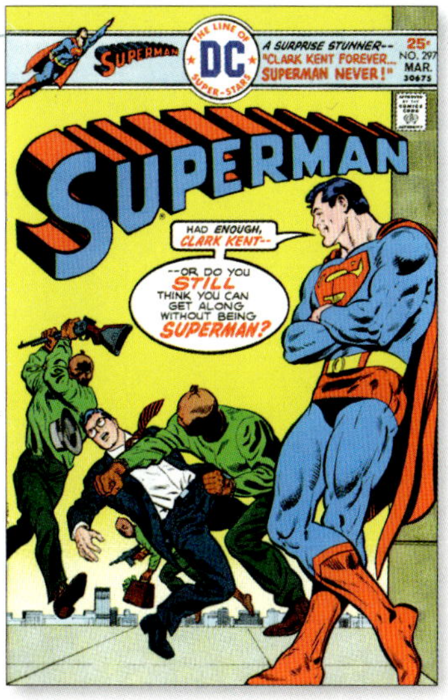

Scripter Elliot S! Maggin and artist Curt Swan crafted a storyline where Superman noticed that his powers were removed while he was dressed as Clark Kent. Assuming that his body was telling him to choose a single identity, Clark found himself becoming less "mild-mannered." He laid out office blowhard, Steve Lombard, yelled at his boss, Morgan Edge, and even dared to pursue his romance with Lois Lane. The two shared a dinner at Clark's apartment. But, unknown to Clark, his altered state was part of an insidious plot to destroy Earth by an alien spy called Xviar posing as his neighbor.

"FOR THE NEXT SEVEN DAYS AT LEAST—AND MAYBE FOREVER—THERE WILL BE NO SUPERMAN... NO MATTER WHAT!"

Clark Kent, *Superman* #297

Lois Lane can't believe she is seeing the usually calm Clark Kent teach Steve Lombard table manners in a Metropolis restaurant.

WELCOME BACK, WONDER WOMAN?

***Justice League of America* #128**

The Justice League officially reinstated Wonder Woman in issue #222 of her own series. However, her meeting with the JLA within the pages of their comic didn't go well, thanks to writer Martin Pasko and artist Dick Dillin. The League had, in fact, decided to disband after each member experienced visions of their own demise. Those visions were being projected by Nekron (no relation to Green Lantern's nemesis), an alien that fed off others' fear. In issue #223, Wonder Woman lassoed her teammates, magically giving them the courage to defeat, Nekron.

March: Elizabeth II of the United Kingdom sends the first royal email.
April: The company Apple Computer, Inc. is formed by Steve Jobs and Steve Wozniak.
April: Punk-rock group The Ramones release their debut self-titled album.
June: Toronto's CN Tower, the world's tallest freestanding structure, is completed.

APRIL

BATTLE OF THE CENTURY
***Superman vs. the Amazing Spider-Man* #1**

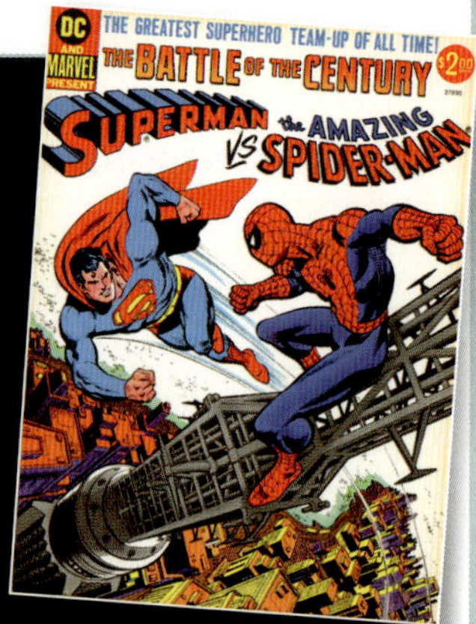

Unquestionably, *Superman vs. the Amazing Spider-Man*, in which DC and Marvel pitted two of their greatest icons against each other, was truly "The Battle of the Century!" The two publishers had collaborated on *MGM's Marvelous Wizard of Oz* less than a year earlier, but this was a major crossover event—a treasury edition-sized tale that merited the comic-book hype it generated.

The tale was written by Gerry Conway and drawn by Ross Andru, both among the few to ever have worked on both Superman and Spider-Man. The ninety-six-page story put the heroes into conflict with each other following the malevolent maneuverings of Lex Luthor and Doc Ock.

The diabolical duo kidnapped Lois Lane and Mary Jane Watson, then somehow made Superman and Spidey think the other was involved. Luthor and Doc Ock also imbued the unknowing web-spinner with a temporary boost of power so that he could hold his own against the Man of Tomorrow—and give readers a more even-sided fight. Fortunately, once that wore off, cooler heads saw reason. Joining forces, the heroes tracked down their enemies just as Luthor was about to take control of the world's weather. Naturally, Doc Ock betrayed his ally, giving Spider-Man the advantage he needed to apprehend him and Luthor while Superman stopped a tidal wave from laying waste to the East Coast.

Many talents from both DC and Marvel contributed to this landmark publication—in addition to inker Dick Giordano, Neal Adams provided several re-drawings of Superman while John Romita, Sr. worked on numerous Peter Parker/Spider-Man likenesses.

The book itself, spearheaded by Carmine Infantino and Stan Lee, also went through several edits on both sides. The result was a defining moment in Bronze Age comics, and set a precedent for many more future company crossovers.

In a 2009 interview in *Death Ray* magazine, writer Gerry Conway describes *Superman vs. the Amazing Spider-Man* as "a touchstone. It was pretty important as the first acknowledgement that the Marvel and DC Universes could co-exist."

APRIL

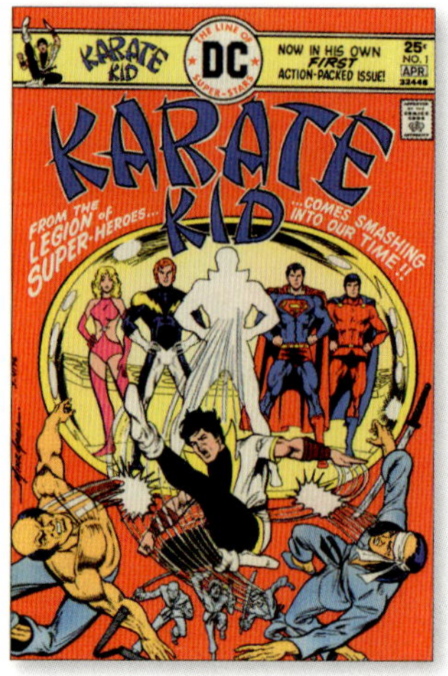

MARTIAL AWE
***Karate Kid* #1**

Writer Paul Levitz and artist Ric Estrada kicked Karate Kid out of the Legion of Super-Heroes—and the thirtieth Century—so that he could headline his own series. Karate Kid Val Armorr, a master of every martial art, traveled 1,000 years into the past in pursuit of Nemesis Kid, a Legion adversary who spontaneously developed any power he needed. Karate Kid emerged triumphant and was so intrigued by his twentieth-century experiences, that he sent his quarry back home, and for a while lived in the past.

JUNE

DISHONOR-BOUND
***The Secret Society of... Super Villains* #1**

Scribe Gerry Conway and artist Pablo Marcos assembled a group of DC's most wanted for an ongoing series. The unscrupulous bunch, including the Wizard and Sinestro, became the Secret Society of Super-Villains. Über-villain Darkseid initially took orders from a clone of the deceased Manhunter, who sought to channel the villains' energies in more positive ways. However, Darkseid eventually revealed himself as the society's benefactor. Too evil even for their tastes, the members disbanded.

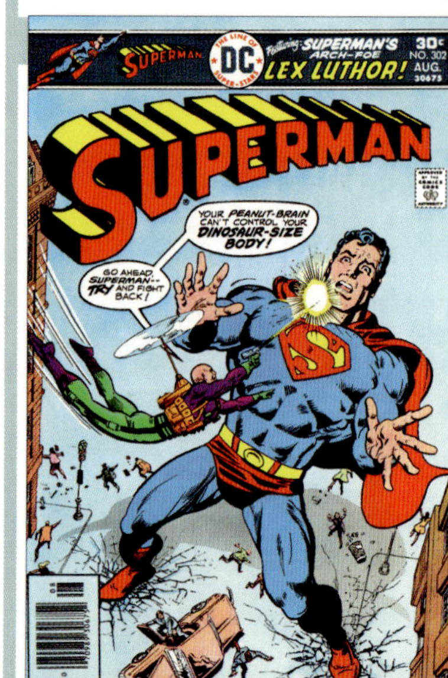

AUGUST

CREDIT WHERE IT'S DUE
***Superman* #302**

For the first time since 1947, Jerry Siegel and Joe Shuster's names were back in *Superman* comics, and listed as the Man of Steel's co-creators. In the story "Seven-Foot-Two… And Still Growing" by writer Elliot S! Maggin and artist José Luis García-López, Superman's arch-nemesis Lex Luthor employed a device that exponentially increased Superman's size while decreasing his mental acuity. The Man of Steel received some super-sized help from his friend, the Atom, to reverse the effects and defeat Luthor.

IN THE REAL WORLD...

July: From coast to coast, the United States celebrates the 200th anniversary of the Declaration of Independence.

July: The 1976 Summer Olympics begin in Montreal, Quebec, Canada.
August: Jacques Chirac resigns as prime minister of France.

SEPTEMBER

BACK TO THE RING

***Green Lantern/Green Arrow* #90**

After a four-year hiatus, Green Lantern's ongoing series made a triumphant return to DC's publishing schedule. Archer Green Arrow joined his emerald ally again, having teamed up for the first time in issue #89 in May 1972. Returning writer Denny O'Neil partnered himself with artist Mike Grell, choosing to focus the title on sci-fi and super-heroics.

In "Those Who Worship Evil's Might," the intergalactic police force—the Green Lantern Corps—were granted new and improved power ring weapons by their founders, the Guardians of Oa.

Meanwhile, nuclear testing in the Nevada desert uncovered a centuries-old spaceship and awoke its inhabitants. Green Lantern and Green Arrow rescued an alien from his supposed aggressors, the Halla's. But, before long, the alien—Jinn—revealed himself as a criminal and Green Arrow discovered that the Halla's were actually predecessors to the Green Lantern Corps. Using a re-energized gun, Jinn nearly eliminated his captors and the Green Arrow, but Green Lantern arrived back on the scene, stopping Jinn with his new power ring.

On the moon Callisto, Green Lantern recharges his ring as he is about to be attacked by Jinn, the alien he is trying to help.

TATTERED TALES

***Ragman* #1**

Ragman's debut was, like the shabby vigilante himself, an underrated gem. Writer Robert Kanigher's origin of the frayed hero was pieced together into moody, coarse segments by Joe Kubert and Nestor, Frank, and Quico Redondo. Vietnam veteran Rory Regan's father and three friends were electrocuted by gangsters after uncovering stolen millions in a mattress. Rory tried to pull them to safety and the electrical current transferred their strength and skills into him. Donning an outfit of rags, the "Tatterdemalion of Justice" was born.

NOVEMBER

SMASHING OUT OF THE TV SCREEN

***The Super Friends* #1**

Since 1973, Alex Toth's renderings of the JLA had dominated Saturday morning television. In fact, Hanna-Barbera's animated *Super Friends* proved so successful that DC brought the concept full circle, adapting the show into a comic. Scribe E. Nelson Bridwell and artist Ric Estrada crafted the inaugural issue, pitting "the most powerful forces of good ever assembled" against a band of self-proclaimed "Super Foes." Although not considered DC canon, *Super Friends* enjoyed nearly a five-year run in comics form, lasting for forty-seven issues.

CLASS CLOWNS

***Welcome Back, Kotter* #1**

High school sitcom *Welcome Back, Kotter* was a smash hit for ABC-TV in 1975. In 1976, DC made the group of juvenile delinquents—the Sweathogs—hit the books (for a change), bringing their classroom antics into their own sit-comic. The first issue, written by Elliot S! Maggin with spot-on likenesses rendered by Jack Sparling, actually gave teacher Mr. Kotter an opportunity to transfer out of Brooklyn's James Buchanan High School. However, his wife Julie and the Sweathogs intervened.

TITANS REUNITE

***Teen Titans* #44**

More than three years since *Teen Titans* was canceled, writers Paul Levitz and Bob Rozakis, with artist Pablo Marcos, revived the series. Strangely, it was the villainous Dr. Light who called for the reunion of Robin, Kid Flash, Wonder Girl, Speedy, and the non-superpowered Mal Duncan. Dr. Light faked an emergency call to Titans Lair so that he could trap the teens and use them as bait against the Justice League. The illuminated antagonist might have succeeded had he not been so dimwitted about Mal, who used a strength-enhancing exo-skeleton to revive the team and power down Dr. Light.

ALSO THIS YEAR: In February, editor and cover artist Joe Kubert helmed *BLITZKRIEG* #1, a unique anthology about World War II as seen through the eyes of the enemy. The first issue featured stories by writer Robert Kanigher, artist Ric Estrada, and storyteller Sam Glanzman... Twin brothers Burr—one good (Jason), the other a cult leader (Jeffrey)—shared a psychic bond and a hatred for each other in March's *KOBRA* #1 by writers Jack Kirby, Steve Sherman, and Martin Pasko, with art by Kirby and Pablo Marcos... In March's *1ST ISSUE SPECIAL* #12 Mikaal Tomas defended Earth as the third Starman in a story from writer Gerry Conway and artist Mike Vosburg...

September: The Irish rock band U2 is formed after drummer Larry Mullen, Jr. posts a note seeking members for a band on the notice board of his school in Dublin, Ireland.

October: The chimpanzee is placed on the list of endangered species.
December: The album *Hotel California*, by The Eagles, is released.

1977

"... THE SECOND TIME I STRIKE —IT'S FOR KEEPS!"

Black Lightning, *Black Lightning* #1

DEFINING MOMENTS

DC Comics was working non-stop toward regaining the strength that for decades not only led the comic book industry, but defined it. The company's new "bullet" logo, designed by Milton Glaser, boldly revamped DC's image. Continuing to increase its output, DC launched twelve new titles, bringing the total up to forty-nine since 1975.

By 1977, comic book cover prices had increased to thirty-five cents and DC had reduced their amount of story pages to seventeen. Publisher Jenette Kahn decided to create Dollar Comics, which focused on more story for the price and, ultimately, dropped the ads.

DC also kept up with its maturing audience by producing life-changing developments for its champions, such as Aquaman and Batman. Furthermore, the publisher was intent on introducing heroes that were offbeat, like Shade, the Changing Man, and socially diverse, such as Black Lightning.

FEBRUARY

TOMORROW IS YESTERDAY
***Wonder Woman* #228**

Writer Martin Pasko and artist Jose Delbo detailed the first chronological meeting between Earth-1's modern-day Wonder Woman and her Earth-2 equivalent during World War II. The comic's time and Earth shifts were actually dictated by ABC-TV's popular Wonder Woman TV series, set during World War II, and they continued in this era for the next fifteen issues—even after CBS-TV placed *The New Adventures of Wonder Woman* in a contemporary setting later that year.

ON TV THIS MONTH: *THE NEW ADVENTURES OF BATMAN* saw the Dark Knight return to Saturday morning TV, joined by Robin, Batgirl, and Bat-Mite. The series lasted for sixteen episodes...

MARCH

WAR ENDS... FOR SOME
***Star Spangled War Stories* #204**

After nearly a quarter-century and 204 issues, comicdom said goodbye to *Star Spangled War Stories*. However, writer Bob Haney and artist Dick Ayers had no intention of terminating the Unknown Soldier, the series' star of more than fifty issues, despite the title of the issue's lead story—"The Unknown Soldier Must Die." The man whom no one knows, but is known by everyone, thwarted Nazi attempts to brainwash ally Chat Noir into killing him, allowing DC to rename the following series after the Unknown Soldier, starting with issue #205 in May.

APRIL

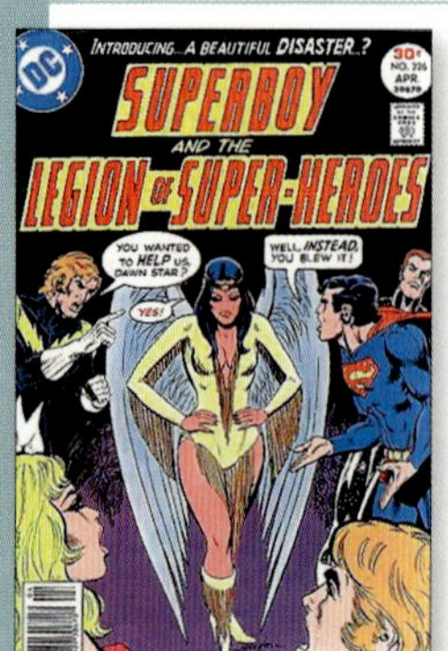

DAWNSTAR TRACKING
***Superboy and The Legion of Super-Heroes* #226**

As soon as Wildfire was named leader of the Legion of Super-Heroes he recruited the young Dawnstar from the Legion Academy, in a story by scribe Paul Levitz and artist James Sherman. Dawnstar was entrusted to help track down the Resource Raiders, an alien conclave of pillagers. A winged ancestor of Earth's Native American Indians, Dawnstar's tracking ability guided the Legionnaires outside the galaxy to locate the Raiders. Later, Wildfire offered Dawnstar Legion membership, though it was clear that he was guided by his own romantic feelings toward her.

IN THE REAL WORLD...

January: *Roots* begins its phenomenally successful run on U.S. TV.
February: Fleetwood Mac's Grammy-winning album *Rumours* is released.

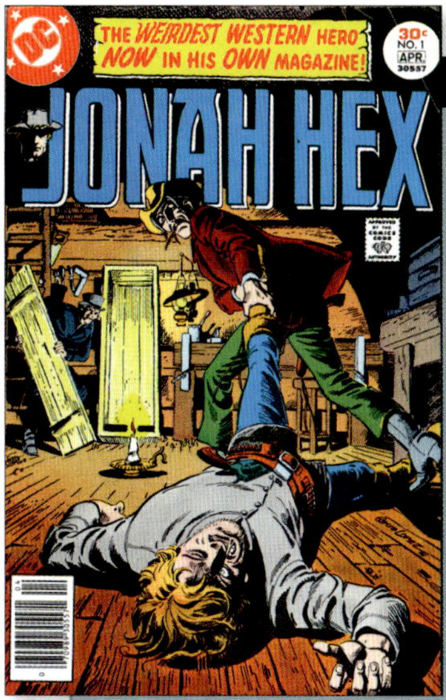

JONAH ON HIS OWN

***Jonah Hex* #1**
In true nomad fashion, disfigured gunman Jonah Hex rode his horse out of *Weird Western Tales* and into his own comic. It was a testament to the character's popularity, considering how conventional western-themed comics had all but galloped off into the sunset. Then again, nothing was ever conventional about Jonah Hex.

Longtime Hex scribe Michael Fleisher and artist José Luis García-López detailed the bounty hunter traveling to Whalenberg, Tennessee, to locate Tommy Royden, the kidnapped son of a plantation owner. He eventually found Tommy, who had died after being forced to compete in a fight club-type promotion by racketeers Blackie LeClerc and Charlie Mange. After being apprehended and sealed in a coffin by Tommy's kidnappers, Hex escaped, then forced the promoters to fight at the edge of a cliff, where both fell to their deaths. Returning to the plantation with Tommy's coffin, Hex didn't wait around for payment this time. Witnessing a mother grieve over her son's coffin, he realized that the family had already paid too much.

With a mean streak that is uglier than even his disfigured face, Jonah Hex punches out violent racketeer Blackie LeClerc.

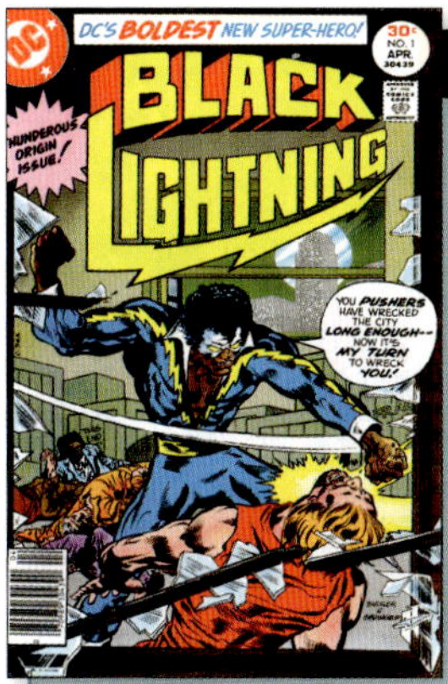

JUSTICE LIKE LIGHTNING

***Black Lightning* #1**
As Black Lightning, Jefferson Pierce became DC's first African-American super hero to headline his own title. A former Olympic athlete, Pierce returned to Metropolis' Suicide Slum as a high school teacher, in order to help the kids.

Both the school and neighborhood were firmly in the grip of the 100 criminal organization and its leader, an African-American albino named Tobias Whale. Refusing to be intimidated, Pierce sent Whale's goons fleeing from the school when they tried to assault him for interfering in their drug-pushing racket. Unfortunately, they turned their attention toward Pierce's students—in particular, Earl Clifford, the school's basketball star. Running from Whale's men while helping Pierce, Earl was killed and suspended from the school gym's basketball net as an example to all.

Blaming himself for Earl's death, Pierce turned to family friend, tailor and inventor Peter Gambi, who urged that the neighborhood needed a symbol to take back the streets. Gambi designed a costume with a force field belt, mask, and wig so that Pierce could become that symbol without those closest to him paying the price. Writer Tony Isabella and artist Trevor von Eeden provided the creative juice for Black Lightning after DC scrapped plans for another African-American character, the Black Bomber.

Black Lightning removes the mask and wig that stop his enemies from recognizing him as teacher Jefferson Pierce.

HE WHO IS LESS THAN HUMAN

***Weird Western Tales* #39**
With scarred gunslinger Jonah Hex riding off into his own series, writer Michael Fleisher and artist Dick Ayers produced a new outcast to headline *Weird Western Tales*. Scalphunter was "a man who lived in two worlds, but was at home in neither." A white child who had been abducted by the Kiowa tribe, Brian Savage was raised as Ke-Who-No-Tay (He Who is Less Than Human). Framed for murder, Scalphunter evaded the U.S. Cavalry in between dispensing retribution against the real killers, who were cowboys that raided a Kiowa burial ground for gold, and meeting the dying biological father he never knew.

JULY

NEW GODS, NEW START

***The New Gods* #12**
The New Gods series and its original numbering was revived after a five-year break, with a story written by Gerry Conway and drawn by Don Newton. Conway and Newton balanced Jack Kirby's bombastic Fourth World opus about the adventures of the New Gods with more traditional comic book anguish. Fan favorites Lightray, Metron, and Orion were joined by new allies like Jezebelle as the New Gods and Darkseid raced to locate six Earth people, each believed to possess portions of the sought-after Anti-Life Equation. The quest lasted eight issues before the series was canceled.

April: Optical fiber is first used to carry live telephone traffic.
May: Scientists report using bacteria in a lab to make insulin for the first time.
June: Jubilee celebrations are held in the United Kingdom to celebrate twenty-five years of Queen Elizabeth II's reign.

JULY

FUGITIVE FROM META
***Shade, the Changing Man* #1**

Steve Ditko returned to mainstream comics with *Shade, the Changing Man*. Joined by co-writer Michael Fleisher, Ditko unveiled the story of Rac Shade, a secret agent-turned-fugitive from the extra-dimensional world of Meta. Framed for treason and sentenced to death, Shade stole a Miraco-Vest to escape from Meta to Earth and clear his name. All the while, he was hunted by Meta's authorities, as well as by his former lover, Mellu Loron, the daughter of Meta's dictator.

POINT OF ORIGIN
***Justice League of America* #144**

Green Arrow thought he had learned the Justice League of America's origin back in issue #9 (February 1962), when he was told of seven meteors transporting aliens to Earth. Now, he found inconsistencies in the story. Writer Steve Englehart and artist Dick Dillin revealed the truth as told by former JLA member J'onn J'onzz (Martian Manhunter). Back in 1959, a White Martian invasion of Earth prompted J'onzz to covertly guide the Flash into bringing together more than thirty heroes. The heroes rescued J'onzz from the White Martians pursuing him, averted the threat, and ultimately introduced J'onzz as a member of their new team.

AUGUST

OCCUPATIONAL HAZARD
***Men of War* #1**

Writer David Michelinie and artist Ed Davis presented an atypical war hero in Ulysses Hazard. In his debut issue, Hazard enlisted in the army for frontline duty during World War II, but was permanently assigned to digging ditches for fallen soldiers on the battlefield. This was not because of the polio he suffered as a child (which he had trained to overcome), but simply because he was black. Hazard contested his treatment all the way to the Pentagon, where the Joint Chiefs of Staff, impressed by his determination, made him a classified one-man platoon in the European Theater with the codename Gravedigger. *Men of War* #1 also included a back-up feature about the popular German World War I pilot Enemy Ace, written by David Kanigher and with pencils by Ed Davis.

AUGUST

DARK DETECTIVE
***Detective Comics* #471**

In just eight issues together on *Detective Comics*, first-time collaborators writer Steve Englehart and artist Marshall Rogers firmly entrenched Batman in his dark, pulp roots. Amazingly, this brief but celebrated collaboration almost didn't happen.

Englehart had agreed to write *Detective Comics* for just a year, as he intended to move overseas. His plan was to plot out his stories in advance, then dialog the artwork. However, a change in artists after two issues prompted Englehart to write his stories with full script for the first time in his career. "It allowed me to control the pacing of my stories exactly," he wrote, "and with Batman, so heavy on atmospherics, that worked to the stories' benefit."

Englehart didn't see the benefit until months later, when he received a package while living in Mallorca. He, like the fans reading *Detective Comics*, was blown away by the renderings of newcomer Marshall Rogers (whose first Batman art appeared in issue #468 in April). According to Englehart, Rogers' work "defined a man, a city, and an *ambience*."

Their first issue together made a major foe of Professor Hugo Strange, who hadn't appeared in a comic in nearly thirty-seven years. Strange had been running a sanitarium for the wealthy, secretly injecting his patients with a growth hormone that turned them into monsters. An unsuspecting Bruce Wayne—recovering from radiation burns suffered at the hands of Dr. Phosphorus—checked himself in. Before long, Strange discovered Wayne was Batman, and kept him sedated while he assumed both super hero and alter ego identities for his own nefarious causes.

Bruce Wayne checks into Graytowers, a sanitarium for the wealthy from where several millionaires have disappeared. However, it is Batman himself who uncovers the strange and monstrous goings-on within the exclusive establishment.

IN THE REAL WORLD...

June: Spain has its first democratic elections, after forty-one years of the Franco regime.
June: American Roy Sullivan is struck by lightning for the seventh time.
July: The New York City blackout of 1977 lasts for twenty-five hours, resulting in looting and other disorder.

SEPTEMBER

RESURFACED RAGE
***Aquaman* #57**

The Sea King's fans were thrilled to see their hero resurface in his own title, though Aquaman unquestionably wished it were under happier circumstances. One month earlier, in *Adventure Comics* #452, Black Manta murdered Aquaman's son, Arthur Curry, Jr. Therefore, it was understandable, when scribe David Michelinie and artist Jim Aparo chronicled Aquaman's pursuit of his nemesis, to claim a life for a life. Aquaman finally earned his opportunity for revenge, but the true hero in him granted his sniveling foe the one thing of which Arthur, Jr. had been deprived: mercy.

Aquaman demands "A Life for a Life" against his son's murderer, Black Manta. However, the monarch of the sea cannot bring himself to claim final retribution.

DOOMED AGAIN
***Showcase* #94**

Writer Paul Kupperberg and artist Joe Staton revived DC's "try-out" series from its seven-year slumber by resurrecting the super hero team, Doom Patrol—sort of. Months after the team had perished in a huge explosion, most of Robotman washed ashore on a beach. Fitted with a new body by the Metal Men's creator, the upgraded Robotman returned to his former headquarters and encountered a new Doom Patrol lineup. He joined this team of outcasts, who battled each other nearly as much as their enemies.

ESCAPIST ENTERTAINMENT
***Mister Miracle* #19**

Writer Steve Englehart and artist Marshall Rogers, having garnered acclaim for *Detective Comics*, picked up *Mister Miracle* where the series had ended three years prior: with newlyweds Mister Miracle and Big Barda honeymooning on New Genesis. However, Granny Goodness, Virman Vundabar, Kanto, and Dr. Bedlam broke up the holiday, abducting Barda to Earth and forcing Mister Miracle, the master escape artist, to battle without his Mother Box supercomputer. By the time the pair reunited, they were stranded on the moon and Barda had been brainwashed.

ORIGINS OF THE JUSTICE SOCIETY
***DC Special* #29**

The genesis of comics' first super hero team, which included the Flash and Green Lantern, had been a mystery since the JSA's debut thirty-seven years ago. Writer Paul Levitz and artist Joe Staton decided to present the definitive origin story. At the behest of President Franklin D. Roosevelt, the era's champions united to thwart Hitler in his attempts to invade England and assassinate FDR. Despite the team's success, Hitler wielded the immeasurably powerful Spear of Destiny, which prevented the JSA from invading Nazi-occupied territories in the future.

DECEMBER

HUNTRESS ON THE PROWL
***DC Super-Stars* #17**

With new blood pumping through the JSA, adding a Batman-character to the team seemed natural. While writer Paul Levitz and artist Joe Staton introduced the Huntress to the JSA in this month's *All Star Comics* #69, they concurrently shaped her origin in *DC Super-Stars*. Helena Wayne was the daughter of Earth-2's Batman and Catwoman. She took on the identity of Huntress when her mother died after being blackmailed by villain Silky Cernak. While Bruce Wayne burned his Batman costume in grief, Helena burned for revenge.

ALSO THIS YEAR: While "The Master Plan of Dr. Phosphorus" made Gotham City's inhabitants nauseous, scripter Steve Englehart and artist Walter Simonson introduced Bruce Wayne to the future love of his life, Silver St. Cloud, in June's *DETECTIVE COMICS #470*... In October's *SUPER FRIENDS* #7 twins Zan and Jayna, and their pet "space monkey" Gleek made their comic book debut, as did the Global Guardians, when scribe E. Nelson Bridwell and artist Ramona Fradon issued "The Warning of the Wondertwins!"... In *DC SUPER-STARS* #16 in October, the global-ruling Corporation manipulated Donovan Flint and his band of Star Hunters to locate and destroy the Somaii, the race responsible for sparking life on Earth in a story by writer David Michelinie and artist Don Newton...

August: Elvis Presley, the king of rock and roll, dies from a drug overdose at his home in Graceland, aged 42. Around 75,000 fans line the streets of Memphis for his funeral.

November: San Francisco elects City Supervisor Harvey Milk, making him the first openly gay elected official of any major city in the U.S.

1978

"HEADS UP, NEW YORK! MAKE WAY FOR FIRESTORM!"

Firestorm, *Firestorm, the Nuclear Man* #1

BIG BANG THEORIES

With new books and expanded page counts, coupled with the heavily anticipated release of *Superman: The Movie* in December, 1978 should have been the year of the "DC Explosion."

Superman: The Movie soared above all expectations, but even the Man of Tomorrow was unable to overcome the disastrous events that led to the now-infamous "DC Implosion."

On top of the decreasing sales and increasing printer costs caused by the recession, horrific winters along the East Coast affected distribution to the point where thirty-one titles had to be terminated by year's end.

The great tragedy of the DC Implosion was how it had effectively collapsed a year of great promise. Exciting new characters like Firestorm, the Nuclear Man had emerged, and the Man of Steel—besides becoming a box-office powerhouse—had entered the ring with boxing's Muhammad Ali.

JANUARY

AIR APPARENT
***Green Lantern/Green Arrow* #100**
For their 100th issue, Green Lantern discovered a fellow hero in the family, while Green Arrow found new purpose as Oliver Queen. In the first story, writer Denny O'Neil and artist Alex Saviuk introduced Hal Jordan, Green Lantern, to another Hal Jordan, son of the elder Hal's late uncle Larry and successor to the mantle of Air Wave. The issue's second tale, by scribe Elliot S! Maggin and artist Mike Grell, saw archer Green Arrow urged by the Mayor to run for office after defusing a gang of bombers.

FEBRUARY

BEGINNINGS AND ENDINGS
***The Teen Titans* #53**
On the day that the Teen Titans super hero team decided to disband, it seemed only fitting that they should reminisce about the adventure that encouraged them to form. While reviewing the Teen Titans Casebook, the Guardian and Bumblebee happened across the team's untold origin, which was vividly transcribed by writer Bob Rozakis and artist Juan Ortiz. Teen Titans Robin, Kid Flash, Speedy, Aqualad, and Wonder Girl initially united when their Justice League mentors inexplicably went on a crime spree. The reason resided within the League's Secret Sanctuary—an alien called the Antithesis was mentally manipulating the senior heroes into committing crimes, which in turn made the entity increasingly powerful. That is, until the teens defeated all of the Antithesis' "champions," thereby forcing him to dissipate.

PARLOR TRICKERY
***Doorway to Nightmare* #1**
Those seeking guidance against the supernatural found it inside Madame Xanadu's fortune-telling parlor in New York's Greenwich Village. Writer David Michelinie and artist Val Mayerik introduced Madame Xanadu as she helped a young woman rescue her boyfriend from a 1,000-year-old priestess who devoured men's souls to stay young. *Doorway to Nightmare* didn't remain open for very long, lasting only five issues. However, the series—produced by a different creative team every issue—gave Madame Xanadu a permanent residence within the DC Universe.

IN THE REAL WORLD...

January: The Copyright Act of 1976 takes effect, making sweeping changes to United States copyright law.

MARCH

MAKE WAY FOR FIRESTORM

***Firestorm, the Nuclear Man* #1**

If inventiveness is the fusion of ideas, then Firestorm was one of the most original characters to emerge from a comic book in years. Penned by Gerry Conway and drawn by Al Milgrom, the Nuclear Man was a genuine sign of the times—the explosive embodiment of a nuclear world.

Firestorm was the forced synthesis of high school student Ronnie Raymond and Nobel Prize-winning physicist Professor Martin Stein. As told through flashbacks, Ronnie, in an effort to impress a girl, joined the Coalition to Resist Atomic Power, a local activist group run by Edward Earhart. Unfortunately, Earhart was also a terrorist who planned to frame Ronnie for blowing up the fully automated Hudson Nuclear Power Plant, designed by Professor Stein.

Learning of Earhart's plans, Ronnie tried to stop him, but both he and Stein were knocked unconscious and left to perish near several pounds of explosives that were about to detonate. Ronnie recovered and tried to drag Stein out of the building, but he was too late. The ensuing radioactive blast fused Ronnie and Stein into an amalgamated being. As Firestorm, the Nuclear Man, the duo discovered that they could fly and alter the constitution of non-organic materials.

Firestorm managed to stop Earhart from striking again, though he would be unable to absorb the impact of DC's implosion after five issues. Thankfully, the character remains a vibrant source of adventure in the DC Universe.

The energetic personality of teenager Ronnie Raymond shines through in the body of Firestorm, the Nuclear Man, which also houses the mind of physicist Martin Stein.

MARCH

FORGED FOR WAR

***Steel, the Indestructible Man* #1**

Thanks to scripter Gerry Conway and artist Don Heck, the red, white, and blue shone like never before—on the steel-alloyed suit of the World War II cyborg, Steel. A biology student who had become a U.S. Marine, Hank Heywood nearly died in an explosion on his military base, however his college professor, Gilbert Giles, literally pieced him back together. In addition to fitting Heywood with micro-motors and steel compounds to replace ravaged bone, muscle, and organ tissue, Giles infused his former student with a bioretardant formula to induce rapid skin growth over his charred body.

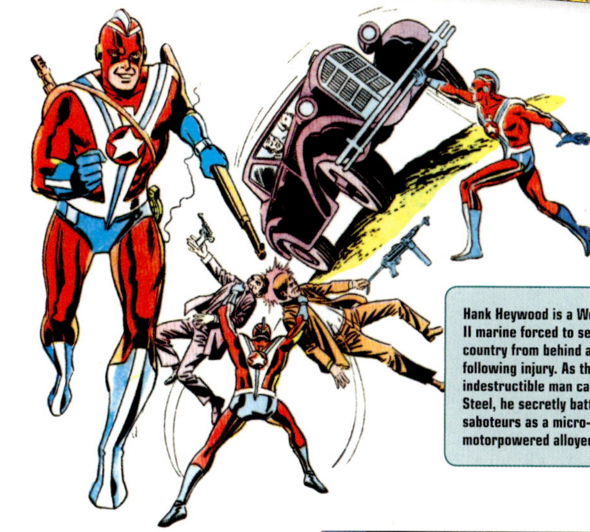
Hank Heywood is a World War II marine forced to serve his country from behind a desk following injury. As the indestructible man called Steel, he secretly battles saboteurs as a micro-motorpowered alloyed force.

WEDDED BLITZ

***All New Collectors' Edition* C-55**

Only an oversized treasury edition could have contained Superboy and the entire Legion of Super-Heroes' battle with the Time Trapper (a trip back to 1978 to restore the United Nations and a tampered thirtieth Century to its proper timeline) and the long-awaited wedding of Lightning Lad and Saturn Girl. Thankfully, Legion favorites Paul Levitz and Mike Grell were up to this enormous challenge with the popular tale "The Millennium Massacre," a story that has since been regarded by fans as one of the team's definitive adventures.

February: The Northeastern United States is hit by blizzards lasting three days.
February: United States Senate proceedings are broadcast on radio for the first time.

March: Zulfikar Ali Bhutto, Prime Minister of Pakistan, is sentenced to death by hanging for ordering the assassination of a political opponent.

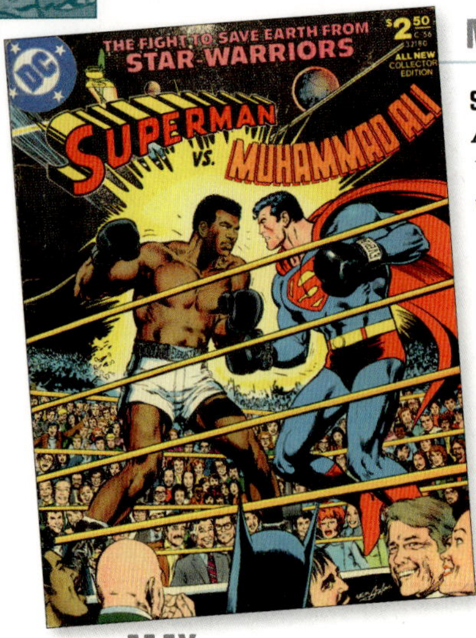

MARCH

SUPER PUNCH-OUT

***All New Collectors' Edition* C-56**

Writer/artist Neal Adams proclaimed that *Superman vs. Muhammad Ali* was "the best comic book" he and co-writer Denny O'Neil had ever produced. With its wraparound cover studded with real-world and DC Universe stars, it told the story of Rat'Lar of the alien race Scrubb, who challenged Earth's champion to fight his own. Battling for the honor of being Earth's champion, Ali, boxing's World Heavyweight Champion, left a de-powered Man of Steel tasting canvas, before beating the Scrubb champion.

MAY

SHOWCASE EXTRAVAGANZA

***Showcase* #100**

DC's try-out series saved its most daring attempt for its landmark 100th issue: bringing together sixty characters who had debuted or starred throughout *Showcase*'s first ninety-nine installments.

Writers Paul Levitz and Paul Kupperberg had only forty-eight pages to make this crisis large enough to warrant the combined attention of five dozen heroes. They devised an alien weapon that was pulling Earth from its orbit so fast that the time stream began ripping open. As a result, rampaging dinosaurs, cavemen, and Nazis overran the Earth, while volcanoes and other unnatural disasters erupted across the planet.

In a genuine Who's Who of DC comicdom, masterfully rendered by artist Joe Staton, the threat amassed the likes of the Silver-Age Flash, Green Lantern, Atom, the Challengers of the Unknown, Adam Strange, Space Ranger, Tommy Tomorrow, Anthro, the Inferior Five, and even a cameo by Fireman Farrell from *Showcase* #1 (March–April 1956). In the end, though, it took a séance in space with the Phantom Stranger to summon the Spectre, who returned Earth to its proper orbit. Meanwhile, in the Rocky Mountains, unlikely heroes Lois Lane and Angel O'Day managed to trash the alien's device that threatened to destroy the planet.

The Space Ranger teams up with Green Lantern to detect the alien force pulling the Earth from its orbit.

JULY

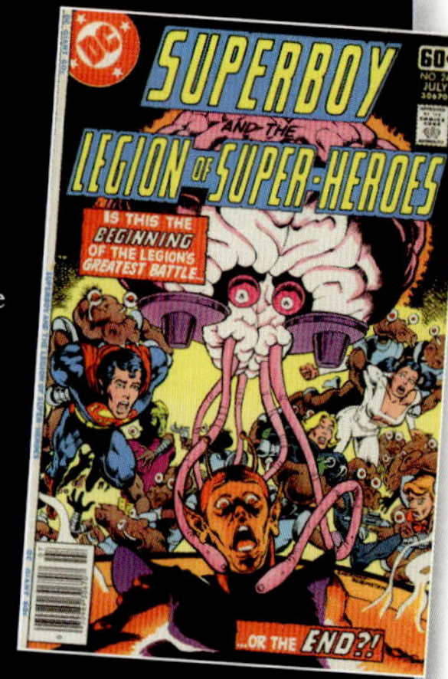

DECLARING EARTHWAR

***Superboy and the Legion of Super-Heroes* #241**

Paul Levitz has been acclaimed as a favorite *Legion of Super-Heroes* writer, his popular "The Great Darkness Saga" (August–December 1982) often being named as a high point in his output. However, he demonstrated his great affinity for the Legion, plus an uncanny ability to structure intricate subplots into a single storyline, four years earlier when he and artist James Sherman waged Earthwar.

"Earthwar" spanned five issues, making it easily one of DC's longest story arcs so far. The ambitious epic significantly magnified the Legion's role as cosmic peacekeepers, the magnitude of their missions—and the consequences.

It all began with the Legion's ranks spread thin amid a series of seemingly unrelated incidents. On Weber's World, Wildfire, Dawnstar, Mon-El, and Ultra Boy uncovered subversives and sabotage at a peace summit between the United Planets and the Dominion. Meanwhile, another contingent of Legionnaires defended Earth from the Resource Raiders, galactic pillagers who were actually advance scouts for Khundian forces planning an assault on the planet.

Levitz's subsequent issues, drawn by Sherman and Joe Staton, revealed other forces that were escalating both problems. Upon taking the fight to Khundia, Superboy and the Legionnaires learned of the involvement of the villainous group Dark Circle. Simultaneously, Earth's final line of defense fell to the retired Legionnaires Lightning Lad, Saturn Girl, Bouncing Boy, and Duo Damsel; Science Police officer Shvaughn Erin (her debut); and the Legion of Substitute Heroes.

When the Legion defeated the Dark Circle, Earthwar's true architect was revealed: longtime Legion foe, Mordru the Merciless. Mordru nearly won the war, but Element Lad transmuted atoms in space to bury him alive—the Legion's greatest victory.

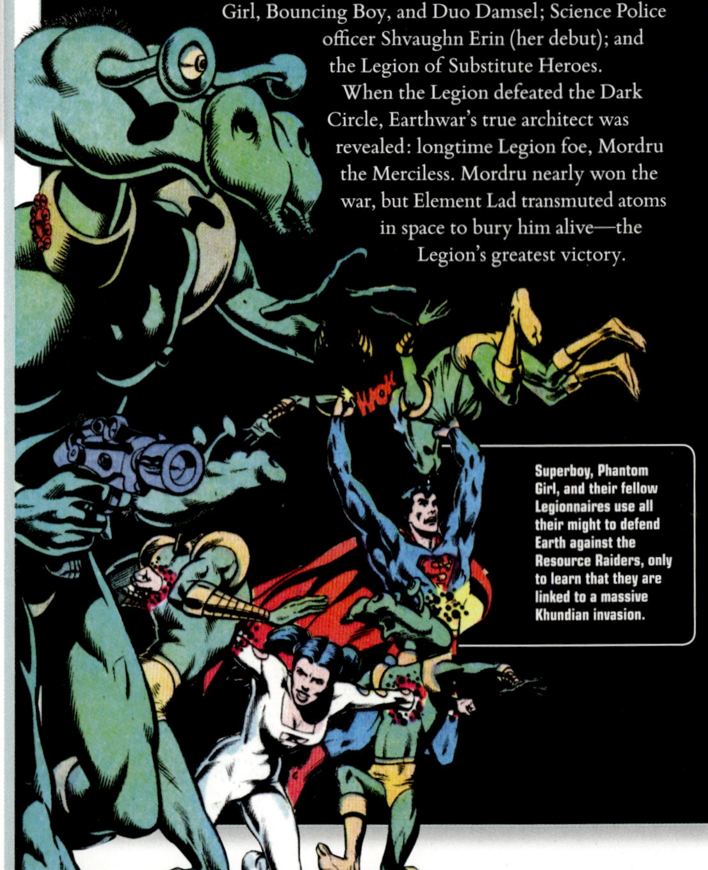

Superboy, Phantom Girl, and their fellow Legionnaires use all their might to defend Earth against the Resource Raiders, only to learn that they are linked to a massive Khundian invasion.

IN THE REAL WORLD...

June: "Garfield," which eventually becomes the world's most widely syndicated comic strip, makes its debut.

June: Argentina defeats the Netherlands 3–1 to win the 1978 FIFA World Cup.

July: Louise Brown, the world's first test-tube baby, is born in Manchester, U.K.

AUGUST

SUPERMAN TEAM-UPS
***DC Comics Presents* #1**

A new *Superman* ongoing series started to mix things up by teaming the Man of Steel with other heroes in the DC Universe. Writer Martin Pasko and artist José Luis García-López launched the inaugural issue, which forced Superman and the Flash into a "Chase to the End of Time." The Scarlet Speedster was coerced into helping the alien Ivlar prevent a billion-year-old civil war between his race—the Zelkot—and the Volkir. Meanwhile, the Volkir recruited Superman to stop Ivlar and preserve the war. Each believed that failure would result either in Earth's destruction, or in Krypton never coming into existence. Thankfully, the champions worked together and ensured that neither tragedy came to pass.

The Flash and Superman are forced onto opposing sides of the eons-old war between the Volkir and Zelkot races.

FACE-TO-CLAYFACE
***Detective Comics* #478**

Writer Len Wein and artist Marshall Rogers vividly depicted Batman's battle with the third Clayface. Preston Payne was an acromegalic—a victim of chronic hyperpituitarism that distorted his body. He believed that he had found a cure after securing a blood sample from the second Clayface, Matt Hagen. But instead of curing Payne, it metabolized his degenerative condition so much that he developed a corrosive touch, which he used to infect others whenever a tremendous fever raged within him. After turning several bodies into oozing puddles of protoplasm, the new Clayface incurred the Dark Knight's wrath.

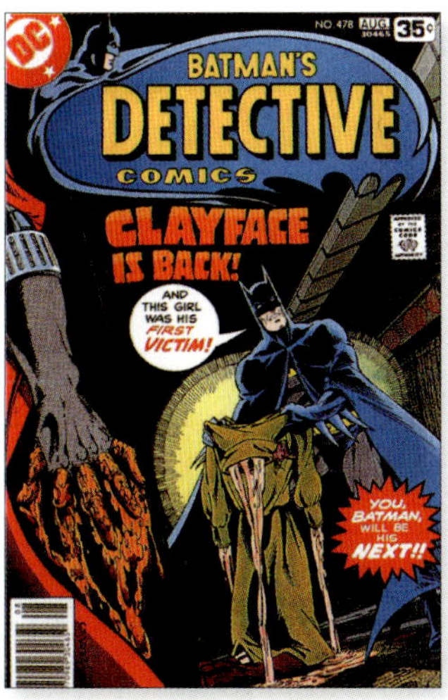

"I HAD HOPED TO AVOID THIS! BUT IF I AM TO SURVIVE, I'M AFRAID YOU MUST NOW FEEL THE TERRIBLE TOUCH OF—CLAYFACE!"

Clayface, *Detective Comics* #478

SUMMER

INDEPENDENT PUBLISHING
***Cancelled Comic Cavalcade* #1–2**

With the devastating "DC Implosion," a majority of the thirty-one titles terminated in 1978 were canceled in the middle of storylines. Therefore, staff members "published," in extremely limited quantites, two volumes of *Cancelled Comic Cavalcade*.

A bleak homage to DC's 1940s anthology series *Comic Cavalcade*, each volume consisted of photocopied stories and covers of the canceled works. These volumes were distributed only to creators of the material, and to the U.S. Copyright office.

Cancelled Comic Cavalcade #1, which included a cover of fallen champions by artist Al Milgrom, a Summer 1978 cover date, and a ten-cent price tag (despite never actually being sold), included the unpublished *Black Lightning* #12 and cover to issue #13; *Claw The Unconquered* #13 and #14; *The Deserter* #1; *Doorway to Nightmare* #6 (though it later appeared in *The Unexpected* #190, April 1979); *Firestorm* #6 (which later ran as back-up stories in *The Flash* #294–296, February–April 1981), and *The Green Team* #2 and #3.

Alex Saviuk covered the unemployed heroes lineup for *Cancelled Comic Cavalcade* #2, which was cover-dated Fall 1978 and sported a mock one-dollar pricetag. Unpublished material that appeared in this issue included *Kamandi* #60 and #61 (with a One Man Army Corps back-up tale); *Prez* #5; *Shade, The Changing Man* #9 (including an Odd Man back-up); *Showcase* #105 and #106, starring Deadman and the Creeper, respectively; *The Secret Society of Super Villains* #16 and #17; *Steel, The Indestructible Man* #6; and *The Vixen* #1. The issue also featured unpublished covers for *Army at War* #2, *Battle Classics* #3, *Demand Classics* #1 and #2, *Mister Miracle* #26, *Ragman* #6, *Weird Mystery Tales* #25 and #26, and *Western Classics* #1 and #2.

ALSO THIS YEAR: The Joker literally killed to get a federal trademark on his smiling Joker Fish in February's *DETECTIVE COMICS* #475… In April's *SHAZAM!* #34 the World's Mightiest Mortal took on a new art style, more sophisticated storytelling—and Captain Nazi, thanks to writer E. Nelson Bridwell and artist Alan Weiss… To reflect the modern setting of CBS-TV's *THE NEW ADVENTURES OF WONDER WOMAN*, scripter Jack C. Harris and artist Jose Delbo produced a story where Earth-1's Amazon helped her Golden Age counterpart apprehend the Angle Man in May's *WONDER WOMAN* #243…

August: Pope John Paul I succeeds Pope Paul VI as the 263rd Pope; he dies in September after only thirty-three days of papacy.

October: The New York Yankees clinch their twenty-second World Series championship, defeating the Los Angeles Dodgers 7–2.

1979

"KRYPTON'S FUTURE LIES IN THE STARS, GENTLEMEN!"

Jor-El, *World of Krypton* #1

AFTERSHOCKS

The effects of the previous year's "DC Implosion" continued to be felt throughout 1979. DC Comics' total output of titles had been cut by more than twenty percent, and DC executives had no intention of adding any ongoing series to the schedule.

Even then, however, positive aspects emerged from what was an incredibly difficult time for the company. DC found great success through the launch of its smaller, digest-sized books, which were filled with stories and compact enough for fans who liked to read while traveling.

DC sought to capitalize on the success of *Superman: The Movie* by publishing more Superman-related titles. They settled on detailing Superman-events—including Krypton's last surviving city, Kandor, breaking out of its bottled shell, and a three-issue limited series, *World of Krypton*, that explored Superman's homeworld.

JANUARY

PRISONER OF LOVE
***Superman* #331**

In a captivating tale, writer Martin Pasko and artist Curt Swan introduced the Smallville prison designer Carl "Moosie" Draper. It was Draper's love for Lana Lang and jealousy of Superman that spurred him to become the gray-costumed incarcerator, the Master Jailer. Pushed over the edge when the Man of Steel made enhancements to his prison for super-criminals, Draper abducted Lana and detained Superman, using a power-siphoning keyring that utilized the abilities of the Parasite, the Atomic Skull, and Metallo. Lana eventually destroyed the keyring, enabling Superman to escape and put the Master Jailer behind bars.

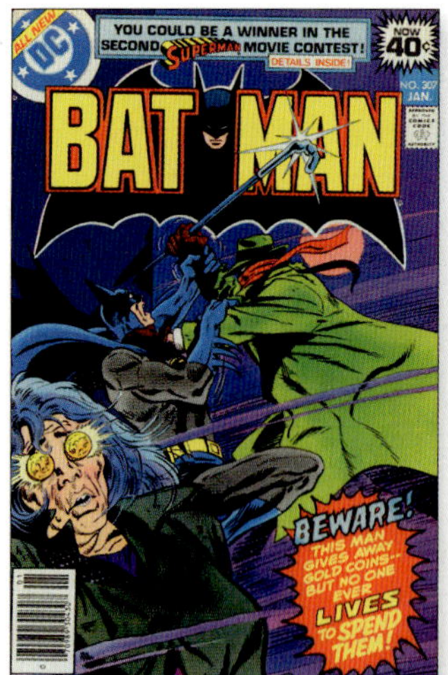

MAKING A KILLING
***Batman* #307**

Writer Len Wein and artist John Calnan introduced Bruce Wayne's new executive, Lucius Fox, in this issue of *Batman*. Handling the Foundation's day-to-day transactions, Fox freed up Wayne's schedule for more Dark Knight duty. With his business in the hands of a man with a "Midas touch," Batman pursued a killer who placed poisoned gold coins over his victims' eyes. Batman discovered that the coin-killer, Limehouse Jack, was Quentin Conroy, whose rich father had abandoned his family for the streets. The unhinged Conroy employed his patriarch's coin collection to become a Dark Messenger of Mercy.

ON TV THIS MONTH: Hanna-Barbera's live-action verison of *THE SUPER FRIENDS* comic, called *LEGENDS OF THE SUPERHEROES*, aired, starring Adam West as Batman and Burt Ward as Robin...

MARCH

TREASURING THE MAN OF REEL
***All New Collectors' Edition* C-62**

DC went to greater lengths with its tabloid-sized *Superman: The Movie* magazine than with prior treasury editions. Instead of containing stories and artwork, it approached the material with a greater eye toward graphic design. The sixty-eight-page magazine included extensive photos, features, actor profiles, comic-to-film comparisons, and extensive behind-the-scenes coverage of the blockbuster film. *Superman: The Movie* was the final DC treasury edition that went under the title of *All New Collector's Edition*.

IN THE REAL WORLD...

February: The Sahara Desert experiences snow for thirty minutes.
March: Philips demonstrates the Compact Disc publicly for the first time.

APRIL

END OF THE KNIGHT

***Adventure Comics* #462**

Writer Paul Levitz and artist Joe Staton shocked both the Justice Society of America and comics enthusiasts everywhere when they did the unthinkable: they killed Batman. Granted, this was Earth-2's Dark Knight, who had retired from crime fighting while daughter Helena assumed the role of Gotham City's guardian, the Huntress. His death was significant nonetheless, as it signaled the end of the Golden Age icon that debuted in *Detective Comics* #27 forty years earlier.

Ironically, it was Bill Jensen, an old enemy of Bruce Wayne's, not Batman's, who would cause his demise. Jensen sought retribution against Wayne (who had become Gotham's commissioner) for allegedly framing and sending him to jail. Sorcerer Fredric Vaux granted Jensen the power to achieve his revenge, and from the top of Gotham Towers, the criminal disposed of the Justice Society of America until Batman arrived on the scene. As the two fought, Batman's mask burned away, revealing the face of the man Jensen swore to destroy. Enraged, Jensen unleashed his full power, killing both himself and Batman, before the horrified eyes of Wayne's daughter. The story's title stated it best: "Only Legends Live Forever."

The Huntress watches her father, Batman, sacrifice himself to stop Bill Jensen from destroying the JSA.

MAY

THIS GOD MUST BE CRAZY

***Detective Comics* #483**

For *Detective Comics*' fortieth anniversary, scribe Denny O'Neil and artist Don Newton told the tale of Batman as he returned to Crime Alley on the anniversary of his parents' murder. The Dark Knight shielded Leslie Thompkins, the good Samaritan who comforted young Bruce Wayne on that tragic night, from the wrath of mob boss Maxie Zeus—a former Greek mythology-obsessed history teacher, who considered himself a god.

JULY

FIRST LIMITED SERIES

***World of Krypton* #1**

Despite a company-wide reluctance to add new ongoing series to DC's schedule, the worldwide success of *Superman: The Movie* motivated the company to publish more Superman-related titles. With that, editor E. Nelson Bridwell oversaw a project that evolved into comics' first official limited series—*World of Krypton*.

Originally slated as a three-issue arc for Showcase and scheduled to coincide with the theatrical release of *Superman: The Movie*, the story was never published as the movie was pushed back and Showcase was canceled. Thankfully, the attention that *Superman: The Movie* garnered would allow the issues to be published as its own miniseries.

Featuring out-of-this-world artwork from Howard Chaykin, Kupperberg's three-issue limited series explored Superman's homeworld in a manner no other Superman title had done. From his Fortress of Solitude headquarters, the Man of Steel reviewed the lost diaries and mind tapes of his father, Jor-El. They revealed Jor-El's childhood, how he achieved his lifetime ambition to become a scientist, and his relationship and marriage to Lara Lor-Van, Superman's mother. The stories also tied together decades of established Kryptonian characters and continuity, including Jor-El's discovery of the Phantom Zone for criminal rehabilitation and Krypton's inevitable destruction.

World of Krypton was never labeled as a limited series, though its publication established many of the new format's parameters. A limited series could properly focus on storylines and characters that would not fit in ongoing titles. Furthermore, as the format's popularity grew, so did the talent pool of writers and artists who wanted to craft stories for their favorite heroes but couldn't commit to an ongoing series.

Jor-El's mind tape recalls Jor-El meeting General Zod and Professor Ken-Dal for a tour around the Kryptonopolis Space Center, having been selected to help oversee Krypton's new space program.

April: Iran's government becomes an Islamic Republic by a ninety-eight-percent vote.
May: Greenland gets home rule.

June: Newly elected Pope John Paul II visits his native Poland, becoming the first Pope to visit a communist country.

JULY

DEATH OF IRIS WEST ALLEN
***The Flash* #275**

Life for the Fastest Man Alive screeched to a halt after writer Cary Bates and artist Alex Saviuk played "The Last Dance" for the Flash's wife, Iris West Allen. Iris had dressed as Batgirl to attend a masquerade party with her husband Barry Allen, who wore his Flash costume. During the party, Barry was drugged, and when he awoke, he discovered killer Clive Yorkin standing over his dead wife. The Flash eventually learned that his wife's murderer was not Yorkin, but the super-villain Reverse-Flash, who had vibrated his hand into Iris' brain at super-speed. Iris would reappear from the future years later, though the tragedy irrevocably altered Barry Allen's life, which ended with his own ultimate sacrifice in the twelve-part maxiseries, *Crisis on Infinite Earths* (1985–1986).

After being drugged at a party, the Flash awakens to find wanted killer Clive Yorkin standing over a murdered Iris West Allen.

AUGUST

KANDOR THINKS BIG
***Superman* #338**

Scribe Len Wein and artist Curt Swan brought in Supergirl to support Superman during his successful restoration of the shrunken Kryptonian city Kandor to full size. Superman coerced the villain Brainiac into shrinking him with the same device that had reduced the city, then reversed the effects with an experimental enlarging gun he had designed. Certain the effects could be reversed, he and Supergirl used the device on Kandor, which broke out of its bottle casing. The Kandorians were ecastatic, even though the city itself crumbled.

> **"YOU MAY HAVE DESTROYED OUR CITY, MY FRIEND—BUT YOU HAVE GIVEN US A WORLD."**
>
> Van-Zee from Kandor, *Superman* #338

SEPTEMBER

ON TV THIS MONTH: Ruby-Spears Productions' animated *THE PLASTIC MAN COMEDY/ ADVENTURE SHOW* provided great range—and "Baby Plas," the limber lawman's springy offspring—to ABC-TV's Saturday morning lineup for two seasons...

OCTOBER

EASY TO DIGEST
***Best of DC Blue Ribbon Digest* #1**

As DC cut back on producing oversized treasury editions, the company leaned toward the digest-sized format that became ideal for stocking on supermarket and newsstand racks. The 100-page *Best of DC Blue Ribbon Digests* were usually comprised of character-related reprints or inventory features. Superman was the focus of the first issue, and many more. The popular format resulted in a second digest series a year later, called *DC Special Blue Ribbon Digest*.

ULTIMATE WARRIORS
***All-Out War* #1**

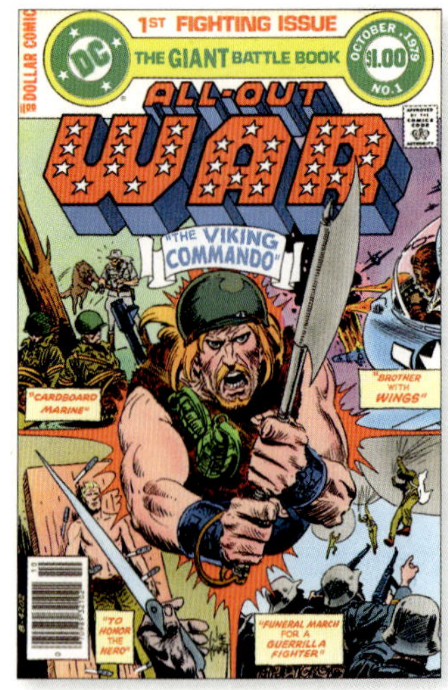

A new anthology declared *All-Out War* with stories featuring both familiar warriors and new combatants. Most notable among the latter was the Viking Commando, whose origin unfolded in "D-Day for a Viking" by writer Robert Kanigher and artist George Evans. During a battle with the Huns, the fifth-century Viking—Valoric—was carried off to Valhalla by the Valkyrie Fey before he died. Upon Odin's command, Valoric awoke on Earth in post-D-Day World War II accompanied by Fey, who was charged with shadowing Valoric until he truly perished. The axe-wielding Valoric was in no hurry to meet his fate.

FOUL PLAY AFOOT
***Justice League of America* #171**

Writer Gerry Conway and artist Dick Dillin crafted a tale of foul play aboard the JLA satellite, during the team's annual get-together with Earth-2's JSA. Mr. Terrific was in pursuit of an old nemesis, the Spirit King, when he was murdered before he could expose a turncoat among the heroes. Not knowing who to trust, the champions from two worlds imprisoned themselves within the satellite until they found the killer. Eventually, it was discovered that the Spirit King had possessed and framed Jay Garrick, Earth-2's Flash.

IN THE REAL WORLD...

August: Michael Jackson releases his first breakthrough album *Off the Wall*, which sells seven million copies in the United States alone, making it a seven-times platinum album.

September: The Entertainment Sports Programming Network (ESPN) debuts in the U.S.
September: The long-running comic strip "For Better or For Worse" begins.

NOVEMBER

TIMELESS TALES

***Time Warp* #1**

The "DC Implosion" had delayed plans to revive the sci-fi tradition that had been censored in the 1950s. DC wanted to bring back *Strange Adventures* (last published in November 1973) as a Dollar Comic-sized anthology. With the renewed popularity of sci-fi films (including *Superman: The Movie*), the series was eventually green-lit, though under a new name—*Time Warp*—that evoked more of a sci-fi feel.

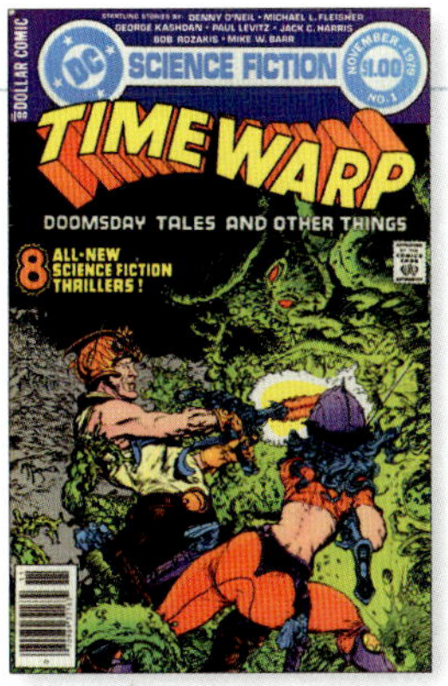

DECEMBER

SOCIETY'S OUTCASTS

***Adventure Comics* #466**

"The Defeat of the Justice Society" was a tale to remember, in which scripter Paul Levitz and artist Joe Staton revealed the reason behind the Justice Society's disappearance in the 1950s. The enemy, as it turned out, wasn't any of the countless foes the Golden Age champions combatted, but the United States government.

The JSA's defeat was recounted by one of its new members, the Huntress, who told the story to Power Girl via flashback. In 1951, after capturing gangsters whose leader was an international spy, the JSA was called before the Joint Congressional Un-American Activities Committee. Senator O'Fallon demanded that the heroes reveal their identities to clear themselves of possible connections to the spy they had captured, and to disprove any further allegations of subversion. Realizing that they would never be truly trusted during that era of political witch-hunts, and that their loved ones would be in constant danger, the JSA members refused, electing to disband instead.

As Green Lantern's power ring transported his fellow JSA members from the room, Hawkman promised that the committee wouldn't hear from the JSA again—a declaration that would remain in effect for more than a decade.

The Justice Society of America members refuse to reveal their secret identities and Hawkman announces the breakup of the team.

DECEMBER

FLYING SOLO AGAIN

***Green Lantern* #123**

After forty-six issues fighting side-by-side with Green Arrow, Green Lantern flew solo once more. Issue #123 reverted from *Green Lantern/Green Arrow* back to *Green Lantern*, although the reasons for the split would only be detailed in the following issue: Hal Jordan had become focused on space missions, which the Green Arrow was not best suited for.

Writer Denny O'Neil, who remained with the series through to issue #129 (June 1980), returned the cosmic element to the emerald warrior's adventures. Whereas any *Green Lantern/Green Arrow* stories had revolved around Earthly, socially relevant topics, the duties of the Green Lantern of Sector 2814 began to take on a more fantastic scope.

Artist Joe Staton joined O'Neil on the series for this new era in Hal Jordan's (Green Lantern's) life. Hal and fortune-teller Kari Limbo had almost married in the previous issue, but called off the wedding after learning that Kari's first love, the presumed dead Green Lantern Guy Gardner, was trapped within the Phantom Zone. Hal tried to save Guy from the clutches of the Kryptonian General Zod and his fellow criminals but Guy was soon abducted by a yellow beam of light. Recognizing the handiwork of Sinestro, Hal battled his arch-enemy and rescued Guy. Unfortunately, his friend's mind had already been torn apart by Sinestro and Hal returned the comatose Guy to Earth. Kari offered to look after her former lover, leaving Hal to hunt Sinestro.

The villainous Sinestro turns Guy Gardner into a puppet to do his every bidding, then mentally tortures the hero and leaves him in a vegetative state.

ALSO THIS YEAR: In May's *JUSTICE LEAGUE OF AMERICA* #166 members of the Secret Society of Super-Villains used a mystical griffin statue to switch bodies with the World's Greatest Heroes, in a tale by writer Gerry Conway and artist Dick Dillin that had repercussions that would continue to be felt more than two decades later… September's *DETECTIVE COMICS* #485 featured five all-new tales with Robin, the Demon, Batigrl, and Man-Bat, though it was the League of Assassins' murder of Kathy (Batwoman) Kane that sent Batman out for revenge in a story by scripter Denny O'Neil and artist Don Newton…

November: The Iran Hostage Crisis begins when 3,000 Iranian radicals, mostly students, invade the U.S. Embassy in Tehran and take ninety hostages.

December: The eradication of smallpox is certified, making smallpox the first, and to date only, human disease driven to extinction.

1980s

THE 1980s WAS a time of inspiration and experimentation, and DC Comics blazed the trail like no other major publisher of the time.

The decade began as merely an extension of what had gone before. The simple hero-versus-villain story told in single or two-part tales was still the norm and super heroes' characters and careers rarely deviated from the status quo. However, the world of comics was already in flux. DC had released its first miniseries, *World of Krypton*, in 1979, and the resultant success inspired more. As comic book specialty stores increased in number, new printing possibilities opened up. Prestige format graphic novels emerged, as well as trade paperbacks that collected favorite tales. Without the pressures of the returnable market of the newsstand, comics could flourish in direct-to-comic-store deluxe formats. The result was higher-quality production values and more dynamic artwork. All of a sudden, comic books started to look less like children's-fare, and more like an untapped storytelling medium. The stage was set for a new era of comic book fiction—the Modern Age.

Right at the start of the decade, writers like Marv Wolfman were already lending a sophisticated ear for dialog to their childhood heroes. Characterization pushed and shoved its way past action as the driving force of the most popular titles. So much so that, by the middle of the decade, comics had suddenly grown up. Sophisticated storytelling accompanied elegant, sometimes gritty plotlines. Works of great insight and intense drama began to emerge. And at long last, the mainstream media began to view comics through a new lens. For the first time in the history of the medium, a comic book had the genuine possibility of being elevated to the level of true literature.

"...WHATEVER'S IN HIM RUSTLES AS IT LEAVES... SIRENS ECHO THROUGH THE TUNNEL... TIRES SCREECH... THE WORLD... IS GROWING DARK... AND COLD...."

Batman witnesses the Joker's death
***Batman: The Dark Knight Returns* #3 (May 1986**

1980

"I WAS IN THE WORLD-SAVING GAME WHEN PEOPLE LIKE *FIRESTORM* AND *BLACK LIGHTNING* WERE STILL IN *DIAPERS*... SO GET *THIS* THROUGH YOUR HEAD, PUNK... I'M *AQUAMAN*, KING OF THE SEVEN SEAS... AND I'M THE *BEST*!"

Aquaman, *Adventure Comics* #475

NEW FACES AND FORMATS

A new decade was dawning, and DC was determined to make it memorable. One of the most experimental times in DC's history, the 1980s began with an influx of fresh faces, both new and reinvented. To insure their creations reached the largest audiences possible, DC also began to take advantage of formats as novel as the ideas they contained.

Chief among these new formats was the preview insert comic. Before a new ongoing series debuted in its premiere issue, DC began to offer a free sixteen-page adventure spotlighting the new title, nestled squarely in the middle of a popular comic that had already proven itself with the readers. This gave fans a risk-free way to sample new characters, and helped DC create a buzz and pique the interest of their fan base. With these special inserts, along with the new concept of the miniseries, DC was expanding its horizons and revitalizing itself as it entered the Modern Age.

JANUARY

THE LEGION STAKES ITS CLAIM
***Legion of Super-Heroes* #259**

After a decade of playing second fiddle to Superboy in *Superboy and the Legion of Super-Heroes*, the Legion finally made a grab for the title's marquee when the Boy of Steel left the 30th Century. In this seminal issue, penned by Gerry Conway and drawn by Joe Staton, Superboy was confronted with a vision of the death of his adoptive parents when he battled with the misguided Rejis Thomak. As he set off for Smallville, Saturn Girl used her telepathic abilities to insure that Superboy would stay in the past and therefore never have to confront a similar vision about his parents' fate when he returned to the future.

STARMAN SHINES
***Adventure Comics* #467**

Adventure Comics was cleaning house and swapping out some of its stars. Out were the adventures of Deadman, Aquaman, the Flash, and the Justice Society, and in were two new features, the first of which restarted the tongue-in-cheek adventures of Plastic Man, written by Len Wein and drawn by Joe Staton. The second debuted a new version of Starman by writer Paul Levitz and illustrator Steve Ditko. Despite bearing a name familiar to readers of DC's Golden Age comics, Starman was an entirely new creation, and he proved a welcome addition to readers.

SUPERBOY GOES HOME AGAIN
***The New Adventures of Superboy* #1**

After recently departing the pages of *Superboy and the Legion of Super-Heroes*, Superboy was free to pursue his own adventures, firmly engulfed in the world of Smallville, Kansas. In this premiere issue written by Cary Bates and illustrated by Kurt Schaffenberger, Superboy faced a threat from immortal aliens who offered him a chance to live forever as a teen. It was an opportunity Superboy might have accepted had he known that his adventures would only continue for fifty-four issues, a number easily surpassed by his old allies, the Legion, in their solo effort.

IN THE REAL WORLD...

March: U.S. President Jimmy Carter announces that the United States will boycott the 1980 Summer Olympics in Moscow.

JULY

UNTOLD BATMAN
The Untold Legend of the Batman #1

After DC released its first-ever miniseries, *World of Krypton,* in 1979, the stage was set for its second offering: another three-issue limited series called *The Untold Legend of the Batman.* As in most cases, Superman had paved the way with the miniseries format, but Batman was hot on his heels. These miniseries soon became standard fare of the comic book industry and allowed stories to be told involving popular characters outside the self-imposed limitations of their current titles' continuity.

Written by Len Wein, with art by John Byrne and Jim Aparo, *The Untold Legend of the Batman* not only delved into the origin of the fabled Dark Knight, but also set up a new mystery, an earmark of most Batman stories of the time. As the first issue began, Batman received an unmarked package in the mail containing the shredded bat costume worn by Bruce Wayne's father years earlier. Thomas Wayne had worn that very costume to a ball during Bruce's childhood, and had been kidnapped by gangster Lew Moxon afterward. Thomas Wayne had eventually escaped Moxon's captivity, and the gangster had sworn revenge, hiring hoodlum Joe Chill to kill both Thomas and his wife Martha. This violent crime had inspired the young Bruce to take up the mantle of the crime fighter known as Batman.

After reliving his tortured past, Batman set out with Robin to discover who had sent the Dark Knight the remnants of his father's costume, sensing it must be someone close to him. As he continued to receive a series of death threats, Batman recounted the origins of Robin, his faithful butler Alfred, the Joker, Two-Face, Commissioner Gordon, and Batgirl, before discovering that the culprit behind the mysterious notes was none other than Robin himself. In an effort to force Batman to confront and defeat his inner demons, Robin had masterminded the elaborate charade. Luckily, it was an effort that paid off, as by the story's end, Batman's war on crime was renewed as he set out once again to protect the citizens of Gotham City.

Batman confronts the memory of revealing his identity to his parents' murderer, Joe Chill, before Chill is killed.

SEPTEMBER

ADDING AQUAMAN
Adventure Comics #475

Despite its two regular features, *Adventure Comics* was in need of a main attraction. While both of its current stories—surrounding Starman and Plastic Man—were popular with the readers, neither told the type of traditional super hero adventure that many comic fans enjoyed. With issue #475, fan favorite Aquaman was added to the lineup, and his first installment was written by J. M. DeMatteis and illustrated by Dick Giordano. Combined with the continued adventures of Starman by writer Paul Levitz and artist Steve Ditko, and the misadventures of Plastic Man by writer Martin Pasko and artist Joe Staton, the appearance of Aquaman meant the chameleon title known as *Adventure Comics* once again changed to better match its environment.

While battling the Scavenger in his opening *Adventure Comics* story, Aquaman quickly reminds his old adversary exactly why he is "King of the Seven Seas."

HUNTRESS' NEW GROUNDS
Wonder Woman #271

The daughter of Batman and Catwoman from Earth-2 found a new home away from home in the pages of Wonder Woman's monthly title. Helena Wayne, perhaps the most popular character from her parallel dimension, donned mask and cape for a regular gig as the back-up feature to the Amazing Amazon's lead story. Handled by writer Paul Levitz and artist Joe Staton, the Huntress faced the villainy of the swamp creature Solomon Grundy in the first part of her new adventures. This landmark issue also saw the return of Steve Trevor to Wonder Woman's life in the main feature by writer Gerry Conway and penciller Jose Delbo.

April: Six Iranian-born terrorists take over the Iranian embassy in London; only one terrorist survives when the SAS retakes the embassy on May 5.

April: Robert Mugabe is elected Prime Minister of Zimbabwe.
May: The movie *Star Wars*: Episode V *The Empire Strikes Back* is released.

OCTOBER

PRESENTING THE NEW TEEN TITANS

***DC Comics Presents* #26**

A special sixteen-page preview section by writer Marv Wolfman and artist George Pérez within *DC Comics Presents* #26 revitalized the stalled franchise of DC's super-hero sidekicks, the Teen Titans. They went on to become DC's most popular comic team of its day. Not only the springboard for the following month's *The New Teen Titans* #1, the preview's momentous story also featured the first appearances of future DC mainstays Cyborg, Starfire, and Raven.

NOVEMBER

THE MACHINATIONS OF MONGUL

***DC Comics Presents* #27**

Artist Jim Starlin displayed his penchant for portraying powerful cosmic villains with the debut of Mongul, a new threat to plague Superman's life, in a story written by Len Wein. After kidnapping Superman's friends Steve Lombard, Jimmy Olsen, and Lois Lane, the alien blackmailed the Man of Steel into retrieving a key buried on New Mars, the home of Superman's former Justice League ally, Martian Manhunter. Forced to battle his friend, Superman defeated the Manhunter but Mongul escaped with the key, and with it, the controls to Warworld, a planet designed for destruction. The issue also had a back-up Congorilla story by writer Bob Rozakis and penciller Romeo Tanghal.

Mongul captures three of Superman's best-known supporting characters in order to successfully bend the Man of Steel to his will.

"I'M AFRAID YOU DON'T PRECISELY UNDERSTAND! I AM NOT ASKING YOU—I AM ORDERING YOU!"

Mongul, *DC Comics Presents* #27

NOVEMBER

TOP TEEN TITANS

***The New Teen Titans* #1**

The spin-off was about to surpass the original. The Teen Titans had been a part of DC Comics lore since their debut in the pages of *The Brave and the Bold* in 1964. Originally grouping sidekicks Robin, Kid Flash, and Aqualad, the team expanded to include Wonder Girl and then gained its own ongoing series in 1966, adding other teen members along the way. Over the course of the years, the teens' popularity began to wane, and after a hiatus and a brief return, the comic was canceled altogether in 1978 at issue #53. But in that title's end, writer Marv Wolfman saw an opportunity for a new beginning.

Joining with artist George Pérez, a detailed craftsman known for his ability to seemingly effortlessly render large casts of characters, Wolfman relaunched the famous team of sidekicks in *The New Teen Titans*. With a mix of familiar heroes like Robin, Wonder Girl, Kid Flash, the Doom Patrol's Beast Boy (now called Changeling), and a few intriguing new faces including the beautiful alien princess Starfire, the mysterious empath Raven, and the half-machine hero Cyborg, *The New Teen Titans* attracted scores of new readers, in no small part due to the quality of the work put into the title.

Wolfman seamlessly blended action and characterization, creating a cast of varied yet easily identifiable teammates, and the New Teen Titans soon climbed to new heights of popularity, scaling right past their mentors in the Justice League to become one of DC's best-selling titles of the day. Readers found themselves not only picking up the comic to witness the Titans square off against new foes like the demon Trigon and the criminal organization H.I.V.E., they also did so to check in on the relationships of the cast, including the budding romance between Robin and Starfire. With a level of sophistication rarely seen in its era, *The New Teen Titans* ran for ninety-one standard issues and spun out into a second series that amassed another 130 issues.

Raven, the mystic daughter of the evil demon Trigon, is responsible for recruiting this new batch of Titans. She remains a mainstay of the DC Universe to this day, along with Wolfman and Pérez's other new creation, Starfire.

IN THE REAL WORLD...

September: Switzerland's St. Gotthard Tunnel, the world's longest highway tunnel, opens.
September: The Robert Redford-directed movie *Ordinary People* premieres.
September: John Bonham of the rock group Led Zeppelin dies of alcohol poisoning.
November: Republican Ronald Reagan is elected President of the United States.

THE CREATURE COMMANDOS IN COMBAT

***Weird War Tales* #93**

A battalion of horror icons created by the U.S. government to aid the American war effort of the 1940s made its debut in an offbeat story by writer J. M. DeMatteis and penciller Pat Broderick. The Creature Commandos, made up of the reanimated, pieced-together corpse of Marine Private "Lucky" Taylor, the manufactured werewolf Warren Griffith, and the vampire Sgt. Vincent Velcro, were unleashed upon unsuspecting German troops to provide the Axis powers with an added element of fear.

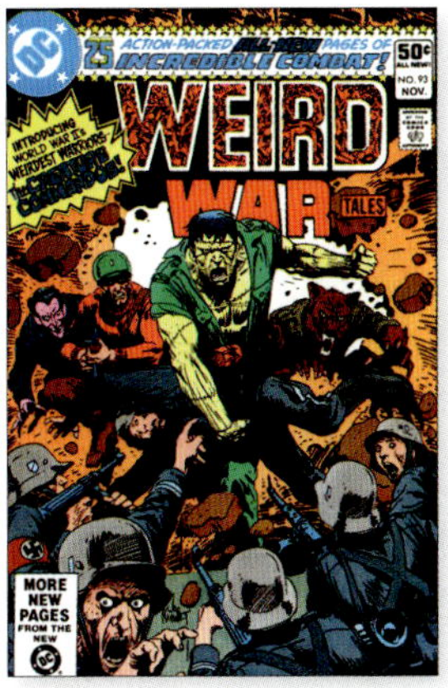

DECEMBER

DEATHSTROKE'S DEBUT

***The New Teen Titans* #2**

When the enigmatic heroine known as Raven assembled the New Teen Titans in issue #1 of their new series, it was in order to battle her demonic father, Trigon. However, on their way to that fight, the Titans met a villain who would play an even bigger role in their lives: the ruthless mercenary Slade Wilson, also known as Deathstroke the Terminator.

Debuting in the shadows of the cover to the team's second issue, written by Marv Wolfman and meticulously illustrated by artist George Pérez, Deathstroke was contacted by the criminal organization known as the H.I.V.E. and asked to kill the Teen Titans. Refusing to work without an advance, Deathstroke turned down the offer, only to see his son Grant Wilson take up the contract using the moniker "the Ravager." Unfortunately, Grant died during the ensuing battle when the H.I.V.E. experiment to increase his brainpower also caused him to age at an accelerated rate. Later, when Deathstroke arrived to collect his son's body, he naturally blamed the Titans for Ravager's death, unwittingly playing right into the H.I.V.E.'s scheme. Deathstroke swore revenge against the Titans and began to plot their deaths—the true goal of the H.I.V.E. all along. Deathstroke would soon become a recurrent thorn in the Titans' side, and he remains an ever-present watchful eye on their activities to the present day.

Deathstroke is a master of a variety of weapons, in addition to having enhanced reflexes, stamina, and agility.

THE CHEETAH'S COMEBACK

***Wonder Woman* #274**

The Amazing Amazon gained a new deadly adversary when Cheetah was reborn, thanks to writer Gerry Conway and artist Jose Delbo. Environmentalist Debbi Domaine's life took an ugly turn when she visited her sickly aunt, Priscilla Rich. Unaware that her aunt had harbored a secret criminal career as the original Cheetah, Debbi watched her beloved relative die in her arms. She was then taken captive and brainwashed into taking up her aunt's nefarious legacy by the criminal organization Kobra. The issue also featured a Huntress back-up tale penned by Paul Levitz and pencilled by Joe Staton.

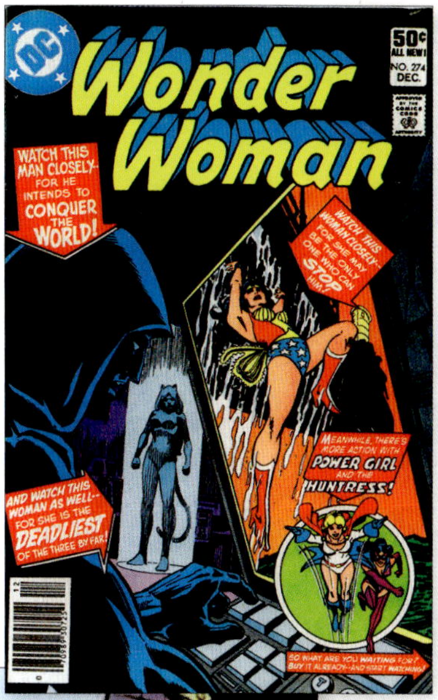

Debbi Domaine is a Cheetah for a new generation. She wears a different costume from the original worn by her aunt, updated with cat-like ears instead of a helmet.

MURDER MISTER E

***Secrets of Haunted House* #31**

Things were changing for the anthology series known as *Secrets of Haunted House*. In the last feature of its thirty-first issue, a story by writer Bob Rozakis and artist Dan Spiegle, a new monster hunter named Mister E was introduced. Designed specifically to give *Secrets of Haunted House* some month-by-month continuity, a proven secret of success in the serial marketplace of comics, Mister E was set to be a new regular feature in the title. Changes were afoot, but issue #31 did also follow the usual format for the title, including horrific tales narrated by the personification of Destiny and featuring the work of writers Arnold Drake and George Kashdan, as well as artists Tenny Henson and J. J. Brozowski.

ALSO THIS YEAR: In November's *GREEN LANTERN* [second series] #134, Marv Wolfman takes over the writing duties on the series as Green Lantern finds himself trapped at the North Pole by Doctor Polaris, all in a tale featuring art by Joe Staton and Anthony Tollin…

November: Millions of viewers tune into the U.S. TV soap opera *Dallas* to learn who shot lead character J. R. Ewing. The "Who shot J. R.?" event is a national obsession.

December: John Lennon is shot and killed by Mark David Chapman in front of the Dakota apartment building in New York City.

SPECIAL TEEN TITANS PREVIEW
DC
WATCH OUT, WORLD! HERE COME...
THE NEW TEEN
TITANS
FREE
ALL-NEW
PREVIEW
OCT.
APPROVED BY THE COMICS CODE AUTHORITY
THE MOST SENSATIONAL SUPER-STARS OF ALL ARE BACK-- IN ALL NEW ACTION!

THE ART OF GEORGE PÉREZ

DC COMICS PRESENTS #26 (October 1980)
This first page of a sixteen-page Special Teen Titans Preview typified the compositional skills and precision of line that made George Pérez one of DC's most popular, successful, and award-winning artists during the 1980s. Pérez helped relaunch and revitalize several super hero "careers," initially making his name with the New Teen Titans.

1981

"THERE'S SOMETHING WRONG HERE—SOMETHING HORRIBLY, INEXPLICABLY WRONG..."

Hawkman, *All-Star Squadron* #1

SUPERMAN OF THE YEAR?

It should have been Superman's year. The highly anticipated sequel to 1978's *Superman: The Movie*, simply titled *Superman II*, was released, and gave movie audiences exactly what they were looking for. Christopher Reeve once again donned the famous red cape and fought several superpowered villains including the evil Kryptonians General Zod (Terence Stamp), Ursa (Sarah Douglas), and Non (Jack O'Halloran). These spectacular battles captured a generation of viewers.

However, DC Comics hadn't quite realized the potential for boosted comic sales that capitalizing on the excitement surrounding the movie had. In fact, there was little added emphasis on the Man of Steel's line of comics at all in 1981. It wouldn't be until the release of director Tim Burton's *Batman* movie in 1989 that DC Comics would time large-scale events to coincide with Hollywood's big-screen efforts.

JANUARY

THE LEGION LOOKS BACK

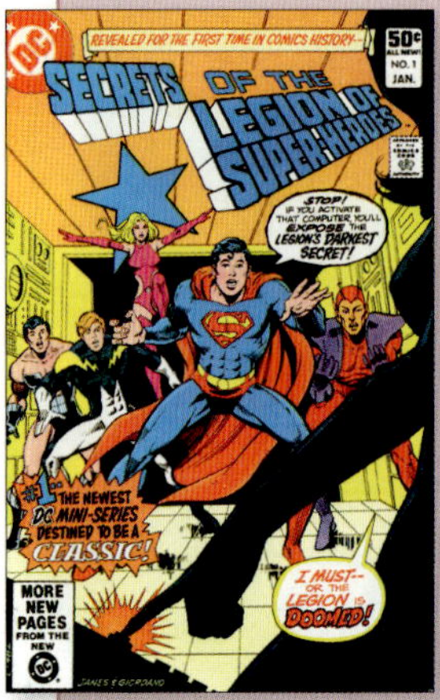

***Secrets of the Legion of Super-Heroes* #1**

This was DC's third foray into the world of the miniseries, and arguably its most revealing to date. A proven hit with the fans, the Legion of Super-Heroes was a natural choice to follow Superman and Batman into the three-issue miniseries format. The star attraction of Superboy (who was proudly present on all three covers) made the experiment even less of a risk for the company.

Plotted by E. Nelson Bridwell, with a script by Paul Kupperberg, *Secrets of the Legion of Super-Heroes* featured the art of penciller Jim Janes, inked by Dick Giordano on the first issue's cover. Giordano then took up the pencilling chores himself on the final two issues' covers. The comic centered around the Legion's financial backer and mentor R. J. Brande, who was on his deathbed due to a rare affliction known as Yorrgian fever. Realizing that the secret to Brande's cure could be within the Legion's computer files, Brande's old friend Marla Latham began to research the origins of nearly every Legionnaire. When he delved into the past of longtime team-member Chameleon Boy, he found that the hero was in fact Brande's son. With this major revelation out in the open, Chameleon Boy cured his father with a simple blood transfusion and began to mend a lifelong family rift.

The pasts of the Legion's founders, Cosmic Boy, Saturn Girl, and Lightning Lad, are explored in this issue.

FEBRUARY

DIALING INTO THE READERS

***Legion of Super-Heroes* #272**

Within a sixteen-page preview in *Legion of Super-Heroes* #272, by writer Gerry Conway and artist Steve Ditko, was "Dial 'H' For Hero," a new feature that raised the bar on fan interaction in the creative process. The feature's story, written by Marv Wolfman, with art by Carmine Infantino, saw two high-school students find dials that turned them into super heroes. Everything from the pair's civilian clothes to the heroes they became was created by fans writing in. This concept would continue in the feature's new regular spot within *Adventure Comics*.

IN THE REAL WORLD...

January: Iran releases fifty-two Americans held hostage for 444 days, ending the Iran hostage crisis.

MARCH

INTRODUCING I… VAMPIRE

***The House of Mystery* #290**

Writer J. M. DeMatteis unveiled vampire/ vampire hunter Andrew Bennett with the help of artist Tom Sutton in *The House of Mystery* #290. A new regular feature in the title, "I… Vampire" told the tale of an unlikely hero and his lifetime in pursuit of vampire Mary Seward. Not a title to give up its anthology format, however, the issue also featured one-off stories by writers Bill Dennehy, George Kashdan, and Don Glut, and artists Ernie Chan, Rubeny, and Dave Manak, all narrated by *The House of Mystery* mainstays Cain and Abel.

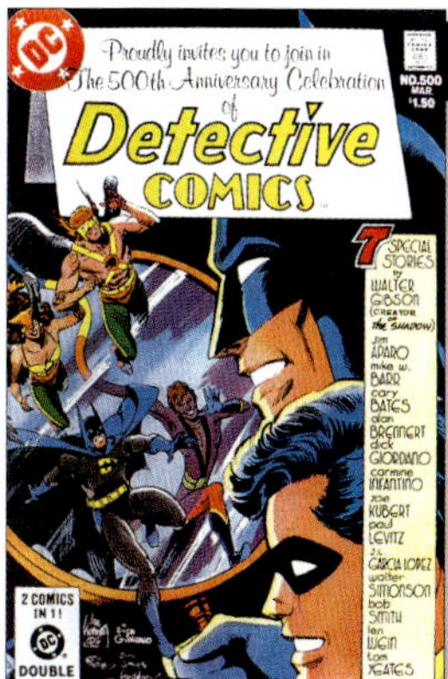

DETECTING A MILESTONE

***Detective Comics* #500**

The comic responsible for DC's name reached its 500th issue with the help of a variety of talented comic book icons. Melding big-name comic professionals with renowned super heroes, *Detective Comics* #500 included seven all-new tales embracing the detecting legacy of the company's flagship title.

Batman claimed the lead feature of the issue. In a dimension-spanning story by writer Alan Brennert and fan-favorite artist Dick Giordano, Batman traveled to an alternate Earth in order to save the parents of a young Bruce Wayne. Next, writer Len Wein and artist Jim Aparo unraveled a Slam Bradley mystery involving nearly every other detective ever featured in the title. Readers were then treated to a short Batman interlude, also by Wein, with the art of Walter Simonson. Writer Mike W. Barr and artist José Luis Garcia-Lopez followed that with an Elongated Man yarn delving into the past of the father of the detective story genre, writer Edgar Allan Poe. After that, writer of pulp icon the Shadow, Walter Gibson, spun a prose story of the Dark Knight, illustrated by Tom Yeates. That feature was followed by a Hawkman tale by writer Paul Levitz and artist Joe Kubert, and then a final story pairing Batman and Deadman, by writer Cary Bates and penciller Carmine Infantino. The entire celebration was capped off by a beautiful collaborative cover by all the artists involved.

The Phantom Stranger gives Batman a chance to travel to a variant Earth to rescue a version of his parents and save another Bruce Wayne from sharing his own tragic fate.

MAY

GREEN LANTERNS AT THEIR GREATEST

***Tales of the Green Lantern Corps* #1**

Green Lantern Hal Jordan gained his own three-issue miniseries by scripter Len Wein, plotter Mike W. Barr, and illustrator Joe Staton. The miniseries recounted the startling origin of Hal's journey to becoming one of the universe's protectors, but it is particularly significant for containing the first appearance of Nekron, the future mastermind of 2009's grand-scale *Blackest Night* miniseries. The first issue also featured the debut of Hal's fellow Green Lantern from Earth's neighboring sector, Arisia of the planet Graxos IV, and a battle with classic foe Krona.

JUNE

OBSERVING THE OMEGA MEN

***Green Lantern* [second series] #141**

Green Lantern Hal Jordan was treating himself to a well-earned vacation at a wilderness retreat with his longtime girlfriend and confidant, Carol Ferris, in *Green Lantern* #141. Unfortunately, the two had no idea that they would stumble upon DC's newest science-fiction franchise, a band of over one hundred aliens called the Omega Men. Led by the enigmatic Primus, this clandestine group of superpowered oddities were from the Vegan planetary system. They gave Green Lantern a run for his money in this issue, written by Marv Wolfman, with art by Joe Staton, and the Omega Men went on to gain their own ongoing series in 1983, which ran for thirty-eight issues. *Green Lantern* #141 also featured an Adam Strange back-up story written by Laurie Sutton and illustrated by Rodin Rodriguez.

As is often the case in comic books, Green Lantern's first encounter with the heroic Omega Men begins in conflict.

AT THE MOVIES THIS MONTH: June 19 saw the release of *SUPERMAN II*, taking the Man of Steel to new heights of action, courtesy of producers the Salkinds, director Richard Lester, and screenwriters Mario Puzo and David and Leslie Newman…

March: U.S. President Ronald Reagan is shot in the chest outside a Washington, D.C. hotel by John Hinckley, Jr.

May: In France, Socialist François Mitterrand becomes President.
June: The first recognized cases of AIDS are reported.

JULY

VYING FOR VIXEN
***Action Comics* #521**

Was she friend or foe? This was a question Superman asked himself on the cover to *Action Comics* #521, when he encountered the new mystery woman known as Vixen for the first time. In a story written by Gerry Conway and pencilled by Curt Swan, supermodel activist Mari McCabe leapt into the Man of Steel's life and proved her heroic intentions when she pursued a band of unscrupulous fur traders to New Delhi in order to shut down their criminal activities. Also included in the issue was a back-up story pairing Aquaman and the Atom, by scripter Bob Rozakis and penciller Alex Saviuk.

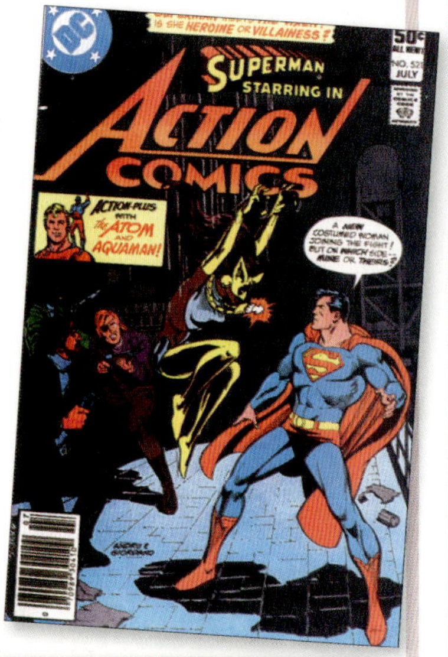

Madame Xanadu crashes a costume party of sorts in order to prevent its attendees from summoning a pair of demonic entities into the Earthly world.

XANADU CASTS HER SPELL
***Madame Xanadu* #1**

With the help of her trusted Tarot deck, the mysterious Madame Xanadu mystically appeared in her own one-shot by a legendary pair of *Batman* alumni, writer Steve Englehart and artist Marshall Rogers. Examining the life and adventures of the sorceress on Christy Street, this special delved into the dark side of magic, and was brought to life by Rogers' playful drawings and sound effects. Not content to simply feature a wrap-around cover by artist Michael William Kaluta, the issue also gave readers a pull-out poster by that same artist, along with an unrelated back-up sci-fi tale by writer J. M. DeMatteis and artist Brian Bolland.

JULY

MEETING OF THE MARVELS
***Marvel Treasury Edition* #28**

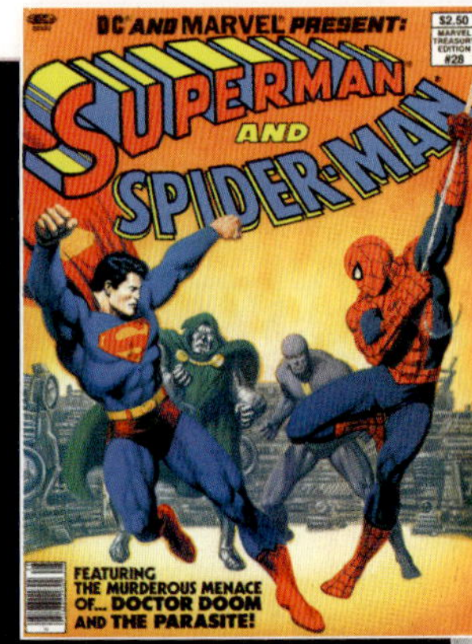

Superman and Spider-Man were teaming up again, and this time they brought their friends along for the ride. In an oversized treasury edition carrying a hefty $2.50 price tag, the Man of Steel paired for the second time with Marvel's iconic web-slinger, after 1976's *Superman vs. The Amazing Spider-Man*. The issue came together thanks to the script of writer Jim Shooter, a bit of plotting assistance by Marv Wolfman, the pencils of longtime Marvel luminary John Buscema, and a veritable fleet of inkers. Reaching from Manhattan's dark corners to the bright city streets of Metropolis, this sixty-four-page blockbuster also featured a painted cover by Bob Larkin over a design by John Romita Sr.

When Fantastic Four arch foe and megalomaniacal super-villain Dr. Doom embarked on his latest attempt at conquering the world, he unleashed the powerhouse known as the Incredible Hulk on the unsuspecting populace of Metropolis. As Superman defeated the Green Goliath by destroying an insect-sized drone emitting an ultrasonic screech that had sent the Hulk into a frenzy in the first place, he failed to notice that the resultant destruction had freed his old foe, the energy-draining Parasite, from his underground cell. Superman soon deduced that Dr. Doom had a hand in the Hulk's attack, and temporarily set up shop in New York in search of him, while Spider-Man, in the guise of Peter Parker, ventured to Metropolis on an assignment for his paper, *The Daily Bugle*.

When Wonder Woman was tricked by Dr. Doom into believing that he and Spider-Man were working together, Wonder Woman battled Spider-Man. Dr. Doom then kidnapped Wonder Woman and Spider-Man found himself in the villain's underground lair after witnessing the attack. In order to free the Amazon Princess and a similarly captured Hulk, Spider-Man and Superman joined forces and thwarted Doom's attempt at setting into motion a planet-wide power outage.

Apart from its large-scale battles and the first clashes between Superman and the Hulk, and Spider-Man and Wonder Woman, this crossover is particularly notable for the inventive handling of Clark Kent and Peter Parker, and their lives as newsmen at opposite ends on the spectrum of success.

Although Spider-Man's reputation is a bit spotty thanks to some manipulative writing in *The Daily Bugle* newspaper, Superman still considers him an ally thanks to their earlier team-up in 1976.

IN THE REAL WORLD...

July: Lady Diana Spencer marries Charles, Prince of Wales.
August: MTV (Music Television) is launched on cable television in the United States.
August: U.S. newspaper *The Washington Star* ceases publication after 128 years.
August: The original PC, Model 5150 IBM, is released in the United States.

SEPTEMBER

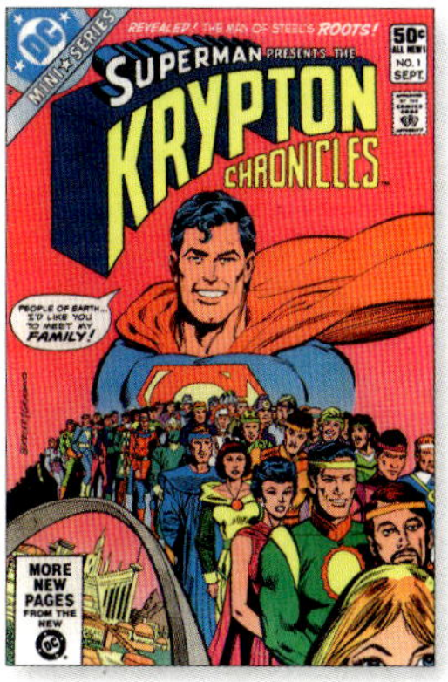

SUPERMAN'S KRYPTONIAN HISTORY

***Krypton Chronicles* #1**

The Man of Steel took a look at his family tree in this three-issue miniseries by writer E. Nelson Bridwell and longtime *Superman* mainstay artist Curt Swan. Reporter Clark Kent set out to discover Superman's family history for a *Daily Planet* story, flying to the restored Kryptonian city of Kandor as his alter ego, Superman. He began researching his lineage, which included architect Gam-El, scientist Tala-El, and general-in-chief Pir-El. The series also contained a handy glossary for dozens of Kryptonian terms.

THE STARS OF EARTH-2

***All-Star Squadron* #1**

The world of Earth-2 was at war. In a dimension not unlike that of the Justice League of Earth-1, the greatest heroes of the 1940s had banded together to form the Justice Society of America, but even that team wasn't enough to battle the Axis powers plaguing their society. So, at the behest of President Franklin D. Roosevelt, a new, larger team was created to help unite the war-torn country. The massive All-Star Squadron was formed, setting up their headquarters in the Perisphere at the heart of New York City's World's Fair.

The creative team of writer Roy Thomas and artist Rick Buckler on *All-Star Squadron* offered readers a nostalgic glimpse back in time, albeit through the slightly distorted lens of Earth-2's history. In this popular series that ran for sixty-seven issues, readers were treated not only to the adventures of the more familiar Justice Society, but also to every other mystery man of the time and dozens of minor heroes from DC's Golden Age, including the speedster Johnny Quick, the patriotic Liberty Belle, powerhouses Robotman and Commander Steel, and the 1940s versions of Batman and Robin. With Thomas' comprehensive knowledge of the heroes and history of World War II-era Americana, the *All-Star Squadron* was a certifiable hit, even if the Earth-2-shattering events of DC's tumultuous *Crisis on Infinite Earths* maxiseries of the mid-1980s took a toll on the book's continuity.

The newly formed All-Star Squadron works tirelessly to keep peace on the home front during World War II.

OCTOBER

THE INCREDIBLE BATMAN

***DC Special Series* #27**

It wasn't exactly what you'd call a fair fight. In yet another landmark crossover between the two comic book publishing giants, the DC Comics and Marvel Comics universes collided in order to offer a treasury-sized panoramic battle between two of the medium's most famous characters. Written by Len Wein and illustrated by José Luis Garcia-Lopez, the comic saw two often-misunderstood icons, Batman and the Hulk, doing battle with both the Joker and Marvel's ultra-powerful Shaper of Worlds.

When the Joker set about pitting the Hulk against Batman in the heart of a Wayne Research plant, the Dark Knight managed to beat the overwhelming odds by forcing the Hulk to inhale a lungful of sleeping gas. However, as fate continued to conspire against the Batman's ongoing manhunt for the Joker, the Clown Prince of Crime managed to unleash the reality-warping Shaper of Worlds, and soon the Dark Knight found himself teaming up with the Hulk in order to end the Joker's onslaught. With cameos by Batman foes Killer Moth, Two-Face, and Scarecrow, and Hulk villains Rhino, the Leader, and the Abomination, this sixty-four-page special served as a fun romp through the mad mind of the Joker, as well as an interesting team-up of a seemingly mismatched pair of comic book legends.

It's brain versus brawn when Batman is forced to battle the self-proclaimed "strongest one there is."

DECEMBER

THE NEW TEEN VILLAINS

***The New Teen Titans* #14**

Writer Marv Wolfman and artist George Pérez began to take a few more liberties in the lives of their successfully revitalized version of the Teen Titans. In this issue, Wolfman and Pérez had the heroes face off against a new version of the Doom Patrol's arch foes, the Brotherhood of Evil. Included in that number, alongside familiar villains Monsieur Mallah and the Brain, debuted the fear-inducing Phobia, voodoo expert Houngan, the location-hopping Warp, and the protoplasmic Plasmus.

ALSO THIS YEAR: Arak, Son of Thunder, debuted in August thanks to writer Roy Thomas and artist Ernie Colón in a free sixteen-page preview comic inside *THE WARLORD* #48, by writer/artist Mike Grell. The same issue also featured a Claw back-up tale by writer Jack C. Harris and artist Tom Yeates...

September: Simon & Garfunkel perform The Concert in Central Park, a free concert in New York City, in front of approximately half a million people.

December: Boxer Muhammad Ali loses to Trevor Berbick in what proves to be Ali's last-ever fight.

1982

"THE DREAM... ALWAYS THE *SAME*...! HOW MANY *YEARS*... HAVE TO PASS... BEFORE I STOP *RELIVING* THAT *HORROR*...?"

Swamp Thing, *The Saga of the Swamp Thing* #1

SEEING WHAT STICKS

It was a time of trial and error. DC was trying a flurry of new projects, relaunching old favorites in their own ongoing series and developing new characters to join them. The miniseries format was still in its infancy, but slowly became a standard way of offering shorter tales that catered more to the direct market of mail order subscribers and fledgling comic book specialty stores than to newsstands. The powers that be at DC would experiment with yet another new format before the year was over.

DC's first-ever maxiseries endeavor, *Camelot 3000*, was a twelve-issue story for the direct market. Besides charting the lengths limited series could stretch to, the popular story was told on Baxter paper, a thicker stock that allowed for brighter colors. Both the mini- and maxiseries formats proved popular with the readers, and many of DC's ongoing titles soon switched over to the higher production value of Baxter stock paper.

JANUARY

IN THE ZONE

***Phantom Zone* #1**

The Man of Steel had accumulated more miniseries than any other DC hero, and he wasn't about to stop now. Despite his heritage already being the focus of two other miniseries (1979's *World of Krypton* and 1981's *Krypton Chronicles*), DC once again shone the spotlight on Superman's alien past in this four-issue miniseries by writer Steve Gerber and artist Gene Colan. Looking at the long and storied past of the mysterious Kryptonian prison dimension known as the Phantom Zone, the comic told the tale of *Daily Planet* production artist and former Phantom Zone parolee Charlie Kweskill. It also featured Batman, Green Lantern, Hawkman, and Wonder Woman.

The Phantom Zone is a ghostly dimension populated by wraith-like Kryptonians, sentenced to the Zone for their heinous crimes against the citizens of their former planet.

FEBRUARY

CAPTAIN OF COMEDY

***The New Teen Titans* #16**

In a sixteen-page bonus preview insert in the middle of the pages of *The New Teen Titans* (written by Marv Wolfman and with art by George Pérez) was the debut story of Captain Carrot and his Amazing Zoo Crew, DC's hilarious new animal comic series. The first furry exploits of the animals of an alternative Earth, written by Roy Thomas and illustrated by Scott Shaw, paved the way for the launch of the animal heroes' ongoing series in March.

MAY

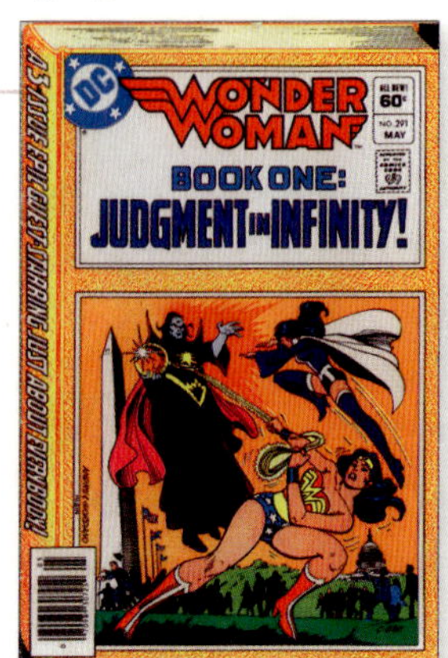

WONDER WOMEN

***Wonder Woman* #291**

In a team-up unlike any other in the past of the Amazing Amazon, Wonder Woman joined forces with the majority of DC's heavy-hitting female super heroes to stop the might of a creature known as the Adjudicator. In a three-part tale by plotter Paul Levitz, scripter Roy Thomas, and artist Gene Colan, Wonder Woman was helped by Zatanna, Supergirl, Madame Xanadu, Black Canary, Starfire, Wonder Girl, and the Earth-2 heroines Huntress and Power Girl to finally overpower the alien.

IN THE REAL WORLD...

February: The European Court of Human Rights rules that it is a breach of human rights for teachers to cane children against parents' wishes.

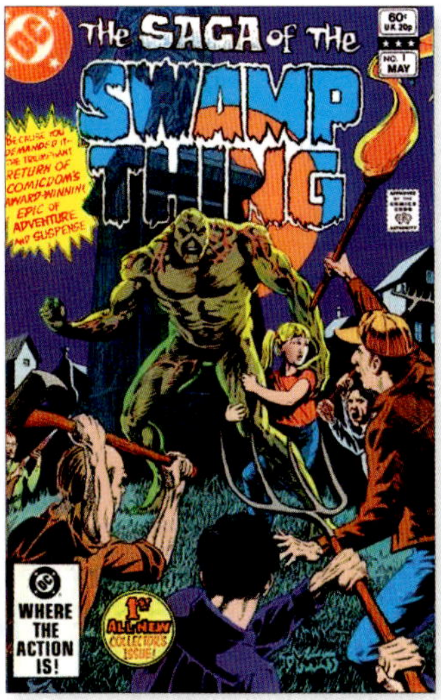

RETURN TO THE SWAMP

***The Saga of the Swamp Thing* #1**

The murky waters of America's swampland were once again occupied by their mysterious guardian as Swamp Thing returned to the pages of a new ongoing series, written by Martin Pasko and drawn by artist Tom Yeates. Created to help draw attention to July's new *Swamp Thing* feature film, this series proved popular with the readers and became a seminal landmark in comic book evolution when writer Alan Moore took over its reins with issue #20. Lasting for an impressive 171 issues, *The Saga of the Swamp Thing* also featured Phantom Stranger back-up stories for its initial thirteen issues, the first of which was written by Bruce Jones, with art by Dan Spiegle.

JUNE

FIRESTORM FIGHTS BACK

***The Fury of Firestorm the Nuclear Man* #1**

Until 1982, Firestorm had been just another casualty of the so-called "DC Implosion." Birthed during the "DC Explosion" of the late 1970s, Firestorm had been handed his own self-titled ongoing series in 1978 but it was canceled by issue #5. Despite having steady sales and a growing fan base, a series of cutbacks at DC had ended the comic's life unexpectedly. But demand for the hotheaded hero continued, and soon Firestorm made his way into *DC Comics Presents*, became a member of the Justice League of America, and gained a back-up feature in the pages of *The Flash*. Firestorm had proven his worth, so DC finally granted the hero a second lease at life with *The Fury of Firestorm the Nuclear Man*.

Written by his Gerry Conway, with art by Pat Broderick, Firestorm continued his carefree adventures in a series that spanned one hundred issues, encountering leagues of new villains along the way. The comic also introduced perhaps the hero's greatest challenge: Firehawk. Debuting in the very first issue of the new series, Lorraine Reilly would prove a longtime love interest of Firestorm's secret identity, Ronnie Raymond, and as Firehawk she would become a dynamic hero in her own right.

The fusion of Professor Martin Stein and student Ronnie Raymond, Firestorm controls the elements to fight a variety of super villains, as well as to play pranks on his classmates.

SUPERMAN GOES GLOBAL

***DC Comics Presents* #46**

The DCU's newest super hero team, the Global Guardians, was formed in this Superman tale by writer E. Nelson Bridwell and penciller Alex Saviuk. When Superman's day off was interrupted by the mystical Doctor Mist, he found himself scouring the globe to secure the villain's magical objects. Teaming with Israel's Seraph, Greece's Olympian, Denmark's Little Mermaid, Ireland's Jack O'Lantern, Brazil's Green Fury, and Japan's Rising Sun, Superman finally defeated the ancient wizard.

TEENAGE TALES

***Tales of the New Teen Titans* #1**

The stars of DC's number one team comic expanded into a four-issue miniseries, written and drawn by their ongoing title's regular writer/artist team, Marv Wolfman and George Pérez. Set during a team camping trip, the series featured detailed origin stories of their four most mysterious heroes: Cyborg, Raven, Changeling, and Starfire. Readers also got a glimpse of the team during their downtime, plus an impressive pin-up drawing of each issue's central character.

JULY

NEW NIGHTMARES

***The New Teen Titans* #21**

The DC Universe grew a little bit darker with the landmark debut of Teen Titans' foe Brother Blood, a crazed cult leader who would plague the young heroes throughout their careers. In addition to this morbid new member of the Teen Titans' Rogues Gallery, this issue by writer Marv Wolfman and artist George Pérez hid another dark secret: a sixteen-page preview comic featuring Marv Wolfman's newest team—Night Force. Chronicling the enterprise of the enigmatic Baron Winters and featuring the art of Gene Colan, Night Force spun out into an ongoing title of gothic mystery and horror the following month.

A recurrent thorn in the Titans' side, Brother Blood is a charismatic religious zealot, relying on the strength of his demented followers to fuel his rage.

AT THE MOVIES THIS MONTH: *SWAMP THING* hit movie theaters on July 30, featuring the directorial talents of Wes Craven and the sex appeal of Adrienne Barbeau, not to mention Dick Durock as the murky monster himself…

March: The United States places an embargo on Libyan oil imports, alleging Libyan support for terrorist groups.

April: The Falklands War begins when Argentina invades the Falkland Islands.
July: Intruder Michael Fagan visits Queen Elizabeth II in her bedroom for a chat.

AUGUST

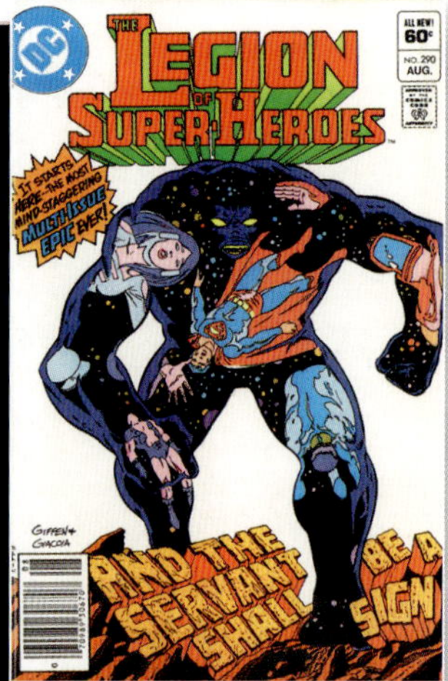

THE GREAT DARKNESS SAGA

***The Legion of Super-Heroes* #290**

Paul Levitz had been writing for the Legion for some time, working hard to earn the trust and favor of the die-hard Legionnaire enthusiasts, notoriously one of comicdom's most dedicated fan groups. However, when he wrote "The Great Darkness Saga," a five-issue epic that pitted the Legion against one of the most notorious villains of DC's long history, he and his artist partner Keith Giffen crafted the most famous Legion story of all time and became fast fan favorites.

It was an election year in *The Legion of Super-Heroes* #290. While the team argued among itself over who would be elected Legion leader, they soon happened upon an outside malicious force that would unite them more than at any other moment in their careers. Mysterious "servants of darkness" were appearing all over the United Planets, wreaking havoc and proudly displaying their vast reservoirs of power. The strongest among the Legion were falling before these demigods, and they had yet to meet the servants' master.

As the attacks continued, Dream Girl was elected leader just in time to help stage a battle on the mystical Sorcerers' World. There, Dream Girl discovered a small infant, a child who had magically appeared during the conflict. In the Legion's custody, the child began to age rapidly as the Legion continued to fight off the servants. When they finally discovered that the villains' enigmatic master was Darkseid himself, the Legion gathered all members past, present, and reserve to attack the dark god in the hope of crushing his scheme of galactic domination. During the Legion's darkest hour, the mysterious child from Sorcerers' World grew completely into a man, finally revealing himself as Highfather, the New Gods' opposite number to Darkseid's evil. With the help of Superboy, Supergirl, and Darkseid's resurrected son Orion (a restored former member of Darkseid's Servants of Darkness), the Legion eventually triumphed, and Darkseid was forced to retreat into the shadows that had spawned him.

Although many of the Legionnaires, like Wildfire, put up a decent fight, Darkseid's Servants of Darkness are more powerful and deadly than any henchmen the team has ever encountered.

SEPTEMBER

BLACKFIRE'S BEGINNINGS

***The New Teen Titans* #23**

The Teen Titans already had their hands full facing off against villains likes Deathstroke the Terminator and the restored Brotherhood of Evil, and they were now confronted with a new threat from one of their number's past. In yet another successful collaboration between writer Marv Wolfman and artist George Pérez, Blackfire, the corrupt sister of new Titan member Starfire, captured her sister and forced the Titans and the Omega Men to come to the young hero's rescue.

OCTOBER

CRISIS ON EARTH-PRIME

***Justice League of America* #207**

The Justice League of America teamed up with the Justice Society of America on a large scale with "Crisis on Earth-Prime," a five-part saga that crossed from the pages of *Justice League of America* into *All-Star Squadron*. The mammoth tale spanned dimensions and the ages as the heroes faced the might of the Crime Syndicate and would-be dictator Per Degaton. A collaboration between writers Gerry Conway and Roy Thomas, and artists Don Heck and Adrian Gonzalez, the saga also featured cover artwork by DC luminaries George Pérez and Joe Kubert.

NOVEMBER

SUPERGIRL STARTS OVER

***The Daring New Adventures of Supergirl* #1**

With the guidance of writer Paul Kupperberg and prolific artist Carmine Infantino, Supergirl found a home in the city of Chicago in a new ongoing series. After a train ride where she was forced to halt a near disaster, Linda Danvers arrived in the Windy City to join the ranks of that metropolis's newest institution of higher learning, Lake Shore University. There, Linda not only stumbled upon a great new apartment, but in true super hero style, she also discovered a new super-villain in the misguided Psi, whom she battled above the rooftops of her newly adopted home.

Unfortunately, this was not exactly the reinvention DC had hoped for, and *The Daring New Adventures of Supergirl* was cancelled after only twenty-three issues.

"IF THERE'S *ONE* THING I'VE LEARNED IN MY LINE OF BUSINESS—IT'S THAT *LUCK* SELDOM HAS ANYTHING TO DO WITH IT!"

Supergirl, *The Daring New Adventures of Supergirl* #1

IN THE REAL WORLD...

October: Walt Disney World in Orlando, Florida, opens its second-largest theme park, EPCOT Center, to the public for the first time.

October: Sony launches the first consumer compact-disc player.

October: The Double Stuf Oreo cookie is first sold.

NOVEMBER

THE UNCANNY TITANS

Marvel and DC Present: The Uncanny X-Men and The New Teen Titans #1

They were the most popular titles on the market. While *The New Teen Titans* had been capturing the attention of DC fans for the past two years, securing them the position as DC's number one team comic, *The Uncanny X-Men* had been doing the same thing over at Marvel Comics. As different as the two titles felt, they were also remarkably similar, both above and below the surface. Both titles starred a team of young heroes. Both teams were a reinvention of a 1960s idea. Both featured a mix of classic and new heroes, living in an almost family-like fashion (although the X-Men were a bit more dysfunctional than the Titans). Perhaps most importantly, both titles featured sophisticated writing and artistic styles that delved into the casts' personal lives as much as they featured cataclysmic battles with old and new foes. The titles were a step above other comics in terms of characterization and artistic endeavors, and both were receiving sales numbers deserving of their high-quality work. Pooling the two teams' efforts made very good sense.

In a $2 deluxe printing spectacular, the X-Men and Titans joined forces to thwart DC's resident evil New God, Darkseid. The issue, written by longtime *X-Men* scribe Chris Claremont and drawn by Walter Simonson, also featured the villainy of Deathstroke the Terminator and the otherworldly entity known as the Dark Phoenix. One of the most well-received crossovers of its time—or of any time for that matter—the team-up was a huge success, and a follow-up sequel was planned. However, as was the case with a highly anticipated Justice League/Avengers crossover of the time, the proposed encore was never completed due to editorial disputes.

The DC and Marvel Universes have merged, and now the Teen Titans and X-Men must also come together to combat the combined threat of their enemies.

DECEMBER

A RATHER GREEN DETECTIVE

Detective Comics #521

Green Arrow netted the coveted position as back-up story to the Dark Knight's adventures in *Detective Comics*. Written by Joey Cavalieri, with art by Trevor Von Eeden, the new feature saw Star City's renowned archer renew his war on crime. He started with a battle against the computer manipulations of Hi-Tek, all the while trying to meet his deadlines as ace columnist Oliver Queen for the *Daily Star* newspaper. The issue also contained a dramatic Batman versus Catwoman confrontation in the lead feature by writer Gerry Conway and artist Irv Novick.

CAMELOT'S SHINING EXAMPLE

Camelot 3000 #1

Writer Mike W. Barr and artist Brian Bolland pushed the limits of the conventional comic book with *Camelot 3000*. DC Comics' first foray into the realm of the maxiseries, *Camelot 3000* was a twelve-issue story printed on vibrant Baxter paper that showcased Bolland's realistic artwork. The story was set in the distant future on an Earth besieged by aliens and featured a resurrected King Arthur Pendragon and the Knights of the Round Table. Touching on mature and formerly taboo themes, the series helped pave the way for the modern graphic novel.

AMBUSH BUG RUNS AMOK

DC Comics Presents #52

Ambush Bug, the sometimes hero/sometimes villain/sometimes ambivalent onlooker, made his debut in the pages of *DC Comics Presents* #52. Eventually becoming a lighthearted adventurer, Ambush Bug interestingly started his career as a fairly ruthless murderer, ending the life of a Metropolis district attorney just to get the public's attention. However, with the combined forces of Superman and the Doom Patrol, and a bit of help from writer Paul Kupperberg and artist Keith Giffen, Ambush Bug was successfully put behind bars, even if he didn't stay there for long.

ALSO THIS YEAR: March saw the debut of Arion, mage of the ancient world of Atlantis, in the back-up feature of *THE WARLORD* #55, by writer Paul Kupperberg and artist Jan Duursema, alongside a lead story by writer Mike Grell and artist Mark Texeira...

November: Michael Jackson releases *Thriller*, the biggest-selling album of all time.
December: The first U.S. execution by lethal injection is carried out in Texas.

December: *Time Magazine*'s Man of the Year award is for the first time given to a non-human: the computer.

1983

"WHETHER BY FATE'S DECREE OR NOT... I FEAR I MAY HAVE GAINED AN ENEMY FOR LIFE!"

Wonder Woman, *Wonder Woman* #305

THE NEXT GENERATION

1983 was a good year for many rookie heroes to get their feet wet. DC was expanding its line and dozens of new crime fighters were getting their chance to prove themselves. With the continued success of *The New Teen Titans* and *The Legion of Super-Heroes*, many new team books started to sprout up. The ongoing series *The Brave and the Bold*, featuring partnerships between Batman and other established characters, was ended to make room for *Batman and the Outsiders*, a team comic starring several new heroes, including Geo-Force, Katana, and Halo. Infinity Inc. made their debut in *All-Star Squadron*, and the Omega Men and the Vigilante made their way from the pages of *The New Teen Titans* into their own ongoing series. Perhaps the year's most notable addition was Jason Todd, who was introduced to the Batman mythos. By the next year, the young circus aerialist would don the familiar costume of Robin the Boy Wonder.

FEBRUARY

WONDER WOMAN AGES GRACEFULLY

***Wonder Woman* #300**

The Amazing Amazon was joined by a host of DC's greatest heroes to celebrate her 300th issue in a seventy-two-page blockbuster. The story featured Wonder Woman and the dream-hopping Sandman as they battled a series of nightmares, one of which playfully included a marriage between the Amazon Princess and Superman. Written by Roy and Dann Thomas, and pencilled by Gene Colan, Ross Andru, Jan Duursema, Dick Giordano, Keith Pollard, Keith Giffen, and Rich Buckler, the issue also had pin-up drawings by George Pérez and Michael Kaluta, and a wrap-around cover by Ed Hannigan.

KILLER CROC MAKES A SPLASH

***Detective Comics* #523**

While battling the Golden Age super-villain Solomon Grundy, Batman had no idea that another sewer-dwelling foe was lurking in the shadows. Though he remained hidden beneath a hat and trench coat throughout the issue, Killer Croc made his mysterious debut in the pages of *Detective Comics* #523, written by Gerry Conway, with art by Gene Colan, which also featured a back-up Green Arrow story written by Joey Cavalieri and drawn by Irv Novick. Croc would soon become a major player in Gotham's underworld, before his intelligence faded and resembled that of his original costar, Solomon Grundy.

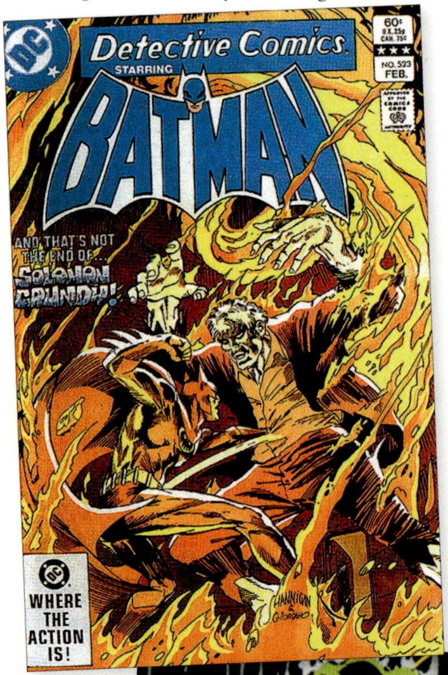

After being depicted as a shadowy figure in his debut appearances, Killer Croc finally reveals his huge physique and reptilian appearance to a startled Batman.

IN THE REAL WORLD...

January: Björn Borg retires from tennis after winning five consecutive Wimbledon championships.

MARCH

REINVENTING ROBIN

***Batman* #357**

It was a familiar story. A circus owner was threatened by a mobster offering a crooked protection racket. Refusing to give in to the criminal's demands, the owner unwittingly put a target on the heads of his star performers, a husband and wife trapeze act. A few days later, a young boy discovered that his parents had been brutally murdered. Taken in by the sympathetic millionaire Bruce Wayne (the secret identity of the Dark Knight Detective known as Batman), the boy submitted himself to a rigorous training schedule and soon joined his new mentor's side as Robin the Boy Wonder. It was a familiar story indeed, but this time it didn't belong to longtime-hero Dick Grayson. This time it was the copycat origin of Jason Todd, the second hero to take on the mantle of Robin.

The red-haired and cheerful Jason Todd first appeared in a circus scene in the pages of *Batman* #357, written by Gerry Conway and illustrated by Don Newton. As the youngest member of the Sloan Circus high-wire act known as the Flying Todds, Jason enjoyed his life in front of an audience alongside his parents, Trina and Joseph. On that fateful night when Jason Todd was to lose his parents at the hands of gang boss Killer Croc, Dick Grayson had attended the Todds' circus act, but he and Batman were too caught up in the gang war between their adversaries the Squid and Killer Croc to prevent history from repeating itself and the Batman from gaining a tragic new partner.

Jason Todd initially wore his circus costume while crime fighting alongside Batman, until Dick Grayson presented him with his very own Robin suit. He would later dye his hair black to match the original Robin, and even have his origin revamped entirely, but readers never really bonded with Jason and he would not reach the heights of popularity of his predecessor. Before the decade's end, he would pay for that with his life.

When facing the villain known as the Squid, Batman is forced to walk an updated version of the plank.

APRIL

EXCAVATING AMETHYST

***The Legion of Super-Heroes* #298**

The other-dimensional Gemworld found a new princess in the form of Amy Winston, an ordinary young girl from a distant reality, in the pages of a special sixteen-page insert comic by writers Dan Mishkin and Gary Cohn, and artist Ernie Colón. As the Legion of Super-Heroes investigated a death in the lead story by writer Paul Levitz and illustrator Keith Giffen, Amy was debuting as the magically powered Amethyst. Standing strong against the forces of the nefarious Dark Opal, Amethyst was gearing up for her own self-titled maxiseries in May.

MAY

GREEN ARROW'S FIRST BULLSEYE

***Green Arrow* #1**

The Battling Bowman fought his way into his own four-issue miniseries at long last, thanks to writer Mike W. Barr and artist Trevor Von Eeden. When his old friend Abigail Horton passed away, Oliver Queen was forced to relive an infatuation from many years ago with her daughter, Cynthia. Inheriting $34 million from Abigail, Ollie became a wanted man and the target of several assassination attempts. After facing his old foe Count Vertigo, Green Arrow finally discovered that the person behind the attacks, and Abigail's death, was none other than his former lover, Cynthia Horton.

DETECTIVE SPANS THE DECADES

***Detective Comics* #526**

Dubbed "an ending—and a beginning," DC celebrated Batman's 500th appearance in *Detective Comics* with a special extra-length anniversary issue. Scripted by Gerry Conway and pencilled by Don Newton, this fifty-six-page finale to the origin story of Jason Todd saw the young teen discover the Batcave for the first time, and even try out an unusual variation on the traditional Robin uniform, before Bruce Wayne made the decision to adopt him. The issue had a roll call of over twenty villains, from the Joker to Signalman, plus appearances from Robin, Batgirl, and Catwoman, and also featured a special pin-up drawing by Batman creator Bob Kane.

January: Seatbelt use for drivers and front-seat passengers becomes mandatory in the United Kingdom.

March: Michael Jackson performs the dance move that will forever be known as the "moonwalk," on stage at the Motown 25 concert.

JUNE

CELEBRATING YEARS OF ACTION
***Action Comics* #544**

After four decades, it was time for super-villains Lex Luthor and Brainiac to change their approach. Both got a complete wardrobe and powers makeover in this double-sized special. In writer Cary Bates and penciller Curt Swan's opening feature, Lex Luthor went to the planet of Lexor and uncovered ancient technology which he used to create a battle suit (designed by superstar George Pérez). In the second story, writer Marv Wolfman and artist Gil Kane chronicled Brainiac's evolution into robot form (designed by Ed Hannigan).

MEETING THE MAIN MAN
***The Omega Men* #3**

When space-bike-riding renegade Lobo made his debut during the "Citadel War" storyline in *The Omega Men*, by Roger Slifer and artist Keith Giffen, he was hardly recognizable as the rebellious anti-hero who would become one of the best-selling DC characters of the 1990s. Lobo's tight purple-and-orange costume was a far cry from the understated black leather jacket he would adopt in later years. However, Lobo was no less formidable than his future self, and the bounty hunter easily bested a shuttleful of powerful Omega Men.

AT THE MOVIES THIS MONTH: June 19 saw Christopher Reeve and company return to the silver screen for *SUPERMAN III*, which also featured the acting talents of Richard Pryor...

THE RAGE OF RONIN

***Ronin* #1**

A lavishly illustrated, six-issue miniseries, *Ronin* was the first DC project to utilize the prestige format (glossy paper with cardstock covers) and proved to be one of the most influential works of its time. A cinematic blending of words and pictures, the science-fiction epic was written and drawn by Frank Miller, a popular comic artist already known for pushing the envelope of visual storytelling in the pages of Marvel Comics' *Daredevil*. A precursor to Miller's groundbreaking work in 1986's *Batman: The Dark Knight Returns*, the Batman "Year One" story arc in 1987, and dozens more best-selling graphic novels and comics in the years that followed, *Ronin* was no less innovative and interesting.

Ronin chronicled the adventures of a heroic masterless samurai from feudal Japan, who was possibly just a construct of the vivid imagination of an psychic idiot savant living in a dystopian future. The comic was an unusual blend of the influences on Miller by French cartoonist Moebius and Japanese Manga comic books, and contained themes and plot elements familiar to fans of Miller's work, such as cannibalism, sewer denizens, leather-clad Nazi gang members, and love and sex in the midst of violence.

Frank Miller's Ronin is a quiet, serious man thrown into a chaotic future world that he can't possibly comprehend.

JULY

CONJURING UP CIRCE
***Wonder Woman* #305**

Diana Prince knew something was wrong, but she couldn't quite put her finger on what. Little did she know that the face she glimpsed in the mirror one morning belonged to perhaps the greatest adversary she would ever know. The sorceress Circe stepped out of the pages of Homer's *Odyssey* and into the modern mythology of the DC Universe in *Wonder Woman* #305, courtesy of Dan Mishkin's script and Gene Colan's pencils. The issue also featured a pin-up drawing by Mike Hernandez and a back-up Huntress story by writer Joey Cavalieri with Hernandez.

"...FOR I HAVE COME FOR YOU, YOUNG PRINCESS, AND I SHALL HAVE YOU YET!

Circe, *Wonder Woman* #305

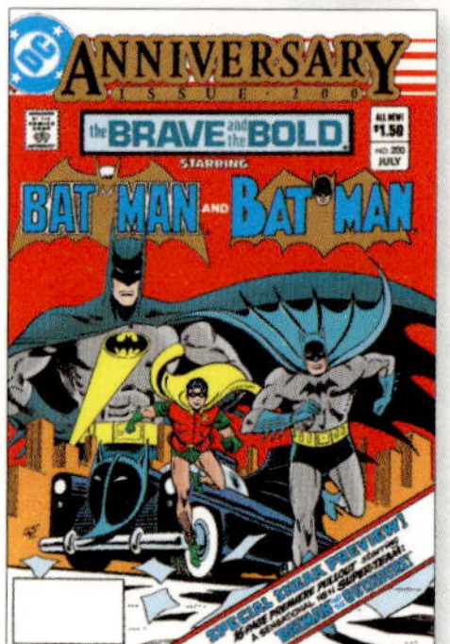

THE END OF THE BOLD
***The Brave and the Bold* #200**

Popular Batman team-up title *The Brave and the Bold* came to its conclusion in a special extra-length anniversary issue. The comic ended with a final pairing: the Batman of Earth-1 with the Batman of the Golden Age world, Earth-2. Written by Mike W. Barr and featuring art by Dave Gibbons, the story continuously shifted art styles to reflect the various eras of the Batman's career, and it was followed by a four-panel Bat-Mite comic strip by Stephen DeStefano. Despite being the final issue of this particular series, the book wasn't closed on Batman's team-ups. Although Batman was through working with partners, it was time to think bigger, and in a special sixteen-page preview insert written by Barr and with art by Jim Aparo, the Outsiders debuted. A super hero team of Batman's own creation, the Outsiders would soon star alongside Batman in the new monthly series *Batman and the Outsiders*.

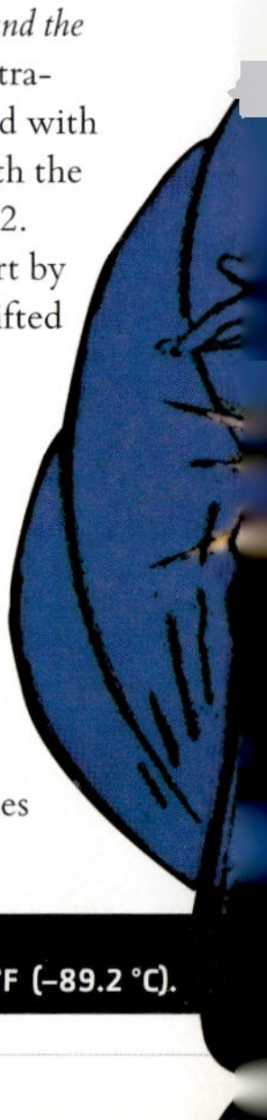

IN THE REAL WORLD...

June: Conservative Margaret Thatcher, Prime Minister of the United Kingdom since 1979, wins election for a second term in a landslide election victory.

July: The Nintendo Entertainment System (NES) goes on sale in Japan.

July: The lowest temperature on Earth is recorded in Antarctica at –128.6 °F (–89.2 °C).

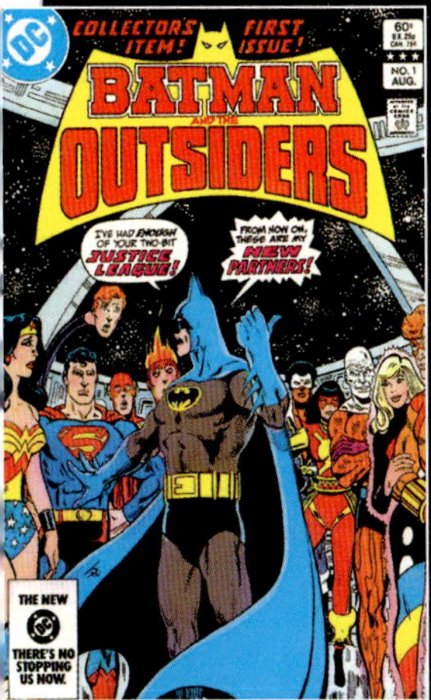

AUGUST

OUTSIDE THE LINES

***Batman and the Outsiders* #1**

The Dark Knight had never been what anyone would call a natural team player. True, he'd had Robin as a partner in his war against crime since near the beginning of his career, but he'd often had trouble meshing with those he considered equals in the Justice League of America. So, when his longtime super-teammates refused to enter the country of Markovia to help Batman rescue Bruce Wayne's longtime employee Lucius Fox, Batman abruptly quit the Justice League and set out for the small European nation on his own.

In the first issue of this new ongoing series by writer Mike W. Barr and longtime Batman artist Jim Aparo, Lucius Fox had been kidnapped by Baron Bedlam, a rebel leader who had already killed the king of Markovia. In an attempt to find Lucius' location, Batman employed the help of his old friend Black Lightning to infiltrate a camp of rebel insurgents in the country. However, when the samurai assassin Katana showed up and killed the rebel general, Batman's plan took a different turn. He encountered the mysterious energy-projecting Halo, the gravity-powered prince of Markovia now calling himself Geo-Force, and his old associate and master of the periodic table of the elements, Metamorpho, who all opposed the forces of Baron Bedlam, and a new plan formed in Batman's mind. After the heroes successfully overthrew Bedlam's reign of terror and saved Lucius Fox, Batman requested that the fledgling team returned with him to Gotham under his leadership. And just like that, the Batman now had his own league of heroes. Only his team would work *outside* the law.

Popular from its inception, *Batman and the Outsiders* ran for forty-six issues (albeit with a slight name change, to *Adventures of the Outsiders*, along the way), and it even spun off into the deluxe Baxter format for a second ongoing title, *The Outsiders*, in 1985. An interesting blend of old and new characters, the team's roster continued to grow over the years, gaining members such as Looker, Windfall, and the Atomic Knight, and facing classic villains including Eclipso, Kobra, and Maxie Zeus.

After resigning from the Justice League of America, the Dark Knight teams up with a host of heroes, including Metamorpho, in an effort to defeat Baron Bedlam and his henchmen.

THE FLASH CROSSES THE LINE

***The Flash* #324**

On his wedding day, Barry Allen was locked in a high-speed chase with his arch-enemy, the Reverse-Flash. Written by Cary Bates, with art by Flash legend Carmine Infantino, the story saw the Reverse-Flash attack Allen's fiancée, Fiona Webb. Flash managed to grab his opponent just in time, but in doing so, he accidentally broke the Reverse-Flash's neck. Allen had saved Fiona's life, but at too high a cost: he lost her affections and broke his own no-killing code in the same instant.

SEPTEMBER

INTRODUCING INFINITY INC.

***The All-Star Squadron* #25**

The children of the original Justice Society of America made their smash debut in this issue by writer Roy Thomas and penciller Jerry Ordway. All that the members of the super-team Infinity Inc. ever wanted to do with their lives was to follow in the footsteps of their Justice Society parents and the patriotic All-Star Squadron of the 1940s. But due to the manipulations of the super-villain known as the Ultra-Humanite, the young heroes instead found themselves displaced in time, battling the men and women they had looked up to since their birth. Projected onto the setting of an America preparing for war against Hitler's Axis forces, Infinity Inc. fought a surprised All-Star Squadron, until Infinity Inc. member Brainwave Jr. finally got the upper hand against the powerful, mind-controlling Ultra-Humanite.

Infinity Inc. proved their strengths and abilities against their elders in this issue, and while their identities remained a secret from the readers for the time being, all was soon revealed when they spun off into their own title set in the present day. An intriguing introduction to a whole new generation of heroes, *The All-Star Squadron* #25 marked the first appearances of future cult-favorite heroes Jade, Obsidian, Fury, Brainwave Jr., the Silver Scarab, Northwind, and Nuklon.

Nuklon withstands the iron blows of Steel, the indestructible man, whose mind is being controlled by the Ultra-Humanite. Eventually the All-Star Squadron members regain control of their thoughts.

ALSO THIS YEAR: The assassin Cheshire first bared her claws in the pages of *THE NEW TEEN TITANS ANNUAL* #2 by writer Marv Wolfman and artist George Pérez… The Omega Men explored the Vegan Star System and beyond in April in their new space-faring ongoing series spanning thirty-eight issues, kicked off by writer Roger Slifer and artist Keith Giffen… In June, *THE LEGION OF SUPER-HEROES* reached its 300th issue in style with a giant-sized anniversary special written by Paul Levitz, with art by a host of Legion artists… November saw the Vigilante take his brand of deadly justice into his own self-titled ongoing series, by writer Marv Wolfman and illustrator Keith Pollard…

September: The Red Hot Chili Peppers launch their self-titled debut album.
October: Microsoft Word is first released.

November: U.S. President Ronald Reagan signs a bill creating a federal holiday on the third Monday of every January to honor American civil-rights leader Martin Luther King, Jr.

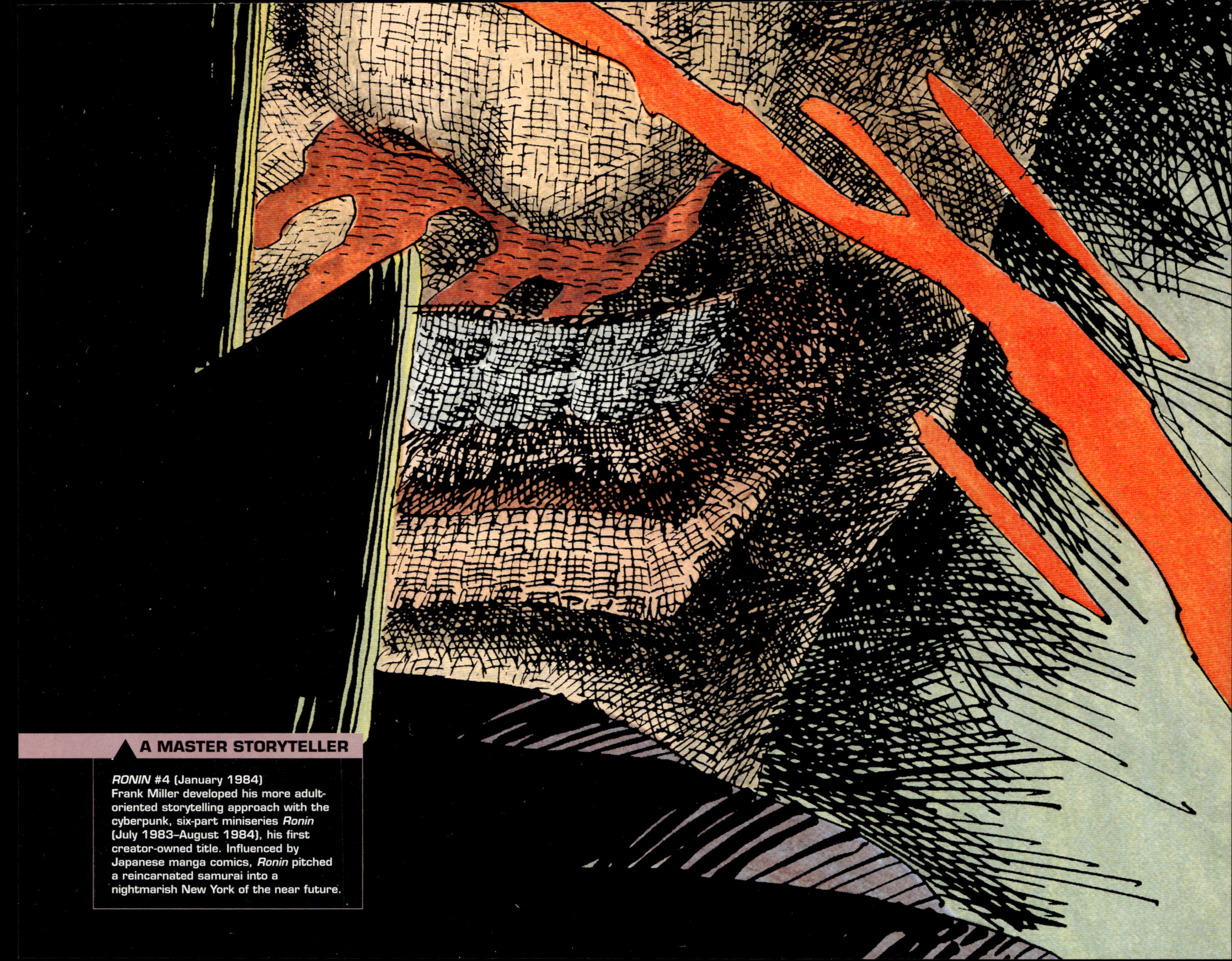

A MASTER STORYTELLER

RONIN #4 (January 1984)
Frank Miller developed his more adult-oriented storytelling approach with the cyberpunk, six-part miniseries *Ronin* (July 1983–August 1984), his first creator-owned title. Influenced by Japanese manga comics, *Ronin* pitched a reincarnated samurai into a nightmarish New York of the near future.

1984

"A *MUTANT*, EH? WELL, WE'VE GOT ALIENS, WITCHES, SHAPE-CHANGERS, AND CYBORGS. SO WHY NOT A MUTANT? 'SIDES, I HEAR YOU GUYS AREN'T HALF BAD."

Nightwing referring to Jericho, *Tales of the Teen Titans* #44

THE NEW DC

By the start of 1984, legendary Batman artist and inker Dick Giordano had been promoted to the position of Vice President/ Executive Editor of the DC Comics line. Giordano made a constant effort to keep his freelance talent happy, and as a result, the quality of the comics under his watch blossomed. With the blessing of DC President Jenette Kahn, Giordano also began to experiment a little. Series were relaunched to take advantage of the vibrant quality of Baxter paper, and a sincere effort was put into making comics fun again. Giordano's further experimentation would lead to some of DC Comics' greatest successes of all time. But little did the DC readers of the time know that the kid gloves would really come off in the next two years, and the medium of the comic book was about to change forever.

FEBRUARY

THE ANATOMY LESSON

***The Saga of the Swamp Thing* #21**
Writer Alan Moore was creating a whole new paradigm, but he had no idea at the time. He was merely attempting to make his mark on the all-too-crowded world of comic books, and telling stories the only way he knew how.

Jumping on board *The Saga of the Swamp Thing* with issue #20, Moore wasted no time in showcasing his impressive scripting abilities. Moore, with help from artists Stephen R. Bissette and Rick Veitch, had overhauled Swamp Thing's origin by issue #21. He had the monster captured and then dissected, proposing that Swamp Thing was not Alec Holland, a scientist caught in an explosion and originally thought to have mutated into the swamp's murky guardian. Holland had indeed perished in the explosion. Swamp Thing was in fact a creature born of plants infected by his consciousness and only believed himself to be the deceased scientist. That major revelation was just the beginning for Moore.

The series went on to truly embrace Swamp Thing's horror roots, and examined the full extent of his vast powers and connection to all plant life. With their adult tone and realistic dialog, Moore's stories were benchmarks in the growing sophistication of American comics, and this series partly inspired the creation of the Vertigo Comics imprint for mature readers, which adopted *Swamp Thing* under its label in 1993.

Swamp Thing lies motionless after being shot and captured, whilst Dr. Jason Woodrue glimpses the being for the first time ahead of his dissection of it.

DC'S FINEST

***World's Finest Comics* #300**
In the tradition of DC's anniversary editions, *World's Finest Comics* #300 was an extra-length issue contributed to by a variety of comic book talent. Written by David Anthony Kraft, Mike W. Barr, and Marv Wolfman, and illustrated by Ross Andru, Mark Texeira, Sal Amendola, and George Pérez, the issue also featured an Ed Hannigan cover. The story saw the World's Finest team of Superman and Batman enlist the help of the Justice League of America, the Outsiders, and the New Teen Titans to help face the dire threat of the Pantheon, a group of superhumans.

IN THE REAL WORLD...

January: The Apple Macintosh computer is introduced.
February: Michael Jackson wins a record eight Grammy® awards.

ROBIN RETURNS

***Batman* #368**

Jason Todd was proving himself as Batman's new partner in his war on crime, but there was one problem: he had no idea what to call himself. That would all change in *Batman* #368, with the help of writer Doug Moench and penciller Don Newton. Dick Grayson—Batman's first sidekick to call himself Robin—paid a visit to the Batcave and revealed that he was retiring the moniker of Robin in order make a new name for himself with the Teen Titans. Dick then graciously passed the mantle of Robin to Jason, who eagerly adopted it.

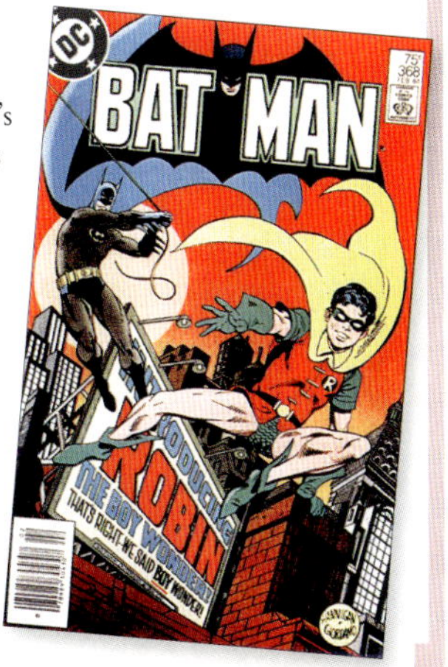

MARCH

INFINITY AND BEYOND

***Infinity Inc.* #1**

On the other dimensional world of Earth-2, the heroes of the Justice Society of America were gathered together for a rare Christmas Eve meeting when a group of brash young costumed heroes burst through their doors demanding membership in the prestigious team. A collection of the sons and daughters of some of the Society's members, the youths nevertheless failed to impress their mentors. Following their rejection by the majority of the Justice Society, the teens decided to band together and form Infinity Inc., a new generation of Earth-2's crime fighters. The group even gained the support of Justice Society member Star-Spangled Kid, who sympathized with Infinity Inc.'s situation so much that he soon joined their ranks.

Written by DC's Golden Age guru Roy Thomas and drawn by Jerry Ordway, *Infinity Inc.* was released in DC's new deluxe format on bright Baxter paper. With the team facing threats like the Ultra-Humanite, Brainwave, Solomon Grundy, and even manipulated versions of the Justice Society themselves, *Infinity Inc.* proved so popular that the title prevailed even after Earth-2 was destroyed during the events of 1985's *Crisis on Infinite Earths*. The comic ran for fifty-three issues, and many of its heroes went on to fight in various other titles, with several eventually graduating as members of the Justice Society of America.

Nuklon, Fury, Northwind, and the Silver Scarab are four of the founders of Infinity Inc. The others are Jade, Obsidian, and Brainwave Jr.

MAY

THE JUDAS CONTRACT

***Tales of the Teen Titans* #42**

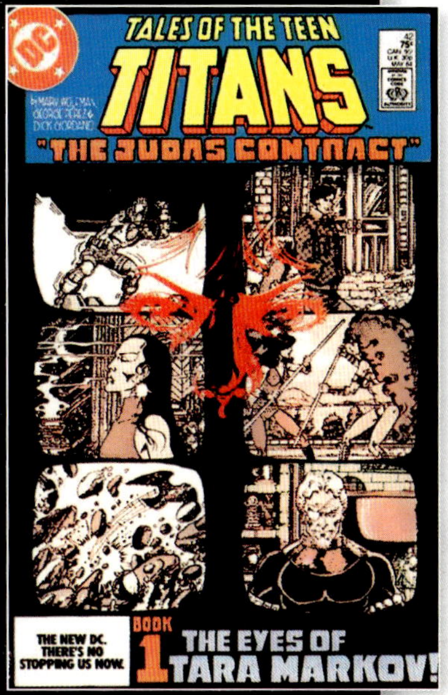

It was almost unthinkable. One of the members of the most popular super hero team book of DC's current line of titles was about to betray the group in spectacular fashion. It was a trial by fire the likes of which the Teen Titans had never seen, and it had been building since the title's inception.

In the four-part story arc "The Judas Contract," writer Marv Wolfman and artist George Pérez created the most memorable of all Titans tales, one that shook up both the team's roster and their lives for years to come. Called "a four-part novel" by its creators, "The Judas Contract" opened on business as usual for the tight-knit group of young heroes as they went about their daily lives and budding relationships. One relationship pairing was between Gar Logan, the Titans' Changeling, and their newest team member, Tara Markov, known as the earth-moving Terra. What the team didn't realize was that Terra had actually been planted in their ranks in order to gain information and their trust by their old adversary Deathstroke the Terminator, who had been plotting his revenge against the Titans since his first appearance in the title (issue # 2).

Armed with the knowledge of the Teen Titans' secret identities, Deathstroke and Terra were able to take out the young heroes one by one, with only Dick Grayson escaping their grasp. No longer calling himself Robin, Dick donned the costume of Nightwing and set out to rescue his friends with the help of a secret weapon: Deathstroke's youngest son, the mute Jericho. Nightwing broke into the headquarters of Deathstroke's employers, the criminal H.I.V.E. organization, and employed Jericho's body-possession powers and his own martial arts abilities to free his friends and destroy the H.I.V.E. complex. As Terra perished in the ensuing battle, the Titans mourned the loss of their teammate but refused to relinquish their optimistic nature, proving that dedication by adopting Jericho into their roster.

Despite her treachery, Terra is still mourned by the Teen Titans, and is buried with dignity as a true member of the team. No member feels her loss more than Changeling, who retains his love for her to this day.

March: A year-long strike begins in the British coal industry.
May: The Soviet Union declares it will boycott the Summer Olympics in LA, California.
June: Indian Army troops storm the Golden Temple at Amritsar, the Sikhs' holiest shrine, killing an estimated 2,000 people.

JUNE

THE DEVIL HAUNTS FIRESTORM
***The Fury of Firestorm the Nuclear Man* #24**

As Firestorm went about his daily business in this issue's lead story (by writer Gerry Conway and artist Rafael Kayanan), he wasn't aware that in the middle of his comic, a sixteen-page preview story marked the debut of fledgling stuntman-turned-hero Blue Devil. An attempt to put the fun back into comics, writers Gary Cohn and Dan Mishkin and penciller Paris Cullins had Blue Devil face the machinations of Flash villain the Trickster in this lead-in to his own ongoing series.

NIGHTWING AND A PRAYER
***Tales of the Teen Titans* #43**

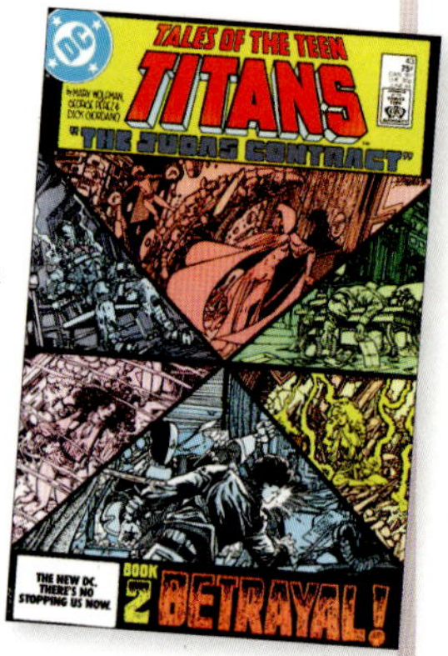

The Boy Wonder had become a man. Having already passed on the moniker of Robin to the Batman's new partner, Jason Todd, Dick Grayson was a hero without a name. It was amidst the chaos of "The Judas Contract," as Deathstroke the Terminator and former hero Terra slowly ravaged the Titan's members, that Dick Grayson adopted a new blue-and-gold costume and appointed himself Nightwing. In this penultimate chapter to the momentous storyline, writer Marv Wolfman and artist George Pérez reinvented one of DC's classic heroes, granting the character a new lease of life and the ability to step out of Batman's dark shadow.

JULY

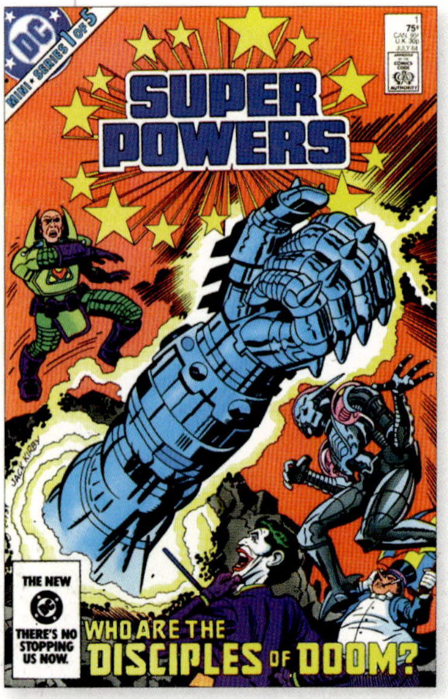

THE POWER OF MERCHANDISING
***Super Powers* #1**

DC's characters were leaping off the printed page. In association with the toy company Kenner, DC released a line of toys called Super Powers, which included modern action figures of Superman, Batman, and many more heroes and villains. Realizing the sales potential of a comic book tie-in, DC soon debuted a five-issue *Super Powers* miniseries plotted by comic book legend Jack "The King" Kirby, scripted by Joey Cavalieri, and with pencils by Adrian Gonzales. Kirby provided covers for all five issues, and even scripted and pencilled the final installment in this effort, which went on to spawn two sequel miniseries.

AUGUST

THE LEGION'S NUMBER ONE
***Legion of Super-Heroes* [second series] #1**

The Legion of Super-Heroes had been around since the late 1950s, but the legendary teens from the future had never starred in their own all-new first issue. The Legion had instead bounced around the pages of *Adventure Comics* and *Superboy*, finally taking over the latter series' title in 1973, a year in which they also starred in a four-issue series featuring reprinted Legion tales from *Adventure Comics*. However, the team had never been treated to the prestige and sales potential of a traditional debut issue. So, as DC began to toy with the idea of relaunching some of their more popular titles using high-quality Baxter paper, the *Legion of Super-Heroes* was an obvious choice.

Utilizing the talents of writer Paul Levitz and artist Keith Giffen, fan-favorite creators ever since their fabled 1982 epic "The Great Darkness Saga," the Legion was off and running in their own new title with a new major storyline. The debut issue introduced a newly united Legion of Super-Villains, a concept that had been building since the Legion of Super-Heroes was born, and a battle royal between the opposing Legions ensued.

Meanwhile, the Legion's other monthly comic changed its moniker to *Tales of the Legion of Super-Heroes* with issue #314. Since the Legion's deluxe new Baxter comic was only available by subscription or in comic specialty stores, DC soon tried an interesting experiment to insure that the regular newsstand fans didn't miss out on the Legion's new adventures. In August 1985, issue #326 of *Tales of the Legion of Super-Heroes* began to reprint the new Baxter stories, but on the normal newsprint paper of DC's standard newsstand editions. This idea was also used with *The New Teen Titans* and *The Outsiders*, two other titles that had made the Baxter transition, but it was nevertheless a short-lived solution, as the Legion's reprint comic was canceled two years later. The Baxter series, however, ran for sixty-three issues until its next relaunch, and remains the high point of the Legion's career in the eyes of many fans.

The might of the Legion of Super-Heroes is matched by that of the full-strength Legion of Super-Villains, but even in the midst of chaos, the bonds between the Legionnaires stand firm.

IN THE REAL WORLD...

September: The United Kingdom and the People's Republic of China sign the initial agreement to return Hong Kong to China in 1997.

October: The Provisional Irish Republican Army (PIRA) attempts to assassinate Prime Minister Margaret Thatcher and the British Cabinet in the Brighton Hotel Bombing.

TITANS TAKE TWO

***The New Teen Titans* [second series] #1**

As one of DC's most popular team books, *The New Teen Titans* was a natural choice to receive the deluxe paper quality and higher price point of the new Baxter format. With their regular newsstand title having already changed its name to *Tales of the Teen Titans* with issue #41, the path was clear for a new comic to once again be titled *The New Teen Titans*. Featuring the trademark writing of Marv Wolfman and the art of George Pérez, this second incarnation was a success from the start, providing readers with the perfect blend of high-quality paper with high-quality storytelling. As the Teen Titans were originally united in order to halt the machinations of Raven's demonic father, Trigon, it only made sense that the demon lord returned for a rematch in the new series' debut issue. During the series, the heroes also met the angel Azrael, fought the Titans of Myth, and encountered a crystal-powered new team member named Kole. With renewed popularity, the series ran for 130 issues, albeit with several rotations made in the art team, as well as a title change with issue #50. In a case rare among comic characters, throughout this series readers were able to witness the Titans age and mature into the adults that continue their heroic mission into the present day.

Trigon is an all-powerful interdimensional demon who has seemingly returned from the dead to attack his daughter Raven and the Teen Titans.

OCTOBER

THE FUTURE OF THE MAN OF TOMORROW

***Superman* #400**

The Man of Steel celebrated his 400th issue in star-studded fashion with the help of some of the comic industry's best and brightest. Written by Elliot S! Maggin and featuring a cover by Howard Chaykin, the extra-long issue featured the art of Frank Miller, Brian Bolland, and Moebius, among others. With a lead story examining Superman's life through the eyes of several future civilizations, the issue also featured a visionary tale written and drawn by Jim Steranko, and an introduction by famous science-fiction author Ray Bradbury.

JUSTICE LEAGUE DETROIT

***Justice League of America Annual* #2**

The prestigious Justice League of America got a bit easier to join, thanks to writer Gerry Conway and artist Chuck Patton. Marking the debut of the camouflaging hero Gypsy, the shockwave-casting Vibe, and the second generation hero Steel, this landmark comic saw many of the more famous League members step down in order to make way for a younger roster to carry on their legacy. Also made up of alumni Elongated Man, Zatanna, Martian Manhunter, and Aquaman, as well as fledgling heroine of *Action Comics* fame Vixen, the Justice League headed in a bold new direction, one many fans unfortunately weren't too happy about.

NOVEMBER

KARATE KID KICKS THE BUCKET

***Legion of Super-Heroes* [second series] #4**

In a surprising start to the Legion of Super-Heroes' new adventures in their Baxter format title, issue #4 saw fan-favorite hero Karate Kid die in action against the Legion of Super-Villains. In a story written by Paul Levitz, with art by Keith Giffen and Steve Lightle, and graced with a powerful Giffen cover hinting at the fate of the young hero, the Karate Kid gave his life heroically while battling Nemesis Kid. Karate Kid's death shocked readers and helped keep fans on the edge of their seats throughout the rest of the series.

JOHN STEWART GOES GREEN

***Green Lantern* [second series] #182**

Architect John Stewart was chosen as Green Lantern Hal Jordan's permanent replacement as guardian of space sector 2814 in this issue by writer Len Wein and artist Dave Gibbons. Hal Jordan had previously quit the Corps, resigning from his longtime position for the woman he loved, Carol Ferris. In doing so, Hal had left his section of space unguarded from any number of threats, and now one of them, Hal's old enemy Major Disaster, decided to make himself known by holding the Baldwin Hills dam hostage. Fortunately, John Stewart was made Green Lantern just in time to thwart Major Disaster's plans.

AT THE MOVIES THIS MONTH: The Girl of Steel flew into theaters with the premiere of *SUPERGIRL*, starring Helen Slater as the title character, along with Faye Dunaway, Peter O'Toole, and Mia Farrow…

ALSO THIS YEAR: Batman was introduced to the Wrath, his evil opposite number, in June's *BATMAN SPECIAL* #1, written by Mike W. Barr and illustrated by Michael Golden… June saw Blue Devil leap from the pages of Firestorm into his own light-hearted monthly comic written by Gary Cohn and Dan Mishkin, with art by Paris Cullins, which lasted thirty-one issues…

October: A famine plagues Ethiopia, where thousands of people have already died of starvation and as many as ten million more lives are at risk.

November: Ronald Reagan defeats Walter F. Mondale in the U.S. presidential election.
November: The Band Aid single "Do They Know it's Christmas?" is released.

THE COMIC BOOK STORE

Comic book stores changed the way that comics could be bought by readers. Before the 1970s, comic books were sold on newsstands at corner markets and grocery stores. Unsold copies were returnable, and the low-risk aspect meant that distributors weren't worried about delivering new issues to the shops quickly, while vendors weren't motivated to push sales. As comics' sales began to fall in the 1970s, a direct market was conceived whereby distributors could purchase specific titles and quantities of comics directly from the publisher for a lower price in exchange for relinquishing the ability to return unsold copies. This innovation led to the creation of comic book stores, specialty outlets that were happy to retain back issues.

In the 1980s, comic book stores began popping up in nearly every small town. Whereas first issues had previously been viewed as a retail gamble—considered by sellers as an untested new product—they now became collectors' items. Stores began to cater directly to fans with an eye for "investments;" rare or first issues became highly sought-after, prompting a trend among publishers for relaunching titles to boost failing sales.

For publishers such as DC, this new, direct market offered many benefits. Limited series became popular and their short publishing life was no longer a problem. More sophisticated printing techniques and better-quality paper became the norm rather than the exception. Higher-priced editions meant more revenue for publishers and specialty stores alike.

For fans, comic stores meant a new level of reliability not found at their local grocery. They could count on purchasing new titles every week, obtaining the issues they needed to complete their collections, often finding those very comics in better condition than at a non-specialist outlet. Comic stores provided the opportunity for camaraderie with like-minded individuals, a more united fan base, and led to the increasing popularity of comic book conventions.

DC took advantage of the direct market early on with miniseries and prestige format specials. The company also took notice of the growing market for trade paperbacks and began producing more reprinted collections than their main competitor, Marvel. DC took advantage of its direct sales program to offer posters, trading cards, and later, statues and action figures exclusively to comic book specialty stores. In addition, the freedom of the direct market made it possible for DC to stretch its creative legs and venture into the world of mature-reader comics.

Although comic books are no longer to be found in supermarket aisles and convenience stores, their life continues elsewhere. The trade-paperback trend is at an all-time high and comics for mature readers are consistently growing in popularity. The number of comic book stores may have decreased in number since the early 1990s as comic book sales have dropped, but they remain the main outlet for comic books and a crucial feature of the industry's landscape.

Left: Sorceress Morgan le Fey was one of the villains of Camelot 3000 *(1982–85), a sci-fi reimagining of the Arthurian legends by writer Mike W. Barr and artist Brian Bolland, and one of DC's first direct market books. Main picture: King Arthur and his knights charge into battle.*

RANG!

1985

"TH-THERE'S HOPE... THERE IS ALWAYS HOPE... TIME TO SAVE THE WORLD!"

The Flash, *Crisis on Infinite Earths* #8

A YEAR IN CRISIS

It was the fiftieth anniversary of DC Comics, and DC decided it was time to prepare older characters for the next generation. With decades of complex continuity under their collective belts, the powers at DC saw that they needed to streamline their comics universe in order to make their titles accessible to new readers. To do that, they'd need more than just one special project.

DC remade the DC Universe in the epic *Crisis on Infinite Earths*, combining the multiple alternate Earths into one playing field. In an unprecedented sweep, hundreds of characters died as a simpler DCU was reborn.

Elsewhere, the monthly maxiseries *Who's Who* began, cataloging the hundreds of players still standing, and the following year, *The History of the DC Universe* limited series would debut to piece together the new timeline. It was a new and improved DCU, but the shake-ups were just beginning.

JANUARY

SOCIETY IN SHAMBLES
***America vs. the Justice Society* #1**
In this limited series by writer Roy Thomas and penciller Rafael Kayanan the JSA was taken to trial, following a modern-day witchhunt. In the other-dimensional world of Earth-2, a diary had surfaced supposedly belonging to the late Batman, who had been killed in the pages of *Adventure Comics* #462 (March 1979). In it the JSA was accused of helping Adolf Hitler. Comprising four extra-length issues, the series retold the JSA's origin and featured the entire roster and many of its Rogues Gallery.

FEBRUARY

WONDER GIRL'S WEDDING
***Tales of the Teen Titans* #50**
Writer Marv Wolfman and artist George Pérez treated Donna Troy (better known as Wonder Girl) and Terry Long to one of the most impressive wedding spectaculars in comic book history. The extra-length fiftieth-issue anniversary of the popular team title featured the entire lineup of Teen Titans, past and present, as wedding guests. Unlike most super hero weddings that are plagued by super-villains, death, and despair, Donna's special day went off without a hitch as she married her mortal husband in a lavish ceremony.

MARCH

WHO TO KNOW
***Who's Who* #1**
Dubbed "The Definitive Directory of the DC Universe," *Who's Who* was a twenty-six-issue illustrated manual to the rich characters and history of DC Comics. The title was written and researched by a variety of comic book historians including Len Wein, Marv Wolfman, Robert Greenberger, Peter Sanderson, and E. Nelson Bridwell. Each character's prose entry was a comprehensive chronicle, garnished with a drawing by one of DC's many talents. Featuring artists such as Joe Orlando, Carmine Infantino, Jerry Ordway, Mike Zeck, Keith Giffen, Gil Kane, Marshall Rogers, Murphy Anderson, and Mike Mignola, the project began with a wraparound first issue cover by George Pérez.

IN THE REAL WORLD...
March: Boxer Mike Tyson makes his professional debut in Albany, New York, a match he wins by a first-round knockout.

APRIL

EPIC CRISIS
***Crisis on Infinite Earths* #1**

Comics didn't get any bigger than this. *Crisis on Infinite Earths* was a landmark limited series that redefined a universe and created a new genre of comic book blockbusters: the crossover. It was a twelve-issue maxiseries starring nearly every character in DC Comics' fifty-year history and written and drawn by two of the industry's biggest name creative talents—writer Marv Wolfman and artist George Pérez. It was a story that saw hundreds of heroes meet their deaths, worlds literally collide, and a bold streamlining of an entire line of super hero books. Not only the biggest event of the year, it would have ramifications way into the future, dividing DC's history into two halves dubbed Pre- and Post-Crisis.

The original idea behind *Crisis* was to create a more fixed universe for the heroes and villains of DC Comics to occupy. Over the years, the formerly exciting idea of parallel universes began to develop into a convoluted mess. The heroes of the Justice League of America lived on Earth-1, while their older counterparts of the Justice Society of America fought crime on Earth-2. Earth-3 housed the Crime Syndicate (evil versions of the JLA) and Earth-Prime was a world where super heroes were relegated to the pages of comic books. There was an Earth for Captain Marvel's exploits, one for the Freedom Fighters, and even one for the funny animal adventures of Captain Carrot. The universes had grown out of control, and so Wolfman and Pérez volunteered to usher in a company-wide spring-cleaning.

Introducing the cosmic threat of the Anti-Monitor, Wolfman and Pérez organized a grand-scale team-up, the like of which no comic company had ever orchestrated. Heroes from all time periods and walks of life united under the guidance of the powerful Monitor. Many heroes sacrificed their lives in the ensuing battles. Finally, the Anti-Monitor was defeated—but at a great cost. In the place of an infinite number of realities, only one remained: a new Earth with an untold story and unlimited potential.

The threat of the Anti-Monitor unites heroes from different worlds, including Earth-2's Superman, Robin, and Green Lantern, and Earth-1's Dr. Light, Kole, and Tempest.

JUNE

CRAFTING CONSTANTINE
***Swamp Thing* [second series] #37**

John Constantine, the master magician and future star of Vertigo's *John Constantine: Hellblazer*, was introduced in a Swamp Thing story from writer Alan Moore, with art by Rick Veitch and John Totleben. While Swamp Thing regrew himself from a seedling into a rooted head and shoulders, Constantine informed him about his status as the greatest Plant Elemental. Soon to be a regular in Swamp Thing's life, the self-serving Constantine was a hit with the readers.

Constantine teaches Swamp Thing a lot about his powers and origins. The information he provides is useful, but he is not always nice about it.

JULY

THE TORNADO TOUCHES DOWN
***Red Tornado* #1**

Writer Kurt Busiek took the Justice League of America's fabled android, Red Tornado, for a spin in this four-issue miniseries drawn by Carmine Infantino. As Red Tornado's fellow teammates of the JLA analyzed his origin, as well as his tenure on their team, they came to a startling decision: to ban Red Tornado from all crime-fighting activity. However, the android hero was forced to ignore this ruling to battle the powerful Construct.

THE DOCTOR IS IN
***Crisis on Infinite Earths* #4**

A series known for its hefty death count, *Crisis on Infinite Earths* also saw the debut of many new heroes. One of them was Kimiyo Hoshi, a scientist studying the antimatter plaguing the Earth's atmosphere. Cold and calculating, Kimiyo was empowered with mastery over light when she had been struck by a ray from the star Vega. Wearing a costume similar to the original villain dubbed Dr. Light, Kimiyo also adopted the doctor's moniker in this saga written by Marv Wolfman, with art by George Pérez.

March: Mikhail Gorbachev becomes de facto leader of the Soviet Union.
March: The professional wrestling event WrestleMania debuts in New York City.

May: Thirty-eight spectators are killed in rioting on the terraces during the European Cup final between Liverpool F.C. and Juventus at Heysel Stadium, Brussels.

SEPTEMBER

THE NEW BLACK

***Detective Comics* #554**

Dinah Lance adopted a new costume tailor-made for the 1980s in the pages of this issue's Green Arrow back-up feature. Written by Joey Cavalieri and drawn by J. K. Moore, Canary's new costume ditched her trademark fishnets in favor of black spiky shoulders and a matching headband. Although the look didn't last very long, it did make its way into the pages of *Justice League* #1 (May 1987), and even inspired an action figure from DC's in-house toy company, DC Direct, in 2009. This issue also featured a Batman lead story by writer Doug Moench and artist Klaus Janson.

THE ONCE AND FUTURE HEX

***Hex* #1**

Transported from the Wild West of the past to a dystopic future society, Jonah Hex had to adapt to the times in this brave new world and series crafted by writer Michael Fleisher and artist Mark Texeira. Escaping his captivity from Reinhold Borsten, the man who had brought him to the future, the famous gunslinger found himself allied with a band of criminal misfits, fighting for survival and trying to avoid the acid rains of this future world. An odd mix of sci-fi and pulp Westerns, *Hex* was canceled after eighteen issues.

BACK TO REALITY

***Superman Annual* #11**

The legendary writer Alan Moore and artist Dave Gibbons teamed up once again with the just-as-legendary Man of Tomorrow for a special that saw Superman face his worst nightmare: the sacrifice of his fantasy life.

It was Superman's birthday. Wonder Woman, Batman, and Robin had flown to the far reaches of his arctic Fortress of Solitude in order to celebrate the birth of the World's Greatest Super Hero. However, they arrived to find Superman held in the sway of the Black Mercy, a rare alien plant life that puts its victim into a dreamlike state where their greatest dreams are realized. As Superman lived out a fantasy life on Krypton, happily married with a wife and child, his friends tried to bring him back to reality, and instead found themselves facing the might of the villain Mongul, the mastermind behind the Last Son of Krypton's current predicament. When Superman finally sacrificed his dream world to wake into his harsh reality, he viciously attacked Mongul, punishing the villain for the shattered life that had seemed so real to him.

A classic tale of heroism over self-interest, this annual quickly became a fan favorite, and years later was even adapted into an episode of the 2004 animated series *Justice League Unlimited*.

Superman's birthday celebrations are seriously disrupted when the scheming Mongul surprises the Man of Steel's friends.

OCTOBER

THE DEATH OF SUPERGIRL

***Crisis on Infinite Earths* #7**

The seventh chapter in the *Crisis* saga saw Supergirl make the ultimate sacrifice. As time itself seemed to unravel all across the globe, new heroes continued to sprout up to face the dire threat posed by the Anti-Monitor, including a new female Wildcat. Writer Marv Wolfman and artist George Pérez assembled a group of heroes from the five remaining Earths and sent them into the antimatter universe to storm the Anti-Monitor's own fortress. While the heroes succeeded in destroying the villain's home, the price was high, as Earth-1's Supergirl was killed in battle.

IN THE REAL WORLD...

July: *Back to the Future*, the first of the successful movie franchise, opens in movie theaters; it becomes the highest-grossing movie of 1985 in the United States.

July: Live Aid pop concerts in Philadelphia, Pennsylvania, and London raise over $75 million (£50 million) for famine relief in Ethiopia.

NOVEMBER

THE FINAL FATE OF THE FLASH

***Crisis on Infinite Earths* #8**

The death of Barry Allen, the legendary Flash, had been hinted at from the opening pages of *Crisis on Infinite Earths* #2 in May. In this issue's dramatic finale by writer Marv Wolfman and artist George Pérez, Allen gave his life in order to destroy an antimatter cannon created by the Anti-Monitor. Literally running himself to death, the Flash was reduced to merely an empty costume. But once the Crisis had been won, Wally West would accept the legacy of his mentor and begin the adventures of the new Flash.

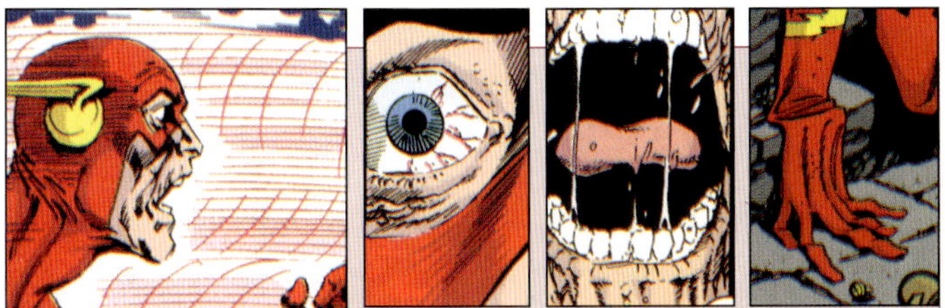

Barry Allen's physical form wastes away to nothing as he runs for his life to destroy the Anti-Monitor's terrible device.

SUPERBOY IN HIS PRIME

***DC Comics Presents* #87**

Superboy, the future spoiled brat turned super-villain of Earth-Prime, made his innocent debut in the pages of this extra-length issue, written by Elliot S! Maggin and illustrated by Curt Swan. Telling two stories that chronicled both the origin of the Boy of Steel from Earth-Prime as well as his first team-up with the Man of Steel from Earth-1, this issue set into motion the life of Earth-Prime's youngest super hero, a major player in the *Crisis on Infinite Earths* saga, and the brutal adversary at the heart of 2005–2006's *Infinite Crisis* limited series.

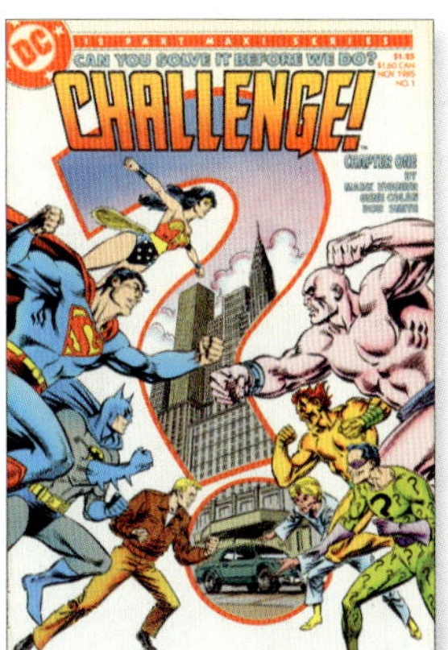

UP TO THE CHALLENGE

***DC Challenge!* #1**

In a playful twelve-issue maxiseries, DC decided to put its writers and artists to the test. With each issue written and drawn by a different team, *DC Challenge!* told a story that was in a constant state of flux. Each issue ended with a cliffhanger, and the writer of the next had to find his way out of it, continue the plot, and also end on a cliffhanger. A mad experiment, *DC Challenge!* was a fun adventure, starring many DC icons. Its debut issue was penned by Mark Evanier and drawn by Gene Colan.

CALIFORNIA DREAMING

***The Outsiders* #1**

Batman's former personal strike force, the Outsiders, departed the doom and gloom of Gotham for the sunny skies of California in issue #1 of their title. The comic saw the popular team given the enhanced quality of a Baxter-format series (printed on high-quality Baxter paper). Written by Mike W. Barr and drawn by Jim Aparo, the landmark debut issue included a special foldout splash page showcasing the ragtag team of adventurers in their new surroundings. Also featuring the costumed debut of new member Looker, this issue pitted the Outsiders against the automatons known as the Nuclear Family, and showed the team's new headquarters in Station Markovia, an oil rig just off the coast of Santa Monica.

The enhanced format of *The Outsiders* main book soon led to a variety of back-up features by many different artists, while the regular newsstand *Batman and the Outsiders* title gave way to *Adventures of the Outsiders* and began to reprint the stories from this Baxter-format title. As the Outsiders battled the Force of July, the People's Heroes, and the Duke of Oil, backup stories featured solo adventures of the characters, fake trading cards, and even a poetic parody of the 1888 baseball verse *Casey at the Bat*. The series finally came to a close after twenty-eight issues, and with its end the team disbanded as well.

Halo shows Metamorpho, Geo-Force, Black Lightning, and Katana an old photograph of the team in action. But the reminiscing gets put on hold when the Outsiders take on the Nuclear Family.

ALSO THIS YEAR: May saw the return of the Winged Wonder in a four-issue miniseries entitled *THE SHADOW WAR OF HAWKMAN* by writer Tony Isabella and penciller Richard Howell… Mr. Bones, future director of the clandestine government agency the D.E.O., debuted in July's *INFINITY INC.* #16, written by Roy and Dann Thomas and pencilled by Todd McFarlane… Also in July future Teen Titan Kid Devil made his costumed first appearance in *BLUE DEVIL* #14 by writers Gary Cohn and Dan Mishkin and penciller Alan Kupperberg… Rick Tyler, the son of Golden Age hero Rex Tyler the Hourman, debuted in the pages of November's *INFINITY INC.* #20, written by Roy and Dann Thomas and illustrated by Todd McFarlane and Michael Hernandez…

September: An 8.1 Richter scale earthquake strikes Mexico City, killing around 10,000 people, injuring 30,000, and leaving 95,000 homeless.

November: The comic strip "Calvin and Hobbes" debuts in thirty-five newspapers. Microsoft Corporation releases Windows 1.0, the first version of Windows.

GEORGE PEREZ

REMAKING HISTORY

CRISIS ON INFINITE EARTHS #1 (April 1985)
Crisis on Infinite Earths straightened out the continuity problems that had beset the major DC characters by unifying different "worlds" into a single universe with a single history. Running for twelve monthly parts, and written by Marv Wolfman with art by George Pérez and Dick Giordano among others, *Crisis* led to many major characters—Batman, Wonder Woman, Superman—being relaunched. It also popularized the "crossover event," a storyline involving many heroes across a number of titles.

1986

"FROGS CROAK LIKE A CARTOON CAR ALARM. CRICKETS PICK UP THE CHORUS. A WOLF HOWLS. I KNOW HOW HE FEELS."

Batman, *Batman: The Dark Knight* #2

THE MODERN ERA

It was what many consider the greatest year in comics. DC debuted two of the industry's most influential works: Frank Miller supplied a gritty take on super heroes with *Batman: The Dark Knight Returns*, while writer Alan Moore brought a literary ear and sophisticated structure to DC's comics with the maxiseries *Watchmen*. DC was *the* publisher to watch in 1986, and it sparked a new age of comics.

The super hero had grown up. Creators across the industry began to realize the limitless potential of graphic storytelling. Many were influenced by the more mature subject matter of *The Dark Knight* and *Watchmen*, and created their own works of powerful art. The modern comic book had been born, ushering in a new level of critical acceptance and acclaim from the mainstream media unseen in the history of the then fifty-year-old medium.

FEBRUARY

GOING FOR GOLD
***Booster Gold* #1**

The DC Universe gained one of its most peculiar stars in the first issue of writer/artist Dan Jurgens's *Booster Gold* ongoing series. Unlike other DCU heroes, Booster couldn't get enough of the media spotlight, and admittedly was in the hero game for the money.

Hailing from the far future, Michael Jon Carter was a promising young athlete who had derailed his career by betting on his own games, ending up as a janitor at Metropolis' Space Museum. So he headed back to the 1980s and began again, with help from some museum pieces. Armed with a Legion of Super-Heroes flight ring, a personal force field, a futuristic suit, and an information droid named Skeets, Booster became a super hero sellout, endorsing any product he could land a deal with and posing for every camera. *Booster Gold* ran for only twenty-five issues, but the character achieved true fame in 1987's *Justice League* series.

APRIL

THE SECRET LIFE OF DC
***Secret Origins* #1**

The heroes of the DC Universe got a little more exposed thanks to the new ongoing effort *Secret Origins*, a title offering new interpretations to the backgrounds of some of comics' biggest icons. With its debut issue featuring the origin of the first true super hero—the Golden Age Superman—by writer Roy Thomas and illustrator Wayne Boring, fans were immediately aware that the complex history of DC's landscape was not to be ignored, despite the recent events of *Crisis on Infinite Earths*. Originally alternating every other issue from a Golden Age character to a Modern Age hero, *Secret Origins* soon blended the two by offering split-features or back-up stories. Nearly every major hero was explored as the series spanned fifty issues.

HAL JORDAN SEES THE LIGHT
***Green Lantern* #199**

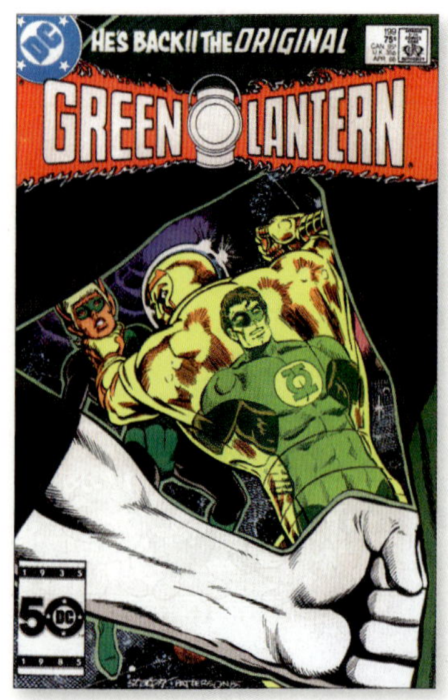

In the opening pages of *Green Lantern* #199, Hal Jordan was once again awarded a power ring and his old familiar uniform as he returned to the ranks of the cosmic police force he had grown so accustomed to. Written by Steve Englehart, with art by Joe Staton, this landmark issue also saw Hal visit Star Sapphire, now leader of the alien tribe known as the Zamarons, and it featured the return of Appa Ali Apsa, a Guardian of the Universe who had encountered both Hal and Green Arrow years before. Fittingly, Hal's return wouldn't be complete without an all-out fight with one of his old foes, the gilded villain Goldface.

IN THE REAL WORLD...

January: The first PC virus, "Brain," starts to spread.
February: Pixar Animation Studios opens.

JUNE

DARKNESS DESCENDS

***Batman: The Dark Knight Returns* #1**

It is arguably the best Batman story of all time. Written and drawn by one of comics' first superstars, Frank Miller (with inspired inking by artist Klaus Janson and beautiful watercolors by Lynn Varley), *Batman: The Dark Knight Returns* revolutionized the entire genre of the super hero.

The Dark Knight was responsible for bringing Batman comics back to their roots. A creature of the night from his first appearance in May 1939's *Detective Comics* #27, the Batman was a violent vigilante, but over the years, the character had lightened in tone. Only in the 1970s did Batman regain a measure of his darkness, but by the mid-1980s he still seemed to be missing a level of grit, replaced instead by the image of Batman as a father figure to Robins Dick Grayson and Jason Todd.

Batman: The Dark Knight Returns changed all that. Dark, shadowy, and a bit rough around the edges, the limited series was the first prestige-format Batman comic book. Through four volumes, Miller produced both a social commentary and a work of escapist fiction, parodying everything from sensationalist media to the presidential term of Ronald Reagan. The comic made waves in the comic book world and the mainstream media, crammed with numerous small TV-screen panels, meticulously designed to control the pacing of the story, and with its first issue showcasing an iconic image of Batman's silhouette overlaid against a backdrop of a flashing bolt of lightning. Not surprisingly, the comic sold out all over the country.

The story featured a retired Bruce Wayne. Now old and gray, Wayne was forced back into the cape and cowl by his own obsession. More violent and unforgiving than ever, Batman began to clean up Gotham City. Showcasing a final fight to the death with the Joker and a partnership with a new female Robin, as well as a pivotal battle with Superman, *Batman: The Dark Knight Returns* painted a noir portrait of Gotham and her guardian and altered the face of the modern-day comic book.

Carrie Kelley, the first female Robin, is a shot of optimism in Batman's grim world. A contrast to Batman in both size and personality, Carrie helps save Batman's life in a fight with the Mutant gang.

JUNE

GREEN FOR GO

***The Green Lantern Corps* #201**

Following the events of the *Green Lantern* bicentennial anniversary issue where the Green Lanterns were forced to police themselves, the adventures of everyone's favorite space cops were given a new title thanks to writer Steve Englehart and artist Joe Staton. Now focusing not just on Green Lantern Hal Jordan, *The Green Lantern Corps* gave an equal spotlight to all of the defenders of space sector 2814 as well as its neighboring sector 2815. With a home base on Earth, *The Green Lantern Corps* showcased the exploits of Hal Jordan, John Stewart and his love interest Katma Tui, the cartoony Ch'p, and the apathetic alien Salakk. The new start to the series also featured the first appearance of Corps member Kilowog, a gigantic brute with a noble heart.

BORN AGAIN BEETLE

***Blue Beetle* #1**

Formerly owned by Charlton Comics, the Blue Beetle swung into his own DC series with the help of writer Len Wein and artist Paris Cullins. The second man to go by this moniker, inventor and millionaire Ted Kord continued the heroic legacy of his predecessor Dr. Dan Garrett, despite not having any superpowers of his own. Armed with his flying beetle-shaped aircraft called simply the Bug, and a gun designed to emit bursts of blinding light, Kord set out as the new Blue Beetle. With no shortage of super-villains plaguing his hometown of Chicago, Beetle's first issue detailed his clash with super-arsonist Firefist, the Incendiary Man.

AUGUST

DC'S TRUE HEROES

***Heroes Against Hunger* #1**

Executive Editor Dick Giordano and the people at DC attempted a feat worthy of super heroes with the one-shot *Heroes Against Hunger*. The World's Finest team had to work together against the machinations of the alien Master, who desired nothing more than the desolation caused by the world's hunger problems. Every two pages were worked on by a different creative team, all volunteering their time, and the proceeds went toward relieving Africa's hunger crisis. Plotted by Jim Starlin, with character designs by Bernie Wrightson, cover by Neal Adams, and back cover by Bill Sienkiewicz, *Heroes Against Hunger* featured nearly every popular DC creator of the time.

April: In Ukraine, a reactor at the Chernobyl nuclear plant explodes, creating the world's worst nuclear disaster.

May: Seven million people form a human chain from New York City to Long Beach, California for the Hands Across America charity event to fight hunger and poverty.

SEPTEMBER

WATCH THIS SPACE

***Watchmen* #1**

"Who watches the Watchmen?" This slogan was everywhere: on the Universal Product Code box of direct market comics; adorning the bottoms of letters columns; and in provocative full-page house ads. DC knew it had its hands on something truly great, and it wanted to whet the appetites of as many fans as it possibly could.

When the first part of the twelve-issue maxiseries *Watchmen* hit the stands, readers weren't quite sure what they were going to get. But when word of mouth began to spread about the quality of both Alan Moore's highly complex script and Dave Gibbons' detailed drawings, *Watchmen* became a fast seller and a surefire hit.

The writer had originally intended for his opus to chronicle the future of the fondly remembered heroes from the defunct publisher Charlton Comics. However, DC soon decided it had its own plans for the heroes, and so Moore created new characters to give *Watchmen* its own distinct universe.

The story itself was a masterful example of comic book storytelling at its finest. As the obsessive Rorschach began to investigate the murder of his old teammate the Comedian, a mysterious conspiracy unraveled that both saved the world and damned it. Filled with symbolism, foreshadowing, and ahead-of-its time characterization thanks to adult themes and sophisticated plotting, *Watchmen* elevated the super hero comic book into the realms of true modern literature. Now regarded as a pinnacle of the medium, *Watchmen* remains one of the best-selling trade paperbacks of all time, was adapted into a motion picture, and was one of *TIME* magazine's top 100 novels since 1923.

Watchmen begins with the brutal murder of the former hero known as the Comedian. The masked vigilante Rorschach investigates the murder only to discover that the killer is a familiar face from his own past.

SEPTEMBER

MAN OF TOMORROW

***Superman* #423**

The seeds had been planted in *Crisis on Infinite Earths*. Superman's career was about to come to an end, but the Man of Steel was not about to go out with a whimper.

In "Whatever Happened to the Man of Tomorrow?", a two-part story written by Alan Moore and illustrated by Curt Swan, the adventures of the Silver Age Superman came to a dramatic close. Beginning in the pages of *Superman* #423 and concluding in *Action Comics* #583, Moore weaved a tale dubbed an "imaginary story." With no restrictions, Moore told his version of the last Superman story and also brought the tale of many of the Last Son of Krypton's villains and allies to an abrupt close.

Superman found himself under attack by his foes. With his identity accidentally exposed to the public, Superman faced an onslaught by villains Metallo, the Kryptonite Man, and a combined version of Lex Luthor and Brainiac. Superman eventually discovered the villain behind his troubles: Mr. Mxyzptlk. Superman defeated his now-deadly foe, then retired from the limelight, marrying Lois Lane and taking up the identity of Jordan Elliot as a tribute to his late Kryptonian father, Jor-El.

The alien entity Brainiac is not to be trusted, even by his criminal allies. Lex Luthor learns this the hard way as the robot takes complete control of his mind and body.

HISTORY 101

***History of the DC Universe* #1**

In an effort to organize the status quo of the DC Universe after the events of the *Crisis on Infinite Earths* maxiseries, artist George Pérez and writer Marv Wolfman collaborated on a two-part prestige-format history of the DCU. Full of detailed illustrations, these two volumes chronicled every major event from the dawn of time through the far-flung future worlds of the Legion of Super-Heroes and the Flash rogue Abra Kadabra. With appearances by nearly every major DC hero, the title put to rest most questions about how the timelines of the various Earths destroyed during *Crisis* now blended into one.

IN THE REAL WORLD...

June: Argentina defeats West Germany 3–2 to win the 1986 FIFA World Cup.
September: Desmond Tutu becomes the first black Anglican Church bishop in South Africa.

October: In the U.S., News Corporation completes its acquisition of the Metromedia group of companies, thereby launching the Fox Broadcasting Company.

OCTOBER

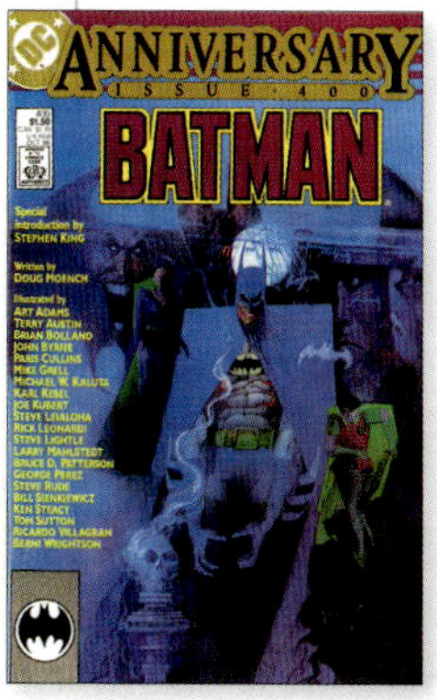

BATMAN'S BREAKOUT BIRTHDAY

***Batman* #400**

Batman celebrated the 400th issue anniversary of his self-titled comic with a blockbuster, featuring dozens of famous comic book creators and nearly as many infamous villains. Written by Doug Moench, with an introduction by novelist Stephen King, the issue detailed a mass breakout at Gotham's Arkham Asylum, orchestrated by Rā's al Ghūl. With nearly every one of Batman's Rogues Gallery on the loose, Batman, Robin, Catwoman, and al Ghūl's daughter Talia had their work cut out for them in this adventure drawn by George Pérez, Bill Sienkiewicz, Arthur Adams, Joe Kubert, Brian Bolland, and others.

A MAN OF TOMORROW

***Man of Steel* #1**

In one of the boldest moves in comic book history, DC decided that its most famous icon was in need of a makeover. The idea was simple. Keep the core themes and elements of Superman's character that had made him popular with the readers throughout his published career, but trim around the edges by removing the outdated concepts and sometimes preposterous situations. The result was a streamlined new Man of Steel that stayed true to the character's personality, but was tailor-made for a modern audience.

In the six-issue miniseries entitled *Man of Steel*, the mammoth task of remaking Superman fell to popular writer/artist John Byrne. Byrne was a lifelong Superman fan and an unbridled success in the comic book industry due to his historic run on Marvel's *The Uncanny X-Men*, among other projects. He made his weighty challenge seem effortless as he fashioned his version of the Last Son of Krypton. Doing away with ideas like Superboy and Krypto the Superdog, Byrne remade Krypton into a cold, sterile world, changed super-villain Lex Luthor into a corrupt businessman, reevaluated the relationship between Superman and Batman, and even reexamined Superman's first clash with Bizarro. The result was an overwhelming success, popular with fans both old and new. Superman had been reborn for the Modern Age of comics, and soon the other icons of the DC Universe would follow suit.

Clark Kent and his father design the famous "S" shield that will serve as Superman's logo. Not to be outdone, Martha Kent supplies the rest of the iconic costume.

NOVEMBER

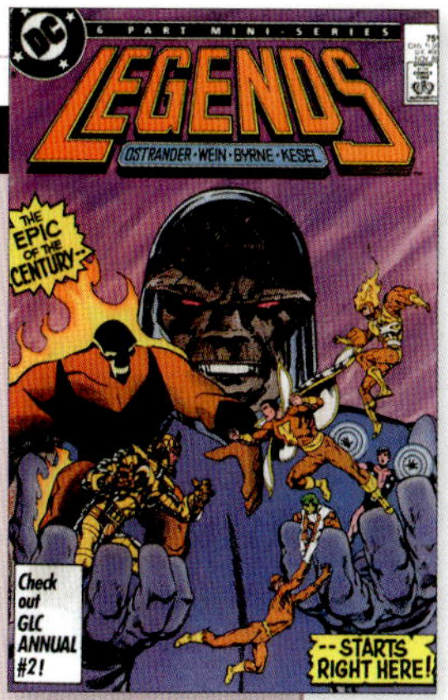

THE LEGENDS CONTINUE

***Legends* #1**

DC's last giant crossover event, *Crisis on Infinite Earths*, was a huge seller and created waves of excitement across the readership. Likewise, artist John Byrne's *Man of Steel* miniseries was another smash success, creating a buzz with DC fans both old and new. Combining these two elements was a recipe for a blockbuster, so it was no surprise that DC's next big crossover showcased John Byrne's pencils on all six of the miniseries' issues.

Entitled *Legends*, this new limited series was plotted by writer John Ostrander and scripted by Len Wein. Just like *Crisis* before it, *Legends* spun its story off into dozens of tie-in issues of DC's other monthly super hero titles, expanding the story for those who chose to dabble in the spin-offs, yet containing the main plot to the core miniseries itself. Weaving the tale of the evil New God Darkseid's latest attack on the heroes of the DC Universe, *Legends* introduced new characters like the titanic monster Brimstone, while also integrating characters like the Blue Beetle and Captain Marvel into the DCU. By the series' end, the stage was set for several new ongoing titles, including revamps of both the concept of the government strike force known as the Suicide Squad, as well as the Justice League.

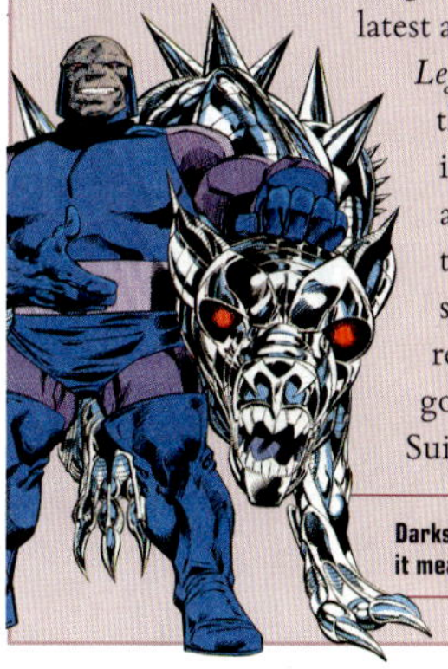

Darkseid's thirst for power can never be quenched, even if it means turning Earth's citizens against its heroes.

DECEMBER

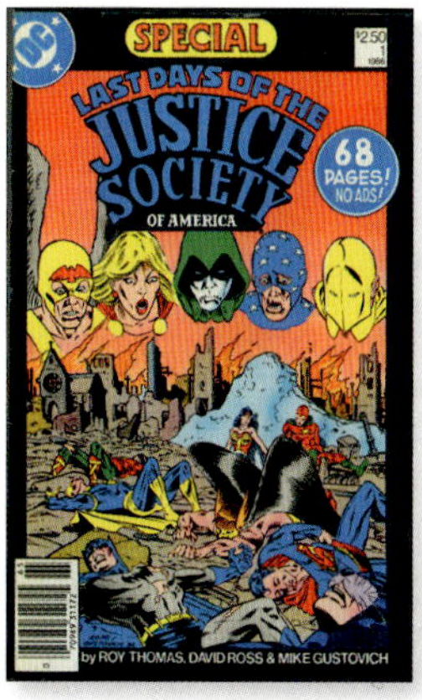

THE FALL OF SOCIETY

***Last Days of the Justice Society of America* #1**

The world's first super-team saw its adventures come to a temporary end thanks to its biggest fan. Writer/editor Roy Thomas acknowledged that, after the devastation of their home dimension in the *Crisis* maxiseries, the JSA seemed no longer relevant. With the help of artist David Ross, Thomas sent the JSA off in a blaze of glory in this stand-alone special, trapping them in the otherworldly Ragnarok, where they would be fated to fight an epic battle for the rest of eternity.

ALSO THIS MONTH: In February, Aquaman donned a blue camouflage costume in a self-titled four-issue miniseries by writer Neal Pozner and artist Craig Hamilton… The Teen Titan franchise expanded with the new monthly comic *TEEN TITANS SPOTLIGHT* in August, with rotating creative teams each tackling a different character… Cosmic Boy saw his own four-issue miniseries debut in December by writer Paul Levitz and pencillers Keith Giffen and Ernie Colón…

November: Chief Justice Rose Bird and two colleagues are removed from the Supreme Court of California in the U.S. by voters for opposing capital punishment.

November: Mike Tyson wins his first world boxing title in Las Vegas.
December: Average per capita income in Japan exceeds that in the U.S.

THE BATMOBILE ATTACKS

BATMAN: THE DARK KNIGHT #2 (April 1986) Subtitled "Dark Knight Triumphant," the second issue of Frank Miller's hugely influential, four-part Batman revamp featured the Dark Knight battling the monstrous Mutant gang for control of Gotham City and destroying the outfit's lair with a tank-like Batmobile. The success of *The Dark Knight* led to heated debates about vigilantism in the press.

THE END OF THE WORLD

WATCHMEN #12 (October 1987)
Midnight: The citizens of New York die in the millions in a faked alien invasion in the final chapter of Alan Moore's comic book masterpiece—but it is all part of a ruthless plan to build "a stronger, loving world." Using a roster of invented heroes, Moore explored and satirized the concept of the super hero in a world heading toward nuclear war.

MADISON SQUARE GARDEN
PALE HORSE
SOLD OUT
NOVEMBER 2ND
G-3265
NOVEMBE
ALE H

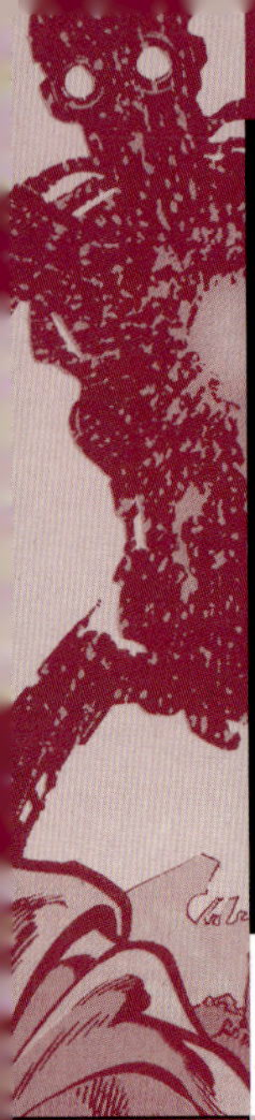

1987

"ONE PUNCH! ONE *PUNCH!*"

Blue Beetle regarding Batman's handling of Guy Gardner, *Justice League* #5

THE ART OF REINVENTION

Crisis on Infinite Earths was just the start. The Earth-shattering maxiseries had left the DC Universe in a malleable state for the first time in years. No longer bogged down by decades of continuity, the powers that be at DC were able to take liberties with their characters, starting the next chapter in their lives with a clean slate not seen since the early days of the Silver Age.

After the success of John Byrne's *Man of Steel* continuity-rewriting miniseries, other characters saw their origins revamped, and in some cases their stories started over. Some characters, like the Flash and Green Arrow, headed off into new directions, while others, like Wonder Woman and the second Robin, Jason Todd, were completely overhauled. First issues were also springing up all across DC's line. The DC properties were more united than ever in a streamlined universe, ripe and accessible for new and old readers alike.

SUPERMAN STARTS OVER

***Superman* [second series] #1**

For the second time in his history, Superman's self-titled comic saw a first issue. Writer/artist John Byrne's successful landmark *Man of Steel* miniseries had rebooted Superman's history, updating him for the modern comic book landscape, and as a result, drastic changes had swept through the Superman line of comics. The original *Superman* title had adopted the new title *The Adventures of Superman*, but continued the original numbering of its long and storied history. Popular writer Marv Wolfman and artist Jerry Ordway handled the creative chores on that particular title. Meanwhile, *Action Comics* continued on, keeping its original numbering as well, but was now written and drawn by John Byrne. And last but not least, a new series was introduced, titled simply *Superman*, again written and drawn by the prolific Byrne.

Not resting on his laurels after the success of the sweeping changes made during *Man of Steel*, Byrne started Superman's new title off with the reintroduction of Metallo, a powerful cyborg with a hatred for the Man of Tomorrow and possessing a kryptonite heart. It was a dangerous new world for the Last Son of Krypton, but the reboot continued to prove an overwhelming success. This second series of *Superman* became a mainstay for DC, running 226 issues before its end in April 2006.

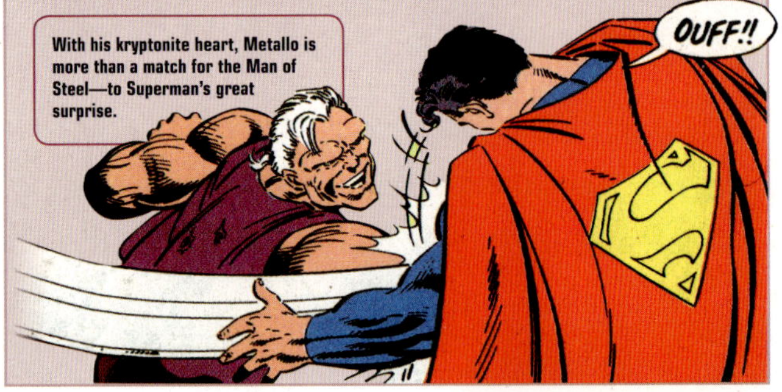

With his kryptonite heart, Metallo is more than a match for the Man of Steel—to Superman's great surprise.

THE END OF THE JLA

***Justice League of America* #258**

Writer J. M. DeMatteis was paving the way for his own Justice League. Alongside artist Luke McDonnell, DeMatteis crafted a dramatic four-part finale to the first series of DC's premier team of super heroes. Consisting of mostly minor characters, with a few older favorites, the JLA was in need of a change. DeMatteis pitted old JLA foe Professor Ivo against the team, resulting in the deaths of Vibe and Steel. The League soon disbanded, setting the stage for the next incarnation of the team.

IN THE REAL WORLD...

January: Aretha Franklin becomes the first woman to be inducted into the Rock and Roll Hall of Fame.

FEBRUARY

BATMAN: YEAR ONE

***Batman* #404**

Writer Frank Miller had already told the last Batman story. In his critical hit *Batman: The Dark Knight*, Miller had delved into the final days of the Caped Crusader and brought Bruce Wayne's legend to a seeming end. A year later, it was time for him to chronicle how it all began.

"Year One" was a four-part saga placed within the monthly *Batman* title. Without explanation or any continuity from previous issues, this impressive flashback tale simply took off running, allowing its beautifully crafted story to stand on its own merits. Illustrated in a shadowy, realistic fashion by artist David Mazzucchelli, "Year One" achieved exactly what its name implied, chronicling the entire first year of Batman's career.

Bruce Wayne had been in training. Obsessed with the idea of waging a war on crime since his parents were shot in front of him, Wayne had traveled the world, honing the skills he would need on his quest, such as martial arts and manhunting. Arriving in Gotham at the same time as new police lieutenant James Gordon, Wayne soon ventured out onto Gotham's streets, injuring himself in a fight with a pimp as he realized he was unable to strike fear into the heart of his opponents. As Gordon wrestled with the police corruption rampant in his new department, Wayne wrestled with a way to frighten criminals and grant him a dark edge. At that exact moment, a bat flew through his window.

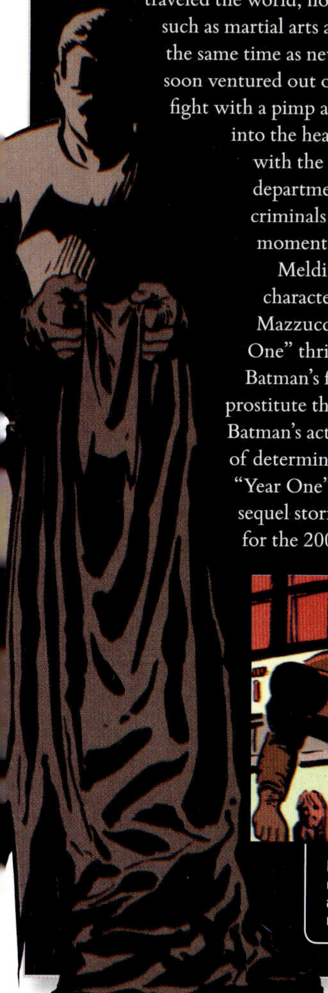

Melding Miller's noir sensibilities, realistic characterization, and gritty action with Mazzucchelli's brilliant iconic imagery, "Year One" thrilled readers and critics alike as it detailed Batman's fledgling career, as well as that of the prostitute that he had met who was soon inspired by Batman's actions into becoming Catwoman. A story of determination, friendship, love, and infidelity, "Year One" inspired hundreds of Batman flashback sequel stories, as well as being one of the influences for the 2005 film *Batman Begins*.

Bruce Wayne's first crime-fighting outing becomes deadly as he fights a vicious pimp. Bruce is arrested and has to escape from a police car, forcing him to realize that he needs an edge over his opponents.

FEBRUARY

WONDER WOMAN'S REWRITE

***Wonder Woman* [second series] #1**

On a trip to DC's editorial offices, artist George Pérez was looking for a few smaller assignments, still reeling from his exhausting work on the *Crisis on Infinite Earths* maxiseries. Learning of Frank Miller's revitalization of Batman and John Byrne's new take on Superman, Pérez naturally wondered who was handling the inevitable relaunch of Wonder Woman. Discovering the reboot of the Amazing Amazon had a writer—Greg Potter—but not an artist, Pérez volunteered for the job, and jumped right back into the frenzied schedule of a monthly book.

Wonder Woman received a complete and utter makeover, even more so than the Man of Steel and the Dark Knight. Her adventures started from scratch, and unlike Superman and Batman's revamped origins, occurred in the present, rather than in flashback fashion. With the help of Pérez's meticulous pencils, as well as his guidance as co-plotter, Wonder Woman was thrust further into the realm of Greek mythology than she'd ever been before. The fledgling heroine was surrounded by ancient legends and characters, and her newest villain was introduced: Ares, the God of War. Even the origin of Paradise Island and the Amazons featured centrally. By the first issue's end, Wonder Woman had been born anew, formed out of the very clay of her island home, and she began her journey into the heart of man's violent world.

Yearning for a child, the Amazon queen Hippolyta forms a baby's likeness out of clay from the seashore. It is then brought to life and empowered by the Greek Gods and Diana, the future Wonder Woman, is born.

RETHINKING THE QUESTION

***The Question* #1**

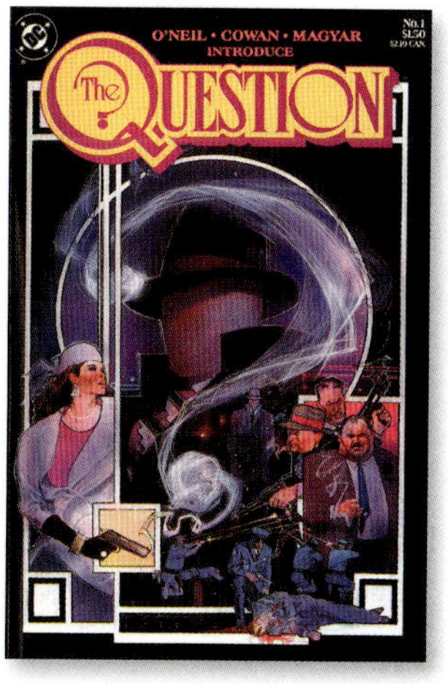

Formerly part of the Charlton Comics line, the Question carved his mysterious niche into the DC Universe with the help of writer Dennis O'Neil and artist Denys Cowan. O'Neil was no stranger to darkening characters from his stint on *Batman* in the 1970s, and he took advantage of the mature subject matter available to him in this new Baxter-format direct market series. O'Neil crafted a different kind of super hero, thrusting Charles Victor Szasz (the Question) into Hub City, a place rampant with corruption, and creating a strong emphasis on philosophy and martial arts.

January: U.S. President Ronald Reagan undergoes prostate surgery, causing speculation about his physical fitness to continue in office.

April: *The Simpsons* cartoon first appears on American television as part of *The Tracy Ullman Show*.

MAY

A LEAGUE OF THEIR OWN

***Justice League* #1**

The Justice League was floundering. With most of its fan-favorite characters on extended sabbaticals, and little more than minor heroes making up its roster, it was clear that the team needed a major overhaul. But no one quite expected how drastic the transformation would truly be in the hands of writers Keith Giffen and J. M. DeMatteis and artist Kevin Maguire.

Instead of embracing the grim and gritty tone set by Frank Miller's *Batman: The Dark Knight Returns* from the previous year and its countless imitators, Giffen and DeMatteis decided instead to do a complete turnaround and crafted a super hero sitcom. While their collaboration resulted in a sophisticated series of well-thought-out fiction, the emphasis was placed on humor over drama, and characterization over violence. Nonetheless, amid the absurd situation and over-the-top super-villains, the pair's humanity shone through brilliantly. With just the right touch of action, the resulting *Justice League* title was a smash success of a comic, a page turner of a different ilk, and DC's original team franchise was restored to its rightful place as king of the mountain.

Spinning out of the events of the *Legends* miniseries, the Justice League reformed, dropping the "of America" part of its name at the insistence of manipulative new backer Maxwell Lord. Comprised of the Martian Manhunter, Black Canary, Captain Marvel, Batman, Green Lantern Guy Gardner, Dr. Fate, Mr. Miracle, Dr. Light, and Blue Beetle, and eventually media promoter Booster Gold, the Justice League battled the likes of the Royal Flush Gang, the Rocket Red Brigrade, as well as each other, changing and shifting their roster, and later adding members Fire and Ice to their ranks. A wonderful example of intriguing storytelling outside the realm of the norm, this new incarnation of the Justice League ran for 113 issues and spawned several spin-off titles in the process.

The League's notorious backer, Maxwell Lord, secretly possesses mind-control abilities, allowing him to be rather persuasive.

The Justice League wades into international waters as it encounters the U.S.S.R.'s answer to the super hero set—the Rocket Red Brigade.

COMMITTING SUICIDE

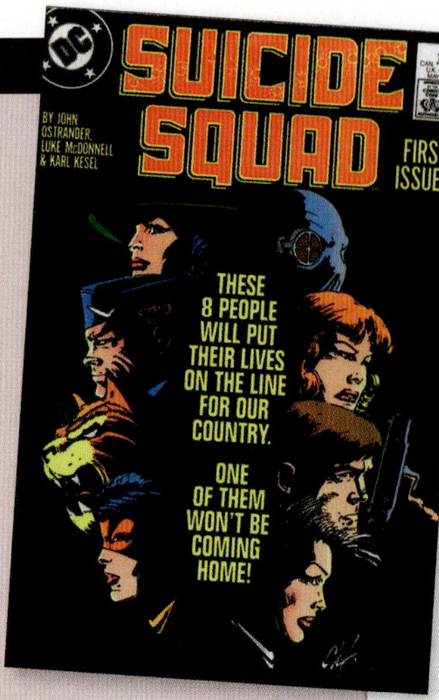

***Suicide Squad* #1**

Writer John Ostrander gave the new Suicide Squad its own series, having brought the team to life in 1986's *Legends* miniseries. In *Legends*, Ostrander paired his concept with a familiar name from DC's history. With the team's own title, Ostrander was helped by artist Luke McDonnell.

The squad was a team of criminals led by government volunteers into impossible missions. The choice was simple: rot away in a jail cell for the rest of their lives or perform black ops missions for the government as part of its clandestine Task Force X. They might not make it back alive. But to the hardened criminals serving time in Belle Reve Federal Prison, it was the chance of a lifetime.

Starring regular cast members Rick Flag Jr., Nightshade, Captain Boomerang, Deadshot, Bronze Tiger, the Enchantress, and Plastique, *Suicide Squad* also featured guest villains, many of whom didn't survive their adventure. Under the watchful eye of the tough Amanda Waller, the Suicide Squad combined super-heroics with international intrigue and tangible suspense. The series ran for sixty-six issues, keeping audiences guessing all the while about which team members would make it safely home.

Team leader Rick Flag Jr. ensures that everybody knows exactly what is involved in being a part of Task Force X.

JUNE

FLASH FORWARD

***The Flash* [second series] #1**

Wally West had outgrown his moniker of Kid Flash and picked up the mantle of his recently deceased mentor, Barry Allen, to become the third Flash. Wally found that he had big shoes to fill, and the task was made difficult by the fact that he could only reach a top speed of 705 miles per hour and required constant sustenance to keep up with his metabolism. Written by Mike Baron, with art by Jackson Guice, the Flash's new adventures began with his twentieth birthday party thrown by his friends in the New Teen Titans.

"HE LEFT ME HIS COSTUMES. AND A PICTURE OF WHAT A HERO SHOULD BE."

The Flash, *The Flash* #1

IN THE REAL WORLD...

May: West German pilot Mathias Rust evades Soviet air defenses and lands a private plane on Red Square, Moscow; he is immediately detained and is not released until 1988.

June: U.K. Prime Minister Margaret Thatcher wins election for the third time.

July: World population reaches five-billion people with a child born in Croatia.

ROBIN RETCON

***Batman* #408**

Batman had been reborn thanks to writer Frank Miller and artist David Mazzucchelli. But now that the fabled "Year One" storyline had come to its dramatic close, the question of how to proceed remained. No longer happy with Jason Todd's copycat origin of the original Robin, editor Dennis O'Neil used the Earth-changing *Crisis on Infinite Earths* maxiseries, as well as Miller's "Year One," as excuses to retroactively alter the continuity of Robin's origin as well.

With the help of writer Max Allan Collins and artist Chris Warner, O'Neil shaped Jason Todd into a street-smart orphan who first encountered Batman when he attempted to steal the tires off the Batmobile. After enrolling the troubled young man into the new Crime Alley-based orphanage run by the aptly named Ma Gunn, Batman was shocked to discover that Gunn's operation was merely a front for breeding a youthful gang of street criminals. With Jason's help, the Batman put an end to Gunn's schemes. Impressed by the young boy's bravery and cunning, Batman took Jason in as his new ward, and soon the boy became the newest Robin to the Dark Knight Detective.

Before he became Batman's trusted sidekick, Jason Todd tried to attack the Dark Knight with the tire iron he had used to steal the Batmobile's tires.

Batman carries the very gun that was used to murder his parents as he contemplates killing the man that caused him a lifetime of misery.

BATMAN: YEAR TWO

***Detective Comics* #575**

Having made history with the "Year One" *Batman* origin story, it was time for the Dark Knight's *Detective Comics* to follow suit. In "Year Two," a four-part sequel set in Batman's second year as a crime fighter, writer Mike W. Barr and artists Alan Davis and Todd McFarlane challenged the Caped Crusader with the threat of the Reaper, a vigilante whose deadly tactics clashed with Batman's no-kill policy. The tale was a welcome addition to the modern mythos of Gotham's Dark Knight, containing a brutal tale of duty and closure as Batman faced the man who killed his parents—Joe Chill.

JULY

AT THE MOVIES THIS MONTH: Christopher Reeve reprised his role as the Man of Steel for the final time in the tepid *SUPERMAN IV: THE QUEST FOR PEACE*, released in theaters on July 24...

AUGUST

THE HUNT FOR GREEN ARROW

***Green Arrow: The Longbow Hunters* #1**

Writer/artist Mike Grell introduced a Green Arrow for the modern comic book reader in the three-issue prestige format *Green Arrow: The Longbow Hunters*. From the opening scene depicting a horrifying murder of a Seattle streetwalker, audiences immediately knew that this wasn't the Green Arrow of old.

As Oliver Queen stalked the Seattle Slasher in a new hooded version of his costume, he crossed paths with Shado, a female assassin with a vendetta against the Japanese mafia known as the Yakuza. Facing problems at home with his longtime love Black Canary, Green Arrow's troubles were magnified when Canary was captured by cocaine traffickers while investigating the drugs trade. As he watched his love being tortured, something inside Queen snapped, and he used his archery skills with deadly force for the first time. Pushed past his breaking point, Ollie began a new stage in his life that would lead into his own series.

An archer whose skill rivals Green Arrow's own abilities, Shado later becomes romantically involved with the hero.

DECEMBER

SON OF THE BAT

***Batman: Son of the Demon* #1**

In an over-sized hardcover graphic novel one-shot, writer Mike W. Barr and artist Jerry Bingham introduced a monumental new character into the life of the Dark Knight—Damian Wayne, the future Robin to Dick Grayson's Batman and son of Bruce Wayne. On a quest to stop the terrorist Qayin, Batman allied himself with extremist Rā's al Ghūl. During this truce, Batman gave in to his feelings for Rā's daughter, Talia. The two had to part ways when Qayin's activities were halted, and Batman and Rā's became enemies again. However, Talia discovered she was carrying a baby—Damian Wayne.

ALSO THIS YEAR: In January, Rocket Red took to the skies in *GREEN LANTERN CORPS* #208, written by Steve Englehart and pencilled by Joe Staton... March debuted the new Captain Atom in his first DC series, by writer Cary Bates and penciller Pat Broderick... In April, Captain Marvel got a limited series—*SHAZAM!: THE NEW BEGINNING*—from writers Roy and Dann Thomas and artist Tom Mandrake... October saw a new Doom Patrol series, by writer Paul Kupperberg and artist Steve Lightle...

July: Guns N' Roses release their debut album, *Appetite For Destruction*.
October: Stock-market levels fall sharply around the world ("Black Monday").

November: Category 5 Typhoon Nina smashes the Philippines with 165 mph (266 km/h) winds and a devastating storm surge, causing destruction and 1,036 deaths.

ONCE UPON A TIME--THERE WAS THE JUSTICE LEAGUE OF AMERICA. BUT THAT WAS ANOTHER ERA, WHEN THE WORLD COULD AFFORD BORDERS AND BOUNDARIES, WHEN HEROES COULD CLAIM NATIONAL LOYALTIES AND FEEL JUSTIFIED IN THEIR CLAIMS.
BUT IN TODAY'S WORLD THERE'S NO LONGER ROOM FOR BORDERS AND BOUNDARIES. THE WALLS BETWEEN NATONS HAVE TO FALL IF OUR PLANET IS TO SURVIVE.
SO, FOR THE NEW ERA-- A NEW LEAGUE:
7

WATCH OUT, WORLD!

JUSTICE LEAGUE INTERNATIONAL #7
(November 1987)
In 1987, a new team of super heroes formed to help a world in crisis. From left: Martian Manhunter, Batman, Black Canary, Booster Gold, Mr. Miracle, Blue Beetle, Guy Gardner, Rocket Red #7, Oberon,

1988

"EVERYTHING ANYBODY EVER *VALUED* OR *STRUGGLED* FOR... IT'S ALL A *MONSTROUS*, DEMENTED *GAG*! SO WHY CAN'T *YOU* SEE THE *FUNNY SIDE*? WHY AREN'T YOU *LAUGHING*?"

The Joker, *Batman: The Killing Joke* #1

FOR THE MATURE READER

Comics were growing up, expanding their subject matter to fully delve into mature stories and themes formerly only skirted around in even the most controversial of past endeavors. With the release of key works like 1986's *Batman: The Dark Knight Returns* and *Watchmen*, the floodgates were opened. Comic creators were embracing the new freedoms that comics suddenly offered, and DC was responding in kind. Rather than censoring some of the adult work, DC created a label that read: "Suggested for Mature Readers."

Not all the new examples of sophisticated work were successful. Some titles across the industry read as pure imitation, focusing on the violence of *The Dark Knight Returns* and *Watchmen* while missing the subtext and innovative storytelling that made those works great. Meanwhile, DC pioneered new frontiers and perfected paths already charted.

JANUARY

JOHN CONSTANTINE BLAZES A TRAIL
***John Constantine: Hellblazer* #1**
Everyone's favorite self-serving mystic stepped out of the pages of *Swamp Thing* into his own comic, courtesy of writer Jamie Delano and artist John Ridgway. An exploration into the dark corners of John Constantine's soul, *Hellblazer* rarely shied away from disturbing imagery and political and social issues. In the first issue's tale of gluttony and addiction, Constantine stumbled across a demon spirit named Mnemoth that cursed its victims with an insatiable hunger. *Hellblazer* was a critical success and inspired a major motion picture in 2005.

A NEW DAWN

***Millennium* #1**
The annual crossover had become a tradition. An idea that started with 1985's *Crisis on Infinite Earths* and then proved itself in 1986's *Legends* had become a standard at DC. A large-scale event that starred dozens of heroes from every corner of the DCU was a surefire hit, and not just for the series that most of the story took place in. Tie-in comics of regular series, labeled as part of the crossover event, sold well too, enticing readers to try titles that they may never have otherwise sampled. Embracing this idea, DC soon released *Millennium*, an eight-part miniseries, written by Steve Englehart and drawn by Joe Staton.

Delivered in weekly installments, *Millennium* centered on an invasion by the predecessors of the Green Lantern Corps, the interstellar robot police force called the Manhunters. Having planted spies among the citizens of Earth (both volunteers and mind-controlled victims), including Superman's former sweetheart Lana Lang and the Flash's father Rudolph West, the Manhunters betrayed the heroes from within their own forces.
Finally, with the intervention of the next stage in human evolution—the New Guardians—Earth's heroes prevailed, and the android conquerors were defeated.

Without consciences and souls, the Manhunters are capable of untold violence against mankind. Fortunately, the Green Lanterns are not lacking in humanity.

IN THE REAL WORLD...
April: The newspaper comic strip "FoxTrot" debuts.
May: The Red Army begins withdrawing from Afghanistan.

FEBRUARY

GREEN ARROW GROWS UP
***Green Arrow* #1**

Mike Grell continued the evolution of the character of Oliver Queen that began in 1987's *Green Arrow: The Longbow Hunters* with an ongoing monthly series. For mature readers, the title examined Oliver's new lethal techniques, as well as the life of the victimized Black Canary, temporarily deprived of her powerful siren call. The series featured pencils by Ed Hannigan, with covers by Grell, although Grell parted ways with the book at issue #80. Following his departure, the book shifted away from its mature readers origins.

MARCH

TEN NIGHTS OF THE BEAST
***Batman* #417**

Throughout his career, Batman had dealt with the worst Gotham City had to offer. In most cases, the villains relied on psychological games to torment the Caped Crusader. But when Soviet assassin the KGBeast came to Gotham, Batman faced a foe who was an equal in combat. Using the Cold War as their backdrop, writer Jim Starlin and artist Jim Aparo crafted the four-part storyline "Ten Nights of the Beast," in which Batman trapped the KGBeast using brains not brawn.

APRIL

THE MAID OF STEEL
***Superman* [second series] #16**

It was less than two years since the relaunch of *Superman*, which had streamlined the world of the last Kryptonian by wiping away all the extraneous elements of the Man of Steel's life. Now, one of those supposed extraneous elements returned in full force. Making her debut on the final page of *Superman* #16, Supergirl sped back into her cousin's busy life thanks to writer/artist John Byrne. In an issue that also reestablished the Prankster for a modern audience, naval explorers discovered a thawing Supergirl at the heart of Antarctica. However, as later issues proved, this Supergirl was not Superman's cousin, but a protoplasmic entity called the Matrix who hailed from a pocket dimension.

In a costume similar to the one that debuted in 1984's *Supergirl* feature film, the Matrix Supergirl is an updated twist on a classic idea.

JULY

THE LAST LAUGH
Batman: The Killing Joke

Batman: The Killing Joke was over four years in the making. Although it was released two years after writer Alan Moore's smash success *Watchmen*, Moore had actually penned the prestige format one-shot years before. The artist on the title, the immensely talented Brian Bolland, wasn't quite as quick as his scripter, but it was well worth the wait. Crafted with meticulous detail and brilliantly expressive art, *Batman: The Killing Joke* was one of the most powerful and disturbing stories in the history of Gotham City.

This monumental forty-eight-page mature readers story was divided into two halves. As the Batman hunted down the escaped Joker, the Clown Prince of Crime's origin was explored more thoroughly than it ever had been in the past. Paying homage to the February 1951 tale from *Detective Comics* #168 entitled "The Man Behind the Red Hood," Moore told the story of the Joker's past. The man who became the Joker was a failed stand-up comedian. Desperate for money, he found himself with no other alternative than to aid a gang in a robbery at the Ace Chemical Factory, donning a mask to become the gang's faux crime boss the Red Hood. When the Batman interrupted the crime, the Red Hood leapt into a vat of chemicals to escape, the event forever bleaching his skin and hair, as well as altering his already frail psyche.

Meanwhile, in the modern-day half of the story, the Joker broke into Commissioner James Gordon's home and shot and paralyzed his daughter, Barbara. Kidnapping Gordon in an attempt to drive him insane, the Joker forced him to enter a twisted funhouse, where photos of a bleeding Barbara were displayed. Batman interrupted the horrific scene, and as usual, bested the disturbed Joker, experiencing a rare moment of understanding about the Joker's tragic life.

Considered perhaps the finest Joker story ever, *The Killing Joke* not only changed the life of Barbara Gordon forever, but was also an influence on director Tim Burton when he brought Gotham City to life on the big screen in 1989's *Batman*.

Barbara Gordon's life is shattered when the Joker pays her a house call, dressed as a twisted tourist.

Brian Bolland's illustrations give the Joker a truly frightening presence, making *The Killing Joke* that much more disturbing.

June: Wembley Stadium hosts a concert to celebrate the seventieth birthday of imprisoned South African ANC leader Nelson Mandela.

August: Mehran Karimi Nasseri, dubbed "The Terminal Man," is stuck in De Gaulle Airport, Paris, where he will continue to reside until August 1, 2006.

AUGUST

BATMAN'S CULT FOLLOWING

***Batman: The Cult* #1**

Writer Jim Starlin took the Dark Knight into the depths of Gotham for the four-issue prestige format *Batman: The Cult*, showing Jason Todd in his greatest act of heroism, and pushing Batman's will to its limits. With horror artist Bernie Wrightson, Starlin wove the tale of Deacon Blackfire, a cult leader bent on conquering Gotham. Taking Batman hostage, Blackfire drugged him in an attempt to gain him as a follower, until Robin rescued his mentor.

THE VENGEANCE OF V

***V For Vendetta* #1**

Alan Moore's first epic effort, the ten-part *V For Vendetta* maxiseries originally began in the pages of England's comics anthology *Warrior* magazine in 1981. After that publication's cancellation, the project was adopted by DC Comics, enabling Moore finally to finish the series seven years after its premiere. A fable of revolution and a cautionary tale of lost freedoms, *V For Vendetta* was a triumph for Moore, this time aided by the shadowy pencils of artist David Lloyd.

The series spanned the complex story of a mysterious vigilante, known only as V and clad as Guy Fawkes, and began as V rescued a young streetwalker named Evey Hammond, and then nonchalantly blew up Parliament. Set in a dystopian vision of England in the then-future of 1997, V was a freedom fighter and hero of the people, protesting against the all-seeing eyes of the Big Brother-like government establishment. Unbalanced and eccentric, V took Evey under his wing after forcing her to undergo a bizarre concentration camp-like experience that tested her resolve and made her understand the high cost and value of freedom.

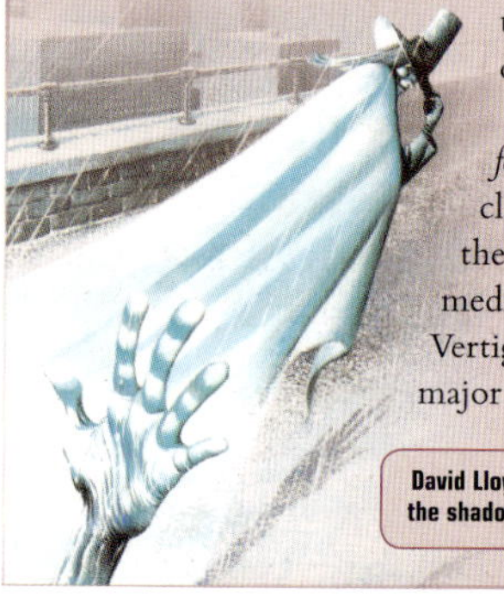

Inspiring, disturbing, and tragic, *V for Vendetta* was another modern-day classic for Moore and further proved the literary potential of the comic book medium. It was later adopted under the Vertigo imprint, and was made into a major motion picture in 2005.

David Lloyd's painted covers serve as a stark contrast to the shadowy world of *V for Vendetta*'s interior.

SEPTEMBER

ANIMAL CRACKERS

***Animal Man* #1**

Writer Grant Morrison was about to go where no writer had gone before: into the pages of his own comic book.

Fans had no reason to think that Animal Man's own ongoing series would be anything other than standard super hero fare. Animal Man had been around since the 1960s, and it only made sense that he should be given his shot at a solo title. But as the series began, Morrison and artist Chas Truog slowly lulled readers into a twisted world of surreal comic book logic and shattered fourth walls.

Morrison's first DC Comics work started innocently enough, describing a world in which Buddy Baker juggled family life with being a minor super hero. As the series progressed, Animal Man not only gained a greater understanding of his powers and his connection to the mystical "Red," a morphogenetic field that united all animal life, but he set out on a journey that would put him face-to-face with his god. In Buddy Baker's case, that god was none other than Grant Morrison himself. A brilliant and innovative metatextual romp, Morrison's time on the title lasted until issue #26 and proved so popular that the series ran for sixty-three more issues.

Able to tap into the morphogenetic field, Buddy Baker can mimic the abilities of any animal, and therefore shares a common bond with all of the creatures of the "Red."

ON TV THIS MONTH: *SUPERMAN* returned to television sets across the country in a new short-lived animated series that ran for thirteen episodes and premiered on CBS on September 17...

OCTOBER

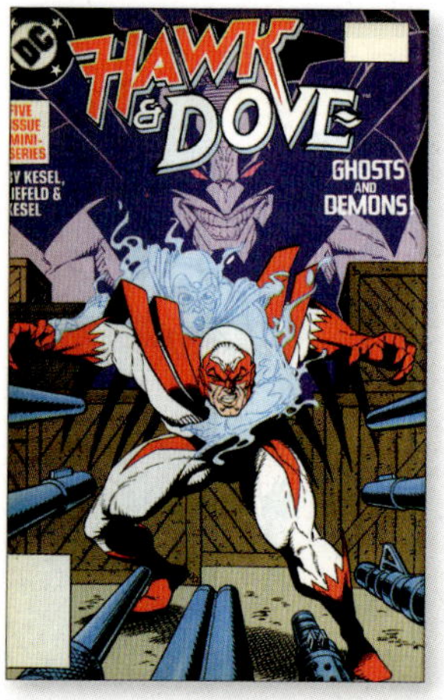

WAR AND PEACE

***Hawk and Dove* #1**

The odd couple of the Teen Titans' defunct West Coast branch, Hawk and Dove, returned in their own miniseries but with a slight change of cast. Since the original Dove had died during the *Crisis on Infinite Earths* maxiseries, Hank Hall was left without a partner and a pacifist voice to cancel out his rage. Fortunately, the lords of order found the crime fighter a new partner—Dawn Granger. Written by Barbara and Karl Kesel and drawn by future superstar Rob Liefeld, this five-issue miniseries reestablished the famous pair for a new generation.

IN THE REAL WORLD...

September: The 1988 Summer Olympics are held in Seoul, South Korea.
October: The video game Super Mario Bros. 3 is released in Japan.
October: Ayrton Senna clinches his first Formula One World Championship with a phenomenal drive in the Japanese Grand Prix.

ON TV THIS MONTH: *THE ADVENTURES OF SUPERBOY* debuted on October 8, marking the return of Clark Kent's live action TV exploits as portrayed by John Haymes Newton (season 1) and Gerard Christopher (seasons 2–4). The 100-episode show spanned four seasons...

NOVEMBER

COSMIC PROPORTIONS
***Cosmic Odyssey* #1**

Writer Jim Starlin and artist Mike Mignola teamed up for a sci-fi miniseries that spanned the DCU. When the New Gods found the Anti-Life Entity, a being bent on destroying the universe, foes Highfather and Darkseid joined together to summon Superman and other Earth-based heroes. Pairing off in groups of two, the heroes had their work cut out for them, none more so than the Martian Manhunter and his arrogant partner, Green Lantern John Stewart. Going it alone, Stewart failed in his mission, resulting in the destruction of an inhabited planet, but the other heroes came through in the end.

Some of Earth's top heroes answer the call of Highfather and Darkseid, including the Martian Manhunter, Starfire, and Superman.

DECEMBER

INITIATING THE INVASION
***Invasion!* #1**

Crossing over with dozens of titles, DC released the three-issue extra-length volumes of *Invasion!* by writers Keith Giffen and Bill Mantlo, with pencils by Giffen, Bart Sears, and Todd McFarlane. When the alien race the Dominators made a pact with the races of the Khunds, Gil'Dishpan, the Psions, the Warlords of Okaara, the citizens of the Citadel, the hawk-people of Thanagar, and the shape-shifting Durlans, the ultimate alien alliance unleashed its wrath on Earth, dropping a gene-bomb that wreaked havoc on those on Earth blessed with superpowers.

ALSO THIS YEAR: In February, the Batman crossed paths with Scarface and the Ventriloquist in *DETECTIVE COMICS* #583 by writers John Wagner and Alan Grant and artist Norm Breyfogle... The sadistic Major Force was birthed in February's *CAPTAIN ATOM* #12, written by Cary Bates and Greg Weisman and pencilled by Pat Broderick... The clandestine government operation Checkmate began its monthly adventures in April in its self-titled ongoing series by writer Paul Kupperberg and artist Steve Erwin... New Starman Will Payton debuted in his own ongoing series in October by writer Roger Stern and artist Tom Lyle... Writer Neil Gaiman scripted the complex *BLACK ORCHID* three-issue prestige format limited series in December, re-envisioning the character with the help of artist Dave McKean...

DECEMBER

A DEATH IN THE FAMILY
***Batman* #426**

Jason Todd hadn't had the best run of luck. To begin with he was saddled with a copycat origin of the original Robin, Dick Grayson, but then Todd had his backstory completely rewritten after the reality-warping events of *Crisis on Infinite Earths*. Re-envisioned as a street punk who had a problem with authority, Todd hadn't exactly found favor with the readers in his newest incarnation, and so the powers that be decided to toy with the idea of getting rid of the second Boy Wonder altogether. They couldn't quite make up their minds, so in a rather unprecedented publicity stunt, DC decided to poll their audiences to see if Jason Todd should live or die. Utilizing a 1-900 number that charged voters 50 cents per call, fans were able to dial in their vote either in favor of Robin surviving, or in favor of his death. It was a close race, but soon it became clear to DC. The fans were out for blood.

In the four-issue "A Death in the Family" saga within Batman's own comic, Robin was captured by the Joker while Todd was on his quest to be reunited with his birth mother. The Clown Prince of Crime savagely beat Jason with a crowbar before blowing up the building in which the Boy Wonder was being held captive. In the third part of this storyline in issue #428, Robin's lifeless body was uncovered by Batman, who was traumatized by the fact he was unable to save his young partner.

Written by Jim Starlin, with art by Jim Aparo and haunting covers by Mike Mignola, "A Death in the Family" proved a best seller with readers in both single-issue and trade paperback form. Prophesized in Frank Miller's *Batman: The Dark Knight Returns* (1986), Jason's death continued to haunt the Batman for years and remains to this day the Dark Knight's greatest failure.

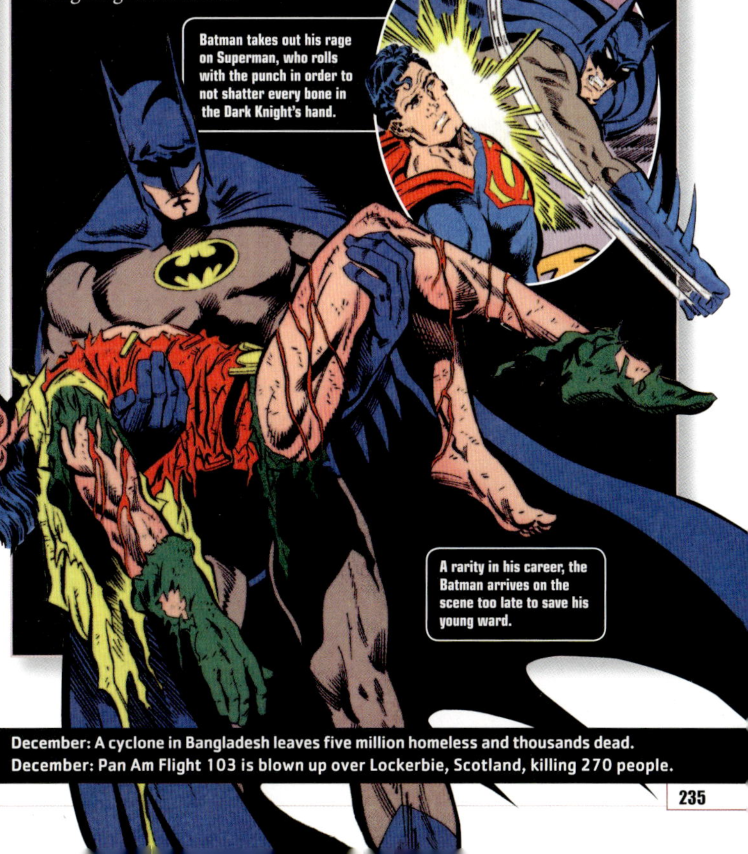

Batman takes out his rage on Superman, who rolls with the punch in order to not shatter every bone in the Dark Knight's hand.

A rarity in his career, the Batman arrives on the scene too late to save his young ward.

October: Republican George H. W. Bush is elected President of the United States.
November: The very first Fairtrade label is launched in the Netherlands.
December: A cyclone in Bangladesh leaves five million homeless and thousands dead.
December: Pan Am Flight 103 is blown up over Lockerbie, Scotland, killing 270 people.

ROBIN® WILL DIE BECAUSE THE JOKER™ WANTS REVENGE. BUT YOU CAN PREVENT IT WITH A TELEPHONE CALL
1-(900) 720-2660
The Joker fails and Robin lives.
1-(900) 720-2666
The Joker succeeds and Robin will not survive.

THE FANS DECIDE

BATMAN #427 (December 1988)
Batman editor Dennis O'Neil let the fans rule on a crucial plot point for the first time. Should Jason Todd (Robin) survive the Joker's bomb blast or die? O'Neil commented: "I saw it as a logical extension of stuff that's been happening in live theater for years and was increasingly happening in the electronic media." Out of 10,000 fans, a narrow majority voted for Jason's death.

1989

"BUT IT'S LIKE I SAID TO DICK. BATMAN NEEDS HELP. BATMAN NEEDS *ROBIN*."

Tim Drake, *Batman* #442

THE YEAR OF THE BAT

Movie audiences had been taught that a Superman could fly. Now it was time for them to see what a Batman could do. Director Tim Burton's *Batman* would be the highest grossing film of the year, a merchandising blockbuster ahead of its time, and it would mark the birth of the modern super hero film. With a mainstream audience still most familiar with the tongue-in-cheek style of the 1966 live-action TV show, millions of viewers were introduced to a darker knight, clad in a black rubber Batsuit. *Batman* showed Hollywood the potential of the modern comic book and was a smash success. On the comic book shelves, DC not only presented the first new solo Batman ongoing title since the 1940s—*Batman: Legends of the Dark Knight*—but also introduced the world to the heir to the Robin mantle, Tim Drake. Batman was the hero on everyone's mind, and DC wanted to make sure that he stayed there.

JANUARY

ENTER SANDMAN
***The Sandman* [second series] #1**

In arguably one of the greatest achievements in serialized modern comic books, writer Neil Gaiman crafted the seventy-five-issue ongoing series *The Sandman*, introducing its readers to a complex world of horror and fantasy. Elaborate, beautiful, disturbing, and poetic, *The Sandman* was a journey through dreams, nightmares, and the darkest corners of the DC Universe.

At the helm of the title was the Sandman himself, a powerful entity named Dream (also known as Morpheus). Lord of the Dreaming, Morpheus was one of seven siblings who each ruled over a different aspect of the universe. Called the Endless, Dream's family consisted of Death, Desire, Delirium, Destiny, Despair, and Destruction, each the living, breathing personification of his or her name, and each a three-dimensional character carefully molded by Gaiman's impressive imagination.

Over the years, *The Sandman* saw a variety of artists grace its pages. Sam Keith drew the first few issues, followed by Mike Dringenberg, Chris Bachalo, Michael Zulli, Kelley Jones, Charles Vess, Colleen Doran, and Shawn McManus, among others. Illustrator Dave McKean's mixed media pieces garnished each cover. Gaiman often adapted his story to the strengths of the title's current illustrator, while still focusing on building up to a transformative conclusion for the title and its main character.

As the series began, Dream escaped a magical prison, having been trapped by a rich businessman, and returned to his home dimension of the Dreaming. After locating several of his mystic possessions and remaking his kingdom, Morpheus resumed his business as usual, helping craft and shape the dreams of the mortal world. With settings ranging from America's heartland to the deepest pit of Hell, and including guest stars Shakespeare, Martian Manhunter, and Lucifer himself, *The Sandman* was a truly original work of fiction, a new direction for the medium of comics. A comic book as accessible to the casual reader as it was to the diehard comic fan, *The Sandman*'s far-reaching success helped to launch DC's Vertigo imprint, and its ten-volume library remains among DC's best-selling titles.

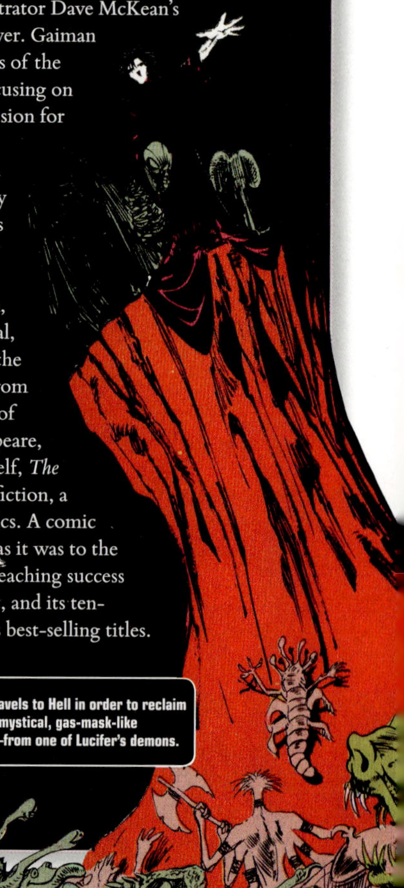

Morpheus travels to Hell in order to reclaim his helm—a mystical, gas-mask-like possession—from one of Lucifer's demons.

IN THE REAL WORLD...

February: The last Soviet Union armored column leaves Kabul, ending nine years of military occupation.

THE ONSET OF ORACLE
***Suicide Squad* #23**

The career of Barbara Gordon, the former Batgirl, had come to a halt when she was shot and paralyzed by the Joker. Despite this, Barbara wasn't quite ready to give up on her life's calling. Barbara set herself up as an information guru, who specialized in the super hero set. Called Oracle, Barbara was recruited by the Suicide Squad in the pages of issue #23 of the Squad's comic, written by John Ostrander and Kim Yale, and pencilled by Luke McDonnell, and took the first step toward life as a super hero advisor.

FEBRUARY

MORRISON GOES ON PATROL
***Doom Patrol* #19**

Writer Grant Morrison decided to lend his unique talents to the Doom Patrol, and the team would never be the same again. With a flair toward the bizarre, and an ability to create three-dimensional personalities even in absurd characters, Morrison was joined by penciller Richard Case. Following the *Invasion!* crossover, in which the Doom Patrol fell apart, Patrol founder Robotman checked into a mental institution, where the former man tried to come to grips with the robot body he had been trapped in for years. Morrison stayed with the title until issue #63, introducing a slew of new members and villains and taking the heroes to the edge of reality.

LETTING THE CAT OUT OF THE BAG
***Catwoman* #1**

Famous cat burglar Selina Kyle finally stole away the spotlight from her heroic counterpart long enough to score a four-issue miniseries for mature readers. Written by Mindy Newell, with art by J. J. Birch, *Catwoman* picked up where Frank Miller's "Year One" story arc left off. *Catwoman* was the story of a reluctant Gotham City prostitute taking charge of her life. It filled in the rest of Selina's origin, telling of her training with Golden Age hero Wildcat, her relationship with her sister Magdalene, and her first kiss with the Dark Knight.

APRIL

A HUNTRESS' MOON
***The Huntress* #1**

The Huntress was the newest of Batman's supporting cast to branch out into her own series. She saw her entire life reinvented to better fit into the streamlined continuity of the DC Universe after the effects of 1985's *Crisis on Infinite Earths* maxiseries. No longer the Earth-2 daughter of Batman and Catwoman, the Huntress was remade into Helena Bertinelli, a mob daughter who witnessed her family's slaughter at the hands of a rival gang. Written by Joey Cavalieri, with art by Joe Staton, *The Huntress* ran for only nineteen issues before being canceled.

EUROPEAN VACATION
***Justice League Europe* #1**

The Justice League was no longer merely America's protector. Spinning out of the pages of *Justice League International*, an offshoot of the Justice League set up camp in Paris. Written by Keith Giffen and J. M. DeMatteis, with art by Bart Sears, the Justice League Europe was made up of members Rocket Red, the Flash, Power Girl, Metamorpho, Captain Atom, Elongated Man, and temporarily Wonder Woman and Animal Man. The team was named in its own ongoing title, which lasted for sixty-eight issues.

MAY

AT THE MOVIES THIS MONTH: *THE RETURN OF SWAMP THING* trudged into theaters on May 12, directed by Jim Wynorski and starring Heather Locklear as Abby Arcane and Dick Durock as Swamp Thing. Durock reprised this role in 1990's *SWAMP THING* TV series…

JUNE

AQUAMAN OF THE PEOPLE
***Aquaman* #1**

Swimming off the pages of his May one-shot special, Aquaman returned to take another lap around Atlantis in his second miniseries. Written by Keith Giffen and Robert Loren Fleming, Aquaman's new five-issue limited series was pencilled by Curt Swan over Giffen's layouts. Returning to Atlantis to lead a prison revolt, Aquaman clashed with his longtime love Mera before overcoming an invasion by an alien aquatic race. Aquaman reclaimed his throne but once again took to the open seas, his true home.

AT THE MOVIES THIS MONTH: Tim Burton's *BATMAN* hit movie theaters on June 23, featuring a screenplay by Sam Hamm and Warren Skaaren and Oscar®-winning set designs by Anton Furst and Peter Young. The movie surprised a nation with its noir sensibilities and its serious take on the Batman…

April: The Hillsborough disaster, one of the biggest tragedies in European soccer, claims the lives of ninety-six Liverpool F.C. supporters.

April: The Motorola MicroTAC, then the world's smallest cellphone, is released.
July: The television show *Seinfeld* premieres.

AUGUST

BATMAN: YEAR THREE
***Batman* #436**

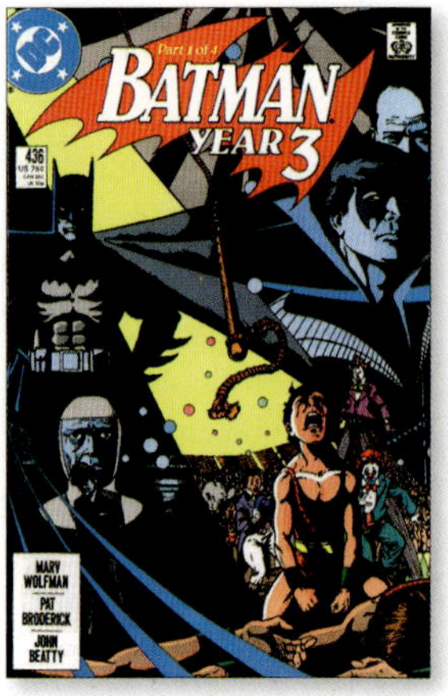

In a modern-day sequel to Frank Miller and David Mazzucchelli's "Year One," the origin of Dick Grayson was revisited, with one minor—but important—detail added into the mix. Written by Marv Wolfman and pencilled by Pat Broderick, the four-issue "Year Three" saga introduced a young boy named Timothy Drake into a flashback sequence starring a young Dick Grayson and his parents. Tim was a fan of the Flying Graysons and watched with horror from the audience as Dick's parents fell to their deaths on a trapeze. While "Year Three" went on to tell the tale of Grayson's progression into the first Robin and later into Nightwing, what fans didn't realize at the time was that Tim Drake would soon become the next Robin.

DEATH BECOMES HER
***The Sandman* [second series] #8**

In the stand-alone story entitled "The Sound of Her Wings" in *The Sandman* #8, Neil Gaiman, aided by penciller Mike Dringenberg, introduced the character Death to a fascinated readership. Peppy, upbeat, and cute as a button, Death, as her name might suggest, was also possessed of the same Goth sensibilities as her younger brother, Sandman. Death was an instant hit and arguably became more popular than the Sandman himself. She went on to star in two eponymous, bestselling miniseries—one of which launched the Vertigo line in 1993—and *The Death Gallery* in 1994, featuring interpretations of the character by artists from across the comic book industry.

BRAVE NEW HAWKWORLD
***Hawkworld* #1**

Writer/artist Timothy Truman fashioned the three-issue prestige format limited series *Hawkworld* in a quest to revamp Hawkman. With an approach similar to that used in Wonder Woman's 1987 relaunch, Truman scrapped Hawkman's history and started over, painting a fantastic and realistic portrait of the alien planet Thanagar. A gritty tale of heroics, addiction, and duty, *Hawkworld* cast wingman ensign Katar Hol as its main character, a natural hunter turned hero who would become the future Hawkman of the planet Earth, and introduced Shayera Hol, his future partner Hawkwoman.

NOVEMBER

RUNNING THE ASYLUM
Batman: Arkham Asylum

Its subtitle said it all: "A Serious House on Serious Earth." Written by Grant Morrison, with painted artwork by Dave McKean, *Batman: Arkham Asylum* was an innovative and complex examination of Batman's Rogues Gallery. Suggested for mature readers, *Arkham* was a terrifying journey into the darkest corners of the human mind.

The inmates had taken over the asylum., and the last item on their list of bizarre demands had just arrived at Arkham's gates: the Batman.

Weaving the tale of Batman's exploration of the asylum, this deluxe hardcover also focused on the history of Arkham's founder, Amadeus Arkham. After the inmate Martin "Mad Dog" Hawkins brutally murdered Arkham's wife and child, Amadeus lost control, remembered that he had killed his mother, and became just another inmate.

Meanwhile, after Batman met psychotherapist Ruth Adams and Arkham's current director, Dr. Cavendish, he was forced to play along with the Joker's mad games, else the patients would kill the asylum staff. Touring the asylum and coming into contact with many dangerous inmates, including Two-Face, Clayface, Scarecrow, Mad Hatter, Maxie Zeus, and Killer Croc, Batman soon discovered that the man behind the breakout was the asylum's Dr. Cavendish, who had been driven mad. With the help of Ruth Adams, Batman managed to bring order to the chaos, as well as maintain his own sanity.

A thinking man's horror story, *Arkham Asylum* marked Grant Morrison's first work on the mythos of Batman, a character he would return to time and time again. Morrison used the title to introduce his theory on the Joker's condition—"super-sanity"—as well as three-dimensional portraits of the Dark Knight's lesser Rogues. *Arkham Asylum* stood the test of time as one of the finest Batman graphic novels ever written.

Dave McKean's terrifying paintings set the eerie mood for *Arkham Asylum*, often depicting the Batman as not much more than a shadow.

IN THE REAL WORLD...

August: Two million indigenous people of Estonia, Latvia, and Lithuania, then still occupied by the Soviet Union, join hands to demand freedom and independence.

November: East Germany opens checkpoints in the Berlin Wall, allowing its citizens to travel freely to West Germany for the first time in decades.

NOVEMBER

LEGENDS IN THE MAKING

Batman: Legends of the Dark Knight #1

The last Batman solo ongoing series had debuted almost fifty years ago, so the powers that be at DC Comics thought it was high time to give it another shot. With the premier issue of *Batman: Legends of the Dark Knight*, DC didn't just give readers another *Batman* comic, they gave them an entirely new animal and helped set trends in formats.

Batman: Legends of the Dark Knight was initially formatted to showcase story arcs across five or six issues. Each arc told a complete story without the hindrance of a direct continuity and was the perfect length to be collected in a trade paperback reprint. A trendsetter in more ways than one, when *Legends of the Dark Knight* debuted, it offered four different colored protective extra covers, each placed over the normal covers. This unwittingly gave birth to the variant comic book cover market when retailers noticed that the different covers led to larger sales.

With most of its tales set in the first few years of Batman's crime-fighting career, "Shaman" (the first five-issue tale) was no exception, itself being a direct sequel to Frank Miller and David Mazzucchelli's "Year One." Written by Dennis O'Neil with art by Edward Hannigan, "Shaman" helped jump-start this popular new title, which ran for an impressive 214 issues.

In the final part of "Shaman," Batman shames the Chubala priest in front of his followers, proving that the Shaman is far from invincible.

LONG LIVE THE LEGION

Legion of Super-Heroes [third series] #1

Fans were given something different with the new *Legion of Super-Heroes* series. Plotted by Keith Giffen and inker Al Gordon, scripted by Tom and Mary Bierbaum, and pencilled by Giffen, this relaunch of the formerly teen team of heroes and heroines broke new ground in the fictional realm of the 30th Century and in the world of super hero comic books. The heroes, now adult, dropped their monikers to fight back against the oppression of the alien Dominators. Sophisticated and mature, this new version of the Legion ran for sixty-one issues before its stars were rebooted back to their teenage roots.

GOTHAM IN A DIFFERENT LIGHT

Gotham by Gaslight #1

An "alternate history of the Batman" was spawned in this dark prestige format one-shot by writer Brian Augustyn and artist Mike Mignola. The story centred around Batman, the World's Greatest Detective, investigating the murders of Jack the Ripper in Gotham in 1888, a meeting that barely seemed possible within the restraints of DC's post-Crisis streamlined reality. When several prostitutes were found killed, the spotlight fell on the mysterious "Bat-Man" as the murderer. Sentenced to hang for the crimes, Bat-Man escaped custody and tracked down the real killer—his uncle Jacob Packer.

DECEMBER

A LONELY PLACE OF DYING

Batman #442

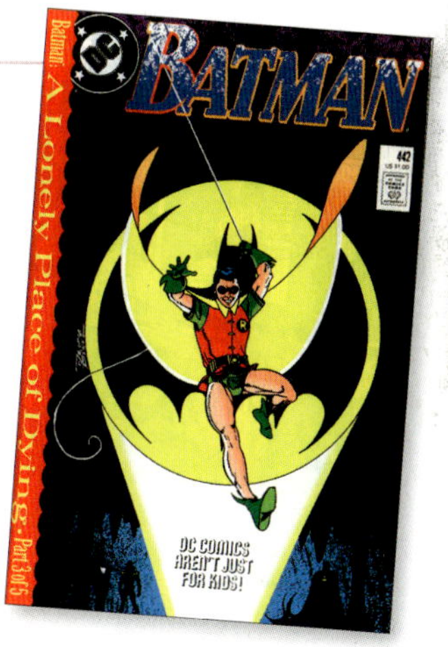

The fans had killed Robin. They'd dialed a 1-900 number and cast their votes, and Robin had died at the hands of the Joker. But that didn't stop writer Marv Wolfman and co-plotter George Pérez from introducing a new Boy Wonder into Batman's life. After all, the Caped Crusader needed a Robin to help keep him sane in his war on crime. With the pencils of Pérez, Jim Aparo, and Tom Grummett, Wolfman concocted the five-issue "A Lonely Place of Dying" that crossed from *Batman* into the pages of *The New Titans*, and ended in *Batman* #442. In it, Tim Drake deduced both Batman and Nightwing's identities and earned his place as the new Robin.

THE DAWN OF A HERO

Green Lantern: Emerald Dawn #1

Superman was the first to have his origins reexamined. Then Batman, Wonder Woman, and even Hawkman followed suit. So when Green Lantern joined these ranks in the six-issue miniseries *Green Lantern: Emerald Dawn*, it shouldn't have come as a surprise. The story of Hal Jordan's ascension to a cosmic cop from a lowly test pilot with a bad record and a DWI was written by Jim Owsley, Keith Giffen, and Gerard Jones, and pencilled by M. D. Bright. Jordan was pitted against the powerful alien Legion, proving Hal's potential as the greatest Green Lantern of all time.

ALSO THIS YEAR: In February, the rebels from *INVASION!* leaped into *L.E.G.I.O.N. '89* #1, a new title by writer/artist Keith Giffen, scripter Alan Grant, and penciller Barry Kitson... *DETECTIVE COMICS* celebrated 600 issues in May with a tribute section by Batman artists and writers... Maxima debuted in September's *ACTION COMICS* #645, written by Roger Stern and George Pérez and illustrated by Pérez...

November: South African President F. W. de Klerk announces the scrapping of the Separate Amenities Act, which had legalized racial segregation in the country.

December: The first full-length episode of *The Simpsons*, "Simpsons Roasting on an Open Fire," premieres on U.S. television.

1990s

THE 1990S WAS AN ERA when style seemed to rule over substance. Comic book stores overflowed with variant editions and limited, foil-enhanced print runs. Holograms seemed to sell a comic better than its title character; fans purchased ten issues of the same poly-bagged comic and filed them away unopened, in the hopes of someday profiting from an increase in value. Comic book artists were elevated to the level of superstars, and were given titles to showcase their strengths. The comic book seemed an entirely new, exciting animal and the readership was expanding. For instance, in 1993, DC capitalized on a growing audience of mature readers by introducing the adult-oriented imprint Vertigo.

During the height of the 1990s comic boom, certain titles sold in the millions. Comic writers and artists left titles if sales dipped below 100,000 readers (now a figure that would rank extremely high on charts). Like it or not, there was something about the trends of the day that worked, and DC Comics soon found itself indulging from time to time in a quick sales gimmick or an eye-catching cover enhancement.

However, despite the short-term benefits of following trends set by their competitors, for the most part, DC chose to go its own way. The company continued to make story and characterization the guiding force of its titles and, in doing so, arrived at an innovative approach to increased sales: the event. Building on the foundation of the 1980s convention of the crossover, DC introduced earthshaking events to their iconic heroes, altering the landscape of their character universe. In the process, DC super heroes gained thousands of new fans, created long-lasting controversies, and proved that the oldest dog in comic book publishing still had plenty of new tricks. As flashy trends ran their course, the end of the decade saw DC once again leading the pack back in the direction of the original classic super hero.

"PLEASE HANG ON! THE PARAMEDICS WILL BE HERE ANY SECOND... PLEASE!"

Lois Lane comforts a dying Superman
***Superman* (second series) #75 (January 1993**

1990

"THE PAST IS ALWAYS KNOCKING AT THE DOOR, TRYING TO BREAK THROUGH, INTO TODAY."

The Phantom Stranger, *The Books of Magic* #1

DIFFERENT DIRECTIONS

As a new decade began, other comic book companies were moving away from a focus on writing in favor of extravagant and attractive art and foil-enhanced covers. It appeared that comic fans seemed not to mind in the slightest. Although DC would later occasionally use embossed covers and hire some of the imitators of this new style of artwork, the company's immediate reaction was simple: concentrate on the story.

After all, DC's focus on groundbreaking storytelling techniques and brilliantly crafted plotlines had helped create the current comic book resurgence in the first place. DC continued to concentrate on sophisticated self-contained miniseries and interesting new directions for its mainstay books. Although the results weren't always flashy, DC was counting on slow and steady to win the race.

FEBRUARY

RUNNING REMATCH

***The Adventures of Superman* #463**

In August 1967's classic *Superman* #199, the Man of Steel and the second Flash, Barry Allen, had run a race in order to decide who was the Fastest Man Alive, once and for all. However, when Barry died saving the world in *Crisis on Infinite Earths* #8 (November 1985) and was replaced by his former sidekick, Wally West, fans were again left wondering who held the title of the world's quickest hero. Writer/penciller Dan Jurgens answered the question with the help of finisher Art Thibert, as he pitted the next generation of super-speedster against Superman in a cross-world sprint that saw the Flash win by a literal nose.

TIME ON HIS SIDE

***Time Masters* #1**

Time-traveling guru Rip Hunter journeyed into the realm of modern-age storytelling for an eight-issue miniseries by writers Bob Wayne and Lewis Shiner. Illustrated by Art Thibert, Hunter's life took a more mature turn from his science-fiction roots as his origin was recounted. Featuring various cameos and supporting characters ranging from Cave Carson and Dr. Fate to Booster Gold and the Justice League, DC's premier guardian of the timeline found himself reinvented for the modern reader and facing off against the villainy of Vandal Savage.

MARCH

STRANGE RETURN

***Adam Strange* #1**

Former star of the long-defunct *Mystery in Space* science fiction series, Adam Strange finally found his name on the marquee in his first three-issue miniseries, delivered in DC's prestige format. Blending a realistic past with a far-fetched present, the series investigated the motives and inner turmoil of a man trapped between two worlds. It also saw the birth of Adam Strange's daughter Aleea and the death (albeit temporary) of his wife, Alanna. Told in a sophisticated voice by writer Richard Bruning, all three volumes were illustrated by brothers and future comics superstars Andy and Adam Kubert.

IN THE REAL WORLD...

February: Nelson Mandela is released from Victor Verster Prison, near Cape Town, South Africa, after twenty-seven years behind bars.

ARCHIVING ATLANTIS
***Atlantis Chronicles* #1**

Paving the way for his legendary relaunch of *Aquaman*, writer Peter David crafted a seven-issue series delving into the history of the mythical people of the undersea kingdom of Atlantis. Aided by the classical style of artist Esteban Maroto, David connected the saga of Arion with that of Aquaman, telling of the sinking of the ancient metropolis, its war between sorcery and technology, and the evolution of its citizens into a water-breathing race. Told in double-length installments, the series also established the curse of Kordax, the legend that would inspire the people of Atlantis to later ban a blond-haired baby named Orin (the future Aquaman) from their city walls.

APRIL

THE DIGITAL DARK KNIGHT
Batman: Digital Justice

DC Comics took a giant step into the digital age with *Batman: Digital Justice*. Featuring the art and writing of Pepe Moreno, this innovative title was DC's first graphic novel using illustrations that were entirely computer-generated. Moreno used a Macintosh II System with an 8-bit/32-bit color board and labored over his work for more than a year. He created a dystopian vision of the Gotham City of the future, plagued by a computer entity calling itself the Joker, and defended by a new Batman, the grandson of Commissioner James Gordon. Moreno's work was groundbreaking for its time, and offered a brief glimpse into technological advances still to come.

MAY

PROGRAMMING THE CYBORG
***The Adventures of Superman* #466**

Cyborg Superman, the villain who would go on to plague both his namesake and Green Lantern time and again, debuted with the help of the script and layouts of Dan Jurgens, and the finishes of Dick Giordano. Scientist Hank Henshaw was trapped in an onslaught of solar flares while aboard a space shuttle with his wife and two friends. Despite gaining amazing new abilities, Hank's entourage suffered fatal effects from the dose of radiation. With Superman's help, Hank's wife survived, but Hank himself seemingly perished, only to be resurrected later as the evil cyborg version of the Man of Steel.

JUNE

A NEW LIGHT
***Green Lantern* [third series] #1**

Hal Jordan was at a crossroads. No longer the carefree flyboy that had easily accepted the role of hero and space cop Green Lantern, Hal was an aging man with white at his temples and the weight of responsibilities on his shoulders. Green Lantern Guy Gardner had taken over Hal's role in the Justice League, a group Hal no longer felt he belonged to. Oa, the home of the Guardians of the Universe, had been destroyed, and Hal's old friend and fellow Lantern John Stewart was on the verge of a nervous breakdown. So Hal set off to see America and find himself, and there was no better place to do it than in a new ongoing series all his very own.

Writer Gerard Jones and penciller Pat Broderick jump-started the further adventures of Hal and company by beginning Green Lantern's third ongoing series, which would last an impressive 181 issues. Although the creative team of the book would change a few times over the years, giving way to the lengthy runs of writers Ron Marz and Judd Winick, the ability of the title to evolve continued to attract readers throughout its entirety.

Over the course of the series, Hal Jordan would find himself plunging headfirst into some of the most dramatic and earth-shattering events of his life. Despite the breakneck pace that was soon to come, the title's debut issue contained a different feel altogether. Depicting Hal's visit with Batman and the current Justice League, a cross-country trip to a small mining town, and a nearly rekindled romance from years past, this initial issue's only action sequence consisted of a fight between Hal and the hotheaded Green Lantern, Guy Gardner. A slow build that would later unfold into tales of cosmic proportion, *Green Lantern* #1 was truly the calm before the storm.

No matter how far he travels, Hal never seems to be able to escape the annoyance that is Guy Gardner.

February: The United Kingdom and Argentina restore diplomatic relations after eight years. The U.K. had severed ties after Argentina invaded the Falkland Islands in 1982.

March: Mikhail Gorbachev is elected as first Executive President of the Soviet Union.
May: The World Health Organization removes homosexuality from its list of diseases.

JUNE

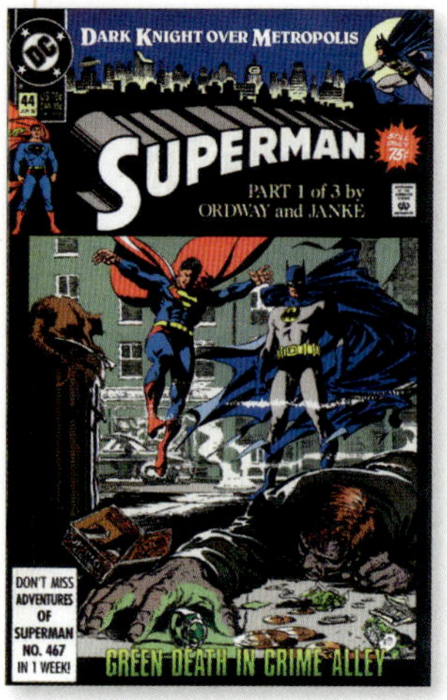

DARK KNIGHT OVER METROPOLIS
***Superman* [second series] #44**

The World's Finest team was revived in a three-part crossover in *Superman*, *The Adventures of Superman*, and *Action Comics*. Written by Roger Stern, Dan Jurgens, and Jerry Ordway, with art by Bob McLeod, Jurgens, Art Thibert, and Jerry Ordway, "Dark Knight over Metropolis" saw Superman accepting Batman's help to solve a murder case involving Lex Luthor, Chiller, Shockwave, and Dr. Moon. The heroes found themselves forming a strong, if uneasy, bond. When Superman found a kryptonite ring, he made Batman its guardian, trusting the Dark Knight to keep him in check should he abuse his powers.

JULY

CHANGES FOR THE CHANGING MAN
***Shade: The Changing Man* [second series] #1**

Writer Peter Milligan, alongside artist Chris Bachalo and psychedelic cover artist Brendan McCarthy, breathed new life into the bizarre world of Shade, the Changing Man, reimagining the obscure Steve Ditko character for a brave new world. Pulling no punches and often rife with controversial topics, Shade explored the adventures of an extra-dimensional hero originally trapped in the body of a serial killer on death row. After befriending Kathy George, the daughter of two of the serial killer's victims, Shade sought to end the cascade of madness that was flowing into reality from his own home dimension of the Meta-Zone.

One of Shade's many foes, the American Scream is a horrifying vision of a patriotic ideal.

ON TV THIS MONTH: ***SWAMP THING*** **took root with television viewers in his own live-action series that debuted on July 27. Spun out of his movie franchise, the show lasted seventy-two episodes over the course of three seasons...**

AUGUST

WORLDS APART

***World's Finest* #1**

On paper, they were an odd pairing: Superman was an alien powerhouse, optimistic by nature, and able to lift mountains with his bare hands, while Batman was a mere mortal, a well-honed human machine with a dark demeanor and a matching outlook on life. The idea of these two icons teaming together made sense in the fledgling days of comics, but writer Dave Gibbons and artist Steve Rude presented a three-issue miniseries in DC's prestige format that proved the World's Finest team of Superman and Batman was still relevant in the cynical modern arena of the 1990s.

Set around Midway Orphanage, located between Gotham City and Metropolis, Gibbons and Rude gave the heroes a common ground while embracing their differences. Its most memorable scenes contrasted Superman's bright, hopeful world with the dark, shadowy life of Batman.

Who better to menace the World's Finest team than arch-villains Lex Luthor and the Joker?

SEPTEMBER

ON TV THIS MONTH: ***THE FLASH*** **started his twenty-one-episode sprint across the airwaves in his new live-action television show debuting September 20 and showcasing the talents of John Wesley Shipp as the title character, not to mention Star Wars' Mark Hamill as the villainous Trickster...**

NOVEMBER

THE MAIN MAN AS THE MAIN ATTRACTION
***Lobo* #1**

The anti-hero of L.E.G.I.O.N. fame, Lobo nabbed his first miniseries with the help of the offbeat plotting and layout skills of Keith Giffen, aided by scripter Alan Grant and artist Simon Bisley. The murdering bounty hunter found himself the escort of Miss Tribb, his fourth-grade teacher from his home planet of Czarnia. Resisting his impulse to kill the one who had brought him misery in his youth, Lobo was duty-bound to protect Tribb in this darkly comedic romp through the outer cosmos.

IN THE REAL WORLD...

June: In Rome, the Three Tenors sing together for the first time; the highlight is Luciano Pavarotti's performance of "Nessun Dorma" from Giacomo Puccini's opera *Turandot*.

July: An earthquake measuring 7.7 on the Richter scale kills 1,600 in the Philippines.

August: Iraq invades Kuwait, an act that eventually leads to the Gulf War.

DECEMBER

SUPERMAN GETS SERIOUS

***Superman* [second series] #50**

Every day Superman is faced with the fantastic. So it was apt that when he proposed to his longtime love Lois Lane, he did so in a modest fashion. In the final issue to the "Krisis of the Krimson Kryptonite" storyline, Clark popped the question at Dooley's, the restaurant below their offices at the *Daily Planet*. Lois accepted and comic book history was made, served up by writer/artist Jerry Ordway and artists Dan Jurgens, Brett Breeding, Kerry Gammill, Dennis Janke, Curt Swan, and John Byrne.

Reality warps for the Caped Crusader as he reels under the influence of the Penguin's hallucinogen.

A NEW DIMENSION TO GOTHAM CITY

Batman: 3D

The Caped Crusader leaped off the pages in all his red-and-blue glory in this over-sized eighty-page special crafted by 3-D expert Ray Zone. Not only did this graphic novel feature an all-new tale written and illustrated by John Byrne, but it also reprinted the classic story "The Robot Robbers" by Sheldon Moldoff and Curt Swan from the 1953 tome *Batman Adventures in Amazing 3-D Action*, which featured 3-D effects by Jack Adler. Boasting a large cast of villains including the Penguin, the Riddler, Two-Face, and the Joker, the issue also showcased eye-popping pinups by such luminaries as Mike Mignola, George Pérez, Alex Toth, Barry Windsor-Smith, and Art Adams, and a pair of punch-out bat-shaped 3-D glasses.

THE MAGIC BEGINS

***The Books of Magic* #1**

Writer Neil Gaiman chronicled the adventures of magic pupil Timothy Hunter in this miniseries. Each issue explored the realms of magic as portrayed by a different painter, just as Hunter's guide changed at the beginning of each new volume. John Bolton and the Phantom Stranger took Timothy through the past; Scott Hampton and mage John Constantine explored the America of the present; Charles Vess and Dr. Occult explored the world of Faerie; and Paul Johnson and the blind monster hunter Mr. E traveled through the future, all the way to the very end of time.

ROBIN'S REDECO

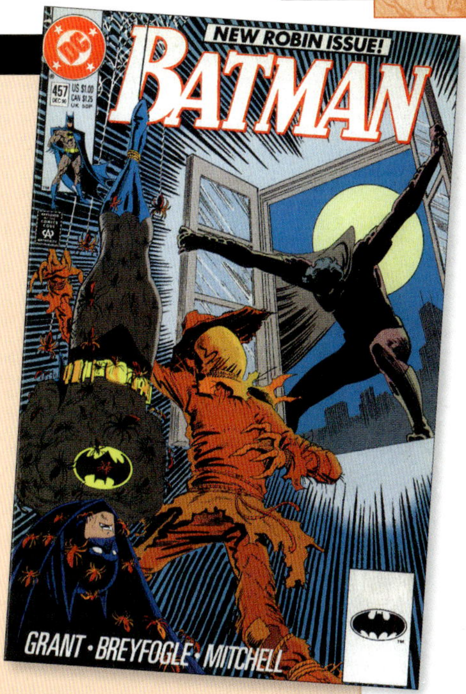

***Batman* #457**

In this tale by writer Alan Grant and artist Norm Breyfogle, Robin finally got a new uniform. As a boy, Tim Drake had deduced that Dick Grayson was the secret identity of the original Robin the Boy Wonder, and as a young teen, he had sought the now-adult Grayson in an attempt to reunite him with his former partner, the Dark Knight. So when Tim rescued Batman from the Scarecrow and officially joined him as the third Robin, it only made sense that he would be the first teen sidekick to put his own individual stamp on the Robin uniform.

When DC editorial made the decision to modify the classic costume of the iconic Boy Wonder, they called upon several artists to put their own spin on it. It was legendary artist Neal Adams who delivered the winning concept. The new design covered up the bare legs of the original Robin costume with green Kevlar, added a more practical black to the back of the yellow cape, and traded the green pixie slippers in for black-toed ninja boots. It was a get-up perfect for fighting crime.

The Robin symbol is converted into a shuriken in this updated costume that would last well into the 2000s.

ALSO THIS YEAR: In June Timothy Truman's *HAWKWORLD* was expanded into an ongoing series, featuring the scripts of John Ostrander and the art of Graham Nolan... Rhyming demon Etrigan returned for a new series in July entitled *THE DEMON*, by writer Alan Grant and artist Val Semeiks, lasting fifty-eight issues... August got a bit hotter with the rise of Blaze, a demonic new foe for Superman and Captain Marvel in *ACTION COMICS* #656, by writer Roger Stern and artist Bob McLeod...

November: Akihito is enthroned as the 125th emperor of Japan.
November: Tim Berners-Lee publishes a formal proposal for the World Wide Web.
November: Margaret Thatcher resigns as Prime Minister of the United Kingdom; John Major succeeds her as Conservative Party leader and is appointed Prime Minister.

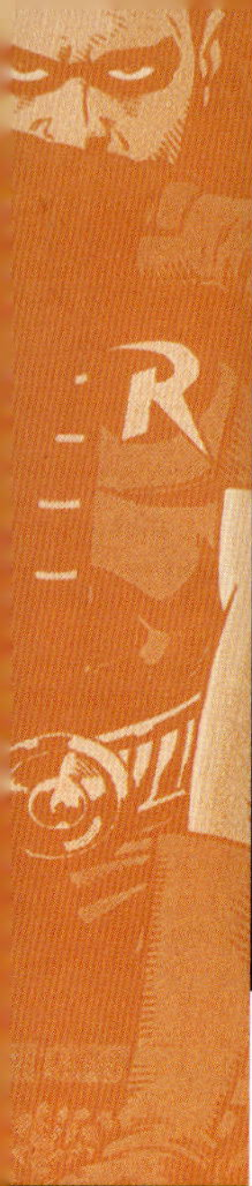

1991

"THE END OF AN ERA. THE START OF ANOTHER. ONE THAT WOULD STRETCH OUT... TO GRIP A WORLD. MY WORLD. MY TIME."

Waverider, *Armageddon 2001* #1

THE COMIC BOOM

The invention of the direct market and its offspring—comic book specialty stores—had given the comic world a much-needed boost. Thanks to the mainstream attention that comics were receiving following the impressive achievements of the late 1980s, the upswing in comic sales was more than doubling. Some of the stigma of being a comics fan was lifted, as the world began to recognize the renewed sophistication of the medium.

Marvel and DC were capitalizing on the heavy foot traffic seen in stores, and numerous new titles began to emerge. However, quality storytelling was still at the forefront of every DC editor's mind. Well-established creators were tapped to spin off well-established characters into their own comics. This method, along with a focus on crossovers to build excitement, helped more minor characters build successful franchises all their own.

JANUARY

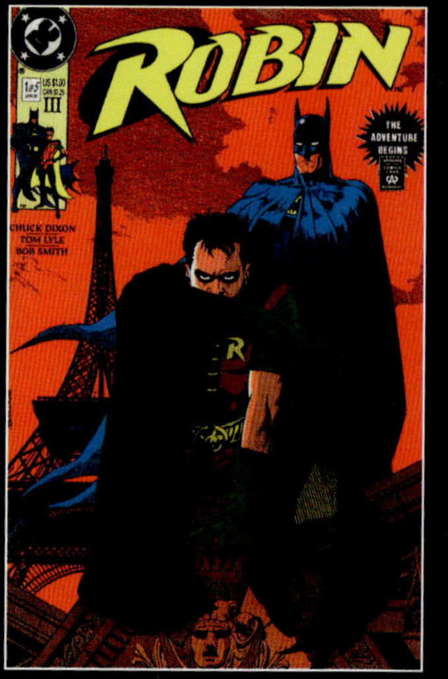

ROBIN FLIES SOLO
***Robin* #1**

Despite being arguably one of the five most famous characters in comic book history, by the start of the 1990s Robin had yet to gain his own title. The first Robin, Dick Grayson, had starred in solo adventures as early as February 1947, when he appeared in *Star Spangled Comics* #65, and he would continue his solo outings through his college years in titles like *Batman Family* and *Detective Comics*. But despite his mainstream fame and popularity, there had never been a single comic entitled simply *Robin*.

Perhaps the time just hadn't been right. Although a fan favorite from his conception, Robin's age and relationship to Batman had proven controversial in the 1950s. By the 1960s, he had become a joke thanks to the popular *Batman* TV show, and in the 1970s and 1980s, both Dick Grayson and his successor, Jason Todd, spent most of their time trying to outgrow that stigma. But by the 1990s, a third Robin, Tim Drake, had accepted the mantle of Batman's sidekick. He wore a new costume reflecting modern sensibilities, and it seemed that the Boy Wonder had finally caught up with the times.

When writer Chuck Dixon, artist Tom Lyle, and cover artist Brian Bolland presented the premier issue of the first *Robin* miniseries, the title was an instant hit, spawning two sequel miniseries and an ongoing series. Complete with a Neal Adams poster stapled to its spine, the first issue featured an apprehensive Robin doubting his place by Batman's side. To give Robin the edge he would need to face the violent world of the Dark Knight, Batman sent him on a globe-trotting training trip, where Robin would study with one of the best martial artists, Lady Shiva. He would also face the blind living weapon known as the King Snake and his accomplice, Lynx. Robin returned to Gotham, confident in his abilities, and ready to serve as the true partner of the Batman.

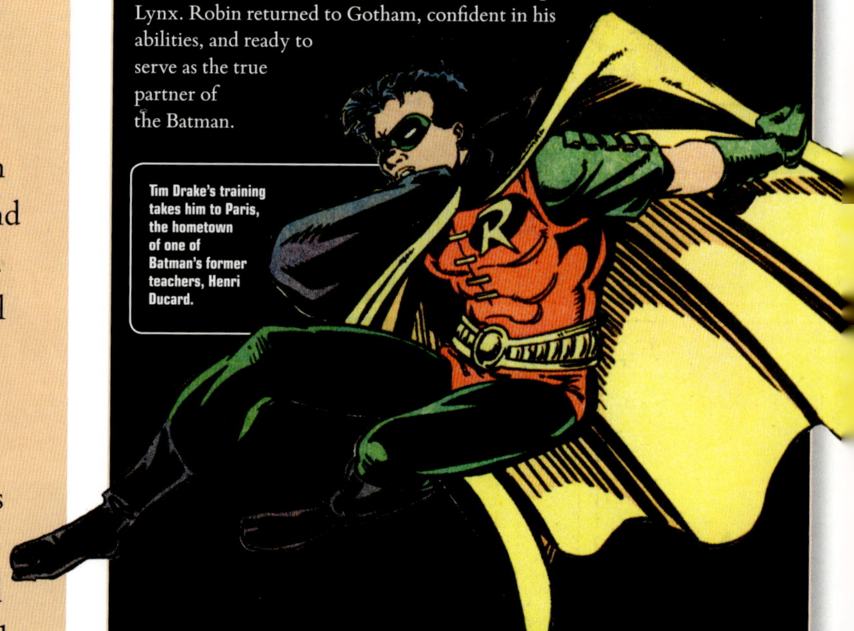

Tim Drake's training takes him to Paris, the hometown of one of Batman's former teachers, Henri Ducard.

IN THE REAL WORLD...

January: The Congress of the United States passes a resolution authorizing the use of military force to liberate Kuwait from Iraq.

FEBRUARY

PANTHA AND PHANTASM PREMIER

***The New Titans* #73**

February saw the debut of a future Titan known as Pantha. The Titans were under siege, and the fans couldn't have been happier. Writer Marv Wolfman had revitalized the Titans franchise yet again, with the help of his new creative partner, artist Tom Grummett. During the "Titans Hunt" storyline that began with issue #71, the Wildebeest Society and its mysterious leader began to target the Titans for assassination or capture. With the Titans falling one by one, the stage was set for the emergence of a few new heroic faces. As the mysterious Phantasm made his debut in issue #73, lurking in the shadows was the ferocious failed experiment of the Wildebeest Society known as Pantha.

CLARK TAKES OFF THE GLASSES

***Action Comics* #662**

For an award-winning reporter, Lois Lane certainly had one blind spot when it came to the biggest story of the year. She had never deduced that her fiancé Clark Kent and Superman were one and the same. With their nuptials looming, Clark thought it was time to reveal his dual identity to the love of his life, in this landmark issue by writer Roger Stern and artist Bob McLeod. A battle with the Silver Banshee made Clark realize the dangers of keeping his secret hidden from his betrothed, so Clark opened his shirt in front of Lois to stand before her for the first time as both Clark Kent and Superman.

MARCH

REINTRODUCING THE BATMAN

***Detective Comics* #627**

In *Detective Comics* #27 (May 1939), writer Bill Finger and artist Bob Kane told "The Case of the Chemical Syndicate," the story that introduced Batman. Six hundred issues later, that story was reprinted with newer versions to celebrate the Batman's changing legacy. This issue also included writer Mike Friedrich and artist Bob Brown's 1969 retelling of "The Cry of Night is – Sudden Death" and two adaptations by the writer/artist teams of Marv Wolfman and Jim Aparo, and Alan Grant and Norm Breyfogle.

APRIL

THE SOCIETY PAGES

***Justice Society of America* [first series] #1**

They were the first super hero team in history, and yet they were all but forgotten. The Justice Society of America had been trapped in limbo since July 1986's climactic *Last Days of the Justice Society* special. Although their endless other-dimensional battle would prevent them from returning to the present for another year, writer Len Strazewski and artist Rick Burchett decided that if the Justice Society wouldn't come to them, they would go to the Justice Society. Together, the pair delivered a flashback eight-issue miniseries set in 1950 that pitted the famous team of heroes against the machinations of their old foe Vandal Savage.

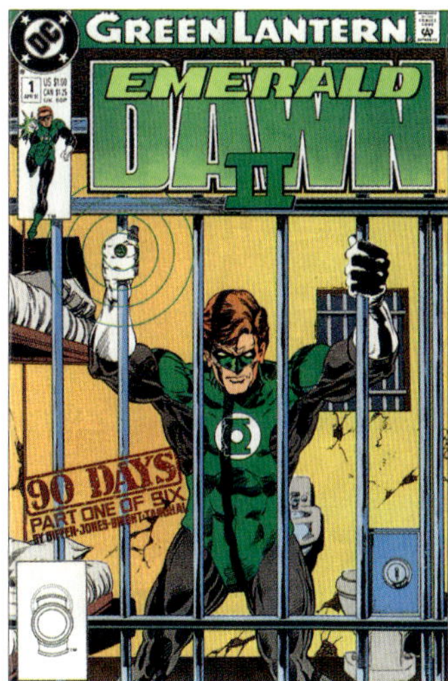

A NEW DAWN

***Green Lantern: Emerald Dawn II* #1**

After the success of the original *Emerald Dawn* miniseries in 1989 and 1990, writers Keith Giffen and Gerard Jones and artist M. D. Bright reunited to delve once more into the past of fabled Green Lantern Hal Jordan. While their last effort skimmed over Hal's time in jail, serving his punishment for a drunk-driving escapade, this six-issue series revealed his prison experience. The limited series also detailed Hal's tutelage at the hands of the corrupt Green Lantern Sinestro. Despite his immaculate record, Sinestro had abused his Guardian-given powers to instill fear into the hearts of his people. However, when an uprising broke out on his home planet due to his absence, Sinestro was dethroned as his world's leader and evicted from the Green Lantern Corps.

Sinestro cannot understand why Hal Jordan feels it necessary to serve his time in jail when he could so easily break out of his prison cell.

ON TV THIS MONTH: ***SWAMP THING*** **regrew his TV fan base in his own animated series, debuting April 20, as well as spawning a Kenner toy line...**

February: The Provisional Irish Republican Army launches a mortar attack on 10 Downing Street during a British Cabinet meeting.

March: Germany formally regains complete independence after the four post-World War II occupying powers relinquish all remaining rights.

Monarch was originally planned to be revealed as Captain Atom, but a leak to fans forced them to rethink the plan.

MAY

THE FACE OF ARMAGEDDON

***Armageddon 2001* #1**

Armageddon 2001 was the DC Comics event of the summer. A massive crossover tale, the story began in its self-titled first issue special and spun off into twelve annuals of the most popular comic titles of the day, before concluding in a second special. Written by Archie Goodwin and Denny O'Neil, and drawn by penciller Dan Jurgens, *Armageddon 2001* chronicled the birth of time-traveling hero Waverider. Hailing from a dystopian possible future in the year 2030, where a super hero had been corrupted and reborn as the dark overlord known as Monarch, Matthew Ryder volunteered for an experiment that gave him the ability to move through time. Now calling himself Waverider, Matthew traveled back to the present to try to stop Monarch before his creation.

By making contact with any given super hero, Matthew experienced a version of that hero's future, and became closer to deducing Monarch's identity. As he moved through the summer's annuals, Waverider saw varied alternate futures. In one timeline, the Joker died while fighting Batman, electrocuting himself by stabbing his metal cane into a socket. In another, Superman was corrupted by his own power and was killed by Batman wearing his kryptonite ring. In yet another, the Martian Manhunter retreated to life high on a mountaintop, dispensing his wisdom to passersby.

But just as Waverider finished a trip into Captain Atom's possible future, his mission was interrupted as Monarch ventured back to the present to destroy him. The heroes united against the dictator, and Monarch was revealed as the former hero Hawk. Corrupted by the death of his partner Dove, Hawk was driven insane and adopted the identity of Monarch, only to be defeated and sent reeling back through the time stream by the power of Captain Atom.

JULY

A WEEKLY DOSE OF SUPERMAN

***Superman: The Man of Steel* #1**

Since the mid-1980s revival of the Superman franchise, the Man of Steel had appeared in stores three times a month in the pages of *Superman*, *The Adventures of Superman*, and *Action Comics*. But as the titles began to carry stories into each others' issues, and triangle numbers appeared on their covers, indicating the order in which to read Superman's exploits, DC editorial saw the chance to give their hero a fourth ongoing monthly book. *Superman: The Man of Steel* was born, with the first issue written by Louise Simonson and with art by Jon Bogdanove, Tom Grummett, Bob McLeod, and Dan Jurgens.

AUGUST

DEATHSTROKE STRIKES

***Deathstroke, the Terminator* #1**

Longtime Teen Titan foe and notorious mercenary-for-hire Slade Wilson began his impressive sixty-issue run with the help of writer Marv Wolfman and artist Steve Erwin. The series' first issue retold Deathstroke's traumatic past and reestablished his relationship with right-hand man Wintergreen. It also served to introduce a new Ravager, a villain bearing the moniker of Deathstroke's deceased son, Grant. As the series progressed, Deathstroke would go on to fight the Dark Knight, join forces with a new female Vigilante, and even make a costume change into a dramatic blue-and-black uniform.

IN THE REAL WORLD...

April: Thieves steal twenty paintings worth U.S.$500 million from the Van Gogh Museum in Amsterdam; they are found an hour later in an abandoned car nearby.

June: In the Philippines, Mount Pinatubo erupts in what will be the second-largest terrestrial eruption of the 20th century; the final death toll tops 800.

JUSTICE BREAKS DOWN

***Justice League America* #53**

The lauded Giffen/DeMatteis era of the Justice League came to a dramatic close with "Breakdowns," a sixteen-part storyline that crossed over through the pages of both *Justice League America* and *Justice League Europe*. When Justice League backer and spokesperson Maxwell Lord was shot, the current team was thrown into disarray by new ambassador Kurt Heimlich before being disbanded by the government altogether. After skirmishes with the Global Guardians, the Extremists, and alien powerhouses Despero and Lobo, the League was shocked by the death of teammate the Silver Sorceress. In the end, the other members went their separate ways in this melancholy epic by writers Keith Giffen, J. M. DeMatteis, and Gerard Jones, and artists Chris Wozniak, Bart Sears, Darick Robertson, and Kevin Maguire.

SEPTEMBER

WORLD WAR

***War of the Gods* #1**

Olympus was under siege in this epic crossover that began in the pages of the first issue of *War of the Gods*. The peaceful home of the Greek gods of ancient myth was stormed by Lord Jupiter and his fellow Roman deities, who all desired a place on what they considered their rightful thrones. Meanwhile, the natural principles of the universe were going haywire. Fireballs plummeted into major American cities. A violent earthquake rocked the peaceful European nation of Markovia. Even the forces of magic seemed to be tearing at the seams, and it was all due to the scheming of the sorceress Circe in her attempt to destroy the world and collect the pieces for herself.

Writer/artist George Pérez crafted this elaborate tale in his detailed style, alongside finishing artists Cynthia Martin, Russell Braun, Romeo Tanghal, Pablo Marcos, Vince Giarrano, and Scott Hanna. Pérez centered the story around Wonder Woman and her world, but still included nearly every major character in the DC Universe. Not only did the action cross over into more than a dozen titles, but three of the four issues in this limited series contained posters of DC characters by the talented Chris Sprouse. Finally, after a series of battles that involved the otherworldly New Gods and the walking dead corpses of former heroes and villains, Circe's reign of terror was ended and Wonder Woman and her allies prevailed.

Hercules and the Son of Vulcan go head to head in battle as the Greek gods clash with the Roman gods.

DECEMBER

BATTLE OF THE BAT-MEN

Batman & Dracula: Red Rain

"In Elseworlds, heroes are taken from their usual settings and put into strange times and places—some that have existed, or might have existed, and others that can't, couldn't, or shouldn't exist. The result is stories that make characters who are as familiar as yesterday seem as fresh as tomorrow." With that mantra, the Elseworlds imprint was born. A series of specials and one-shots, Elseworlds offered a glimpse into fantastic new worlds, and provided readers with a diversion from the continuity of their favorite heroes. Although *Red Rain* wasn't the first title to bear the Elseworlds logo (that was *Batman: Holy Terror* in October 1991), it was certainly one of the most popular.

Written by Batman alumnus Doug Moench, and illustrated with the shadowy pencils of Kelley Jones, *Red Rain* chronicled the clash between Batman and the legendary Dracula. The meeting of these two creatures of the night proved so popular as to inspire two sequel specials, *Batman: Bloodstorm* and *Batman: Crimson Mist*.

The Dark Knight walks away from the battle bitten and boasting his own bloodied fangs.

AQUAMAN GAINS NEW SEA LEGS

***Aquaman* [second series] #1**

For the first time since the 1960s, Arthur Curry, the King of the Seven Seas, was granted his own ongoing series to celebrate the 50th anniversary of Aquaman's first appearance, care of writer Shaun McLaughlin, penciller Ken Hooper, and cover artist Kevin Maguire. The series wasn't quite the success intended, and lasted a mere thirteen issues. However, despite its short lifespan, the comic still managed to feature several mainstay Aquaman villains, including Black Manta and Scavenger, and even featured a memorable tale guest-starring Batman and his Soviet foe, the NKVDemon.

ALSO THIS YEAR: Ragman returned in October, with an updated origin, in an eight-issue miniseries written by Keith Giffen and Robert Loren Fleming, and illustrated by Pat Broderick... November saw Black Canary get her first miniseries, by writer Sarah E. Byam and artists Trevor Von Eeden and Dick Giordano, which lasted for four issues...

June: Croatia and Slovenia declare their independence from Yugoslavia.
September: The Seattle grunge band Nirvana release their hit album *Nevermind*.
October: The first free parliamentary elections are held in Poland.
December: Mikhail Gorbachev resigns as President of the Soviet Union.

1992

"HE CAN MAKE YOU LONELY FASTER THAN ANYBODY ON EARTH."

Commissioner Gordon regarding Batman's disappearing act, *Batman: Sword of Azrael* #1

BATMANIA RETURNS

Three years after Tim Burton's *Batman* motion picture shocked and fascinated moviegoers, Batman continued to be DC's favorite son. With the release of Burton's sequel, *Batman Returns*, "Batmania" was spreading again.

Batman Returns gave stores a chance to push Batman merchandise, from Pez dispensers to action figures, and comic retailers weren't left out of the loop. DC debuted a new series, *Batman: Shadow of the Bat*, and one-shots meant to attract the casual buyer excited about the new movie. Prestige format specials like *Catwoman Defiant* and *Penguin Triumphant* were released to capitalize on the villains from the movie, and there was a comic book adaptation of the film. With the "Knightfall" crossover looming, Batman's top spot seemed secure for the future.

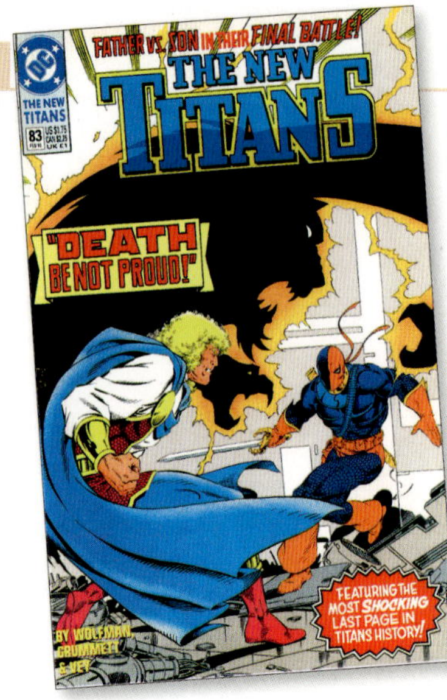

FEBRUARY

THE BATTLE OF JERICHO

***The New Titans* #83**

Writer Marv Wolfman and artist Tom Grummett crafted a grand finale to the epic "Titans Hunt" storyline in the form of the "Jericho Gambit" storyline. Former Teen Titan Jericho was revealed to be the mastermind behind the current string of attacks plaguing the Titans team. In the guise of the leader of the Wildebeest Society, Jericho had hunted down his former teammates and was only stopped when his father, the notorious Deathstroke, led a band of new Titans on a storm of Jericho's extra-dimensional headquarters. Realizing that his son had been possessed by corrupt other-worldly entities, Deathstroke did the unthinkable and impaled his son on his sword, seemingly ending Jericho's threat forever.

THE RAY SHINES

***The Ray* #1**

Longtime DC writer/editor Jack C. Harris reworked the Golden Age character of the Ray into a new hero, assisted by future superstar artist Joe Quesada. In this six-issue miniseries, Ray Terrill was introduced as a tortured boy, forced to live in near-complete darkness due to a condition that made him light-sensitive. Little did he know that his father was the original Freedom Fighters super hero called the Ray, and that he too possessed the Ray's light-based superpowers. With the help of love interest Jenny Jurden, the reluctant new Ray accepted his legacy and became a super hero.

APRIL

SPECTACULAR REVIVAL

***Justice League Spectacular* #1**

The heroes of the Justice League were needed, but did the heroes need the Justice League? This was the question that each individual member was asking him or herself in *Justice League Spectacular* #1, a forty-eight-page special that would completely reset the status quo of both Justice League America and Justice League Europe. With the titles spearheaded by *Superman* mainstay Dan Jurgens, writer Gerard Jones and artists Rick Burchett and Ron Randall jumped on board as well to help revitalize the franchise. By adding Superman to Justice League America, and both Aquaman and Green Lantern Hal Jordan to the European branch in this special, the individual titles were given renewed lives and interesting new directions.

IN THE REAL WORLD...

January: Russian President Boris Yeltsin announces that Russia will stop pointing nuclear weapons at United States cities.

PANIC IN THE SKY

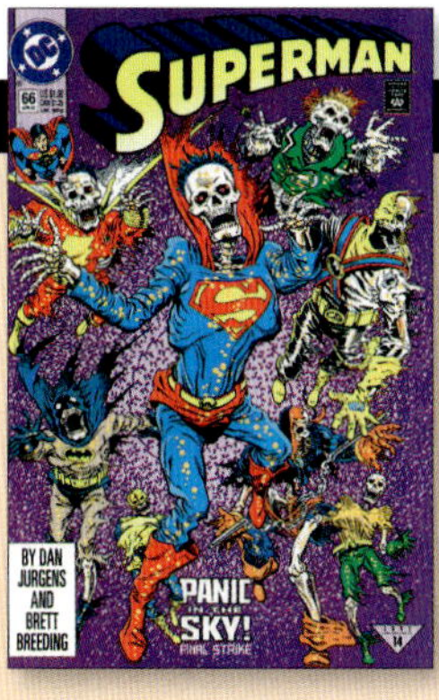

Superman [second series] #66
Superman's old foe Brainiac had taken control of Warworld, a planet designed for battle, and, using its power, had invaded Earth, intent on annihilation. With Supergirl and Maxima under his control, Brainiac was conquering anything in his path, including Orion and Lightray of the New Gods. But Superman knew his old enemy was coming, so he began to gather an army.

In this seven-part adventure that spanned the pages of *Superman*, *The Adventures of Superman*, *Action Comics*, and *Superman: The Man of Steel*, writers Dan Jurgens, Jerry Ordway, Roger Stern, and Louise Simonson, with artists Brett Breeding, Tom Grummett, Jon Bogdanove, and Bob McLeod, assembled many of DC's favorite characters to defend the world from Brainiac's hordes, including the Metal Men and Deathstroke, the Terminator. The heroes beat back Brainiac's forces, overcoming his mind-control of many of their allies. Supergirl and Maxima joined the heroes, and Maxima used her telepathic abilities to reduce Brainiac into a comatose state.

In *Superman* #66's "Final Strike" against Brainiac's forces, Maxima's ruthless nature once again reared its ugly head when she took away Brainiac's most prized possession: his mind.

JUNE

FLIGHT OF THE CONDOR

***Black Condor* #1**
Writer Brian Augustyn and penciller Rags Morales gave the world a new face to bear the name of the Freedom Fighter Black Condor—Ryan Kendall. Kendall gained the power of flight and enhanced senses from his grandfather's corrupt secret organization. However, the new Black Condor failed to hold onto his title, which ran for a mere twelve issues. Before its end, the series managed to squeeze in guest appearances by the Shark, Batman, and fellow Freedom Fighter legacy hero, the Ray.

HOW GREEN WAS MY VALLEY

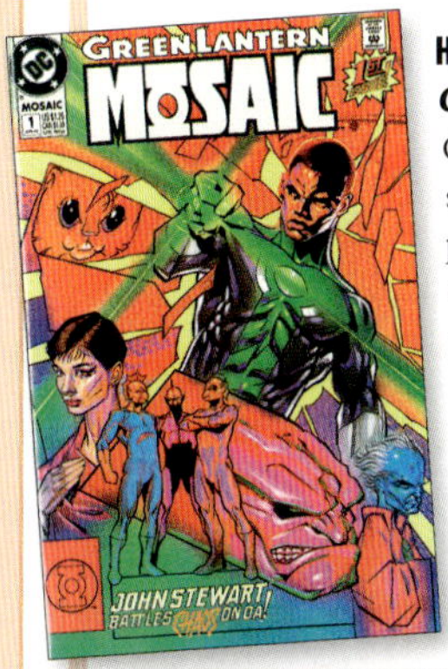

***Green Lantern: Mosaic* #1**
Green Lantern John Stewart finally got his chance to shine in *Green Lantern: Mosaic*. Sold with a promotional glow-in-the-dark plastic Green Lantern ring, the first issue of this unique series saw Stewart preside over the planet Oa. With each section of Oa populated by a different planet's race, complete with its own atmosphere and gravity, the job of peacekeeper proved quite a challenge for the longtime Green Lantern. Yet despite its many possibilities, *Mosaic* was nonetheless short-lived, running for only eighteen issues.

AT THE MOVIES THIS MONTH: Director Tim Burton released his highly anticipated sequel *BATMAN RETURNS*, with Michael Keaton reprising his role as the Caped Crusader opposite Michelle Pfeiffer as the leather-clad Catwoman and Danny DeVito as the sewer-dwelling Penguin...

JUNE

IN THE SHADOWS

***Batman: Shadow of the Bat* #1**
The 1989 *Batman* movie had inspired DC to create the third ongoing Batman title in the character's history, *Batman: Legends of the Dark Knight*. Similarly, DC timed the release of *Batman: Shadow of the Bat* to coincide with the surefire hit, *Batman Returns*. An ongoing series that took place in the Gotham City of the present, *Shadow of the Bat* lasted ninety-four issues. Handled by the former team on *Detective Comics*—writer Alan Grant and artist Norm Breyfogle—the first issue was released in both a newsstand and deluxe polybagged format. While both were essentially the same, down to the Brian Stelfreeze covers, the bagged version included a *Shadow of the Bat* bookmark, mini poster of the covers for the first two issues, an Arkham Asylum pop-up paper model, and a set of blueprints of Arkham's interior.

Shadow of the Bat also offered readers well-crafted tales, jump-starting the title with "The Last Arkham," a four-part story where Batman was checked into Arkham Asylum as a patient. As the tale unfolded, the readers realized that the Dark Knight had arranged for his capture in order to stop the murderous Mr. Zsasz from escaping from the asylum. While Grant stayed on with the book for nearly its entire run, crafting powerful stories featuring minor characters, Stelfreeze left after the forty-ninth issue, and the title seemed to lose its individuality as a result.

To be an inmate in the fabled Arkham Asylum, you have to look the part. So in order to uncover the secrets of the home for the criminally insane, Batman masquerades as a raving lunatic.

February: The Maastricht Treaty is signed, founding the European Union.
February: The English FA Premier League is officially formed.
March: *The Silence of the Lambs* wins the Academy Award® for Best Picture.
April: Disneyland Paris officially opens under the name "EuroDisney."

JULY

TOTAL ECLIPSE

***Eclipso: The Darkness Within* #1**

An obscure villain from a bygone era, Eclipso reared his two-toned face in a new crossover that would establish him as one of the greatest threats in the DC Universe. Told in two fifty-six-page self-titled specials written by Keith Giffen and Robert Loren Fleming, and illustrated by Bart Sears, *Eclipso* told the tale of a cruel lord of chaos, freed from his prison inside the body of adventurer Bruce Gordon.

In Eclipso's debut special (with a plastic black diamond affixed to the cover of the direct-market edition), the master of darkness could take possession of anyone that held black diamond shards while in a state of anger. Using this power, Eclipso amassed an army of the most powerful protectors of Earth, starting with the star-faring hero Valor and the unstable creature of the night known as the Creeper.

As the special bled into summer annuals, roles were reversed and heroes became villains due to the accessibility of the black diamonds. The plague was put to an end when Vril Dox of the L.E.G.I.O.N. and a host of heroes stormed Eclipso's palace. There they fought off their possessed former friends until Starman valiantly sacrificed his life to end Eclipso's reign of terror.

The combination of magic and muscle proves too much for Superman during his first encounter with Eclipso.

ON TV THIS MONTH: Christopher Chance snuck his way onto television screens on July 20 in the new live-action show *HUMAN TARGET*, starring Rick Springfield, that lasted only seven episodes...

SEPTEMBER

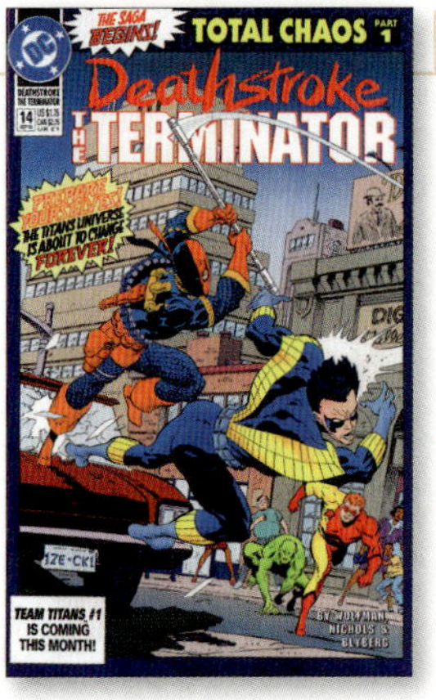

TOTAL CHAOS

***Deathstroke, the Terminator* #14**

The world of the Titans was expanding. Pantha and Red Star had joined the team, and a baby Wildebeest mutation had found its way into their headquarters. But the arrival of Lord Chaos and his opponents from the future, the Team Titans, threatened to complicate the lives of the Titans. The "Total Chaos" story, by writer Marv Wolfman and artist Art Nichols, saw the Titans team up with Deathstroke and other unlikely allies to battle Lord Chaos.

THE ONCE AND FUTURE TITANS

***Team Titans* #1**

As the "Total Chaos" event continued, crossing from the pages of *Deathstroke, the Terminator* into the pages of *The New Titans*, the Titans found themselves at odds with a group of teens from an alternate future. These teens would go on to form the Team Titans and spin off into an ongoing series all their own. Although their series would only last twenty-four issues, the team nevertheless started with a bang, offering five first issue, that each contained a different origin story for every team member. Marv Wolfman supplied the scripts for each issue, while the art was handled by Kevin Maguire, Gabriel Morrissette, Adam Hughes, Michael Netzer, Kerry Gammill, and Phil Jimenez.

OCTOBER

BATMAN IN ANIMATION

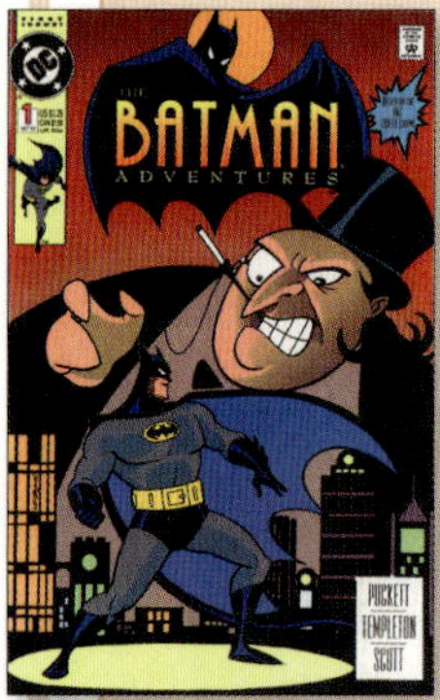

***The Batman Adventures* #1**

The public was starting to take comics more seriously, and it was time for animation to catch up. On September 5, Fox debuted *Batman: The Animated Series* to an audience that would quickly realize the serious potential that super hero cartoons had to offer. The tie-in comic called *The Batman Adventures*, by writer Kelley Puckett and penciller Ty Templeton, emerged a mere month after the series made its TV debut. It was set in the animated universe of the cartoon but contained new stories.

The brainchild of producer/artist Bruce Timm, designer and background painter Eric Radomski, producer Alan Burnett, and writer Paul Dini, among many other artists and writers, *Batman: The Animated Series* took a more serious approach to the Caped Crusader, matching the tone prevalent in the comics of the time. Approaching each episode like a mini-movie, with a live orchestra and fully painted backgrounds, the series also used a dark art deco style for the appearance of Gotham City. The result paid homage to the *Superman* cartoons of the Fleischer Studios from the 1940s, the *Batman* comic books of the late 1970s and early 1980s, and touched on the mood of the two Tim Burton *Batman* films.

The series included the vocal talents of Kevin Conroy as Batman, Mark Hamill as the Joker, and Arleen Sorkin as Harley Quinn, and lasted eighty-five episodes, before moving to the WB network for another twenty-four. *The Batman Adventures* ran for thirty-six issues before being reborn under another title.

The comic book format allows the animated Batman an escape from the TV censors, and doesn't require him to pull any punches.

IN THE REAL WORLD...

May: Jay Leno becomes the new host of NBC's *Tonight Show*.
June: Denmark beats Germany 2–0 to win the 1992 UEFA European Football.
July: The 1992 Summer Olympics are held in Barcelona, Spain.
October: The Toronto Blue Jays become the first Canadian team to win the World Series.

THE GARDNER OF GOOD AND EVIL

***Guy Gardner* #1**

It was Guy Gardner's fondest dream, and most other heroes' greatest nightmare. Not only was the brash former Green Lantern alive and well in his own ongoing series, but now he came armed and ready for battle with a yellow power ring. Kick-started by writer Gerard Jones and penciller Joe Staton, Guy Gardner's new solo exploits proved explosive from the start, as the loudmouth brawler razed a slum simply because he had the power to do so. As his series continued for a respectable forty-four issues, Gardner soon traded in life as a ring-slinger for life as a human weapon, as he realized his alien Vuldarian heritage and became known as Guy Gardner: Warrior.

THE ADVENT OF AZRAEL

***Batman: Sword of Azrael* #1**

Azrael, one of the most important characters of the modern Batman mythos, was dropped right under the noses an unsuspecting reading populace in the debut issue of *Batman: Sword of Azrael*, by esteemed bat-scribe Denny O'Neil, talented young penciller Joe Quesada, and inker extraordinaire Kevin Nowlan.

Heir to a clandestine organization of religious killers called the Order of St. Dumas, everyday college student Jean-Paul Valley found himself donning the garb of Azrael as the order's newest soldier. Utilizing the secret programming he had undergone since infancy, Azrael became a ruthless killer, dispatching opponents using his flaming wrist daggers. But while on a mission to hunt the Order's enemy LeHah, a servant of the dark demon Biis, Azrael overcame his training to rescue Bruce Wayne, who had been kidnapped by LeHah. By this simple act of kindness, the "avenging angel" created a new path for himself and became a staunch ally of the Batman. This loyalty would be put to the test in 1993 in the "Knightfall" crossover event that would have dire ramifications for both Azrael and the Dark Knight Detective.

Jean-Paul Valley's father bore the Azrael mantle before passing it on to his son. His costume lacked the retractable gauntlet blades, as he relied on a traditional sword.

NOVEMBER

DOOMSDAY DEBUTS

***Superman: The Man of Steel* #17**

With advertisements in comics foretelling the coming of Doomsday and cover blurbs on the Universal Product Code box of direct-to-comic store issues, fans knew a wrench was about to be thrown into the works of the Man of Steel. Doomsday made his understated first appearance on the twenty-second page of a comic about Superman fighting a league of freak mutations. While readers awaited the upcoming story, all they were shown was a teaser sequence of panels depicting a fist slamming into a wall. Little did they know that that fist belonged to a creature who would live up to his portentous name.

Doomsday's raw brute strength is not only enough to break out of a seemingly indestructible prison, but it later proves a daunting threat for the Man of Steel.

DECEMBER

THE SPECTRE'S NEWEST HAUNTING

***The Spectre* [third series] #1**

The crime fighter from beyond the grave, the Spectre, was back in a new series by writer John Ostrander and artist Tom Mandrake. With its debut issue featuring a macabre glow-in-the-dark cover and a retelling of detective Jim Corrigan's ascension to the role of Spectre, the stage was set for a gritty series delving into crime and punishment. Ostrander's thought-provoking stories, with Mandrake's shadowy illustrations, meant this series outlasted its two previous attempts, running for sixty-two issues.

THE END OF AN ERA

***Legion of Super-Heroes* [third series] #38**

Writer/artist Keith Giffen was leaving the *Legion* title, and he was determined to go out with a bang. In the future reality of the Legion of Super-Heroes, the Legion and the citizens of Earth had overcome the alien Dominators and ended five years of oppression. Just as everything was getting back to normal, 4,000 people were killed when Tokyo collapsed into a "sinkhole." A Dominator underground explosion had caused a reaction that would rock the planet's core. In a desperate move, the denizens of Earth fled their planet, and watched as Death came to claim their world in a cataclysmic explosion. This powerful prose issue was written by Keith Giffen and Tom and Mary Bierbaum, with pencils by Jason Pearson.

ALSO THIS YEAR: In January, Batman faced an alien Predator who had chosen Gotham City as his hunting ground in *BATMAN VERSUS PREDATOR* #1… October saw a new police force patrol the spaceways in *DARKSTARS*… October also saw the release of *BATMAN: NIGHT CRIES*, a graphic novel looking into the evils of child abuse… In December the Cluemaster's daughter, Stephanie Brown, donned a blue and purple costume and became the Spoiler in *DETECTIVE COMICS* #647…

November: Bill Clinton defeats incumbent President George H. W. Bush to win the U.S. presidential election.

December: Prince Charles and Princess Diana of the United Kingdom publicly announce their separation.

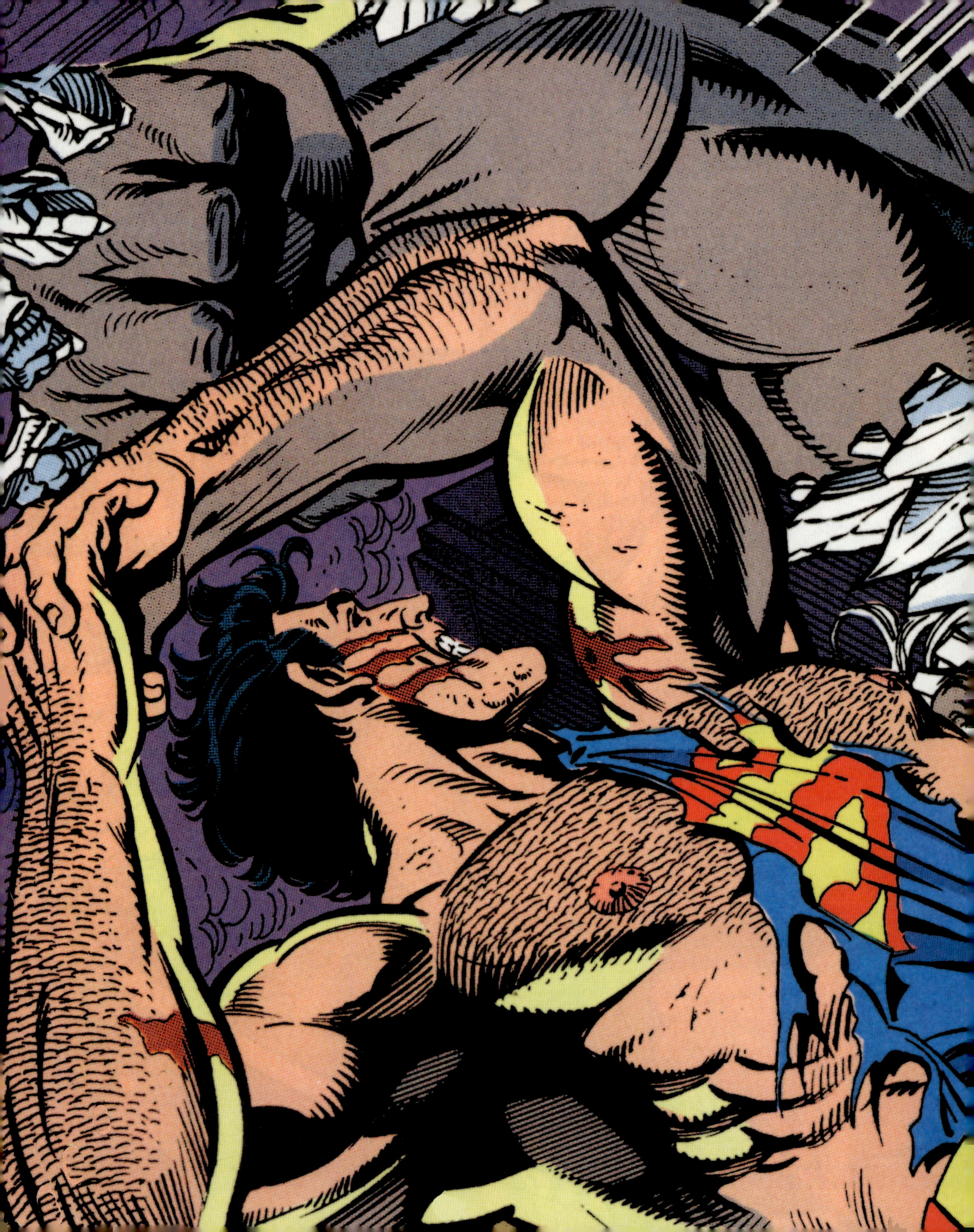

THE DEATH OF SUPERMAN!

SUPERMAN (second series) #75 (January 1993) "Nobody tears apart my city and gets away with it!" Superman and the killing machine Doomsday's final clash on the streets of Metropolis ended with them both seemingly being killed. Written and illustrated by Dan Jurgens, with many full-page panels, Superman's death became a national sensation and *Superman* #75 sold six million copies.

1993

"JUST REMEMBER... NO MATTER WHAT HAPPENS... I'LL ALWAYS LOVE YOU. *ALWAYS.* BUT NOW... *DOOMSDAY* GETS HIS."

Superman to Lois Lane, *Superman* [second series] #75

INTRODUCING THE EVENT

Crossovers were selling, there was no question about that. Ever since 1985's *Crisis on Infinite Earths* maxiseries, DC had realized the sales potential of large-scale stories featuring giant casts of characters and earth-shattering events. Year after year, summer crossovers brought in new readers and convinced regular readers to pick up more comics than usual. With Batman and Superman each featured in four books a month, it was only a matter of time before crossover stories began to revolve around each character.

Superman was first to be given the crossover treatment in "The Death of Superman" saga, which paved the way for Batman's "Knightfall" storyline. Soon, everyone from Wonder Woman to Green Lantern would gain their own crossover epic. It was a new era of shock and consequence, and DC was leading the pack.

JANUARY

THE DEATH OF SUPERMAN

***Superman* [second series] #75**

Clark Kent was making headlines, and it wasn't only in the *Daily Planet*. Superman was now a lead story in the news of the real world. In *Superman* #75, an issue available in a regular newsstand edition and a deluxe edition complete with an obituary, poster, and black armband, DC had killed their icon.

Although the character saw a resurgence in the mid-1980s with John Byrne's miniseries *The Man of Steel*, the hero's books had grown stagnant in many readers' eyes. It was time for the character that paved the way for an entire genre of super hero comics to once again be a trendsetter; and when editor Mike Carlin and the rest of the *Superman* writing staff conceived the "Doomsday" storyline, the character would do just that.

An alien powerhouse from another world, Doomsday had broken free from his ancient prison and carved a bloody swath across America. Now the rampaging beast had come for the Man of Steel. As the pair battled, Superman used up every bit of his strength, and in a dramatic finale delivered in splash images and written and drawn by artist Dan Jurgens, with finishes by Brett Breeding, he had no more to give. He delivered one final blow to the creature, downing his enemy, but at the cost of his own life. Superman was dead, and "The Death of Superman" saga would go on to be the best-selling comic book paperback of all time.

Another crossover, "Funeral for a Friend," would follow later that month, and show a super hero community reeling in shock at the loss of their inspiration. It was in part three of the saga, within *Superman: The Man of Steel* #20, by writer Louise Simonson and penciller Jon Bogdanove, that the heroes displayed their grief to the bewildered public. In a funeral procession more impressive than any president's, the super heroes walked down a crowded Metropolis street swarming with mourners to pay tribute to Earth's greatest champion.

There is no mistaking it: wrapped in his shredded red cape and cradled in the arms of a devastated Lois Lane, Superman lies dead on the streets of his adopted city, Metropolis.

IN THE REAL WORLD...

January: IBM announces a U.S.$4.97 billion loss, the largest single-year corporate loss in United States history to date.

MAY

KNIGHTFALL

***Batman* #492**

"Knightfall" was a nineteen-part crossover event that passed through the pages of *Batman*, by writer Doug Moench and artists Norm Breyfogle, Jim Aparo, and Mike Manley; *Detective Comics*, written by Chuck Dixon and illustrated by Norm Breyfogle, Jim Balent, and Graham Nolan; and the *Showcase '93* Two-Face feature, scripted by Doug Moench and drawn by Klaus Janson. With most of its issues featuring eye-catching covers by relatively new *Batman* artist Kelley Jones, plus a slowly eclipsing numbered bat-logo in the upper right-hand corner, "Knightfall" was instantly recognizable as a major event in the life of Bruce Wayne, and rightfully so.

Conceived at the same time as the "Death of Superman" crossover in the Man of Steel's various titles, "Knightfall" pitted Batman against his deadliest foes, all freed from their cells in Arkham Asylum by a new criminal mastermind: Bane. A deadly combination of brute strength and a brilliant strategic mind, Bane was introduced to readers in January's *The Vengeance of Bane* #1. Bane had spent his entire life in a harsh prison environment and was injected with the steroid serum Venom during a prison experiment, arming him with superhuman strength. He broke free from captivity to hunt down Batman, the man he perceived to be the living embodiment of his inner demon, and during "Knightfall" he became one of the Dark Knight's greatest foes.

As Batman faced the Mad Hatter, the Ventriloquist, the midguided brute strength of Amygdala, and the psychotic slasher Mr. Zsasz, fatigue set in and he became weak. Bane and his henchmen Bird, Trogg, and Zombie slowly began to get a foothold in Gotham's underworld, and the Dark Knight was nowhere close to rounding up all the escaped criminals. Batman hunted Cornelius Stirk, Firefly, Poison Ivy, the Scarecrow, and the Joker, while Robin recruited former assassin Azrael (Jean-Paul Valley) into their war on crime. "Knightfall" was heating up, Batman was wearing down, and just as the Dark Knight felt he could no longer take any more he was forced to fight his way through Bane's inner circle to the end of the line, where stood Bane himself.

In the climactic *Batman* #497, Bane beats the exhausted Batman in a brutal fight. The villain triumphantly lifts the Dark Knight in the air and shatters Batman's spine over his knee.

JUNE

REIGN OF THE SUPERMEN

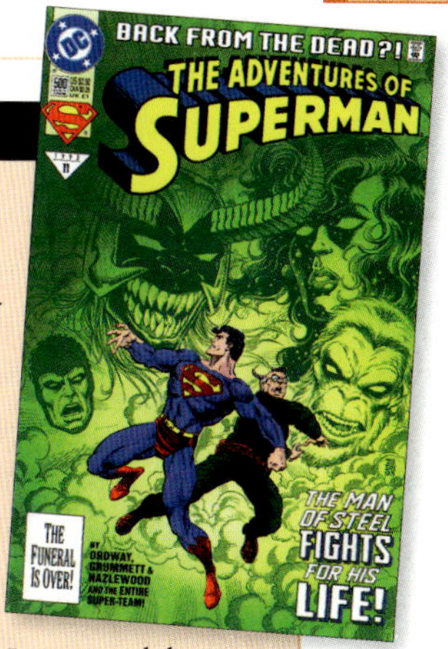

***The Adventures of Superman* #500**

Superman was back from the dead—or was he? The new "Reign of the Supermen" crossover jump-started with this sixty-two-page issue, available in a deluxe edition or a standard newsstand version. As Clark Kent's adoptive father Jonathan lay at death's door in a hospital after suffering a heart attack, he drifted into the afterlife, where his son's soul appeared before him. Together, the two fought their way back to life, and Jonathan awoke convinced that Superman was alive and well. Meanwhile, Lois Lane visited the tomb of her deceased love and discovered Superman's body was missing.

Besides this monumental central story, the issue also featured four teaser comics that introduced a group of contenders all vying for the Superman name. Construction worker John Henry Irons found a new purpose in life as the future Steel in a story by Louise Simonson, with art by Jon Bogdanove. The Eradicator returned in a preview tale by writer Roger Stern and artist Jackson Guice. A cloned Superboy escaped captivity in a yarn by writer Karl Kesel and artist Tom Grummett, and a Cyborg Superman claimed he was the real Man of Steel in a short by storyteller Dan Jurgens. Each character then spun off into his own *Superman* title (*Superman: The Man of Steel*, *Action Comics*, *The Adventures of Superman*, and *Superman*, respectively), complete with a deluxe cover featuring a die-cut S-shield.

Lois Lane is filled with both shock and hope when she discovers Superman's coffin lying empty.

JUSTICE TAKEN TO TASK

***Justice League Task Force* #1**

Writer David Michelinie and artist Sal Velluto introduced a different type of Justice League in their new ongoing series *Justice League Task Force*. With a roster that changed depending on each mission's needs, the series starred such notable characters as the Martian Manhunter, the Flash, Gypsy, Bronze Tiger, Nightwing, and Aquaman. The team even went on a mission with a wheelchair-bound Bruce Wayne, as the former Batman healed from his broken back injury. Despite its potential star power and flexible format, the series underwent a revamp with a new roster before being canceled at issue #37.

January: The Buffalo Bills become the first team to lose three consecutive Super Bowls.

March: North Korea announces that it plans to withdraw from the Nuclear Nonproliferation Treaty and refuses to allow inspectors access to nuclear sites.

AUGUST

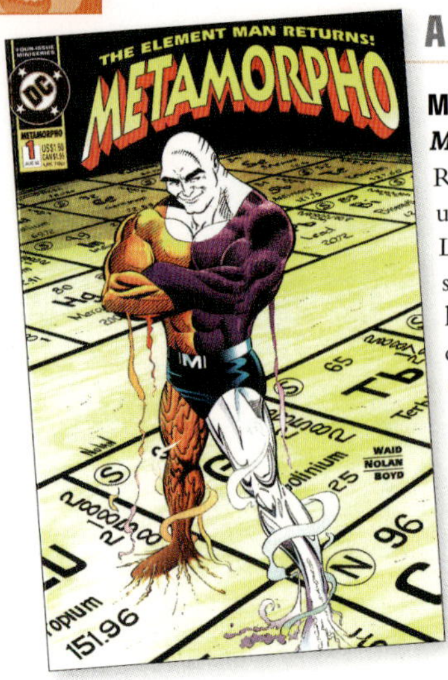

METAMORPHO MAKES HIS MOVE

***Metamorpho* #1**

Rex Mason, the world-famous Metamorpho, used his recent fame as a member of Justice League International to make a return to solo action in the four-issue *Metamorpho* limited series. Written by Mark Waid, with co-plotting and art chores handled by Graham Nolan, everyone's favorite walking chemistry set was in good hands as he not only met and battled another metamorph, but also searched for a cure for his mutated son Joey. In the end, the Element Man restored his son to human condition, and even fixed his own ailing marriage with his true love Sapphire Stagg.

THE CAT CAME BACK

***Catwoman* [first series] #1**

With only one limited series to her credit in her entire fifty-year history, Selina Kyle finally stole the spotlight in her first ongoing series by writer Jo Duffy and artist Jim Balent. Spinning out of the pages of the large scale "Knightfall" crossover, Catwoman's adventures began when the criminal Bane sought to have some control over her. With an emphasis on international intrigue as well as the occasional jewel heist, Catwoman delivered nonstop action for ninety-four issues before being relaunched into a second ongoing series. With the help of later writers like Chuck Dixon and Doug Moench, Catwoman even managed to gain her own Rogues Gallery, which included Hellhound, Cyber-Cat, and She-Cat.

"HELLO, SWEETHEARTS. DID YOU MISS ME?"

Catwoman, *Catwoman* #1

SEPTEMBER

HAWKMAN'S NEW FLIGHT PLAN

***Hawkman* [third series] #1**

Chicago had a guardian angel with armored wings in Hawkman's latest adventures by writer John Ostrander and penciller Jan Duursema. Katar Hol was back in this premier issue with a deluxe gold foil cover. Featuring villains Mustang Suzy and the hitman Deadline, it was the first in a series jammed with guest stars including Wonder Woman, Bloodwynd, and the Eradicator. Hawkman even teamed up with Green Lantern Hal Jordan in issue #2. However, his character would soon be completely reinvented, a fact that may have led to the series' cancelation by issue #33.

Hawkman takes flight using his costume's built-in supply of the gravity-defying "Nth metal" to thwart his enemies.

THE GOLDEN STANDARD

***The Golden Age* #1**

Writer James Robinson brought the Justice Society of America back into the spotlight in this four-issue collaboration with acclaimed *X-Men* artist Paul Smith. The first of several critically praised efforts involving Robinson and the heroes of the 1940s, this Elseworlds series chronicled life behind the scenes for the All-Star Squadron, and detailed the corruption of former hero Dan the Dyna-Mite, then his change into the villainous Dynaman. With realistic characterization and cinematic storytelling techniques, *The Golden Age* broke new ground and helped elevate its author to the realm of comic book star.

ON TV THIS MONTH: Superman's personal life was aired before a TV audience when *LOIS & CLARK: THE NEW ADVENTURES OF SUPERMAN* debuted, showcasing the romantic chemistry between costars Dean Cain (Superman) and Teri Hatcher (Lois Lane)...

OCTOBER

SUPERMAN RETURNS

***Superman* [second series] #82**

In this grand finale to the "Reign of the Supermen" saga by writer/artist Dan Jurgens, a familiar figure appeared in the skies of Metropolis: Superman was back. The story saw the Cyborg Superman quickly prove he was no hero when, in allegiance with the villain Mongul, the Man of Steel's doppelgänger destroyed Coast City. Set to right the situation, the true Superman emerged from a Kryptonian revitalization chamber close to powerless. With the help of his new allies Steel, Superboy, and the Eradicator, plus old friends Green Lantern and Supergirl, the Last Son of Krypton faced down his imitator in Engine City. In a final moment of sheer will, Superman regained his powers and punched a hole through the chest of the Cyborg Superman, seemingly defeating the creature.

THE NEW BATMAN'S KNIGHTQUEST

***Batman* #500**

Batman was broken. Luckily, Bruce Wayne had been grooming his replacement: the former assassin Azrael. By *Batman* #500, the last chapter of the "Knightfall" saga by writer Doug Moench and artists Jim Aparo and Mike Manley, Azrael was truly his own Batman. He now wore a customized costume with gauntlet claws and a chest light that displayed Batman's symbol on his intended target. This crueler Batman had also defeated Bruce Wayne's nemesis Bane and embarked on his own set of adventures, sparking the new crossover "Knightquest," which continued throughout the *Batman* titles. A seminal moment in *Batman* history, the issue was available in both a standard newsstand and a deluxe edition, featuring the cover art of Kelley Jones and Joe Quesada, respectively.

Batman puts the claws on his new armored costume to use.

IN THE REAL WORLD...

April: Tennis star Monica Seles is stabbed in the back by an obsessed fan of rival Steffi Graf at a tournament in Germany.

May: A Tamil Tigers suicide bomber assassinates President Ranasinghe Premadasa of Sri Lanka.

NOVEMBER

INSIDE THE OUTSIDERS

***Outsiders* [second series] #1**

The Outsiders made their return in a new series courtesy of writer Mike W. Barr and artist Paul Pelletier, beginning with two first issues: Alpha and Omega. Alpha described the first meeting of veteran hero Geo-Force and newcomers Technocrat, Faust, and Wilde, and Omega dealt with the re-teaming of familiar faces Katana, Halo, and Looker. Later joined by the Eradicator and Windfall, the team fought the vampire Roderick as well as Lady Shiva, Felix Faust, and the forces of Kobra. With guest appearances from Batman, Superman, the Teen Titans, and the New Gods, plus cameos by old friends the Atomic Knight, Metamorpho, and Black Lightning, the series ran for twenty-four issues.

Travis Charest illustrated the covers for both first issues of *Outsiders*, showcasing new costumes for Katana and Geo-Force. Looker and Halo would also gain new uniforms during the series.

THE SIDEKICK GOES SOLO

***Robin* #1**

Tim Drake had grown up idolizing the Batman. A brilliant young mind, Tim earned his place by the Dark Knight's side by deducing Bruce Wayne's dual identity, and then proving his own ingenuity. When Batman's back was shattered by the criminal known as Bane, and Jean-Paul Valley (alias Azrael) took over the mantle of the bat, it didn't take Robin long to realize that it is not the Batsuit that makes the man.

As Batman, Valley insisted that he didn't need a partner, and continued to prove his point by bricking up Tim's private entrance to the Batcave. So, in the debut issue of his own ongoing series, Robin fired up his sleek sports car named the Redbird and embarked on a solo career, with the help of writer Chuck Dixon and artist Tom Grummett, not to mention a deluxe embossed cover.

The series was an immediate success. Although his relationship with Batman ebbed and flowed over the years, and Dixon left the title after a remarkable one-hundred-issue run, Robin's series lasted for 183 issues before being given a name change and reboot. Tim Drake proved a reader favorite, and paved the way for other ongoing titles like *Azrael*, *Nightwing*, and *Batgirl*.

The new Batman isn't shy about letting Robin know that his services are no longer needed.

DECEMBER

THE SHORT HALLOWEEN

***Batman: Legends of the Dark Knight Halloween Special* #1**

Editor Archie Goodwin was on to something when he paired Jeph Loeb and Tim Sale on the first holiday special of the popular *Batman: Legends of the Dark Knight* series. The writer/artist team had worked together on a *Challengers of the Unknown* miniseries, but it wasn't until they charted the adventures of the Dark Knight together that they seemed to really hit their stride. Mixing a haunting Scarecrow tale with a bit of tragic romance in Bruce Wayne's personal life, the holiday special was so popular that it earned two sequel specials and several hit miniseries, including *Batman: The Long Halloween*.

THE COMING TIDE

***Aquaman: Time and Tide* #1**

Writer Peter David journeyed below the waves to chronicle the next era of Atlantean history in Aquaman's newest miniseries. Drawn by Kirk Jarvinen, this flashback story chronicled Aquaman's first meeting with the Flash, his first encounter with his lover Kako, and his first high-profile public appearance. Pitting young Orin Aquaman against his half-brother Ocean Master, as well as the Trickster, this series served as a history lesson on Aquaman's life and a foundation for David's upcoming *Aquaman* ongoing series.

DRAWING BLOOD

***Bloodbath* #1**

Despite the large-scale crossovers in the *Superman* and *Batman* titles, DC still found time for a summer crossover running through many of their super hero annuals. "Bloodlines" detailed an attack from shape-shifting aliens that fed off the spinal fluid of their human prey. However, many of the aliens' victims survived, and developed superpowers as a result. These "new blood" heroes joined forces with Superman, Batman, and other DC faces for a final showdown with the aliens in the pages of *Bloodbath*, a series of two specials by writer Dan Raspler and pencillers Chuck Wojtkiewicz, Bill Willingham, Sal Velluto, and Val Semeiks.

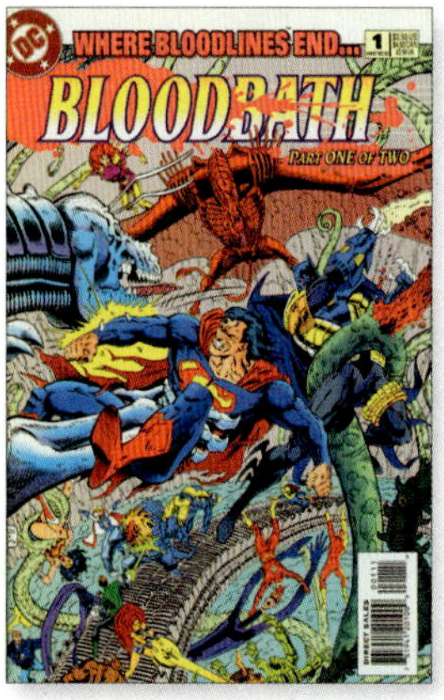

ALSO THIS YEAR: DC acquired humor institution *MAD MAGAZINE* and took the popular publication under its publishing wing… As part of an ongoing expansion of titles, DC began to publish new titles under the Milestone imprint, placing a much-deserved emphasis on diversity with heroes such as Static, Icon, and Shadow Cabinet… Christmas Day saw the theatrical release of *BATMAN: MASK OF THE PHANTASM*, an animated feature film set in the world of *BATMAN: THE ANIMATED SERIES*, which was originally intended for the direct-to-video market… Brash anti-hero Lobo, created to mock comic stereotypes and trends, muscled his way into his own ongoing series by writer Alan Grant and artist Val Semeiks in December, complete with a rather appropriate foil cover enhancement on his crotch…

June: Kim Campbell is appointed as the nineteenth Prime Minister of Canada. She is the first female ever to hold Canada's highest office.

December: id Software releases *Doom*, a seminal first-person shooter video game that uses advanced 3-D graphics.

VERTIGO

VERTIGO'S VISION

Death was only the beginning. In March 1993, DC Comics debuted a three-issue miniseries entitled *Death: The High Cost of Living*. The upbeat, living embodiment of death who had debuted in *The Sandman* #8 (August 1989) was now starring in her own series. Written by Neil Gaiman and drawn by future comics superstar Chris Bachalo, *The High Cost of Living* had one notable trait besides a brilliant story: its cover bore a new logo. With this debut, DC's provocative new mature-reader imprint, Vertigo, was born.

DC Comics was no stranger to experimentation, and many mature-reader titles had hit the market in previous years. Even before the so-called "British invasion" of talent in the 1980s, DC had prided itself on putting the story first. When Alan Moore conceived his masterpiece *Watchmen*, when Grant Morrison wrote himself into his own comic stories, starting with *Animal Man* #26 (August 1990), and when Neil Gaiman crafted the mythos of the Dreaming in *The Sandman* #1 (January 1989), DC was the natural publishing house for these writers' output.

By 1993, it was time to branch out. Neil Gaiman's *Sandman* series was a runaway critical and commercial success, as were Grant Morrison's reinventions of *Animal Man* and *Doom Patrol*, and writer Peter Milligan's *Shade, the Changing Man*. *Swamp Thing* was continuing its own revolutionary run, along with the book that got started in its pages—*Hellblazer*. An alternative market was forming for edgier, more sophisticated books, and editor Karen Berger decided to pursue it. With a sidebar emphasizing its logo on each issue's cover and an advisory label stating that the comic was "Suggested for mature readers," Vertigo debuted. Since Berger decided not to restart the numbering on ongoing series, the transition was simple. The comics maintained their storylines, but continued their drift away from the DC Universe into the Vertigo line.

New titles soon began to appear. *Sandman Mystery Theatre* started its seven-year run, bringing a period noir sensibility to the imprint. Gaiman's *The Books of Magic* began as a miniseries and led into an ongoing title; Gaiman's *Black Orchid* followed suit. Creator-driven titles, such as *The Invisibles* and *Preacher*, also appeared under the Vertigo label, and minor characters from other Vertigo titles were granted their own miniseries. The imprint was a commercial and critical success, and DC Comics would attempt to recapture the magic formula that produced this proud offspring.

Also in 1993, DC had experimented with another imprint, Milestone, a super hero line starring minority characters. DC later launched Paradox Press, a series of black-and-white graphic novels that included *Road to Perdition* and *A History of Violence* (both of which inspired hit movies), as well as the acclaimed *Big Book* anthology series. 1997 saw the birth of the sci-fi line Helix, which published *Transmetropolitan*, a book later adopted by Vertigo. None of these efforts, however, found a big audience. But DC had latched on to a shooting star with Vertigo, propelled by a host of brilliant writers and artists, and because of this, the imprint continues to this day.

Death: The High Cost of Living *#1 (March 1993): Dave McKean's superb gothic cover art set the tone perfectly for new mature-readers imprint Vertigo. The story followed the adventures of sixteen-year-old Didi (alias Death) on the day, once every century, she becomes a living person.*

1994

"THEY SAY YOU CAN'T MAKE AN OMELET WITHOUT BREAKING A FEW EGGS... SO I HAD TO ERASE ALL EXISTENCE TO BUILD A NEW AND FAR BETTER REALITY."

Parallax, *Zero Hour* #0

NEW BEGINNINGS

It was a time of reinvention. Popular heroes like Green Lantern, Hawkman, and Green Arrow were getting modern facelifts. New characters like Superboy, Azrael, and the Eradicator from DC's successful crossovers were beginning their own individual franchises. Even the concept of time itself was subject to change. DC wasn't about to rest on its laurels and a new year meant new crossovers and character shake-ups. A new age of heroes was beginning, and the zero issues that accompanied the summer's blockbuster crossover *Zero Hour* would cement that idea.

But despite the ever-shifting status quo, DC never lost sight of its roots. The true Superman was safely back in Metropolis, Bruce Wayne returned to Gotham City (if only briefly) and even in those comics that seemed to be ever-changing like *The Flash* and *Aquaman*, telling a good story still ranked higher than shocks and clever marketing.

JANUARY

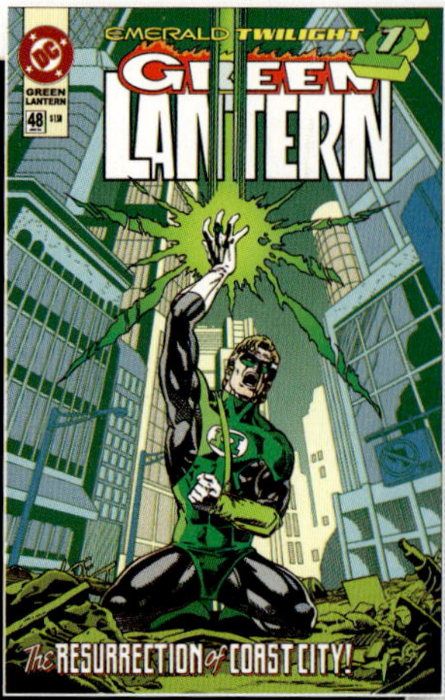

EMERALD TWILIGHT

***Green Lantern* [third series] #48**

The editors at DC had found a pattern that worked. Take a major super hero icon, have that hero stretched beyond his limits and then replace him with a younger model (or four). Having already scored a tremendous success with Superman and Batman, DC applied this theory to Green Lantern with the same result—although, perhaps, a bit more controversy.

In "Emerald Twilight," a three-issue saga penned by new writer Ron Marz and drawn by artists Bill Willingham, Fred Haynes, and Darryl Banks, longtime Green Lantern Hal Jordan set out to right the wrongs done to him. During the "Reign of the Supermen" storyline over in the Superman titles, Green Lantern's hometown of Coast City had been completely decimated. As a result, beginning in *Green Lantern* #48, Hal sought to gain more power from the keepers of the Green Lantern energy, the Guardians of the Universe, in order to restore his home. Fighting his way through an army of his friends and fellow Lanterns, Hal resorted to violent tactics, even seemingly killing his old friend Kilowog.

In the climactic final part of this epic, contained in the fiftieth anniversary issue of *Green Lantern* (which was garnished with a dynamic glow-in-the-dark cover and backed by a gallery section), Hal faced off with his old enemy and disgraced former Green Lantern, Sinestro. Apparently killing this last-ditch guardian of the Green Lantern central battery core, Hal then absorbed the battery's awesome power to become the entity later known as Parallax. As quickly has he'd come, Hal flew away, ready to "fix" his city, and then perhaps the world. But what Hal didn't know was that one Guardian had survived his onslaught. Armed with the last power ring in existence, the Guardian Ganthet traveled to Earth and randomly selected the final bearer of the Guardian's power: everyman Kyle Rayner. Inexperienced and undisciplined, artist Kyle quickly embraced his new legacy, and by the next issue he had even adopted a costume more fitting to his unique tastes. The sunset of Hal Jordan was over, but there was a new dawn for Green Lantern.

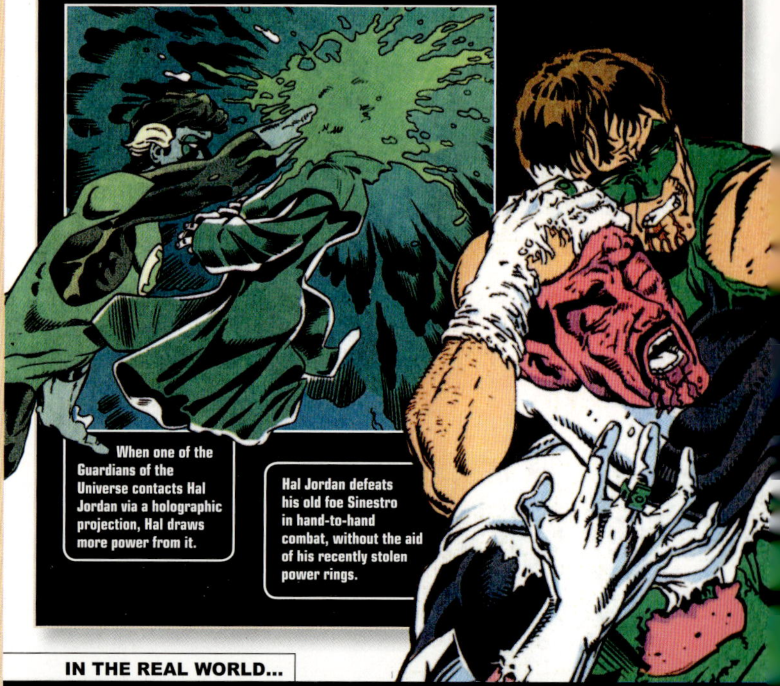

When one of the Guardians of the Universe contacts Hal Jordan via a holographic projection, Hal draws more power from it.

Hal Jordan defeats his old foe Sinestro in hand-to-hand combat, without the aid of his recently stolen power rings.

IN THE REAL WORLD...

January: The Irish government announces the end of a fifteen-year broadcasting ban on the Provisional IRA and its political arm, Sinn Féin.

FEBRUARY

LOVESICK

The Batman Adventures: Mad Love

Fresh from their work on *Batman: The Animated Series*, writer Paul Dini and artist Bruce Timm partnered for a special set in the animated world of the Dark Knight. Revealing the origin of the Joker's lover, popular made-for-TV character Harley Quinn, the storytelling duo crafted a sweetly disturbing award-winning tale. When psychologist Harleen Quinzel treated the Joker at Arkham Asylum, she first fell madly in love with him, and then became mad herself. She soon became the Joker's tortured and abused sidekick, with delusions of romance that were as unhealthy as her mental outlook.

STEEL FORGES A PATH

***Steel* #1**

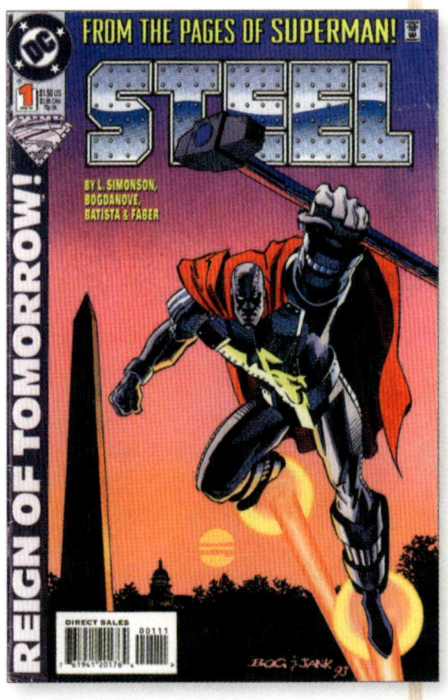

Originally setting out to replace Superman, Steel finally stepped out of Superman's shadow in his own ongoing series by writers Jon Bogdanove and Louise Simonson, and artist Chris Batista. Returning home to Washington D.C., John Henry Irons reunited with his family but was instantly caught up in gang violence. Debating putting his life of superheroics behind him, Irons instead forged a new version of his suit of armor, and set out to protect his hometown as the hero Steel. Although he retained the red cape and his trademark sledgehammer, gone was his chest S-shield. Now Steel was truly his own man, and his series ran for fifty-two issues.

SUPERBOY MEETS WORLD

***Superboy* [third series] #1**

It was spring break all year round for the Boy of Steel as Superboy set up camp in picturesque Hawaii in his new ongoing title written by Karl Kesel and with art by Tom Grummett. Along with his supporting cast fresh from the depths of the clandestine organization known as Project Cadmus, the young clone of Superman made his mark on the super hero world with his brash actions and laid-back teenage attitude. Fighting villains like Sidearm and the voluptuous Knockout, Superboy quickly found a home in this exotic locale and on the comic book stands, lasting an impressive one hundred issues, and even spawning a second title, the short-lived *Superboy and the Ravers*.

JULY

KNIGHTSEND

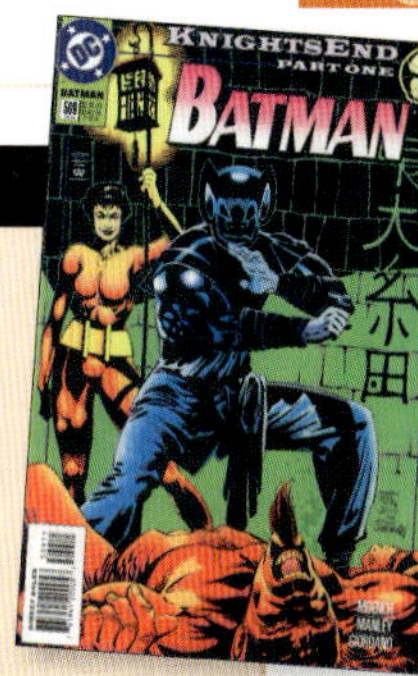

***Batman* #509**

It was time for Bruce Wayne to reclaim his mantle as Batman. The only problem was, Jean-Paul Valley had no intention of giving it back. In "KnightsEnd," the dramatic crossover conclusion to both the "Knightfall" and "Knightquest" epics, Bruce Wayne's journey back to Batman spanned the pages of not only *Batman* and *Detective Comics*, but also *Batman: Shadow of the Bat*, *Batman: Legends of the Dark Knight*, *Robin*, and even *Catwoman*. Chronicled by writers Doug Moench, Alan Grant, Chuck Dixon, Jo Duffy, and Denny O'Neil, as well as artists Mike Manley, Bret Blevins, Ron Wagner, Tom Grummett, Jim Balent, Graham Nolan, and Barry Kitson, the storyline consisted of ten chapters and two epilogues.

As Jean-Paul Valley slowly descended into madness, a victim of a lifetime of brainwashing, a now-healed Bruce Wayne began training under the guidance of martial-art expert Lady Shiva in order to confront his violent heir. Finally ready to take on his crazed successor, Bruce Wayne donned his familiar cape and cowl and battled Valley over the streets of Gotham in a fight that eventually led to the deepest recesses of the Batcave. Forced to abandon his suit of armor to fit through the small crevices of a particular tunnel, Valley finally saw what kind of monster he had become when faced with the cold light of day. He then relinquished the role of the Batman to its rightful owner, and Bruce Wayne was back.

Bruce Wayne wears a ninja disguise, the Mask of Tengu, before donning the original Batsuit once more.

IMPULSE'S INITIATION

***The Flash* [second series] #92**

The brainchild of writer Mark Waid and artist Mike Wieringo, Impulse burst onto the scene at quite a pace. Young Bart Allen, the grandson of the Silver Age Flash, Barry Allen, was raised in a future timeline where his hypermetabolism imprisoned him inside a virtual environment, the only thing capable of keeping up with his accelerated growth rate. Already looking like a teenager when he turned two, Bart was stolen from his government captors by his grandmother Iris Allen, who took him back to the past to find a cure. There Bart found a way to stabilize his system, and he also became the Flash's new sidekick, using the moniker Impulse.

February: Edvard Munch's painting *The Scream* is stolen in Oslo; it is recovered on May 7.
March: Apple, Inc. releases the first Macintosh computers with PowerPC microprocessors.
March: *Schindler's List* wins seven Oscars® including Best Picture and Best Director.
April: The Rwandan Genocide begins in Kigali, Rwanda.

JULY

COLD AS ICE

***Justice League Task Force* #14**

It was judgment day for the Justice League in this penultimate part of the "Judgment Day" crossover. The Justice League's old foe, the immensely powerful Overmaster, had returned. The League had defeated the entity before, but apparently it had only been testing the team. As they gathered for the battle, team members were devastated to see hero Ice seemingly murdered by the Overmaster's beams of pure energy. In the very next issue, the other heroes gathered once more to finally defeat their cruel opponent.

AUGUST

AQUAMAN LENDS A HAND

***Aquaman* [third series] #1**

Writer Peter David had been building toward this series for years now. After revealing the ancient history of Aquaman's underwater home in the 1990 miniseries *Atlantis Chronicles*, as well as touching on the high points of young Orin's early life in *Aquaman: Time and Tide* from December 1993, David was finally ready to put all his backstory to practical use in the new monthly *Aquaman* title. With the help of artist Martin Egeland, and later Jim Calafiore, David molded Aquaman into the regal king he had been intended to be, adding a beard and long hair to give Aquaman an Arthurian impression of authority.

But David's dramatic changes didn't stop there. By issue #2, he had Aquaman lose his hand to a host of frenzied piranhas as the villain Charybdis held his hand in the water. By the following issue, Aquaman was sporting a harpoon where his hand used to be, and by issue #5, he had traded in his orange uniform for a metallic chest piece and two-toned tights. Aquaman was a new man, gruff and regal, and charting new waters every issue. Peter David stayed with the character for nearly fifty issues before stepping down to allow for new regular writer Erik Larsen to take over. Dan Jurgens would carry the book to its conclusion at issue #75 in January 2001.

Aqualad, in a supporting role, tried to snap his mentor out of his grim funk by attacking him.

SEPTEMBER

HOUR OF RECKONING

***Zero Hour* #4**

It began at the end of time. A powerful force had started a countdown to the destruction of the DC Universe, a mystery man out to reform time itself. And his identity would send shockwaves through the comic book community.

In DC's newest summer blockbuster *Zero Hour*, writer/artist Dan Jurgens and finisher Jerry Ordway crafted a five-issue story that began with issue #4, and counted backward to zero. As the timeline began to be altered, the resulting time anomalies began to cross into most of the DC titles. Time was going haywire, and only the combined forces of Earth's super heroes showed any hope of righting it.

Rather appropriately, Superman was the one who gathered them all together, with the exception of the aged heroes of the Justice Society. They were away at the Vanishing Point, a realm out of time's reach, opposing the seeming villain behind the crisis in time: an entity calling himself Extant who was a corrupted future version of the time-traveling hero Waverider. As the Golden Age incarnations of the Atom and Dr. Fate perished at Extant's hands, and the future of the Legion of Super-Heroes began to crumble before those heroes' eyes, a group of heroic icons finally gained the upper hand against their foe, only to realize that Extant wasn't the true mastermind behind the time disturbances. The true villain was former Green Lantern Hal Jordan, now calling himself Parallax. Mad with grief after the destruction of his hometown of Coast City, Hal had set out to recreate the universe into one he himself could live with.

In the end, Hal realized the folly of his ways when he was confronted by his old friend Green Arrow, Oliver Queen. Ollie shot Parallax in the chest during a dramatic encounter at the very beginning of time itself. Once Hal had seemingly died, relative newcomer Damage used his explosive powers to create a new Big Bang, which restarted the timeline that Hal had altered. By *Zero Hour* #0, time had righted itself, and a newly streamlined world was born as a result. The DC Universe was granted a fresh start and, as if to prove that point, nearly every DC title was given a special #0 origin issue.

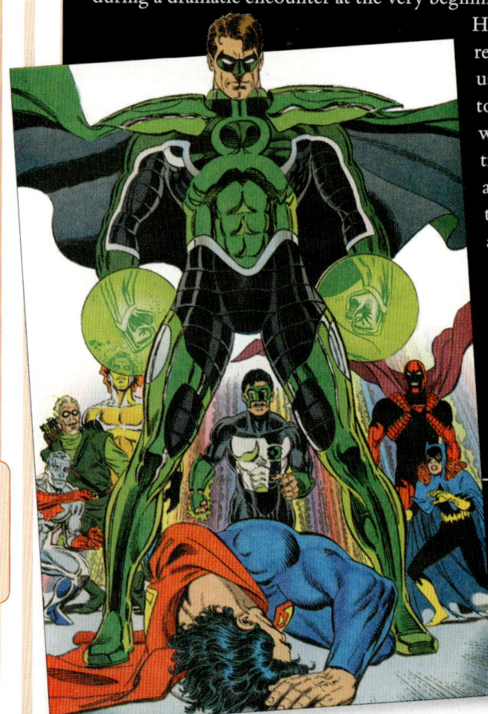

As Parallax, Hal Jordan is prepared to go to extremes to change the world. Armed with the power of the Green Lantern central battery, he tries to "fix" time and undo the destruction of Coast City.

IN THE REAL WORLD...

May: Three-time Formula One world champion Ayrton Senna is killed in an accident during the San Marino Grand Prix in Imola, Italy.

May: The Channel Tunnel, which took 15,000 workers over seven years to complete, opens between England and France.

OCTOBER

REACHING FOR THE STARS

***Starman* [second series] #0**

The original Starman, Ted Knight, had retired, and it was up to his son to carry on his legacy. In this ongoing series by writer James Robinson and artist Tony Harris, a new Starman was unleashed on the world, but it wasn't who the Knight family expected. When Ted's oldest offspring, David Knight, was killed on one of his first outings in costume, his reluctant younger brother, Jack, was forced to defend his lauded Opal City against the son of the villainous Mist. Wearing vintage goggles and a star-garnished leather jacket, Jack became the new Starman, even befriending the former villain known as the Shade along the way. With realistic dialog and characters set against fantastic situations and adversaries, Robinson captured critical acclaim with his new series and Starman journeyed across eighty issues before Jack Knight retired.

CONNOR HAWKE LEAVES THE NEST

***Green Arrow* #0**

Another product of DC's Zero Month, future Green Arrow Connor Hawke debuted in the zero issue of *Green Arrow*, courtesy of scripter Kelley Puckett and penciller Jim Aparo. The forgotten son of Oliver Queen, Connor was reunited with his father when he was a student at a monastery where Ollie himself had trained. Connor had inherited all his father's potential in archery and the martial arts, but none of his temper and gruff behavior. But when the two joined forces to help foil the plan of a few bloodthirsty mercenaries, they realized they had more in common than they knew, and set out together to find the mastermind behind the hired guns.

BACK TO THE FUTURE

***Legion of Super-Heroes* [third series] #0**

The Legion of Super-Heroes had no future; Parallax had seen to that. The previously uninterrupted adventures of the team from the 30th Century had ended in the chaos of *Zero Hour*. But in this zero issue written by Tom McCraw and Mark Waid and drawn by Stuart Immonen, a new incarnation's adventures were only just beginning. With the slate wiped clean, the Legion's origin was reset in a story that would carry over into the heroes' sister title, *Legionnaires*. A mix of old and new, the rebooted Legion featured new monikers for most of the familiar faces, plus new characters like the speedster XS.

THE ULTIMATE HAWKMAN

***Hawkman* [third series]#0**

Although it took its toll on many, the streamlined time effects of *Zero Hour* hit Hawkman harder than most. In that miniseries, Golden Age Hawkman Carter Hall had melded mind and body with Thanagarian space cop Katar Hol, as well as the original Hawkgirl, to form a brand new hero—a Hawkman with all their shared memories. Now part hawk, with real feathered wings that could retract inside his back, Hawkman fought a new string of dark adventures with the help of writer William Messner-Loebs and artist Steve Lieber, not to mention the impressive cover art supplied by Lee Weeks.

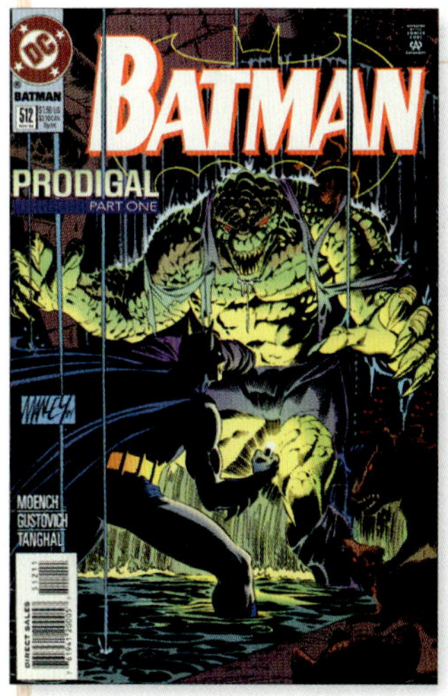

NOVEMBER

PRODIGAL

***Batman* #512**

In this twelve-part aftermath to the "Knightfall" crossover, Bruce Wayne reclaimed the mantle of the Batman from his unstable successor, Jean-Paul Valley, and passed it to the former Robin and current Nightwing, Dick Grayson. Written by Doug Moench, Alan Grant, and Chuck Dixon, with artists Bret Blevins, Lee Weeks, Phil Jimenez, Graham Nolan, and Ron Wagner among others, the "Prodigal" crossover ran Dick Grayson through a gauntlet of old foes and the titles of *Batman*, *Batman: Shadow of the Bat*, *Detective Comics*, and *Robin*.

DECEMBER

THE SPAWN OF THE DARK KNIGHT

***Spawn/Batman* #1**

In a highly anticipated comic book event, Spawn teamed up with the Dark Knight in a gritty tale of cyborgs and the undead. But it was the creative talent behind the special that excited fans. This prestige one-shot marked Frank Miller's return to *Batman*, and was labeled as a companion piece to his classic 1986 work, *Batman: The Dark Knight Returns*. The issue was drawn by Todd McFarlane, one of the most popular artists in comic book history. Fans were also treated to a companion special entitled *Batman/Spawn* (May 1994), by writers Doug Moench, Chuck Dixon, and Alan Grant, and artist Klaus Janson.

ALSO THIS YEAR: Writer Grant Morrison's intriguing tale of rebellion and conspiracy began in September with the debut of Vertigo's *THE INVISIBLES*, featuring the art of Steve Yeowell... Justice Leagues America and International combined in October to create *JUSTICE LEAGUE AMERICA* #0, a *ZERO HOUR* tie-in that showcased the newest incarnation of the famous team by writer Gerard Jones and artist Chuck Wojtkiewicz...

May: Nelson Mandela is inaugurated as South Africa's first black President.
May: Jacqueline Kennedy Onassis dies in her home from non-Hodgkin's lymphoma.
September: The car ferry MS *Estonia* sinks in the Baltic Sea, killing 852 people.
November: George Foreman becomes the oldest heavyweight champion in history.

1995

"SO HE WAS A HOUND AND A ROGUE AND AN UNAPOLOGETIC WOMANIZER. BUT HE DIED AS HE LIVED. HE WAS WHAT *ALL* OF US STRIVE TO BE EVERY DAY. OLIVER QUEEN WAS A HERO."

Zatanna, *Green Arrow* #101

ANTI-HEROES VS. HEROES

The DC Universe had grown darker. As other companies found success in comics featuring big guns and violent anti-heroes, the trend slowly seeped into the world of DC's icons. Superman and Batman had already been replaced by more bloodthirsty successors, and Wonder Woman was next. Heroes were trading in bright costumes for heavy suits of armor, and a new breed of edgy characters emerged. But there was one small problem: the fans weren't happy.

Although DC's large-scale crossovers attracted a slew of new readers, longtime fans were upset by some of the company's recent decisions. Fortunately, the editors could not have agreed more, and they exhaled a collective sigh of relief when the fans rallied and showed overwhelming support for DC's original icons. DC had recognized the fad for what it was, and while they teetered on the brink, they managed to avoid plummeting into the dark abyss.

JANUARY

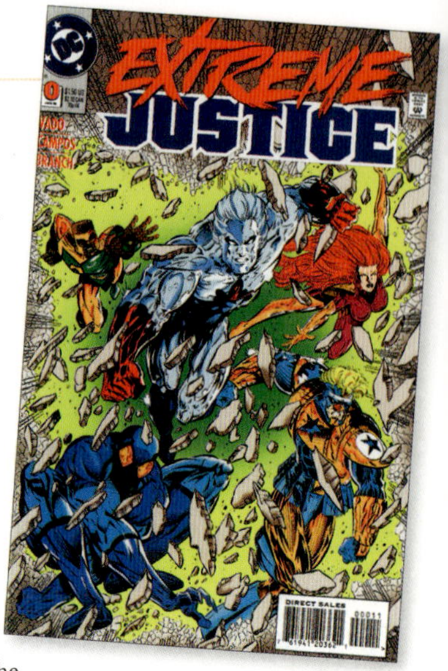

THE EXTREME APPROACH

***Extreme Justice* #0**

In what many considered an example of pandering to the darker trends of the day that had led to big sales for other companies, DC launched an "edgier" Justice League in *Extreme Justice*, a new ongoing series by writer Dan Vado and penciller Marc Campos. As Captain Atom grew unhappy with the direction of the League in the wake of his fellow hero Ice's death, he formed his own team with the help of villain-turned-heroine Maxima, fledgling crimefighter Amazing-Man, Blue Beetle, and a newly armored version of Booster Gold. Despite the additions of Firestorm and even the Wonder Twins, the title only lasted up to issue #18, going through several creative team changes in the process.

WONDER WOMAN'S MAKEOVER

***Wonder Woman* [second series]#93**

Diana, the Amazons' longtime ambassador to Man's World, lost the right to call herself Wonder Woman in this issue by writer William Messner-Loebs and artist Mike Deodato, Jr. When Diana's mother, Queen Hippolyta, had a vision of Wonder Woman dying she sought to protect her daughter. She called for a contest among the Amazons to choose a new Wonder Woman. A red-haired siren named Artemis was the winner.

Hailing from an Amazon splinter group called the Bana-Mighdall, Artemis had first appeared only three issues earlier. Perceived as savage by most of her peers, Artemis nevertheless became the new Amazing Amazon. Donning her Wonder Woman costume for the first time, Artemis sported the famous tiara and magic lasso along with a pair of flying sandals from the Greek god Hermes and the magical strength-increasing bracelets of Atlas. Meanwhile, not one to take defeat lightly, Diana refused to retire from her life as a hero and adopted a black spandex costume and matching jacket to continue her adventures.

With or without her classic uniform, Diana's heroic crusade continues, even versus the likes of the Cheetah.

IN THE REAL WORLD...

January: The World Trade Organization (WTO) is established to replace the General Agreement on Tariffs and Trade (GATT).

FEBRUARY

BACK IN BLACK

Batman #515

In the first issue of the four-part "Troika" crossover by writers Doug Moench, Alan Grant, and Chuck Dixon, with artists Kelley Jones, Barry Kitson, Graham Nolan, and Tom Grummett, the true Batman had finally returned to Gotham City. To mark this special occasion, *Batman* #515 sported a deluxe embossed cover crafted entirely in shades of black, with artwork by Kelley Jones. As the "Troika" storyline passed through the pages of *Batman: Shadow of the Bat* #35 and *Detective Comics* #682 that month, both boasted similarly dark covers, and through each of them Batman's image slowly stepped from the darkness into the light. By *Robin* #14, the story's last installment, it was evident: Batman was wearing a new costume.

On his return to Gotham, Bruce Wayne had begun to make changes to his classic costume, starting with gray gloves and leg spikes on his gray pants. When this Russian mafia tale concluded, however, Bruce had lost the all-gray bodysuit in favor of his traditional outfit, albeit without his trademark blue underwear. While the colorists made every effort to ensure Batman's blue-and-gray costume was as dark as possible, the all-black cover to *Batman* #515 was merely an artistic statement. The all black-on-black Batman uniform would not be seen in comics, and would instead remain exclusive to the silver screen.

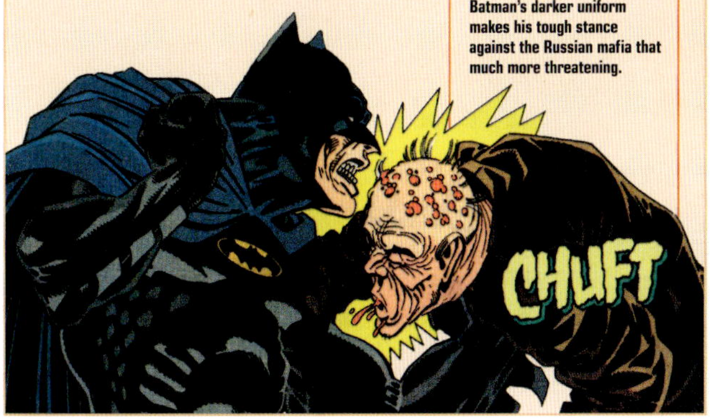

Batman's darker uniform makes his tough stance against the Russian mafia that much more threatening.

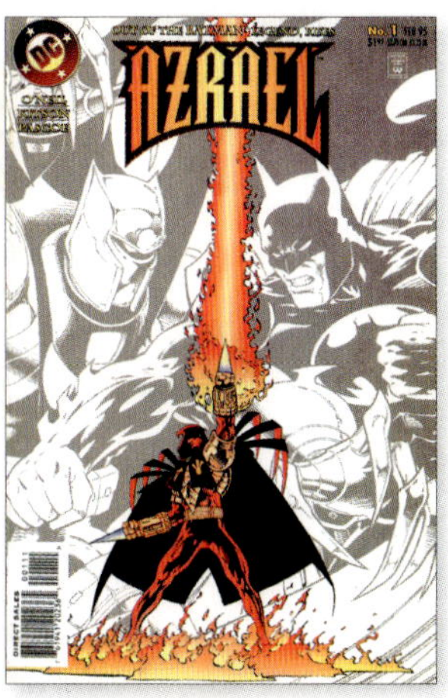

AZRAEL'S ADVENTURES

***Azrael* #1**

Longtime writer/editor and Azrael co-creator Denny O'Neil picked up the pieces of the life of former Batman Jean-Paul Valley in a new ongoing effort, aided by artist Barry Kitson. Homeless and without direction, Jean-Paul reclaimed his role as Azrael with the help of Batman and set out to discover his roots as he waged war against the shadowy ancient Order of St. Dumas. Well-received by fans, the title ran for one hundred issues, with O'Neil reestablishing Azrael as an agent of Batman in a new costume with issue #50. Jean-Paul seemingly gave his life in order to defeat an imposter in his final issue, concluding his mission and his story, but not his legacy.

LIGHTNING CRASHES

***Black Lightning* [second series] #1**

Writer Tony Isabella returned to his prized character, Black Lightning, in an ongoing series with artist Eddy Newell. Updating the classic 1970s hero and Outsiders alumnus with a new costume, Isabella threw teacher/hero Jefferson Pierce into the gritty new surrounding of Brick City, an area seemingly devoid of hope and in need of a guiding light. Black Lightning began to clean up the town with the help of familiar faces such as Gangbuster, and later Batman himself. The comic was short-lived and ended at issue #13. However, Black Lantern's new costume went on to gain a bit of immortality in plastic, as this series inspired Black Lightning's first action figure courtesy of toy company Kenner's *Batman: Total Justice* line.

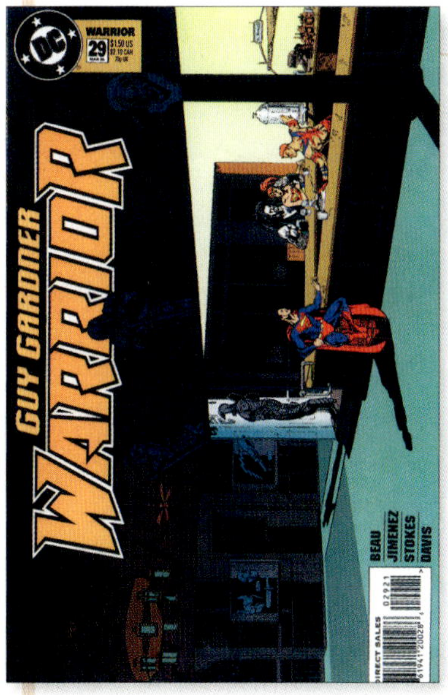

MARCH

WARRIORS' GRAND OPENING

***Guy Gardner: Warrior* #29**

Served up in a cover depicting an empty bar, inspired by Edward Hopper's *Nighthawks,* and in a deluxe edition with doors that opened to reveal a crowd of super heroes, *Guy Gardner: Warrior* #29 marked the opening of Warriors, Guy Gardner's bar for super heroes. With an interior that mimicked real-world theme franchises like Hard Rock Cafe, Warriors was Guy's attempt to cash in on his fame. In this issue by writer Beau Smith and artist Phil Jimenez, nearly every hero in the DCU came to get a look at Guy's new place, as well as a ringside seat to its first inevitable super-brawl.

CAP'S COMEBACK

***The Power of Shazam!* #1**

Writer Jerry Ordway chronicled the further adventures of Billy Batson, the World's Mightiest Mortal, in the new ongoing effort *The Power of Shazam!*, alongside artists Mike Manley and Peter Krause. Ordway managed to recapture the innocence and appeal of Captain Marvel's classic adventures, an effort that did not go unappreciated by fans. The series ran for an impressive forty-seven issues as a result, and featured guest appearances by Batman, Starman, Plastic Man, and the Justice League, as well as a host of classic villains including Mr. Mind, Captain Nazi, and Black Adam. The series also managed to reestablish heroes Mary Marvel, Captain Marvel Jr., and even Bulletman.

January: A magnitude 7.3 earthquake, named the "Great Hanshin earthquake," occurs near Kobe, Japan, causing extensive damage to buildings and killing 6,434.

February: Barings Bank, the U.K.'s oldest investment banking firm, collapses after securities broker Nick Leeson loses U.S.$1.4 billion on the Tokyo Stock Exchange.

APRIL

JESSE CUSTER'S LAST STAND

***Preacher* #1**

One of Vertigo's main goals was to explore new avenues. Premier titles like *The Sandman*, *Swamp Thing*, and *Animal Man* had proved very successful for the imprint since its launch in the 1980s, but Vertigo was now poised to extend its reach in new directions, especially ones that were creator-driven. What they ended up with was a smash hit that spoke not only to established comic book fans, but also to many people who had never before set foot in a comic book store.

Writer Garth Ennis and artist Steve Dillon (along with cover artist Glenn Fabry) gave Vertigo one of its greatest dark comedies and social satires in the ongoing series *Preacher*. Following the adventures of the hard-drinking former Texas preacher Jesse Custer, *Preacher* told an edgy tale of one man's literal search for God and country. No subject was taboo for the quirky new title as Ennis took hard looks at the church, law enforcement, sex, and even America itself.

As the story began, preacher Jesse Custer was possessed by the offspring of an angel and a demon, which bestowed him with the word of God but simultaneously killed his entire parish. By speaking simple commands in his newly biblical voice, Custer found he could compel others to follow his orders, a talent that came in handy as he set out to find God. It turned out that the man upstairs had quit his day job, and Jesse intended to set things right. He was accompanied on his mission by his gun-toting flame Tulip, as well as the self-serving vampire Cassidy. With the mystical Saint of Killers on his trail, and a lengthy list of deadly enemies in his path, Custer and company had their work cut out for them in this sixty-six-issue series. As disturbing as it was darkly humorous, *Preacher* proved a bestseller in the trade paperback market, and spawned a *Saint of Killers* miniseries in 1996, plus a handful of specials before its finale. A book of its covers was also released, along with a line of action figures from DC's new in-house toy company, DC Direct.

Being possessed by the spawn of a demon and an angel is an understandably difficult predicament. The deadly result leaves Jesse Custer a changed man.

APRIL

ACTING ON IMPULSE

***Impulse* #1**

Writer Mark Waid and artist Humberto Ramos unleashed Impulse in his own series, just a few short months after the character's initial debut. In this new ongoing title, young Bart Allen set up camp in the town of Manchester, Alabama under the guidance of speedster guru Max Mercury. Combining a lighthearted feel with interesting new villains, *Impulse* was a gamble that paid off, running eighty-nine issues. The character of Impulse himself later earned a place on the super hero teams Young Justice and the Teen Titans.

TERMINAL VELOCITY

***Flash* [second series] #100**

The Flash's latest epic battle, the six-part "Terminal Velocity," came to a screeching halt courtesy of writer Mark Waid and artists Salvador Larroca, Carlos Pacheco, and Oscar Jimenez. The landmark issue, available in both a deluxe foil Centennial Edition and a standard edition by cover artist Mike Wieringo, saw the villainous cult leader Kobra unleash a deadly earthquake on Keystone City. But when Wally West (the Flash) returned from the grave after witnessing the mysterious Speed Force energy field firsthand, he pulled off a miracle and put an end to Kobra's reign of terror.

JUNE

AT THE MOVIES THIS MONTH: Director Joel Schumacher took over the *BATMAN* movie franchise with *BATMAN FOREVER*, starring Val Kilmer as the Dark Knight Detective, Chris O'Donnell as Robin, Tommy Lee Jones as a rather comedic Two-Face, and Jim Carrey stealing the show as the Riddler…

JULY

FALL OF AN AMAZON

***Wonder Woman* [second series] #100**

Diana reclaimed her famous moniker as Wonder Woman in another in the series of Centennial Edition comics, available in both a foil deluxe edition and a newsstand version with a cover drawn by Brian Bolland. Written by William Messner-Loebs and drawn by Mike Deodato, Jr., the issue depicted Artemis' final struggle with a horde of demons and the maleficent Cheetah. Eventually, the Hell-spawn proved too much for the new Wonder Woman, but Artemis bestowed her strength-enhancing bracelets on Diana before she died. Diana was now back where she had fought hard to be, but losing her friend was too high a price to pay for the role.

IN THE REAL WORLD…

May: U.S. President Bill Clinton indefinitely closes part of the street in front of the White House to vehicular traffic in response to the Oklahoma City bombing on April 19.

May: Jacques Chirac is elected President of France.

June: The most active hurricane season in sixty-two years begins.

SEPTEMBER

NIGHTWING'S NIGHT OUT

***Nightwing* #1**

The original Boy Wonder, Dick Grayson, finally saw his name on the marquee in this four-issue miniseries by writer Denny O'Neil and artist Greg Land. Still reeling from his time as Batman during the "Prodigal" storyline, Nightwing hung up his old costume, convinced that he was done with the hero game. Unfortunately, an ominous letter from the principality of Kravia brought him back to the front line as he began to investigate a new detail of his parents' death. Destined for a life of heroics, Grayson soon adopted a new blue-and-black Nightwing costume designed by Batman's mute mechanic/computer whiz Harold, and once again followed in his adoptive father's footsteps.

OCTOBER

GREEN ARROW'S PARTING SHOT

***Green Arrow* #101**

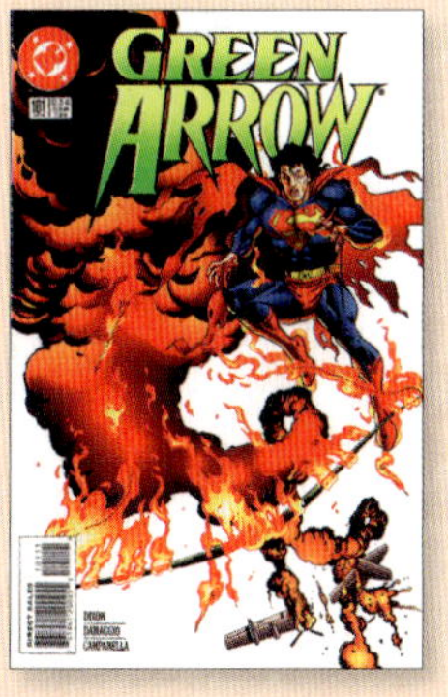

As the "Where Angels Fear to Tread" five-part saga continued to run through Green Arrow's title, writer Chuck Dixon and artists Michael Netzer, Jim Aparo, and Rodolfo Damaggio were putting longtime Green Arrow Oliver Queen through his paces—and it got a whole lot worse for the hero, as by issue #101, Ollie was forced to sacrifice his life.

Oliver Queen had been through a lot lately. After being forced to seemingly kill his best friend, Hal Jordan, Ollie was shocked when Hal visited him, alive and as powerful as ever. But it was Hal's news that was the greatest shock to Ollie—it turned out that Ollie's own protégé, Connor Hawke, was his son. Not only was Oliver Queen forced to deal with his ever-growing family, but he also had to face the menace of a new Force of July, a reunion with his former sidekick Arsenal, and a crazed new love interest going by the name of Hyrax.

As Green Arrow uncovered Hyrax's plan to raze the city of Metropolis, he realized he had to take a stance against this environmental extremist. On board a plane with a powerful bomb set to destroy Metropolis, Green Arrow activated a dead man's switch, giving him a choice: he could lose his arm to escape the inevitable explosion, or lose his life altogether. In the end, Oliver Queen chose death, paving the way for Connor to take his place as the new Green Arrow.

Superman offers to save Green Arrow's life by severing his arm, but Ollie opts for death. This is a nod to Frank Miller's *Batman: The Dark Knight Returns*, where a one-armed Green Arrow nurses quite a hatred for the Man of Steel.

NOVEMBER

EXPLORING THE UNDERWORLD

***Underworld Unleashed* #1**

The villains of the DCU underwent their own extreme makeovers in *Underworld Unleashed*, a three-issue miniseries by writer Mark Waid and artist Howard Porter. In this crossover saga, the powerful demon Neron tempted heroes and villains alike with the promise of enhanced powers in exchange for their mortal souls.

As many infamous characters accepted the terms of Neron's dark deal, they saw their appearances upgraded and their power levels spike. Villains like Mr. Freeze, Copperhead, Major Disaster, and even Killer Moth became heavyweight contenders with new and improved costumes and abilities. Accompanying them were Neron's inner council, made up of Abra Kadabra, Lex Luthor, Circe, Dr. Polaris, and the Joker, each having made his or her own deal with the devil. In fact, in keeping with his character, the Joker sold his soul for a mere box of cigars. But villains weren't the sole beneficiaries of Neron's bargaining. The hero Blue Devil also submitted to Neron's twisted deal, upping his own powers at the cost of the death of a dear friend.

A popular crossover, the miniseries' story passed through many titles of the time, spawned four tie-in specials, and even employed a new fluorescent green ink color not seen before in DC's printing pallet.

Neron organizes a mass prison break. The prison villains are then teleported to Neron's quarters when they light magic candles that burn with a green flame.

ALSO THIS YEAR: A team of "new blood" heroes fresh from the "Bloodlines" crossover starred in the first super hero reality show in March, in the pages of the four-issue miniseries *BLOOD PACK* by writer Charles Moore and penciller Christopher Taylor… July granted the Dark Knight a new quarterly anthology title that would run for twenty-three issues with the release of *THE BATMAN CHRONICLES* #1, by Batman mainstay writers Chuck Dixon, Alan Grant, and Doug Moench, and featuring the art of Lee Weeks, Stewart Johnson, and Brian Apthorp… In summer, Superman gained a new quarterly title to ensure his weekly appearance on comic book store racks in the short-lived *SUPERMAN: THE MAN OF TOMORROW* #1, by writer Roger Stern and penciller Tom Grummett…

September: The DVD, an optical-disc computer-storage media format, is announced.
September: The online auction site eBay is founded.

October: French woman Jeanne Calment reaches the confirmed age of 120 years and 238 days, making her the oldest person ever recorded.

1996

"REGULAR HITMEN KILL REGULAR PEOPLE. I AIN'T REGULAR HITMEN."

Hitman, *Hitman* #1

THE GREAT AMALGAM

Who was stronger, DC's Superman or Marvel's Incredible Hulk? Could the Justice League of America defeat the X-Men? Fans had argued over questions like these for years. Despite a few memorable team-ups between DC and Marvel in the past, the meetings of each company's respective icons were rare.

However, that had all changed by the mid-1990s. Specials featuring clashes between DC and Marvel characters were becoming commonplace. DC and Marvel had reached a level of unheard-of cooperation, and they soon dropped their biggest bombshell: the four-issue miniseries *DC versus Marvel Comics*.

Spinning out of that series, DC and Marvel launched the Amalgam Comics imprint and published a series of specials showcasing combined versions of their characters. Working together, DC and Marvel ended many arguments between fans but also sparked a few new ones by creating a brand new universe.

FEBRUARY

THE SHOWDOWN OF THE CENTURY

***DC versus Marvel Comics* #1**

DC and Marvel were about to give the fans what they wanted, so they had to be sure to get it right. In an unprecedented cross-company production, the two major comic book publishers joined together to pit their icons against one another in a no-holds-barred match of strength and skill. To keep the contest as fair as possible, DC and Marvel let the readers decide the victors.

Written by Peter David and Ron Marz with art by Dan Jurgens and Claudio Castellini, this four-issue miniseries event consisted of five major battles voted on in advance by reader ballots distributed to comic stores, as well as several other minor fights that saw the writers choose the outcome. Forcing the champions of each universe to fight in order to solve a cosmic battle of superiority, *DC versus Marvel Comics* also saw the creation of Access, a gatekeeper between the Marvel and DC Universes.

With the framework set, the battles began. Thor defeated Captain Marvel, Aquaman bested Namor, and the Flash triumphed over Quicksilver. Robin got the drop on Jubilee, the Silver Surfer proved too much for Green Lantern, and Elektra beat Catwoman. In the balloted bouts, Wolverine trounced Lobo, Storm took out Wonder Woman, Spider-Man beat Superboy, Superman clobbered the Incredible Hulk, and Batman outfought Captain America. Before the heroes could reflect on their victories or losses, they found their universes suddenly combined—the Amalgam Age of Comics had now begun.

Familiar heroes and villains meet for the first time in this landmark series. Spider-Man Ben Reilly faces down the Clown Prince of Crime, the Joker.

MARCH

CONTAGION

***Batman: Shadow of the Bat* #48**

In the latest crossover to shake up Batman's universe, a manufactured virus nicknamed "the Clench" was unleashed on the public of Gotham City. The fatal infection leaked into Batman's hometown from the corrupt Order of St. Dumas in this saga by writers Alan Grant, Chuck Dixon, Denny O'Neil, and Doug Moench, and artists Vince Giarrano, Tommy Lee Edwards, Mike Wieringo, Barry Kitson, Jim Balent, Dick Giordano, Kelley Jones, and Graham Nolan. The plague ran its course through the pages of *Batman: Shadow of the Bat*, *Detective Comics*, *Robin*, *Azrael*, *Catwoman*, and *Batman* before the Dark Knight discovered the antiviral formula that saved his city.

IN THE REAL WORLD...

February: Chess computer Deep Blue defeats world chess champion Garry Kasparov.

APRIL

AMALGAM'S FIRST LADIES
***Assassins* #1**

Spinning out of the pages of *DC versus Marvel Comics* was a series of specials jointly published by DC and Marvel. These one-shots saw combined versions of characters from each company's respective universe granted new lives and origins in the fledgling Amalgam Universe. Daredevil veteran writer D. G. Chichester and artist Scott McDaniel paired up for *Assassins*, which spotlighted the partnership of Dare (the female amalgam of Deathstroke and Marvel's Daredevil) and Catsai (a combination of Catwoman and Marvel's Elektra).

DC'S LATEST HIT
***Hitman* #1**

Following in the dark-humored footsteps of *Preacher*, writer Garth Ennis' newest effort unleashed a hard-drinking, gun-toting anti-hero on the DC Universe proper. Alongside artist John McCrea, Ennis took hitman and "Bloodlines" character Tommy Monaghan from the pages of *The Demon* and placed him in harm's way time and again for a rip-roaring sixty-issue romp. With guest stars like Batman, Catwoman, and Superman, and such new offbeat characters as Six-Pack and Dogwelder, *Hitman* was an enjoyable cult favorite that approached the iconic world of super-heroics from a cynical and often hilarious viewpoint.

JUNE

BLACK AND WHITE AND READ ALL OVER
***Batman: Black and White* #1**

In a beautiful four-issue miniseries composed completely without color, editors Mark Chiarello and Scott Peterson assembled a virtual who's who of comic book superstardom in order to create an anthology collection of short stories revolving around the life of the Dark Knight. Boasting covers by legendary artists Jim Lee, Frank Miller, Barry Windsor-Smith, and Alex Toth, as well as pinups by other accomplished visionaries like Moebius, Alex Ross, and Neal Adams, this well-received series had no shortage of powerful visuals.

These alternative visions of Batman are by artists Joe Kubert, Ted McKeever, and Howard Chaykin.

JULY

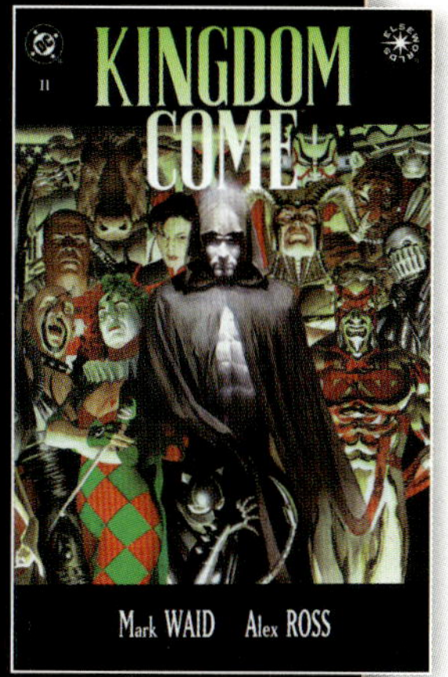

PAINTING A KINGDOM
***Kingdom Come* #1**

Painter Alex Ross had been looking for a new project. Already lending his realistic depiction of super heroes to an unsuspecting public in Marvel Comics' *Marvels* miniseries, Ross was ready to bring his stylish brush over to the DCU, and an eager readership awaited him.

Alongside writer Mark Waid, Ross developed a complex future story for DC's icons in the four-issue prestige-format *Kingdom Come* miniseries. Under the limitless possibilities of DC's Elseworlds label, Ross and Waid crafted a tale of biblical proportions. Ross fleshed out a reality in which a reader could become fully immersed, creating new costumes for nearly every character, while attempting to stay true to each character's roots and personality. He also added dozens of characters of his own creation, including some designs from his childhood. It was a world that was as real and as fantastic as Ross's paintings themselves.

In the DC Universe of the near future, Superman had retired from the life of fighting crime after the death of Lois Lane, and a new generation of superpowered beings had risen to prominence. Without the guidance of their elders, the younger characters spent their days in a series of violent skirmishes rather than protecting the innocent. This was Ross and Waid's commentary on the modern state of violent anti-heroes prevalent in the comics of the time, and the chaos of this dystopian future spoke to the readers.

Superman was coaxed back into action by Wonder Woman in order to rein in the new generation of heroes. Restored to his rightful role as the inspiration to millions, Superman and his fellow allies of the Justice League attempted to right the wrongs of the youth, until Superman's new battle escalated with the involvement of Lex Luthor and his mind-controlled puppet, the powerful Captain Marvel. In a final dramatic conflict, heroes battled anti-heroes even as a nuclear bomb killed the majority of the players on each side. Superman survived, however, and with the help of Wonder Woman and Batman, began to carve out a better, more peaceful world for the survivors to call home.

Kingdom Come unfolds in front of the eyes of priest Norman McCay, a character based on the likeness of Alex Ross's own father.

February: Canadian singer Alanis Morissette wins the top honor, the Album of the Year award, at the Grammy® Awards; she is the youngest person ever to receive it.

March: A gunman opens fire at Dunblane Primary School, Dunblane, Scotland, killing sixteen students and one teacher before fatally shooting himself.

AUGUST

BATMAN'S LEGACY
***Detective Comics* #700**

The horrific "Clench" virus that plagued Gotham had not been eliminated. With this deadly threat hanging over his head, Batman sought out the mastermind behind the epidemic, Rā's al Ghūl, in "Legacy," a seven-part story that spanned the pages of *Detective Comics*, *Batman: Shadow of the Bat*, *Batman*, *Catwoman*, and *Robin*. Written by Alan Grant, Doug Moench, and Chuck Dixon, and illustrated by Dave Taylor, Jim Aparo, Graham Nolan, Jim Balent, and Staz Johnson, this story kicked into full speed in the anniversary issue of *Detective Comics* (#700), which came with a unique envelope wrapping.

SEPTEMBER

JOURNEY TO THE JLA
***Justice League: A Midsummer's Nightmare* #1**

It had been years since the icons of the DC Universe had served on the Justice League together. In the three-issue miniseries *Justice League: A Midsummer's Nightmare*, writers Mark Waid and Fabian Nicieza and pencillers Jeff Johnson and Darick Robertson pitted DC's big seven heroes (Superman, Batman, Wonder Woman, Aquaman, Martian Manhunter, the Flash, and Green Lantern) against the reality-warping powers of Dr. Destiny and his manipulator Know Man. A precursor to the following year's *JLA* ongoing series, *A Midsummer's Nightmare* not only saw the return of major characters to DC's premier team, but was also one of the first major DC titles to feature enhanced computer effects.

ON TV THIS MONTH: Superman followed in Batman's footsteps as Bruce Timm and company granted him his own TV series, *SUPERMAN: THE ANIMATED SERIES*, which debuted on September 6, lasted fifty-four episodes, and featured the voice talent of Tim Daly as the Man of Steel...

SUPERGIRL GETS REAL
***Supergirl* [third series] #1**

The Girl of Steel flew back into an ongoing series at long last, courtesy of fan-favorite writer Peter David and artist Gary Frank. At the start of the first issue, Linda Danvers had been kidnapped for a demonic sacrifice by the mysterious Buzz. To save Linda, the protoplasmic entity from another dimension known as the Matrix Supergirl merged her form with Linda's, creating an all-new Supergirl. When she did this, she found herself feeling pain for the first time, as well as a slew of new emotions. Adjusting to life as both human and superhuman, Supergirl was met with a whole new set of challenges and enemies, not the least of which was Buzz.

OCTOBER

NIGHTWING TAKES WING
***Nightwing* [second series] #1**

Following his September 1995 miniseries, Dick Grayson was rewarded for years of heroic service with his own ongoing series, written by Chuck Dixon and with art by Scott McDaniel. Setting up camp in Blüdhaven, a city close to his Gotham City home and twice as corrupt, Nightwing quickly acquired quite a Rogues Gallery. From underworld boss Blockbuster to the acrobatic Lady Vic to the twisted former cop Torque, Nightwing battled his way to respect in his new town, and the fans took notice. A hit from the start, *Nightwing* lasted 153 issues.

NOVEMBER

THE DCU PASSES ITS FINAL TEST
***The Final Night* #1**

In this four-issue miniseries by writer Karl Kesel and artist Stuart Immonen, the heroes of the present united with the Legion of Super-Heroes and the New Gods in an attempt to stop a "sun-eater," a black mass that absorbs all light and energy, that was heading toward the solar system. As the Earth grew darker and colder, only one man could reignite its dying sun: Parallax, the former Green Lantern Hal Jordan. Sacrificing himself so that his world would live, Hal flew valiantly into the sun, and a new day dawned.

DECEMBER

GREEN LANTERN'S LIGHT BURNS ON
***Green Lantern* [third series] #81**

Writer Ron Marz and artist Darryl Banks assembled an impressive cast of DC's stars to bid farewell to Green Lantern Hal Jordan in this memorable issue, available in both a regular newsstand and deluxe tombstone edition, and including a second feature by writer John Broome and artist Gil Kane. After the heroes of the present day gathered in an emerald construct church to pay their respects to the life of a hero, Swamp Thing used his mastery of plantlife to create a green paradise in the once-desolate Coast City. With the added tribute of a green eternal flame from former Green Lantern Alan Scott, and an energy construct sculpture of Hal in his prime by the new Green Lantern Kyle Rayner, Hal's legacy was set to shine forever.

An artist in his civilian life, Green Lantern Kyle Rayner immortalizes his predecessor Hal Jordan by crafting a dramatic statue in his honor.

IN THE REAL WORLD...

May: Swede Göran Kropp reaches the Mount Everest summit alone and without oxygen, having bicycled there from Sweden.

July: Dolly the sheep, the first mammal to be successfully cloned from an adult cell, is born at the Roslin Institute in Midlothian, Scotland.

DECEMBER

TAKING THE PLUNGE

Superman: The Wedding Album #1

With their wedding nearly sixty years in the making, Clark Kent and Lois Lane finally tied the proverbial knot in a ninety-one-page one-shot that let readers delve right into their special day. Not an imaginary story and not a dream sequence, *The Wedding Album* delighted fans as DC finally married off its most renowned icon. Written and drawn by a slew of the most influential people in the Man of Steel's life, the issue was delivered in style, available in a newsstand edition featuring a cover by John Byrne—the writer/artist who reinvented Superman for a new generation in 1986's *The Man of Steel*—as well as in an all-white, embossed prestige-format version.

The behind-the-scenes talent on this monumental issue appropriately spanned several generations of the Man of Tomorrow's career. Written by Dan Jurgens, Karl Kesel, David Michelinie, Louise Simonson, and Roger Stern, the one-shot featured the pencils of John Byrne, Gil Kane, Stuart Immonen, Paul Ryan, Jon Bogdanove, Kieron Dwyer, Tom Grummett, Dick Giordano, Jim Mooney, Curt Swan, Nick Cardy, Al Plastino, Barry Kitson, Ron Frenz, and Dan Jurgens. A highlight of the art was the final three-page pull-out image, featuring Clark and Lois' first kiss as husband and wife in a church full of real-life DC Comics professionals, including editor Mike Carlin, President Jenette Kahn, and Publisher Paul Levitz.

Superman: The Wedding Album told the tale of a recently de-powered Clark Kent, who was still feeling the effects of *The Final Night* events, and featured a unique story chock-full of characterization. As Lois searched for the perfect dress and recounted Superman adventures of days gone by, Superman was paid a visit by Batman, who assured his old ally that Metropolis would be cared for during Clark's upcoming honeymoon. After a quick visit from the extra-dimensional imp Mr. Mxyzptlk, Clark and Lois finally tied the knot, surrounded by their closest friends and family.

Clark's best man is long-time sidekick Jimmy Olsen, and Lois' maid of honor is none other than her sister, Lucy Lane.

DECEMBER

BATMAN TAKES A HOLIDAY

Batman: The Long Halloween #1

The acclaimed team of writer Jeph Loeb and artist Tim Sale reunited to chronicle a dark year of the Dark Knight's past with *Batman: The Long Halloween*, a thirteen-part limited series. Comprising two bookend prestige-format issues that sandwiched eleven regular-length deluxe issues complete with cardstock covers, this series carried a rather hefty price tag for the time. Yet Sale's beautiful artwork, complemented by Gregory Wright's powerful colors, seemed to more than make up for it.

Beginning and ending on Halloween, this maxiseries told the story of the mysterious Holiday Killer who was slowly murdering all the members of the Falcone mob family. Each month, the enigmatic killer would strike on a major holiday and that issue's cover would spotlight the holiday in question. While this was going on, the fledgling Dark Knight was busy forming an alliance with Commissioner Gordon as well as District Attorney Harvey Dent (the future villain Two-Face). Featuring a laundry list of Batman villains including the Joker, Catwoman, Riddler, Poison Ivy, and even Solomon Grundy, this murder mystery kept audiences guessing while simultaneously retelling the origin of Two-Face.

A critical and financial success, *The Long Halloween* spawned two sequel miniseries and a line of action figures from DC Direct.

Catwoman shows an interest in the Falcone crime family during *Batman: The Long Halloween*. It is later revealed that Carmine Falcone may be her father.

ALSO THIS YEAR: Future Wonder Girl Cassie Sandsmark debuted in January's *WONDER WOMAN* [second series] #105, thanks to writer/artist John Byrne... In April, writers Grant Morrison and Mark Millar introduced Aztek in a self-titled ongoing series that ran for a mere ten brilliant issues... In the style of the bygone preview inserts of the 1980s, a new group of Teen Titans [destined for their own ongoing title] debuted in the pages of *SUPERMAN* [second series] #116, written and pencilled by Dan Jurgens, interrupting a Superman tale also written by Dan Jurgens and with art by Ron Frenz...Writer Chuck Dixon and artist Gary Frank paired two birds of a feather in December's special *BLACK CANARY/ORACLE: BIRDS OF PREY* #1...

October: The government of New Zealand pays the U.S. $130 million in compensation for the loss of land suffered by the Maori population between 1844 and 1864.

December: The United Nations Security Council elects Kofi Annan as the next Secretary-General of the United Nations.

THE ART OF ALEX ROSS

KINGDOM COME #2 (June 1996)
Alex Ross' gouache artwork (which took him almost two years to complete) and writer Mark Waid's storyline made the four-part miniseries *Kingdom Come* a DC landmark. The miniseries also signaled Ross' breakthrough as a major comic book artist. Described as "the last stand of the super heroes" by Ross, *Kingdom Come* featured just about every DC super hero.

1997

"NO SWEAT KIDS. THE CRISIS IS OVER. THE BIG GUY'S ON THE CASE."

Metamorpho regarding Superman, *JLA* #1

HITS AND MISSES

It was a year of trial and error. DC was in the process of reinventing its line, experimenting with new concepts and characters. The readers seemed tired of large-scale crossovers and flashy events, so DC began to adapt, with many editors taking different approaches.

While the *Superman* titles bestowed the Last Son of Krypton with a strange new costume and powers, the *Batman* books were steered into a series of stand-alone issues and smaller storylines. Some editors fell back on what worked and developed more DC/Marvel crossovers, while others trialed new characters or revitalized old concepts—the most prominent of which was *JLA*, a modern regrouping of the icons of the DC Universe into the premier team of the Justice League. A runaway success, *JLA* proved that classic heroes were still a viable commodity.

JANUARY

THE JUSTICE LEAGUE RETURNS
***JLA* #1**

The Justice League of America had been struggling for years. Faded from the attention of the mainstream, the League was composed of mostly second- or third-string characters that, while possessing a following, certainly weren't attracting the attention of the casual comic buyer. But all that was about to change.

It started with Mark Waid and Fabian Nicieza's *Justice League: A Midsummer's Nightmare* miniseries that once again grouped DC's big seven heroes, a teaming that hadn't occurred in decades. Starring Batman, Superman, Wonder Woman, Aquaman, Martian Manhunter, and the next generation of Flash and Green Lantern, the miniseries had attracted much attention from the fans, and had featured an ad for the new *JLA* ongoing series in its final issue in September 1996. A few months later, *JLA* #1 hit the stands, enthralling readers with its compelling, fast-paced story by writer Grant Morrison, and showcasing the art of the talented relative newcomer Howard Porter. With Porter's modern sensibilities, the League appeared contemporary and fresh, and Morrison's innovative scripts quickly showed the world why they had always needed their greatest heroes.

After the defeat of the second-tier characters of the current Justice League, the big seven reunited again when a mysterious team known as Hyperclan appeared on the scene. Although Hyperclan displayed a heroic façade, their nefarious intentions were soon clear as they defeated the reunited Justice League one by one, until only Batman remained. Deducing the clan's identity as a band of ruthless white Martians, Batman exploited the villains' vulnerability to fire and set his allies free. Soon the Justice League was able to triumph over this new threat.

Renewed as one of DC's most popular titles, *JLA* ran for 125 issues before its next relaunch. Earning countless spin-off miniseries and specials, the Justice League reclaimed its place atop DC's hit titles list, receiving more attention than it had garnered in nearly ten years.

The Hyperclan arrive on Earth in style, tricking the American public into thinking they are benevolent heroes.

As white Martians, the Hyperclan possess the ability to shapeshift, although their weakness is a vulnerability to the effects of fire.

IN THE REAL WORLD...

February: Divorce becomes legal for the first time in Ireland.
March: Rapper The Notorious B.I.G. is killed in a drive-by shooting.

MAY

RESURRECTION CONNECTION

***Resurrection Man* #1**

The writing team of Andy Lanning and Dan Abnett alongside the art of Jackson "Butch" Guice introduced readers to a new kind of hero in *Resurrection Man*. Chronicling the adventures of amnesiac drifter Mitch Shelley, the ongoing title enticed readers with its unique premise: every time Mitch died, he not only came back from the dead—he did so with a different superpower in tow. A hit with critics and fan publications, *Resurrection Man* nevertheless ended after a mere twenty-seven issues, having never found the readership that it deserved, despite guest appearances by the JLA, Batman, the Phantom Stranger, Deadman, and even the Forgotten Heroes.

SUPERMAN'S "SHOCKING" NEW LOOK

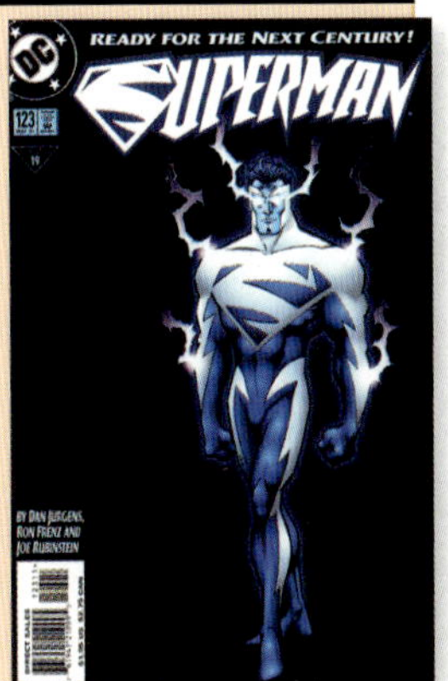

***Superman* [second series] #123**

He was a hero composed of pure energy, with blue skin and a flashy containment suit; not quite the Superman the world knew and loved. In a startling fallout from *The Final Night*, Clark Kent quickly evolved into a different kind of Superman after losing his powers. Bullets didn't bounce off this new Superman—they passed through him. He could now deliver bursts of energy to his opponents, as well as fly at much faster speeds. He was the Superman for the next generation.

In *Superman* #123, an issue available in both a newsstand and deluxe glow-in-the-dark edition, Superman debuted his new blue-and-white costume with a little help from scripter Dan Jurgens and penciller Ron Frenz. In a story that made headlines in the real world as well as in the DC Universe, Superman's powers began to go haywire during a conflict with the monstrous villain Scorn. As his flesh turned blue and his body's energy began to disperse, Superman flew to S.T.A.R. Labs, where he was given an experimental containment suit developed by LexCorp. After a few stylistic additions, including a jagged version of his familiar "S" symbol, Superman was reborn.

Superman struggles to control his new powers, to the dismay of Lois Lane and Perry White.

JUNE

AMALGAM

***JLX Unleashed!* #1**

Part of the second batch of Amalgam specials jointly published by DC and Marvel Comics, *JLX Unleashed!* was written by Christopher Priest and pencilled by Oscar Jimenez. Plagued by the Hellfire League of Injustice (an amalgam of the Injustice League and Marvel's Hellfire Club), the JLX (the Justice League of America combined with Marvel's X-Men) teamed with Amazon (an amalgam of Wonder Woman and Marvel's Storm) to stop the Hellfire League's creation, Fin Fang Flame (a fusion of Brimstone and Marvel's dragon Fin Fang Foom).

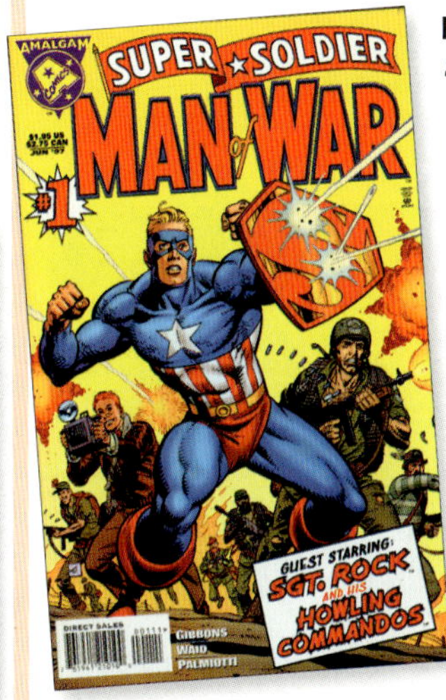

MARCHING ON

***Super-Soldier: Man of War* #1**

Super-Soldier (an amalgam of Superman and Marvel's Captain America) returned in his second Amalgam one-shot, by writer Mark Waid and penciller Dave Gibbons. Part of the All-Star Winners Squadron (the All-Star Squadron and Marvel's All-Winners Squad combined), Super-Soldier used his fantastic abilities to help the allied powers during World War II. The issue also guest-starred Aqua-Mariner (an amalgam of Aquaman fused with Marvel's Sub-Mariner), Whiz (a combination of the Golden Age Flash and Marvel's Whizzer), and Human Lantern (the Golden Age Green Lantern combined with Marvel's original Human Torch).

THE SPIRIT OF MR. TERRIFIC

***The Spectre* [third series] #54**

The Spectre ongoing series was nearing its end, but that didn't stop writer John Ostrander and artist Tom Mandrake from pooling their creative forces to create one of the DCU's newest shining stars. Michael Holt, a former Olympic athlete and one of the smartest minds on the planet, was distraught over the death of his wife, Paula, and was about to throw himself from a bridge when he was visited by the Spectre. Michael was talked out of committing suicide when he heard the Spectre's tale of the original Golden Age hero Mr. Terrific. An inspired and reborn Holt then picked up the mantle of Mr. Terrific, determined to leave the world a better place than he had found it.

AT THE MOVIES THIS MONTH: Director Joel Schumacher's *BATMAN & ROBIN*, a big-budget movie starring George Clooney as the Dark Knight, Chris O'Donnell as Robin, Uma Thurman as Poison Ivy, Arnold Schwarzenegger as Mr. Freeze, and Alicia Silverstone as Batgirl, was released...

April: The Red River of the North breaks through dikes and floods Grand Forks, North Dakota and East Grand Forks, Minnesota, causing U.S.$2 billion worth of damage.

May: The Labour Party ends eighteen years of Conservative rule in the U.K. by winning the 1997 general election with a landslide majority.

AUGUST

THE DEATH OF WONDER WOMAN

***Wonder Woman* [second series] #124**

It seemed Wonder Woman had breathed her last in *Wonder Woman* #124, thanks to writer and artist John Byrne. Ripped from the streets of Gateway City and taken to the realm of the underworld by the demon Neron, Princess Diana and fellow Amazonian Artemis, along with Diana's friend Helena Sandsmark and Helena's daughter Cassie, found themselves prisoners of the dark lord. During the resulting conflict, the Amazing Amazon was struck down by a powerful magic blast from Neron and killed on the spot. In the following issue, Diana's body was transported back to Earth, where her allies in the Justice League were completely powerless to help her.

AT THE MOVIES THIS MONTH: Basketball star Shaquille O'Neal suited up to act the role of John Henry Irons in director Kenneth Johnson's movie *STEEL*, released in theaters on August 15...

SEPTEMBER

JLA ROCKS THE AGES

***JLA* #10**

Writer Grant Morrison and artist Howard Porter upped the ante to cosmic proportions in *JLA* #10, the first part of the six-issue "Rock of Ages" storyline. With new members Green Arrow (Connor Hawke) and Aztek in tow, the JLA faced off against solid hologram doppelgängers of themselves as well as the malicious Darkseid, all in an attempt to prevent the misuse of the reality-warping Philosopher's Stone. After the dust settled and the heroes prevailed in the double-sized issue #15 in February 1998, the next issue ushered in new team members, including Zauriel, Plastic Man, Huntress, Steel, Orion, Big Barda, and Oracle, as well as debuting the notorious villain Prometheus.

Lex Luthor assembles an impressive inner circle to challenge the Justice League, including Dr. Light, Mirror Master, the Joker, Circe, and Ocean Master.

TRANSMETROPOLITAN AVOIDS LABELS

***Transmetropolitan* #1**

In an attempt to once again broaden its publishing scope, DC Comics formed a science-fiction line of titles under the imprint Helix. Its lead title was *Transmetropolitan*, a dark comedy set in a future urban dystopia by writer Warren Ellis and artist Darick Robertson. Helix was retired in 1998, but *Transmetropolitan*'s story of renegade journalist Spider Jerusalem was able to reach its natural conclusion under Vertigo's watch. Running for sixty issues, *Transmetropolitan* caught the attention of critics and fans, and sprouted a line of reprint trade paperbacks.

OCTOBER

THE GENESIS OF THE DCU

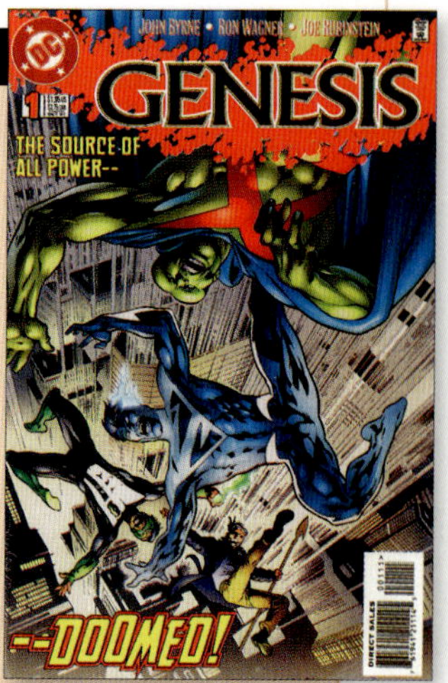

***Genesis* #1**

The energies of the DC Universe were being altered. In *Genesis*, a four-issue cosmic crossover event written by John Byrne and drawn by Ron Wagner, with covers by Alan Davis, The Flash was losing his speed, Green Lantern's ring was malfunctioning, and Captain Marvel had lost his magic. All over Earth, super heroes' powers were going haywire, and only the gods knew what was going on.

The planet's heroes gathered to ponder their current situation, but found their world attacked by a panicking alien armada. Then, just as the violence was about to escalate, Highfather of the New Gods appeared before the assembled forces and explained the situation.

The Godwave, the force that created all known life in the universe, had passed twice across the universe—creating gods and planets on its first pass, and superhumans on its second—and it was now contracting. A natural force of power, the Godwave was preparing to explode outward and erase all life in the universe. The only way to stop the grand extinction was to send a small party of heroes inside the mystical Source itself to combat the threat. As the citizens of Earth rioted and despaired, a band of heroes led by New God Takion journeyed beyond the walls of the Source and helped remake the entire cosmos.

Highfather is an endless fountain of wisdom for the New Gods. Here he shares his knowledge with Orion and Takion.

IN THE REAL WORLD...

June: J.K. Rowling's *Harry Potter and the Philosopher's Stone* is published.
July: The United Kingdom hands sovereignty of Hong Kong to China.
July: Andrew Cunanan shoots fashion designer Gianni Versace to death outside Versace's Miami, Florida residence.

NOVEMBER

THE LEGENDS CONTINUE

***Batman: Legends of the Dark Knight* #100**

Batman's anthology title reached its hundredth issue in this extra-sized anniversary edition featuring a painted cover by superstar Alex Ross. The issue included a revised Robin origin story by fabled *Batman* writer Denny O'Neil alongside penciller Dave Taylor, plus a Jason Todd tale by writer James Robinson and artist Lee Weeks. A gallery section of past issue covers, and a pinup section by an array of the industry's top professionals, such as Frank Miller, Gene Ha, Walt Simonson, and Joe Quesada, also featured in the issue.

CREEPING INTO THE NIGHT

***The Creeper* #1**

Writer Len Kaminski and penciller Shawn Martinbrough put a modern slant on a classic DC character with the short-lived *The Creeper* series. Canceled after issue #11, the series was an attempt to rescue the off-kilter hero from his status in comic book limbo and place him firmly in the realm of the DC Universe. As such, its first issue participated in DC's "Faces of the DC Universe" cover theme, showcasing a closeup headshot of the star of each respective issue. Offering a psychological examination into the depths of the mind of Jack Ryder, the Creeper's alter ego, *The Creeper* still failed to attract enough readers, even with the added attraction of guest stars Batman and the Joker.

DECEMBER

GOING OFF ON A TANGENT

***Tangent: The Atom* #1**

It was an experiment that hadn't been attempted since the 1950s. Take a recognizable DC Comic character's name and scrap nearly everything else. Start from the ground up and create a new character around the super hero moniker. The first time this strategy was employed in the 1950s, the Silver Age of Comics was born, giving an excited readership characters like the Barry Allen Flash and Hal Jordan Green Lantern. The second time it was tried years later, the result was Tangent Comics.

A series of nine one-shots springing from the imagination of writer/artist Dan Jurgens, the Tangent Comics imprint introduced an entirely new universe of heroes, with the Atom ironically standing the tallest among them. Now an atomic-powered icon in the Tangent Universe, with similarities to Superman, the Atom was the heir to a legacy of super heroes, as detailed in his self-titled special written and pencilled by Dan Jurgens. Sharing a universe with many altered faces, including an optimistically bright Flash, a grave-walking Green Lantern, a rebellious female Joker, and a clandestine operation called Nightwing (who all featured in their own Tangent specials), the Atom soon helped super hero team the Secret Six found their own one-shot title (written by Chuck Dixon and drawn by Tom Grummett). In the end, the Tangent Universe proved quite popular with the readership and it soon earned a second round of nine specials the following year, and even a twelve-issue miniseries ten years later.

The Atom is the Tangent Universe's equivalent to the Man of Steel. He even looks similar to Superman, thanks to the pencils of longtime Superman artist Dan Jurgens.

THIS IS YOUR LIFE

***The Life Story of the Flash* #1**

Writers Mark Waid and Brian Augustyn, with illustrators Gil Kane, Joe Staton, and Tom Palmer, recounted the life and times of the Silver Age Flash Barry Allen in this ninety-six-page hardcover. The mostly prose special issue was designed to read like a tell-all biography of a nonfiction celebrity, and was supposedly written by photojournalist and Flash's longtime love interest Iris Allen. It boasted a realistic cover by painter Glenn Orbik, too, to help add to its pretense. Also featuring sequential comic sections, this touching tribute spanned Barry's entire career, from his origin until his death during the grand-scale *Crisis on Infinite Earths* maxiseries.

A stray lightning bolt and a dash of chemicals transform scientist Barry Allen into the Fastest Man Alive.

ALSO THIS YEAR: Writer Howard Chaykin and painter Daniel Brereton delivered the three-issue Elseworlds miniseries *THRILLKILLER* in January, starring Batgirl and Robin… April saw the release of *ADVENTURES IN THE DC UNIVERSE*, an ongoing series set in the universe of the Batman and Superman animated series and featuring a host of DC characters, written by Steve Vance, with art by John Delaney… The Shade, now enjoying renewed popularity from his appearances in *STARMAN*, nabbed his first miniseries in April, courtesy of writer James Robinson and artists Gene Ha, J. H. Williams III, Bret Blevins, and Michael Zulli…

August: Diana, Princess of Wales, dies following a car accident in the Pont de l'Alma road tunnel in Paris.

September: Mother Theresa of Calcutta dies of heart failure in Kolkata, India.
December: James Cameron's epic movie *Titanic*, premieres.

1998

"ID, EGO, AND SUPEREGO UNLEASHED. I COULD EXPLAIN IT IN MORE DETAIL, BUT I'LL NEED A SLIDE PROJECTOR AND SOME CHARTS."

Red Tornado, *Young Justice* #1

SPREADING JUSTICE

It had seemed impossible only a few years earlier. After 1987's *Justice League* series brought minor characters into the team, the idea of DC's biggest icons working together as the JLA seemed a thing of the past. But by 1998, writers Mark Waid and Grant Morrison had restored the Justice League to their 1960s "big gun" status. Now a reinvigorated franchise, DC planned to expand the property as much as the industry would allow.

Besides a variety of direct *JLA* spin-offs, a new crossover event was planned in *DC One Million*, which involved concepts originating in the *JLA* title. Longtime Leaguer Martian Manhunter was given his own ongoing series, and new team titles like *Young Justice* appeared. The strategy was working, and DC would continue the plan throughout the rest of the decade with titles like *Titans*, *Hourman*, and *JSA*.

JANUARY

START-UP LEAGUE

***JLA: Year One* #1**

The new JLA was a clear hit, but its past was somewhat foggy. Since the team debuted in the 1960s with a lineup consisting of Superman, Batman, Wonder Woman, Martian Manhunter, Aquaman, the Flash, and Green Lantern, the timelines of half its founding fathers had been reinvented. 1985's *Crisis on Infinite Earths* maxiseries, along with the subsequent relaunches of the Superman, Batman, and Wonder Woman franchises, had led to the history of DC's premier team becoming a bit jangled. In an early attempt to clear up the JLA's timeline, November 1988's *Secret Origins* #32 (written by Keith Giffen and Peter David, with art by Eric Shanower) confirmed that Superman, Batman, and Wonder Woman were no longer founding members of the team, and inserted the Silver Age Black Canary into the mix in their place. With only this brief glimpse of the team's beginnings, fans were left wondering exactly how the Justice League began.

It was up to writers Mark Waid and Brian Augustyn and artist Barry Kitson to fill in the blanks. With their twelve-issue maxiseries *JLA: Year One*, the trio examined the early days of the team. Involving clashes with classic foes, great characterization, heroic guest stars, and a grand-scale alien invasion, *JLA: Year One* proved a success, and cleaned up decades of convoluted comic history.

Appearing on the scene when super heroes are a rare sight in the DC Universe, the JLA quickly gains an impressive fan base.

CHASE SCENE

***Batman* #550**

As a springboard for her upcoming ongoing series *Chase*, agent Cameron Chase debuted in the pages of *Batman* #550. The issue was available in a deluxe edition with a Kelley Jones cover and Chase trading cards, and in a newsstand version sporting a J. H. Williams III cover. In this stand-alone story by writer Doug Moench and pencillers Kelley Jones and J. H. Williams III, Batman met Chase, an agent for the secretive Department of Extranormal Operations (D.E.O.) with hidden superpowers all of her own. Teaming up to help stop the rampaging Clay-Thing, the offspring of Batman foe Clayface III and Lady Clayface, the two formed an uneasy alliance as they defeated the tragic young monster.

IN THE REAL WORLD...

January: On American television, U.S. President Bill Clinton denies he had "sexual relations" with former White House intern Monica Lewinsky.

FEBRUARY

EXPANDING THE LEGENDS
***Legends of the DC Universe* #1**

Batman: Legends of the Dark Knight, the ongoing title about Batman's early years, had been a solid seller for some time, so it only made sense for DC to explore the rest of the super hero spectrum in *Legends of the DC Universe*. Superman took center stage in the series' debut story, penned by James Robinson and drawn by Val Semeiks. As the series continued, many other heroes would get their moments in the spotlight, including the Justice League, Teen Titans, the Flash, and Wonder Woman.

SUPERMAN'S SPLIT PERSONALITY

***Superman Red/Superman Blue* #1**

Superman was fast becoming a man of two minds. In the extra-sized *Superman Red/Superman Blue* one-shot, the former Man of Steel was stretched beyond his limits when he split in half to form two separate heroes. It paid homage to the classic Silver Age story *Superman* [first series] #162 (July 1963), an "imaginary story" in which two versions of the Last Son of Krypton patrolled the universe. The special was written by Dan Jurgens, Stuart Immonen, Karl Kesel, and Louise Simonson, with pencils by Stuart Immonen, Ron Frenz, Tom Grummett, Paul Ryan, and Jon Bogdanove. Appropriately, a red-and-blue 3-D cover drawn by Dan Jurgens was released along with a regular full-color newsstand version of the cover. Packaged with a pair of 3-D glasses, the issue also came with a separate reprint issue entitled *Superman 3-D*.

Still getting used to his energy-based powers and his blue containment suit, Superman was annoyed to learn his old foe the Toyman had broken out of prison. To make matters worse, the Toyman soon joined forces with the Cyborg Superman and the two captured Metropolis' guardian, locking him in a machine designed to disperse and contain Superman's energy. However, the device overloaded, and Superman was split into two different individuals: an aggressive red version and a more contemplative blue version.

Superman Red is much more aggressive than his mellow blue half, often charging into battle without weighing the consequences.

APRIL

CATACLYSM

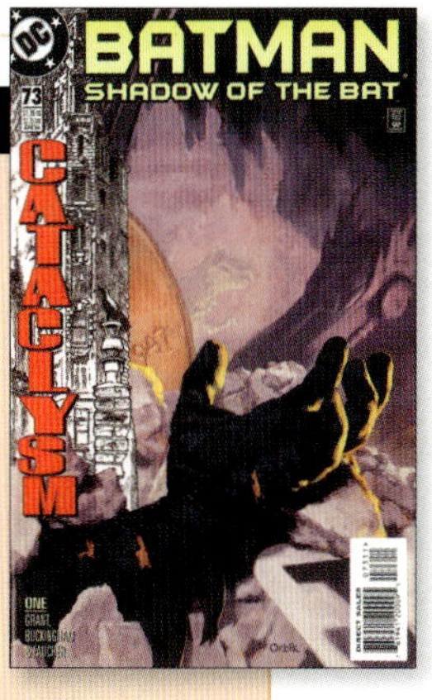

***Batman: Shadow of the Bat* #73**

Gotham City had been through a lot lately. Always plagued by society's worst criminal minds, the city was still recovering from the widespread infection of the deadly, manufactured "Clench" virus. It was unprepared for another large-scale crisis, especially one of natural origin.

A tale of heroism in the face of chaos, the seventeen-part "Cataclysm" storyline showed a Gotham City devastated by an earthquake. It was written by Alan Grant, Chuck Dixon, Doug Moench, Dennis O'Neil, Devin Grayson, Chris Renaud, Rick Burchett, Klaus Janson, and Kelley Puckett, and illustrated by Mark Buckingham, Scott McDaniel, Klaus Janson, Roger Robinson, Graham Nolan, Jim Balent, Staz Johnson, Jim Aparo, Marcos Martin, Chris Renaud, Alex Maleev, Rick Burchett, Eduardo Barreto, and Dave Taylor. The story began in the pages of *Batman: Shadow of the Bat* #73, and continued in *Nightwing, Batman, Azrael, Catwoman, Robin*, and *The Batman Chronicles*, and through three specials entitled *Batman: Blackgate – Isle of Men, Batman: Arkham Asylum – Tales of Madness*, and *Batman: Huntress/Spoiler – Blunt Trauma*.

Wayne Enterprises is diligent about reinforcing its skyscrapers in case of an earthquake. However, historic Wayne Manor hasn't been built with the same precautions.

JUNE

FOREVER UNITING THE RED AND BLUE STATES
***Superman: Forever* #1**

The classic Superman was back in style, and flying off the pages thanks to a painted cover by Alex Ross. Available in both a standard and deluxe version with a lenticular cover that gave the illusion of Clark Kent changing into the Man of Steel, this special was written and illustrated by a host of Superman talent, including Karl Kesel, Dan Jurgens, and John Byrne. After saving the world from destruction by plunging one of his two current energy forms into the very core of the Earth, Clark Kent was miraculously restored to his original form in this issue, starting a new era of truth, justice, and the American way.

February: Karla Faye Tucker is executed in Texas, becoming the first woman executed in the United States since 1984.

April: The Belfast Agreement (also known as the Good Friday Agreement) is signed by the Irish and British governments.

AUGUST

WONDER WOMAN FINDS HER HUMANITY

***Wonder Woman* [second series] #136**

Writer/artist John Byrne was leaving *Wonder Woman*. Having worked on the title for the past three years, Byrne had ushered in a new era of the Amazing Amazon's adventures, as well as several new characters. But before he could move on to other projects, there was one final thing Byrne still had to do: bring Wonder Woman back from the dead. Having perished at the hands of the demon Neron and been granted divinity as the Greek goddess of truth, Diana flew back to Earth and returned to her island home of Themyscira in order to help save the life of the former Wonder Girl, Donna Troy.

FOR WANT OF A NAIL

***Justice League: The Nail* #1**

Writer/artist Alan Davis examined a DC Universe without a Superman in an innovative Elseworlds three-issue limited series. Based around the simple premise of a nail puncturing Jonathan and Martha Kent's tire and therefore preventing their discovery of the baby Kal-El, this series showed how the Justice League's lives would be forever altered without their main source of inspiration. In this brave new world, Green Arrow had been paralyzed in a fight with the villain Amazo, Lex Luthor was the lauded mayor of Metropolis, and Black Canary headed up the Outsiders alongside the so-called "Man of Iron," Geo-Force. However, in perhaps the Earth's greatest crisis, a familiar-looking Amish farmer stepped up to join the fight, and Superman finally stood revealed to the world.

Even in a world without Superman, some things remain the same. One such thing is the animosity between Batman and his arch-enemy, the Joker.

““WHAT A PARTY POOPER. BUT THEN YOU NEVER DID HAVE A SENSE OF HUMOR.”

The Joker, *Justice League: The Nail* #1

SEPTEMBER

'TIS THE SEASON...

***Superman: For All Seasons* #1**

Writer Jeph Loeb and artist Tim Sale had achieved comic superstardom with their critically acclaimed miniseries *Batman: The Long Halloween* and its precursor *Batman: Legends of the Dark Knight* one-shot Halloween specials. So when they decided to lend their particular talents to the Man of Steel's early years, the resulting effort was a smash hit. Complemented by the beautiful pastel hues of colorist Bjarne Hansen, this four-issue prestige-format series was a bright counterpoint to Loeb and Sale's noir *Batman* collaborations.

As each volume centered on a different season, fans were treated to a glimpse into the young life of Clark Kent as he developed his powers and made the momentous decision to move from Smallville, Kansas to the big city of Metropolis. In "Spring," Clark explored the picturesque Norman Rockwell setting of Smallville with his high-school sweetheart Lana Lang. As his powers developed, simple, mundane chores like having a haircut turned into near impossible feats. After proving his abilities in a tornado, Clark decided to put his powers to good use and moved to Metropolis to adopt the identity of Superman. By "Summer," Superman was a Metropolis fixture, attracting the attention of beautiful *Daily Planet* reporter Lois Lane, as well as corrupt business mogul Lex Luthor. As "Fall" rolled around, Metropolis fell victim to a virus, forcing Superman to ask Luthor for help combating this new threat. In "Winter," Clark retreated to Smallville, defeated and blaming himself for the viral attack. However, after once again proving his worth in his hometown, Clark returned to the big city, confident that the world truly needed a Superman.

For All Seasons served as a bold coming-of-age tale, and delved into the often-overlooked human side of the most powerful of all super-beings.

Having a son with super-strength makes work around the farm fairly easy for Jonathan Kent.

IN THE REAL WORLD...

June: Microsoft releases the first edition of Windows 98.
July: France defeats Brazil 3–0 to win the 1998 FIFA World Cup.
August: The Real IRA detonates a car bomb in Omagh, Northern Ireland, causing the greatest loss of life in a single incident throughout The Troubles.

SEPTEMBER

SIDEKICKS UNITED

***Young Justice* #1**

When the Justice League originally debuted with impressive sales in 1960, it didn't take long for the powers that be at DC to realize the potential for a team featuring the sidekicks of those iconic heroes. By 1964, the Teen Titans were formed, and DC discovered it had two blossoming franchises on its hands. However, in the wake of the 1997 *JLA* relaunch, the Titans had long since grown up. Luckily, a new generation of sidekicks had appeared on the scene in recent years, and out of the lessons of the past came *Young Justice*, a new ongoing series starring Robin (Tim Drake), Superboy, and Impulse.

Written by Peter David and illustrated by Todd Nauck, *Young Justice* succeeded in finding its fan base, just as the Teen Titans had in the 1960s. The trio of young friends soon gained a mentor in JLA alumnus Red Tornado, and later fleshed out their roster with the addition of a few female heroes: Wonder Girl (Cassie Sandsmark), the ghost-like Secret, and archer Arrowette. The series ran for fifty-five issues, even sparking the company-wide crossover "Sins of Youth" along the way, before the team finally graduated to the fabled Titans status.

Despite their very different personalities, the founders of Young Justice get along surprisingly well.

OCTOBER

THE WORLD'S FASTEST WEDDING

***The Flash* [second series] #142**

At last, Wally West was going to marry his longtime love interest Linda Park. When the terrorist organization Kobra decided to wage war on Keystone City that same day, the Flash wasn't impressed with their timing. Despite the obstacles, the ceremony went ahead, thanks to writers Mark Waid and Brian Augustyn, and artist Pop Mhan. Wally placed a ring on Linda's finger and recited his vows. Then everything changed: Linda vanished, and the Flash appeared in his living room, with no memories of his new wife, and being manipulated by an unknown foe lurking in the shadows.

MY FAVORITE MARTIAN

***Martian Manhunter* #0**

The fan-favorite team of writer John Ostrander and artist Tom Mandrake, fresh off their lengthy run on *The Spectre*, were ready to take on another caped powerhouse with *Martian Manhunter* #0, a special introductory issue to J'onn J'onzz's first ongoing series. Springing from the pages of *JLA*, this origin issue recounted J'onn's original battle with Ma'alefa'ak, his fellow Martian and the creator of a telepathic virus that annihilated all of J'onn's race. Chronicling the Manhunter's journey to Earth and his adoption of the identity of police detective John Jones—as well as many other human identities—this reinvention of a classic character ran until issue #36.

NOVEMBER

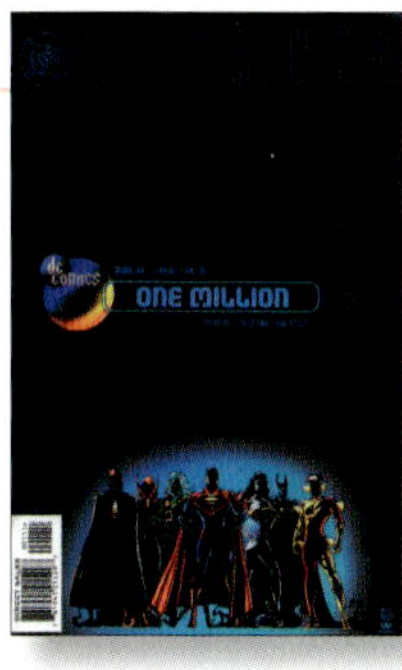

DC'S MILLION-ISSUE MARCH

***DC One Million* #1**

Writer Grant Morrison headed back to the future with the crossover event *DC One Million*, a glimpse into the future world of the 853rd century. Starring the Justice Legion A, the future counterparts to the JLA of the present, the series also spotlighted the new android Hourman, a character who had made his debut in the "Rock of Ages" storyline in Morrison's *JLA* title. Drawn by Val Semeiks, this four-issue miniseries spun off into a series of specials, each with a cover number of #1,000,000, for nearly every DCU title. These created interesting bookends to the #0 issues that were released with 1994's *Zero Hour* crossover event, and solidified a fascinating future that still could be.

DECEMBER

CLASH OF THE TITANS

***JLA/Titans* #1**

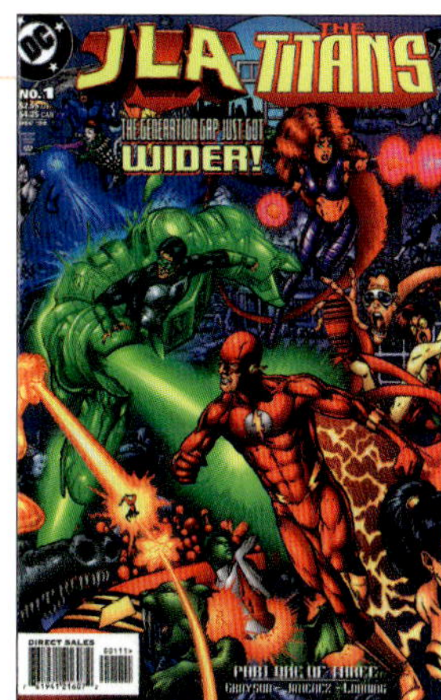

Writer Devin Grayson and artist/co-plotter Phil Jimenez revived another stalled DC property in the *JLA/Titans* miniseries. As ex-Titan Cyborg—now possessed and controlled by the alien collective Technis and calling himself Cyberion—took root on the moon and captured members of the Titans, the JLA staged a rescue attempt. However, the Titans refused to let the League attack their former teammate and a battle between heroes and mentors erupted. Ultimately, the founding Titans reunited and traveled to the heart of the Technis collective to free their friend from its dark influence.

ALSO THIS YEAR: Hero Jakeem Thunder debuted in *THE FLASH* [second series] #134 in February, by writers Grant Morrison and Mark Millar and penciller Paul Ryan... December saw the "Road to No Man's Land" crossover begin in a flipbook issue of *AZRAEL: AGENT OF THE BAT* #47/*BATMAN: SHADOW OF THE BAT* #80, by writers Denny O'Neil and Alan Grant and artists Mark Buckingham and Roger Robinson...

September: Google Inc. is founded in Menlo Park, California, by Stanford University Ph.D. candidates Larry Page and Sergey Brin.

October: Sky Digital satellite television and radio service launches in the U.K.
November: The European Court of Human Rights is established.

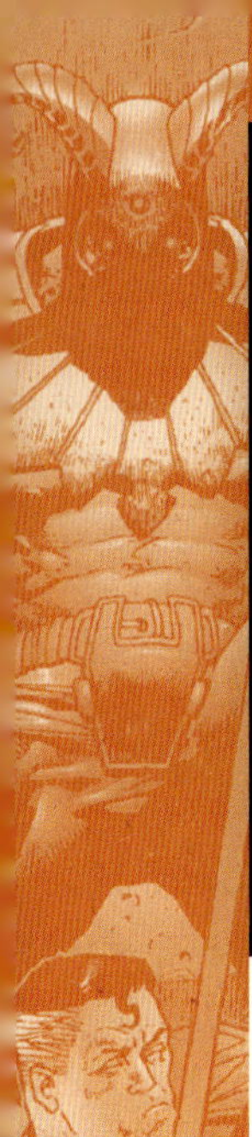

1999

"I HAVE TO ADMIT THIS WAS *AMUSING*... THE HISTORY LESSON PART."

Mordru, *JSA* #1

BACK TO BASICS

Everything old was new again. Heroes had returned to their proper roles and costumes. Teams from bygone days had reunited with rosters that paid homage to the past, while embracing the next generation of super-heroics. The flashy trends of the 1990s were coming to a close, and an industry-wide emphasis was being placed back on storytelling and characterization.

But DC still tried out new ideas. Editor Denny O'Neil and the rest of the *Batman* staff introduced the largest multi-part event in Batman's history in "No Man's Land." New characters sprang up across the DCU, as old monikers were adopted by fresh faces. And in a landmark deal, DC purchased Jim Lee's WildStorm imprint, gaining another super hero universe. Under DC's watchful eye, WildStorm would later branch out into videogame and movie properties, as well as a string of creator-owned titles. Despite all the players being familiar, this was the beginning of a whole new ballgame.

JANUARY

A QUEST FOR PEACE
Superman: Peace on Earth
Comic's own Norman Rockwell—the critically acclaimed painter Alex Ross—teamed up with writer Paul Dini, lauded for his work on *Batman: The Animated Series*, to tell a powerful story of the Man of Steel. In this beautiful sixty-four-page oversized one-shot, meant to emulate the grand-scale feel of DC's large tabloid comics of the Bronze Age, Superman fought a battle even he couldn't truly win: the war on poverty and hunger. A tragic tale of the limitations of power, *Peace on Earth* was so well received by readers that it inspired an entire string of these oversized painted works and several lithographs by Ross and Dini over the next few years, starring the biggest names from the DC Universe.

CATCHING THEIR PREY
***Birds of Prey* #1**
After proving their worth in a series of specials and a miniseries, Oracle and Black Canary were finally rewarded with their own ongoing series by scripter Chuck Dixon and penciller Greg Land. With an emphasis on world travel, the series saw the former Batgirl and current computer expert Oracle team up with field operative Black Canary to carry out a variety of secret missions for the betterment of society. During the series' 127-issue run, more operatives were added to Oracle's entourage, including the Huntress, Lady Blackhawk, and Misfit. The series also ignited the long-awaited romance between Oracle and Nightwing.

ON TV THIS MONTH: ***BATMAN BEYOND*****, a fifty-two-episode animated series by producer Bruce Timm that offered a glimpse into the future of the Caped Crusader, premiered on the WB Television Network...**

FEBRUARY

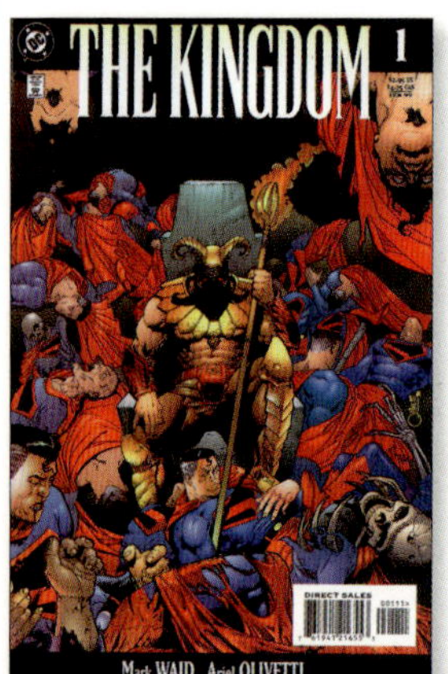

KEYS TO THE KINGDOM
***The Kingdom* #1**
Writer Mark Waid returned to the kingdom he helped envision with this series of specials designed as a sequel to the hit miniseries *Kingdom Come*. With two bookends entitled *The Kingdom* (illustrated by Ariel Olivetti and Mike Zeck), and five specials focusing on various characters or locations from the possible future reality, these one-shots provided updates to the lives of the *Kingdom Come* characters, and detailed the first meeting of the *Kingdom Come* universe and the DC Universe proper. They also introduced the concept of Hypertime, an interconnected web of parallel timelines.

IN THE REAL WORLD...
January: The euro (€), the official currency of the European Union, is established.

MARCH

GOTHAM GHOST TOWN

***Batman: No Man's Land* #1**

Gotham City was on its knees. First the "Clench" virus took its toll upon Gotham's populace, and then a 7.6-level earthquake shook the very foundations of the unprepared city. After the machinations of the one-man political movement Nicholas Scratch during the recent "Road to No Man's Land" crossover, the United States had made up its mind: Gotham City was to be declared a disaster zone and officially abandoned by its own country. Gotham's citizens were ordered to leave, walls were erected around the city's borders, and National Guard soldiers were in turn positioned around them. The city's bridges were then destroyed, and no one was permitted in or out. Only the brave, the stubborn, and the insane stayed in Gotham City, and the Batman was nowhere to be found.

The *Batman: No Man's Land* one-shot, written by Bob Gale and illustrated by Alex Maleev, with both a deluxe lenticular cover and a standard version by painter Alex Ross, kicked off the enormous crossover event "No Man's Land," which showcased the talent of dozens of writers and artists new to Gotham City. A monumental storyline for the Dark Knight, the four monthly *Batman* titles (*Batman*, *Detective Comics*, *Batman: Legends of the Dark Knight*, and *Batman: Shadow of the Bat*) worked in tandem like never before, in effect each serving as a weekly dose of the connecting "No Man's Land" plot. Numbering eighty-five comics officially labeled as part of the crossover, including four specials and various issues of *Robin*, *Catwoman*, *The Batman Chronicles*, and *Azrael*, "No Man's Land" created a Gotham City never seen before, a streamlined new world with its own set of laws and rules.

In Batman's absence, Gotham began to be divided up by various criminals, crime fighters, and even the remaining members of the police force, each group marking their territory by means of graffiti tags. When Batman finally returned after his mysterious time away, he lead the heroes into an all-out war for law and order, and the city was eventually saved with the help of a surprise benefactor—Lex Luthor.

With a skeleton crew police force spread thin amongst the wreckage of a destroyed Gotham, the inmates of Arkham Asylum cause chaos.

MARCH

TITANS TOGETHER

***The Titans* #1**

Writer Devin Grayson, alongside artist Mark Buckingham, relaunched the Titans in a new ongoing series, featuring a roster composed of members from nearly every incarnation of the team. Led by the now-adult founding members Nightwing, Troia, Arsenal, Tempest, and the Flash, the team also featured Cyborg and Starfire from *The New Teen Titans* era, as well as Damage and Argent from later versions of the team, and new member Jesse Quick. With the older members serving as mentors to the younger generation, the Titans were reborn, and the series ran for fifty issues.

MAY

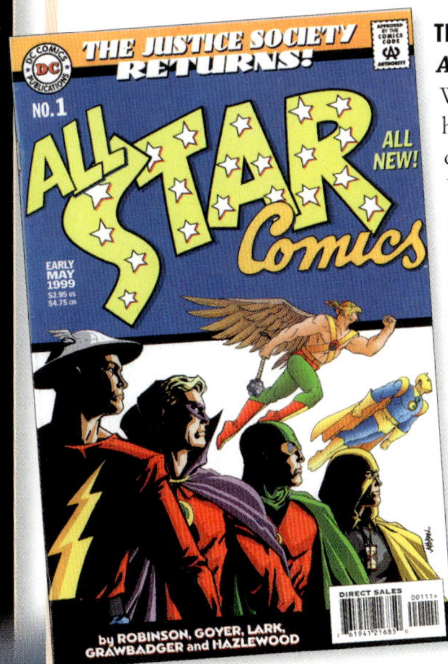

THE ALL STAR GAME

***All Star Comics* #1**

Writer James Robinson had proven he could entrance audiences with characters from DC's Golden Age. With a successful *Starman* revamp and acclaimed Elseworlds limited series *The Golden Age* already under his belt, Robinson had set the stage for his newest opus—the return of the Justice Society of America. With this first in a series of nine specials bearing nostalgic titles from years past on their covers, Robinson and writer David Goyer, with artist Michael Lark, told a classic tale of the team. They concluded the story in the event's other bookend, *All Star Comics* #2, featuring art by William Rosado and the first glimpse of the modern JSA.

JUNE

SUPERMAN'S REIGN

***Superman: King of the World* #1**

Superman had gone too far. He had unleashed a horde of Superman robots to patrol the world for him in search of the villain Dominus, as he sat on a throne at his new Metropolis command center. As the public began doubting their protector, the young hero Outburst found that Superman had already captured Dominus. But when Lex Luthor freed the villain, he discovered Dominus had switched places with the Man of Steel, perverting his heroic image. In this extra-length one-shot by writer Karl Kesel and penciller Doug Braithwaite, the true Superman eventually defeated his crafty foe and regained the trust of his beloved public.

March: Bertrand Piccard and Brian Jones become the first people to circumnavigate the Earth in a hot-air balloon.

April: In a Columbine, Colorado high school, two teenage students open fire, killing twelve of their classmates and one teacher, before committing suicide.

JULY

STAR-SPANGLED BANTER
Stars and S.T.R.I.P.E. #0

Writer Geoff Johns showed his love for the obscure corners of the DCU with his title, *Stars and S.T.R.I.P.E.* With penciller Lee Moder, Johns recreated the Golden Age pairing of the Star-Spangled Kid and his adult sidekick Stripesy by creating a new Star-Spangled Kid—Courtney Whitmore. Whitmore was a fan favorite from the start, as she teamed with her stepfather, the original Stripesy, who now wore a robotic suit of armor and called himself S.T.R.I.P.E. Courtney joined the new JSA and was later renamed Stargirl.

A BRAVE NEW BATGIRL
Batman #567

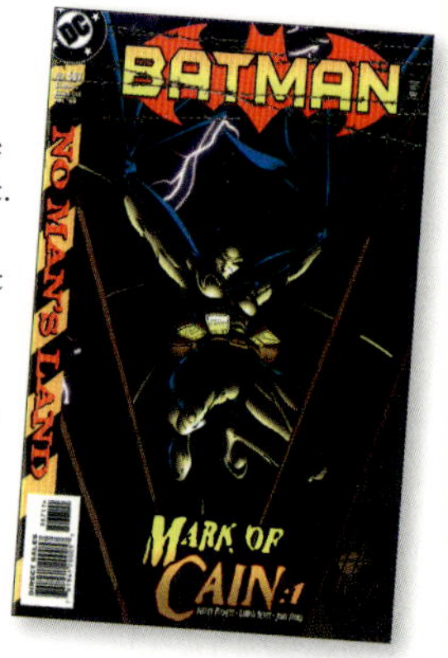

Cassandra Cain couldn't talk or read, but the one thing the new Batgirl could do was fight. Trained only in the language of violence since birth, Cassie grew up learning how to predict her opponent's next move and read body language better than anyone alive. Rejecting her father's ways after she was forced to commit murder, Cassie took off on her own and soon met former Batgirl and current Oracle Barbara Gordon during the "No Man's Land" event, as chronicled by writer Kelley Puckett and artist Damion Scott in *Batman* #567. After Batman rejected the Huntress' claim on the title of Batgirl, Cassie assumed the role and joined the ranks of the Dark Knight's trusted inner circle.

AUGUST

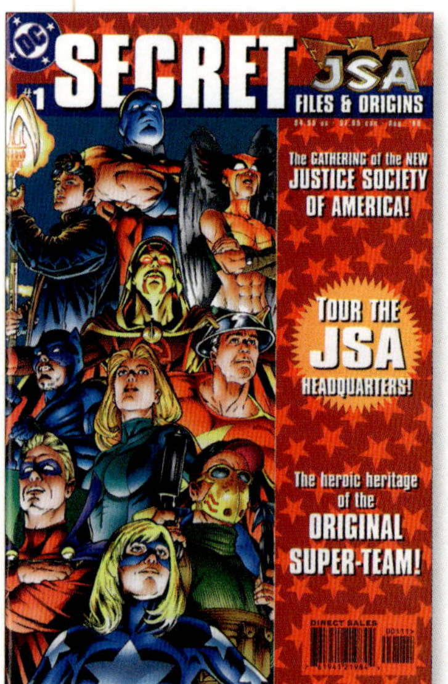

THE SECRET ORIGIN OF HAWKGIRL
JSA Secret Files & Origins #1

Although released the same month as *JSA* #1, which updated the JSA team roster, the first *JSA Secret Files & Origins* special had the privilege of introducing readers to the newest woman to take up the mantle of Hawkgirl—Kendra Saunders. Kendra was a young woman who commited suicide, and when her soul left her body, she became possessed by the reincarnated spirit of the Hawkwomen who came before her. She became the highflying heir to her Thanagarian legacy in a story penned by writers James Robinson and David Goyer and pencilled by Scott Benefiel. Also featuring the death of longtime Sandman Wesley Dodds, this issue featured a JSA timeline chronicling the actions of the team from the Golden Age to the present, a JSA headquarters schematic, two back-up features, and a gallery of profile pages detailing the background of the new team by a variety of creative talent.

AUGUST

JUSTICE IS SERVED
JSA #1

Writers James Robinson and David Goyer, along with penciller Stephen Sadowski, gave readers an update on the founding fathers of the super-team with *JSA* #1, the first of a new ongoing series starring a roster hailing from various generations. Besides founding Golden Age heroes Green Lantern (Alan Scott), Wildcat (Ted Grant), and the Flash (Jay Garrick), the team also featured a host of newcomers and second-generation heroes. Black Canary (Dinah Lance) joined the group, straight from the Silver Age, as did grown-up Golden Age hero Sand, and former Infinity Inc. member Atom Smasher (formerly Nuklon). Starman joined the fledgling team as well, along with other newcomers Hourman (from the pages of *JLA*), Hawkgirl, and the new Star-Spangled Kid. It was an impressive lineup that would shift and change over the course of the title's successful eighty-seven-issue run, as members of the team passed the torch to other new members. Perhaps more importantly, the title's original writers would also pass the torch along to a new writer.

After an initial arc that involved a battle against a younger version of Legion of Super-Heroes villain Mordru, and a stand-alone Sand story, James Robinson left the title in the capable hands of Goyer's new writing partner, Geoff Johns. Soon to be a DC phenomenon, Johns' knowledge of super hero continuity and characterization propelled the comic for nearly the rest of its tenure, and later guided the super-team into a successful relaunch.

Over the course of the title's run, the JSA battled many villains, including the likes of the Ultra-Humanite, Eclipso, Extant, and the Gentleman Ghost. The series saw new members Hawkman, Captain Marvel, Jakeem Thunder, the second Mr. Terrific and Hourman, a new Dr. Fate, and even the supposedly reformed villain Black Adam. The title also debuted a new and deadly Crimson Avenger and delved into the nine lives of team member Wildcat.

The Justice Society of America's Dr. Fate is Hector Hall, the son of founding father Hawkman.

IN THE REAL WORLD...

June: Apple, Inc. releases the iBook, the first laptop computer designed specifically for the average consumer.

July: Off Martha's Vineyard, New England, a plane piloted by John F. Kennedy, Jr., son of the former U.S. President, crashes, killing him, his wife, and his wife's sister.

OCTOBER

HERE'S HARLEY!
***Batman: Harley Quinn* #1**
Harley Quinn finally made her way into the DC Universe in her own one-shot prestige-format special by writer Paul Dini alongside artist Yvel Guichet, with a dramatic painted cover by Alex Ross. She was originally created by Dini and producer Bruce Timm as the sidekick of the Joker in the fan-favorite TV show *Batman: The Animated Series*. *Harley Quinn*, an unofficial part of the "No Man's Land" crossover saga, detailed Arkham Asylum intern Dr. Harleen Quinzel's descent into madness at the hands of her love, the Joker. Unlike her animated counterpart, however, this Harley was given a special formula by her friend and fellow Batman rogue Poison Ivy, that enhanced her agility and strength and made her a much more dangerous threat to the Caped Crusader.

NOVEMBER

THE SPECTRE GETS HIS DAY
***Day of Judgment* #1**
For better or for worse, Hal Jordan, the deceased former hero Green Lantern, was now the Spectre, and a new era of his heroic legacy was about to begin. *Day of Judgment* saw a team of the world's greatest magicians come together for the first time when the heroes of the DCU faced the wrath of Hell itself as God's Spirit of Vengeance, the Spectre, merged with the fallen angel Asmodel. Calling themselves the Sentinels of Magic, the team helped lead bands of heroes into Heaven and Hell and succeeded in dethroning Asmodel, finally replacing him with the soul of Hal Jordan. Writer Geoff Johns continued his rise to the ranks of DC superstar in this five-issue miniseries, which was pencilled by artist Matt Smith.

BATMAN WAGES WAR
Batman: War on Crime
The second in the oversized prestige-format tabloid collaborations between writer Paul Dini and painter Alex Ross, *Batman: War on Crime* was just as successful as its predecessor, and just as beautiful. Beginning with a two-page origin story, this fully painted one-shot was told in a storybook format. Like *Superman: Peace on Earth*, this story pitted its protagonist against seemingly insurmountable odds, in this case the cruel realities of those victimized by violent crime. A dark tale augmented by a bittersweet glimmer of hope, *War on Crime* was a tragic glimpse into the life of the man behind the mask.

DECEMBER

A SHADOWY TALE

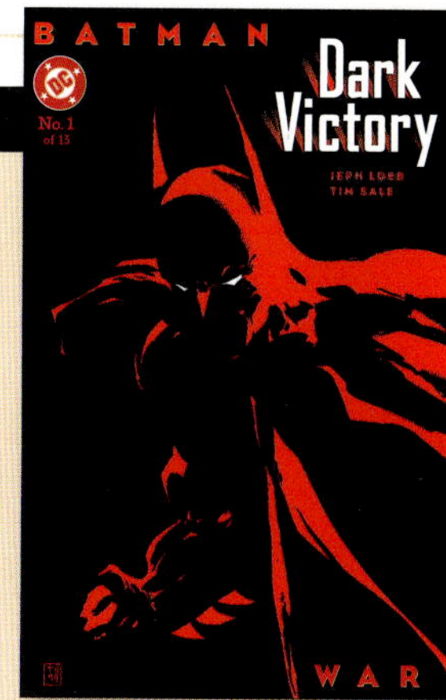

***Batman: Dark Victory* #1**
The superstar team of writer Jeph Loeb and artist Tim Sale was back, and just as dark as ever. In this thirteen-issue sequel to the pair's acclaimed *Batman: The Long Halloween* maxiseries, the creative team picked up right where they left off during Batman's early years. Once again beautifully colored by Gregory Wright and complemented by two forty-eight-page prestige-format specials to sandwich the other eleven issues, this series featured memorable and dynamic Tim Sale covers. Since the story once again focused on a variety of *Batman* villains, Sale illustrated a different character on each cover, shrouded in shadows and highlighted by a single bold color.

Another complex murder mystery, *Dark Victory* detailed the exploits of Gotham's newest serial killer, the Hangman. More importantly, the series also reexamined the origin of Dick Grayson (Robin) and Batman's acceptance of the boy first into his home at Wayne Manor and later into his life as a crime-fighting partner. In the end, the Hangman killer was revealed to be mob daughter Sophia Falcone Gigante, and Robin was sworn into service by the Batman after proving himself in a Batcave battle with many of the Dark Knight's deadliest rogues.

Batman faces off with Solomon Grundy, an undead swamp creature who was the foe of the Golden Age Green Lantern.

ALSO THIS YEAR: The Flash raced alongside nearly every super-speedster ever in "Chain Lightning," a six-part storyline by writers Mark Waid and Brian Augustyn and artist Paul Pelletier, beginning in February in *THE FLASH* (second series) #145 and introducing a new look (albeit temporary) for the Fastest Man Alive… Batman and Superman reunited in April in the ten-issue limited series *WORLD'S FINEST*, which examined their relationship over the course of their careers. The series was written by Karl Kesel and illustrated by Dave Taylor, Peter Doherty, Graham Nolan, and Tom Morgan, and complemented by prestige-format first and final issues… The L.A.W. (Living Assault Weapons) partnered the heroes of Charlton Comics' fame for a six-issue miniseries by writer Bob Layton and penciller Dick Giordano in September…

July: Cyclist Lance Armstrong wins his first Tour de France.
August: A total solar eclipse is seen in Europe and Asia.

December: The U.S. turns over complete administration of the Panama Canal to the Panamanian government, as stipulated in the Torrijos-Carter Treaty of 1977.

WONDER WOMAN [second series] #150 (November 1999)
Adam Hughes remains one of the best known and distinctive comic-book cover artists. His celebrated four-year run on *Wonder Woman* began in 1998. In the process, his elegant, beautifully composed portraits transformed Wonder Woman from a rather straitlaced seeker of truth into a strong, sensual super hero, as charismatic as Superman and Batman.

THE ART OF ADAM HUGHES

2000s

As millennium fever subsided and a new century dawned, DC Comics was in great shape. With top creatives joining the company, the first decade of the 21st Century heralded an era of remarkable creativity across multiple genres. The movies *Batman Begins* and *The Dark Knight* smashed box office records, and *Smallville* became one of the longest running sci-fi TV shows, making comics a bigger part of mainstream popular culture than ever before—with DC's iconic stars taking center stage.

The decade's optimistic start was soon overshadowed by global terrorism, economic concerns, and conflict in the Middle East—all of which made the world feel less stable and more dangerous. The change was reflected in comics: heroes and storylines grew darker, exemplified by the best-selling *Identity Crisis* series, which ran from August 2004 to February 2005. With readers eager for innovation, but wary of too jarring a change, creative talents—writers especially—became increasingly important to DC. Geoff Johns, Mark Waid, and Grant Morrison re-imagined many of the company's greatest heroes and shook up the very universe they lived in—while remaining true to seventy-five years of continuity.

At the same time, the company led the way in exploring new formats and markets, introducing titles like the weekly *Wednesday Comics* and the Vertigo Crime line. Collections of DC's stories were stocked in most bookshops, including everything from high-quality, hardcover "Absolute Editions" of classics such as *The Sandman* to collections of main titles, with *Superman: Brainiac* topping *The New York Times* bestseller list.

By the end of the decade, the company had restructured, gaining a new name—DC Entertainment—a new president—Diane Nelson—and giving top talent more power. With its comic books topping the charts, its writers and artists winning awards, and its heroes breaking out across a variety of media, DC Entertainment was ready for the challenges of the ensuing decades of the 21st Century.

"YOUR BONES WILL SNAP. YOUR BLOOD WILL FILL MY BELLY."

Killer Croc, *Batman* #608 (December 2002

2000

"YOU GET THE BEST SEAT IN THE HOUSE FOR ARMAGEDDON."

The Joker to Harley Quinn as he turns her into a constellation, *Action Comics* #770

A BRAVE NEW ERA

With the start of the new decade and a new millennium, DC Comics was making plans for the future. While other comic book companies had jumped headfirst into the Nineties trend of special cover after special cover, DC had always put its stories first. In 2000, writers and artists who would go on to provide the company with some of their all-time great stories were pushing boundaries and revitalizing established characters. Whether it was future megastar writer Geoff Johns on *The Flash*, established writer/artist Walt Simonson on *Orion*, or writer Grant Morrison and artist Frank Quitely on *JLA: Earth 2*, it was clear that DC had every faith in the talent who were working on their books. These individuals, and other future stars, would take DC's titles to whole new levels of excitement over the next decade and make the company *the* place for today's creative talent.

JANUARY

ANIMAL MAGIC
***Beast Boy* #1**

Beast Boy (a.k.a. Garfield "Gar" Logan) found himself in deep trouble during his first miniseries, courtesy of writers Ben Raab and Geoff Johns, with art by Justiniano. Having left the Teen Titans to find himself, Gar tried to rebuild his acting career, after appearing in *Space Trek 2020*. Instead he was framed for murder. With his old friend Nightwing and Titans West's Flamebird helping him, Beast Boy learned that the enemy who had set him up was Gemini, the daughter of old Doom Patrol villain Madame Rouge. Gemini blamed Gar for her mother's death and wanted revenge.

FEBRUARY

WILD HORSES
Preacher: Tall in the Saddle

As Vertigo's *Preacher* neared its conclusion, writer Garth Ennis and artist Steve Dillon turned the clock back to tell a story of a younger Jesse Custer and Tulip O'Hare. Published as a prestige format one-shot, *Tall in the Saddle* followed Jesse, Tulip, and their friend Amy as they joined forces with a retired Texas Ranger to bring down a gang of cold-blooded horse thieves. Filled with *Preacher*'s usual great dialog and bracing, over-the-top violence, *Tall in the Saddle* was a fantastic glimpse into the lives of Jesse and Tulip when the couple were first together.

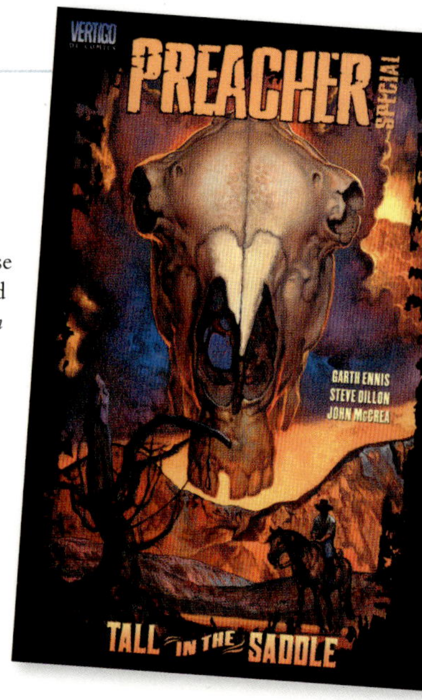

Jesse Custer rides off into the sunset at the end of *Preacher: Tall in the Saddle* after hanging the horse-eating villain Napoleon Vichy.

IN THE REAL WORLD...

January: The world enters a new millennium without serious, widespread computer failures, despite fears to the contrary.

FEBRUARY

THE CRIME SYNDICATE RETURNS

JLA: Earth 2

Writer Grant Morrison and artist Frank Quitely brought the Crime Syndicate of America back to DC continuity in *JLA: Earth 2*. The Crime Syndicate was a twisted mirror image of the Justice League and had first appeared in *Justice League of America* #29 in August 1964. The group continued to cause trouble from its homeworld of Earth-3 until reality was destroyed in *Crisis on Infinite Earths* (1986). Post-*Crisis*, a variation of the group had appeared in Summer 1992's *Justice League Quarterly* #8 but had very little to do with the original team—unlike Morrison's makeover.

Published as a graphic novel, *JLA: Earth 2* started with an heroic Alexander Luthor having escaped from the antimatter world ruled by the Crime Syndicate to the Earth of the JLA, wanting to enlist the JLA's help to free his home. Crossing over to the antimatter universe, the JLA hoped to inspire people to rise up against the Crime Syndicate. The Crime Syndicate's members were updated versions of the original 1964 incarnations: Ultraman (Lieutenant Clark Kent, an astronaut given amazing powers by aliens); Superwoman (a superpowered Lois Lane); Owlman (Thomas Wayne Jr., son of Police Commissioner Thomas Wayne); Johnny Quick (a Flash-like speedster); and Power Ring (based on the Green Lantern). However, when the JLA moved to Earth-2, the Crime Syndicate found itself transported to the Earth of the JLA, to balance out the two realities. Morrison had fun with the premise of an antimatter Earth and its history, changing major events on the antimatter world. On the Earth of the Crime Syndicate, President Benedict Arnold had declared war on the British colonies when they had announced their independence from Amerika in 1776, while the president lived in the Black House. With the Crime Syndicate running amok on Earth, the JLA returned to stop them. However, the JLA realized it couldn't win on the antimatter Earth because in that reality evil always triumphed. A variation on the Crime Syndicate returned years later in the final issue of *52* (May 2007).

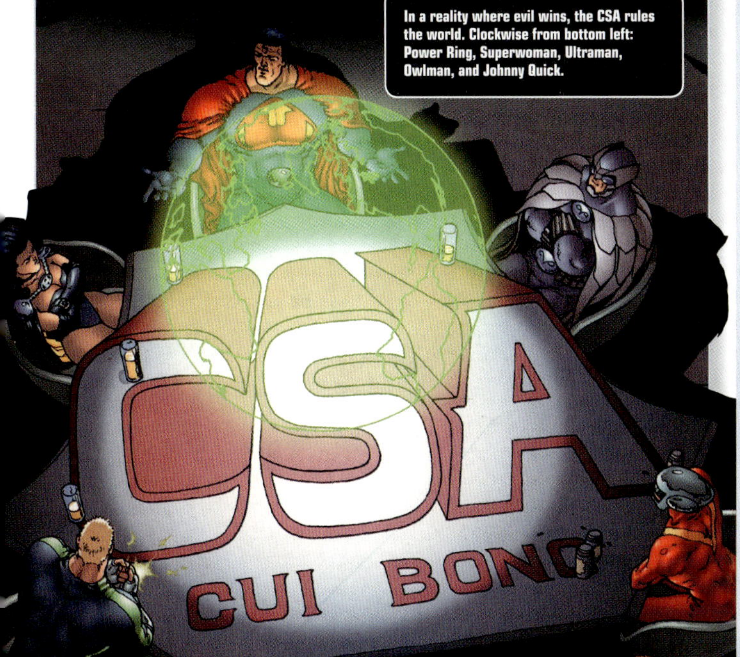

In a reality where evil wins, the CSA rules the world. Clockwise from bottom left: Power Ring, Superwoman, Ultraman, Owlman, and Johnny Quick.

APRIL

BATGIRL BEGINS

***Batgirl* #1**

Cassandra Cain became the first Batgirl to star in a regular series after her successful appearances alongside Batman during 1999's "No Man's Land" saga. The new series was plotted by Scott Peterson and Kelley Puckett, with the latter handling the script, and featured art by Damion Scott. *Batgirl* followed Cassandra's attempt to become a full-fledged crime fighter as Batman and Oracle (the original Batgirl) watched over her and provided help when needed. The opening issue dealt with Cassandra's troubled past and her brave attempt to overcome her upbringing as a would-be assassin.

MAY

RETURN OF THE MONSTERS

***Creature Commandos* #1**

The Creature Commandos returned to service thanks to writer Timothy Truman and artist Scot Eaton. The new team of the Bogman, Aten the Mummy, Medusa, Velcoro (a vampire-like creature), Patchwork (similar to Frankenstein's Monster), and Wolfpack (a werewolf) were joined by a cyborg called Gunner. It was hinted that Gunner was from the "Gunner and Sarge" story from *Our Fighting Forces* #45 in May 1959. The new team was formed in time to stop an invasion from a parallel world.

THE FEMALE OF THE SPECIES

***Swamp Thing* #1**

Writer Brian K. Vaughan and artist Roger Petersen unleashed a new Swamp Thing in the shape of Abby Holland's daughter, Tefé. John Constantine and Tefé's father, the original Swamp Thing, had helped a young Tefé replace a terminally ill girl called Mary Conway, altering Tefé's body so she looked like the dying child. It was the only way to protect Tefé from her own elemental powers. Tefé forgot who she was and lived as Mary until she saw her boyfriend with another girl. The shock brought her elemental nature to the fore and she exacted a bloody revenge on her boyfriend before faking her own death and going off in search of her destiny.

February: The final original "Peanuts" comic strip is published following the death of its creator, Charles Schulz.

March: Prime Minister Vladimir Putin is elected president of Russia.
May: The billionth living person in India is born.

JUNE

THE FOURTH WORLD RETURNS
***Orion* #1**

Comic book legend Walt Simonson brought his unique vision to one of Jack Kirby's greatest heroes on *Orion*, the first ongoing series to feature the most prominent of the New Gods. Simonson was writer and artist on the series, with John Workman providing his usual outstanding lettering job. The new series opened with Orion questioning his own origins, including whether he really was Darkseid's son, and trying to track down Darkseid to gain answers. Unknown to Orion, Darkseid was on Earth, with deadly plans of his own.

JULY

WHAT'S UP, DOC?
***Superman & Bugs Bunny* #1**

Two worlds were set on a collision course when Mr. Mxyzptlk helped bring the DC Universe together with the world of Bugs Bunny and his cartoon pals. Writer Mark Evanier and artist Joe Staton produced a cool and wacky adventure that featured many of DC's greatest heroes and their cartoon counterparts. Highlights included the Flash meeting Speedy Gonzales, and the Green Lantern facing off against Marvin the Martian. Meanwhile, Daffy Duck and the Tasmanian Devil caused Mr. Mxyzptlk problems, especially when Taz tried to eat Superman's old foe.

The first issue ended on a cliffhanger, as Mr. Mxyzptlk decided to use his power to replace Superman with Elmer J. Fudd. Later issues of the four-part series featured Elmer as Superfudd, a Clark Kent with an urge to hunt rabbits, and a new take on Batman when Daffy Duck became the Duck Knight.

DC's finest heroes go head-to-head with the stars of Looney Tunes as two worlds collide—including a not-to-be missed confrontation between the Green Lantern and Marvin the Martian!

SEPTEMBER

EMPEROR JOKER
***Superman* [second series] #160**

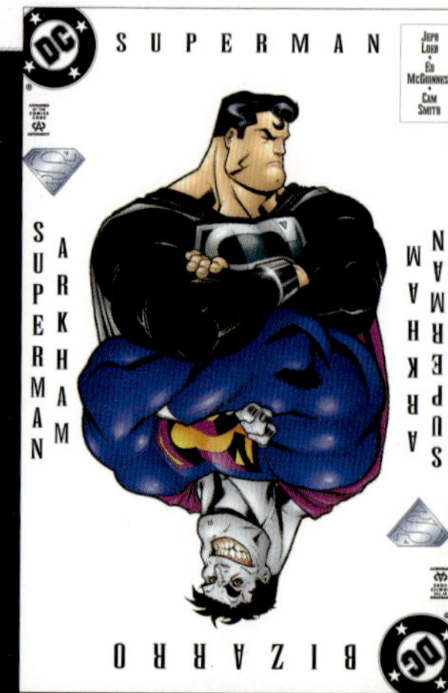

Superman was a criminal, breaking out of jail every night to terrorize the people of Metropolis. That was just the start of Superman's biggest epic of the year. In a nine-part saga that stretched over all the Superman titles, starting in *Superman* #160 with script by Jeph Loeb and art by Ed McGuinness, the escaped Superman was eventually taken back to jail by Bizarro and given over to the jail's governor—Solomon Grundy. Over the next three chapters it became clear that something was very wrong with the world. People were living in dread, Superman was a wanted man, and Mr. Mxyzptlk was repeatedly being killed by falling weights and runaway trains. The identity of the villain behind the chaos was kept secret until the end of the fourth chapter when Superman looked down on Earth only to see a square world imprinted with the Joker's face on every side. At the time of publication, it was a shocking twist and one most readers didn't see coming. It transpired that the Joker had stolen the power of Mr. Mxyzptlk and was now in charge of reality, bending it to his every insane whim. Through sheer force of will, Superman opposed the Joker and, thanks to Mr. Mxyzptlk, learned who the Joker's one weakness was—Batman. Despite the Joker killing the Batman every night and then bringing him back to life the following day, he couldn't wipe Batman from existence. By pointing out the "white elephant" in the Joker's universe, Superman destroyed the Joker's hold on Mr. Mxyzptlk's power and Mr. Mxyzptlk rebuilt reality as it had been before the Joker's interference. The saga's intelligent climax was perfect for such a twisted tale, as was the final scene of a straitjacketed Joker whispering "rorepme rekoj" again and again.

The Joker packs more than a punch when he reshapes reality to suit his own crazy desires, with Superman as the world's leading super-villain.

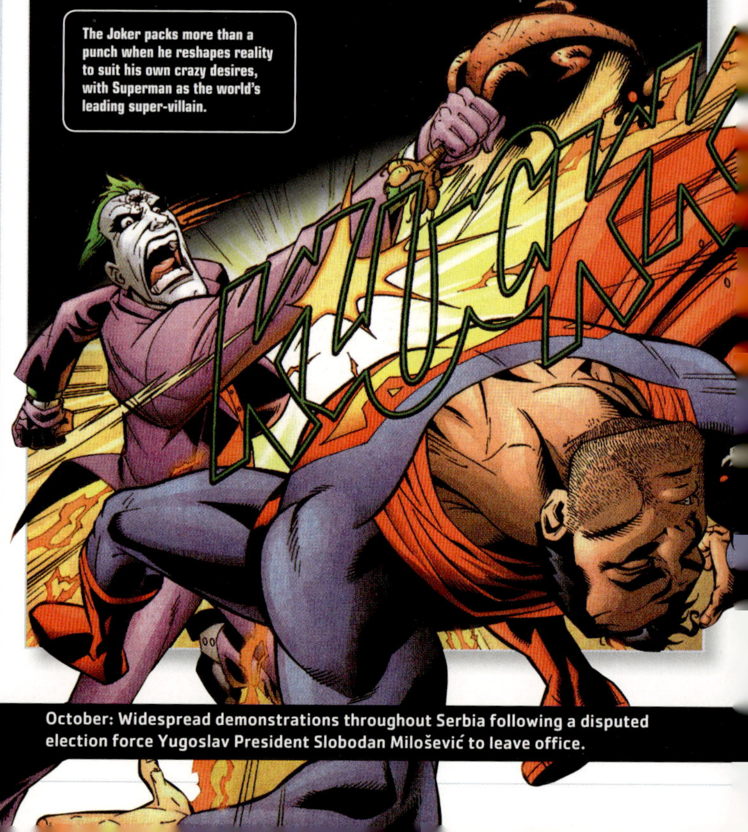

IN THE REAL WORLD...

July: An Air France Concorde aircraft crashes into a hotel in Gonesse, Paris.
September: The Summer Olympics are held in Sydney, Australia.

October: Widespread demonstrations throughout Serbia following a disputed election force Yugoslav President Slobodan Milošević to leave office.

SEPTEMBER

OLD MAN CONSTANTINE

***Hellblazer Special: Bad Blood* #1**

Writer Jamie Delano, who chronicled John Constantine's adventures when *Hellblazer* was first released, returned to the character for a four-part miniseries, with art by Philip Bond. *Bad Blood* was a dark comedy set in 2025 that followed an aging Constantine's attempts to save his friend Dolly from being touted by makers of a reality TV show as the true heir to the British throne. A satirical take on modern society, the series ended on Dolly revealing she was pregnant with Constantine's child, giving him the option of seeing his offspring become Britain's ruler.

NOVEMBER

HIGHWAY TO HEAVEN

JLA: Heaven's Ladder

The JLA took part in one of its greatest adventures when Earth was stolen by a race of aliens in search of the meaning of life. Artist Bryan Hitch made full use of the book's extra-large format, illustrating amazing scenes featuring not just Earth but other planets collected by the god-like scientists behind Earth's theft. Written by Mark Waid, *Heaven's Ladder* dealt with religion and the afterlife and proved to be one of the JLA's most cosmic stories ever.

OCTOBER

WAR STORIES

***Adventures in the Rifle Brigade* #1**

Writer Garth Ennis brought his dark sense of humor to World War II as he teamed up with artist Carlos Ezquerra on *Adventures in the Rifle Brigade*. The story followed one of the toughest and strangest squadrons of the British army on their adventures behind enemy lines. Led by Captain Darcy, a stiff-upper-lipped officer of the realm, the group was a dangerous collection of psychos and oddballs consisting of Second Lieutenant Cecil Milk, a weedy old Etonian; Sergeant Crumb, the largest soldier in the British army; Corporal Geezer, a psycho who had killed 413 before joining the army; Hank the Yank, a cigar-stomping caricature of old World War II heroes; and finally the Piper, a Scottish bagpiper whose music was so bad it made people's ears bleed. The Rifle Brigade was caught by the Gestapo but escaped and blew up a V2 research facility before making it back to Blighty. Full of over-the-top humor, *Adventures in the Rifle Brigade* proved to be one of the funnier takes on World War II. After completing a second series, Ennis turned his hand to more serious war tales in Vertigo's *War Stories* in 2001.

Captain Darcy, leader of the Rifle Brigade, sharpens his knife and readies for action behind enemy lines.

DECEMBER

THE BOY WONDER

***Robin: Year One* #1**

The original Robin, Dick Grayson, gained the *Year One* treatment courtesy of writers Chuck Dixon and Scott Beatty, with art by Javier Pulido and Marcos Martín. The four-issue prestige format series followed Dick's attempt to prove his worth to Batman. In the first volume, Dick broke up a child-smuggling ring operated by the mind-controlling Mad Hatter. Later issues followed Dick as he joined the League of Junior Assassins and became involved in a plot to kill Two-Face. The series not only charted Dick's growth as a hero but also the beginnings of his partnership with the Dark Knight.

LOVE HURTS

***Harley Quinn* #1**

While Harley Quinn had appeared in comics before—most notably in 1994's *Mad Love* graphic novel—she finally got her own regular title eight years after her debut in TV's *Batman: The Animated Series*. Written by Karl Kesel and drawn by Terry Dodson, the double-sized first issue dealt with Harley's twisted relationship with the Joker, as she disguised herself as Poison Ivy to help break him out of Arkham Asylum. After nursing the Joker back to health, Harley tried to impress him by sabotaging a fairground based on heroes and villains only to nearly be killed by the Joker in the process. By the end of the issue, Harley had stopped the Joker's plans and was beginning to question her love for the Clown Prince of Crime.

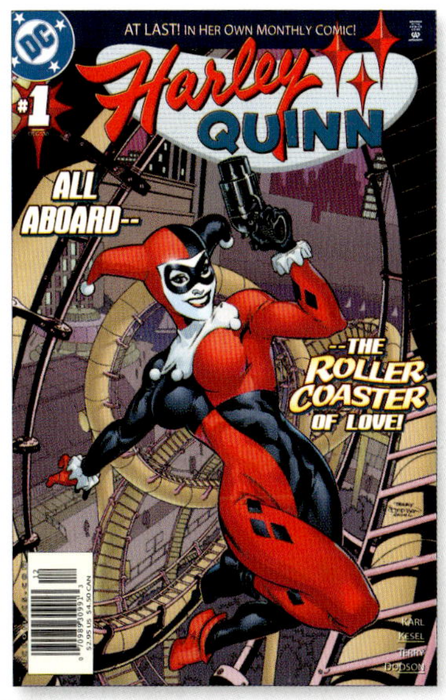

ON TV THIS MONTH: In December, the animated *BATMAN BEYOND: RETURN OF THE JOKER* was released direct to DVD, featuring the vocal talents of Kevin Conroy as Batman and Mark Hamill as the Joker... **ALSO THIS YEAR:** In February, Imperiex made his first appearance in *SUPERMAN* #153... A new version of the Injustice Society appeared in *JSA* #10 in May... Lucifer gained his own eponymous Vertigo series in June... *PREACHER* ended with a bang in October after sixty-six issues...

October: The New York Yankees defeat the New York Mets 4–1 to win their twenty-sixth World Series title.

November: Republican Texas Governor George W. Bush defeats Democratic Vice President Al Gore in the closest U.S. presidential election in history.

2001

"'BACK IN ACTION?' WHAT DO THEY MEAN? I NEVER LEFT."

Green Arrow, *Green Arrow* #2

HEROES AND VILLAINS

2001 started on a shocking note for DC with the election to high office of a corrupt politician who had used his wealth and media connections to usurp political power... Lex Luthor became President of the United States. The surprising rise to the White House of Superman's arch-enemy was to dominate the DC Universe for the next few years, and his influence was felt across many comic book titles. Perhaps the biggest creative shock of the year, however, was Stan Lee, the mastermind behind Marvel Comics, writing his first books for DC. The *Just Imagine* series teamed Stan Lee up with some of the world's best artists for his own reimagining of DC's greatest heroes. Elsewhere, two old favorites reappeared as Hal Jordan and Oliver Queen returned to the DC Universe as heroes. Oliver Queen's dramatic "rebirth" would pave the way for other characters later in the decade.

JANUARY

GODS OF GOTHAM

***Wonder Woman* [second series] #164**
Chaos came to Gotham City in the form of three children of Ares, the God of War. Phobos (the God of Fear), Eris (Goddess of Discord), and Deimos (the God of Terror) possessed the Scarecrow, Poison Ivy, and the Joker respectively. The "Gods of Gotham" storyline marked the start of Phil Jimenez's run on the series as artist and writer (with J. M. DeMatteis on board as co-scripter for the first arc). Wonder Woman joined forces with Batman to stop the trio's plans to remake Gotham into a place fit for their father. Over the following issues, the danger increased as Batman found himself possessed by Phobos, bringing terror to everyone in Gotham City—good and bad alike. Fortunately, Wonder Woman was on hand to help Batman drive the spirit of Phobos out. In Jimenez's stories, Wonder Woman reconnected with her mythical roots while also remaining true to previous continuity. It was just the start of one of Wonder Woman's greatest eras.

Wonder Woman faces off against a Batman possessed by Phobos, the Greek God of Fear.

PRESIDENT LUTHOR
***Superman: Lex 2000* #1**

Lex Luthor's campaign for the White House concluded in the *Superman: Lex 2000* one-shot. Consisting of four short stories written by Jeph Loeb and one by Greg Rucka, the special showed the buildup to the announcement of Luthor's victory and its effect on his enemies. The stories included a piece by WGBS TV reporter Catherine Grant on Lex's life (with art by Tony Harris); Batman warning Luthor that he would be watching (pencilled by Dwayne Turner); and Superman taking his rage out on a passing comet (art by Ed McGuinness). The election result made Luthor more menacing—as he had the whole government behind him.

IN THE REAL WORLD...

January: Wikipedia, the online encyclopedia, is launched on the Internet.
March: *Gladiator* wins Best Picture at the 73rd Annual Academy Awards®.

FEBRUARY

GIRL POWER
***Zero Girl* #1**

Teenager Amy Smootster had a problem: Every time she was embarrassed her feet grew wet, circles seemed to give her strange powers, and squares were trying to kill her. Writer and artist Sam Kieth's tale of teenage alienation was both surreal and touching as outcast Amy struggled to understand her peculiar connection to circles and her growing feelings for Mr. Foster, the guidance counselor at her school. It was also further proof of Sam Kieth's unique vision as a storyteller.

MARCH

HAL JORDAN RETURNS
***The Spectre* #1**

The new Spectre gained his own series following on from 1999's *Day of Judgment*. Writer J. M. DeMatteis and artist Ryan Sook brought a more human aspect to the Spectre who, under Hal Jordan's influence, began to use his god-given power to redeem people rather than punish them. Jordan was accompanied by the spirit of Abin Sur (the Green Lantern Hal originally inherited his ring from), and the series followed Jordan not only judging the guilty but also seeking answers about his own troubled existence.

GORDON SHOT
***Batman* #587**

The seven-part "Officer Down" storyline stretched over the *Batman* family of titles as Commissioner Gordon was shot and left for dead. The first chapter, written by Greg Rucka and drawn by Rick Burchett, began with Gordon celebrating his birthday in a bar and ended with an image of Gordon in a pool of blood, with three bullet holes in his back. The only witness was Catwoman, who was accidentally shot and injured by Gordon as he collapsed. Gordon's allies rallied to find the culprit. He was revealed to be ex-Mafia member Jordan Reynolds, whom Gordon had arrested years earlier. While the police failed to make Reynolds pay, a final shot in *Gotham Knights* #13 (March 2001) showed Reynolds' apartment empty with a bloodstain on the floor.

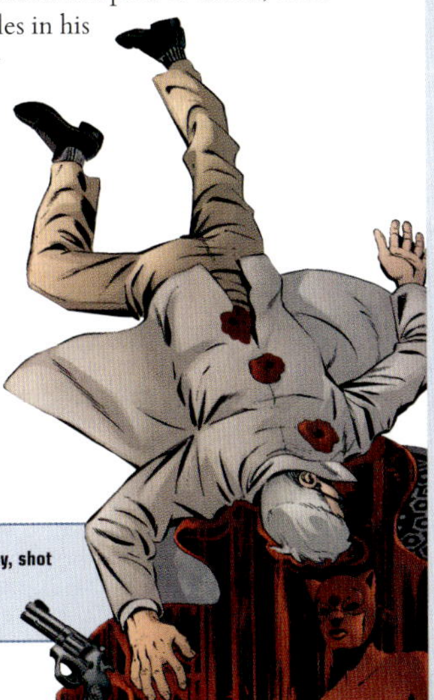

Commissioner Gordon lies in a Gotham City alleyway, shot in the back by a mystery assailant, an injured Catwoman the only witness.

APRIL

BACK FROM THE DEAD
***Green Arrow* [second series] #1**

Oliver Queen had died saving Metropolis from a terrorist attack in *Green Arrow* #101 (October 1995). While his successor, Connor Hawke, had his own fans, most readers still wanted Oliver Queen as the Green Arrow. Enter Kevin Smith, writer and director of the 1994 cult movie *Clerks*. Smith teamed up with artist Phil Hester and accomplished the impossible—they brought Oliver Queen back from the dead and did so in a way readers not only accepted but also applauded.

"Quiver," the ten-part story that helped launch the new series, opened with a cinematic view of Oliver Queen's life and showed how those who cared for him were still coming to terms with their loss. The first issue ended with a green-garbed figure launching an attack on a seedy party run by a corrupt councillor. However, it wasn't until issue two that a living Oliver was seen in all his glory, saving the future Speedy, Mia Dearden, from the councillor before returning to his temporary home, the brownstone of his friend Stanley Dover.

Over the course of "Quiver," Smith revealed that it was Oliver's old friend Hal Jordan who had returned him to life while Hal had been endowed with cosmic powers. There was one problem though—Oliver lacked a soul. With the help of Hal (now in the form of the Spectre), Oliver journeyed to Heaven to meet his soul. However, it wasn't until a climactic fight with Stanley (who turned out to be a devil-worshipping child-killer) that Ollie's soul returned to Earth and Ollie's body, making the Green Arrow whole once more.

Back from the dead, Green Arrow faces off against child-killer Stanley Dover.

April: In the Netherlands, an Act allowing same-sex couples to legally marry goes into effect.

May: Bayern Munich wins the UEFA Champions League.

July: The world's first self-contained artificial heart is implanted in a patient.

AUGUST

A LITTLE BIT OF DELIRIUM

The Little Endless Storybook

Child versions of Morpheus (a.k.a. the Sandman) and his family, known as the Little Endless, had first appeared in *The Sandman* #40 (August 1992), and proved to be exceptionally popular with fans. This made a Little Endless story almost inevitable. *The Little Endless Storybook*, written and lovingly illustrated by Jill Thompson in the style of a young children's picture book, told the story of the Endless's Delirium and her dog, Barnabas, in which he was separated from his strange mistress and tried to find her. His quest took him to the realms of Delirium's brothers and sisters—including Death and Morpheus.

OUR WORLDS AT WAR

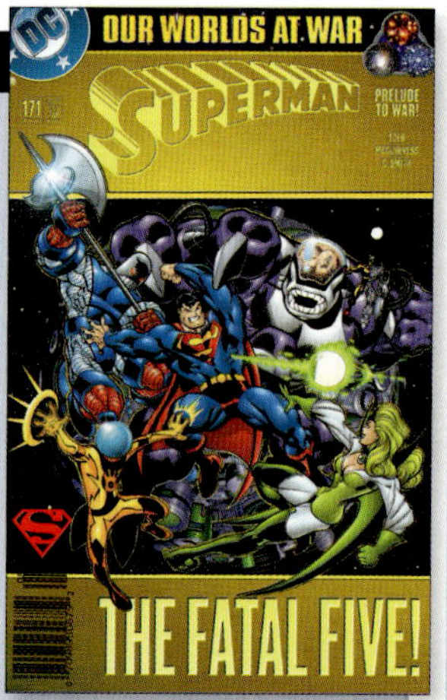

***Superman* [second series] #171**

Superman and many of the world's most powerful heroes went to war as the cosmically powered Imperiex threatened the whole galaxy. The multipart story "Our Worlds At War" dominated the Superman books for the August and September cover dates and also included Wonder Woman's title and a number of one-shots. While the central threat to Earth appeared to be Imperiex, the war was actually a manipulation by Brainiac 13 who had planned to use the heroes to steal Imperiex's power and take over the universe. The opening chapter, written by Jeph Loeb and drawn by Ed McGuinness, began with Superman investigating the missing Pluto, which had been replaced by Warworld (a battleworld created by aliens and first seen in 1980's *DC Comics Presents* #27). While exploring the planet, Superman came under attack from the Fatal Five, only to realize they were projections of Warworld itself. It was the opening barrage of a war that would involve the New Gods and conclude with Superman sending Imperiex and Brainiac 13 back in time to the Big Bang, the only way of destroying them without annihilating the universe.

Superman takes the fight to Imperiex only to find the galaxy-destroying entity is more than a match for even his amazing strength.

SEPTEMBER

IMAGINE THIS

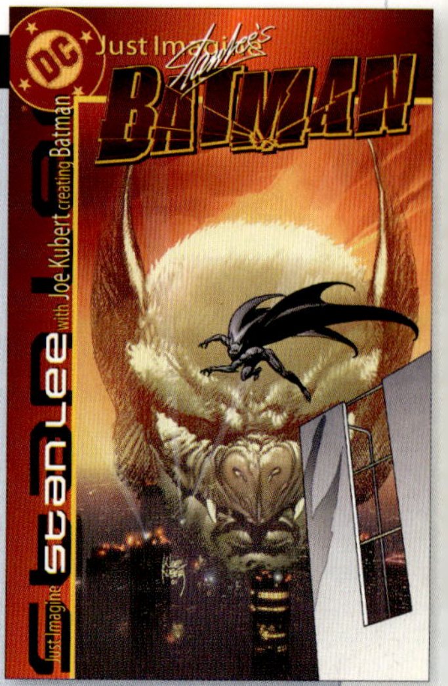

Just Imagine: Stan Lee's Batman

It was quite a coup. Stan "the Man" Lee, ex-Editor-In-Chief of Marvel Comics and the writer responsible for co-creating most of Marvel's greatest heroes swapped sides to write for DC. Teaming up with comicdom's top artists, Lee put his own unique take on DC's iconic heroes. The series consisted of thirteen prestige format books and started with Batman, drawn by art legend Joe Kubert. Lee's Batman was Wayne Williams, a black teenager jailed for a crime he didn't commit. Wayne wanted revenge for the murder of his father by the local mobster called Handz. In jail, Williams was befriended by Frederick Grant who urged Wayne to make more of himself. After several years, Wayne was released. He still wanted to bring Handz to justice but needed money to put his plans into action. Creating a new identity for himself, Wayne became a professional wrestler called the Batman, soon becoming rich and famous. Wayne used his wealth to hire Grant, who upgraded his wrestling costume, so it could be used to help Wayne fight crime. At long last he confronted Handz, who fell to his death during their fight. A subplot ran through each book as the Reverend Darkk tried to bring his evil master, Crisis, to Earth. After introducing his take on Batman and then Superman, Stan Lee brought the JLA together for a series of adventures as they tried to save the world from the Reverend Darkk's plans and ultimately from the demonic Crisis.

Wayne Williams bases his Batman alter ego on his wrestling identity, using an advanced version of the costume to fight crime.

OCTOBER

ON TV THIS MONTH: *SMALLVILLE* started on The WB TV. The show, developed by Alfred Gough and Miles Millar, was based on the adventures of Clark Kent (played by Tom Welling) before he became Superman, as he learned to come to terms with his powers and his Kryptonian origins. Joined in the early seasons by Lana Lang (Kristin Kreuk) and Lex Luthor (Michael Rosenbaum), the show proved to be a ratings smash and was still going strong in 2010 after nine seasons. In later episodes, *SMALLVILLE* also introduced other DC heroes to TV such as the Green Arrow, the Martian Manhunter, and even the Justice Society of America...

IN THE REAL WORLD...

July: The twenty-seventh G8 summit takes place in Genoa, Italy amid massive demonstrations from anti-globalization groups.

September: Almost 3,000 people are killed in the September 11 terror attacks at the World Trade Center in New York City and the Pentagon in Washington.

NOVEMBER

TANK COMMANDER
***War Story: Johann's Tiger* #1**

Garth Ennis, the writer behind *Preacher*, brought his keen knowledge of World War II to bear on *War Story: Johann's Tiger*, the first of four sixty-four-page stand-alone tales set during the conflict. Each issue was illustrated by a different artist, with Chris Weston drawing the first, entitled *Johann's Tiger*. Set during the last days of World War II, *Johann's Tiger* followed the attempt of Nazi tank commander Johann Kleist to get his squad to the American lines, so they could surrender to enemies more friendly than the invading Soviets. The grim and realistic story wasn't afraid to show the true horrors of war, with Johann traumatized by the terrible acts he had committed. He felt that he deserved to die as punishment for his war-crimes, but only after he had given his squad, who were guilty only of being in the wrong place at the wrong time, a chance to live. The story ended on a tragic note as his crew died fighting Soviet forces, but saving Johann's life in the process. Future *War Story* titles dealt with the D-Day Dodgers (following the invasion of Italy), the last days of Easy Company, and a tragic story about the war at sea.

Tank Commander Johann Kleist recalls the many acts of evil he has committed in the name of the Third Reich. His only wish is to help his innocent tank crew survive the war.

DECEMBER

HE WHO LAUGHS LAST
***Joker: Last Laugh* #1**

After discovering he had a deadly brain tumor, the Joker decided to go out with a bang and take the world with him. Opening with the Joker coming to terms with his mortality, part one followed his escape from the Slab (a prison for meta-humans). Meanwhile, Barbara Gordon took a night off from being Oracle to have dinner with Dick Grayson (Nightwing) and wasn't there to react to the Joker's escape. Published weekly and written by Chuck Dixon and Scott Beatty (with art in issue #1 by Pete Woods), *Joker: Last Laugh* crossed over into all the mainstream DC titles as the world's heroes tried to stop the Joker's plan to use his Joker Venom on the world.

ON TV THIS MONTH: The Justice League finally gained their own animated television show. The series ran for five seasons, ending in 2006.

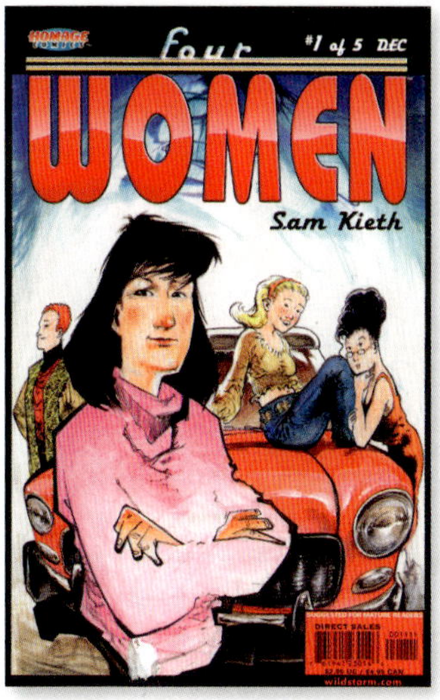

BREAKDOWN
***Four Women* #1**

Writer/artist Sam Kieth's work had always been slightly edgier than most, even when working on mainstream books. This was especially true on *Four Women*. Published by Homage, *Four Women* was a tough thriller about sexual assault and survivor guilt. The story was told in flashback as Donna gave her psychiatrist details of a vicious attack that had happened while she was on her way to a wedding with three female friends. Sam Kieth's realistic story made the horrific acts even more disturbing.

FURTHER ADVENTURES OF THE DARK KNIGHT
***The Dark Knight Strikes Again* #1**

Writer and artist Frank Miller returned to one of his greatest works in *The Dark Knight Strikes Again*, a follow up to 1986's *Batman: The Dark Knight*. Released as three prestige-format books, it was set three years after the original and followed the aging Batman as he led a revolution against a totalitarian state ruled by Lex Luthor and Brainiac. The series proved controversial as Miller experimented with style and color and turned Dick Grayson into a new incarnation of the Joker.

ALSO THIS YEAR: Star Trek came to WildStorm in February with *STAR TREK: THE NEXT GENERATION*... Slam Bradley, a private eye barely seen since the 1940s, reappeared in a back-up strip in *DETECTIVE COMICS* #759 in August on the lookout for Catwoman... Doom Patrol returned with a new series in December...

September: Letters containing deadly anthrax spores are mailed from Princeton, New Jersey to several U.S. news channels and newspapers, killing five people.

October: The United States invades Afghanistan, with participation from other countries.
October: Michael Schumacher wins the Formula One World Championship by a record margin.

CREATIVE FORCE

The 2000s were significant years for many important DC creative talents, and the decade also planted the seeds of change for DC Comics as a company.

Writer/artist Jim Lee became an overnight comic book sensation after producing his first art for Marvel Comics in the late 1980s. He soon became one of the X-Men's most popular artists before leaving to form Image Comics with six fellow creators. Lee established the WildStorm imprint at Image to publish such hit titles as *WildC.A.T.S* and *Gen^{13}*.

Over the next decade, WildStorm produced several critically acclaimed comics, including *The Authority* and *Planetary*, and became a home to Alan Moore's award-winning ABC imprint. Although Lee was successful, he missed his first love—illustration. He joined DC Comics in 1998, bringing his WildStorm imprint with him. Lee went on to produce some of the best work of his career at DC, including *Batman: Hush*, *Superman: For Tomorrow*, and *All Star Batman and Robin, the Boy Wonder*, all in the 2000s.

Almost paralleling Jim Lee's career path, Geoff Johns quickly rose through the DC ranks, becoming one of the company's most trusted writers. He penned *Stars and S.T.R.I.P.E.* and enjoyed a critically acclaimed run on *The Flash* before writing two of DC's most significant series of the decade: *Infinite Crisis* (December 2005–June 2006) and *Blackest Night* (June 2009–May 2010).

The link between creative success and chart success was clear in the 2000s, and DC Comics began the next decade with this in mind. A company restructure led to two of the five new top positions being given to creatives: Jim Lee became Co-publisher and Geoff Johns became Chief Creative Officer. While creatives had held executive positions before—artist Carmine Infantino had been Editorial Director then Publisher from the late 1960s to the mid-1970s and writer Paul Levitz had been President and Publisher in the 2000s—the new appointments felt like something different. Comic fans sensed that DC's new president, Diane Nelson, was giving the talent more of a say in the company's direction than ever before.

The appointment of Lee and Johns reflected DC's acknowledgment of the vital importance of artists and writers to its continued success. The company made a conscious effort to build on the creative successes of the past and use them to expand far beyond comic books. In fact, Lee and Johns are due to oversee the transition of Green Lantern from the printed page to the big screen in 2011, as DC Entertainment takes its first steps into big-screen moviemaking.

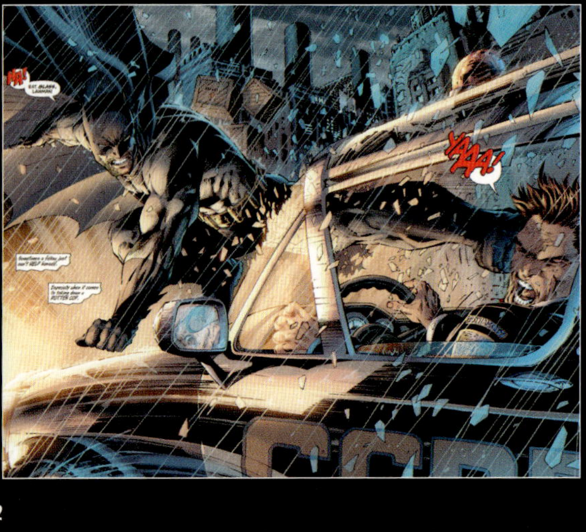

Left: "Ha! Eat glass, Lawman!" Superstar creators writer Frank Miller and penciller Jim Lee teamed up for All Star Batman & Robin, the Boy Wonder, *a series retelling the story of Bruce Wayne's famous ward. Main picture: Jim Lee's pencils for the same image (from #6, September 2007) reveals his mastery of the medium.*

GOTHAMCITY

2002

"YOU KNOW YOU CAN'T RESIST ME. NO MAN—OR WOMAN—CAN."

Poison Ivy, *Batman* #608

ONCE UPON A TIME

2002 was the year DC went into overdrive. Both DC and its Vertigo imprint stepped up a gear to create some of their best series to date. Vertigo launched *Fables* and *Y: The Last Man*, two titles that would go on to garner both critical praise and numerous awards, and Grant Morrison produced *The Filth*, one of his most coolly bizarre works since 1994's *The Invisibles*. In the mainstream DC Universe, Jim Lee produced his first major story arc for DC since his WildStorm imprint joined the company in 1999. Entitled "Hush," the arc started in *Batman* #608 and was written by Jeph Loeb. Lee and Loeb's work on this twelve-part epic put *Batman* back on top of the sales charts and set up plotlines that would echo through the rest of the decade. Along with all this, Catwoman reappeared with a new look and a brand new series. It was just the beginning of DC's resurgence.

JANUARY

DARK END OF THE STREET

***Catwoman* [second series] #1**

One of DC's longest running characters got a makeover courtesy of writer Ed Brubaker and artist Darwyn Cooke as *Catwoman* was relaunched. Catwoman had already gone through several changes since her first appearance in *Batman* #1 (Spring 1940), but Brubaker's was one of the most dramatic. Her first solo series had ended after ninety-four issues in July 2001 with Catwoman's apparent death at the hands of Deathstroke, the Terminator. Since then Selina Kyle had been keeping a low profile, with many believing her to be dead. "The Trail of the Catwoman," a back-up strip in 2001's *Detective Comics* #759–762, had private investigator Slam Bradley searching for proof that Catwoman was alive. Kyle visited Bradley to explain her actions and urge him not to reveal the fact that she had faked her own death. The new series started a short time after and had Selina going through some major changes. She hadn't used her Catwoman costume for six months, and was seeing Leslie Thompkins, a therapist recommended by Batman, to talk through her problems. With her hair cut short, Selina ditched her old outfit for a slinky and (according to an approving Batman) more sensible black leather one.

The opening story arc, "Anodyne," dealt with Catwoman's return to her old neighborhood of Gotham's East End and her worries that she might revert to her old ways. The main villain was a shape-changing serial killer who had been bringing terror to the East End's prostitutes. With Brubaker's tight, noir-like scripting and Darwyn Cooke's stylish artwork, *Catwoman*'s new direction made the character more popular than ever.

The new-look Catwoman takes to the streets of Gotham City's East End, trying to protect some of her old friends from predators.

IN THE REAL WORLD...

January: Euro banknotes and coins are launched in twelve countries.
January: The No Child Left Behind education act is signed into law in the U.S.

JANUARY

ANIMATED HEROICS

***Justice League Adventures* #1**

Fresh from the success of their animated show, the Justice League gained a new title produced in the style of the 2001 hit Cartoon Network series. The first issue was written by Ty Templeton and illustrated by Bruce Tim. It saw the Justice League battling an alien trying to save his people by finding a way of stopping his mortal enemy, only for his quest to threaten Earth with destruction. The mini-epic was graced with a vivid Alex Ross cover.

MARCH

BATMAN: MURDERER

***Batman: The 10 Cent Adventure* #1**

Batman's alter ego was framed for murder in the first part of his latest epic. The first issue cost 10 cents and was the perfect introduction for new and old readers. On returning home from a night fighting crime, Bruce Wayne discovered the body of Vesper Fairchild, his ex-girlfriend, in Wayne Manor. The police were there far too quickly and Bruce was framed for murder. Eventually Lex Luthor was revealed as the mastermind behind the frame, but it took some time for Batman to clear his alter ego's name.

MEET ALEX LUTHOR

***The Adventures of Superman* #600**

To celebrate the 600th issue of *The Adventures of Superman*, the Man of Steel had a super-sized anniversary issue pitting him against Lex Luthor—or Alex Luthor. Superman's old enemy (and now President of the U.S.A.) went missing from the White House after an assassination attempt. Wearing a wig, Lex became Alex Luthor, a reckless version of Lex that he had always kept buried in his subconscious. With a script by Joe Casey and art by Mike Wieringo, the issue included a twelve-page poster section and a humorous take on the Superman newspaper strip.

Superman races to stop Alex Luthor after the Man of Steel's nemesis has a personality change and allows his more dangerous side loose.

A STORY TO REMEMBER

9-11: September 11th, 2001

Following the terrorist attacks on America on September 11, 2001, comic creators from all companies produced benefit books for the victims. DC Comics coordinated the launch of their title with Dark Horse Publishing to reach as many readers as possible. The full title of DC's book was *9-11: September 11th, 2001 (The World's Finest Comic Book Writers and Artists Tell Stories to Remember) Volume Two*. Dark Horse had published volume one. It brought together many of the company's top creators for an anthology of stories based on or around the events of 9/11. Made up of different sections, each with their own distinctive style, creative talent included Will Eisner, Michael Moorcock, Dennis O'Neil, George Pérez, Marv Wolfman, Neal Adams, Geoff Johns, Alex Ross, Paul Levitz, and Jim Lee. Neil Gaiman contributed a new story of the Endless entitled "The Wheel" (drawn by Chris Bachalo), while Amanda Conner and Jimmy Palmiotti created "Silver Linings in Big Clouds of Dust." The stories ranged from those dealing with the attack itself and the aftermath to more super heroic and fantasy-based tales. Everyone involved in the title's creation worked for free, with all of the profits that were made benefitting The New York State World Trade Center Relief Fund, Survivors of the National Campaign Region, and The September 11th Fund of the New York Community Trust among others.

DC Comics' top creators come together for a special 9-11 charity book.

MAY

OLD TESTAMENT

King David

Writer and artist Kyle Baker created a unique version of one of the Old Testament's best known stories, David and Goliath. Based on the life of the King of the Israelites, the graphic novel remained true to the source material while also being fresh and full of attitude. Baker's artwork added drama to every page, especially in his use of color. The story included the major events from King David's life, starting with the fight with Goliath and finishing with the birth of his son after his affair with Bathsheba.

February: Kidnapped U.S. newspaper reporter Daniel Pearl is murdered in Karachi, Pakistan.
March: *A Beautiful Mind* wins Best Picture at the 74th Annual Academy Awards®.

April: The funeral of Queen Elizabeth, the Queen Mother of the United Kingdom takes place in Westminster Abbey, London.

JULY

HAPPILY EVER AFTER

***Fables* #1**

Vertigo published the first issue of writer Bill Willingham's contemporary take on the fantastical characters from fairy tales in what would become one of the imprint's best-loved publications, *Fables*. With artist Lan Medina on board for the first story arc, Willingham introduced a host of characters mostly living in Fabletown, an almost-hidden district of New York. The series opened with a mystery: Snow White's sister Rose Red had gone missing and was believed to have been murdered. Fabletown's head of security, Bigby Wolf (better known as the Big Bad Wolf), was sent in to investigate—and uncovered a number of suspects for the murder, including Jack (the Giant Killer) and the often-divorced Prince Charming (ex-husband of Snow White, Sleeping Beauty, and Cinderella). The first issue introduced some of *Fables'* vast cast, including Beauty and the Beast. The happy couple had problems, as Beast's curse would return when his wife was annoyed with him, turning him beast-like again and making it hard to blend in with New York's residents. Future issues revealed more of Fable history, and introduced their main enemy, the Adversary, who had driven them from their homelands. *Fables* went on to win many awards, including a 2003 Eisner award for Best New Series.

The Adversary faces off against the Fables during the creation of his Empire, forcing many Fables to flee the Homelands to New York.

AUGUST

VERY WEIRD TALES

***The Filth* #1**

Even by writer Grant Morrison's standards, *The Filth* was wonderfully strange. With artwork by Chris Weston and Gary Erskine, it followed the adventures of Officer Slade, an agent for an inter-reality agency known as the Hand. The first issue showed Slade hiding out from the Hand in a para-personality of Greg Feely, only to be tracked down by ex-colleague Nil and forced to return to duty. With highly designed covers by Segura Inc., *The Filth* pushed the boundaries of storytelling.

THE ORIGINAL GREEN LANTERN

Green Lantern: Brightest Day, Blackest Night

Written by Steven T. Seagle and painted by John K. Snyder III, the prestige-format *Brightest Day, Blackest Night* turned the clock back to 1944 to show the original Green Lantern in action against the Nazis and Solomon Grundy. As Nazi spies attempted to steal the Zeta Wave machine, which could make their forces invisible, they made a fatal error of landing in Slaughter Swamp, home of Solomon Grundy. Before long, Grundy was on their trail, like a dark force of nature. The Golden Age Green Lantern, Alan Scott, was caught in the middle as Grundy and the Nazis fought. Ultimately a train put an end to Grundy, and Green Lantern's allies in the JSA helped him to remove the Nazis from U.S. soil.

Alan Scott, the original Green Lantern, confronts Solomon Grundy while the Nazis wait in the wings.

SEPTEMBER

KRYPTON LIVES

***Superman* [second series] #184**

Superman met his father Jor-El in the first part of "Return to Krypton." The story started in *Superman* #184 as Jor-El escaped to Earth to request his son's superhuman help to fight fascist zealots close to taking over Krypton. Scripted by Geoff Johns and illustrated by Pasqual Ferry, the story delivered an emotional punch as Superman and his father were reunited. Superman was suspicious, though, as it all seemed too good to be true. Traveling to Krypton with his father and Krypto, Superman joined in the fight against the fascists before realising the terrible truth—the whole of the planet was a trap created by Brainiac 13. The story continued in *The Adventures of Superman* #606 and *Superman: The Man of Steel* #128, and concluded in *Action Comics* #793, with a touching finale as Jor-El gave his life to stop Brainiac 13's plans.

IN THE REAL WORLD...

May: The U.S.State Department releases a report naming seven state sponsors of terrorism: Iran, Iraq, Cuba, Libya, North Korea, Sudan, and Syria.

June: Brazil wins the FIFA World Cup for a record fifth time.

July: The International Criminal Court is established.

GENDERCIDE

***Y: The Last Man* #1**

Written by Brian K. Vaughan and illustrated by Pia Guerra, *Y: The Last Man* was one of Vertigo's most original series in years. It told the story of life after every male creature in the world had been wiped out by a mysterious plague—every male apart from would-be escape artist Yorick Brown and his pet monkey, Ampersand. The first page threw the reader straight into the moment that men died before flashing back twenty-nine minutes to introduce the main cast: Yorick, Ampersand, a tough spy known as Agent 355, and Doctor Allison Mann, who was about to give birth to her own male clone. Over the course of the sixty-issue series, Vaughan showed a world slowly rebuilding itself from disaster, as some women managed to handle the chaotic aftermath of the gendercide better than others. With distinctively painted covers by J.G. Jones, Yorick's quest to reach his fiancé, Beth Deville, in Australia proved gripping right up to its touching and thoughtful conclusion.

As the last male alive in the world, escape artist Yorick Brown finds himself a wanted man, with new groups like the Amazons willing to go to any lengths to capture or kill him.

MARTIAN MAN HUNTERS

***The League of Extraordinary Gentlemen* [second series] #1**

The first series of *The League of Extraordinary Gentlemen* had launched Alan Moore's America's Best Comics (ABC) line in 1999, and it proved to be one of the writer's most popular works. With Kevin O'Neill outdoing his own high standards on the art, series two continued the adventures of Allan Quatermain's band of adventurers. This time the group faced invaders from Mars. The first issue set the scene, with John Carter and Lt. Gullivar Jones defeating the aliens on Mars and driving them off the planet to Earth.

DECEMBER

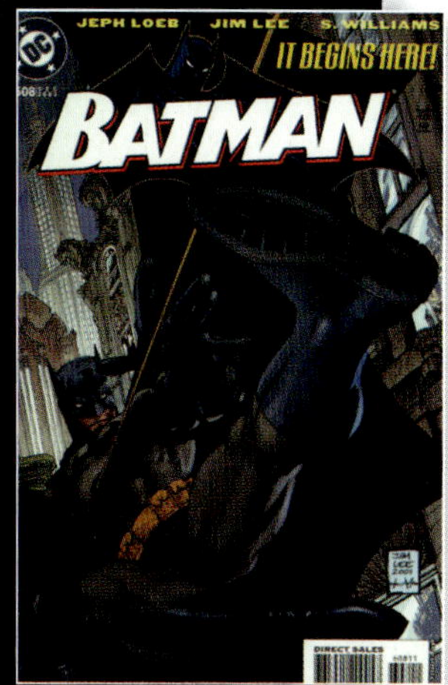

JIM LEE UNLEASHED

***Batman* #608**

The "Hush" story arc in *Batman* #608 was artist Jim Lee's first major work since he joined DC as Editorial Director in 1999. Written by Jeph Loeb, "Hush" brought profound changes to the life of the Dark Knight. The twelve-part saga was the comic book equivalent of a movie blockbuster, with breakneck speed and dynamic art. The first issue was packed with action as Batman took on a rampaging Killer Croc before pursuing Catwoman across Gotham City. When someone cut Batman's cable and the Dark Knight fell to Gotham's streets, fracturing his skull, Catwoman left him to his fate.

Thomas Elliott, a childhood friend of Bruce's and now a brain surgeon, saved Batman's life and the Dark Knight began to investigate. He found that Poison Ivy had been controlling Catwoman and was now controlling Superman, yet did not appear to be the mastermind behind a wave of crimes committed by Batman's enemies. Neither was Rā's al Ghūl, who was for while implicated in what seemed to be an anti-Batman plot.

Loeb provided various misdirections to the true identity of the mastermind—Hush—before the culprit was revealed to be Thomas Elliott. Or at least, Hush claimed to be Elliott. As a child, he had tried to kill his mother for her inheritance but Bruce Wayne's father had saved her life. Learning of Bruce's identity, Elliot had decided to take revenge on the Batman. As Hush and Batman fought, Hush was shot by Two-Face, his body crashing into the waters near Gotham. The series had two more twists: Batman worked out that the real instigator of events had been the Riddler and Jason Todd's grave was empty.

The young Bruce Wayne plays chess with his childhood friend Thomas Elliott, whose return years later would coincide with the arrival of the mysterious Hush, one of the deadliest villains Batman has ever faced.

ALSO THIS YEAR: Writer Doug Moench and art legend Paul Gulacy produced the futuristic thriller *S.C.I. SPY* for Vertigo in April… Artist Darwyn Cooke handled the writing and art for October's graphic novel *CATWOMAN: SELINA'S BIG SCORE*… Writer Garth Ennis and artist Glenn Fabry gave the Authority their toughest time yet as they met ex-SAS operative Kev in *AUTHORITY: KEV* in October…

October: The Beltway snipers of Washington, D.C. are arrested.
November: United Nations weapons inspectors, led by Hans Blix, arrive in Iraq.
December: United Airlines, the second-largest airline in the world, files for bankruptcy.
December: The U.N .Population Division calculates forty million people are infected with HIV.

2003

"I'M ABOVE ALL THIS. WAY ABOVE IT."

Conner Kent, *Teen Titans* #1

NEW DIRECTIONS

2003 was a year of renewal for DC Comics. Some of the company's most popular titles, such as the *Teen Titans,* were reinvigorated with strong new creative teams and bold new directions. In a similar vein, Superman and Batman teamed up as heroes of their own regular title for the first time since the demise of *World's Finest Comics* in January 1986. Writers were rapidly increasing in importance, and their roles would be vital to the company's success in the years that followed. With *Superman: Birthright*, writer Mark Waid reimagined the Man of Steel for a new generation, creating a contemporary and exciting take on Superman's early years, while at the same time bringing in elements from the successful *Smallville* TV series. By the end of the year, DC's titles were gaining praise from across fandom, and the scene was set for even greater commercial and creative success in the years to follow.

JANUARY

Amy Smootster was all grown up in the follow up to Sam Keith's Zero Girl—but squares were soon causing her problems.

ZERO THE HERO

***Zero Girl: Full Circle* #1**

The follow-up to writer and artist Sam Kieth's cult classic was set fifteen years after the events of the 2001 series. This version shifted the focus from Amy Smootster and her guidance counselor Tim Foster to Tim's fifteen-year-old daughter, Nikki. Nikki proved to be just as confused as Amy had been in the original series. However, Nikki was drawn to squares rather than circles, and when her dead mother returned, she found her life taking a very strange turn. With its expanded cast and stylishly surreal artwork, Sam Kieth again proved himself to be one of comicdom's best storytellers.

FEBRUARY

GOTHAM'S FINEST

***Gotham Central* #1**

Police procedurals had always been big business on TV, but they were rare in comics. *Gotham Central* changed that with hard-hitting stories set on Gotham's mean streets. Presented by writers Ed Brubaker and Greg Rucka, with art by Michael Lark, the series followed the night and day shifts of the Gotham City Police Department. The writers split the stories between them, with Brubaker taking on tales of the night shift and Rucka the day. They worked together on the first story, an investigation into the murder of police officer Charlie Fields at the hands of Batman's old foe Mr. Freeze. Featuring a cameo from the Dark Knight, the series was nominated for several Eisners.

A NEW BOX OF TRICKS

***Hellblazer Special: Lady Constantine* #1**

First seen in *The Sandman* [second series] #13 in February 1990, Lady Constantine finally gained her own title courtesy of writer Andy Diggle and artist Goran Sudzuka. The four-issue series was set in 1785 and followed the quest of Joanna Constantine to retrieve a mysterious box, with an immortal witch trying to prevent Constantine from doing so. Featuring a cameo from an ancestor of the Swamp Thing (called Jack-in-the-Green), *Lady Constantine* was a swashbuckling addition to the Constantine mythos.

IN THE REAL WORLD...

March: The World Health Organization issues a global alert on SARS disease.

GORDON GOES SOLO

***Batgirl: Year One* #1**

Scott Beatty and Chuck Dixon came together to pen the story of Barbara Gordon's first year as Batgirl. With stylish art from Marcos Martin, the nine-part series saw Batgirl fighting Killer Moth while also detailing her reasons for becoming Batgirl. Prevented from joining the Gotham City Police Department by her father, James Gordon, and too short to join the FBI, Barbara decided to fight crime like the other masked heroes appearing in her city. The series, while light in tone, also foreshadowed Barbara's eventual fate at the hands of the psychopathic Joker.

JUNE

COMRADE OF STEEL

***Superman: Red Son* #1**

Mark Millar was never a writer to shy away from a controversial topic or from taking a unique concept to its shocking conclusion. With *Superman: Red Son*, he did both by presenting Superman as a communist and giving the conclusion a surprise twist. With art by Dave Johnson and Kilian Plunkett, *Red Son* was released as three prestige format books, each set in a different decade of the alternative Superman's life. The first book, "Red Son Rising," opened with the Soviet Union announcing Superman's existence in the 1950s through a political broadcast.

Superman's appearance triggered a new arms race as the U.S. government employed Lex Luthor to develop America's response. Superman, as Stalin's right-hand man, concluded that he could only make the world a better place by taking over the Soviet state. By the second volume ("Red Son Ascendant"), set in the 1970s, Superman was in control of the government. Soviet influence had spread across the globe, with only America and Chile holding out. In the final book, "Red Son Setting," Luthor's plan to defeat the Man of Steel came to fruition in the early 21st century, and Superman met his apparent death saving the world from an out of control Brainiac. The series contained a final twist as Earth's far future was revealed to be Superman's home world. A variation of the communist Superman later appeared in *Countdown to Infinite Crisis* and *Final Crisis*.

The communist Superman defeats a Bizarro clone created by Lex Luthor.

JULY

SCHOOL'S OUT

***Titans/Young Justice: Graduation Day* #1**

Big changes occurred to Young Justice and the Titans in *Graduation Day*, a three-issue miniseries written by Judd Winick and pencilled by Alé Garza. After an attack from the future by a damaged robot, the Titans and Young Justice joined forces to stop it. The machine, later called Indigo, set a Superman robot on the heroes, and it killed Omen and Donna Troy. The robots were stopped, but the deaths led to both teams splitting up. Some members, such as Nightwing and Arsenal, became part of a new Outsiders lineup, while the core of Young Justice graduated into a new Teen Titans group.

ON TV THIS MONTH: The Teen Titans got a stylish animated series on Cartoon Network. It lasted for five seasons, ending in 2006...

AUGUST

WARCRIMES

***The Losers* #1**

Writer Andy Diggle and artist Jock's new version of *The Losers* had nothing to do with the 1970s original group that appeared in *Our Fighting Heroes*. Stylish and violent, the new Losers were an ex-CIA Black Ops team betrayed and left for dead by their own handlers. Their motivation was simple—to clear their names and find the shadowy figure responsible for ordering their executions. The team consisted of Franklin Clay, a hardhearted and ruthless corporal; his right-hand man, Roque, a cold and treacherous killer; Jensen, a savvy and smart-mouth computer technician; Cougar, a cowboy-hat wearing sniper; and Sgt. Linwood "Pooch" Porteous, the team's pilot.

In the opening issue the renegades were joined by the mercenary Aisha, who was raised on the Afghan/Pakistan border and spent most of her childhood fighting (and killing) the Soviet invaders. The title lasted for thirty-two issues and was an intelligent mix of action, dark humor, and political conspiracies. A movie version appeared in 2010.

Franklin Clay is the leader of the Losers. Motivated by a clear sense of right and wrong, he wants to reveal the CIA's illegal activities to the world.

March: Land troops from the United States, United Kingdom, Australia, and Poland invade Iraq.

May: In Casablanca, Morocco, thirty-three civilians are killed and more than one hundred are injured in a series of terrorist attacks.

SEPTEMBER

TITANS TOGETHER

Teen Titans [third series] #1

The Teen Titans had been one of DC's most popular teams of the 1980s, and while successive series had been well-received, none had reached the heights of the Marv Wolfman and George Pérez era until writer Geoff Johns and artist Mike McKone's relaunch.

Following the events of *Titans/Young Justice: Graduation Day*, Cyborg and Starfire decided to form a new team of Teen Titans to train the next generation of heroes. The team was partly made up of the former members of Young Justice: Robin (Tim Drake), Wonder Girl, and Impulse (who renamed himself Kid Flash shortly after joining). The new lineup was eventually completed with the return of Raven. The first story arc, "Child's Play," put the new team through their paces as their old foe Deathstroke set out to kill them. The team soon learned that Deathstroke was being possessed by his son, Jericho, an old Titan long thought dead. Jericho was insane and wanted to stop the team reforming, hoping to prevent more deaths like his own. The series succeeded in pleasing fans of all eras with its mix of old and new characters. Writer Geoff Johns also brought characterization to the foreground, making the reader feel empathy toward the teenage heroes. It wasn't long before *The Teen Titans* was one of DC's bestselling titles once again.

The new lineup of the Teen Titans included (clockwise from bottom left) Beast Boy, Robin, Starfire, Raven, Cyborg, Superboy, Kid Flash, and Wonder Girl.

SEPTEMBER

SUPERMAN BEGINS AGAIN

***Superman: Birthright* #1**

Superman's post-*Crisis on Infinite Earth*'s origin had remained lore since John Byrne's seminal *Man of Steel* series in 1986, but by 2003 it was time for an update. Writer Mark Waid was joined by artists Leinil Francis Yu and Gerry Alanguilan to create the twelve-part story charting Superman's first appearance. While remaining faithful to the basic tenets of Byrne's version, Waid's version had a few new additions—the most notable being that the Kents were now younger and Lex Luthor was now a childhood acquaintance of Clark's (as he had been in Superman's pre-*Crisis* origin). The story moved between Clark's childhood in Smallville and his first appearance as a hero in Metropolis, adding Clark's missing year spent in West Africa. It was Clark's time in West Africa that inspired him to become a hero and utilize his Kryptonian heritage in a dramatic costume. The series packed a real emotional punch, with the new childhood connection between Clark and Lex making their now enmity all the more powerful, and Superman coming across as more "human" than ever before. The crux of the story involved Lex seeking to utilize Kryptonian technology and imagery (gained by a sub-space communicator he created) to establish a link between Earth and Krypton. Luthor's aim was to strengthen his hold on Metropolis and discredit Superman by launching a fake Kryptonian invasion of the city. Superman (helped by Jimmy Olsen and Lois Lane) saved the day, revealing the truth behind the invasion and Lex's treachery. The series ended touchingly, with Superman's Kryptonian parents receiving a message from Kal-El telling them that their son had arrived on Earth safely.

A young Clark Kent saves his friends and learns some hard lessons about the world while traveling through Africa.

IN THE REAL WORLD...

August: Global oil production begins a four-year plateau (and subsequent decline) in the face of rising demand, causing price increases.

October: The Concorde makes its last commercial flight, bringing the era of airliner supersonic travel to a close.

COSMIC TEAM-UP!

***JLA/Avengers* #1**

It was an event that had taken over a decade to come to fruition and proved to be one of the biggest and best of the DC and Marvel crossovers, incorporating many of the two companies' greatest heroes and villains. The crossover had originally been planned for 1983, with artist George Pérez having drawn thirty pages before the book was postponed. While Pérez still handled the art for the 2003 version, the script was by Kurt Busiek, a writer with an encyclopedic knowledge of both DC and Marvel history. It was clear from the opening that both talents were going to have fun with the concept.

With the JLA facing off against Avengers' foe Terminus and the Avengers facing Starro, it wasn't long before more elements of both universes started to cross over. Each team became unwittingly embroiled in a fight between the Grandmaster (one of Marvel's cosmic Elders of the Universe) and Krona, a DC immortal with the power to destroy galaxies. The two teams were at first pitted against each other to gain twelve powerful artifacts, but they soon realized the scale of the threat and united to stop it. Filled with high drama and enough nods to continuity to please even the most rabid fanboy, the cover image of the final volume, with a battered Superman holding Captain America's shield and Thor's hammer, was one of the most powerful images of the decade.

Superman fights to save two universes, armed with Thor's hammer—Mjolnir—and Captain America's shield.

KILLER ON THE LOOSE

***Red* #1**

Writer Warren Ellis' three-issue miniseries was short, sharp, and extremely brutal. *Red* was a violent take on the story of an ex-operative coming out of retirement. Paul Moses, a troubled ex-CIA agent, returned to the violent ways of his past when the CIA placed a kill order on him to prevent him returning to their ranks. The story followed Moses' blood-soaked path to CIA headquarters to track down those individuals responsible for the order. Cully Hammer's art provided the perfect foil for Ellis' tight script, and the series was soon optioned for a big-screen adaptation for release in 2010, starring Bruce Willis, Morgan Freeman, and John Malkovich.

THE WORLD'S GREATEST HEROES?

***Formerly Known as the Justice League* #1**

For many, the 1987 Justice League series was a highlight of that decade. In 2003, writers J. M. DeMatteis and Keith Giffen and original artist Kevin Maguire worked on a six-part series reuniting the team. Maxwell Lord was again the brains of the group, seeing the team as a way of making money by marketing them as heroes of the common man. The squad members soon found themselves in an intergalactic arena fighting for their lives before stopping an invasion from their old foe Manga Khan.

OCTOBER

WORLD'S FINEST

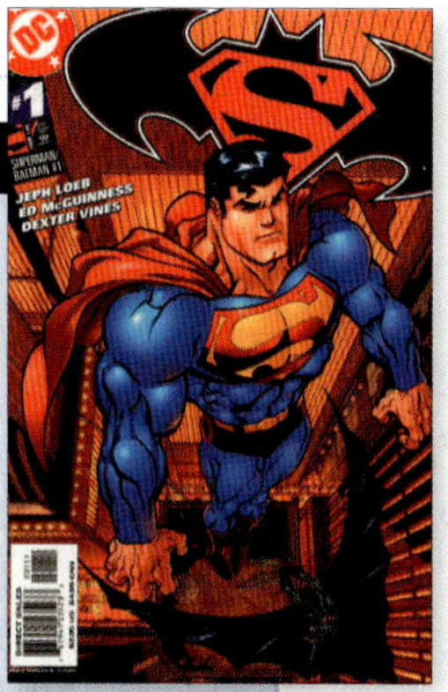

***Superman/Batman* #1**

Superman and Batman once headlined *World's Finest Comics* and were close allies, but in the reality that followed the end of *Crisis on Infinite Earths* in 1986, they had been portrayed as uneasy allies at best. *Superman/Batman* changed that and brought two of DC's biggest stars back together on a regular basis. Writer Jeph Loeb and artist Ed McGuinness created a tale befitting such A-list characters in "Public Enemies," the six-part story that launched the new series. Opening with a recap of both Batman and Superman's origins, "Public Enemies" emphasized the two heroes' different backgrounds before bringing them together to fight Superman's old enemy Metallo. The first issue ended on a dramatic note when Superman was shot with a kryptonite bullet by Metallo and buried alive with Batman. After escaping the grave, the two heroes uncovered a conspiracy by Lex Luthor to destroy Superman once and for all. A gigantic kryptonite meteorite was heading for Earth, and President Luthor, rather than enlisting Superman's aid, declared the Man of Steel responsible for its arrival and placed a bounty on his head. After saving the planet, Batman and Superman teamed up to bring Luthor to justice and finally brought his reign as president of the United States to an end.

Batman and Superman fight for their lives as a host of super-villains attempt to claim the reward promised by President Luthor for their capture.

ALSO THIS YEAR: John Byrne presented *SUPERMAN/BATMAN: GENERATIONS III* in March… *DIAL H FOR H-E-R-O* returned with a new direction in April, simply entitled *H-E-R-O*… Matt Wagner's *TRINITY*, a three-issue prestige format series charting Batman and Superman's first meeting with Wonder Woman, began in August… In October, a new series of *HUMAN TARGET* began…

October: The Florida Marlins win their second World Series title.
November: In the Rugby World Cup, England defeats Australia 20–17 after extra time.
December: Saddam Hussein, former president of Iraq, is captured in Tikrit, Iraq by the U.S. Army.

2004

"ANYONE WHO PUTS ON A COSTUME PAINTS A BULL'S EYE ON HIS FAMILY'S CHEST."

Ralph Dibny, *Identity Crisis* #1

DEATH IN THE FAMILY

In 2004 , two major series blew DC's competition out of the water and set new standards of storytelling—*Green Lantern: Rebirth* and *Identity Crisis*. *Rebirth* provided Green Lantern with his best reviews in decades and revitalized the Green Lantern Corps, while *Identity Crisis* gave DC's heroes and villains a darker tone and was not afraid to deal with contentious and startling topics. Both series also heralded the rise in importance of writers to the company. Story had always been the main force behind DC's success, but as the decade progressed, writers of the caliber of Grant Morrison, Mark Waid, Brad Meltzer, and Geoff Johns became increasingly important to the company's direction. Such writers plotted the future, not just of one year but several, bringing themes, subtext, and subplots to their work that would pay off in the years that followed.

FEBRUARY

THE QUANTUM EFFECT

***The Authority vs. Lobo: Jingle Hell* #1**

Lobo met his match in the form of the Authority's three-year-old Jenny Quantum in this one-shot special, which proved another classic addition to Lobo's adventures. Plotted by Keith Giffen, scripted by Alan Grant, and drawn by Simon Bisley, the story saw Wildstorm's Authority cross paths with Lobo when Jenny Quantum (the superpowered reincarnation of former Authority hero Jenny Sparks) came across a copy of the 1991 comic *Lobo Paramilitary Christmas Special*. Its tale of Lobo killing Santa Claus sent her into a rage, and she demanded that the Authority made Lobo pay. Her tantrum also flipped reality and made it possible for Lobo to cross over into the Wildstorm universe on his own mission—to kill the Authority. As Lobo arrived on the Authority's interdimensional carrier, a brutal yet comical confrontation took place. It only came to an end when Lobo found a copy of the comic Jenny had been reading and took her to the North Pole to see the destruction there, pointing out that she had read about it in the comic and then created it in reality. She had, in effect, killed Santa Claus. This realization made Jenny's power explode, knocking Lobo out cold.

Lobo might be the main man, but he met his match in the Authority's three-year-old Jenny Quantum.

APRIL

PULP HORROR

Lovecraft

Adapted by Keith Giffen from a screenplay by Hans Rodionoff, with beautifully painted artwork by Enrique Breccia, Vertigo's *Lovecraft* was a fictional horror novel based on the life and work of H.P. Lovecraft, one of the twentieth century's most famous pulp writers. The graphic novel combined real events from Lovecraft's life, such as his parents' insanity and his failed marriage, with a horror story about Lovecraft's fight against creatures let loose by the Necronomicon. The book could be read two ways—as the story of the writer trying to protect reality from nightmarish demons or as one man's struggle with insanity.

IN THE REAL WORLD...

January: A dead whale explodes in Tainan City, Taiwan, while being transported to a university for tests.

MAY

SWAMP THING RETURNS
***Swamp Thing* #1**

British writer Andy Diggle and artist Enrique Breccia returned *Swamp Thing* to its roots and gave Vertigo's most famous monster a new lease of life in its fourth series. With echoes of writer Alan Moore's legendary run on the comic, Diggle made Swamp Thing the villain of the first six-part story. John Constantine, the main character of *Hellblazer*, raised Dr. Alec Holland from the dead in order to place his soul in the Swamp Thing's body, thus protecting the planet from the creature's inhuman rage. The horrible sight of the rotting Holland hidden in a trench coat remained with the reader long after the story's conclusion.

AUGUST

THE BATMAN PRESENTS...
***Scratch* #1**

Writer and artist Sam Kieth presented a new hero for the DC Universe in the form of Scratch, a misunderstood teenage werewolf. When fifteen-year-old Zack believed himself to be deformed, he fled his home. He was soon befriended by a "deformed" girl called Sage, and later learned he was in fact a werewolf. With the help of Batman, the two teenagers solved the mystery of a missing child and a monster lurking near the town. *Scratch* was a bizarre and touching tale of deformity and acceptance, and continued Sam Kieth's run of brilliantly inventive work for DC.

Batman comes face to face with Scratch as the Dark Knight tries to decide if the teenage werewolf will be a force for good or become one of his most dangerous foes.

AUGUST

DARK SECRETS
***Identity Crisis* #1**

Written by award-winning novelist Brad Meltzer, with art by Rags Morales, *Identity Crisis* was a dark super hero whodunit that set the tone for much of what was to follow in the DC Universe. The story opened with the brutal murder of Sue Dibny, wife of the Elongated Man, who brought together his old Justice League teammates to help him track down the villain he believed responsible—Doctor Light. Shockingly, it was revealed that the team had in the past operated in a questionable way. Years before, Sue had been raped by Doctor Light, who gloated that he would return to repeat the crime. To prevent this, the Justice League had, unbeknown to Elongated Man, asked Zatanna to erase Light's memory and alter his mind, thus depowering him. They had also partly wiped Batman's mind when the Dark Knight objected, and in a separate incident had mind-wiped Flash's Rogues. Now the League sought out Light, believing he had regained his powers, but it seemed Sue's killer was somebody else: an attack on Atom's ex-wife, Jean Loring, proved near-fatal, and Tim Drake's father, Jack, was killed by hired assassin Boomerang. The truth came out when Doctor Mid-Nite and Mister Terrific performed an autopsy on Sue's corpse and found that her death was not caused by the burns on her body, but by a cerebral infarction due to miniature footprints on her brain. Doctor Mid-Nite and Mister Terrific, along with Batman, realized that the killer must have had use of the Atom's shrinking technology. It could only be one person: Jean Loring. She had faked the attack on her and paid Boomerang to attack Jack Drake, hoping to win back her husband by making him believe her life was in danger. After Jean's crimes were revealed she was taken to Arkham Asylum, while a distraught Atom shrank almost out of existence, unable to deal with his ex-wife's heinous actions.

DC's greatest heroes, including Superman, Flash, Aquaman, and Green Arrow, pay their respects to Sue Dibny, wife of the Elongated Man. Sue's brutal murder changes the lives of many heroes forever.

Zatanna and her fellow members of the Justice League of America harbor a dark secret that will tear the team apart.

February: The CIA admits that there was no imminent threat from weapons of mass destruction before the 2003 Invasion of Iraq.

March: Simultaneous terrorist attacks, with bombs in four rush-hour trains in Madrid, kill 190 people.

AUGUST

POWER PLAY

***Ex Machina* #1**

Mixing politics and superpowers, *Ex Machina* was crafted by the award-winning team of writer Brian K. Vaughan and artist Tony Harris. WildStorm's multilayered saga followed the life of Mitchell Hundred, formerly super hero the Great Machine, as he became mayor of New York. The first story combined flashbacks to the Great Machine's origin with Hundred's first days as mayor. It ended on a dramatic image of a lone, post-9/11 Twin Tower, with Mayor Hundred pointing out that if he had been a real hero, he would have saved both towers from destruction. *Ex Machina* is planned to last for fifty issues and has proved to be a big success, winning a 2005 Eisner Award for Best New Series.

SEPTEMBER

A TRIBUTE TO JULIUS SCHWARTZ

DC Comics Presents

When DC Comics' icon Julius Schwartz sadly passed away in February 2004, some kind of major tribute was required. Schwartz had joined DC (then National Comics) in 1944 and his creativity, vision, and editorial skill were instrumental in the company's success. To celebrate his life, DC revived the *DC Comics Presents* series, producing eight one-shots in which DC writers and artists put their own twists on covers inspired by Schwartz and reimagined classic Silver Age stories featuring Green Lantern, Mystery in Space, Hawkman, Batman, Superman, Flash, the Atom, and the Justice League of America. Grant Morrison, Brian Bolland, J. H. Williams III, and many more top DC names lined up to pay their respects to one of comics' all-time greats.

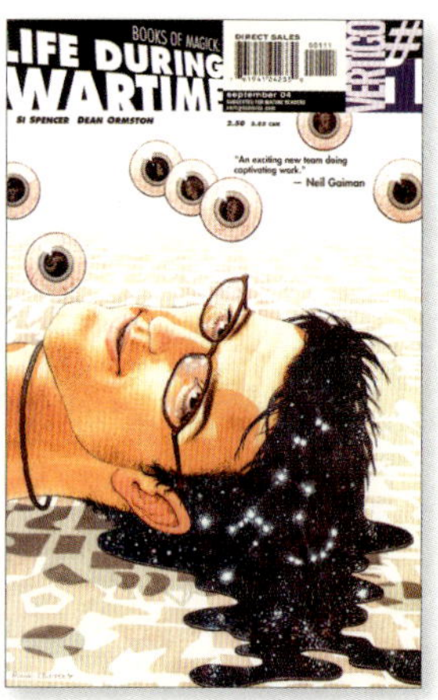

A NEW BOOK OF MAGICK

***Books of Magick: Life During Wartime* #1**

Life During Wartime presented a new Timothy Hunter to readers, one considerably different from the young hero of the previous *Books of Magic* ongoing series, which ended in 2000. This Timothy Hunter was older and more powerful. So powerful, in fact, that he had created a whole world for himself to hide in, away from his home where two factions warred—the Bred (humans) and the Born (various Faerie-related creatures). Creator Neil Gaiman worked with writer Si Spenser on the story, while Dean Ormston provided darkly evocative art.

OCTOBER

THE HUNT BEGINS AGAIN

***Manhunter* #1**

Federal Prosecutor Kate Spencer was the latest hero to use the Manhunter name, as writer Marc Andreyko and penciller Jesus Saiz gave the world a very different take on the hero, with only minor links to those who had gone before. Kate, a prosecutor, became a ruthless vigilante after watching yet another superpowered criminal escape justice—the mutated cannibal known as Copperhead. After Copperhead avoided the death penalty and escaped from police custody, Spencer stole impounded equipment (including a Darkstar powersuit and a staff that chiefly came from 1980s Manhunter Mark Shaw) to help her track down and kill Copperhead. As a chain-smoking mother who put her job before her child, and with a dramatic costume that covered her whole body, this Manhunter was a fresh take on super heroes and gained a loyal following.

ANIMAL LIBERATION

***WE3* #1**

Writer Grant Morrison and longtime artistic collaborator Frank Quitely presented one of the year's most touching and original stories in *WE3*. The three-issue series opened with a brutal assassination carried out by three cybernetic animals—a dog, cat, and rabbit named 1, 2, and 3 by their creators at Project AWE. "WE3" was the code name given to the animals, who had gained the power of speech via cybernetic implants. Each animal had a specialist role: the dog was effectively a tank, the cat was used for stealth, and the rabbit was trained to deliver mines and poisoned gas. When the three animals were marked for extermination, their handler Roseanne Berry helped them to escape. The second issue followed the increasingly brutal attempts of Project AWE to recapture the animals, as WE3 desperately tried to find a place to call their home. Finally, the last chapter of the series depicted a savage confrontation between the animals and a ferocious, cybernetically modified mastiff.

WE3, survivors of animal testing by the U.S. military for Project Awe, find freedom for the first time as they search for a place they can call home.

IN THE REAL WORLD...

July: Former Iraq President Saddam Hussein appears in court for the first time on charges of crimes against humanity.

August: *Confessions, Pt. II*, by Usher, is the best-selling album of the summer.

October: Japan is hit by a 6.6-magnitude earthquake.

NOVEMBER

ROMAN HOLIDAY
***Catwoman: When in Rome* #1**

After the success of *Batman: The Long Halloween* (1996–7), writer Jeph Loeb and artist Tim Sale returned to the Batman universe for a six-issue murder mystery starring Catwoman. As with the Batman series before it, *When in Rome* took place early in the protagonist's career as she traveled to Italy's capital to settle a score with the Falcone crime family, while also attempting to learn the truth about her parentage. The series continued Loeb and Sale's winning streak with DC, and proved to be a stylish and captivating thriller.

DECEMBER

TRUTH, JUSTICE, AND THE BRITISH WAY

Superman: True Brit

Comedy legend John Cleese joined forces with artist John Byrne, inker Mark Farmer, and writer Kim Johnson for a unique take on the Superman story. *Superman: True Brit* saw Kal-El's rocketship land on a farm near Milton Keynes in the U.K., rather than Smallville, and Kal-El raised by a nervous British couple called the Clarks. The graphic novel was played strictly for laughs as the young Kal-El (named Colin by his adopted parents) was taught to hide his superpowers from the world at large—and especially the neighbors. Needless to say, Kal-El's powers made that hard to do, as he used his abilities to milk the cows at super-speed (much to the alarm of the cows) and warm up tea with a simple blast of heat vision. Colin also got himself into a spot of bother by making an enemy out of Batman, so named because the superpowered Colin accidentally lodged a cricket bat in his chest during a cricket game. Eventually, like his Earth-1 counterpart, Colin found himself working as a reporter, only this time for a sleazy tabloid called the *Daily Smear,* instead of the *Daily Planet*. When Colin eventually took on the role of Superman, the new hero quickly became a celebrity, before falling foul of the British press. The story ended with a parallel to John Cleese's own celebrity experience, as Superman decided to emigrate to America and start a new life, away from the prying eyes of the British media.

Batman, with a cricket bat stuck in his chest, returns to take revenge for his injury on the superpowered Colin Clark.

DECEMBER

THE RETURN OF HAL JORDAN
***Green Lantern: Rebirth* #1**

Writer Geoff Johns took one of DC's greatest heroes to the top of the best-seller list with *Green Lantern: Rebirth*. The six-part miniseries not only returned Hal Jordan to his rightful role as the Green Lantern of Sector 2814, but it also re-established the Green Lantern Corps as major players in the DC Universe. Since causing the destruction of the Corps (in *Green Lantern* [third series] #48–50, released during January–March 1994), Hal Jordan had been a pariah, first as the destructive Parallax and later as the new host for the Spectre. Both incarnations had not really clicked with the readers, however, and Johns now managed to put Hal back where he belonged while also keeping continuity buffs more than satisfied.

The first issue opened with an echo of Hal Jordan's origin as Green Lantern Kyle Rayner crashed to Earth in a spacecraft, talking of an impending threat. It went on to show a Hal Jordan struggling with his new role as the cosmically powered Spectre, and established a number of mysteries from the reappearance of the destroyed Coast City to the sudden loss of ex-Green Lantern Guy Gardner's Warrior powers (by which he could transform his body into a range of weapons). These mysteries would later be solved when the threat behind Kyle Rayner's warning was revealed: Parallax. The issue also introduced subplots that would carry on into future issues, with the Black Hand's attack on Green Arrow and a cameo by longtime Green Lantern enemy Hector Hammond.

Johns' wonderfully crafted science-fiction tale solved many problems that bringing Jordan back as a hero could have caused. Parallax was no longer merely an insane Hal Jordan but the living embodiment of fear, a massive yellow creature that, millennia before, was imprisoned in the central power battery by the Guardians. The creature was also used by a revived Sinestro to test the Corps. By the end of the series, Hal was free of both Parallax and the Spectre, and restored to his role as Green Lantern, leading to a new, stronger Green Lantern Corps being formed. Geoff Johns' story was beautifully brought to life by penciller Ethan Van Sciver and managed to unite several continuity strands into an epic tale of redemption and rebirth.

Hal Jordan returns to life and helps re-establish the Green Lantern Corps as a major force in the galaxy, while also learning the Corps' darkest secret.

ALSO THIS YEAR: *BITE CLUB* brought vampires to Vertigo in June... Garth Ennis' smart-mouthed ex-SAS officer was back in *THE AUTHORITY: MORE KEV* in July... November saw fantasy writer Michael Moorcock teamed up with artist Walt Simonson to produce *ELRIC: THE MAKING OF A SORCERER*... In December movie director George Romero introduced zombie thriller *TOE TAGS*...

October: Australian and Indonesian archaeologists unearth 18,000-year-old skeletons of a tiny, "hobbit-like" species of human on a remote island in Indonesia.

December: A series of tsunamis in the Indian Ocean devastates coastal areas in fourteen countries and kills close to 230,000 people.

HAL JORDAN'S RETURN

GREEN LANTERN: REBIRTH #6 (May 2005)
All the main players in the Green Lantern Corps (from left: Guy Gardner, Kyle Rayner, Hal Jordan, Kilowog, and John Stewart) appeared on this inspiring cover by Ethan Van Sciver. The six-part "Rebirth" storyline touched on sixty years of Green Lantern history and rehabilitated Hal Jordan, the Silver Age Green Lantern. He had previously been linked to the parasitic villain Parallax and then became the new Spectre.

2005

"THIS SHOULD GET ME KILLED. BUT IT WON'T."

Robin, *All Star Batman & Robin, The Boy Wonder* #1

YEAR OF CHANGE

By the middle of the decade, a change was taking place across the DC Universe. Many titles started to take on a darker, edgier tone following the events of *Identity Crisis*. The shocking conclusion to 2004's hit series set off a chain of events that reverberated across the whole of DC's continuity and began the buildup to *Infinite Crisis* and beyond. Jim Lee followed up his work on *Batman: Hush* by joining forces with legendary writer Frank Miller for *All Star Batman & Robin, The Boy Wonder*. 2004 also brought the Dark Knight back to the big screen with the award-winning *Batman Begins*. The movie starred Christian Bale as Bruce Wayne and was directed by Christopher Nolan, and many fans saw it as the best cinematic version of *Batman* to date. The year also saw the creation of a live-action pilot of *Global Frequency*, based on Warren Ellis's hit WildStorm comic.

JANUARY

DARKEST KNIGHT

***Detective Comics* #800**

Detective Comics' 800th issue was extra large to celebrate the comic's anniversary and set up a new direction for the Dark Knight. After the tragic climax of the "War Games" storyline, Batman found himself alone and at the top of Gotham's Most Wanted list. His sidekick, Stephanie Brown, had died, vigilantes were now outlawed, and the Black Mask had gained control of all the city's gangs. Scripted by Andersen Gabrych and pencilled by Pete Woods, the issue took Batman back to basics—solo and fighting crime in a Gotham more dangerous than ever.

FEBRUARY

NEW DIRECTIONS

***Legion of Super-Heroes* [fourth series] #1**

Top writer Mark Waid and artist Barry Kitson joined forces to relaunch one of DC's best-loved super-teams. The second reboot of the Legion (after the 1958 original and the 1994 Post-*Zero Hour* versions) took the team back to its teenage roots. The heroes, including Ultra Boy, Lightning Lad, Karate Kid, Saturn Girl, Colossal Boy, Star Boy, Sun Boy, and Shadow Lass, not only protected the universe, but also fought against the stifling, regimented society around them. Readers had enjoyed a glimpse of the new-look Legion in the *Teen Titans/Legion Special* the previous November, and while the team still consisted of the core stars, their unofficial number had expanded to the thousands as teenagers across the galaxy joined them. The first story arc, "Teenage Revolution," saw the Legion become a major power as they went to the aid of their young followers on the distant world of Lallor, after an attack by the planet's adult rulers. While the Legion succeeded in its mission, it planted the seeds for further trouble with the governments of both Earth and the United Planets, as more teenagers flocked to the Legion's cause hoping to change society.

Colossal Boy, Sun Boy, and their fellow Legionnaires take their teenage revolution to the world of Lallor.

IN THE REAL WORLD...

January: Cancer is now the largest cause of death in people under 85.
April: Pope John Paul II dies at the Vatican, aged 84.

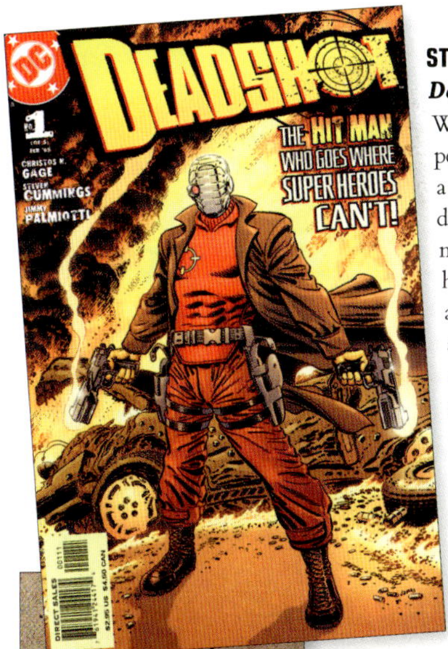

STREET CRIME
***Deadshot* #1**

Writer Christos N. Gage joined penciller Steven Cummings to portray a more heroic version of one of DC's deadliest villains in Deadshot's second miniseries. Deadshot found out he had a daughter in "Urban Renewal," and the story followed the hitman's attempts to find her. When he discovered her neighborhood was suffering due to a crime wave, he cleaned up the streets. Brutal and darkly humorous, the story showed the assassin in a new light, as a reluctant—but still deadly—hero.

Deadshot meets the daughter he never knew he had for the first time, and decides to clean up the crime-ridden section of Star City where she lives.

MAY

DEATH OF THE BLUE BEETLE
***Countdown to Infinite Crisis* #1**

The prequel to *Infinite Crisis* was a collection of short stories connected by the narrative thread of Blue Beetle investigating the theft of funds from his company. Different artists worked on the individual stories, which were written by Geoff Johns, Greg Rucka, and Judd Winick. The issue reached a shocking climax as Blue Beetle traced the theft to Maxwell Lord, who then killed him. This was just the first of many deaths to follow in *Infinite Crisis*.

JUNE

THE SPECTRE UNLEASHED
***Day of Vengeance* #1**

Some of the most far-reaching changes leading up to *Infinite Crisis* happened in the *Day of Vengeance* miniseries. Written by Bill Willingham and illustrated by Josue Justiniano and Ron Wagner, the series dealt with Eclipso corrupting the Spectre. Shadowpact joined forces with Captain Marvel to stop the duo—only for the Spectre to kill the wizard Shazam, thereby removing the Marvel Family's superpowers. The repercussions continued into *The Trials of Shazam!* series.

AT THE MOVIES THIS MONTH: ***BATMAN BEGINS*** **hit movie theaters in the U.S. Directed by Christopher Nolan, it had an all-star cast including Christian Bale as Batman, Michael Caine as Alfred, Gary Oldman as Jim Gordon, and Liam Neeson as Henri Ducard. It won countless awards including an Oscar for Wally Pfister's cinematography...**

APRIL

MORRISON'S MASTERPIECE
***Seven Soldiers of Victory* #0**

Writer Grant Morrison's imagining of the *Seven Soldiers of Victory* was one of DC's most adventurous titles. Referred to by the writer as a megaseries due to its complex structure, it went on to win an Eisner Award for Best Limited Series. The story started in *Seven Soldiers of Victory* #0 and continued in seven four-issue miniseries—*The Bulleteer*, *Frankenstein*, *Mister Miracle*, *Zatanna*, *Shining Knight*, *Manhattan Guardian*, and *Klarion*—before concluding in *Seven Soldiers of Victory* #1. In the opening chapter, Shelley Gaynor had taken on the identity of the Whip from her grandfather and was asked to join a new team of Seven Soldiers by original team member Vigilante. As well as the Vigilante and the Whip, the new lineup consisted of I, Spyder, Gimmix, Little Boy Blue, Dyno-Mite Dan, and the Bulleteer. The Vigilante asked the heroes to investigate the Buffalo Spider, a creature he thought he had defeated years before but now believed had returned. The team learned too late that the mission was a trap by the Sheeda, a race of aliens who fed on humanity over the centuries, leaving behind just enough for humans to rebuild from so the Sheeda could one day feed again. Issue #0 finished with the Seven Soldiers apparently killed and a group of mysterious strangers admitting they had one last chance to stop the Sheeda—by finding seven new soldiers. Over the next seven miniseries, the new lineup of the Seven Soldiers was revealed, leading to the battle with the Sheeda in *Seven Soldiers of Victory* #1.

The new Seven Soldiers of Victory fight their battle against the Sheeda. From left to right: Klarion, Shining Knight, Zatanna, Frankenstein, Manhattan Guardian, Bulleteer, and Mister Miracle.

May : Tony Blair becomes the first British Labour Party Prime Minister to win three successive terms in office.

July: London is hit by a series of coordinated terrorist attacks on the transport system during the morning rush hour, causing fifty-six deaths and injuring hundreds.

JULY

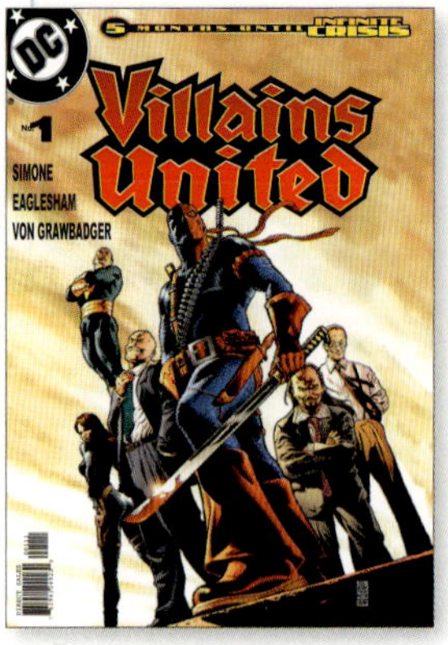

THE BUILDUP TO WAR
***Villains United* #1**

As the buildup to *Infinite Crisis* intensified, various villains maneuvered for top position. In *Villains United*, writer Gail Simone and artist Dale Eaglesham introduced a new Secret Six—consisting of Deadshot, Catman, Scandal Savage, Parademon, Ragdoll, and Cheshire. The villains teamed up for work they couldn't handle alone, but soon found themselves facing Lex Luthor's Secret Society of Super-Villains when they refused to join his new army. *Villains United* was a huge success and gained a second series post-*Infinite Crisis*.

THE GREEN LANTERN IS BACK!
***Green Lantern* [fifth series] #1**

After successfully bringing Hal Jordan back as the Green Lantern in *Green Lantern: Rebirth*, writer Geoff Johns remained at the helm for Hal Jordan's further adventures. The fifth series' first story, illustrated by Carlos Pacheco, delved further into the history of the Corps and its predecessors, the Manhunters.

Following the shocking events of *Green Lantern: Rebirth*, a reborn Hal Jordan is as fearless as ever as a member of the revitalized Green Lantern Corps.

DESOLATION TESTED
***Desolation Jones* #1**

Writer Warren Ellis added a new bizarre hero to his repertoire with Desolation Jones. Michael Jones was an agent of MI6 when he took part in the Desolation Test. The test changed him physically and mentally, turning his hair white and giving him a very personal view of reality. The first story arc involved a conspiracy theory and the legacy of the Third Reich in a superbly twisted cyberpunk-style tale illustrated by J. H. Williams III.

POST-WAR RECONSTRUCTION

Top 10: The Forty-Niners

A graphic novel prequel to the award-winning *Top 10* series, *The Forty-Niners* proved to be one of the best books of the year. Writer Alan Moore and artist Gene Ha continued the high-quality work of the original series and also introduced a host of new heroes. The book turned the clock back to post-World War II Neopolis and introduced the city through the eyes of sixteen-year-old war-veteran Steve Traynor—better known as Jetlad, and previously seen as an old police captain in *Top 10*—as he first arrived in a city being built to contain all the world's science heroes and villains. The main story followed Steve and German War-hero Leni Muller (a.k.a. Sky Witch) in their attempts to fit in to the new city, as Leni joined the newly formed police force and Steve became a mechanic for the Skysharks (a group of WWII air aces). The new city faced a number of dangers—including gangster vampires, time-traveling Nazis, and an attempted military coup by members of the Skysharks. The story also served as a coming-of-age—and coming out—story, as the teenage Steve struggled to come to terms with his feelings toward the leader of the Skysharks, Wulf.

Moore's script proved to be as original and brilliant as ever, and Ha's amazing artwork was the perfect combination of retro and futuristic.

The Sky Witch takes out one of the deadly gangster vampires threatening to take over the city of Neopolis.

AUGUST

GAIMAN ADAPTATION
***Neverwhere* #1**

Originally broadcast on the BBC in the United Kingdom as a six-part TV series and then turned into a novel by Neil Gaiman, *Neverwhere* was adapted into comic form by writer Mike Carey, with art by Glenn Fabry. The nine-part series followed the adventures of city worker Richard Mayhew as he became involved with a mysterious group of people who lived in a magical city beneath the streets of London. Fabry's imaginative art brought Gaiman's fantastical characters to life, while adding extra menace to the saga.

IN THE REAL WORLD...

August: New Orleans, Louisiana is hit by Hurricane Katrina, a Category 3 storm, which causes levees to break and flooding throughout the city.

October: Angela Merkel becomes Germany's first female Chancellor.
October: Riots erupt in Paris suburbs after two teenagers are killed.

SEPTEMBER

ALL STAR LINEUP

***All Star Batman & Robin, The Boy Wonder* #1**

The concept of DC's new All Star comic imprint was to team up the medium's best writers and artists and let them loose on DC's leading characters without the constraints of traditional continuity. Writer Frank Miller and artist Jim Lee got things started in the first release for the new imprint—*All Star Batman & Robin, The Boy Wonder*. According to Miller, the series should be treated as a prequel to the seminal graphic novel *The Dark Knight Returns* (1986), and it proved to be just as brutal as that title in its depiction of Batman. The first issue opened with a reinterpretation of Robin's origin, as the young Dick Grayson's parents were shot dead in front of him during their circus act. Seeing an echo of his own tragic childhood in Dick's plight, Batman rescued the twelve-year-old from corrupt Gotham police who were about to kill him. The series followed the Dark Knight's training of his young assistant and their investigation into the murder of his parents, which took them through Gotham City's corrupt streets and into contact with members of the Justice League and Batman's nemesis, the Joker. It suggested that, without the humanizing influence of Robin, Batman, might have become too dark and brutal to be a true hero. While the series proved controversial due to its violence and harsh dialog, it was also a huge hit.

Batman coldly hoists the young Dick Grayson up in the air. He isn't yet used to working with children.

OCTOBER

UP, UP, AND AWAY!

***Supergirl* [fourth series] #1**

Following her reintroduction to the DC Universe in *Superman/Batman* #8 (May 2004), Superman's cousin Kara Zor-El received her own title. Written by Jeph Loeb and illustrated by Ian Churchill, the fourth series featured a Supergirl still getting accustomed to her life on Earth. In the first issue she met the Justice Society, only to be attacked by member Power Girl. When the conflict ended, Power Girl warned Kara that she sensed a growing darkness in her, something that was explored fully in later issues.

DECEMBER

INFINITE CRISIS BEGINS

***Infinite Crisis* #1**

The follow-up to the classic *Crisis on Infinite Earths* had a lot to live up to. Its predecessor was one of the most important limited series in the history of DC and reset the DC Universe by decades. *Infinite Crisis*, the second in what was to become the *Crisis* trilogy (ending with 2008's *Final Crisis*) made a similar dramatic shift to the reality of the DC Universe, bringing back the Multiverse, killing several major characters, and introducing a number of new heroes and villains. Several other titles led directly into the double-sized opening issue, which showed an Earth on the edge of destruction from Lex Luthor's Secret Society of Super-Villains. At the same time, Batman, Wonder Woman, and Superman met to discuss just how far apart they had all grown. With the Earth (and the universe) heading for destruction, some long-lost heroes came out of their self-imposed exile to help—Superboy-Prime, Superman of Earth-2 (Kal-L), and Alexander Luthor (sole survivor of Earth-3, where his father Lex was the only hero). As the saga continued, it transpired that Alexander Luthor had planned the crisis in an attempt to recreate his own lost reality. By the end, Superboy-Prime had established himself as one of DC's most persistent villains; he had also killed Kal-L and Conner Kent, before being captured and imprisoned by the Green Lantern Corps. Many others were changed forever. A new Blue Beetle (Jaime Reyes) was created (replacing the deceased Ted Kord); the Spectre left in search of a new host body; and Batman, Wonder Woman, and Superman were allies once more, paving the way for a relaunch of *Justice League of America* in 2006.

An insane Alexander Luthor attempts to recreate the Multiverse using the Anti-Monitor's corpse and several trapped heroes as a power source.

Kal-L, Superman of Earth-2, grieves the loss of his beloved wife, Lois.

ALSO THIS YEAR: Renee Montoya gained her own series as *THE QUESTION* in January... Vertigo's Hellblazer made it to the big screen in February with Keanu Reeves as *CONSTANTINE*... *DAY OF VENGEANCE* brought some of DC's greatest supernatural heroes and villains together in June... Some of the U.K.'s classic comic stars reappeared in *ALBION* in August... In the same month, a much-loved Titan came back from the dead in *DC SPECIAL: THE RETURN OF DONNA TROY*...

December: Millions of Iraqis turn out to cast votes to elect a new parliament, the first since the overthrow of former Iraq President Saddam Hussein.

December: Gwen Stefani's "Hollaback Girl" is downloaded 1.7 million times, making it the most downloaded song of the year.

SUPERBOY DIES

INFINITE CRISIS #6 (May 2006)
A hugely successful, seven-part miniseries, *Infinite Crisis* was a sequel to 1985's *Crisis on Infinite Earths*. Written by Geoff Johns with art by Phil Jimenez, George Pérez, Jerry Ordway, Ivan Reis, and Andy Lanning, *Infinite Crisis* was an epic crossover that revamped the DC Universe, revising the histories of many DC heroes and killing off others. One hero who died was Superboy Conner Kent, a victim of Superboy Prime.

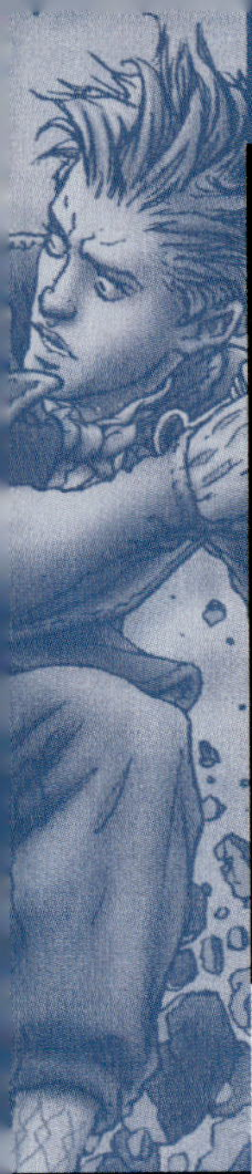

2006

"WE BROKE IT, CLARK. WE SHOULD BE THE ONES TO PUT IT BACK TOGETHER."

Batman, *Justice League of America* #1

CREATIVE FORCES

2006 was a year of flux in the DC Universe. Almost every title had a sense of impending change—from the cosmic climax of *Infinite Crisis,* with the deaths of Conner Kent and Kal-L (the Superman of Earth-2), through to the start of *52*, DC's first weekly series for years. The influence of major talents was also making an impact, with Grant Morrison and Frank Quitely unleashing one of the best Superman series for decades with *All Star Superman*, and Morrison beganning his epic run on *Batman*. WildStorm ended the year on a horrific note with the first of their New Line horror titles, *A Nightmare On Elm Street*. Meanwhile, Vertigo gave everyone's favorite rogue, Fable, a series of his own in *Jack of Fables* and the tragic *Pride of Baghdad* set new standards for graphic novels. Beyond the comic world, the Man of Steel finally hit the big screen again with *Superman Returns*.

JANUARY

SUPERMAN MUST DIE
***All Star Superman* #1**

Writer Grant Morrison and artist Frank Quitely unveiled one of the most original and well-received Superman series for years as they combined high-concept science-fiction elements with classic Silver Age concepts in their *All Star Superman* series. The opening issue started with high drama. After Superman rescued a group of astronauts attempting to harvest energy from the sun, he found himself falling into a trap set by arch-enemy Lex Luthor. To save the astronauts' lives, Superman was forced to extend his own bioelectric field but, in doing so, exposed himself to critical levels of stellar radiation. Lex Luthor had finally found a way to kill the Man of Steel, and Superman was left with just one year to live. He decided to make the most of his remaining time, and started by revealing his secret identity to an astonished Lois Lane.

Future issues reimagined classic Silver Age characters for a whole new generation, such as a temporarily superpowered Lois Lane, the Supermen of the future, and a monstrous Jimmy Olsen (taking on the form of Doomsday to stop a Superman-turned-bad). The vision of Metropolis produced by Morrison and Quitely made it a true city of tomorrow, and a city inspired by Superman's heroics to greater and better things. This inspiration was most clearly seen in the work of Mister Quintum, mastermind behind a new DNA P.R.O.J.E.C.T. (itself first seen in Jack Kirby's seminal run on *Superman's Pal, Jimmy Olsen* in the 1970s). The second release in DC's All Star line (after 2005's *All Star Batman & Robin, The Boy Wonder*), *All Star Superman* proved to be a smash hit and won many awards, including two Eisners for Best New Series (2006) and Best Continuing Series (2007).

Jimmy Olsen is Metropolis' only hope of stopping a Man of Steel who has turned evil following a dose of personality-altering black kryptonite.

N THE REAL WORLD...

February: A Danish newspaper prints negative cartoons depicting the Muslim prophet Muhammad, leading to angry demonstrations.

JANUARY

WILD WEST HERO

***Jonah Hex* #1**

Writers Justin Gray and Jimmy Palmiotti brought Western hero Jonah Hex back to the mainstream DC Universe after several well-received Vertigo miniseries. The newest version of *Jonah Hex* returned the anti-hero to his hard-core Western roots, providing a series of tough, violent, and atmospheric tales set at various times during Hex's life. The opening issue set the tone for what was to follow, as Hex was hired to find a missing boy—only to uncover a circus using captured children to fight dogs for the amusement of the crowd. Luke Ross's gritty art was the perfect match for the grim tales of DC's most famous bounty hunter.

MAY

ONE YEAR LATER

***Detective Comics* #817**

After the conclusion of *Infinite Crisis*, all of DC's main titles jumped forward by one year. While the story of the missing year was told in *52*, the main titles showed the after-effects of the time without Batman, Superman, and Wonder Woman, as well as the events upon their return. Some titles, such as *The Flash* and *Wonder Woman*, were eventually relaunched with new first issues. The darkest events during that period took place in a six-part crossover that started in *Detective Comics* #817 (and continued in *Batman* #651). Batman had left a reformed Harvey Dent as guardian of Gotham, but Dent collapsed under the pressure and his self-scarring Two-Face persona returned to plague Batman and Robin as they reemerged in the city. The "One Year Later" stories provided a great jumping-on point for new readers, while also giving an air of mystery and complex drama for existing ones.

With Batman and Robin away, a reformed Harvey Dent brings justice to the streets of Gotham City, but the madness of Two-Face is always close.

BRAVE NEW WORLDS

***52* #1**

While DC had used the weekly format before (most notably with *Action Comics* in April 1988), *52* was their first attempt to launch a new title as a weekly. Set in the time between the end of *Infinite Crisis* and the "One Year Later" storylines, *52* dealt with the events of the missing year—a year without Superman, Batman, and Wonder Woman. The title was masterminded by writers Geoff Johns, Grant Morrison, Greg Rucka, and Mark Waid, with Keith Giffen providing art breakdowns. Its weekly publication meant several artists had to handle the art, starting with Joe Bennett on the first four issues. A massive saga spanning the whole DC Universe (and beyond), *52* introduced several new heroes and villains, including a new Question and Batwoman, before the big reveal of a new multiverse of fifty-two realities, each containing an alternate Earth. The story had a huge impact on the DC Universe, affecting everything from Black Adam's *World War III* spin-off, to Booster Gold's post-*52* reality-spanning adventures. It also led into *Countdown to Final Crisis* and left the DC Universe a dramatically different place.

With Superman nowhere to be found, Booster Gold brings justice to the streets of Metropolis, taking out the super-villain Blockbuster in the process.

JUNE

THE LAST GUARDIAN

***Ion* #1**

The first story arc of a new *Ion* series explored how the traumatic events of *Rann-Thanagar War* and *Infinite Crisis* had affected Kyle Rayner. He had once again found himself endowed with powerful cosmic forces, but they seemed to have driven him insane. The true villain of the piece was later revealed to be Kyle's old nemesis, Alex Nero, who had been impersonating him. Writer Ron Marz and artist Greg Tocchini reestablished Kyle Rayner as Ion and provided him with a new role—protector of the Guardians' power.

AT THE MOVIES THIS MONTH: The Man of Steel returned to movie screens at long last in *SUPERMAN RETURNS*. Directed by Bryan Singer, Brandon Routh took on the role of Superman, with Kevin Spacey portraying his arch-enemy, Lex Luthor...

March: *Crash* wins the Academy Award® for Best Picture.
June: Gardasil, a new vaccine to prevent cervical cancer, is approved for use in the U.S.

July: A series of bombs is detonated during evening rush hour on commuter trains in Mumbai, India, killing and wounding hundreds.

SEPTEMBER

A NEW SAGA BEGINS

***Batman* #655**

The first story arc of Grant Morrison's award-winning run on *Batman*, "Batman and Son" set the standard for what was to follow for the Dark Knight and introduced elements that would later prove to be vitally important. The first issue started with a brutal confrontation between the Dark Knight and the Joker—one of the few Batman foes still free following the Dark Knight's return to Gotham. After capturing all of the escaped Arkham Asylum villains, Batman was exhausted. Bruce traveled to London for a charity event, but came across a flustered Kirk Langstrom, creator of the Man-Bat formula. Unbeknownst to Bruce, Langstrom had been blackmailed by Talia al Ghūl to help her turn the League of Assassins into an army of deadly ninja Man-Bats. The story not only brought Talia al Ghūl back into Bruce Wayne's life but also introduced a major new character: Damian Wayne, Batman's son. Jezebel Jet, an actress and future girlfriend of Bruce Wayne, also made her first appearance. Andy Kubert provided some of the most dramatic and atmospheric art of his distinguished career in "Batman and Son," as Grant Morrison's arrival signaled one of the most powerful and important sagas in the history of the Dark Knight.

The Joker has Batman at his mercy—although in Gotham City, things are seldom as they appear.

LEGENDARY

***Jack of Fables* #1**

Vertigo's award-winning *Fables* gained a lighthearted spin-off focusing on fan favorite Jack. *Jack of Fables* followed the eponymous hero's adventures after his banishment from Fabletown and the loss of his movie studio. Jack found himself imprisoned in the Golden Boughs Retirement Community and confronted with an ex-girlfriend: Goldilocks. *Fables* writer Bill Willingham was joined by long-time writing partner Matthew Sturges on the scripting for the series, with Tony Atkins providing suitably imaginative artwork.

OCTOBER

THE JUSTICE LEAGUE, RELAUNCHED

***Justice League of America* [second series] #1**

After the success of *Identity Crisis*, best-selling novelist Brad Meltzer was given the job of relaunching the *Justice League of America* in the title's second series. With Ed Benes providing the pencils, Meltzer stripped the Justice League back to basics, building on the humanity of DC's greatest heroes and combining it with a sense of epic adventure.

This was reflected in the first story arc, "The Tornado's Path," which brought back one of the team's most popular members—Red Tornado. Destroyed during *Infinite Crisis*, Red Tornado gained a new mortal body with the help of Deadman, the robotic shell of his old body being used by an intelligent Solomon Grundy to create a new Amazo. The Tornado's time as a living, breathing human and the ensuing loss of his mortal body gave the first story its emotional core. Even the revelation that Solomon Grundy was the mastermind behind Amazo's return had an element of humanity to it, as Grundy revealed he was attempting to end his own cycle of death and rebirth by making himself immortal.

Meltzer used his skill as a novelist to weave three separate storylines together: Red Tornado's rebirth; Wonder Woman, Batman, and Superman's meeting in the Batcave to vote on new members; and Green Lantern and Black Canary's own attempts to build a new League. By the end of the seven-part story, the new Justice League was assembled. Its lineup consisted of previous members Batman, Wonder Woman, Superman, Green Lantern, Black Canary, Red Tornado, Vixen, and Hawkgirl, with new members Black Lightning and Red Arrow (formerly known as Speedy) joining them. It was the start of a new era of greatness for DC's premier super hero team.

A vast group of super heroes were available for selection to join the new Justice League of America.

IN THE REAL WORLD...

August: Astronomers rule that the planet Pluto is no longer a true planet, but a "dwarf planet," after a new definition of the term "planet" is agreed by scientists.

September: Steve Irwin, the famous animal conservationist and daring "Crocodile Hunter," dies when he is stung in the chest by a stingray.

OCTOBER

THE NEW CAPTAIN MARVEL

The Trials of Shazam! #1

Captain Marvel got a new look in *The Trials of Shazam!*, written by Judd Winick and drawn by Howard Porter. Captain Marvel Jr. (Freddy Freeman) had lost his powers, but after Captain Marvel replaced the wizard Shazam, Freddy attempted to replace Captain Marvel. The series followed Freddy as he tried to prove to the gods behind Captain Marvel's power that he was worthy of the role. In the end, he achieved his goal, but chose a new name: Shazam!

COSMIC TALES

***Mystery in Space* #1**

Mystery in Space had been one of DC's best-selling titles of the 1950s and 1960s, showcasing a series of first-rate science fiction adventures. The title returned for an eight-issue run featuring Captain Comet, and was written by Jim Starlin and drawn by Shane Davis. It also contained a back-up strip starring the Weird, written and drawn by Starlin. Reborn in a younger body, Captain Comet was forced to hunt for his own corpse, ultimately learning that telepathic clones were being grown from it. The Weird joined Captain Comet in the saga's explosive finale.

NOVEMBER

WAR STORIES

Pride of Baghdad

Written by Brian K. Vaughan, the award-winning writer of *Y: The Last Man*, and beautifully illustrated by Niko Henrichon, *Pride of Baghdad* was a touching and emotional tale that revealed the brutality and desperation of war. It was based on the true story of four lions that escaped from Baghdad Zoo during the invasion of Iraq. The story followed the lions as they struggled to survive in the war-torn city after the bombing of the zoo, their story reflecting the plight of humans during wartime. Led by Zill, a haughty male lion, the pride included the lioness Noor, her cub Ali, and the wise, old, one-eyed lioness Safa. The pride's journey in search of safety took them through the streets of Baghdad and into one of Saddam Hussein's destroyed palaces, where they found a chained lion and a wild, dangerous bear. Attacked by the bear, the lions used their hunting skills to eventually bring it down. The story ended tragically, just as in the true story that inspired it. The book went on to win the IGN Graphic Novel of the Year award.

Zill and his pride of lions find there is a world beyond the confines of their zoo.

DECEMBER

THE FABLES' GRAPHIC NOVEL

Fables: 1001 Nights of Snowfall

The first *Fables* graphic novel was set in the early days of the Fables' arrival on Earth and followed Snow White's journey to meet the Arabian Fables and her imprisonment by a local sultan. To save her life, Snow White took on the role of Scheherazade, and charmed the sultan with numerous tales of the Fables. Written by Bill Willingham, the framing sequence was illustrated by Charles Vess and Michael William Kaluta, and artists of the caliber of John Bolton, Mark Buckingham, Tara McPherson, and Brian Bolland brought Snow White's enchanting stories to life.

DREAM EVIL

***A Nightmare on Elm Street* #1**

A Nightmare On Elm Street was the first of New Line's horror titles to be published by WildStorm, with *Friday the 13th* and *The Texas Chainsaw Massacre* following in 2007. The opening story arc introduced a new group of teens for Freddy Krueger to hunt, including Jade Arnstrum, who had witnessed Freddy killing her brother in a dream. With her father's help, Jade attempted to save her friends from Freddy and rescue a comatose girl from his dreamworld. Chuck Dixon's script and Kevin J. West's pencils helped to create a suitably nightmarish start for Freddy's latest incarnation.

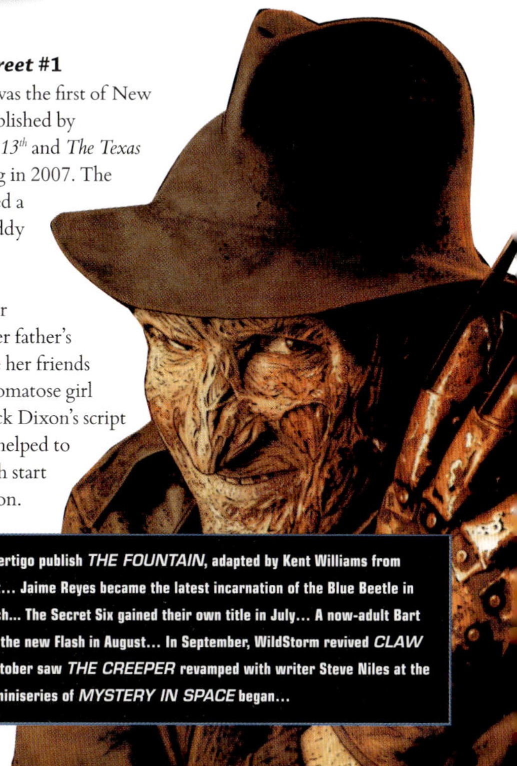

ALSO THIS YEAR: January saw Vertigo publish *THE FOUNTAIN*, adapted by Kent Williams from Darren Aronofsky's movie script... Jaime Reyes became the latest incarnation of the Blue Beetle in *INFINITE CRISIS* #5 in March... The Secret Six gained their own title in July... A now-adult Bart Allen began his short career as the new Flash in August... In September, WildStorm revived *CLAW THE UNCONQUERED*... October saw *THE CREEPER* revamped with writer Steve Niles at the helm... Also in October, a new miniseries of *MYSTERY IN SPACE* began...

November: The Nintendo Wii home video console, complete with a remote control that detects players' movements, is launched.

December: "Godfather of Soul" James Brown dies age 73 from congestive heart failure.
December: Former Iraqi President Saddam Hussein is executed by hanging in Iraq.

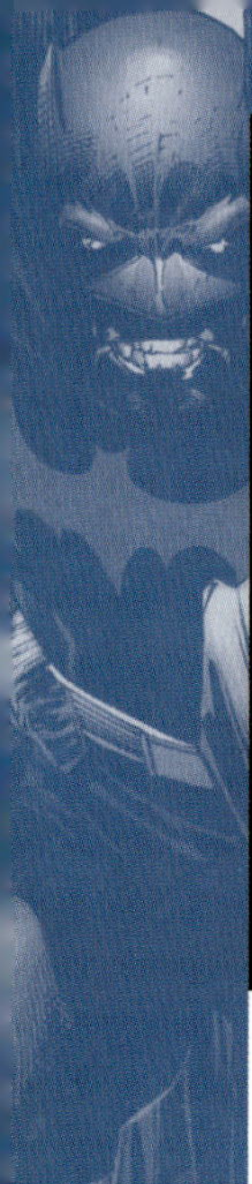

2007

"THE WORLD NEEDS BETTER GOOD GUYS."

Wildcat, *Justice Society of America* [third series] #1

THIS MEANS WAR

Comics often reflect the world around them, and in 2007, as the real-life wars in Iraq and Afghanistan continued, conflict seemed to erupt across the whole DC Universe. Whether it was in the midst of *52*, where Black Adam launched a brutal attack against the entire world, an Amazonian invasion of Washington, D.C. in *Amazons Attack!*, or the start of the crossover Sinestro Corps War, harsh times and dark storylines enveloped the mainstream books. Continuity between titles was tighter than ever and the grimmer the stories became, the more fans seemed to love them. It was as if many of the main titles were preparing for a final crisis the following year. Elsewhere WildStorm expanded their horror line with *The Texas Chainsaw Massacre* and *Friday the 13th*, while Vertigo produced the hard-hitting thriller *Scalped,* one of the year's best-received new titles.

JANUARY

SUPERMAN: THE EARLY YEARS...
***Superman Confidential* #1**

Superman Confidential turned the clock back to the early days of the Man of Steel's career. Each story arc was handled by a different team. Writer Darwyn Cooke and artist Tim Sale began with "Kryptonite," a six-part tale of Superman's first contact with the energy-sapping green element. The story revealed a less-confident Man of Steel who was trying to work out the limitations of his powers and his place in the world while dealing with Lex Luthor and casino boss Tony Gallo. Gallo harbored a secret—a block of kryptonite containing an alien entity who had recorded Krypton's final hours.

PSYCHO KILLERS
***The Texas Chainsaw Massacre* #1**

A Nightmare on Elm Street had launched WildStorm's horror imprint and was joined by New Line stablemates *The Texas Chainsaw Massacre* and *Friday the 13th* in January and February respectively. The first *Texas Chainsaw Massacre* arc, "Americarnivore," was a direct sequel to 2003's movie, with a vengeful FBI agent investigating his missing niece while Leatherface and family had some new guests for dinner. Writers Dan Abnett and Andy Lanning were joined by artist Wes Craig, and the team created a suitably gruesome tale of Southern inhospitality.

FEBRUARY

DARK KNIGHT BEGINS
***Batman Confidential* #1**

The new Batman title focused on the early days of the Dark Knight's career, revealing a hero still working out the best way to fight crime, just as its companion book did with the Man of Steel in *Superman Confidential*. The first story arc, "Rules of Engagement," was written by Andy Diggle with art by Whilce Portacio, and it brought Batman face-to-face with Lex Luthor. Superman's arch-enemy had stolen WayneTech secrets for military weapons and used them to create an army of G.I. Robots with which he planned to take over the United States.

IN THE REAL WORLD...

January: The number of nations in the European Union reaches twenty-seven, as Bulgaria and Romania join.

THE NEXT GENERATION OF HEROES

***Justice Society of America* [third series] #1**

Writer Geoff Johns and artist Dale Eaglesham relaunched the JSA, with Alex Ross providing covers for the series. "The Justice League is a strike force. The Justice Society is a family," Batman told surviving Society members Wildcat, Flash (Jay Garrick), and Green Lantern (Alan Scott). The latest version of the JSA mixed the experience of older heroes with the enthusiasm of newer ones, such as Damage and Starman. The team soon had their first case to solve when Mr. America crashed through the roof of their base, assassinated while investigating the murder of his own family.

MARCH

NO RESERVATIONS...

***Scalped* #1**

Writer Jason Aaron and artist R.M. Guéra mixed crime and Native American culture in *Scalped*. The Vertigo series began as undercover agent Dashiell "Dash" Bad Horse as he returned home to the Prairie Rose Reservation to infiltrate the tribal leader's criminal organization. Hired to be a cop on the reservation, Dash soon found himself caught up in the reservation's problems and became conflicted between life as an FBI agent and as a tribe member. *Scalped* remains a brutal noir thriller that is not scared to reflect the grim reality of life for many modern-day Native Americans.

APRIL

A CLASSIC TITLE RETURNS

***The Brave and the Bold* [third series] #1**

Writer Mark Waid and artist George Pérez teamed up to relaunch one of DC's best-loved titles, *The Brave and the Bold*. The first story was a six-issue space epic in which several of DC's greatest heroes attempted to retrieve the Book of Destiny (a magical tome that contained every event—past, present, and future). The first issue opened with Green Lantern (Hal Jordan) finding a human corpse floating beyond Earth's atmosphere. Copies of the same body had been found across the world—including by Batman inside the Batcave. Batman and Green Lantern teamed up to investigate, and were joined in later issues by Supergirl, Blue Beetle, and Lobo.

JUNE

A CALL TO ARMS

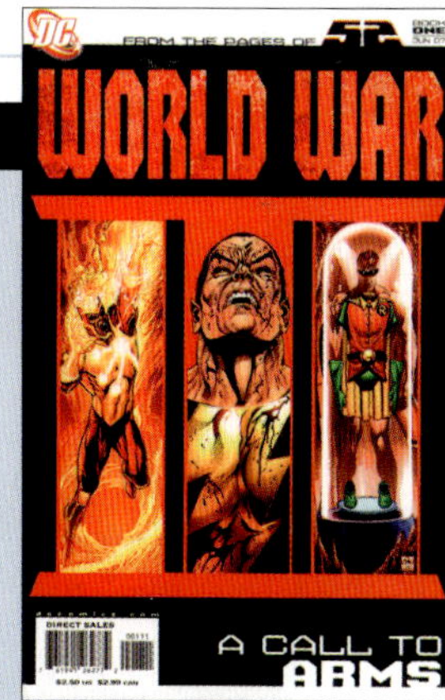

***World War III* #1**

World War III focused on Black Adam's rage over the savage death of his family and the aftereffects of his attack on Bialya, the nation he held responsible. It opened with an attempt by J'onn J'onzz, the Martian Manhunter, to stop Black Adam in the ruins of Bialya. J'onzz, traumatized after the villain allowed him to telepathically see every man, woman, and child killed during his attack, fled into space to deal with the disturbing images and Black Adam continued his rampage. By the main part of the story, set during week 50 of *52*, Black Adam was tearing an even bloodier path across the world. He savagely ripped the face off Father Time, hurled an aircraft carrier at New York City (which was saved from devastation by Firestorm, who turned the carrier to snow), destroyed the leaning tower of Pisa, and killed Terra while battling the Titans. When Black Adam's rampage reached China, the country's main super hero team—the Great Ten—proved helpless against him. The Chinese government eventually allowed the waiting Justice Society in to confront Black Adam. Joined by a host of other heroes, a massive final battle took place. A returned J'onn J'onzz mentally wounded Black Adam by showing the villain images of the pain he himself had faced due to the loss of his entire civilization, as well as the pain suffered by his victims. In a final confrontation with Captain Marvel, Black Adam's powers were stripped from him and he disappeared. Black Adam's alter ego, Theo Adam, was glimpsed in *52*, week 50, as he began his quest to regain his lost powers—a storyline that was explored further in Black Adam's own series in October.

The Justice Society of America combine with other heroes to stop the grief-stricken Black Adam.

INVASION U.S.A.

***Amazons Attack!* #1**

The Amazons invaded America in this six-issue miniseries by writer Will Pfeifer and artist Pete Woods. The story opened with a violent attack on Washington, D.C. by Queen Hippolyta and her Amazonian warriors. The brutal soldiers were soon met by the Justice League as the conflict escalated. The series ended on a shocking note when the goddess Athena was revealed to be Darkseid's accomplice, Granny Goodness, paving the way for *Final Crisis* and Darkseid's conquest of reality.

February: The U.S. ups its military presence in Iraq by sending a further 30,000 troops. The French government bans cigarette smoking in public places.

April: Eight sailors and seven marines, all British, are freed after being detained by Iran's military for twelve days for allegedly straying into Iranian waters.

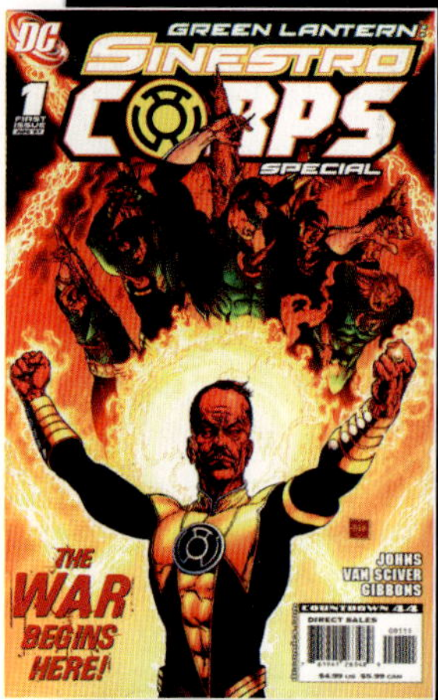

AUGUST

TOTAL WAR

Green Lantern: Sinestro Corps Special #1

The Green Lantern Corps was plunged into an intergalactic war when renegade Corps member Sinestro created his own paramilitary force. Using fear as a power source, the universe's deadliest and most feared beings were selected to join the Sinestro Corps, including the Anti-Monitor, Superboy-Prime, Cyborg Superman, and an all-new Parallax, who was now possessing the Green Lantern's most powerful member, Kyle Rayner (Ion).

The double-sized special by writer Geoff Johns and artist Ethan Van Sciver saw Sinestro muster his forces as yellow rings selected members from across the universe and brought them to Qward, a world deep in the anti-matter universe. Over the course of the eleven-part epic (which continued in *Green Lantern* [fourth series] #21 in September and *Green Lantern Corps* #24 in July 2008) the conflict spread across the entire galaxy. The Guardians argued about the best course of action and Ganthet and Sayd left, opposing the group. The Guardians of the Universe rewrote their own code of laws, creating ten new laws—including use of lethal force against the Sinestro Corps. As many of Earth's heroes—including the Justice League and Teen Titans—came to fight alongside the Green Lanterns, one of the Guardians was scarred trying to stop the Anti-Monitor, who himself was thrown into deep space by a crazed Superboy-Prime. Another Guardian gave up his life-force to send Superboy-Prime back to his home universe and, as the Sinestro Corps fled, Sinestro himself was defeated and arrested by Hal Jordan. Sinestro's plan wasn't to win the war, however, but to make the Guardians change their laws to allow their members to kill. The series ended on an ominous note, with a final image of a giant black lantern on the anti-matter world of Qward, waiting for the rise of the Black Lanterns. The series proved to be another successful epic in the Green Lantern saga, one of DC's most popular titles since Geoff Johns' revamp of the hero in 2002.

Sinestro, Hal Jordan's former mentor-turned-nemesis, leads a new Corps dedicated to bringing fear to the whole galaxy.

AUGUST

SWIMMING WITH THE FISHES

Silverfish

David Lapham, author and artist of the critically acclaimed self-published series *Stray Bullets*, brought his unique vision to Vertigo for a stylish graphic novel. When teenager Mia Fleming and her friends found a phone book belonging to Mia's stepmother, Suzanne, they used it to make prank phone calls and found themselves in unexpected danger from a serial killer. He was a man with whom Suzanne had once been involved and now, thanks to the actions of Mia and her friends, he returned to wreak revenge on Suzanne and anyone close to her. The title came from the killer's belief that he was being told what to do by demonic fish living inside his ear. A fast-paced noir thriller, *Silverfish* was further proof that David Lapham was one of the most skillful creators to cross over from indie to mainstream comics.

Mia Fleming uncovers a dark secret from her stepmother's past, starting a terrifying chain of events that will end in violence and murder.

SEPTEMBER

SURVIVIOR...

Green Arrow: Year One #1

Writer Andy Diggle and artist Jock took Ollie Queen back to the beginning in *Green Arrow: Year One*, an updated version of Green Arrow's origin. Oliver Queen was a bored playboy with a Robin Hood fixation who was betrayed by his closest friend, Hackett, and left close to death and stranded in the ocean. Ollie washed up on an island used by Hackett's paymaster—China White—as a heroin farm. Using his Robin Hood-like skills with a bow and arrow to survive, Ollie was given the name "Auu Lanu Lau'ava" (or Green Arrow) by China White's slaves. As Green Arrow helped the slaves win freedom and destroy the heroin farm, Ollie discovered his true calling as a swashbuckling hero.

IN THE REAL WORLD...

May: Nicolas Sarkozy is elected as the twenty-third President of France.
June: Tony Blair steps down as U.K. prime minister and is succeeded by Gordon Brown.
June: Apple Inc. releases the iPhone, an Internet- and multimedia-enabled cellphone.
July: Buenos Aires, Argentina sees its first snowfall in eighty-nine years.

HOW THE WEST WAS RUN...

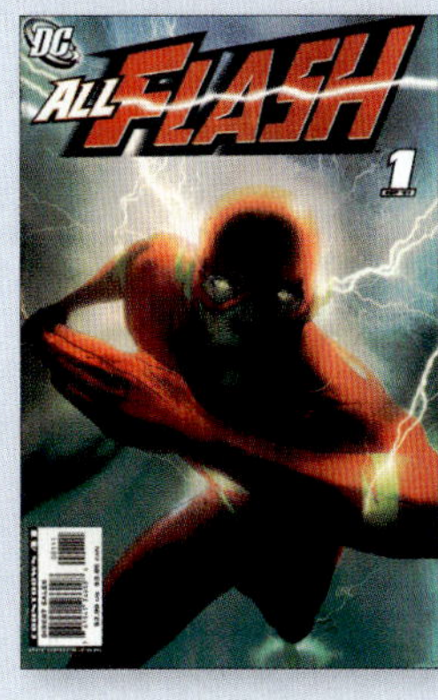

***All Flash* #1**
Following the murder of Bart Allen in the last issue of Bart's own short-lived series, Wally West returned as the Flash in *All Flash* #1. The one-shot picked up Wally's tale from the end of *Justice League of America* [second series] #10 in August 2007, where Wally and his family had returned from an alternate reality. Shocked at the news that his protégé had been murdered, Wally wasted no time in tracking down the main culprit—Inertia. While West couldn't execute the villain, he froze Inertia in time, placing him in the Flash Museum to stare at a memorial statue of Bart.

The following month the regular Flash series returned to its pre-Bart numbering and continued Wally's story with #231. Both the one-shot and the regular series were written by Mark Waid, whose amazing run on the title was still held in high regard by fans and was one of the reasons Wally West was many people's favorite incarnation of the hero. The one-shot was illustrated by a number of artists including Karl Kerschl, Ian Churchill, Mañuel Garcia, Joe Bennett, and Daniel Acuña.

Wally West returns as the Flash, accompanied by his two superpowered children.

ALSO THIS MONTH: Warner Bros.' successful straight-to-video launch of animated films continued with *SUPERMAN: DOOMSDAY*, featuring the vocal talents of Adam Baldwin as Clark Kent and Superman, Anne Heche as Lois Lane, and James Marsters as Lex Luthor...

OCTOBER

BLACK ADAM'S REVENGE
***Black Adam: The Dark Age* #1**

After the destructive events of *World War III*, *52*, and *Countdown*, Black Adam was powerless, his kingdom destroyed and his family slain. *The Dark Age* followed Black Adam's attempt to bring his lover, Isis, back to life. While a villain, Black Adam's role in the DCU had been that of an anti-hero. His own series showed him at his most savage, but it also revealed a man mourning for the loss of his lover. The series ended with a beaten Black Adam in his ruined palace, little suspecting that the villain Faust had succeeded in raising Isis from the dead.

NOVEMBER

COLD FEET...
***Green Arrow and Black Canary Wedding Special* #1**

Two of DC's best-loved characters were married in the *Green Arrow and Black Canary Wedding Special*—or so it seemed. As the big day arrived, a host of heroes turned up for the ceremony. However, the service was gatecrashed by villains aiming to wipe out all their enemies in one go. The bad guys were defeated and the pair wed—but there was a twist to the tale. On their honeymoon, a crazed Green Arrow attacked Black Canary and tried to strangle her, forcing Dinah to kill her new husband. The shock ending led into the *Green Arrow and Black Canary* ongoing series, where the truth was revealed—the Amazon Goddess Athena had replaced Ollie with shape-changer Everyman.

DECEMBER

GOTHAM'S NEW PROTECTOR...
***Simon Dark* #1**
Gotham City gained a different protector as Steve Niles (writer of *30 Days of Night*) brought a new hero to the DCU. Aided by artist Scott Hampton, Niles produced a brooding mystery as Simon Dark protected the people of the Village (a section of Gotham) while uncovering the events of his origins. The dark tone for the series was set in the opening pages when this hero saved a man from being sacrificed. Later issues revealed Simon's tragic beginnings when a mixture of science and magic brought him to life by using the bodies and souls of twenty innocent children.

FALL OF THE FOURTH WORLD...
***The Death of the New Gods* #1**

Writer and artist Jim Starlin helmed this eight-part series as a mysterious force brought destruction to the inhabitants of the Fourth World. The first issue opened with the death of the Black Racer and ended with the death of Big Barda, wife of Mister Miracle. Over the course of the series, all the New Gods met their end. The eventual killer was revealed to be the Source (a mysterious energy predating the New Gods), which sought to bring about a Fifth World. By the end of the series, even Darkseid had apparently been killed, and both Apokolips and New Genesis merged into one world. Darkseid's final destiny was revealed in *Final Crisis*.

ALSO THIS YEAR: *52* led into a new weekly series, *COUNTDOWN*, debuting in July... Both Booster Gold and the Metal Men gained their own new series in October... November saw Vertigo release *SENTENCES: THE LIFE OF MF GRIMM*, the autobiography of hip-hop artist Percy Carey...

November: The Writers Guild of America, representing 12,000 writers, begins strike action, ceasing production on many U.S. prime-time comedies and dramas.

December: *I Am Legend* breaks the box-office record for a December weekend debut. The U.S. wins its first Davis Cup since 1995.

2008

"HAVE NO FEAR. HERE IS KNOWLEDGE."

Metron, *Final Crisis* #1

DEATH AND DESTRUCTION

In 2008 the complex stories and subplots that DC Comics' top writers had been planning for years came to fruition at last. With *Countdown to Final Crisis* following directly after *52*, the expectations of comic book readers were that something major would happen in the DC Universe—and they were not disappointed. Writer Grant Morrison had planted warnings of the *Final Crisis* to come in his *7 Soldiers of Victory* titles in 2006, and when writer and artist Jim Starlin started to kill off all the New Gods, there was a definite sense of impending doom for all of DC's finest. As the events of *Final Crisis* impacted across the DC Universe, many heroes and villains found themselves changed forever—and one DC staple even died! All of this high drama in a year when *The Dark Knight* movie ruled at the box office and Grant Morrison's dramatic run on *Batman* came to a shocking climax.

JANUARY

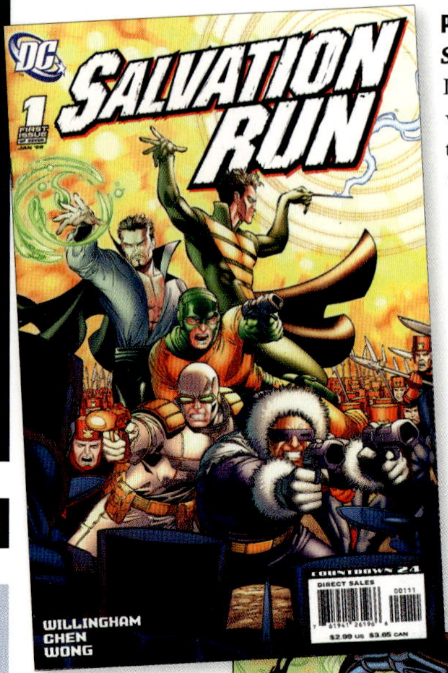

PRISON WORLD

***Salvation Run* #1**

In the limited series *Salvation Run*, the world's deadliest villains found themselves exiled from Earth and trapped on a hostile world. The prison planet, known as Salvation, had been selected to house Earth's most dangerous superpowered criminals. In the first issue, written by Bill Willingham with art by Sean Chen, new arrivals—including the Joker—struggled to survive. Later, the villains would form two rival sides—one led by the Joker, the other by Lex Luthor. The story had a shocking climax as the Martian Manhunter was revealed to be one of their number, masquerading as the villain Blockbuster.

Two of the Flash's Rogues, Kadabra and Captain Cold, struggle to survive on the deadly and inhospitable prison world of Salvation, where they are exiled.

Ash, hero of the *Evil Dead* movies, finds himself facing *A Nightmare on Elm Street*'s Freddy Krueger and *Friday the 13th*'s Jason Voorhees as the three horror icons finally meet.

CLASH OF THE PSYCHOS

***Freddy vs. Jason vs. Ash* #1**

WildStorm teamed up with Dynamite Entertainment to release the story horror fans the world over had been waiting for as *Evil Dead* hero Ash found himself up against two iconic horror villains—*Nightmare on Elm Street*'s Freddy and *Friday the 13th*'s Jason. Jeff Katz provided the story, James Anthony Kuhoric the script, and Jason Craig the art as Ash again found himself the reluctant hero when Freddy sought to increase his nightmarish powers far beyond Elm Street.

IN THE REAL WORLD...

January: After a disputed presidential election, violence erupts in Kenya, leading to many deaths and the displacement of thousands.

FANTASY UNLEASHED
***World of Warcraft* #1**

The online role-playing sensation of the decade hit the comic book world courtesy of Walt Simonson, with art by Ludo Lullabi and Sandra Hope and a stunning cover from Jim Lee. Set in the Warcraft universe and published by WildStorm, *World of Warcraft* quickly became a hit. Originally planned for two six-issue story arcs, its run was expanded after its rip-roaring success.

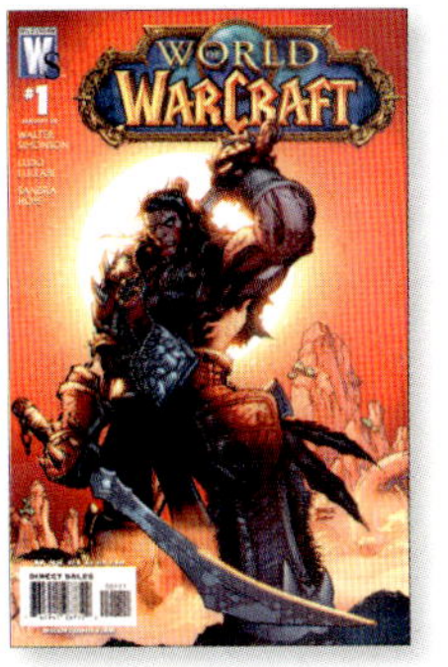

MARCH

THE GREAT ESCAPE
***Y: The Last Man* #60**

One of Vertigo's best-loved titles *Y: The Last Man*, reached its conclusion in March. Writer Brian K. Vaughan's epic tale of Yorick Brown had won fans far beyond the average comic reader. With Pia Guerra deftly handling the artwork, the final issue jumped forward sixty years from the traumatic events of the previous issue to provide a glimpse of the world's future. It was a time when clones of Yorick were walking the world, and Yorick's daughter was president of France and keeping watch over her suicidal father. The strong images of an old straitjacketed Yorick in a room full of cloned monkeys, known as Ampersands, and his lone straitjacket blowing free in the sky helped bring Yorick's story to a satisfying and touching end.

JUNE

TITANS TOGETHER
***Titans* #1**

Writer Judd Winick and penciller Ian Churchill produced a Titans series to please both modern-day fans and those of the classic Marv Wolfman/George Pérez era. A prologue had occurred in the *Titans East Special* in January as Cyborg attempted to form a new team, only for them to be destroyed by a mysterious foe. Power Boy was killed and Cyborg himself left dismantled and close to death. With Titans the world over under threat, the original lineup reformed to investigate and soon believed the danger stemmed from Raven's demonic father, Trigon. Later issues revealed the true danger to be from his evil offspring.

THE CRUCIAL THREE
***Trinity* #1**

Hot on the heels of *52* and *Countdown*, DC continued its success in the weekly comic market with *Trinity*, teaming up its Big Three heroes—Superman, Batman, and Wonder Woman— in a massive story arc. Writer Kurt Busiek and artist Mark Bagley (in his first project for DC) guided the travails of the three heroes as they struggled to find the secret of a cosmic force that was threatening to destroy them—and Earth.

JUNE

R.I.P.
***Batman* #676**

Writer Grant Morrison and artist Tony Daniel's run on *Batman* reached its climax with the story arc "R.I.P.," which made headlines across the globe with the apparent death of Batman. In this epic tale, Batman was driven insane by Dr. Simon Hurt and the Black Glove, a criminal group created to destroy everything Batman held dear. Through the course of the story (which branched out into other titles, including *Robin* and *Nightwing*), Bruce Wayne found many of the foundation stones of both his and Batman's life in danger of being overturned. One of the biggest bombshells was Dr. Hurt's claim that he was Bruce Wayne's father, Thomas, and that it was he who ordered the murder of his own wife. Morrison also brought back the Batman of Zur-En-Arrh. Originally seen in February 1958's *Batman* #113, Morrison re-imagined the character from an amusing alien version of the Dark Knight into a subconscious safeguard Bruce Wayne had created in the event of an enemy driving him mad or wiping his mind. "R.I.P." followed Batman's fall from grace and betrayal by his then-girlfriend Jezebel Jet, herself a secret member of the Black Glove and one of the few women to learn Batman's true identity.

The story arc left no one close to Batman untouched and brought to an end Bruce Wayne's career as the Dark Knight. It also led into the equally shocking *Final Crisis* #6 in January 2009, and was followed by *Batman: Battle for the Cowl* in May 2009, as several heroes and villains fought to replace Bruce Wayne as the Batman.

Dr. Simon Hurt creates the Black Glove to destroy everything Batman believed in. He also claims to be Bruce's father, Thomas Wayne, who was thought to have been killed years before.

February: *Ratatouille* wins the Academy Award® for Best Animated Picture.
February: Kosovo declares independence from Serbia.
May: A cyclone devastates Myanmar (Burma), killing tens of thousands.
May: Israel celebrates the sixtieth anniversary of its founding.

JULY

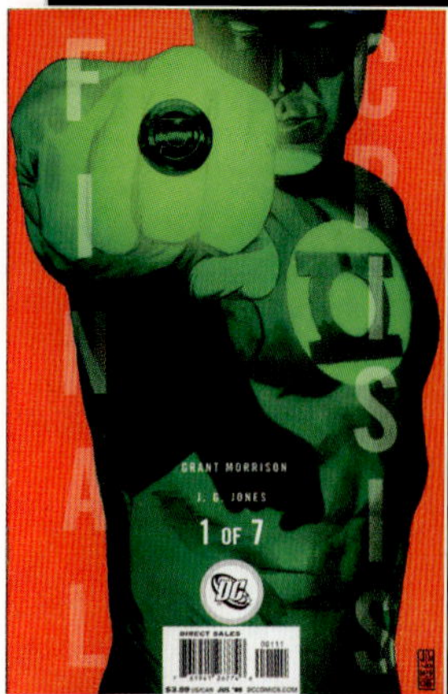

EVIL WINS!
***Final Crisis* #1**

Grant Morrison's most ambitious epic for DC affected the whole of the DC Universe and was the end result of years of careful planning. In the opening issue, the murder of the New God Orion hinted at the apocalyptical events to follow. Orion's murder was investigated by both Detective Dan Turpin and the Green Lantern Corps, while the issue also featured the brutal murder of the Martian Manhunter by the mysterious villain Libra. The Martian Manhunter's death signaled the beginning of an all-out war between good and evil.

Marketed with the tagline "Evil Wins," the series lived up to its premise, as the later issues revealed a twisted version of an Earth firmly under Darkseid's control. The main series, with art by J. G. Jones (joined on later issues by Carlos Pacheco and Doug Mahnke), had a visually dramatic conclusion as an army of pan-dimensional Supermen teamed up to save the world from the effects of Darkseid's Anti-Life Equation.

The story spread out into several miniseries under the *Final Crisis* banner, many of which added an extra layer of depth to the central storyline. These included *Final Crisis: Rogues' Revenge*, in which Flash's arch-enemies sought out Inertia for payback in making them complicit for the death of Bart Allen; *Final Crisis: Legion of 3 Worlds*, in which Superman-Prime attacked the Legion of Super-Heroes; and *Final Crisis: Superman Beyond 3D*, highlighting Superman's other-dimensional journey through time and space to save a mortally injured Lois Lane. As well as the various miniseries, several one-shots were published, including *Final Crisis: Requiem*, covering the aftermath of the Martian Manhunter's murder, and both *Final Crisis: Submit* and *Final Crisis: Resist*.

Detective Dan Turpin discovers the body of Orion, one of the greatest of the New Gods, in Gotham City Harbor. The death is just the first of many.

JULY

AT THE MOVIES THIS MONTH: The follow-up to 2005's *BATMAN BEGINS* hit the cinemas. Directed by Christopher Nolan, *THE DARK KNIGHT* reunited nearly all the cast from the first film, with Maggie Gyllenhaal replacing Katie Holmes as Rachel Dawes. The movie also included an Oscar-winning performance from Heath Ledger as the Joker and broke box-office records...

AUGUST

WITCHY WOMAN
***Madame Xanadu* #1**

Matt Wagner came back into the fold as writer for Vertigo following his work on the long-running *Sandman Mystery Theatre* by helming a relaunch of 1981's *Madame Xanadu*. Madame Xanadu was a relatively minor player in the DC Universe, but Wagner, assisted by stunning art from Amy Hadley, crafted a first-class tale looking back over the centuries into her past. The series began with Madame Xanadu's time in Arthur's Camelot, where she was known as Nimue, the witch who beguiled Merlin. Her story involved many of Vertigo and DC's supernatural characters, including the Phantom Stranger, Zatara, and Death herself.

SEPTEMBER

A WAR IN HELL...
***Reign in Hell* 1**

DC's version of Hell erupted into all-out war when the rulers of Purgatory, Blaze, and Satanus, invaded Neron's infernal domain. Written by Keith Giffen, with art by Tom Derenick and Bill Sienkiewicz, the war grew worse as both sides called on heroes and villains from the mortal realm to help them. Shadowpact, Etrigan the Demon, Dr. Fate, and even Lobo found themselves drawn into the conflict, which left Lady Blaze in control.

MAGIC
***Billy Batson and the Magic of Shazam!* #1**

Writer and artist Mike Kunkel took Shazam well and truly back to his roots in one of the more popular Johnny DC titles, an imprint aimed at a younger audience. Stylish art and a fast-paced, action-packed story helped to put some magic back into the adventures of Billy Batson's superpowered alter ego, Captain Marvel.

IN THE REAL WORLD...

August: The summer Olympic Games are held in Beijing, China.
August: The Russia–Georgia War begins when Georgia attacks South Ossetia.
September: A succession of hurricanes—named Fay, Gustav, Hanna, and Ike—hits Haiti, killing 600 people.

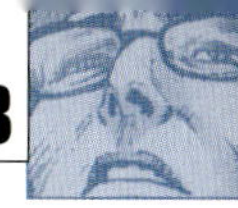

OCTOBER

LOST ISLAND
***Air* #1**

One of Vertigo's most original series, *Air* followed the travails of flight attendant Blythe. After an encounter with a mysterious but charming passenger (and possible terrorist), Blythe found herself in the strange lost country of Narimar and a target for a violent anti-terrorist group known as the Etesian Front. Dealing with war, terrorism, and the nature of reality itself, *Air* was created by writer G. Willow Wilson and artist M. K. Perker, who had previously worked together on the critically acclaimed original graphic novel, *Cairo*.

DECEMBER

A BRAVE NEW WORLD
***Action Comics* #870**

In *Action Comics*' story arc "Brainiac," writer Geoff Johns and artist Gary Frank added another definitive chapter to one of the most iconic runs in the history of the comic. Superman's latest battle with the deadly Brainiac came to a bittersweet end as the Man of Steel and Supergirl teamed up to stop the villain's plan to shrink Metropolis to the size of a bottle. Their joy at finding the lost city of Kandor was tempered by the tragic death of Clark's adopted father, Jonathan Kent. The story led into the *Superman: New Krypton Special* #1, in December, where the people of Kandor realized the potential of their Superman-like powers, and Superman left Earth for New Krypton.

Tragedy soon follows Superman's victory over Brainiac when Jonathan Kent, Superman's adoptive father, has a heart attack and dies before Superman can fly home to be with him.

WAR IS HELL
***Unknown Soldier* #1**

Vertigo's revamped *Unknown Soldier* moved the story of the bandaged anti-hero from World War II to modern-day Uganda. Writer Joshua Dysart and artist Alberto Ponticelli produced a series that wasn't afraid to confront the brutal horror of war on the African continent, and dealt with child soldiers, religion, despair, and hope. It was nominated for a prestigious Eisner Award for Best New Series and was hailed by many as the best horror book of the year.

BEST SELLER

***Gears of War* #1**

One of the best-selling comics of the year was WildStorm's adaptation of the hit computer game *Gears of War*. Created for the Xbox 360 by Epic Games, *Gears of War* was the fastest selling console game of 2006, and its highly visual content made it a clear choice for a comic book spin-off.

Seen through the eyes of new Delta Squad recruit Jace Stratton, the first six-part story arc, "Hollow," introduced the violent, post-apocalyptic world of Sera and the main Gears of Delta Squad—including the legendary hero Marcus Fenix. The story opened with the main Gears in the thick of the action. They were fighting the alien Locust as Delta Squad attempted to find other surviving Gears in the Badlands surrounding Jacinto, one of the few surviving human cities in a world ravaged by Locust.

Joshua Ortega's action-packed strip and Liam Sharp's atmospheric testosterone-fuelled art helped the comic become a massive hit. The first issue of *Gears of War* sold over 400,000 copies, partly due to it being sold in Blockbuster and Games stores across America, as well as in traditional comic shops.

Marcus Fenix, legendary leader of Delta Squad, leads the fight against the deadly Locust.

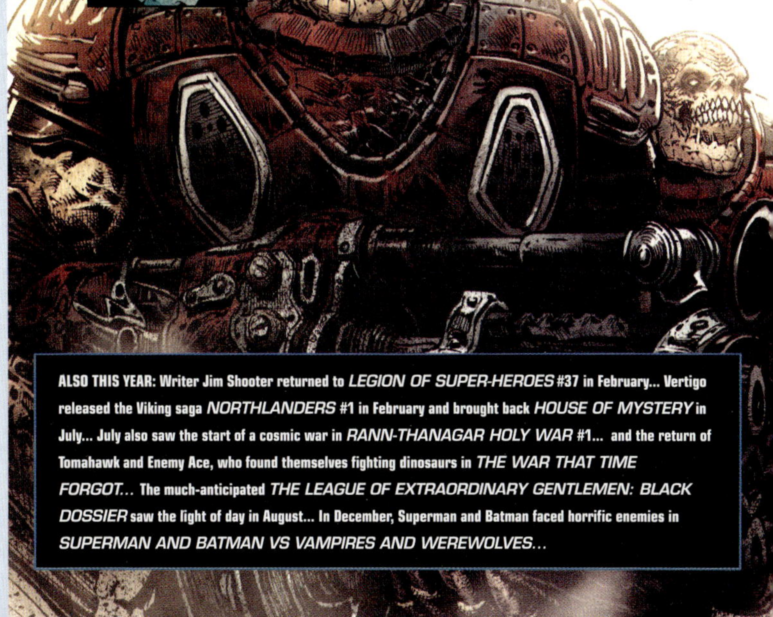

ALSO THIS YEAR: Writer Jim Shooter returned to *LEGION OF SUPER-HEROES* #37 in February... Vertigo released the Viking saga *NORTHLANDERS* #1 in February and brought back *HOUSE OF MYSTERY* in July... July also saw the start of a cosmic war in *RANN-THANAGAR HOLY WAR* #1... and the return of Tomahawk and Enemy Ace, who found themselves fighting dinosaurs in *THE WAR THAT TIME FORGOT*... The much-anticipated *THE LEAGUE OF EXTRAORDINARY GENTLEMEN: BLACK DOSSIER* saw the light of day in August... In December, Superman and Batman faced horrific enemies in *SUPERMAN AND BATMAN VS VAMPIRES AND WEREWOLVES*...

November: Barack Obama becomes the first African American to be elected President of the United States, in an election with the highest voter turnout in forty years.

November: A cholera epidemic in Zimbabwe kills thousands.
December: Coldplay's *Viva La Vida* is the best-selling album of the year.

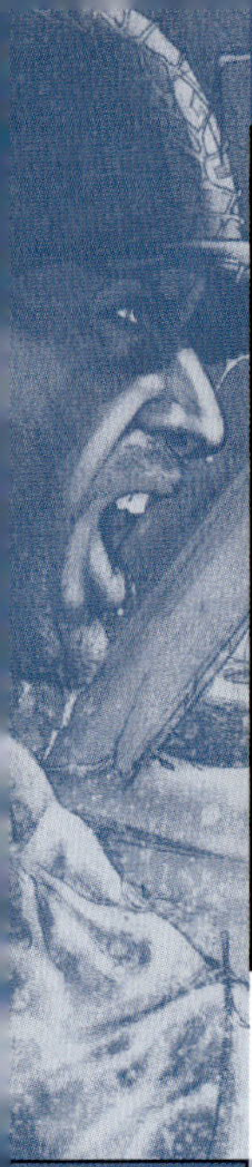

2009

"BARRY ALLEN. YOU OWE ME YOUR LIFE. YOU ALL DO."

Nekron, *Blackest Night* #4

THE DEAD RETURN

2009 was a year in which DC dominated the sales charts with hit after hit. It was also a year that saw DC taking the comic medium into bold new directions with exciting formats such as the stylish *Wednesday Comics*. Meanwhile, Geoff Johns' Green Lantern saga exploded into the DC Universe with the crossover event *Blackest Night*. Promotional Black Lantern rings were given away with the first printing of *Blackest Night* #1 and became every comic fan's must-have accessory for the year. They were soon followed by rings for each of the other Corps. Eventually a special boxed set of rings was released. Elsewhere, Grant Morrison's run on *Batman* started a new chapter as Dick Grayson assumed the Dark Knight's mantle. With many of the dark stories of previous years heading toward their climaxes, DC was ending the decade both stronger and more popular than ever before.

JANUARY

OMAHA BEACH

***Sgt. Rock: The Lost Battalion* #1**
Billy Tucci took on both the writer and artist roles to return Sgt. Rock and Easy Company to action. Tucci's six-part story was based on the true-life story of the last stand of U.S. infantrymen trapped behind enemy lines following the Omaha Beach landings of World War II. Tucci blended real-life facts with tough war action to create something extra special, as he told the story through the eyes of a cartoonist crossing paths with Sgt. Rock, providing a different take on DC's greatest war hero. The story opened with a drawing of Rock in the style of Joe Kubert, the artist most closely associated with the hero. The series' fact-based background led to it being featured in the *Army Times*, a weekly newspaper for U.S. Army personnel.

Sgt. Rock and Easy Company face heavy fire during the landings on Omaha beach in World War II.

FEBRUARY

GHOST IN THE MACHINE
***Haunted Tank* #1**

A popular war story, *Haunted Tank* returned with an updated setting. The ghost of cavalry commander Jeb Stuart had originally appeared in *G.I. Combat* in 1961, set during World War II. Now, Stuart haunted an M1 Abrams tank that was fighting in the second Iraq war. Published by Vertigo, the five-issue series writer by writer Frank Marraffino and artist Henry Flint dealt with war and racism as the ghost of General Stuart (who fought for the South in the Civil War) met his latest descendent—an African-American tank commander.

IN THE REAL WORLD...

January: A U.S. Airways pilot manages to land his ailing plane on the icy waters of the Hudson River, New York, saving all on board.

MARCH

JUSTICE LIKE LIGHTNING

***Black Lightning: Year One* #1**

Black Lightning was given the *Year One* treatment courtesy of writer Jen Van Meter and artist Cully Hamner. The six-issue series told the story of ex-Olympic athlete Jefferson Pierce's return to his home of Suicide Slum, an impoverished district of Metropolis. The district was under the thrall of a criminal gang known as the 100, and a mysterious force was at work preventing Superman from helping the residents. When one of Pierce's students was brutally killed, Pierce decided to use his previously hidden meta-human powers to clean up the neighborhood, giving birth to a new hero.

NO REST FOR THE WICKED

***Faces of Evil: Solomon Grundy* #1**

Evil took over DC for many of the March titles as the bad guys gained their own lead stories. From Lex Luthor in *Action Comics* #873 to Hush in *Detective Comics* #852, the villains were placed firmly center stage. Some, such as Kobra, Promethea, and Solomon Grundy, gained their own one-off titles. *Faces of Evil: Solomon Grundy* was co-written by Geoff Johns and Scott Kolins, with Kolins also providing the artwork as Grundy's dark origins were explored.

AT THE MOVIES THIS MONTH: Alan Moore and Dave Gibbons' epic *WATCHMEN* was released. Directed by Zack Snyder, the movie was accompanied by the release of *WATCHMEN: TALES OF THE BLACK FREIGHTER* as an animated, straight-to-DVD film…

APRIL

ELEGY FOR THE DARK KNIGHT

***Batman* #686**

Writer Neil Gaiman and art legend Andy Kubert teamed up to present a touching imaginary tale of a wake for the dead Batman. The Dark Knight's ghostly form looked on as both his friends and enemies—including the Joker and Superman—paid Batman their final respects. A love song to the Dark Knight's long history, this comic's storyline, "Whatever Happened to the Caped Crusader?," concluded in *Detective Comics* #853, also in April. It went on to win *SFX*'s Best Comic award in 2010.

MAY

A NEW DARK KNIGHT BEGINS

***Batman: Battle for the Cowl* #1**

Tony Daniel took on the writing tasks and the art for the three-issue follow-up to *Batman: R.I.P.* With Bruce Wayne believed dead, Gotham's criminals were running wild, and a new Black Mask was trying to make things even more chaotic. The opening issue had Dick Grayson struggling with his destiny while Jason Todd cut a swath through Gotham's criminals as a new gun-toting Batman. By the end of the series, Dick had defeated Jason and assumed the identity of Batman, heralding a new beginning for the Dark Knight.

JUNE

FAST JUST GOT FASTER

***Flash: Rebirth* #1**

Writer Geoff Johns and artist Ethan Van Sciver, the team behind the seminal *Green Lantern: Rebirth* of 2004 and 2005, joined forces again to relaunch Barry Allen as the Flash. Hot on the heels of Barry's dramatic re-entry to the DC Universe at the end of *Final Crisis* #3 (September 2008), Johns was given the job of reintroducing Barry Allen to the world. It was a difficult line to walk, as many fans held Wally West close to their hearts. The first issue opened with the celebrations for Barry's return while also dealing with the disconnection he felt upon returning to a world that had changed so much since he had joined the Speed Force years before. It also reintroduced the Flash "team" of Wally, Bart Allen (himself brought back from the dead during *Final Crisis*), and Jay Garrick, while also introducing a mystery when Barry accidentally turned Wally's old enemy Savitar to dust with just a touch. *Flash: Rebirth* was a runaway success, the first issue selling out within days of its release. Not only was Barry Allen back, but the whole Flash family had joined him for the start of a new era.

Barry Allen races to save his own history as he tries to solve the mystery of his return.

February: Australia sees the deadliest wildfires in its history, as homes across the state of Victoria are destroyed and hundreds of people are killed or injured.

February: *Slumdog Millionaire* wins the Academy Award® for Best Picture.
June: Music icon Michael Jackson dies at the age of 50 after suffering a cardiac arrest.

JUNE

THE LOST WORLD

***Warlord* [third series] #1**

Writer and artist Mike Grell was back at the helm for the return of DC's greatest sword-and-sorcery hero—Travis Morgan, the Warlord. During its late-1970s heyday, the title had been one of DC's best sellers. The new series followed on from the end of Grell's original run, ignoring 2006's failed attempt at a reboot. Opening with a new group of explorers finding their way to the lost world of Skartaris, the action soon reintroduced Travis and his trusted sidekick Shakira, as the Warlord became involved in helping his old friend Machiste retake the entire Shadow Kingdom. Joe Prado provided the interior art, with Mike Grell producing the covers and script.

THE LOST GIRL...

***Power Girl* #1**

Writers Justin Gray and Jimmy Palmiotti, together with artist Amanda Conner, emphasized the fun of Power Girl in her first ongoing series. Power Girl had suffered a great deal more than most heroes since her first appearance in *All Star Comics* #58 in February 1976. Originally the cousin of Earth-2's Superman, she had her origins retconned following *Crisis on Infinite Earths* #12 (March 1986) to make her the granddaughter of Arion of Atlantis. After the events of *Infinite Crisis*, her original Earth-2 Kryptonian origin was back, but the hero now found herself on New Earth—as a new Earth-2 had its own version of Power Girl. Set in New York, *Power Girl* #1 saw the hero trying to start a new life as Karen Starr, until an old JSA foe, the Ultra-Humanite, attacked, hoping to place his consciousness in Power Girl's body.

JULY

A BOLD NEW FORMAT

***Wednesday Comics* #1**

52 had given DC its first major success with the weekly format, but with the publication of *Wednesday Comics*, DC took the concept to new creative heights. Named after the day that new comics arrive in U.S. comic shops, *Wednesday Comics* was a broadsheet anthology created to be reminiscent of the comic section in Sunday newspapers. It also brought together some of the medium's top creators. The first issue contained fifteen continuous stories, including a new Sgt. Rock saga drawn by the legendary Joe Kubert and written by his son Adam; "Metamorpho," scripted by Neil Gaiman and illustrated by Michael Allred; "Superman," with a script by John Arcudi, and art by Lee Bermejo; "Wonder Woman," scripted and illustrated by Ben Caldwell; "Kamandi: The Last Boy on Earth," with a script by Dave Gibbons and art by Ryan Sook; and "Batman," with a story by Brian Azzarello and art by Eduardo Risso. The new format proved a massive success, with the first few issues quickly selling out and the Superman story being reprinted in *USA Today*. The series ended in September after twelve issues.

Green Lantern, Hawkman, and Kamandi all feature in the first series of *Wednesday Comics*, DC's bold new weekly anthology.

AUGUST

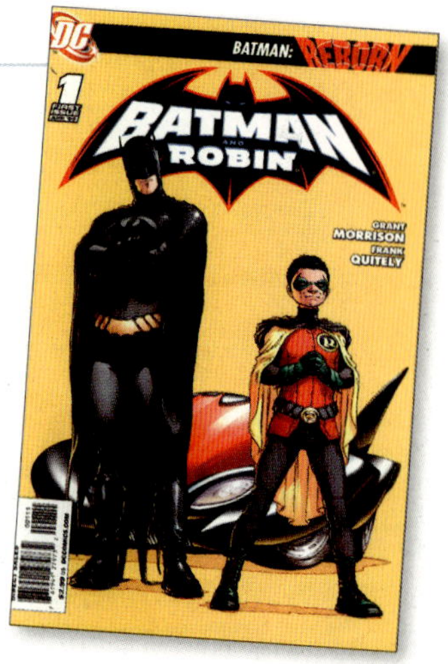

THE NEW DYNAMIC DUO

***Batman and Robin* #1**

After the critical acclaim of their *All Star Superman* series, writer Grant Morrison and artist Frank Quitely teamed up once again to unleash a new Dynamic Duo on Gotham City. Following the events of *Batman: R.I.P.* and *Batman: Battle for the Cowl*, Bruce Wayne was believed to be dead, and Dick Grayson had taken on his mantle, with Damian Wayne now functioning as Robin. The new team had a vibrant synergy, with the smart-mouthed Damian convinced of his own abilities while also believing that Dick wasn't up to assuming Batman's role. The new series also emphasized Gotham City's strange inhabitants and introduced a new foe for the Dark Knight in the form of the strange and twisted Professor Pyg, who could control people by molding strange doll-like masks onto their faces. Future issues brought back Jason Todd (as the Red Hood) with a new sidekick named Scarlet, the duo being a dark and twisted version of Batman and Robin. The series was another brilliant chapter in Grant Morrison's epic run on the Dark Knight.

Dick Grayson and Damian Wayne, the new Batman and Robin, take to the streets (and skies) of Gotham City, with a bizarre array of villains lying in wait for them.

IN THE REAL WORLD...

August: U.S. Senator Edward "Ted" Kennedy, youngest brother of Former President John F. Kennedy, dies from brain cancer at his home.

September: An undersea earthquake causes a series of tsunamis to hit the Samoan islands of the Pacific, killing over 100 people.

SEPTEMBER

RISE!

***Blackest Night* #1**

By 2009, readers of both DC and Marvel were becoming immune to the surprises that the big summer series brought on an almost annual basis—changes that were often reversed within a couple of years. So for an event title to shock and thrill readers, it had to be something extra special. *Blackest Night* was just that. Flowing naturally out of writer Geoff Johns' legendary run on *Green Lantern*, the seeds of *Blackest Night* had been planted at the start of *Green Lantern: Rebirth* (December 2004) and it took an eight-issue series of its own to tell.

The opening issue was filled with foreboding and a sense of impending doom as people across the world remembered fallen heroes, including the seven million killed when the tyrant Mongul and the Cyborg Superman destroyed Coast City. At the same time, something was emerging from the mysterious Sector 666—black rings with the ability to apparently raise the dead. With the Guardians of the Universe themselves unable to stop the long-predicted Blackest Night, the rings connected with dead heroes and villains and returned them to life—or rather a twisted version of sentience that made them want to "recruit" living friends into the Black Lantern Corps by tearing out their hearts. Artist Ivan Reis handled the vast array of characters with amazing skill, bringing out the emotional core of Johns' brilliant script. The truly shocking final scene of the first issue saw Hawkman and Hawkgirl brutally murdered by Black Lantern versions of Elongated Man and Sue Dibny (for years DC's happiest and brightest couple). The savage deaths ramped up the feeling that this was one threat that would leave a permanent mark not only on the Green Lantern Corps, but the whole of the DC Universe.

Heroes and villains alike rise from the dead to become Black Lanterns, the deadliest threat the Green Lantern Corps has ever had to face.

NOVEMBER

UP, UP, AND AWAY

***Superman: Secret Origin* #1**

While 2003's *Superman: Birthright* had dealt with the Man of Steel's first appearance in Metropolis, his origin hadn't been told since 1986's *Man of Steel* miniseries by John Byrne. By 2009 it was time for the story to be told again. Writer Geoff Johns and artist Gary Frank approached the story from a different angle than previous envisioners. They brought out the distinctly human (and Kryptonian) side of the Man of Steel's story.

The first issue dealt with the young Clark Kent struggling to come to terms with his powers in Smallville, his first kiss with Lana Lang, and his first contact with a young Lex Luthor (now also a native of Smallville)—not to mention his first time flying. By the issue's end, Martha Kent had fashioned a costume for her adopted son from the Kryptonian blankets found in his rocket ship. Clark wasn't impressed however, declaring, "Today is the last time I ever wear this." Future issues covered Clark's adventures with the Legion of Super-Heroes, his arrival in Metropolis, and the effect Superman's first appearances had on the city—especially on the *Daily Planet*'s Lois Lane. *Superman: Secret Origin* was a smash hit, satisfying old and new Superman fans alike, and cementing the Man of Steel's origin for the 21st century.

The young Clark Kent starts to learn of his Kryptonian origins when a hologram of Jor-El and Lara appears before him and his adoptive father, Jonathan.

ALSO THIS YEAR: *SEAGUY* returned to Vertigo for a new limited series in June... August saw Tim Drake gain a new name and a new series in *RED ROBIN*... In the same month *GOTHAM CITY SIRENS* followed the exploits of Catwoman, Harley Quinn, and Poison Ivy... Best-selling author Ian Rankin penned Hellblazer graphic novel *DARK ENTRIES* in October for Vertigo...

December: A United Nations conference on climate change is held in Copenhagen.
December: "Poker Face" by Lady Gaga is the best-selling single of the year.

December: Pope Benedict XVI is knocked down by a woman with a history of psychological problems during the start of his Christmas Eve mass at St. Peter's Basilica.

2010s

It was time for DC Comics to evolve. After years of successful movies, animated and live-action television series, and merchandising that kept well ahead of even the most dedicated collectors, DC decided it was in need of rebranding on a global level to help better encompass its various endeavours. Publisher Paul Levitz stepped down, making way for new Co-Publishers Dan DiDio and Jim Lee. DC also formed the overarching brand name of DC Entertainment, spearheaded by President Diane Nelson. It was a bold move, but with an experienced team onboard, fans could be confident that DC's new direction would stay true to the roots of its characters and its rich history.

The start of the decade heralded the first significant change. A company-wide shakeup saw much of the DC offices relocate from New York to a new home in Burbank, California. Then, in late 2011, DC brought to a close its entire line of comics, and released 52 new titles that now featured characters existing in a streamlined revision of the past 75 years of continuity. Although several titles had reached landmark numbers—including the 900th issue of *Action Comics*—the new initiative offered a total reboot of the line, providing fans with a fresh take on the characters. With each title now beginning at issue number one, DC was confident that it would give new readers a clean slate without the burden of decades of backstory. The changes in the characters' continuity lit up message boards and social media platforms with debate and excitement, and there was still more to come. The true innovation of the *New 52* lay in its digital initiative. For the first time in the history of the medium, every title that DC offered would be available for digital download on the same day that its physical counterpart hit comic book stores. The move would prove that DC was fearless and innovative in its attempts to keep the business of comic books serving the audience of the future.

"WHO THE HELL IS BRUCE WAYNE?"

A *New 52* era Bruce Wayne reveals his identity to Green Lantern for the first time in *Justice League* #5 (January 2012)

2010

"BREAK AWAY FROM THE PAST AND THE BLACKEST NIGHT AND HEAD INTO TOMORROW."

Hal Jordan, *Blackest Night* #8

BRIGHTEST DAY

2010 was a year of change, rebirth, and celebration for DC Comics. The epic *Blackest Night* came to its conclusion, leading into the mystery of *Brightest Day*. Three classic titles reached milestones with *Superman* and *Batman* reaching their 700th issues and *Wonder Woman* her 600th. However, the event that outshone all others was the company's own—DC Comics celebrated its 75th anniversary.

The company wasn't living off past successes, however. Publisher Paul Levitz stepped down, and Co-Publishers Dan DiDio and Jim Lee, along with DC Entertainment Chief Creative Officer Geoff Johns, teamed up to helm DC Comics. With DC Entertainment President Diane Nelson promising more movies based on DC Comics' heroes, the future has never looked brighter.

APRIL

AT THE MOVIES THIS MONTH: Vertigo's thriller *THE LOSERS* hit the big screen, directed by Sylvain White and starring Jeffrey Dean Morgan as Clay and *THE WIRE*'s Idris Elba as Roque...

MAY

HOLLYWOOD BABYLON
***American Vampire* #1**
Vertigo has a proven track record of cutting-edge horror—much like best-selling novelist Stephen King. When the two came together, the title was always going to be special, and *American Vampire* was just that. The first five double-sized issues consisted of two stories, illustrated by Rafael Albuquerque. Scott Snyder wrote each issue's lead feature, and Stephen King wrote the back-up tales. The opening tale in issue #1 was set in 1920s Hollywood, mixing the glitz and glamor of the period with the literal bloodsuckers of the film world. King's tale provided background to the first story, set decades before in the Wild West, and introduced Skinner Sweet, the first American Vampire.

LET THERE BE LIGHT

***Blackest Night* #8**
Written by Geoff Johns and illustrated by Ivan Reis, *Blackest Night* proved to be the darkest hour for many of DC's finest heroes. The saga reached a suitably epic climax in May, with DC's heroes joining forces to defeat Nekron and end his connection with Black Hand. The series' conclusion had one final major shock for readers as the White Lantern raised several heroes and villains from the dead. The gatefold pullout of the reborn heroes and villains—including Aquaman, the Martian Manhunter, Firestorm, and Hawkman—set up the mystery of the *Brightest Day* saga that followed. This saga would go on to explore why these heroes and villains, including a now living Deadman, were the ones chosen to be reborn. The end of *Blackest Night* concluded themes stretching back almost a decade through *Green Lantern: Rebirth* and the events of the Sinestro Corps War, and paved the way for a new chapter in the history of the DCU.

Ivan Reis' impressive gatefold featured (left to right): Maxwell Lord, the Reverse-Flash, Hawk, Jade, Captain Boomerang, Firestorm, Martian Manhunter, Aquaman, Hawkman, Hawkgirl, Deadman, and Osiris, back from the dead and ready to take part in the *Brightest Day*.

IN THE REAL WORLD...

April: In one of the worst ecological disasters in U.S. history, a BP oil rig explodes in the Gulf of Mexico and creates a devastating oil spill.

JUNE

AT THE MOVIES THIS MONTH: Western hero Jonah Hex got the big-screen treatment with the release of a self-titled feature film starring Josh Brolin and directed by Jimmy Hayward.

JULY

A NEW DAY DAWNS

***Brightest Day* #1**

The *Blackest Night* might have been over but it left in its wake a mystery—12 heroes and villains resurrected by the white light expelled from within the center of the Earth. This enigmatic white light later transformed into a lantern that no one was able to move. The most changed of the reborn heroes was former Deadman Boston Brand, now very much alive and in possession of a white ring that gives the user powerful control over the physical world. Co-written by Geoff Johns and Peter J. Tomasi, and illustrated by Ivan Reis, Patrick Gleason, Ardian Syaf, Scott Clark, and Joe Prado, *Brightest Day* was the start of the next chapter in the history of the DC Universe.

CLAN OF THE BAT

***Batman: The Return of Bruce Wayne* #1**

Writer Grant Morrison continued his epic run chronicling the Dark Knight's adventures with *Batman: The Return of Bruce Wayne*. The six-part series followed an amnesiac Bruce Wayne as he was slowly pulled through time to the present, each issue taking part in a different period of history and illustrated by a different artist.

The first issue followed on from the end of *Final Crisis*, where Bruce Wayne had been thrown back in time by Darkseid's Omega Beams, rays of energy that sent the recipient into progressively worse alternate lives. Trapped in the prehistoric past, Wayne helped the Deer People tribe, who was fighting its neighbors, led by Vandal Savage. Wayne took up the mantle of the bat again, albeit it in a more primitive form, as depicted on the cover. Subsequent issues included Batman as a pirate, a cowboy, and an investigator, before he returned to the present day.

There was also a mystery to solve. What had the Omega Beams actually done to the Dark Knight? Batman's allies Rip Hunter and the Time Masters joined Superman to track their friend down. At the literal end of the universe, they learned that Darkseid had used Batman as a doomsday device who was set to destroy the world when Wayne returned to the present. It was an epic tale, reintroducing Bruce Wayne to the present, while providing a unique look at the history of the DC Universe.

An amnesiac Bruce Wayne, unaware of his life as Batman, is pinned to the ground in the desert and left to die by Vandal Savage after appearing in prehistoric times.

LEVITZ'S LEGION

Legion of Super-Heroes* #1 *[fifth series]

Stepping down from his long tenure as the Publisher at DC Comics, Paul Levitz proved to fandom that he had no intention of retiring from the comic book world as he stepped up as writer to both a new *Legion of Super-Heroes* revitalization as well as the recently resurrected *Adventure Comics* title. With the Legion firmly resurrected to their original incarnation and continuity thanks to the efforts of writers like Brad Meltzer and Geoff Johns, Levitz was able to pick up right where he left off with his favorite heroes with the help of artist Yildiray Cinar. The two instantly shook up the 31st century's status quo by inducting the villain Earth-Man into the Legion's hallowed ranks.

BIRD WATCHING

Birds of Prey* #1 *[second series]

Before the end of its run, the original *Birds of Prey* series was one of the longest running DC comics with a female lead, second only to *Wonder Woman*. So with the theme of renewed life permeating the DC Universe during the *Brightest Day* event, it only made sense to bring back the title with fan-favorite writer Gail Simone at the helm. With the help of artist Ed Benes, Simone threw Oracle, Black Canary, Huntress, and Lady Blackhawk back into the thick of the action, this time joined by recently resurrected hero Hawk.

The Birds quickly ran afoul of the Penguin, and a mysterious new martial artist calling herself the White Canary.

A dark figure battles the Huntress and the Black Canary when they come to the aid of the Penguin in a dark alleyway. The Birds are curious about this skilled fighter who calls herself the White Canary.

April: Apple launches its iPad tablet computer in the U.S.
April: Polish President Lech Kaczynski is killed in a plane crash in Russia.
April: An ash cloud created by the eruption of a volcano in Iceland brings chaos to the European air industry by grounding flights for seven days.

AUGUST

A NEW BEGINNING

***Batman Beyond* #1 [second miniseries]**

The Batman of the future, Terry McGinnis, made the fulltime leap from animation to the world of comic books, courtesy of writer Adam Beechen and artist Ryan Benjamin. While the hero had previously made a handful of guest appearances in other comics, as well as in his own 1999 miniseries and an ongoing title that tied into his cartoon series, this new six-issue miniseries was the first real attempt to bind the world of *Batman Beyond* to the DC Universe. Fighting crime in the future, with the aid of his elderly mentor Bruce Wayne, Terry's adventures took place in an amalgam of the comic book and animated continuities and proved so popular that the series blossomed into its own regular title.

A STAR IS REBORN

***Green Arrow* #1 [third series]**

Life was never boring in Green Arrow's hometown of Star City. After being devastated by an attack orchestrated by the super-villain Prometheus, the city experienced a bizarre rebirth during the Brightest Day event when a star-shaped forest instantly formed out of the wreckage. Under the direction of writer J. T. Krul and penciller Diogenes Neves, Green Arrow found himself now a modern-day Robin Hood, an outlaw seeking refuge in that very forest, only to learn of its mystical properties. Green Arrow's new debut issue was celebrated with a painted cover by Mauro Cascioli and a variant edition by Ethan Van Sciver.

FROM ROBIN TO RED HOOD

***Red Hood: Lost Days* #1**

Jason Todd, the notorious corrupted second Robin, was finally awarded a miniseries of his own with the help of writer Judd Winick and artist Pablo Raimondi. No stranger to chronicling the adventures of the now-adult Todd, Winick took full advantage of the six-issue series to fill in the gaps between the character's resurrection in the pages of *Infinite Crisis*, to his reemergence in Batman's world in the popular *Batman: Hush* storyline. The result was a tale of a hero's decent into the realm of anti-hero, aided and abetted along the way by other notorious Gotham villains, including Rā's and Talia al Ghūl and the Joker.

UP, UP, AND AWAY!

***Superman* #700**

The 700th issue of *Superman* was 56 pages long, with two special covers to celebrate DC's 75th anniversary. The main cover was by Gary Frank, with a variant by Eduardo Risso. Inside, three of comicdom's most talented writers created very special Superman tales. Dan Jurgens, the writer who had once killed off Superman, returned to the Man of Steel for the first time in years. Writer James Robinson brought his epic run to an end with a touching tale that brought Superman back to Lois Lane after his time on New Krypton. Lastly, new *Superman* writer J. Michael Straczynski gave a preview of his much-anticipated run that would begin in the following issue.

AMAZON ANNIVERSARY

***Wonder Woman* #600**

Wonder Woman was renumbered to mark the Amazing Amazon's 600th issue, with writer J. Michael Straczynski joining a host of top talent to celebrate. The 56 page special was released with two covers, the main one illustrated by comics legend George Pérez, which introduced the Amazon Princess' new costume. Writers Geoff Johns and Gail Simone and artists Phil Jimenez and Don Kramer also supplied their talents. J. Michael Straczynski's tale gave an insight into the direction he would take the title when assuming control from issue #601. Straczynski was one of the most hotly anticipated writers to work on the title since George Pérez's run following *Crisis on Infinite Earths*.

IN THE REAL WORLD...

August: The first ever Summer Youth Olympics—the 2010 Summer Youth Olympic Games—are held in Singapore.

September: An undersea earthquake causes a series of tsunamis to hit the Samoan islands of the Pacific, killing over 100 people.

NOVEMBER

SUPERMAN EARTH ONE
Superman: Earth One

DC had previously introduced a fresh non-canonical approach with its All Star line, setting the adventures of Superman and Batman outside of the DC Universe continuity. The change meant that each book was more focused on having a distinctive voice and a bolder approach, rather than restarting the characters' adventures to inspire a modern audience. But there was still a market for a revitalized-style line of DC books.

That's where writer J. Michael Straczynski and artist Shane Davis came in. Well known for his work on the TV series *Babylon 5*, as well as for having helped breathe new life into Marvel's famed web-slinger in the pages of *Amazing Spider-Man*, Straczynski's cinematic storytelling was just the modern voice DC was looking for. Alongside the art of rising star Shane Davis, already a headliner in DC's popular *Justice League of America* and *Superman/Batman* titles, the stage was set to reinvent the first of what would possibly be a long line of super hero revitalizations. And there was no better or bolder place to start than with Superman.

Utilizing the graphic novel hardcover format rather than a monthly issue-by-issue series that would later be collected, DC attempted to show their readers that what they were about to experience was something new, told in a self-contained fashion. The story began when a young Clark Kent headed to Metropolis for the first time, unsure of where his life would take him. With unlimited physical and mental capabilities, the future was wide open for the teen. However his fate soon came into focus when an invading alien force attacked the city, searching for the last living son of Krypton. Forced to become a man before the readers' eyes, Kent stepped up to the plate as valiantly as ever, debuting Superman to a stunned city and setting the stage for future chapters in Superman's new dramatic story.

An alien mothership arrives in Metropolis, and several other cities, with a hoarde of smaller ships. Clark learns that the invaders are enemies of Kyptonians from the planet Dheron.

Tyrell has spent years searching for the last survivor of Krypton, and he won't stop until his enemy is destroyed. The resulting battle is a huge test for the Man of Steel, who must stop Tyrell before he destroys Earth.

DECEMBER

THE BRITISH BATMAN
Knight and the Squire #1

In a series spinning out of writer Grant Morrison's take on the classic British equivalent of Batman and Robin, writer Paul Cornell and artist Jimmy Broxton embraced some of the lesser known facets of English culture as they charted the adventures of London's own Dynamic Duo. As the Knight and his sidekick Squire participated in offbeat adventures ranging from pub brawls to mystical encounters at Stonehenge, Cornell sprinkled in dozens of authentic details from his native country. In fact, there were so many cultural references that DC included a "translation" page of sorts in the back of the issues, letting American readers in on many of the comic's inside jokes.

Magic keeps villains and heroes at peace with each other—Jarvis Poker, the British version of the Joker, is actually against crime—but when this force is disrupted, the Knight and Squire must retain the peace.

FACED WITH DEATH
Action Comics #894

One of best-selling writer Neil Gaiman's creations, favored by fans, was given new life in the DC Universe when writer Paul Cornell and artist Pete Woods brought Death into an issue of *Action Comics* to meet Superman's arch foe, Lex Luthor. The upbeat living personification of life's final stage greeted Luthor in trademark style when the villain was injured and thought dead. Since Gaiman's Sandman characters had made few appearances in the continuity of the DCU after the birth of the Vertigo Comics imprint, many fans wondered if those characters still co-existed in the same world as heroes like Superman and Batman. Death's appearance in *Action Comics* seemed to cement this idea, although the true re-merging of the Vertigo and DC worlds wouldn't occur until the following year during the dramatic events of the miniseries *Flashpoint*.

As Lex Luthor's body lies motionless, seemingly dead, he has an out-of-body experience observing the scene from a point outside time where he encounters the ominous teenager, Death. Death uses her powers to show him the intricacies of his past life.

December: A United Nations conference on climate change is held in Copenhagen.
December: "Poker Face" by Lady Gaga is the best-selling single of the year.

December: Pope Benedict XVI is knocked down by a woman with a history of psychological problems during the start of his Christmas Eve mass at St. Peter's Basilica.

BATMAN #700 (August 2010)
With cover art by David Finch, a script by Grant Morrison, and art by Tony S. Daniel, Andy Kubert, Frank Quitely, Finch, and Richard Friend, this milestone issue of *Batman* featured an all-star roster of talent. *Batman* #700 was an oversized special that featured stories spotlighting Batmen from different eras: Bruce Wayne; Bruce's troubled son, Damian Wayne; and Dick Grayson, who, in 2009, had taken on the mantle of Batman.

FINCH

2011

"YOU KNOW THE DEAL, METROPOLIS. TREAT PEOPLE RIGHT OR EXPECT A VISIT FROM ME."

Superman, *Action Comics* #1 [second series]

THE NEW 52

Fans had heard whisperings, but no one had any true idea of the DC Universe shakeup that would occur toward the end of 2011. While interest had begun to grow at the launch of DC's new large-scale crossover mini-series *Flashpoint*, it was the release of the fifth issue of *Flashpoint* that peaked online chatter and fan excitement. Suddenly, the DC Universe had been drastically altered, with every title in the line coming to a close in order to make way for 52 new monthly titles. Characters' backstories were altered, heroes' wardrobes were overhauled, new writers and artists emerged while old favorites were shuffled around, and a bold same-day digital release initiative began. Both the real life and fictional worlds of DC Comics had been given a facelift for a new generation, one that would spark controversy, and draw attention on a worldwide scale.

JANUARY

BATMAN GOES GLOBAL
***Batman Incorporated* #1**

Acclaimed writer Grant Morrison's multi-tiered Batman saga took a dramatic turn with *Batman Incorporated # 1*, the next step in the evolution of Batman's war on crime. A new ongoing series written by Morrison with art by Yanick Paquette, *Batman Inc.* sprang from the pages of the *Batman: The Return of Bruce Wayne* mini-series, the events in the series *Batman and Robin*, as well as the one-shot special *Batman: The Return*, which was also written by Morrison, with art by superstar David Finch. Now safely home from an adventure spiraling through time due to the machinations of the villain Darkseid, Batman had seen a glimpse of the future, and decided to prepare for the darkness ahead. He organized Batman Incorporated, a global operation that would set up a Batman in strategic locations and countries all around the world. And to give his decision that much more impact, Bruce Wayne himself had announced this initiative at a press conference, revealing that he had been financially backing Batman's actions and would continue to do so into this new phase.

With the help of other artists including Chris Burnham and digital renderer Scott Clark, Morrison explored this idea of a corporate team of Batman heroes, recruiting many of the characters that had appeared before in Morrison's previous run on the Batman title, as well as in other past comic books. Characters like the Knight, Squire, Man-of-Bats, and Raven Red joined the fray, as did longtime Batman associates Catwoman, Oracle, Batgirl, Robin, and Dick Grayson (still serving as Gotham's Batman during Bruce Wayne's travels). New heroes related to Batman, such as Nightrunner and Batwing, were introduced, and characters like the Hood were dug up from relative obscurity. Even members of Batman's old hero team, the Outsiders, were brought into the fold in the Dark Knights' battle against a new corrupt worldwide organization calling itself Leviathan.

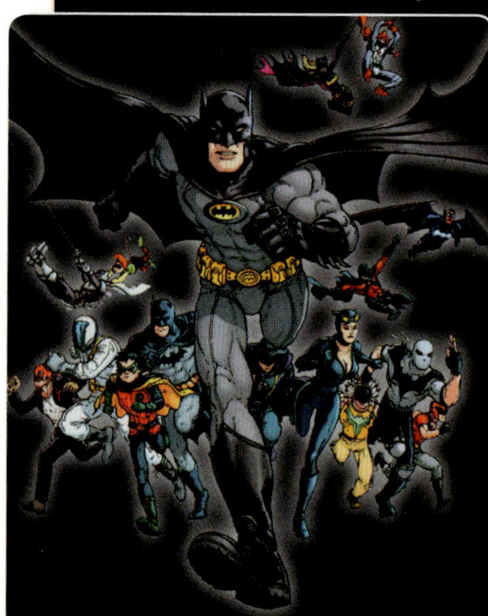

Batman leads an international group of handpicked vigilantes who will each take on the work of Batman across the world. The team includes Robin, Catwoman, Red Robin, Batgirl, Batwoman, The Hood, El Gaucho, Nightrunner, Batwing, and Mr. Unknown.

Through the series' eight-issue run, Morrison continued to write in the style that had made him the top Batman author since his return to the character in 2006. He combined modern storytelling with past and present Batman continuity, updating long-lost tales for a contemporary audience without alienating new readers. He even reintroduced the original Batwoman from the 1950s into the series, despite the character being deemed outdated and non-canon. Morrison's interpretation of Batman continued to be the version to watch, no matter what title he happened to be working on.

IN THE REAL WORLD...

January: Violent protests, part of the "Arab Spring," result in the fall of the Tunisian government.

JANUARY

BATMAN'S DARK SIDE

***Batman: The Dark Knight* #1**

David Finch had established himself as a favored artist among fans while working for Marvel on characters such as the X-Men and New Avengers. So when he made the move to DC, he was granted his own new Batman title to draw, but was also given free reign to write the comic. Finch's meticulous style brought about largely positive changes, accompanied by impressive sales figures and increased popularity. With a tale that featured a romance from Bruce Wayne's childhood intertwined with a demonic supernatural secret, *Batman: The Dark Knight* proved worthy of its title's adjective, showcasing a shadowy, foreboding Gotham City to match its guardian.

There is animosity at first, but feelings between Dawn Golden and Bruce Wayne ignite when they are thrown together following the death of his parents.

THE LIGHTER KNIGHT

***Detective Comics* #871**

While *Batman Incorporated* and *Batman: The Dark Knight* celebrated the return of the original Caped Crusader, Bruce Wayne, both *Batman* and *Detective Comics* focused on the continued adventures of Gotham's other Batman, Dick Grayson. Having taken over from his mentor when Bruce Wayne was thought murdered by Darkseid, Grayson was a more optimistic Dark Knight, despite the grim world he was thrown into. And there were few people better to chronicle Grayson's exploits than new writer Scott Snyder, whose tight plotting and fresh voice combined with striking art by Jock and Francesco Francavilla to create one of the most memorable and critically praised runs on *Detective Comics* in recent years.

THE NEW BATWOMAN

***Batwoman* #0**

Kate Kane made her long-awaited breakthrough into her own monthly series with the zero issue of *Batwoman*, written and illustrated by an artist quite familiar with the character, J. H. Williams III, with co-writing by W. Haden Blackman and additional art by Amy Reeder. While Batwoman's series wouldn't begin its monthly installments until the dawn of the *New 52*, this special introductory issue followed Bruce Wayne as he observed Batwoman, discovering for himself the kind of hero that she had become.
With breathtaking rendering and impressive page design, *Batwoman* was a visual tour de force, placing a welcome spotlight on a distinctive female protagonist.

APRIL

ONLINE OPUS

***DC Universe Online Legends* #1**

Writers Marv Wolfman and Tony Bedard piloted the adventures of some of the biggest heroes in the DC Universe in this new 26 issue biweekly comic. Tying into the premise of DC's new shared multi-player video game in the tradition of other hits like *World of Warcraft*, *DC Universe Online Legends* promised a tale as epic as its source material. With the premise of a desperate Justice League ravaged by Brainiac's forces in a dystopian future, the debut issue of this saga featured art by JLA star Howard Porter as well as Adriana Melo.

MAY

WAR OF THE GREEN LANTERNS

***Green Lantern [third series]* #64**

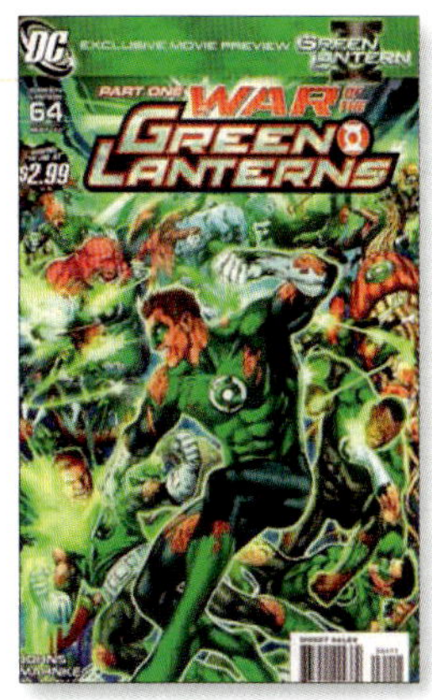

In chapter one of a new Green Lantern event timed to coincide with Warner Bros.' blockbuster *Green Lantern* movie, writer Geoff Johns and penciler Doug Mahnke began the "War of the Green Lanterns" crossover. This epic ten-part battle would begin in the pages of Green Lantern's own title, and continue into the other GL titles: *Green Lantern Corps* and *Green Lantern: Emerald Warriors*. This action-packed first chapter began as Hal Jordan and the other lead representatives of the color spectrum went searching for renegade Guardian Krona. While the rest of Hal's team were sucked into the magical *Book of the Black*, Hal found himself facing an army of mind-controlled Green Lanterns taken over by the power-seeking Krona.

April: An earthquake and subsequent tsunami hit the east coast of Japan, killing several thousand. Tsunami warnings are issued in neighboring countries.

April: Prince William and Catherine Middleton marry in a large ceremony held in Westminster Abbey, London.

JUNE

AT THE MOVIES THIS MONTH: Actor Ryan Reynolds took to the stars as Hal Jordan in director Martin Campbell's new movie, *GREEN LANTERN*, finally throwing a mainstream spotlight on the DC hero.

A HERO RETURNS
***Action Comics* #900**

After a brief journey across the country, Superman was back in Metropolis in time for *Action Comics'* landmark 900th issue. The first comic book title to reach such an epic milestone, Action Comics' anniversary was celebrated with a 96-page spectacular. The issue featured the conclusion to the Lex Luthor tale that writer Paul Cornell had been crafting since issue #890, and also segued into the title's new story arc, *Reign of the Doomsdays*. With a main story featuring art by Pete Woods, Dan Jurgens, Rags Morales, Ardian Syaf, Jamal Igle, and Gary Frank, the issue also featured back-up stories by a variety of creators, including writers Damon Lindelof, Paul Dini, Geoff Johns, David S. Goyer, Richard Donner and Derek Hoffman. Illustrating the scripts was an equally talented array of artists, including Ryan Sook, R.B. Silva, Gary Frank, Miguel Sepulveda, and Matt Camp. As an added bonus, a particularly fun two-page spread showcased Superman's evolution from the 1930s to present day, produced by artist Brian Stelfreeze.

SEPTEMBER

WAITING GAMES
The New Teen Titans: Games

It was a project that was over twenty years in the making. The legendary pairing of writer Marv Wolfman and artist George Perez reunited on the team that rocketed them to superstardom in the 1980s. While the team had begun work on Games late in that same decade, it had proven to be a taxing project for Perez's extremely detailed artistic style. Due to the labor-intense nature of the story and changes in editorial staff at DC, both Wolfman and Perez postponed this hardcover in favor of other projects before finally returning to finish this espionage epic nearly two decades after its original conception, altering the story in the process.

JULY

GONE IN A FLASH
***Flashpoint* #1 [second miniseries]**

Writer Geoff Johns had been reinventing the DCU for some time now, having revived the classic Silver Age Green Lantern, Hal Jordan, and returned him to his place as a DC icon through his popular ongoing series and the *Blackest Night* miniseries. So when Johns helped resurrect Silver Age Flash, Barry Allen, it made sense that he would then place the character at the center of a giant crossover event that would see the Flash as the main protagonist. But restoring Barry Allen's fan base was only the tip of the iceberg for this five-issue miniseries drawn by superstar Andy Kubert. It was accompanied by many tie-in miniseries and one-shots, such as the critically acclaimed three-issue series by fellow superstar writer Brian Azzarello and artist Eduardo Risso, *Batman: Knight of Vengeance*.

The main *Flashpoint* series began as Allen woke up in a reality far different than the one he'd been accustomed to. It was a world in which Aquaman and Wonder Woman were at war with one another's forces, devastating the common man in the process. It was a world where Superman was a frail, meek captive, and Cyborg was a top-tier heroic force for good. A world in which Bruce Wayne was murdered by a fateful mugger, forcing his father Thomas Wayne to adopt the mantle of a more violent and jaded Batman. It was the world of *Flashpoint*, and Barry Allen had no idea how to get back to his own universe.

After joining forces with Batman, Cyborg, new heroine Element Woman, and a handful of other rebel heroes to combat the warring Atlantis and Amazon factions, the Flash soon learned that he himself was the reason that history had been altered. In mourning for his mother, the Flash had raced to the past to stop his foe, the Reverse-Flash, from murdering her. The resultant energies Barry carried with him from the Speed Force had changed reality into the dystopia of *Flashpoint*. Knowing what he had to do, Barry raced back in time to undo his mistake, and then sped forward again, in the hope of returning to a restored DC Universe.

However, on the journey back, something was different. Instead of just one reality, the Flash witnessed three: the DC, *Wildstorm*, and *Vertigo* universes. As he continued toward the present, the Flash glimpsed a hooded, mysterious figure who seemed to be watching the events as they transpired. In the end, Barry Allen managed to arrive back in the present day, but unbeknownst to him, the universe had changed again. And this time, it seemed to be permanent.

Life as Barry Allen knows it is turned on its head when he wakes to find the world a very different place. His mother is alive and Superman has been replaced by Subject 1, an unfamiliar character being kept in a government cell.

IN THE REAL WORLD...

May: President Barack Obama announces that Osama bin Laden has been killed during an American military operation in Pakistan.

June: New York becomes the sixth state to legalize same-sex marriage.

July: Atlantis returns to Earth, concluding NASA's space shuttle program.

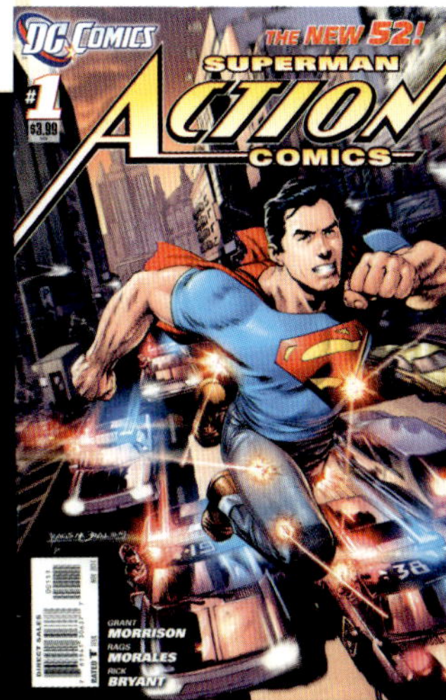

Action Comics #1 [second series]

The renumbering of *Action Comics* meant a story change that proved to be very popular with fans. *Action Comics* #1 debuted as one of the *New 52*'s strongest sellers, even with its bold diversions from past incarnations. Writer Grant Morrison and artist Rags Morales' retelling of the Man of Steel's early career combined fast-paced sequences, worthy of its title, with an inexperienced, cockier version of Superman, who was just six months into his career.

Batman #1 [second series]

Writer Scott Snyder paired with superstar artist Greg Capullo in this second volume to create modern flair and indisputable energy. As one of the heroes whose backstory was minimally affected by the revamp of the DCU and the events of *Flashpoint*, the title began with business as usual for the Caped Crusader: stopping a riot at Arkham Asylum. But as Snyder's story progressed, Batman would soon find himself at war with a secret society and their enforcers known as Talons.

NOVEMBER

THE SENSATIONAL SEVEN

Justice League #1

Employing midnight release parties all over the United States, DC proudly debuted the first of its *New 52* comics in this dynamic premier issue written by Geoff Johns and drawn by Jim Lee. With a powerhouse creative team and an arguably more powerful roster of DC's biggest name heroes (Superman, Batman, Wonder Woman, Green Lantern, Flash, Aquaman, and Cyborg), the Justice League was back with a bang, ushering in the new reality of the post-Flashpoint DC Universe.

Taking place approximately five years ago, Justice League began with a six-issue story set to retell the original meeting of these icons. While later stories would shift to present-day adventures of the hero team, this initial tale began with Batman's first meeting with Green Lantern, both on the trail of a mysterious alien creature called a Parademon. Batman and Green Lantern traveled to Metropolis to recruit the help Superman. Soon joined by the Flash, Wonder Woman, Aquaman and the young Cyborg, the unlikely allies quickly discovered that the Parademons were actually invading troops sent by an other-dimensional god named Darkseid. In their triumph, they had unintentionally formed the Justice League.

A runaway hit for DC, *Justice League* served as the first indication of the continuity changes that were to affect the DCU. This revamped team was to be a band of younger heroes; it was a *Justice League* intended for a new generation, and a monumental flagship title for the *New 52*.

Wonder Woman #1 [fourth series]

Brian Azzarello took the reigns to write Wonder Woman's newest volume of chronicles. Partnering with Azzarello on this new title was Cliff Chiang, whose take on Wonder Woman employed a looser artistic hand, allowing the violence of the story and the motion of the action to take center stage. A new costume, sans flash, was debuted for the heroine, and fans also noticed the mystical and complex world of intrigue and horror that Azzarello created as he intertwined realistic characters with fanciful gods of myth.

ALSO THIS YEAR: October saw the final release of *JUSTICE SOCIETY OF AMERICA* #54 where Alan Scott seemingly gave his life to defeat a foe, saving friends and family in the process. In November, Barbara Gordon, who was paralyzed by a gunshot wound, resumed her former role in *BATGIRL* #1. In the same month, Geoff Johns and Ivan Reis reinvented *AQUAMAN*, turning the character into a force to be reckoned with. Also in November, *ANIMAL MAN* #1 by writer Jeff Lemire and artist Travel Foreman, was released.

September: Occupy Wall Street protests begin in the United States. This develops into the Occupy movement, which spreads to several countries by October.

December: The United States formally declares an end to the war in Iraq.
December: Tropical Storm Washi causes flash flooding in the Philippines.

THE 52 PICK-UP

There have been periods of waning sales as well as spans of renewed interest throughout comic book history. In the early years of the Golden Age, comics sold in the millions and were often traded and re-read by kids eager to experience the new idea of the super hero. The 1960s saw another boom in popularity spearheaded by the mania of the 1966 *Batman* TV show. The 1990s saw an unprecedented return to sales in the millions with the height of direct market and comic book stores. But as of 2011, comics weren't selling as well as they had in the past, even as super hero movies topped the box-office charts. This was a different age, and comics would need to adapt.

This was the environment that birthed DC Entertainment, and soon after, the *New 52*; the launch of 52 new ongoing comic titles, some that restarted old series, and some that featured new takes on familiar characters or concepts. The resulting changes to continuity and issue numbering may have been controversial, but there was no denying the heightened interest it granted DC in 2011.

While costume overhauls were pretty much a universal change, the continuity adjustments made to each character were done on a case-by-case basis, with an eye toward stimulating each franchise. Batman's world was nearly unchanged as creators were merely shifted around with one or two new additions. Nightwing, Batwing, and Catwoman received their own titles, and the Birds of Prey continued their mission while Red Hood and the Outlaws began theirs. Meanwhile, Harley Quinn shifted over to the pages of the new title *Suicide Squad,* by writer Adam Glass and artist Federico Dallocchio, where she was given a new costume alongside her super-villain teammates. The history of Green Lantern was also virtually unaltered, although it did continue to expand in the pages of not just *Green Lantern*, but also *Green Lantern: New Guardians, Green Lantern Corps*, and the violent title *Red Lanterns* by writer Peter Milligan and artist Ed Benes.

Superman's world was drastically revised, as *Action Comics* retold the Man of Steel's origin, while *Superman* chronicled more recent events. Superman and Lois Lane were no longer married in this brave new reality, they had never even dated, an idea that freed the Man of Steel up for many new love interests. Meanwhile, Superboy's story was restarted by writer Scott Lobdell and artist R. B. Silva, tying his origins in further to the Teen Titans, a super-team whose continuity was also severely altered, essentially starting the group's exploits from the ground up. Supergirl also began from square one, and Green Arrow's costume was altered to match that of his counterpart in the *Smallville* television series.

The Justice League titles expanded to include *Justice League International* as well as writer Peter Milligan and artist Mikel Janin's *Justice League Dark*, which featured the adventures of magic-based heroes banding together. And while The *Savage Hawkman* saw writer Tony S. Daniel and artist Philip Tan continue Hawkman's exploits and *The Flash* saw writer/artist Francis Manapul do the same with Barry Allen with the help of co-writer Brian Buccellato, DC also experimented with a few new genres, including writer Paul Cornell and artist Diogenes Neves' take on medieval times in *Demon Knights*. War and horror genres were explored, and Jonah Hex even starred in *All Star Western*, courtesy of writers Justin Gray and Jimmy Palmiotti and artist Moritat.

There were hits and misses for the *New 52*, but DC was prepared to be innovative in an attempt to give the industry the fuel it needed. Only time would tell what other drastic changes awaited the DC Universe.

Below: The New 52 *series threw up a good deal of changes for Clark Kent. In this new reality, Clark is no longer married to Lois Lane. Clark visits Lois at home to apologize for his recent behavior and unwittingly disturbs her evening with a new boyfriend.*

2012

"THE WHOLE WORLD'S CHANGING FAST AND GETTING WEIRDER. THAT MEANS OPPORTUNITY, CLARK."

Jimmy Olsen, *Action Comics* #3 *(second series)*

TURNING THE PAGE

The *New 52* was just the beginning. Not prepared to slow the hectic pace that had been set by recent changes, DC Comics continued to test new concepts and shake up its recently relaunched titles. Creative teams were altered as editors looked at ways to improve the new titles. Six publications were brought to a close, though each one was immediately replaced with a new title to keep the 52 initiative going strong, and to test out other untried concepts.

The DC logo also underwent reconstructive surgery. The new logo, called 'The Reveal,' featured the letter C, partially covered by a "peeling" D, which created a page turn effect. It was a bold statement and just one of the many indicators that DC was looking toward the future.

JANUARY

BRINGING THE THUNDER
T.H.U.N.D.E.R. Agents [third series] #1

The agents of The Higher United Nations Defense Enforcement Reserves (T.H.U.N.D.E.R.) were a fondly remembered team published by Tower Comics in the 1960s. After DC finally obtained the rights to the characters, writer Nick Spencer came aboard in 2010 to write a ten-issue series primarily illustrated by artist Cafu. But due to the sweeping changes of the *New 52*, fans were left wondering if these cult classic characters would return to comic book limbo for the foreseeable future. Fortunately for them, Spencer and the T.H.U.N.D.E.R. agents returned for a new six-issue miniseries, this time featuring the artwork of Wes Craig.

FEBRUARY

COMING TO LIGHT
The Ray* #1 *[second miniseries]

A popular character from *Quality Comics* in the 1940s, the Ray had been reinvented time and time again to suit an ever-changing modern audience, first as a member of DC's Freedom Fighters in the 1970s, and then as a solo act when his son took over his super heroic mantle in the 1990s. And while another hero briefly picked up the reigns in the 2000s, writers Justin Gray and Jimmy Palmiotti decided the time was right once again to introduce a new Ray, this time into the world of DC's *New 52*. With a bold new look thanks to the interpretation of artist Jamal Igle, the Ray burst onto the scene in the form of good-humored lifeguard Lucien Gates.

Lifeguard Lucien Gates is enjoying the sun when he is hit by a particle beam. His friend, Darius Williams, runs to his aid, but it is too late—Lucien has undergone a startling change.

IN THE REAL WORLD...

January: The European Union imposes a trade embargo against Iran following its attempts to enrich uraniaum.

DARKSEID LIVES!

Justice League #4

The first major threat to the safety of the post-*Flashpoint* DC Universe arrived in dramatic fashion thanks to writer Geoff Johns and artist Jim Lee. In a story set five years in the past at the Justice League's original formation, the heroes were busy facing a hoard of aliens from an unknown origin called Parademons. As each hero proved his worth on the battlefield, none was quite prepared for the god-like creature that would suddenly greet them from an extra-dimensional wormhole in space and time called a Boom Tube. The creature announced himself without the slightest tinge of fear of the powerful beings standing before him. He was Darkseid, and the fledgling Justice League's troubles had just begun. Sporting a new costume designed by Jim Lee with an overt omega design theme, arguably the greatest villain in the DC Universe was reestablished after his high profile death in the pages of 2008's *Final Crisis*. While the evil god's fate is uncertain in the world of the *New 52*, Darkseid's appearance as the Justice League's first adversary seemed a perfect fit for the blockbuster Johns and Lee were assembling.

Notorious god, Darkseid, lives on. He appears before the Justice League who were unaware of the imminent arrival of this dangerous nemesis.

HOSTILE TAKEOVER

Batman Incorporated: Leviathan Strikes #1

In a story set firmly in the reality before the changes brought on by the *New 52*, writer Grant Morrison and artists Chris Burnham and Cameron Stewart finished the latest chapter in the saga of *Batman Incorporated*. In this oversized special that was originally intended to be several issues of the regular *Batman Incorporated* series, fans saw a stand-alone Batgirl solo adventure followed by a dramatic confrontation between Batman's forces and those of Dr. Dedalus, a battle that ended with a shock as Robin was forced to kill the villain in order to save Batman's life. But Morrison had more surprises in store for his audience. On the issue's final splash page, he revealed the mastermind behind the forces of Leviathan as none other than Batman's old flame and Robin's mother, Talia al Ghūl.

FORGING STEEL

Action Comics #4 [second series]

Writer Grant Morrison and artist Rags Morales granted John Henry Irons, the well-known hero called Steel, a new origin in this issue of *Action Comics*. In this new incarnation, John Henry Irons' former origin involving his life as a construction worker was reworked, and Henry was established as a scientist and inventor who donned his metal battle suit to aid the young Superman during a bout against corrupted government employee, John Corben. Corben was wearing experimental Metal-Zero mechanized armor, but had lost control due to the machinations of an alien force. And so, like the true hero he was, Irons charged off into battle, helping Superman and ending Corben's violent rampage—the details of which were explained further in this issue's back-up story by writer Sholly Fisch and artist Brad Walker.

Steel was just one of the many characters given new life in the world of the *New 52*. Superboy and Supergirl were also given familiar yet reworked origins in their own respective titles, making the landscape of Superman's own particular corner of the DC Universe vastly different to its pre-*Flashpoint* counterpart.

John Corben, wearing a mechanized suit, attacks Superman. John Henry Irons is called to don his own armor in order to help the super hero.

MARCH

OLD FRIENDS

Action Comics #5 [second series]

While the Legion of Super-Heroes had been introduced to the post-*Flashpoint* DC Universe in the pages of its own title written by Paul Levitz with art by Francis Portela, as well as the new series *Legion Lost*, written by Fabian Nicieza and drawn by Pete Woods, their first appearance in Superman's newly revised history was revealed in *Action Comics* #5, thanks to writer Grant Morrison and artist Andy Kubert. Also featured alongside the debut of Cosmic Boy, Saturn Girl, and Lightning Lad was Superman's fully realized new origin, a modern reinterpretation of how baby Kal-El was sent rocketing to planet Earth.

February: Queen Elizabeth II celebrates her Diamond Jubilee, marking the 60th anniversary of her accession to the throne.

February: Acclaimed American singer and actress Whitney Houston is found dead in her hotel, the night before she is due to attend the Grammy Awards ceremony.

MARCH

BEWILDERING THE BATMAN

***Batman* #5 [second series]**

When Batman awoke to find himself in a secret labyrinth underneath Gotham City, he finally realized the extent of the power held by his opponents, the Court of Owls. Writer Scott Snyder and artist Greg Capullo were making life quite difficult for everyone's favorite Dark Knight, as Batman became a pawn in a larger game, running like a rat in a maze for the entertainment of this shadowy group of Gotham's elite. Drugged and pursued by the violent enforcer known as Talon, Batman limped through his bizarre surroundings, while the panels of the comic itself began to run sideways and then upside down, giving the reader a similarly disorienting effect to that which Batman was experiencing. Told through beautiful artwork depicting the true horror of the Dark Knight's situation, this issue was the perfect penultimate chapter in Batman's first encounter with the Court of Owls, and a clear indicator of the level of creative thought being put into Snyder and Capullo's well-crafted run.

APRIL

BEYOND BATMAN

***Batman Beyond Unlimited* #1**

Despite having his animated series canceled years ago, *Batman Beyond* continued to thrive in the comic book world as a fan-favorite version of the future Caped Crusader. With the shakeup of the *New 52* inspiring another reboot of his title, *Batman Beyond* returned in a series that would not only chronicle his own adventures, but also those of the *Justice League Beyond*, his superpowered teammates. Comprised of two stories in each issue, the first half of the comic featured a solo *Batman Beyond* story written by Adam Beechen with art by longtime Batman artist Norm Breyfogle. The second story focused more on the adventures of the JLB, written by Derek Fridolfs and Dustin Nguyen, with Nguyen also serving as the story's penciller.

CHALLENGERS OF THE UNKNOWN

***DC Universe Presents* #6**

The anthology format of *DC Universe Presents* was set up to be an introduction of sorts to some of the more obscure reaches of the *New 52*. The title started strong with its opening five-issue arc starring Deadman, written by Paul Jenkins and illustrated by Bernard Chang. And while Deadman was by no means a first-tier DC character, the next heroes to take the center stage in the book were even lesser known. Written by Dan DiDio with art by mainstay Jerry Ordway, a new interpretation of the *Challengers of the Unknown* crashed into their own storyline, updating a classic idea for the modern-day DCU.

MAY

INTRODUCING SHAZAM!

***Justice League* #7**

Captain Marvel was given facelift in the first chapter of his new series of back-up stories that appeared after the main *Justice League* tale. Geoff Johns and guest artist Gene Ha wrote the issue's lead story, while Johns tackled the back-up with the help of artist Gary Frank. In a series that would not only tweak Captain Marvel's costume, but also change his name to simply "Shazam," readers were given a glimpse at a new Billy Batson, presenting a character considerably less of a boy scout than his pre-*Flashpoint* counterpart. The new Billy was mischievous, bouncing from foster home to foster home, while dealing with the loss of his parents.

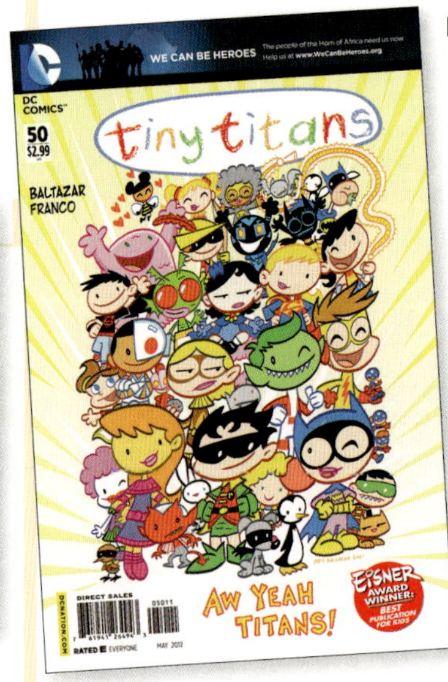

LAST OF THE TITANS

***Tiny Titans* #50**

Writer/artist Art Baltazar and co-writer Franco's popular children's comic hit its 50th issue with this final installment in the offbeat adventures of the reimagined *Teen Titans*. Often filled with inside jokes for older diehard comic book readers, but told in a simplistic style that attracted generations too young for other DC titles, *Tiny Titans* was a breath of fresh air, essentially discovering an untapped market DC hadn't approached since its days experimenting with funny animal comics. It was a winning formula that Baltazar and Franco would carry on into the pages of their newest kids' comic, *Superman Family Adventures*, which would debut just two months after the *Tiny Titans* finale.

JULY

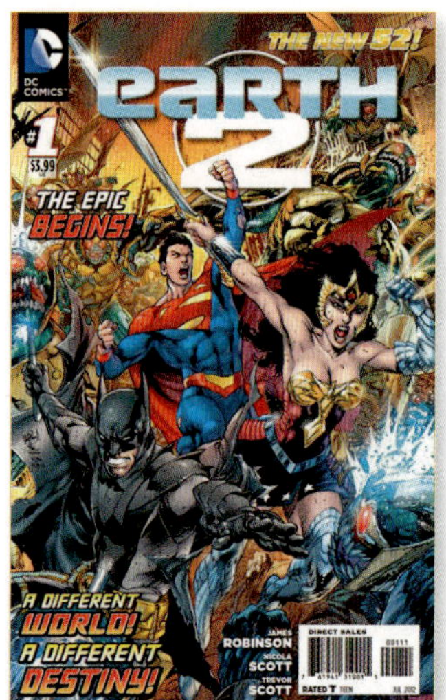

TALE OF TWO EARTHS

***Earth 2* #1**

After the events of *Flashpoint*, and the creation of a brave new world for DC's host of characters, writer James Robinson set out to define the status quo of the multiverse with the help of the talented penciler Nicola Scott. The cover featured a dynamic image of Superman, Batman, and Wonder Woman of Earth 2 diving into action, but none of these three heroes would survive the issue. Although they defeated the Parademon invasion of their home, the Earth 2 counterparts of DC's fabled trinity were all killed in action, making way for a new breed of hero—reinvented characters from DC's Golden Age.

IN THE REAL WORLD...

March: Well-known publication Encyclopaedia Britannica discontinues its print edition with plans to focus on its online edition.

March: The President of Mali, Amadou Toumani Touré, is ousted in a coup d'état.
May: The 2012 World Expo is held in Yeosu, South Korea.

NEXT GEN

***The Ravagers* #1**

Penned by former Marvel scribe Howard Mackie, with art by Ian Churchill, was the newest ongoing addition to the *New 52*, *The Ravagers*. A melding of *Wildstorm*'s popular *Gen 13* title and characters from the Teen Titans franchise like Rose Wilson, Terra and Beast Boy, *The Ravagers* spun directly out of the events of *"The Culling"* a crossover involving other young characters, including the Teen Titans and Superboy. The series' debut issue featured a variant cover to help link the title to the current *Teen Titans* series.

FRESH INC.

Batman Incorporated* #1 *[second series]

Writer Grant Morrison returned to the Batcave to continue his opus with art by Chris Burnham. In this revival of the former hit series, Morrison began the next chapter in Batman's battle against the forces of Leviathan with a bout with an assassin named Goatboy. Folding his work into the reality of the *New 52*, Morrison continued his fresh approach to the Batman mythos, jumpstarting these adventures with the reveal of Leviathan's secret mission. The series debut was celebrated by a variant cover by former *Batman and Robin* artist, luminary Frank Quitely.

DIALING IT BACK

***Dial H* #1**

As six titles of the original *New 52* line-up ended, six new ongoing comics debuted including *Dial H*, a revitalization of the *Dial H for Hero* concept of the 1960s. While updating this particular strip wasn't a new idea and had been attempted fairly recently in 2003's *HERO*, this particular incarnation, written by Hugo award winning novelist China Mieville and illustrated by Mateus Santolouco, promised to explore the very boundaries of reality itself.

LIEFELD AND LOBO

Deathstroke* #9 *[second series]

Everyone's favorite 'bastich,' Lobo, made his *New 52* debut when he discovered another tough DCU gun for hire, Deathstroke, hot on his trail. With this issue, Rob Liefeld moved from the recently canceled *Hawk and Dove* title to take over for writer Kyle Higgins and artist Joe Bennett as both the writer and artist of Deathstroke's ongoing series. And in order to make his debut as dramatic as possible, Liefeld brought with him Lobo, the nearly indestructible intergalactic biker with a chip on his shoulder. The result was a flashy dose of mayhem as only the main man could deliver.

GIRL POWER

***World's Finest* #1**

Fans of Power Girl and the Huntress had been seeing the groundwork for the revelation of the other dimensional *Earth Two* in the lives of their heroines almost since the start of the *New 52*. Readers had been spotting hints of another Earth in the pages of *Mister Terrific*, by writer Eric Wallace and artist Gianluca Gugliotta, surrounding supporting character Karen Starr (Power Girl's alter ego), as well as in writer Paul Levitz and Marcus To's recent *Huntress* miniseries. It all built up to this newest take on the *Worlds' Finest*, a dramatic pairing of these two dimensionally-displaced heroines written by Levitz with art by George Pérez and Kevin Maguire.

THE WAR EFFORT

G.I. Combat* #1 *[second series]

The relaunch of the DC Universe allowed the company to experiment with other genres that had proven popular in years past. One of those was the unfortunately still-relevant world of real-life combat. In the first batch of *New 52* titles, DC had debuted the action drama *Men of War*, written by Ivan Brandon and Jonathan Vankin with art by Tom Derenick and Phil Winslade, as well as the more fantastic special forces thriller *Blackhawks* by writer Mike Costa and penciller Graham Nolan. And although both of those titles were canceled as of their eighth issues, DC decided to once again invest in the art of war with *G.I. Combat* by writers J. T. Krul, Justin Gray, and Jimmy Palmiotti, and featuring the art of Ariel Olivetti and Dan Panosian. Alongside commentary on the realities of modern day warfare, this series also rekindled two classic DC properties, the *War That Time Forgot* as well as the *Unknown Soldier*.

SOMEBODY SAVED HIM

***Smallville Season 11* #1**

When Bryan Q. Miller's *Batgirl* run ended, fans were sad to see an end to the writer's take on the character, as well as the unique brand of youthful humor he was able to bring to the title. And when the popular WB live-action Superman television series *Smallville* ended, many fans were also disappointed to see this particular take on the Boy of Steel's growth into the Man of Steel conclude. Luckily for both camps, DC decided to continue the *Smallville* series in comic book form in this new title written by Miller, with art by Pere Perez, picking up where the show's tenth TV season had left off.

July: The Summer Olympics begin in London, England.
August: The Mars Science Laboratory (Curiosity rover) is scheduled to land on Mars.
December: The Mayan Calendar comes to an end; for some, the date signifies the end of the world.

EARTH 2 #1 (MAY 2012)
Longtime readers of *DC Comics* were in for a shock with the release of the new *Earth 2* series by writer James Robinson and penciler Nicola Scott. Previously, this alternate dimension had tended to feature gentler heroes. However, in this new post-*Flashpoint* reality, Earth 2 was proving to be just as dark and foreboding as the rest of the *New 52*. This is hinted at in this variant cover for the first issue, penciled by artist Ivan Reis.

EARTH 2

2013

"YOU KNOW, I'VE BEEN LOOKING FORWARD TO THIS FOR A LONG TIME, SUPERMAN..."

Wraith, *Superman Unchained* #3

NEW DIRECTIONS

By 2013, the New 52 was no longer so "new." Once readers became familiar with the updated incarnations of beloved heroes (and villains), DC Comics' talented writers and artists wove complicated storylines that showed that this new universe would become just as rich, complex, and rewarding as in previous decades. Writers pushed their heroes to the brink, and tested their loyalties and strengths to the limit.

Batman and his world were shaken to the core, and Superman embarked on a dangerous new mission in the new *Superman Unchained* series. In other corners of the DC Universe, Wonder Woman, Aquaman, Green Lantern, The Flash, and Green Arrow held their own as events unfolded that culminated in the epic Trinity War. The series' villainous aftermath would be felt for months—if not years—to come...

JANUARY

DEATH OF THE FAMILY

***Batman* [second series] #16**
The Joker returns to Gotham City and gets his revenge in this 23-issue storyline, illustrated by a host of celebrated comic book artists and written by Scott Snyder. Spanning the *Batman* family of titles, including *Batman*, *Detective Comics*, *Batman and Robin*, *Batgirl*, *Nightwing*, *Red Hood and the Outlaws*, and *Teen Titans*, its title is a play on the seminal storyline from the 1980s in which the Joker murdered the then-current Robin, Jason Todd.

After being sent to Arkham Asylum by Batman, the Joker has his face surgically removed by the villain Dollmaker, who then pins it to the wall of the Joker's cell after the Joker escapes. The Joker finally returns to Gotham City, threatening Batman and those he holds dear. Claiming they have made the Dark Knight weak, the Joker vows to kill Batman's allies. Batman believes that the Joker may have discovered the location of the Batcave. The secret identities of Robin, Nightwing, Batgirl, and the others have been compromised. Batman's worst fears are realized when the Joker makes his way into the Batcave, threatening the lives of Batman's friends. Luckily, Batman escapes and thwarts the Joker. Batman realizes that the entire series of events was one of the Joker's twisted ploys, and he tells the villain that he knows his true identity. But the Joker escapes before anything is revealed.

Despite the Joker being thwarted, Batman's allies feel betrayed by the danger the Dark Knight placed them in. One of the most affected of Batman's allies is Batgirl, aka Barbara Gordon. After Barbara's mother is kidnapped, she receives a call from someone she thinks is the Joker, warning her that they know she is Batgirl. Batgirl decides to kill the Joker—breaking Batman's cardinal rule. But following a series of dark events, Batgirl faces certain death. A haunting tale of rebirth, secrets, lies, and trust, "Death of the Family" shook Batman and his friends and family to the core, and remains a turning point in the New 52 chronology of the Dark Knight.

Batgirl was prepared to defy Batman and break his no-killing rule. She viewed the Joker as the ultimate menace. She agreed to become the Joker's bride in order to gain his trust and then kill him. But she became his prisoner instead.

IN THE REAL WORLD...

February: Pope Benedict XVI resigns amid controversy within the Catholic Church. His successor, Francis I, is elected the next month.

MARCH

THRONE OF ATLANTIS

***Aquaman* [seventh series] #16**

Encompassing Aquaman's own title and several issues of Justice League, "Throne of Atlantis" chronicles the fight for the rule of the kingdom of Atlantis. When a Navy warship incites the wrath of the Atlanteans after it accidentally attacks Atlantis, the villainous Ocean Master (the current king of Atlantis) declares war on the surface world. Aquaman calls upon his allies, including Superman, Batman, and Wonder Woman. The Justice League is captured, except for Cyborg, in the battle that follows. Cyborg enlists help from Green Arrow, Hawkman, and others. The combined efforts of the heroes stop Ocean Master. Aquaman is saddened to learn that his faithful assistant, Vulko, was behind the bombing.

APRIL

THE DEATH OF DAMIAN WAYNE

***Batman Incorporated* [second series] #8**

Writer Grant Morrison's epic run chronicling Batman and his world comes to its shocking conclusion in this unforgettable issue. As the deadly Leviathan wages war on Gotham City, the situation becomes critical. Not one to stand idly by, Robin (Batman's son Damian) joins the fray. Damian flies into the lobby of Wayne Tower and fights off hordes of the Leviathan's henchmen until they outnumber him, but Nightwing arrives and saves him. The two reminisce, and Damian admits that Nightwing is his favorite crime-fighting partner. Robin and Nightwing then re-engage and defeat the henchmen, but the Heretic knocks Nightwing out. The Heretic challenges Robin to a fight to the death, with the winner being declared Talia al Ghūl's true son. Robin accepts. Batman, in the meantime, is locked in a safe that is submerged in a pool on the roof of Wayne Tower. Here, Talia taunts him about Damian being a failed creation of theirs. After eventually freeing himself, Batman is attacked by Man-Bats on his way to find Robin. When he arrives, Batman is devastated to find that Damian has been slain by Heretic.

Batman's son, Damian, struggles to defeat the villainous Heretic, but he is tragically murdered.

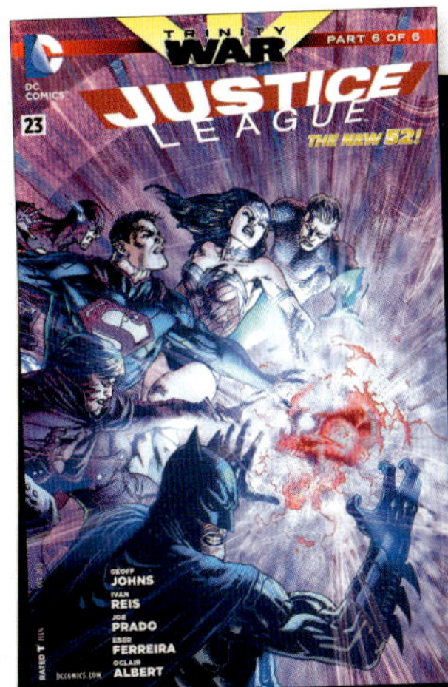

AUGUST

TRINITY WAR

***Justice League* [second series] #23**

Since the launch of the New 52, readers have been trying to figure out the story behind Pandora, the mysterious figure responsible for the restructure of the DC Universe. Involving just about every DC Comics character, and spanning eleven issues, *Trinity War* answered many long-awaited questions and led directly into *Forever Evil*, another mini-series that changed the status quo of the DC Universe.

When Pandora is informed that her box can only be opened by either the purest or darkest of hearts, it sets off a series of events involving the three distinct Justice League teams. The box changes hands several times before Madame Xanadu tells Pandora that the box is in fact a doorway, not a vessel as previously thought. The mysterious figure known as the Outsider reveals his presence to Earth's Super Heroes and informs them that the box is not magic, but science, and was created on his home world. What's more, it can only be opened by someone from his world. The box opens a gateway to another universe known as Earth-3. The Outsider opens the box, breaking it in the process. The Earth-3 iteration of the Justice League, known there as the Crime Syndicate, emerges: Ultraman, Super Woman, Owlman, Johnny Quick, Power Ring, and Deathstorm. The Outsider himself is revealed to be Earth-3's Alfred Pennyworth. The Crime Syndicate claims Earth as their own, and their rule of absolute terror begins.

Writers Geoff Johns and Jeff Lemire's dense and complex reveal is filled with enough twists and turns to keep even the most detail-oriented reader guessing, and together with several of DC Comics' finest artists, they crafted one of the defining stories of the year, one whose repercussions are still being felt a year later.

All the members of the Justice League, Justice League of America, and Justice League Dark race to open Pandora's box before an unknown terror can be unleashed on Earth in this stunning triptych by acclaimed artist and fan favorite Doug Mahnke.

ALSO THIS YEAR: "Wrath of the First Lantern" runs throughout the Green Lantern family of titles from April to July and chronicles the rise of the mysterious space alien known as Volthoom. *Forever Evil* kicks off in November with a seven-issue mini-series that focuses on the takeover of Earth by the Crime Syndicate of Earth-3 and the banding together of Earth Prime's villains to combat the superpowered menace. Writer Geoff Johns and artists David Finch and Richard Friend are the team responsible for turning deadly villains into unexpected heroes.

April: The oldest remains of dinosaur embryos from a species that lived approximately 190 million years ago are uncovered in China.

July: Tennis player Andy Murray claims his second Grand Slam title and becomes the first British male champion of the Wimbledon Championships in the UK in 77 years.

AUGUST

SUPERMAN UNCHAINED

***Superman Unchained* #1**

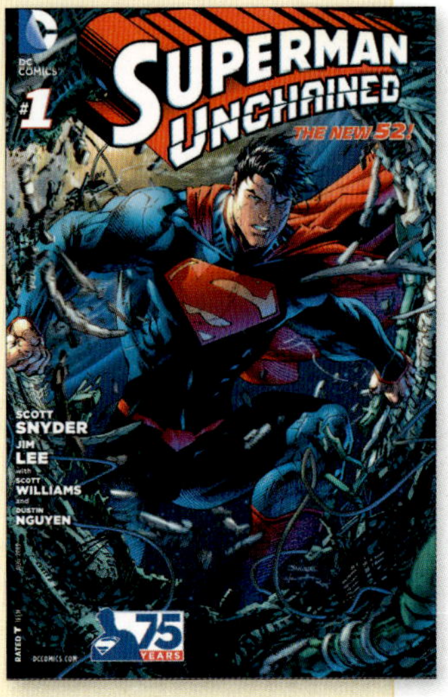

2013 was a big year for Superman. Not only was it his 75th anniversary, but Zack Snyder's blockbuster Superman reboot, *Man of Steel*, starring Henry Cavill as Clark Kent/ Superman and Amy Adams as Lois Lane was also released. As part of the anniversary celebration, DC Comics announced a new ongoing series of Superman by popular writer Scott Snyder, and illustrated by comics legend Jim Lee. Titled *Superman Unchained*, the series' first issue was released with eight variant covers, each in the style of a previous decade of the Man of Steel's comic book history. This trend continued for all of the issues of the series, but the real attraction of the first issue was a massive four-page illustration (by Lee) of Superman smashing several rogue satellites to pieces before they reached Earth.

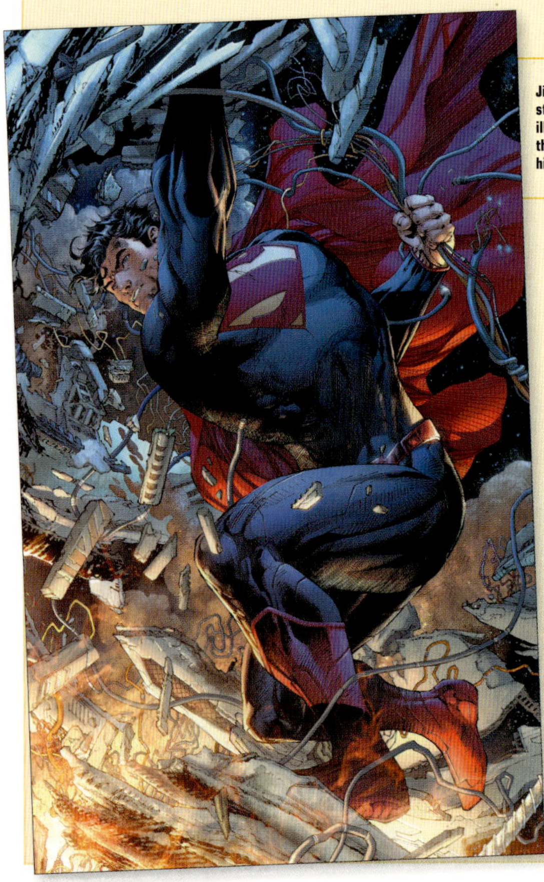

Jim Lee's stunning multi-page illustration celebrates the Man of Steel in all his iconic glory.

CROSS WORLD

***Batman/Superman* #1**

Writer Greg Pak and artist Jae Lee introduce the story of the fateful first meeting between Bruce Wayne/Batman and Clark Kent/Superman when the latter comes to Gotham City to investigate a series of murders involving several Wayne Enterprises employees, but things take a strange turn when both Super Heroes come face-to-face with alternate versions of themselves, leading to the memorable introduction of a new villain known as Kaiyo the Trickster. As Batman and Superman of Earth Prime learn to work with and understand their Earth-2 counterparts—as well as deal with the literal differences in their worlds—they begin to trust each other.

Superman and Batman's first meeting is an aggressive and confrontational one, as each is mistrustful of the other. The fight between the two is the polar opposite of the amicable relationship they will forge five years into the future.

DARK DAYS AHEAD

***Green Lantern* [fifth series] #21**

A new Green Lantern story arc begins as Hal Jordan assumes leadership of what has become the most feared and hated group of individuals in the universe: The Green Lantern Corps. The reputation of the Corps has suffered, and with Hal Jordan now in charge, it's unclear if things will get better or worse. It's a new start, as Hal Jordan struggles to undo damage and restore the good name of the Green Lanterns.

IN THE REAL WORLD...

July: Prince George is born to William and Catherine, the Duke and Duchess of Cambridge, at St. Mary's Hospital, London.

September: A five-day siege at a mall in Kenya terrifies a country and grips the world. The terrorists are finally thwarted by the Kenyan government.

ZERO YEAR

***Batman* [second series] #21**

"Zero Year," a 12-issue look at Bruce Wayne's first months as Batman, kicks off with part one of "Secret City" by series writer Scott Snyder and series artist Greg Capullo. Set six years before the current time, the story reveals a Gotham City ravaged by destruction and damage, with Bruce Wayne apparently dead and Batman gone. Crime has once more grown rampant, and the Red Hood Gang reigns supreme. Despite the fact that he has been declared legally dead, Bruce Wayne is alive and well, although he has not yet gone public with his return. Instead, Bruce decides to remain legally dead, insisting that he would be better able to take down the Red Hood Gang as Batman, without the distraction of being Bruce Wayne. Batman then makes his anticipated return.

These events set in motion a gripping tale of action, suspense, and mystery, and surprise after surprise. Despite multiple versions of Batman's origins in decades past, "Zero Year" is the definitive origin of the Batman of the New 52. Readers also learn the origins of Batman's enemies and allies, and those first crucial twelve months of their various careers. Masterfully plotted and beautifully illustrated, "Zero Year" is Batman at his most fascinating—and best.

A younger and greener Bruce Wayne starts his dangerous new life as the crime-fighting hero soon to become known as the Batman!

OCTOBER

WAR

***Wonder Woman* [fourth series] #23**

Writer Brian Azzarello and artist Cliff Chiang continue their unique and acclaimed run on the Amazon Princess' flagship title. After an intense visit to New Genesis and an adventure with the New Gods, Wonder Woman returns to her home base of London to find that the city has been destroyed by the First Born and his army, as part of his quest to conquer Mount Olympus. Wonder Woman wants justice. She removes her Bracelets of Submission and unleashes her full power against the First Born. She subdues the First Born, but kills War in the process. A penitent Diana seeks War's forgiveness before he dies. He absolves her, and says he would have done the same.

NOVEMBER

IN REVERSE

***The Flash* [fourth series] #24**

The "In Reverse" storyline, which started in issue #20, reaches its emotional conclusion in The Flash #24, written and illustrated by the talented Francis Manapul. Having discovered that the Reverse Flash is his friend Iris West's brother Daniel, the Flash is thrown back in time with the villain. By stealing the Flash's Speed Force energy, Daniel can go back in time to execute his master plan: the murder of his abusive father. The Reverse Flash is stopped when his younger self begs him to leave his father alone. Daniel relents and decides to move forward with his life. The Flash then drains Daniel of his energy.

DECEMBER

POWER COUPLE

***Superman/Wonder Woman* #1**

The surprise romance of the New 52 has been Superman's developing relationship with Wonder Woman. While Superman's marriage to Lois Lane was the status quo for decades, their relationship is one of deep friendship in this new universe, and the Man of Steel only has eyes for the Amazon Princess—so far. The new series highlights the differences and similarities between the two, and shows what that means for them as Super Heroes, and as a couple. Add in some deadly adversaries from Kyrypton and beyond, and this issue provides an action-packed look at two of the most powerful heroes on Earth.

In this dynamic gatefold cover, the respective cast of characters of Superman and Wonder Woman's worlds shows the complexity of the two leads.

November: A super typhoon hits the Philippines, causing unprecedented death and destruction across the country.

December: Freedom fighter, and former South African president, Nelson Mandela dies at the age of 95.

2014

"IF I'D WANTED TO KNOW WHO WAS UNDER ALL THOSE CAPES, I WOULD MAKE IT MY BUSINESS."

Commissioner Gordon, *Batgirl* [fourth series] #26

WORLD'S GREATEST

The spring of 2014 brought with it the announcement of several new ongoing weekly series. The first of these was the game-changing event known as "Future's End," which takes place in the future of the DC Universe.

The year also celebrates Batman's 75th anniversary, with a host of titles—both new and ongoing—to mark the occasion. A new creative team on *Detective Comics*, Francis Manapul and David Buccellato, was introduced in addition to a new weekly series entitled *Batman Eternal* and a special edition of *Detective Comics* #27, which commemorates Batman's first appearance in 1939.

DC Comics also unveiled a special anniversary logo for Batman. After 75 years, Batman remains the World's Greatest Detective.

JANUARY

THE DEATH OF KON-EL
***Superman* [third series] #25**
Following the events of "Forever Evil," the speedster *Johnny Quick* hurled the Teen Titans forward in time. After he is separated from the Titans, Kon-El encounters Jon Lane Kent, the villainous future son of Superman and Lois Lane. Kon-El is revealed to be a clone of Jon Lane Kent, created by Harvest (founder of N.O.W.H.E.R.E.), so that a cure could be found for the illness that is slowly killing Jon. During their battle, Jon Lane Kent is seriously injured. Kon-El falls through a portal, and is transported to Argo City on Krypton during the planet's past. He arrives only days prior to Krypton's destruction. Kon-El uses his powers to lift Argo City off of the dying Krypton, so that Supergirl can arrive on Earth as she destined to do. Kon-El dies when Krypton explodes.

THE DARK AGE
***Earth-2* #17**
The new Batman makes a big reveal on Earth-2, as a new story arc begins. Superman, distraught at the death of his wife Lois Lane, defeats Steppenwolf, attacks the Earth-2 "wonders" (Super Heroes), and decimates a city. Meanwhile, General Lane uploads Lois' consciousness into the body of an android named Red Tornado. He then dies in her arms shortly after. Batman infiltrates the World Arkham Base and enters the chamber in which the criminals are held in stasis. Batman declares that the prisoners may need to be released in order to save the world from Superman's fury. Earth-2's Batman is not Bruce Wayne, but rather, Thomas Wayne, Sr., who became the Dark Knight in order to avenge his son's death. However, Wayne, Sr.'s age and physical limitations have led him to use the Miraclo serum for super-strength, and he has since become addicted to it.

ALSO THIS YEAR: In April, "Zero Year" begins its final story arc, "Savage City," with the publication of Scott Snyder and Greg Capullo's Batman #30. "Forever Evil" reaches its shocking conclusion with issue #7, published in April.

IN THE REAL WORLD...
January: Bill de Blasio is sworn in as the 109th Mayor of New York City.

FEBRUARY

THE OUTSIDERS WAR
***Green Arrow* [fifth series] #26**

"The Outsiders War" storyline begins as Green Arrow recovers from the attack by Count Vertigo. The man who murdered Oliver's father, Komodo (who, it turns out, is alive), is still at large with Shado's daughter and Oliver's half-sister. Despite Oliver's protestations, Shado travels to the island, which Oliver was stranded on for years before he became Green Arrow, to destroy Komodo.

BATGIRL, WANTED
***Batgirl* [fourth series] #26**

Barbara Gordon feels lost after the death of her brother. Her one friend and confidant was shot by her father, so she seeks an outlet for her anger. She eventually finds one when she learns that the villain Knightfall is sending a cadre of his criminal followers to capture and torture Commissioner Gordon. What follows is an emotionally raw wrap-up to a story arc that saw Jim Gordon blame Batgirl for his son's death, and seriously placed the commissioner's faith in costumed heroes in doubt. But Barbara holds on to the hope for good, which led her to become Batgirl in the first place.

APRIL

RED DAUGHTER OF KRYPTON
***Supergirl* [sixth series] #28**

Young Kara Zor-El has not had an easy time since coming to Earth. Everything that has happened to her over the past few months has left her confused, frustrated, and angry. That anger becomes the perfect target for the Red Lanterns, who are in need of some new members. After a knockdown fight with the Czarnian bounty hunter Lobo, Supergirl expresses her anger with those around her. After she beats Lobo into submission, a Red Lantern ring takes notice and acquires a new target: Supergirl. Supergirl gives in to her rage, and becomes the newest Red Lantern. She accepts the ring and thus begins a shocking new chapter in the Girl of Steel's troubled life, courtesy of writer Tony Bedard and artists Vildiray Cinar and Ray McCarthy.

MAY

DARK KNIGHT WEEKLY
***Batman Eternal* #1**

Batman gets a new weekly series—one of several new weekly titles launched this year—written by the team of Scott Snyder, James Tynion IV, John Layman, Ray Fawkes, and Tim Seeley. Each writer takes a turn writing the lead story, while various artists, including Jason Fabok, Dustin Nguyen, Andy Clark, and Guillem March, provide vibrant illustrations. The first three-issue story arc introduced a Gotham City where the police are no longer allies with Batman—with Commissioner Gordon on the wrong side. The buzz surrounding this issue proved that Batman is an unending source of excitement.

JUNE

FUTURE DRAMA WEEKLY
***The New 52: Future's End* #1**

In this debut issue of The New 52's weekly series, written and illustrated by a talented team of writers and artists, the DC Universe is reeling from a war with another Earth. Set five years from now, the war leaves the world unprepared for an approaching evil, which threatens to destroy the future. Together with a time-traveling Batman, a huge cast of Super Heroes from the DC Universe attempt to avert the impending apocalypse. Packed with action and surprises, the heroic Grifter turns against humanity, and a member of the Justice League perishes.

Written by comic book superstars Jeff Lemire, Brian Azzarello, Dan Jurgens, and Keith GIffen, *Future's End* #1 is illustrated by Patrick Zircher and boasts a gorgeous cover by artist Ryan Sook, with a variant cover by John Romita, Jr. (featuring his first work for DC Comics before his start on *Superman* with writer Geoff Johns) and Klaus Janson.

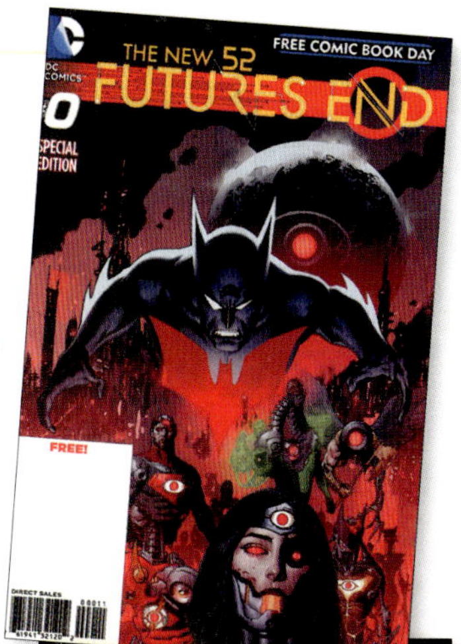

Grifter turns his back on humanity as the shocking and far-reaching events of "Future's End" begin in the first issue of the new weekly series.

January: Former Prime Minister of Israel, Ariel Sharon, is buried on his ranch in southern Israel, following a state funeral.

February: The XXII Olympic Winter Games 2014 begin amongst much controversy in Sochi, Russia.

JUNE

"ICARUS" Begins

Detective Comics [second series] #30

Batman's flagship title gets a new creative team in the form of writer Brian Buccellato and artist Francis Manapul—both fresh from their acclaimed run on *The Flash*.

Detective Comics #30 introduces new characters and challenges for Bruce Wayne and Batman. The story is set against the growing dark side of Gotham City's underworld, which is usually overlooked when the Dark Knight is focusing on the super-villain of the day. The issue introduces a new drug, Icarus, which has hit the streets of Gotham City. A murder case involving the drug grabs the attention of Batman and police detective Harvey Bullock. While the two characters may have a mutual respect for the other's work, their personal feelings for each other can be summed up in one word: hate. In a "Zero Year" issue of *The Flash*, Bullock was introduced to Icarus when he lost a partner to the drug. When the drug reappears in the murder case and incriminates Bruce Wayne, Detective Bullock is determined to seek justice—or perhaps revenge instead.

Between the top-notch writing and Manapul's stunning art, *Detective Comics* #30 showcases two storytellers at the top of their game. This issue ushers in a new and thrilling era for Batman. It is the perfect exclamation point on the past 75 years, and firmly creates an exciting template for the next 75.

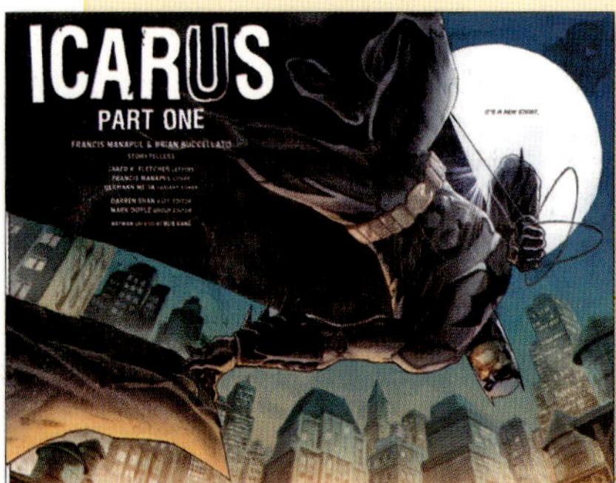

Batman swings across the nighttime skies of Gotham City looking for trouble, courtesy of artist Francis Manapul, in this breathtaking and instantly iconic image.

THE RETURN OF WALLY WEST

***The Flash Annual* [fourth series] #3**

In the future, The Flash is a broken man. His powers have failed him again and again at a great cost to him—and the city he has sworn to protect. In this issue, The Flash returns to 2014 to stop the event that destroyed his life. Meanwhile, in the present, Barry Allen contends with thieves who are trying to capitalize on the devastation of "Forever Evil." Wally West makes a highly-anticipated return in his New 52 debut.

JULY

THE RACE OF OUTLAWS

***Catwoman* [fourth series] #30**

Catwoman is in an ideal situation to show off her thieving skills in this exciting issue. Selina Kyle has tried to stop herself, but she loves being Catwoman. Selina dons the catsuit once more when she hears about a globetrotting contest that's right up her alley—a competition to prove that she's the best thief in the world. The Race of Outlaws begins in this action-packed story, written by Ann Nocenti with illustrations by Pat Olliffe.

DOOMED

***Superman: Doomed* #1**

Writers Greg Pak, Charles Soule, and Scott Lobdell re-introduce Doomsday into Superman's life with this miniseries, which redefines one of the Man of Steel's greatest and most iconic villains. The return of Doomsday crosses over into the Action Comics, Superman, and Superman/Wonder Woman titles, culminating in a showdown with the Kryptonian monster that tests Superman and those he loves. The story also features some of the characters best known to Superman fans, including Lois Lane, Supergirl, and Steel. The writers have stated that this is not simply a retelling of the classic "Death of Superman" storyline, but instead the events point the two key players in a pivotal new direction.

A NEW KIND OF JUSTICE

***Justice League United* #1**

Writer Jeff Lemire unveils the newest team of Canadian-based Super Heroes with Justice League United—a new ongoing series starring Stargirl, Martian Manhunter, Hawkman, Green Arrow, Animal Man, Supergirl, Adam Strange, and a new Cree Nation hero called Equinox. The first arc of the series takes place in the rural communities of Moose Factory and Moosonee. In the first arc, the story focuses on the post-"Forever Evil" fallout that causes the team to move to Northern Ontario, while the second arc takes the heroes to Thanagar for a story centered around Hawkman.

IN THE REAL WORLD...

June: Brazil hosts the 2014 FIFA World Cup, which kicks off on June 12.

July: Events are held around the globe to commemorate the start of World War I on July 28, 1914—100 years ago.

AUGUST
The Man of Tomorrow
***Superman* [third series] #32**
Geoff Johns returns to the Superman family when he takes over as writer for the Kryptonian's self-titled series with *Superman #32*. First-time DC Comics artist John Romita, Jr. joins him as they reshape the Man of Steel in a story arc titled "The Man of Tomorrow."

MAN OF TOMORROW

INDEX

T

ARTIST AND WRITER ACKNOWLEDGMENTS

Jack Abel, Daniel Acuña, Art Adams, Neal Adams, Daniel Adell, Dan Adkins, Jack Adler, Gerry Alanguilan, **Oclair Albert**, Rafael Albuquerque, Alfredo Alcala, Mike Allred, Sal Almendola, Bob Almond, Marlo Alquiza, Brad Anderson, Murphy Anderson, Ross Andru, Jim Aparo, Sergio Aragones, **Ulisses Arreola**, Terry Austin, Tony Aviña, Chris Bachalo, Kyle Baker, Art Baltazar, Bernard Baily, Michael Bair, Matt Banning, Darryl Banks, Eduardo Barreto, Eddy Barrows, Sy Barry, Moose Baumann, Mark Beachum, John Beatty, Terry Beatty, C. C. Beck, David Michael Beck, Ed Benes, Mariah Benes, Joe Bennett, Javier Bergantiño, Lee Bermejo, D. Bruce Berry, Jerry Bingham, Simon Bisley, Steve Bissette, Tex Blaisdell, Jon L. Blummer, Will A. Blyberg, Jon Bogdanove, Brian Bolland, Henry Boltinoff, Brett Booth, Wayne Boring, Ron Boyd, Timothy Bradstreet, Ken Branch, Brett Breeding, Mark Bright, Norm Breyfogle, Pat Broderick, Bob Brown, Jimmy Broxton, Joe Brozowski, Brian Buccellato, Mark Buckingham, Rich Buckler, Rick Burchett, Chris Burnham, Jack Burnley, Ray Burnley, John Buscema, Rick Bryant, John Byrne, Don Cameron, Robert Campanella, Marc Campos, Giuseppe Camuncoli, Greg Capullo, Nick Cardy, Mauro Cascioli, Paul Cassidy, Barbara Ciardo, Claudio Castellini, Joe Certa, Jim Chambers, Ernie Chan, Bernard Chang, Howard Chaykin, Sean Chen, Cliff Chiang, Frank Chiaramonte, Mark Chiarello, Ian Churchill, **Vincente Cifuentes,** Chris Claremont, Matthew Clark, Andy Clarke, Dave Cockrum, Olivier Coipel, Gene Colan, Vince Colletta, Ernie Colon, Darwyn Cooke, Richard Corben, Charles Cuidera, Paris Cullins, Steven Cummings, Rodolfo Damaggio, Tony Daniel, Alan Davis, Dan W. Davis, Ed Davis, Shane Davis, Geof Darrow, Mike DeCarlo, Jose Delbo, John Dell, J. M. DeMatteis, Mike Deodato, Hi-Fi Design, David DeVries, Tony DeZuniga, Dick Dillin, Steve Dillon, Steve Ditko, Ed Dobrotka, Rachel Dodson, Terry Dodson, Luis Dominguez, Arnold Drake, Bill Draut, Mike Dringenberg, Jan Duursema, Kieron Dwyer, Dale Eaglesham, Scot Eaton, Martin Egeland, Lee Elias, Randy Elliot, Whitney Ellsworth, Gabe Eltaeb, Bill Ely, Mike Esposito, Ric Estrada, Gary Erskine, Mark Evanier, George Evans, Nathan Eyring, Carlos Ezquerra, Jason Fabok, Glenn Fabry, Nathan Fairbairn, Mark Farmer, Wayne Faucher, Derek Fridolfs, David Finch, Lou Fine, Bill Finger, Virgil Finlay, Derek Fisher, Ken Fitch, Creig Flessel, John Forte, Gardner Fox, Ramona Fradon, **Gary Frank**, Ron Frenz, Richard Friend, Carl Gafford, Kerry Gammill, Manuel Garcia, Jose Luis Garcia-Lopez, Alex Garner, Carlos Garzon, Drew Geraci, Frank Giacoia, Dave Gibbons, Ian Gibson, Joe Giella, Keith Giffen, Dick Giordano, Archie Goodwin, Al Gordon, Rube Grossman, Jerry Grandenetti, Jamie Grant, Mick Gray, Dan Green, Sid Greene, Mike Grell, Tom Grummett, Pia Guerra, Jackson Guice, Mike Gustovich, Gene Ha, Phil Hale, Scott Hanna, Ed Hannigan, Tony Harris, Frank Harry, Doug Hazlewood, Russ Heath, Don Heck, Niko Henrichon, Everett E. Hibbard, Bryan Hitch, Phil Hester, Sandra Hope, **Adam Hughes**, Rian Hughes, Dave Hunt, Jamal Igle, Stuart Immonen, Carmine Infantino, Frazer Irving, Mark Irwin, Dennis Janke, Klaus Janson, Kirk Jarvinen, Oscar Jimenez, Phil Jimenez, Geoff Johns, Dave Johnson, Drew Johnson, J. G. Jones, Kelley Jones, Malcolm Jones, Ruy Jose, Dan Jurgens, Josue Justiniano, Mike Kaluta, Bob Kane, Gil Kane, Robert Kanigher, Rafael Kayanan, Stan Kaye, Karl Kerschl, Karl Kesel, Sam Kieth, Jack Kirby, Leonard Kirk, Barry Kitson, George Klein, Scott Kolins, Ray Kryssing, Andy Kubert, Joe Kubert, Michel Lacombe, Harry Lampert, Greg Land, Andy Lanning, David Lapham, Ken Lashley, Paul Lauretta, Bob Layton, Jae Lee, **Jim Lee**, Steve Leialoha, Rob Liefeld, Steve Lightle, David Lloyd, Jeph Loeb, Aaron Lopresti, Tom Lyle, Mike Machlan, Kevin Maguire, Rick Magyar, Larry Mahlstedt, Doug Mahnke, Guy Major, Alex Maleev, Francis Manapul, Tom Mandrake, Mike Manley, Esteban Maroto, Cynthia Martin, Shawn C. Martinbrough, Jose Marzan Jr., Francesco Mattina, Randy Mayor, Sheldon Mayer, David Mazzucchelli, Brendan McCarthy, Ray McCarthy, John McCrea, Scott McDaniel, Luke McDonnell, Dave McKean, Ted McKeever, Mike McKone, Ed McGuinness, Frank McLaughlin, Bob McLeod, Al McWilliams, Lan Medina, Paco Medina, Brad Meltzer, **Jesus Merino**, Mike Mignola, Al Milgrom, Frank Miller, Steve Mitchell, Lee Moder, Sheldon Moldoff, Jim Mooney, Alan Moore, Rags Morales, Ruben Moreira, Pepe Moreno, Grant Morrison, Win Mortimer, Dean Motter, Todd Nauck, Martin Naydel, Paul Neary, Mark Nelson, Don Newton, **Diogenes Neves**, Martin Nodell, Graham Nolan, Paul Norris, Irv Novick, Kevin Nowlan, Eddy Newell, Dustin Nguyen, Peter Nguyen, Bob Oksner, Ariel Olivetti, Pat Olliffe, Leo O'Mealia, Denny O'Neil, Kevin O'Neill, Glen Orbik, Jerry Ordway, Joe Orlando, Andy Owens, **Carlos Pacheco**, Tom Palmer Sr., Tom Palmer Jr., Jimmy Palmiotti, Yanick Paquette, Charles Paris, James D. Pascoe, Ande Parks, Sean Parsons, **Allen Passalaqua**, Bruce Patterson, Chuck Patton, Paul Pelletier, Mark Pennington, Shea Anton Pensa, George Pérez, Mike Perkins, Rich Perrotta, Harry G. Peter, Sean Phillips, Al Plastino, Howard Porter, Joe Prado, Bruno Premiani, John Prentice, Javier Pulido, Howard Purcell, Jack Purcell, Joe Quesada, Joe Quinones, Frank Quitely, Humberto Ramos, Rodney Ramos, Norm Rapmund, Fred Ray, Paul Reinman, **Ivan Reis**, **Rod Reis**, Eduardo Risso, Andrew Robinson, Jerry Robinson, Kenneth Rocafort, Denis Rodier, Anibal Rodriguez, Rodin Rodriguez, Marshall Rogers, Prentis Rollins, John Romita, John Romita Jr., **Alex Ross**, David Ross, George Roussos, Mike Royer, Joe Rubinstein, Steve Rude, Nei Ruffino, P. Craig Russell, Matt Ryan, Paul Ryan, Bernard Sachs, Stephen Sadowski, Jesus Saiz, Tim Sale, Alex Saviuk, Kurt Schaffenberger, Julius Schwartz, Lew Sayre Schwartz, Damion Scott, Nicola Scott, Bart Sears, Mike Sekowsky, Val Semeiks, Hal Sharp, Liam Sharp, Hal Sherman, Howard Sherman, James Sherman, Jim Shooter, Joe Shuster, Jon Sibal, Jerry Siegel, Bill Sienkiewicz, John Sikela, Tom Simmons, Joe Simon, Walter Simonson, Mark Simpson, **Alex Sinclair**, Joe Sinnott, Bob Smith, Cam Smith, Matthew Dow Smith, John K. Snyder III, Ray Snyder, Cat Staggs,Ryan Sook, Andrea Sorrentino, Jack Sparling, Dick Sprang, Frank Springer, Chris Sprouse, Al Stahl, Jim Starlin, Joe Staton, **Peter Steigerwald**, Marvin Stein, Brian Stelfreeze, Dave Stewart, E. C. Stoner, Karl Story, Lary Stucker, Vincent Sullivan, Curt Swan, Romeo Tanghal, Ty Templeton, Mark Texeira, Art Thibert, Jill Thompson, Bruce Timm, Alex Toth, John Totleben, Timothy Truman, Chas Truog, Billy Tucci, Michael Turner, **Ethan Van Sciver**, Brad Vancata, Rick Veitch, Sal Velluto, Al Vey, Dexter Vines, Trevor Von Eeden, Wade Von Grawbadger, Matt Wagner, Ron Wagner, Mark Waid, Brad Walker, Chris Warner, Lee Weeks, Joe Weems, Len Wein, Al Wenzel, Kevin West, Chris Weston, Glenn Whitmore, Bob Wiacek, Mike Wieringo, J. H. Williams III, **Scott Williams**, Bill Willingham, Marv Wolfman, Basil Wolverton, Walden Wong, Wally Wood, Pete Woods, Berni Wrightson, Ira Yarbrough, Tom Yeates, Cliff Young, Leinil Francis Yu, Mike Zeck.

The artwork featured on the jacket is credited to the artists whose names appear in bold on this page.